LOYALTIES

Also By Thomas Fleming

FICTION
Over There
Time and Tide
The Spoils of War
The Officers' Wives
Promises to Keep
Rulers of the City
Liberty Tavern
The Good Shepherd
A Cry of Whiteness

NONFICTION
1776: Year of Illusions
The Man Who Dared the Lightning
The Man from Monticello
West Point: The Men and Times of the U.S. Military Academy
One Small Candle
Beat the Last Drum
Now We Are Enemies

THOMAS FLEMING

LOYALTIES

= A NOVEL OF WORLD WAR II =

HarperCollinsPublishers

HarperCollins books may be purchased for educational, business, or sales promotional use. For information, please write: Special Markets Department, HarperCollins Publishers, Inc., 10 East 53rd Street, New York, NY 10022.

FIRST EDITION

Designed by C. Linda Dingler

Library of Congress Cataloging-in-Publication Data
Fleming, Thomas J.
    Loyalties : a novel of World War II / Thomas Fleming. —1st ed.
        p.   cm.
    ISBN 0-06-017709-8
    1. World War, 1939–1945—Fiction. I. Title.
PS3556. L45L69 1994
813' .54—dc20   93-41000

94 95 96 97 98 ❖/HC 10 9 8 7 6 5 4 3 2 1

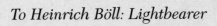

To Heinrich Böll: Lightbearer

For historians ought to be . . . unprejudiced, and neither interest nor fear, hatred nor affection, should cause them to swerve from the path of truth, whose mother is history, the rival of time . . . the monitor of the future.

MIGUEL DE CERVANTES

This war . . . is one of those elemental conflicts which shake the world once in a thousand years and usher in a new millennium.

ADOLF HITLER

While in high places there is eternal alternance of victory and defeat, those in the depths pray, pray with that mighty piety of the Second Religiousness that has overcome all doubts for ever. There, in the souls, world-peace, the peace of God . . . is become actual—and there alone.

OSWALD SPENGLER

CHRONOLOGY

1939

August 23—Hitler and Stalin sign Nonaggression Pact.

September 1—Germany invades Poland. Britain and France declare war.

September 27—Warsaw surrenders. Poland partitioned between Russia and Germany.

1940

April 9—Germany invades Denmark and Norway.

May 10—Germany invades Netherlands, Belgium and Luxembourg. Winston Churchill becomes British Prime Minister.

May 12—Germany invades France. Blitzkrieg swiftly shatters French army.

May 26–June 4—British army evacuated from Dunkirk.

June 10—Italy declares war on Britain and France.

June 14—German troops enter Paris.

September 3—United States gives Great Britain fifty destroyers in swap for naval bases.

September 27—Germany, Japan and Italy sign Tripartite Pact.

November 11–12—British planes surprise Italian fleet at Taranto.

November 14—German planes smash Coventry.

1941

January 10—United States launches lend-lease program to aid Great Britain.

April 6—Germany invades Greece and Yugoslavia.

April 9—United States begins secret talks with Japan to prevent war.

June 22—Germany invades Russia.

July 7—United States occupies Iceland.

August 12—Roosevelt and Churchill meet in Newfoundland to discuss war aims and issue the Atlantic Charter.

September 16—U.S. Navy begins escorting convoys to Mid-ocean Meeting Point (MOMP), 600 miles west of Iceland.

October 31—U.S. Destroyer *Reuben James* sunk.

November 15—Saboro Kurusu, special Japanese envoy, arrives in the United States with new proposals for deadlocked negotiations.

November 26—U.S.-Japanese negotiations break down.

December 4—Leak of Rainbow Five, the United States' top-secret war plan.

December 7—Japan attacks Pearl Harbor.

December 8—United States and Britain declare war on Japan.

December 11—Germany and Italy declare war on the United States, which immediately declares war on them.

1942

January 21—German offensive in North Africa threatens Cairo and Suez Canal.

February 15—British surrender Singapore.

April 9—U.S. forces on Bataan surrender; Philippines fall.

May 4–8—Battle of Coral Sea stops Japanese assault on Australia.

May 30—First RAF 1,000 plane raid on Cologne.

June 4–8—U.S. Navy victory at Midway throws Japan on the defensive in the Pacific.

August 19—British lose 50 percent of their force in raid on Dieppe.

August 25—German Army drives on Stalingrad and nears Grozny oil fields in Cacausus.

October 23—British victory at El Alamein drives Germans out of Egypt.

November 8—Anglo-American army lands in North Africa.

November 19–22—Russian counteroffensive stuns German Army in Stalingrad.

1943

January 26—Roosevelt and Churchill meet at Casablanca, declare unconditional surrender to be their war policy.

February 2—Moscow announces German surrender at Stalingrad.

March 2—British bombers hit Berlin with 900 tons of high explosives.

May 13—German Army in North Africa surrenders.

July 9–10—Allies invade Sicily.

July 25—Mussolini resigns as Italian premier.

September 9—Allies land at Salerno in southern Italy. Germans occupy Italy and a nine-month military stalemate begins.

November 6—Russian troops recapture Kiev, capital of the Ukraine.

November 28—Roosevelt, Churchill and Stalin confer at Teheran. The British and Americans promise to launch a second front in France in 1944.

December 24—Dwight Eisenhower named Allied commander for the invasion.

1944

January 21—RAF raids Berlin with 800 planes.

March 15—Allied planes drop 3,500 tons of bombs on Cassino but fail to dislodge Germans.

June 4—Allied offensive captures Rome.

June 6—D-Day: Allied army lands in Normandy.

June 13–14—German V-1 pilotless planes attack Britain.

July 20—German anti-Nazi conspirators fail to kill Hitler in bomb attack at his headquarters.

August 25—Paris liberated.

September 8—German V-2 rockets hit London.

September 17—Allied airborne attack on Arnhem fails. Attempt to invade Germany from the north repulsed.

December 16—Germans launch Ardennes counteroffensive—Battle of the Bulge.

1945

February 4–11—Stalin, Roosevelt and Churchill meet at Yalta.

March 7—U.S. First Army crosses the Rhine, invades Germany.

April 11—Americans liberate first concentration camp.

April 12—U.S. Ninth Army reaches Elbe River, fifty miles from Berlin, but does not advance beyond it, in accordance with Yalta agreement.

April 12—Roosevelt dies of cerebral hemorrhage. Harry S Truman becomes president.

April 30—Hitler commits suicide in Berlin bunker.

May 2—Berlin falls to Russians.

May 7—Germany surrenders unconditionally.

August 6—First atomic bomb dropped on Hiroshima, Japan.

August 9—Second atomic bomb dropped on Nagasaki.

August 14—Japan surrenders.

BOOK ONE

1

ANGEL IN THE DEPTHS

Past whales and sharks and dolphins the submarine glided with surreal menace. It was at home in this world of icy darkness, which could snuff life out of a human body in an instant with its implacable cold, its crushing weight. At home in a world of death.

The submarine was designed for only one purpose: to inflict death. Its grayness, its projectile shape, reeked of death, of evil incarnate. But on its conning tower it displayed a symbol of nobility, courage: the head of a knight in armor, painted a glowing white.

There were men inside that metal tube. Brave men, who faced death with the tenacity of mythic heroes. Laughing men, who exchanged rough jokes with each other. Feeling men, who read letters from home with tears in their eyes. Religious men, who sang songs of joy and faith at Christmas time. Men who were proud of the symbol on the conning tower, who called the submarine *Das Ritterboot*—the Knight's Boat.

How could such evil and such humanity coexist in the same vessel? Half-dreaming, half-awake in her mother-in-law's villa in the Berlin suburb of Wannsee, Berthe von Hoffmann twisted in torment, trying to understand. Above all she struggled to accept this mingling of nobility and murderous purpose on the resolute face of Ernst von Hoffmann, her husband, the commander of the Ritterboot.

Then Berthe saw the depth charges. Shaped like garbage cans, they spun and tumbled in the gloom. *Wabos*, the men called them, short for *Wasserbomben*—water bombs. Their simultaneous blast engulfed the Ritterboot in lethal orange flame. It tilted up like a fish with a hook in its throat, then toppled sideways like a mortally wounded soldier in no-man's-land.

Berthe was inside the submarine now. She saw the icy water surging through the compartments. Saw the writhing men, their faces pressed against the steel overhead, gasping for one more breath of life. Weeping, she swam down the length of the boat until she was in the conning tower, where the Ritterboot's commander met the flood with stoic despair.

Oh, oh, oh, wept Berthe. How could she prevent it? How could she place herself between that beloved face and its doom? She had kissed those lips in this very bed. She had accepted his flesh within her body, she had carried his children in her womb. She had suggested painting the knight's head on the conning tower as proof of her faith in his honor, her devotion to Germany's cause.

Then Berthe saw the angel. A great white creature, as long as the submarine, he swam out of the deep's icy darkness and cradled the dying boat in his immense arms. His staring eyes emanated compassion. On his mouth was transfixed the hieratic smile of a Byzantine saint. The whales, the sharks, the dolphins swarmed around him unafraid.

The Path, Berthe thought. *The angel was part of the Path.*

Below, the old clock in the front hall bonged 7 a.m. It was November 9, the third anniversary of the worst day of her life. Berthe arose and braided her thick blond hair and pinned it carefully into a severe chignon at the nape of her long slender neck. Dressing with her usual care, she went downstairs to have breakfast with her two children, Georg, seven, and Greta, four. Georg was a miniature rendition of his father—the same bold blue eyes and blond hair and determined mouth. He was carrying a toy submarine under his arm.

"Georg," Berthe said. "Take that back to your room. We don't bring toys to the table."

Stumping into the room on her cane, Berthe's mother-in-law, Isolde von Hoffmann, contradicted her, as usual. "Let him keep it in his lap. It makes him feel close to his father."

If ever a human being had been misnamed, it was Isolde von Hoffmann. She did not have a trace of romance in her soul. Her life was consumed in the details of housekeeping, managing the family's money and promoting the careers of her sons. At eighty, the flesh on her gaunt face was almost transparent, but she exuded the same fierce will that had enabled her, the daughter of a minor bureaucrat, to acquire a titled husband, a young hero of the Franco-Prussian War who won fame as a general in Russia in the last war. Her oldest son had died on the battlefield in France in 1918. Yet she had committed her two remaining sons to the current war without so much as a flicker of hesitation. There were times when Berthe admired her resolution. More often she was appalled by it.

They sat down to their usual Sunday breakfast of sausage and eggs. Isolde von Hoffmann turned on the radio in the parlor next to the dining room and they listened to the communiqués from the fighting fronts. In Russia, the panzer divisions were within striking distance of Moscow and Leningrad. In Egypt, the Afrika Corps, though recently forced to retreat, still threatened Cairo and the Suez Canal. England had been punished with another heavy air raid on her west coast ports. The Ubootwaffe reported another thirty-six ships, totaling 400,000 tons, had been sunk.

"Heil the U-boats," Georg roared. Berthe suppressed a terrific impulse to shush him. She could not afford to waste any more of her strength on minor matters today.

"Are you going to that church again?" Isolde von Hoffmann said, as the aged cook served coffee.

"Yes," Berthe said.

"I've told you before, Berthe. The wife of a naval officer should have nothing to do with that ranting cleric. If you were a shopgirl from the back alleys of Berlin, it would make no difference. Saving their souls adds a dimension to their mediocre lives."

"I've already told you my answer, Frau von Hoffmann. I have no other choice."

Ich kann nicht anders. In her mother-in-law's contemptuous glare, Berthe wondered how much longer she could cling to her claim to spiritual kinship with Martin Luther, the man who had made that profession of faith a turning point in the history of Germany and the world. The words had leaped to her lips the first time Isolde von Hoffmann had assaulted her for attending the small church where the pastor, Friedrich Bruchmuller, preached the Christian's need to resist the powers of this world—and criticize the government of Adolf Hitler.

"In fact," Berthe said, as her children's eyes registered amazement at her defiance of *Grossmutter*, "today I'll be gone until dark, at least. We're having an afternoon of reconciliation after the regular Sunday service."

"What does that mean?" Isolde von Hoffmann snarled.

"We'll discuss the need to avoid the—the sin of hating our enemies—the English, the Russians."

"And the Americans?" asked Georg with cheerful indifference to what his mother had just said. "Grandmother says they're the worst. They must be destroyed after the Russians. We'll sink all their ships!"

He aimed his submarine at the pitcher of milk in the center of the table and released an imaginary torpedo. Four-year-old Greta clapped with glee. With a terrific effort, Berthe remained calm. "We're not at war with the Americans. If they attack us, we'll defeat them in battle, of course. But we must not hate them. They're people like us. They have boys and girls who play with submarines and sink milk pitchers."

"Nonsense!" hissed Isolde von Hoffmann. "I've told them how despicable the money-grubbing Americans are. Cowards who stay out of a war until both sides are exhausted and then claim the victory. I've told them how they killed their father's brother. How they betrayed Germany at the peace conference in 1919. How can you say we shouldn't hate such people? Hate is good for the soul. It strengthens pride, increases courage!"

"I'm sorry, Frau von Hoffmann, I don't agree."

"I've also told them to ignore your ridiculous opinions!"

Berthe struggled for acceptance. It was unbelievably humiliating, to be dismissed as a fool in front of her children. Was this part of the Path? She remembered the angel cradling the submarine in its gigantic arms and wondered if she was in the same superhuman embrace.

The whole thing was too mysterious to understand. She was a Schonberg, a name almost synonymous with gaiety, frivolity, cynicism among the German aristocracy. For generations they had been the wits, the patrons of the arts, in the otherwise dour court of the Hohenzollern kaisers. Her father and his brothers gambled away millions at Monte Carlo and even managed to shock Paris with their escapades. When Germany's defeat in 1918 tumbled the last Kaiser into history's dustbin, most of the Schonbergs went with him. They lost the rest of their dwindling fortune in the financial chaos of the 1920s and became that most pathetic of social entities, impoverished aristocrats.

Berthe had turned the family's disarray into an opportunity. She browbeat her father into sending her to the university—an almost unheard of thing in prewar Germany, where women of the lower classes were catechized on *kirche kuche kinder* (church, kitchen, children) and those of the upper classes were raised like expensive dogs or horses only for breeding purposes.

Berthe von Schonberg defiantly chose as her patron saint Friedrich Schliermacher, whose eighteenth-century *Catechism of Reason for Noble Women* urged them to "lust after men's education, art, wisdom and honor"—an idea that the pervasive leaden respectability of the nineteenth century had expunged from the fatherland's consciousness. She had graduated with honors from the University of Berlin and plunged into the artistic and intellectual ferment of the 1920s.

In a Europe desolated by the catastrophe of the Great War, Berlin was the capital of the continent's nihilism for ten chaotic years and no one mocked respectability and solemnity more artfully than Berthe von Schonberg. The list of writers she edited at Ullstein's publishing house were the cleverest, the wittiest, the most cynical talents in Germany. Her blond beauty decorated more than one cover of the racy magazines that reported Berlin's high and low life.

It seemed logical that Berthe would choose a swaggering naval officer like Ernst von Hoffmann. An aristocrat, of course—but a sailor, presumably with a sailor's morals. No one knew that behind her mask of mocking laughter the playgirl had fallen in love with a man who talked of Germany's destiny in a naive yet heroic way that stirred a peculiar resonance in her uncertain soul.

That was in 1932. Nine years ago. The following year, Adolf Hitler became the ruler of Germany. At first there was no discernible change in the Hoffmanns' lives. Ernst graduated from the U-boat school at Kiel and he and Berthe were married on the terrace of this house. Her mother-in-law disapproved of the marriage because Berthe brought neither a dowry nor a reputation to the family. But Ernst, the youngest son, had always been the defiant one—perhaps resenting the attention his older brothers received. Early on, he had declared his intention to join the navy rather than the army. He took a certain pleasure in flaunting his masculine freedom to choose a wife in his mother's frowning face.

As a professional military officer, Ernst was forbidden to participate in politics and his interest in the grubby world of vote hunting was minimal—except where such matters affected his career. From that viewpoint, Hitler's determination to undo the humiliation of the Versailles Treaty was a godsend. As the Führer trumpeted defiance of France and England and began to rebuild the Ubootwaffe, his name was invoked with enthusiasm in the Hoffmann household. The Navy's expansion had not a little to do with Ernst's rapid promotion from *oberfahnrich zur see* (ensign) to *kapitanleutnant* (lieutenant commander), while his older brother Berthold rose to colonel on the expanding army's general staff.

With two children in three years, Berthe had quit her job at Ullstein's and immersed herself in motherhood. Hoping to placate her mother-in-law—and tempted by the comforts of the Wannsee villa— she had accepted her invitation to live with her, rather than struggle to survive on Ernst's puny naval salary. She did not pay much attention to what was happening inside Germany under Hitler at first. She only saw her circle of literary friends sporadically. They thought the ranting little chancellor was hopelessly déclassé. They made wry jokes about him and his crew of louts from Bavaria, who spoke German as if they had mouthfuls of strudel.

Like most Berliners, Berthe and her friends disagreed with Hitler's hysterical attacks on Jews, but they expressed their disgust privately. Berlin cosmopolitans were not anti-Semitic—Berthe's favorite poet, Else Lasker-Schuler, was Jewish—but they were also not involved in the ugly details of politics. Besides, the Nazis, with their brawling brownshirted stormtroopers, were more than a little frightening. People who spoke out against them were beaten up—or disappeared into mysterious concentration camps.

Then came November 9, 1938. Ernst was on maneuvers in the North Sea. Berthe drove to central Berlin for dinner with Else Lasker-Schuler and Helen Widerstand, an editor at Ullstein's. They were meeting to discuss how to raise funds for Lasker-Schuler, who had been beaten up twice by Nazi thugs because of her denunciations of National Socialism. At sixty-seven, with her books and plays banned, this woman, whose poems were in anthologies beside those of Goethe and Schiller, was in danger of starving to death. She had tried living in Zurich and found the Swiss almost as anti-Semitic as the Nazis.

The moment Berthe reached the center of the city, she sensed something was wrong. Berlin's orderly demeanor had vanished. Crowds of Nazi *Sturm Abteilung* surged along the sidewalks. The air was thick with smoke. Everywhere there was broken glass, shards and shards of it.

At the Café des Artistes on Fasanstrasse, she found a terrified Lasker-Schuler and an infuriated Helen Widerstand. In Paris, Helen told Berthe, a young German Jew, deranged by his family's persecution, had shot a German diplomat, and the Brownshirts were storming through the city, burning synagogues, smashing up Jewish shops, beating up anyone on the street who looked Jewish. The frantic proprietor of the Café des Artistes urged them to leave. He was a well-known Jew.

As they hesitated, a half-dozen Brownshirts burst into the restaurant roaring: "Jewish pigs shouldn't feed in public!" They flung a chair through the front window and began smashing up the bar. Food on the tables was hurled against the walls. Berthe, Helen and Lasker-Schuler headed for the street.

"Is she a yid?" a beefy Brownshirt at the door asked, seizing Lasker-Schuler's arm. Her delicate features had a distinctly Jewish cast.

"She's my sister, you miserable thug," Helen Widerstand said. "Take your hands off her or I'll break your neck." Helen was six feet tall, with a heavyweight boxer's physique and a temperament to match it. A Marxist since her student days, she detested Nazis and Nazism.

"I'll have what's left of you arrested," Berthe said. "My husband is a naval officer, the son of General von Hoffmann."

"What the hell are you doing in a Jewish restaurant?" the lout bawled.

A few blocks away, flames gushed from the windows of the Central Synagogue. Helen Widerstand rushed back to Ullstein's to rescue some manuscripts. Berthe put her arm around Lasker-Schuler and offered to drive her home. The poet numbly assented and they began walking down Fasanstrasse to the side street where Berthe had parked her car. On the next block, they found a woman squatting on the glass-strewn sidewalk, cradling a man's bloody head in her lap.

"Help me please!" she cried. "My husband needs a doctor!"

No one in the crowd showed a trace of sympathy. There were too many Brownshirts among them. They had beaten the man, who was at least seventy, and smashed his jewelry shop. When the woman tried to reach a telephone on the corner, they shoved her back, screaming awful insults. On Berthe's arm, Else Lasker-Schuler was trembling with an explosive combination of fear and rage.

Seemingly from nowhere a slim, incredibly handsome young man in the dark suit of a clergyman shoved his way through the crowd. He put a coin in the telephone and called a doctor. One of the crowd asked a friend: "Who's that guy?"

"Bruchmuller, one of the Confessing crowd."

They were talking about a split in the German Lutheran church between pastors who accepted the Nazis' racial laws and those who declared they violated the confession of faith. Until this moment, the disagreement had meant little to Berthe. Schonbergs seldom darkened the doors of churches—nor were the Hoffmanns much more devout.

Pastor Bruchmuller came back from the telephone and knelt beside the old man. With infinite tenderness, he wiped the blood from his forehead and face and told the woman a doctor would soon be there—a man from his congregation.

On Bruchmuller's face was something Berthe had never seen before. It was more than courage, more than pride, more than nobility. She had seen all these things on her husband's face, mingled in his case with heartbreaking boyishness. As she groped for a word, Else Lasker-Schuler muttered in her ear: *"Einer Lichtrager."* A lightbearer.

Thus did Berthe encounter *Kristallnacht* (plate glass night)—when Hitler declared all-out war on the Jews. She drove Else Lasker-Schuler to her shabby rooming house in the Kreuzberg district, listening to her sobbing monologue. "This settles it. I'm going to move to Palestine. The thought horrifies me. Living in a country where almost no one speaks German. I don't know whether I can do it. I may kill myself instead. I'm German to the lining of my intestines, Berthe! I think, I feel, I pray in German!"

The next day, the newspapers shouted the news of Kristallnacht. In Berlin, twenty-three out of twenty-nine synagogues had been gutted. Virtually every Jewish business in the city had been smashed and looted. The scale of the hatred was so vast, the government's attitude so unrelenting, Berthe wondered if there was anything a mere housewife could do, beyond helping friends like Lasker-Schuler emigrate.

She turned on the radio and Adolf Hitler's coarse voice filled the parlor with ugly phrases, congratulating the stormtroopers for their night's work. Suddenly the air was so thick with a putrefying smell, Berthe almost fainted. It was a mixture of sulphur and offal, as if a flaming sewer had emptied into the placid parlor, with its oriental rug and stolid nineteenth-century furniture.

What was happening to her? Isolde von Hoffmann sat listening matter of factly to Hitler's sneering words. She had a low opinion of the "Austrian," an insult, in her private terminology, even worse than "Frenchman." She had already expressed her abhorrence of the brutality of Kristallnacht. But as long as the German Army and Navy supported the Führer, she would never breathe the stench of evil in his livid words.

That was when Berthe decided to visit Pastor Bruchmuller's church. The visit had led to additional visits and the sense of a Path down which she had been groping all her life, a winding, twisting trail that had led her to the small white-walled building where this committed man preached faith in a caring God.

Now, on the morning of November 9, 1941, Berthe kissed her children and put on her coat and hat for the walk to the Schnellbahn, the rapid transit line that would take her to Alexanderplatz, the working class section where Bruchmuller's church was located. She waited until she was at the door to say goodbye to her mother-in-law.

"There's something else we're going to do at the day of reconciliation," she said. "Something even more important than the call for loving regard for our enemies."

"What's that?" snarled Isolde von Hoffmann.

"It's November ninth. The third anniversary of Kristallnacht. We're going to call on the Führer and the country to repent and do penance for persecuting the Jews."

She fled down the lawn to the street. But her mother-in-law was not going to let her have the last word. "I'm going to tell Ernst about this!" she shouted from the open door. "You have responsibilities to him, to your children. To the family of the von Hoffmanns. You have no right to endanger his career!"

Isolde von Hoffmann was correct, of course. She never said anything that was not correct. But the Path that Berthe had discovered in Pastor Bruchmuller's church beckoned her irresistibly onward. She walked toward a future that was plunged in darkness as blank as the depths in which the Ritterboot prowled. Yet somehow, somewhere, the angel incomprehensibly promised sunlight, warmth, peace.

2

PROPHET WITHOUT FAITH

"Approaching MOMP, Captain," said the Quartermaster of the Watch.

Lieutenant Commander Jonathan Trumbull Talbot, better known to his Annapolis classmates as Zeke, beat his arms against his sides in a vain attempt to restore some circulation to his fingers. The temperature in the wheelhouse of the USS *Spencer Lewis*, DD107, was ten degrees above zero. November on the North Atlantic, Talbot thought. November 9, 1941, to be exact—a date which had no significance whatsoever to him—simply another day in the undeclared war he was being ordered to fight against his better judgment.

The deck beneath Talbot's feet abruptly tilted thirty degrees as a mountainous wave spilled tons of freezing gray-green water on the bow of the ancient destroyer. Sheets of icy rain beat against the wheelhouse windows. Along the dawning horizon, a half-dozen merchant ships wallowed toward England, part of Fast Convoy HX170, which the *Lewis* and three other U.S. destroyers had been escorting for the past five days.

The Americans were bringing HX170 to MOMP, which was 600 miles west of Iceland and stood for Mid-ocean Meeting Point. It was also known as CHOP, for Change of Operational Command. There the plodding merchantmen would be passed to the vigilance of British destroyers of the Western Approaches Command, most of them ancient four stackers like the *Lewis*, built in American ship-yards in 1918, too late to get into World War I. Last year fifty of these relics had been hauled out of mothballs and handed to England in a historic swap that gave the United States some bases in the Atlantic and Caribbean that the overextended British fleet could not use. Talbot liked to point out that the transfer incidentally violated every concept of neutrality in the history of international law.

"Pass the word to keep a sharp lookout for the Limeys," Talbot said.

"Aye-aye, Captain," said the telephone talker. He transmitted the message to foul-weather jacketed lookouts freezing in the *Lewis*'s superstructure.

"Also remind them to keep what's left of their eyeballs peeled for Unterseebooten," Talbot said.

"Captain?" said the telephone talker, who was not very bright.

For several weeks, Talbot had been telling everyone on the bridge that they ought to start learning German. He spoke it fluently, thanks to five boyhood years when his father had been American ambassador to Berlin.

"U-boats. Watch for U-boats. This is their favorite time to attack."

It was the fifth convoy the *Spencer Lewis* had theoretically protected with her four-inch popguns and depth charges since the President of the United States, Franklin D. Roosevelt, met with the prime minister of England, Winston Churchill, at Placentia Bay in New-foundland on August 9, 1941, and issued a spate of Woodrow Wilson-ish rhetoric called the Atlantic Charter.

Less well known was a by-product of that meeting, Navy Opera-tion Order No. 7-41, issued by Admiral Ernest J. King, Commander-in-Chief, Atlantic Fleet, better known as Cinclant, on September 15, 1941. For a nation theoretically at peace, Order No. 7-41 had some very strange language in it. U.S. warships were told to "destroy hos-tile forces which threaten shipping of U.S. and Iceland flags." The order was soon verbally extended to protect ships flying any and all flags, including British, within the vast swath of the Atlantic the Pres-ident had designated as a U.S. "defense zone." The destroyers were ordered to attack "when potentially hostile vessels are within sight or sound of such shipping."

Every time Lieutenant Commander Jonathan Trumbull Talbot

thought of Order No. 7-41, he ground his back teeth until his jaw ached. In late September, an American destroyer, the USS *Greer*, had survived near misses from two torpedoes. The President had voiced public outrage and announced U.S. warships would now "shoot on sight" at any German submarine—as if this was a new idea and Order No. 7-41 did not exist. He also conveniently neglected to mention that the *Greer* had been tracking the U-boat for three hours and reporting its position to nearby British planes. In early October the USS *Kearny* had taken a torpedo in her engine room and limped home with eleven dead men in ballast. Two weeks later, the USS *Reuben James* had been broken in half by another torpedo, leaving 115 men dead in the freezing Atlantic. The President's wrath rose to heights matched only by the depths of his hypocrisy.

Lying to the American people was basic to Roosevelt's style, in Zeke Talbot's scathing opinion of his commander-in-chief. Talbot's grandfather had been one of the founders of the Republican party in Connecticut. His father had been a Congressman from the State of Steady Habits, then an ambassador and foreign policy architect under four Republican presidents. To some extent Talbot's animus toward Roosevelt was ancestral, part of his bloodline. But his antipathy had been exponentially increased by being forced to risk his ship and perhaps his life in obedience to the President's attempt to edge the country into a war against Germany without a mandate from the American people.

"I don't understand why Congress is letting him get away with it," Talbot growled to his executive officer, Lieutenant Charlie Cartwright, a stocky swarthy southerner whose Annapolis nickname was the Pirate. "In the latest poll eighty percent of the voters said they were against getting into this goddamn thing."

"Ah hell, Zeke, wouldn't you rather be out here maybe seein' some action than at some borin' dinner dance with your wife at the NOB?"

NOB was shorthand for the Norfolk Operating Base Officers' Club. Talbot ruefully admitted to himself that lately he would rather be almost anywhere than with the Lady of Shalt-Not, the secret name he had begun calling his wife. At home all he got were corrections of his political opinions and criticisms of his refusal to kiss the Democratic asses selected by her congressman father to win faster promotion in Franklin D. Roosevelt's navy.

"If I have to get my tail blown off, I want it to be for the country, not for some amateur strategist in the White House," Talbot said. "Roosevelt's got forty percent of the fleet in the Atlantic now. Meanwhile he's telling the Japanese to behave or else. Or else what? That's what they're saying in Tokyo, I guarantee you. We don't have enough ships out there to fight a decent battle with them. Roosevelt's doing exactly what Wilson did in the last war—talking tough without anything to back him up. A lot of guys around our age are going to get killed if things go wrong."

A southerner and thus presumably a Democrat, Cartwright said nothing in reply. Did he really prefer the North Atlantic in November to his wife's company? Estelle was one of those honey blondes who seemed to ooze sex. Maybe the Pirate too was discovering hot sheets were not enough to keep the home fires burning.

Or was Cartwright thinking that now he knew why the Annapolis class of 1928 had nicknamed Jonathan Trumbull Talbot Zeke, short for Ezekiel, the prophet who specialized in lamentations about the awful present and predictions of a dire future? Talbot occasionally admitted there was some basis for the nickname—but he stubbornly insisted it was the way ordinary mortals, in particular his wife, viewed a man who was determined to tell the truth about the world around him and damn the consequences.

"My brother was killed in the first war," Talbot said. "He died because the United States, the country that invented the airplane, did not have a single plane to send to Europe with her fliers. They had to train in French discards, flying coffins that killed more pilots than the Germans—"

A second later Talbot sensed the torpedo. There was no physical possibility that he or any of his lookouts could detect it in that foaming, running sea. But he felt that murderous mechanical thing racing toward the vitals of his ship. "Hard left rudder!" he roared to the helmsman.

Too late. The torpedo buried its gyroscopic nose in the vitals of the *Spencer Lewis* just aft of the first stack and exploded with a savage boom that flung Talbot and Cartwright flat on their backs.

"Jesus H. Christ!" Cartwright said.

As Talbot stumbled to his feet, he felt the deck tilt in a remorseless way that had nothing to do with the heaving ocean.

"Captain," the helmsman croaked. "The forward half of the ship's gone."

Talbot stared dazedly at the sea swirling beneath the superstructure at the base of the wheelhouse. For a moment he felt as if the amputation had happened to his own body. His legs seemed to vanish. He clutched an overhead stanchion and said: "Abandon ship."

Abandon ship? No, it was impossible. Abandon his first serious command? He discounted his captaincy of Minesweeper 222, which his wife, with her usual combination of wit and savage sarcasm, accurately called "Two-two-two-small." Talbot was flooded with memories of the pride he had felt when he stepped aboard the *Spencer Lewis* and saluted the flag on her aged fantail. A poor thing but mine own, he had told himself, gazing up at the four fragile stacks, knowing the rusty armor plate was too thin, the ancient power plant ridiculously weak.

Now he was losing the *Spencer Lewis*, losing his crew. A third of them were probably dead already in the flooded engine rooms and other belowdecks compartments. The catastrophe confirmed Talbot's basic intuition that the world was a meaningless place, with no trace whatsoever of a caring God.

"Come on, Zeke," Lieutenant Cartwright shouted, thrusting a life jacket at him. "This old girl is goin' goin' gone. No one expects you to go with her."

The wheelhouse was empty. The sea gushing into the torn hull of the after two-thirds of the *Spencer Lewis* was tilting her inexorably on her side. "Did you send an SOS? Fire rockets?" Talbot asked, following Cartwright out the after hatch.

"Yeah," Cartwright said. "Here goes one more." He raised the Very pistol in his hand and pulled the trigger. A geyser of yellow light rose into the leaden sky. Flipping the pistol into the sea, the Pirate pointed to one of the gray rescue rafts that had been lashed against the *Spencer Lewis*'s superstructure. The well-trained deck crew had cut them loose when they heard the order to abandon ship. "If I don't make it, Zeke, and you do, tell Estelle I loved the hell out of her right to the finish," he said.

Cartwright leaped into the wind-whipped ocean and began swimming toward the bouncing spinning raft. A dozen other crew members were thrashing in the same direction. Talbot wished them luck and worked his way along the tilted superstructure. The *Lewis* was all the way over on her port side now. On her beam ends, as they said in the days of fighting sail. He wanted to make damn sure he was the last man off his ship. Climbing up on the starboard side of the superstructure, he found an open hatch and shouted down the dark ladder. "Anybody need help down there? This is the Captain!"

Out of the shadows emerged the round pale face of an engine room sailor, a fireman named Klein. Kosher Klein, they called him. He was the only Jew aboard the *Spencer Lewis*. "I got a buddy down there. I've been carrying him. But he's too heavy to get up this ladder," Klein said.

A deep groan, obviously a death shudder, rose from the bowels of the *Spencer Lewis*. His heart pounding, Talbot descended the ladder with Klein and found a sailor stretched on the deck—or more exactly, the port bulkhead, which had become the deck. He was a machinist mate named Kelly, who had made numerous appearances at Captain's Mast on drunk and disorderly charges. "He got knocked out by the explosion," Klein said. "We just come out of our compartment. Goin' on watch."

Cursing, grunting, heaving, they got Kelly up the ladder to what passed for the outer deck. He was at least six feet, and a dead weight. Talbot did most of the lifting. At Annapolis, he had been the star of the wrestling team's 160-pound division. As they dragged the unconscious man onto the superstructure, he realized Kelly was not wearing a life jacket. "Where the hell is his jacket?" he roared.

"I thought I put it on him," Klein said dazedly. "It must have fallen off."

The fireman took off his jacket and tied it on the unconscious man. "He's the best friend I got on this ship, Captain," he said.

"Hang onto him and to me," Talbot said.

With Kelly between them, they climbed out on the tilted superstructure. Icy water lapped around their feet. A man could not live more than a half-hour in the North Atlantic in November. Talbot hoped the other destroyers in the convoy were racing toward them in response to their SOS and distress signals.

For another moment the Lieutenant Commander thought of that faker in the White House, telling the American people his biggest whopper of the 1940 presidential election campaign: "I promise you I will never send American boys to fight in a foreign wahr." He wondered what the great man would call the sinking of the *Spencer Lewis*.

With a lurch, Talbot led Klein and dragged Kelly into the racing foaming sea. Instantly he was blind, choking, gagging. Oil from the ship's ruptured fuel tanks lapped around and over them. Simultaneously, he felt as if he had ceased to exist from the neck down. The water's stunning cold demolished all sensation in his body.

"Oh God, oh God," Klein wailed.

"Forget the prayers!" Talbot roared. "We're going to make it. We'll find a raft."

Over the next swell spun a raft, making him an instant prophet in Klein's eyes. Unfortunately it was upside down and no amount of heaving by Talbot and Klein, encumbered by the unconscious Kelly, could right it.

An instant later, with the loudest death shudder yet, the rear two-thirds of the *Spencer Lewis* sank. "Get up on the raft," Talbot said. "The depth charges—"

Somehow he clambered aboard the raft's slippery bottom and dragged the oil-soaked fireman after him. Ten seconds later, a series of tremendous explosions sent water cascading skyward as the *Lewis*'s depth charges detonated. Kelly, trailing behind them in Klein's grip on the straps of his life jacket, awoke with an agonized cry. It was echoed by other screams of anguish around the swirling whirlpool created by the sinking ship. Bolts of deadly force from the exploding depth charges were rupturing men's kidneys and blood vessels. Blood drooled from Kelly's mouth. "What happened?" Klein screamed.

"He's dying. Take his life jacket," Talbot said.

"No!"

"That's an order, goddamn it!"

With immense difficulty they stripped the jacket from the semi-conscious Kelly and let him slip beneath the surface. Talbot furiously knotted the life preserver onto the sobbing Klein. "Lash one of those to your jacket," he said, pointing to the tangled trailing ropes around the edge of the raft.

Klein obeyed. A freezing cascade of water almost washed Talbot off the raft and he took his own advice, lashing himself to another rope. The rain squall increased in fury and the waves grew bigger. The raft proved amazingly buoyant, but there was no protection against the icy water or near-zero temperature. Talbot began to feel the blank drowsiness that preceded hypothermia—death by freezing. Klein was a whimpering huddle.

In the distance Talbot heard the whoop of a ship's siren. Searchlights probed the dark turbulent ocean. The other destroyers had arrived. He pounded Klein awake and they shouted and screamed. But the wind snatched their words away. Why the hell had he let Cartwright fire off that last Very rocket? He should have ordered him to keep it. Or give it to him. Had he screwed up?

There were so many ways to screw up in the U.S. Navy. From the day he went to Annapolis, against his father's advice, Talbot had been haunted by fear of failure. He had driven himself to near frenzies of effort to escape it. Now failure was all around him, viscous, sickening, burning his eyes, fouling his mouth, numbing his body with the presage of death. He had lost his ship, his crew. All he had managed to save was one miserable sailor.

The sirens, the flashing searchlights vanished. The Atlantic spun Talbot and Klein across its foaming blankness, confirming once more his intuition of an uncaring universe. They were like ants clinging to a random chip of wood on the sea's freezing immensity. Violent chills shook the Lieutenant Commander's body, followed by renewed drowsiness, the prelude to death. Curled into the fetal position, Klein babbled prayers to an absent God.

Talbot wished somehow he could send a farewell message to his son. He did not particularly care what his wife thought. They had quarreled so often lately, she would probably disagree with anything he said out of pure spite. What could he tell his son?

Vote Republican? They were only marginally better than the Democrats. Never trust a politician? As a politician's son he rejected that idea. There was no alternative to trusting them. Someone had to run the country and somehow extract from the prevailing mediocrity America's promise to the world. Suddenly Talbot remembered a boyhood moment—his mother, his father, his older brother and himself and a dozen other Americans around a piano on the Fourth of July in Berlin in 1912, singing "My Country 'Tis of Thee." He remembered the swelling pride he had felt in his young heart, pride he saw reflected on his brother's face and his father's face, at the soaring praise of America, land of the Pilgrim's pride, where freedom rang from every mountainside.

My Country 'Tis of Thee. Somehow that said it all. He had tried to love his country, to serve it in the proud tradition of earlier generations of Trumbulls and Talbots. He wanted his son to know how hard he had tried, in spite of the desolation of the Great Depression, which had destroyed faith in America for so many voters and exposed them to the wiles of a demagogue like Franklin D. Roosevelt. He wanted his son to feel proud of his father's devotion to their country, even if his death in an undeclared war was meaningless. He wanted him to transfer that pride to America, to somehow regain the fervent faith he had once felt in her destiny.

An instant later, Talbot brushed oil and salt water from his eyes and stared disbelievingly at the shape that loomed out of the murky dawn. Painted dark gray, the submarine slithered with preternatural silence through the surging Atlantic, its deck awash. In the center of the hull loomed a conning tower with a white head of a knight in armor painted on it. Although Talbot had seen many American submarines, the sudden appearance of this boat, the knowledge that it had just sunk the *Spencer Lewis*, gave it an aura of murderous evil beyond the imagination of his favorite author, that master of the sea's malevolence, Herman Melville.

Human figures moved at the top at the conning tower. "You on the raft," said one of them in accented English. "What ship are you from?"

"The USS *Spencer Lewis*," Talbot said.

"Throw him a line," the man said in German. He wore a white hat.

A line whipped across Talbot's body. He seized it and strong arms pulled the raft against the submarine. "We thought you were British," the white hat said. "That's what happens when you share your ships with the wrong people."

Talbot saw no need to comment on the white hat's sarcasm. For one thing, he agreed with him.

"What is your name and rank?"

Talbot told him.

"You were the captain?"

"Affirmative."

"We'll take you aboard. Who is the other man?"

"One of my engine room crew."

"We have no room for him. He'll have to take his chances."

"Either you take both of us—or neither of us."

There was a muttered exchange on the conning tower. The white hat spoke sharply in German. "I will take responsibility!" Bearded crewmen wearing gray-green oilskins and sou'westers clambered down the conning tower and reached out to Talbot. He ordered Klein to go first. Then he let them hoist him aboard. When he tried to stand up, his flesh seemed to be mostly pulp and his bones seemed made of lead. He would have toppled into the sea if one of the crewmen had not seized him and, with some help from two others, dragged him up the ladder to the submarine's bridge.

After another struggle, Talbot found himself inserted into the tiny hatch and lowered into the interior, where he collapsed on the deck. Klein soon appeared and collapsed beside him. Looming above them was a slim man in dripping oilskins. On his head was the visored white cap that distinguished him on the bridge. He had a tight smile on his blond-bearded angular face and a mocking superiority in his blue eyes.

"I'm Kapitanleutnant Ernst von Hoffmann. Welcome to U-Boat Five Five Five. We call her *Das Ritterboot*."

"Heil Hitler," Talbot snarled. The German may have just saved his life. He may call his submarine the knight's boat and see himself as a crusader. But he had also sunk Talbot's ship and killed most of his crew. He saw no reason to be nice to the son of a bitch.

"I hope when you get home, Commander, you'll teach that greeting to your children. It may come in handy in four or five years."

There was a rumble of uneasy laughter from the figures surrounding them. "Funny you should say that," Talbot replied, speaking German to make sure the rest of the crew understood him, "a few minutes ago, when I was expecting to freeze to death within the hour, I kept wanting to say something to my son that would help him in the future."

"What did you decide?" Kapitanleutnant von Hoffmann asked.

"My Country 'Tis of Thee. Sweet land of liberty."

For a moment Hoffmann's blue eyes clouded with something indefinable, perhaps anger, perhaps doubt. "We too have a slogan," he said. "One people, one fatherland, one leader."

Ein Volk, ein Vaterland, ein Führer. Somehow it sounded more declarative, more menacing, in German. Gazing into Hoffmann's determined face, Talbot was seized by an unnerving premonition. He and this man, who had just torpedoed not only his ship but possibly his naval career, were destined to become implacable personal enemies in the war that was now almost certain to erupt between their countries.

3

KNIGHT AT SEA

Goddamn it, Ernst, you've done it this time, thought Kapitanleutnant von Hoffmann as he watched his sailors lead the two slimy Americans aft to be washed and clothed. *You've sunk an American warship. A violation of nothing less than an order from the Führer. It was bad enough to have a wife who defends Jews and criticizes Hitler in the name of some crazy vision of Martin Luther's God. They may take your boat away from you.*

Hoffmann did not show a trace of this inner turmoil to those around him. He gestured at the oily mess on the conning tower deck and ordered it cleaned up. With quick vigorous motions he returned to the bridge to take charge of the Ritterboot. Cruising on the surface this close to Iceland required the strictest vigilance against lumbering British Sunderland patrol planes, "tired bees," as the men called them. These bees were loaded with depth charges. A U-boat that could not dive in thirty-five seconds became their prey.

His first officer, bearlike Oskar Kurz, was on the bridge, along with the usual three lookouts. "Are we going after that convoy, Herr Kaleu?" he said, using the shortened form of Hoffmann's rank.

"Of course. We've still got three torpedoes left."

"I'm glad you picked up those Americans," Kurz said. "In another hour they would have been dead."

"You think there's an ethical dimension to our work, Number One?"

"There are ethical moments, Herr Kaleu," Kurz said.

"Perhaps. But that was not one of them. If they had been British, I would have left them to die. The gesture was purely political. To show our apologetic side for sinking an American warship."

"Ah," said Kurz, with a hint of disappointment. A Bavarian, he was secretly devout. One night Hoffmann found him asleep in his bunk with a rosary twined around his thick hands. Hoffmann began calling him "Saint Oskar," which the crew had shortened to the Saint.

Lieutenant Wolfgang Griff, the official naval correspondent who was making his first submarine voyage with them, emerged from the hatch with a concerned expression on his narrow bony face. Like his idol, Propaganda Minister Joseph Goebbels, Griff was a small skeletally thin man, overcharged with nervous energy. Hoffmann had feared he would go to pieces in the confined world of a U-boat but he had handled himself well so far.

"Herr Kaleu," he said, "I have some very disturbing news. The enlisted American is named Klein. He's a Jew."

Calm, you must and shall remain calm, Hoffmann told himself. It was no different from being under attack by an enemy destroyer. Griff's father was high in the Gestapo. He was going to write a story for the official Nazi party newspaper, the *Volkischer Beobachter*, about his voyage aboard the Ritterboot. He could do great things for Kapitanleutnant von Hoffmann's reputation—and he could also ruin him.

"What do you expect me to do about that, Lieutenant?" Hoffmann said.

"I don't know," Griff said, with the unnerving mixture of obsequiousness and superiority that he frequently displayed toward the Ritterboot's commander. "If you wish to conceal it, Herr Kaleu, I assure you of my cooperation. I've come to admire you so deeply, I would hate to see you incur any official disapproval for an action which was, on the whole, humanitarian—and politically astute."

Calm, you will remain calm, Hoffmann insisted. The voice of the Lion, Admiral Karl Dönitz, Commander-in-Chief of the Ubootwaffe, spoke in his head. *A man must first command himself if he hopes to command other men.*

Could he trust Griff? Hoffmann asked himself. The answer was unequivocally no. If he bluntly told him he thought the Führer's campaign against the Jews was irrelevant to the business of winning the war, he might find himself denounced instead of glorified in the *Volkischer Beobachter*. "The man is a fact, Lieutenant Griff. We can't eliminate him from the record."

Griff chewed his protruding lower lip. "Both men are in poor physical condition, Herr Kaleu. They could easily die. There would be no need to mention them in your KBT."

Griff was talking about the U-555's war diary, the *Kriegstagebuch*. It was personally examined by Admiral Dönitz after every voyage, usually in the boat commander's presence. The thought of giving the man he most admired in this world a faked KBT stirred Hoffmann to fury.

"Who is going to kill them, Herr Griff? You? You'll do me this favor?"

Griff expanded his concave chest and stiffened his drooping jounalist's shoulders. "If you give me an order, Herr Kaleu, I'll do it with the greatest pleasure. I have a supply of cyanide capsules which I brought along for the use of myself and a few friends in the crew, in case we were trapped on the sea bottom. They could be administered quite casually—"

Calm. You must remain calm. Was Berthe right? Were these people infecting Germany with an evil that would undo the most righteous war a nation ever waged? A war against the betrayal of the two million dead of the first war at that infamous palace of Versailles? No. She saw everything through the glaze of her bizarre female mysticism. The Nazis were an epiphenomenon on the map of history, a minor turbulence in the onward march of the German volk. They could be dealt with by the cool, calm intellect, the resolute will.

"I will give you no such order, Lieutenant Griff. I disagree with your political tactics. In the submarine service, we live by those three great maxims of Admiral Dönitz, Attack! Strike! Sink! We've done nothing which we need to conceal in such an underhanded way. We met the Americans' ship on the open seas in fair combat and sank her because our tactics, our weapons, were superior. We should make that clear when we produce the Jew and his captain at a press conference in Berlin to placate American public opinion."

Griff's smile again combined that unnerving mixture of submission and superiority. "Only time will tell which of us is right, Herr Kaleu."

"Goddamn it, Griff! It was the decent thing to do, Jew or no Jew!" the Saint roared.

"Herr Kaleu! Tired Bees!" cried the forward lookout. Barely visible in the lowering clouds, the bulbous shapes of two Sunderlands headed toward them. They were less than a half mile away, traveling at 250 miles an hour. "Alarm!" Hoffmann shouted over the voice tube that connected the bridge to the rest of the boat.

Griff vanished down the hatch so quickly he might have evaporated. The three lookouts went next, then the Saint, wasting precious seconds as always as he stuffed his bulk through the minimal opening. Hoffmann went last, slamming the hatch and furiously whirling the hand wheel that made it watertight. Below him, bells were clanging and readiness reports poured into the tower.

"Flood!" Hoffmann said. "Crew to the bow!"

"All vents clear!" Chief Engineer Walter Kleist reported from the Zentrale, or control room, beneath the tower.

Feet thudded on metal as every man who was not on duty rushed to the bow to hasten the U-555's descent. The hydroplane operators had already set the forward plane hard down and the Chief Engineer and his team opened the emergency evacuation tanks. A terrific roar swirled through the boat as the air in the tanks escaped and the submarine tilted into the depths.

Hoffmann glanced at his watch as the last waves sloshed over the bridge and the U-555 vanished below the surface. Forty seconds had passed. "Not good enough," he said to the Saint.

Ten seconds later a series of thunderclaps rocked the U-555 as the Sunderlands' depth charges exploded nearby. They were close— but not critical. Kapitanleutnant von Hoffmann watched the dial on the depth manometer until it reached one hundred meters. Around them the sea remained silent. British pilots usually dropped their entire load on the first run, the charges set at shallow numbers in the hope of a quick kill. After five minutes, Hoffmann rose to thirteen meters and used his sky periscope to scan the heavens. The Sunderlands were gone.

He immediately ordered the U-555 back to the surface to continue their pursuit of the convoy. Below the surface, running on batteries, a submarine could only make six knots. Above, with its two powerful diesels, three times that speed. More than enough to catch even so-called "fast" convoys whose top speed was nine knots. They were soon beyond range of the Sunderlands' patrols and he let the Saint take command of the bridge.

In the Zentrale, Hoffmann found a pale exhausted-looking Talbot slumped in Walter Kleist's seat, sipping hot coffee, politely listening to a lecture from the Chief Engineer on the array of dials and switches confronting him. Kleist had outfitted Talbot with a blue workshirt and faded blue pants from his wardrobe. The Chief's courtesy and consideration, though it was in accord with naval tradition, irked Hoffmann.

"This fellow speaks better German than I do!" Kleist said.

"That doesn't mean you should tell him all the secrets of our boat, Chief," Hoffmann said.

"Ah! There are no secrets here. Just good engineering," Kleist said.

"Where did you learn our language so well, Commander?" Hoffmann asked.

"At the Franzosisches Gymnasium in Berlin," Talbot said.

"The FG!" Hoffmann said, unable to believe it. "One of my brothers went there. He graduated in 1905. I went to the Kreuze Allee. When were you there?"

"From 1907 to 1912."

"Did you play soccer?"

"Sure."

"We must have played each other. I was a forward. "

"I was a wing."

The conversation was unreal. He was talking to an enemy, a man from a country bent on destroying his fatherland, about some of the most precious memories of his life, the Germany that existed before the catastrophe of the first war. Hoffmann was almost relieved when his red-haired radioman, Ruhle, interrupted them. "Message from BDU, Herr Kaleu." BDU was short for *Befehlshaber der Unterseeboote* (Commander-in-Chief, U-Boats).

"You'll have to excuse me," Hoffmann said. "I must decode this."

Leaving Talbot in the Zentrale, he followed Ruhle down the passageway to the tiny radio station, directly opposite the cubicle that served as Hoffmann's office and quarters. On Ruhle's desk was the Schlussel M cipher machine—a metal case with a typewriter keyboard and above it a panel that replicated the keyboard's letters. When the keys were pressed, the alternative letters that glowed on the panel became the ciphered message. The best cryptanalysts in Germany had designed this wonder to make radio traffic with BDU impenetrable.

The message was the one Hoffmann had expected before he was drawn into that disconcerting conversation with Talbot. The deciphered version read: REPORT AMERICAN DESTROYER SUNK IN YOUR PATROL AREA. CONFIRM OR DENY IMMEDIATELY.

Pain gnawed in Hoffmann's belly. He could almost see the Lion pacing his headquarters, insisting that Kapitanleutnant von Hoffmann would never do anything as stupid as disobey a führer order. Hoffmann gulped a monosodium glutinate tablet to quiet the turmoil in his stomach and wrote out his answer for Ruhle to send on the Schlussel. DESTROYER USS SPENCER LEWIS DD107 SUNK AT 4:45 A.M. SIX HUNDRED MILES WEST OF ICELAND. PRESUMED BRITISH. RESCUED CAPTAIN AND ONE CREW MEMBER AS GESTURE OF COMPASSION.

"Excuse me, Herr Kaleu." Lieutenant Commander Talbot was standing in the passageway, looking with mild interest at the cipher machine. Hoffmann struggled to control his exasperation. Technically the American was not a prisoner of war. He could not be confined aboard the U-555—and there was no room to put him or his Jewish fireman anywhere in the first place.

He decided to make light of the intrusion. The American and British navies undoubtedly knew the existence of the Schlussel. They were probably expending thousands of man hours trying to crack it, just as the German Navy B-Dienst (radio intelligence men) were trying to crack the British code. "Are you interested in cryptanalysis, Commander?" he asked, handing the message to Ruhle and casually blocking Talbot's view of the Schlussel.

Talbot shook his head. "Even if you were, it would take you the rest of your life to solve the codes this thing creates," Hoffmann said.

"I'm looking for my fireman," Talbot said. "I hope he's okay."

"Why shouldn't he be?" Hoffmann bristled. Was Talbot implying that all Germans were Jewbaiters?

"He was in worse shape than I was," Talbot said.

"Coming through, Herr Kaleu." The Ritterboot's cook had a bowl of steaming soup on a tray.

"Who's that for?" Hoffmann asked.

"The American seaman, Herr Kaleu. He needs something hot in his stomach."

In another time and place, Hoffmann might have made a rueful remark about the solidarity of the enlisted ranks. While Talbot made do with Chief Kleist's lukewarm coffee in the Zentrale, the crew was ordering up a gourmet treat for their fellow proletarian. He and Talbot followed the cook along the narrow passageway to the bow compartment. In a lower bunk surrounded by a half-dozen torpedomen about his age lay Klein, propped on one elbow, speaking some kind of German dialect to his audience.

"Hello, Captain," he said to Talbot. "You're just in time to help me convince these guys. They think Jews own the USA and they can't figure out why I'm not an admiral and my father's not richer than Rockefeller."

"What language are you using?" Talbot said.

"Yiddish," he said. "It's mostly German. They get it pretty good. But they don't believe a word of what I'm saying."

The cook deposited the soup on a small table beside the bunk with a flourish worthy of a waiter at a good Berlin restaurant. "Eat up!" he said. "Tell us whether German Navy chow is better than American."

Klein swung his feet into the passageway and tasted the soup. "Fantastic! Where can I join up?" he said, giving Talbot a conspiratorial wink.

"Is it true what he says, Herr Kapitanleutnant?" one of the torpedomen asked Talbot. "The Jews are not in control of America?"

"Hardly," Talbot said. "My wife is half-Jewish. Her father's a congressman. He takes all his orders from a fellow named Kelly, an Irish-American. He runs Chicago the way the Führer runs Germany."

"Marlene Dietrich is his favorite actress," another torpedoman said, obviously regarding Klein as some sort of exotic species.

"She's mine too," Talbot said. "I've seen *The Blue Angel* six times."

"These guys say Herr Kaleu's wife is better looking than Dietrich," Klein said.

For a moment Hoffmann was irritated by the thought of his sex life being discussed in the torpedo room. But there was something to be said for having a beautiful wife. It impressed other men—especially other sailors.

"We will eat dinner at noon, Commander," Hoffmann said. "I hope you'll join me and my officers in what passes for our wardroom. The food won't be up to the style of the old Berlin restaurants like Kranzler's but the conversation will be lively."

They left Klein talking Yiddish to the torpedomen and went back to the Zentrale, where Hoffmann spoke to the Saint on the bridge and was reassured that all was well. He sent up hot coffee for him and the three-man watch and informed the cook that Talbot was joining the officers for dinner. Radioman Ruhle handed Hoffmann another message from BDU. IMPERATIVE YOU OBTAIN STATE-MENT OF APPRECIATION FROM RESCUED AMERICANS. IF POSSIBLE ADMISSION THEY WERE IN WAR ZONE.

The Chief Engineer and the Second Officer, a lean son of East Prussia named Werner, joined them for dinner, along with Lieutenant Griff, whom Hoffmann introduced as a war correspondent. As they waited for the food, Hoffmann drew Griff back into the Zentrale. "The man is far from hostile," he said. "I think we can obtain a statement from him that will put us in a favorable light. You could include it in a dispatch."

"Excellent," Griff said. "This may redound to both our credits, Herr Kaleu."

The cook produced a moderately decent dinner, boiled beef with horseradish sauce. Hoffmann drew a bottle of schnapps from beneath his bunk, jokingly telling Talbot that he was revealing another secret of the U-555. He claimed that the Chief Engineer would give a half year's pay to find out where he hid the stuff. Kleist grinned, good-naturedly acknowledging that between voyages his drinking was legendary.

"I can't drink this myself. I have a bad stomach," Hoffmann said. "I give everyone else a snort to celebrate a kill."

"Have you given many on this voyage?" Talbot asked.

"Quite a lot," Griff said. "We've only got three torpedoes left and we haven't wasted one yet. We've sunk an estimated two hundred and fifty thousand tons. Kapitanleutnant von Hoffmann is certain to find a Knight's Cross waiting for him when we get back."

Hoffmann felt a flush of pleasure at this praise, even if the tonnage estimate was grossly inflated. So far they had sunk ninety thousand tons. A hundred thousand was usually enough to win a Knight's Cross.

Hoffmann was not pouring the schnapps in a spirit of joie de vivre. Talbot looked more and more exhausted; his eyes drooped, his lips were a bloodless gray. Hoffmann hoped the liquor would hit him twice as hard as the rest of them and loosen his tongue. Talbot took a hefty swallow of the pale liquid. "American officers can't get a drink aboard their ships no matter how many tons we sink," Talbot said. "The U.S. Navy has been dry since 1914, when Woodrow Wilson appointed an idiotic Southern Baptist as Secretary of the Navy and he banned liquor from the wardrooms."

"Interesting, the problems the American Navy has with your politicians," Hoffmann said.

"We're still having them," Talbot said, gulping down more schnapps. It was not hard to imagine how good it felt coursing through his still half-frozen interior. "Now we've got a president who talks about 'my navy' and treats it like a personal possession. A lot of us don't think we have any business out here on the North Atlantic fighting you people to rescue the goddamn British empire again."

Hoffmann could hardly believe his ears. Second Officer Werner and Chief Engineer Kleist stared in astonishment. Griff looked as if he might have an orgasm on the spot.

"I'm happy to hear you hold no grudge against us for sinking your ship, Commander," Hoffmann said.

"Why should I? You didn't know you were shooting at Americans. You wouldn't have been shooting at us—if we had a president who obeyed our Constitution."

"You say this opinion of the war is widespread among Navy officers?" Griff said.

"Very widespread."

"Including those of flag rank?" Hoffmann asked.

"Of course. I could give you a half-dozen names. But I won't," Talbot said, with a nervous laugh. "I've probably talked too much already."

"Nonsense," Hoffmann said, refilling his glass. "We have a very positive attitude toward America in the German Navy. We've always felt the British lied you into the last war. We fear they'll do the same thing this time."

"Your problem is Hitler," Talbot said. "If you got rid of him, I guarantee you the possibility of war between us would vanish overnight. What do you fellows think of him?"

Hoffmann gazed unblinkingly at Griff. Calm, you will remain calm, he ordered himself. "He embodies the Führer principle, a form of government the German people find useful for the time being," he said. "He's displayed rare talent for rallying the nation from the despair and humiliation of Versailles. "

Hoffmann could almost hear the rage gurgling in Griff's throat at this tepid endorsement of Adolf Hitler. The stolid Werner was now gazing at his commander with astonishment. The Chief Engineer, who made no secret of his loathing of the Nazis when he was drunk, regarded Hoffmann with a mixture of fatherly pride and concern. A glow of triumph ignited Hoffmann's flesh. For a moment he could envision the pride on Berthe's face as he told her the story.

But would he tell her the rest of it? His cool reassurance to Griff, later, that his dismissal of Hitler was mere tactics, to keep the American talking freely. Hoffmann let Talbot's response smother this question. "If that message could somehow be communicated to the American people, it would change a great many things," he said.

"Perhaps you should also communicate the bitter suspicion of the German people, when you tell us to get rid of Hitler. You told us to get rid of the Kaiser in the last war. We trusted you and signed the armistice. Then your president, Wilson, collaborated with our enemies to inflict the treaty of Versailles on us."

"My father has often said that treaty was the most atrocious document ever signed by an American president," Talbot said. "He especially criticized the war guilt clause, blaming the whole thing on Germany."

The man was unbelievable. If they had not plucked him from the freezing Atlantic by sheer accident, Hoffmann would have been tempted to believe he was an agent provocateur, sent to seduce Germans into believing Americans were their friends. "Let us drink a serious toast to peace and understanding between two great peoples," he said.

They raised their glasses again for hearty swallows. Hoffmann poured another round, though he wished he could skip Kleist, who licked his lips in anticipation. A drunken chief engineer could mean disaster when they attacked the convoy tonight.

"Did you serve in the last war, Commander?" Hoffmann asked.

Talbot shook his head. "I was too young. Fifteen. My brother volunteered for the air service but he never saw action. He was killed learning to fly one of those French Nieuports—the worst plane ever designed by the mind of man."

Again, Hoffmann was assailed by an unwanted sense of identity with this man. "My brother—my oldest brother, Hans—died fighting the Americans in the Argonne. He was an infantry captain."

"Needless deaths," Talbot said. "They're the hardest to accept."

The cook served coffee and one of his specialties, *pannkuchen*, a pancake filled with honey. "Now I advise you to get some rest, Commander," Hoffmann said as they finished the meal. "You won't get much tonight. We hope to use those last three torpedoes."

"Where do I bunk? In a torpedo tube?" Talbot said. "This thing makes an American submarine look like a luxury liner."

The schnapps had him swaying in his seat now. His mouth sagged, his eyes were glazed. But Hoffmann was not inclined to excuse his implication that American submarines were superior. "You may use the First Officer's bunk," he snapped, glad to regain his fundamental hostility to this man and his double-talking country.

Griff followed Hoffmann back to the conning tower, where he alternated between flattery and political posturing. First he gleefully assured Herr Kaleu that they had gotten just what they needed from the loose-lipped American, then urged him to correct the statement he had made about the Führer as quickly as possible with the Chief Engineer and Second Officer. Hoffmann curtly assured him that he would take care of the matter—though he had no doubt they understood the game they were playing.

Griff began lecturing him on the preeminence of führer loyalty. Hoffmann was on the point of telling him to shut up when the Saint's excited voice came down the intercom from the bridge. "Herr Kaleu. Smoke on the horizon. It's probably our convoy."

"Reduce engines to half-speed. I want to catch up to them at dusk."

Hoffmann turned his back on Griff and his führer loyalty and pondered the chart of the Atlantic on the small table beside the periscope. It was divided into a series of numbered squares that enabled Admiral Dönitz to send his U-boats like chessmen against his floundering opponents. They were back to the only thing that mattered—winning the war.

4

DAYDREAMER

Anna Richman Talbot, known to her friends as Annie, began the day in her two-bedroom stucco house on a back street of Norfolk by prodding her eleven-year-old son Butch onto the schoolbus. That required repeated orders to get dressed and stop reading a book on binomial equations his father had given him for a birthday present. Sometimes a child with an IQ of 170 was more trying than a juvenile delinquent.

The great maternal task completed with the grinding of the schoolbus's gears, Annie settled down with the Washington *Post*. Her first item was a column opposite the editorial page, "Behind The Headlines," by Jack Richman. Her older brother's rugged good looks were displayed above a paean to the courage of the RAF pilots who were fighting the Germans for control of the skies over England. Annie agreed wholeheartedly with the sentiments; she seldom if ever disagreed with anything Jack wrote. Simultaneously she enjoyed the delicious speculation that Jack's pro-English passion was inspired by his latest inamorata, a svelte brunette named Daphne, who performed obscure duties at the British Embassy in Washington, perhaps including the seduction of influential columnists.

Effortlessly, Annie slipped into the Navy wife's favorite pastime— the daydream. She was working for Jack, one of his backup staff, coolly strolling into the State Department and the War Department to interview diplomats and generals and admirals. *Off the record, what do you think of the President's foreign policy?* Or lunching at the Mayflower Hotel with some tall rangy general's aide, leaning toward him across the white table. *How secure are the Philippines from Japanese attack?* Invariably, the victim blanches, amazed by the boldness of this small determined woman, with her black hair trimmed around her ears like a helmet. Perhaps intrigued by the possibility of something more exciting than newsbreaks in her sultry green eyes—he babbles the truth.

Later in the daydream, she sidled into a room deep in the Navy building and found Lieutenant Commander—or maybe Commander—Talbot hard at work on some top secret orders. She nibbled his ear before he knew she was there and inevitable reprimands cascaded from those no-nonsense lips.

Damn it, Annie, what the hell do you think you're doing?

All I want to know is why six battleships have transited the Panama Canal in the last six days?

Do you seriously expect me to compromise the security of the Atlantic fleet?

She shut the door and pirouetted into his lap. Inserting her tongue deep in his mouth, she whispered: *Yeth.* With a groan he told her everything. He could not resist the promise of that tongue traveling elsewhere around and down his hard-muscled body.

Tonight? he whispered.

Maybe, she replied.

What was wrong with a daydream of seducing information out of your own husband? Absolutely nothing—except the suggestion that there might be something desperately wrong with this marriage.

Braaaaang! The telephone jolted Annie back to reality. It was Estelle Cartwright, fellow celibate thanks to the endless cruise of the *Spencer Lewis*, asking Annie's opinion of how the officers' club should be decorated for the Christmas dance. The wife of the admiral in command of the base had delegated Estelle to round up ideas—while contending that the sixteen-inch candy canes and Santa Clauses in sailor suits they had used last year were in perfect condition and could be used again. Everyone below the age of fifty-five—Mrs. Admiral's age—thought they were corny, but no one had the nerve to say so. Annie exchanged badinage with Estelle about the idiocy of it all, which may have cheered them both up, although it was hard to tell.

This abrupt reminder that she was an unpaid adjunct of the U.S. Navy persuaded Annie to find the courage to call the local garage and find out how much the latest surgery on their disintegrating 1935 Chevrolet was going to cost. "'Bout two hunnert," the mechanic drawled, obliterating all hopes for a new dress this year.

Gloomily, she hauled out a bag of Butch's socks she had been vowing to darn for the past two weeks. Among his other deficiencies, the boy genius seldom cut his toenails. Sewing was Annie's most hated household chore. It made her feel like a candidate for the poorhouse—which was not too far from the truth, as she struggled to control the expensive tastes she had acquired in her youth and somehow live genteelly on Zeke's minuscule Navy salary.

Within minutes, the needle sat unthreaded in Annie's fingers and she was staring out at the street, brooding over her ongoing argument with her husband about the moral desuetude of the Democratic party and the deceitful foreign policy of Franklin D. Roosevelt. Once upon a happy time they had joked about such things. Now Zeke lashed out at her with a painfully personal animus. It had begun last year, when Roosevelt decided to seek a third term. Until that point, Zeke had alternated between grudging admirer and half-hearted critic of the thirty-second president. FDR had, after all, rescued the country from the worst depression in its history.

Roosevelt's decision to seek a third term, shattering the precedent laid down by Washington and Jefferson, had concentrated all the latent hostility in Zeke Talbot's Republican psyche. Almost as bad was the way FDR had won the nomination—by relying mostly on the support of left wing Democrats in the labor movement and the big city machine politicians. At the convention in Chicago, Boss Ed Kelly of the Windy City and Boss Frank Hague of Jersey City had packed the galleries and roared "We want Roosevelt" over hidden microphones until the dazed delegates surrendered. In Zeke's outraged opinion, it was mobocracy in action, the investiture of a potential dictator.

In an ideal world, Annie Talbot, summa cum laude graduate of Washington D.C.'s Trinity College, America's premier school for Catholic women, would probably have agreed with him. Her education had attuned her to the moral dimensions of politics and history. But in the real world of 1940, Annie Talbot also happened to be the daughter of Ulysses S. (Uncle Sam) Richman, for the past seventeen years the reigning congressman from Chicago's North Side and one of the pillars of Illinois's political establishment. So good old Boss Ed and Boss Frank had packed the house and more or less stolen the convention? That was how they had been doing things in Chicago for fifty or sixty years. A political machine might be a little bit harmful to some people—such as Republicans who tried to vote on election day and wound up in the hospital—but when you have grown up enjoying the delicious taste of the machine's power, it was awfully hard to criticize it.

What was wrong with Zeke Talbot anyway? Republicans had no sense of humor. That was Annie's original contention as she tried to control the explosive anger that was threatening to demolish her marriage. Staring into the gray November morning, Annie had to admit this long patented formula was not working very well. She knew why. In her far from humble opinion, she had uncanny insights into people's motivations, including her own.

America had been rich and getting richer in 1928, the year she and Zeke Talbot met. The stock market was soaring into the stratosphere, Zeke's father, Roger Sherman Talbot, had just returned from a series of successful ambassadorships in Europe to become undersecretary of state with a very good chance of rising to secretary of state, the third highest officer in the American government. Beyond that, who knew what the future might hold? Secretaries of state often became presidents. In the glow of his father's celebrity, Zeke Talbot could dismiss trivial details like Annie Richman belonging to the wrong political party and having a déclassé Irish-Jewish bloodline. He could concentrate on more important things, like the cleavage in the skintight blue tank suit she wore when they went swimming at Virginia Beach.

On January 19, 1930, the Archbishop of Washington granted a special dispensation to permit Jonathan Trumbull Talbot, with his ten generations of stubbornly unconverted Protestant blood, to marry Anna Fitzmorris Richman at the main altar of the Trinity College chapel. Normally such ceremonies were performed in obscure back rooms to underscore the Church's disapproval of mixed marriages. But Congressman Richman had barely needed to tug the prelate's sleeve, much less twist his arm, to get a waiver. It was a sign of the way the political wind was blowing. The stock market had crashed and America was sinking like a disabled battleship into the Sargasso Sea of the Great Depression.

For the Talbots, it was the worst imaginable news. Zeke's father's chances of becoming secretary of state in President Herbert Hoover's second term were evaporating along with most of the Talbots' money. In another two years, Franklin D. Roosevelt was president and Sam Richman was no longer an obscure congressman from Chicago's North Side. He was on his way to becoming a senior member of an overwhelming Democratic majority while Roger Sherman Talbot slunk back to his ancestral home in Connecticut with barely enough money to maintain a facade of affluence. The rest of the Republican party shrank into insignificance with him.

This was the primary wound that had been festering and oozing into their marriage for a long time. It was the real reason for Zeke's outrage when FDR, after solemnly promising to stay out of the war in Europe, abruptly reversed his course and ordered Destroyer Division 12 onto the North Atlantic with orders to sink German submarines on sight. She quailed before the memory of Zeke's farewell shout, after another argument had ruined their last night together. "I hope I don't have to get killed to prove I'm *right*."

With a sigh Annie threw aside the undarned socks and began reading the final pages of Mary Ritter Beard's *On Understanding Women*. She was hoping to persuade Zeke to read this book. Mary Beard was one of her heroines, something of an oddity because Annie did not agree with one word her husband, the famous historian, Charles A. Beard, had ever written. In fact, he had recently published a ferocious blast at FDR for trying to sneak the country into the war. Maybe she could work out a Chicago-style political deal and give Zeke a copy of Charles A.'s diatribe by way of bribing him into reading Mary.

Soon she was in another daydream. Zeke had resigned from the Navy around the time her brother Jack, his Annapolis roommate, had figured out that promotions would be slow and the pay would remain dismal for the foreseeable Depression-devastated future. Instead of going into journalism, Zeke had headed for academe. With a Ph.D. in history, he had crafted three or four vivid books on early America, using Talbot family papers and reams of other material that she, his devoted helpmate and researcher, had dug out of the National Archives and the bowels of the Library of Congress. The books were blazing refutations of Beard and Marx and their crude economic determinism—fierce affirmations of the importance of ideas and idealism in history.

Finally Annie was ready to write her book: *The Old and the New: America's Impact on Europe.* It would be a brilliant reversal of standard scholarship, which endlessly blah-blahed about Europe's influence on America. There was a cornucopia of material to demonstrate that it worked both ways. With immense generosity, and not a trace of patronizing, Jonathan Trumbull Talbot announced he would be *her* researcher. *She's forgotten more about European history than I'll ever know,* he said to a swarm of scribbling reporters as they boarded the *Queen Mary* for their foray to the archives of the Old World.

Stewards shouting "all ashore," then the long low moan of the foghorn as the great liner slipped past Sandy Hook into the Atlantic mist. In their stateroom on the first deck, Mr. and Mrs. Talbot were making delirious historical love . . .

Clack Clack Clack! Someone was practically breaking the knocker through the cheap pine planks of the front door. Was it Estelle Cartwright, coming to pick her up for the committee meeting? She had a car that actually ran, thanks to her rich ole Southern Daddy. Annie was still in sloppy slacks and one of Zeke's discarded shirts. She yanked the door open, apologies on her lips, to find Mrs. Admiral and Mr. Admiral, the commander of the Norfolk base. He was small and compact in navy blue, she was large and uncompact in funereal black. Both wore grave expressions.

"Has something happened to Zeke?" Annie said.

They told her something had happened to the *Spencer Lewis.* The Germans had sunk her with virtually all hands. Only forty-nine men had been rescued. Zeke was not one of them. "We have to presume he's gone, Mrs. Talbot," said the Admiral, whose name was Bunker.

"I suppose you'd like to see the Chaplain," Mrs. Admiral said. She had a sweet Southern manner, which beautifully disguised a will of iron.

Annie shook her head. She simply refused to believe it. How could that lean blazing-eyed Connecticut Yankee who had left this house two months ago in a raging fury at her and Franklin D. Roosevelt be dead? It was all a rather tasteless joke, in which Zeke had enlisted Admiral and Mrs. Bunker to teach his argumentative bitch of a Chicago wife a lesson. Any moment he was going to come grinning in the door and she would hurl herself into his arms, weeping, begging his forgiveness. She would be reduced to a total yes-woman for the rest of her life but that was all right. She told God she would never argue with Zeke again, she would never say a single word that was not immediately prefaced or followed by "yes, dear, you're right, dear."

But of course God was not listening. Annie had more or less eliminated God from the equation. It was part of her postwedding game plan to make herself totally adorable to her taciturn, moody husband. She forgot about the promise to raise Butch as a Catholic, forgot about having sex only on safe days, roughly four or perhaps five a month, in the Vatican-approved rhythm method of birth control. She bought a diaphragm and was available every time he looked in her direction. She stopped going to Mass and accepted, even applauded, Zeke's sullen accusatory attitude toward God for killing his brother in World War I. She went him one better and read Ernest Renan's *Life of Jesus* and other books that proved Christianity was utter nonsense, a compound of Greek myths and Jewish hysteria.

"He isn't really dead, is he?" she whined to Admiral Bunker.

"Oh my dear. Would you like to pray with me?" Mrs. Bunker said. "I lost a brother in the last war. I know what you're going through. You have to ask God for acceptance."

Never never never, Annie vowed. All she wanted to do was be alone and smash things. "Thank you very much," she said. "I'm going to call my father—"

"I've already called him. He and your mother are on their way from Washington," Admiral Bunker said. Congressman Richman was vice chairman of the House Military Affairs Committee, which made him well known to the Navy's higher ranks.

No, not her mother, Annie begged God or Admiral Bunker, someone, anyone, with the power to countermand the visit. Mother would transfix her with those unsmiling Irish eyes, telling her this was her punishment for practicing birth control and never going to Mass and raising her son as an atheist and failing to convert her husband to the one true faith even though she, Helen Fitzmorris, had spectacularly failed to convert *her* husband. But that was permissible because Sam Richman was more electable as a Jew on the North Side where everyone remembered his father, "Honest Abe" Reichman, the family's Moses, who had migrated from points east to Germany to New Orleans and finally to Chicago where he streamlined his name and made a modest fortune selling suits and lost it all on the Chicago Commodity Exchange in the Panic of 1893, dying two days later murmuring "Don't blame America."

"Your brother Jack's coming too," Mrs. Bunker said, the gleam in her crafty eyes suggesting she hoped Jack would write a column in which Admiral Bunker would be prominently quoted.

The Admiral's thick lips curled into something approximating a snarl. "They never had a chance. It's a hell of thing, sending men into a war zone in ships that are ready to fall apart. When a German torpedo hits one of those old destroyers—"

"The President must know that. He was assistant secretary of the Navy when those dreadful things were built," Mrs. Bunker said.

More Roosevelt haters. Were they waiting for her to make a full confession? Admit she had sent her husband out to die in the name of the great shibboleth of Chicago politics, you've got to go along to get along? "Get out of here," Annie screamed. "Get out of here before I go crazy!"

5

PERILS OF A PASSENGER

Groggy from his belts of schnapps, Jonathan Talbot dozed fitfully in First Officer Kurz's bunk; genuine sleep was impossible. Footsteps thudded, voices echoed in the passageway. The air was fetid with a hundred unpleasant odors. He was uneasily aware that the Ritterboot was on its way to another attack on Convoy HX170. He might soon be a reluctant witness to more deaths in the freezing Atlantic.

The clang of the diving alarm interrupted this meditation. Hoffmann's voice crackled over the loudspeaker. "All hands, battle stations!" As the Ritterboot slid into the depths, Talbot pulled on his shoes and strolled to the Zentrale, where Kapitanleutnant von Hoffmann stood before the massive main periscope. "What a view!" he said. "At least thirty of them, rocking like elephants. Too bad we've only got three torpedoes left."

"Can I take a look?" Talbot asked.

"Of course, Commander," the Kapitanleutnant said.

Talbot pressed his forehead against the rubber cushion of the eyepiece. Through the periscope's swiveling lens, he saw close up a half-dozen freighters, wallowing in a heavy sea. Beyond them in the twilit gloom were the bulky shadows of at least a dozen more. There was not a sign of a destroyer. The low thumping knock of the freighters' piston engines, the chirping of their turbines, the grinding of their propellers, resounded through the Ritterboot. It was dismaying that a submarine could get this close without detection.

"Are you going to attack?"

Hoffmann shook his head. "We'll wait until dark and attack on the surface. Would you like to join me on the bridge?"

"Why can't you pick them off from here?"

"We could only get one. The rest would scatter and the escorts would be after us. On the surface at night, we can get close enough to make every torpedo count and get away before the escorts know what's happening."

A new sound. The grinding of a much faster propeller. Talbot spun the periscope and saw a destroyer lunging wolfishly through the cresting swells, coming straight at them. He was able to read the big white number on her bow: 413. "USS *Wilson Smith*, bearing three two zero, distance one thousand yards," he said.

"Goddamn it!" Hoffmann all but shoved him out of the way and seized control of the periscope. "Rudder full left, new course, due south," he shouted. "Dive, Chief. Bring her down fast. Prepare for depth charges!"

With a shudder, the Ritterboot dove for the ocean floor. Talbot clung to a nearby handgrip to keep from being thrown on his face. He was again in imminent danger of a watery death. Nevertheless he enjoyed the anxiety on Kapitanleutnant von Hoffmann's face as the *Wilson Smith's* propellers grew to an ominous roar.

"Level off at 170!" Hoffmann called to Chief Kleist.

Within sixty seconds, they were cruising horizontally, the soft purr of the electric motors the only sound in the boat. Then came the *ping* of the *Wilson Smith's* sonar as the soundwaves struck the submarine's hull. *Ping, ping, ping.* If the sonarman was listening closely, the next sound they heard might be the crash of depth charges.

Who was he rooting for? Talbot wondered. Under the circumstances, it was definitely not the *Wilson Smith*, even though a classmate, Harry Mullhouse, was the captain.

Ping. Ping. Piiiing. The potentially fatal noise tailed off, along with the thrashing of the destroyer's propellers. Sonar detection was a notoriously unreliable science. It depended on the alertness and judgment of the sonarman, who might have his mind on his last fling with his girlfriend or what he ate or did not eat for lunch. Or he may have recently gotten his ass chewed by his chief petty officer for being too quick to report every echo he picked up from passing whales and the uncertain terrain of the sea bottom. The advantage was unquestionably with the submarine.

Hoffmann ordered Chief Kleist to bring them up to periscope depth. With a curse, the Kapitanleutnant reported the convoy had zigzagged and was now far to the south. "We'll surface as soon as it's dark," Hoffmann growled. He repeated his invitation to join him on the bridge for the attack. Talbot coolly accepted, though he was aware that Hoffmann was almost too eager to show him just how good the Ritterboot—and by extension the entire Ubootwaffe—was at their business. He might learn something that would be useful when and if he found himself commanding another destroyer in Roosevelt's undeclared war.

Hoffmann put on dark sunglasses and gave Talbot a pair. "To build up your night vision," he explained.

For a half-hour they chatted casually about the war, which Hoffmann was supremely confident Germany would soon win. With the French defeated and the Russians close to collapse, the Wehrmacht was supreme in Europe. The Navy was going to starve the English to their knees by sinking ships at an unparalleled pace. By the end of next year the Ubootwaffe would triple in size. They had developed new tactics—as many as a dozen submarines would soon be attacking a convoy simultaneously.

Abruptly, Hoffmann turned to the periscope to check conditions on the surface. Satisfied that darkness had fallen, he called: "Stand by to surface. E motors full ahead. Blow out main ballast tanks by diesel!"

The Ritterboot soon broached in the heaving sea. Clad in borrowed oilskins, Talbot climbed to the bridge with Hoffmann and the attack crew, which included First Officer Kurz, Second Officer Werner, and two petty officers. Talbot arrived just in time to get several dozen gallons of freezing salt water in the face.

"Both engines ahead full," Hoffmann barked over the speaker-tube to the Zentrale. They pounded south through the black foaming ocean. There was no moon and only a scattering of stars through scudding clouds. Again and again waves broke over the tower, sending icy water sluicing under Talbot's foul weather gear while the freezing wind congealed his flesh. Hoffmann ordered Talbot and the others to buckle themselves into safety harnesses while he peered into the darkness. Suddenly he whacked Talbot on the shoulder and shouted: "There they are!"

To port and starboard, the shadowy shapes of a half-dozen merchant ships loomed around them, less than 500 yards away. They had burst into the convoy from the rear, undetected. The wolf was in the center of the flock.

"Engines ahead one-third!" Hoffmann said. "Use one torpedo to a target, Number Two. Take the farthest and fattest first. The nearest last."

The Second Officer peered through a range finder mounted on the conning tower rail and began feeding data below: "Angle right seventy, distance five hundred, speed eleven knots—"

A gasp from one of the petty officers. "Destroyer bearing three forty, angle zero!"

To port, less than a thousand yards away, the blurry whitish gray shape of a destroyer was racing toward them. "The hell with him," Hoffmann said. "He won't spot us in this sea."

Talbot watched the destroyer close the gap. With the Ritterboot's decks awash, and nothing but her gray conning tower above the surface, she was close to invisible on the dark ocean. "Whether he sees you or not, if he rams you the results will be unpleasant," Talbot shouted into the wind.

"We'll take the chance, Commander," Hoffmann shouted back.

Second Officer Werner began repeating his data to the fire control computer operators in the Zentrale. "Let them have it, Number Two!" Hoffmann said.

"Tube one—ready—launch!" Werner said. "Tube two—ready—launch!" Turning to port he gave the same command to tube four, aimed at the nearest ship.

They waited in the howling wind and spray for at least sixty seconds. "Destroyer approaching attack position," the terrified petty officer said.

"Close tube doors. Three times full ahead," Hoffmann roared down the speakertube. "Hard right rudder!"

An instant later, three tremendous explosions sent geysers of flame hurtling toward the black sky. The night was filled with the hollow boom of collapsing bulkheads and the shriek of toppling masts. A new series of explosions aboard the nearest ship sent a cascade of molten steel into the air. Above it soared a rainbow of distress rockets. "How do you like that, Commander?" Hoffmann bellowed.

Talbot was not sure he liked it but he could not deny the excitement beating in his body. Flames from the burning ships flickered eerily on their faces. He felt weirdly exultant—and simultaneously ashamed of the emotion. A lot of British and Canadian sailors were dying out there in those flaming explosions. But the effrontery, the cool knowhow of Hoffmann's attack was paramount. In a strange way, he had almost become part of the Ritterboot's crew.

Would the destroyer see them now? The sharp turn to starboard had swung them out of her path. The black night, the submarine's low silhouette, still favored the wolf over the shepherd.

Down from the starless sky drifted at least a dozen parachute flares, illuminating the sea around them with the blazing clarity of a tropic noon. The destroyer let out a series of action station whoops and veered to attack them. Hoffmann watched impassively, hoping they could outrun her in the heavy sea. But this destroyer was not a World War I relic that could barely match the submarine's eighteen knots in such weather. It was one of the new 1,640 tonners launched in 1940. They were capable of twenty-six knots in a full gale.

"Hard right rudder," Hoffmann shouted, as the last of the parachute flares sizzled into the water. But the destroyer—it was DD413, the *Wilson Smith* again—promptly fired a cluster of star shells that returned everything to high noon. The distance rapidly closed. Flames spurted from the destroyer's forward five-inch gun mount. Shells whined over the conning tower to explode a hundred yards ahead of them.

"Get below, we're going deep," Hoffmann yelled. Talbot plunged down the ladder to the inner tower, Kurz, Werner and the petty officers crashing after him, stepping on his half-frozen hands. The diving alarm was shrieking as they landed on the deck, closely followed by Hoffmann. "Down into the cellar fast!" he shouted to Chief Kleist in the Zentrale. "Crew to the bow!"

The Chief ordered the diving planes shoved to their sharpest angle. The Ritterboot slanted into the depths while the crew stampeded forward to accelerate the process. Talbot followed Hoffmann and the others down to the Zentrale as the grinding of the destroyer's propellers reached a crescendo above them. A terrific explosion lifted the bow of the submarine and shook her like a bone in the mouth of an angry mastiff. The blast flattened everyone in the Zentrale and knocked out the lights. Talbot lay there in the darkness, thinking: *what a lousy way to die.*

He was amazed when he heard Chief Kleist say in a perfectly ordinary voice: "Emergency lighting. Blow tanks three and five. Both planes up."

In a moment they emerged from their dive. Feeble lights illuminated the Zentrale. The Chief, his diving plane operators and other technicians were still sitting calmly before their dials and gauges. "Rig for silent running," Hoffmann said. "Port motor seventy revolutions, starboard sixty."

That arrangement would angle them away from the site of their dive. Once more, Talbot was forced to admire the coolness of the Kapitanleutnant and his crew. But the men on the surface were equally cool about the business of destruction. The *ping ping ping* of the sonar probed the depths for their exact location. Down came another spread of depth charges to shake the Ritterboot with violent fury.

Ping ping ping went the deadly fingers. The *Wilson Smith*'s propellers threshed to a coruscating howl, the engines hammered. Instinctively, the Ritterboot's crew stared up at their invisible adversary. Three deafening explosions tore the depths off their stern to starboard.

"Maybe we should send up Seaman Klein with a message," one of the diving plane operators said. "He'd tell them what wonderful fellows we are."

"Where is he?" Talbot asked.

"In the after torpedo room, saying his prayers like the rest of us."

"No talking," Kapitanleutnant von Hoffmann said. "The sonar can pick up the slightest sound."

Ping ping ping. Hoffmann ordered another change of course. But the sonar pursued them. A spread of at least sixteen depth charges exploded above the conning tower. Gauges spewed broken glass onto the deckplates. The submarine groaned like a wounded beast. The emergency lighting flickered and went out. Through the darkness drifted the odor of leaking oil.

Reports flowed into the Zentrale.

"Water in forward torpedo compartment."

"Starboard motor out of order."

"Rudder jammed."

"Take her down as far as you can go, Chief," Hoffmann said.

The Ritterboot slanted into the depths again as more charges boomed above them. Talbot watched the needle move from the green part of the diving gauge to the red zone. Kleist stopped at 250 meters—over 750 feet. "What's the design limit of this class sub?" he asked the Chief.

"Two twenty-five," Kleist said. "But we've gone to three hundred more than once."

"No talking, even at this depth!" Hoffmann hissed.

The emergency lighting flickered on again. The second officer reported the rudder had been repaired, the leak in the torpedo compartment contained. Hoffmann ordered another change of course. Outside the Ritterboot, water pressure of four hundred pounds per square inch held them in a King-Kong grip, relentlessly attempting to rupture seams, crack the steel hull. More depth charges boomed above them but they barely shook the boat. No one in the American or British navies knew a submarine could operate at 225 meters. Aboard the *Spencer Lewis* 150 meters had been the maximum setting on their depth charges.

A tremendous roar rushed through the submarine. It sounded as if a runaway locomotive were coming at them. "Inboard air induction valve has ruptured!" shouted a voice from the passageway. The submarine lost trim and began sinking by the stern.

"Are you ready to work one of your miracles, Chief?" Hoffmann said.

"We'll fix it, Herr Kaleu," Kleist said and lunged out of the Zentrale toward the stern. Talbot followed him, concerned for Klein's safety. In the engine room, he was amazed to find the Fireman up to his waist in surging water, handing tools to three petty officers who were taking turns diving under the oily surface to struggle with the spurting pipe. "The head valve is jammed," Klein said to Talbot. "We'll have it replaced in a few minutes."

As a deck officer, Talbot's knowledge of the mysteries of the engine room was close to zero. He watched as the Chief Engineer joined the petty officers in the underwater contest. "These guys are great machinists," Klein said, continuing to hand them various wrenches on demand. "Old Kelly used to say he could fix anything in an engine room with a screwdriver and two wrenches. I think these guys could do it with one wrench."

In five minutes the Germans had replaced the valve and began pumping the water into the Ritterboot's bilge tanks. Talbot followed the dripping Kleist back to the Zentrale. "That Jewish kid knows his way around an engine room," the Chief said. "I'm glad that Nazi swine Griff didn't poison him."

"What the hell are you talking about?" Talbot said.

"Forget I said that, Commander," Kleist said.

Back in the Zentrale, Kleist reported the emergency over and quickly shifted water from stern to bow tanks to bring the submarine back into trim. A hundred meters above them, depth charges continued to rumble. Talbot noticed the way Hoffmann thanked Kleist for his fast repair job. Although the Kapitanleutnant was clearly in command, he had a son's respect in his voice when he spoke to the balding sardonic Chief Engineer.

For another hour they sprawled on the deckplates in the dim emergency lighting with the air growing more and more foul, while the sonar pinged and the depth charges boomed above them. Suddenly a much larger boom penetrated their underwater coffin, followed swiftly by a second one of the same dimensions. "Those are torpedoes!" Kleist said.

"Another U-boat's attacking the convoy," Hoffmann said. "I sent BDU a signal when we sighted them."

The *Wilson Smith*'s depth charges and sonar abruptly ceased. Her propellers dwindled as she charged away to hunt this new killer. Hoffmann waited another half hour and ordered Kleist to bring the Ritterboot to periscope depth. He found an empty ocean and quickly surfaced. Wintry air poured through the submarine's fetid compartments. Talbot joined the Kapitanleutnant on the bridge to survey the dark Atlantic.

"Homeward bound?"

"It depends on what Kleist tells us about our damage."

The Chief appeared with a glum look on his face. "It's much worse than I thought, Herr Kaleu," he said. "The starboard E motor is knocked off its foundations. The after ballast tank is ruptured, and the starboard propeller shaft is badly bent. I recommend stopping at the Canaries for emergency repairs. I wouldn't want to get caught in the Bay of Biscay with the boat in this condition."

Hoffmann nodded. "Tell the navigator to set a course immediately."

As Kleist went below, Talbot could not repress a question. "Don't the Canary Islands belong to Spain?"

Hoffmann smiled condescendingly at his naïveté. "Surely you know the part Germany played in defeating the Russians in the Spanish Civil War. My brother Berthold commanded a tank brigade in the final attack on Madrid in 1939. Without our help, General Franco would be a fugitive today."

As a man who had spent a lot of time studying charts of the Atlantic, Talbot knew that the seven Canary Islands were about 700 miles south of Gibraltar, and about a 100 miles off the coast of Spanish Morocco. For the next three days, the Ritterboot limped southeast on the surface. In daylight, she looked in need of a complete overhaul. Her protective red undercoat showed in streaks through the splintered gray surface paint. Rust had formed everywhere, even around the barrel of the heavily greased 8.8 millimeter gun on the foredeck. There was a sheen of light green algae on the wooden deck that covered the steel hull.

The weather grew increasingly kind as they left the bitter winds of the North Atlantic behind them. Talbot spent a lot of his time on the bridge with Hoffmann or his first and second officers in the rotating watch. More than once he was tempted to ask them to explain Kleist's remark about poisoning Klein but he did not want to embarrass the Chief Engineer. Instead they discussed neutral topics—sports, schools, women.

When Lieutenant Griff joined them, they often got a monologue about the glories of National Socialism, to which everyone listened, Talbot thought, with almost visible impatience. Griff also quizzed him about his opinion of the Ritterboot and her crew. Talbot said he admired the ferocity with which Kapitanleutnant von Hoffmann attacked his targets and the skill with which he evaded pursuit.

On the morning of the fourth day, the green hills of Grand Canary Island appeared on the horizon. In the distance loomed towering cloud-shrouded El Tiede, the ten-thousand-foot-high mountain on the island of Tenerife. Talbot was on the bridge with Hoffmann as they passed the harbor of Las Palmas, Grand Canary's chief port. Over their heads skimmed a four-motored white seaplane to make a perfect landing on the placid sunny water. "Pan American!" Talbot said. "You don't have to lug me and Klein all the way back to Germany, Herr Kapitanleutnant. We can get home from here."

Discomfiture, even dislike, distorted Hoffmann's handsome face. "I'll have to consult with Berlin before I can agree to that proposal,

Commander. In a certain sense, you're a prisoner of war."

"In an equally certain sense, I'm nothing of the sort. Unless you want to start a war between Germany and the United States on your own. I thought we agreed this was the last thing either of us wanted, from a personal point of view."

"We're already fighting a war! The difference is, you're doing it in the most cowardly possible way, pretending to be neutral while you depth charge us at sea and ship your weapons to our enemies."

The words burst out of Hoffmann with a savage venom that left Talbot momentarily dismayed. His premonition was coming true. Here was a man whom, in almost any other time and place, he would gladly call a friend. Instead, Roosevelt's secret war had turned them into enemies.

"There's some truth in what you say," Talbot said. "But it doesn't change my determination to get off this submarine here—in the Canary Islands. I formally request your permission to go ashore and consult with the American consul on my status. For one thing I'd like to let my wife and son know I'm still alive. There's a very good chance I've been reported missing and presumed dead. Klein's family has probably been told the same thing."

"That message can be arranged," Hoffmann said. "But I refuse to allow you off this boat until I discuss the matter with Berlin."

A dozen miles down the coast from Las Palmas, the Ritterboot nosed into a much smaller harbor. Along the shore were the thatched roofs of a fishing village. Tied up to a pier inside the palm-tree-lined curve of the harbor's mouth, invisible from the sea, was a weather-beaten brown tanker. Another submarine was lashed to her outboard side. Workmen swarmed over the U-boat, using power tools connected to a tangle of lines snaking from the tanker's deck. The sound of riveting guns, the whine of metal cutters echoed from the hull.

"Goddamn it," Hoffmann said half humorously. "That's Popke in the Five Five Eight. Didn't he know I had a reservation?"

Talbot sensed an advantage. "Surely you're not going to keep me here as a prisoner for a couple of weeks while you both undergo surgery. Be reasonable, Herr Kapitanleutnant."

Hoffmann said nothing. Talbot wondered if there was more involved in his status than Berlin's approval—something to do with Griff and poison.

They tied up outboard of the 558 amid cheerful waves and calls from both the U-boat and the tanker. Hoffmann and Kleist went over to the tanker to discuss their troubles with the experts. Returning, Hoffmann adjourned to his cubicle, where he prepared a lengthy message for the radioman to encode and send to Berlin. At lunch, the Kapitanleutnant glumly informed his officers that 558's repairs would take at least a week, which meant the Ritterboot would not leave for home for two full weeks.

"I've radioed Berlin, asking permission for some shore leave. I've heard Las Palmas is a very civilized little city," he said.

"Spanish women can be charming," Griff said, with a hungry leer. "When we occupy Spain—a decision which may come at any moment—I hope to spend a lot of time there."

"My brother Berthold enjoyed himself in Madrid," Hoffmann said. "The women were grateful for their liberation from the Russians. They told wonderful stories of their Mongolian stupidity and barbarism."

"The Spanish are a moderately superior race, considering their Mediterranean gene pool," Griff said. "They got rid of their Jews a long time ago."

Again, Talbot saw a flicker of repugnance on several faces, particularly Kleist's, as Griff portentously explained why the Nordic race was superior to the southern races. The radioman interrupted the monologue. "Message from BDU, Herr Kaleu," he said, handing a piece of yellow paper to Hoffmann.

"Here's good news for you, Commander," he said to Talbot. "Berlin has accepted my recommendation. You and Fireman Klein will be turned over to Spanish authorities in Las Palmas and will undoubtedly soon be on your way home. I hope, as a man of honor, who has declared his personal desire for genuine neutrality in this war, you won't reveal the presence of the repair ship here."

"Of course I won't," Talbot said, carried away by a rush of gratitude.

"A Spanish official will pick you up in about an hour," Hoffmann said.

"This calls for another round of schnapps, Herr Kaleu," Kleist said.

"Why not?" Hoffmann said. "There's not much left. We might as well kill it."

On their way to the Canaries, he had distributed a round of

schnapps for the crew at dinner to celebrate their triple kill against Convoy HX170. He poured the officers and Talbot the last of the final bottle.

"To homecoming," Kleist said.

"To peace," Hoffmann said. Instead of looking at Talbot, his eyes seemed to seek Griff's face.

The Nazi's smile made Talbot uneasy. It was closer to a sneer. "I hope your confidence in Commander Talbot's honor is not misplaced, Herr Kaleu," he said.

"You have nothing to worry about, Lieutenant!" Talbot said. "When an American makes a promise he keeps it." He was tempted to add: "Unlike Herr Hitler." But he saw no point in stirring acrimony when Kleist and Hoffmann were trying to end their voyage on a friendly note.

Exactly an hour later, a messenger from the tanker announced the Spanish official's arrival. Talbot shook hands with Kleist and Hoffmann and led a very happy Fireman Klein across the deck of U-boat 558 and the tanker to the dock. The Spaniard was an army major in a wrinkled tan uniform. He welcomed them to Spain with grave courtesy and drove them to a white-walled house in the hills behind Las Palmas without saying another word. Talbot's attempts to converse with him in his rusty Spanish won only monosyllables in reply.

A tall beaknosed American of indeterminate middle age was waiting at the gate of the house's courtyard. "Talbot?" he said in a Maine accent. "I'm Shaw Snyder, the consul here."

They shook hands and Talbot introduced Klein. Snyder thanked the major in Spanish and signed some sort of document. He led them across the courtyard to a study with the drapes drawn against the tropic sun. "I thought it was best to meet you here, Commander, rather than at the consulate. I've gotten orders to sequester you from any and all visitors."

"Why?" Talbot asked.

Shaw shrugged. "This arrived about three hours ago." He handed Talbot a cablegram.

COMMANDER TALBOT IS TO BE HELD INCOMMUNICADO
UNDER STRICT ORDERS NOT TO SPEAK TO ANY REPORTER

OR OFFICIAL OF THE SPANISH GOVERNMENT WITHOUT A
MEMBER OF THE AMERICAN CONSULAR STAFF IN ATTEN-
DANCE.

ERNEST J. KING

COMMANDER-IN-CHIEF, ATLANTIC FLEET

"I don't know what's going on, Commander," Shaw Snyder said.
"But I've been in this business long enough to suspect you're in deep
shit."

6

IN A DARK WOOD

"Frau von Hoffmann? I wonder if I could see you today. It's urgent."

It was Pastor Bruchmuller. For the past five days, Berthe had been bracing herself for a call of some sort—but not from him. On the third anniversary of Kristallnacht, she and forty-two other members of Bruchmuller's congregation had signed a statement, calling on the government of the Reich to repent for Germany's persecution of the Jews.

Each of them knew they might be arrested. Not all of them—that was not the style of the *Geheime Staats Polizei*, better known as the Gestapo. But a half-dozen of them might be designated the ringleaders of this nefarious plot to embarrass the Führer and his followers. Her mother-in-law had been stalking her like a tigress all week, trying to find out what Bruchmuller had done with the petition. Fortunately, Berthe had no idea.

"Is it about the protest to the government, Herr Bruchmuller?" she asked.

"Yes and no. The Gestapo is now following me everywhere. Are you being followed?"

"I don't think so."

"Good. I'll manage to lose my pair of bloodhounds in the subway and meet you in front of the Siegessäule at two o'clock. Dress warmly. We may have to remain out of doors for several hours."

As usual, with gasoline severely rationed, Berthe walked to the Wannsee terminus for the trip to the center of Berlin. As she boarded the green, scrupulously clean Schnellbahn cars, she heard a man's voice jovially calling her name.

Smiling up at her from a seat beside the door was Lothar Engle. Typically, he did not get up to greet her. With a swoop of his long muscular arm, he seized her by the wrist and drew her down beside him. She gazed into the familiar face, dominated by a nose that was almost a falcon's beak, and saw the usual mockery in his gray eyes, the same cynicism on his wide smiling mouth. Once she had allowed that mouth to kiss her everywhere. Was there a part of her body, her soul, that clever tongue had not explored?

Lothar Engle belonged to the night world of Berlin's Kurfursten-damn, where Berthe von Schonberg had once prowled, determined to amuse and be amused. There seemed to be no other purpose in life.

Lothar's father had been a professor of history at the University of Berlin. The Engles came from a long line of professors, stretching back to the eighteenth century. But Lothar's year on the Western front in 1918 had convinced him that the world had changed forever. He became a newspaperman, one of the most savage, slashing columnists in Germany, feared and propitiated by politicians of all parties.

Lothar was wearing the black uniform and shroud-like cloak of an oberführer (colonel) in the *Schutzstaffel*—the elite corps of the Nazi party, usually called the SS. Above the visor of his cap gleamed the *Totenkopf*—death's head—which was their best-known trade-mark. Above that, just below the brim, the German eagle sur-mounted a swastika. After laughing at Hitler as an Austrian buffoon, Lothar had discovered amazing virtues in the Führer when he became Reich chancellor. By the time the war began, Lothar was an intimate advisor to Hitler's Minister of Information, Joseph Goebbels.

"Why is an oberführer using public transportation?" Berthe said, while Lothar held both her wrists, forcing her to face him.

"It's a purely honorary title," Lothar said. "Goebbels has given me the job of improving the SS's image. It's like trying to make a matinee idol out of Frankenstein's monster. To demonstrate his hostility, Herr

Himmler has refused to give me a car. How are you, my beautiful one? Is married life still agreeing with you?"

"Absolutely," Berthe said, forcing defiance into her voice.

"You enjoy the company of your esteemed mother-in-law?"

"Immensely," Berthe said.

Lothar made a clownishly skeptical face. "Even my mother, who could reduce an entire dinner table to insensibility with the recitation of her recipe for sauerbraten, considered her boring. You're convincing me that marriage can truly transform the character. Do you sit around with Frau von Hoffmann reciting 'The Song of the Bell'?"

This famous poem by Schiller was an endless paean to *die zuchtige Hausfrau* (the disciplined housewife). It was cordially hated by every German woman who sought a modicum of education and independence. It portrayed the ideal housewife teaching her daughters, controlling her sons, spinning and weaving and filling drawers with shimmering woolens and snowy linens—and never resting.

"It's a perfect portrait of me," Berthe said. "I never rest. Not even at night. I sleep with one eye open."

"I sleep the same way," Lothar said. "My open eye is fixed on a certain painting which I keep in my room, the way the devout hang portraits of Jesus or the Virgin."

Berthe knew exactly what he was talking about. It was a painting for which she had posed in one of her wilder moments in 1930. The painter, a witty Bohemian named Richard Ziegler, had approached her in the Romanisches Cafe one night to reveal that she haunted his dreams. With Lothar's help he persuaded her to come to his studio and pose until dawn. The result was "The Young Widow."

Ziegler stood Berthe before a half-length mirror, naked except for a garter belt, and painted her in the glaring colors and violent lines of German expressionism. Her skin was as white as housepaint, her hair as yellow as sulphur. Her hands were cupped beneath her breasts, shoving them together, her buttocks were lifted, tight and round as beachballs. Her mound gleamed in the shadowy bottom of the mirror. On her head, across her face, was a black veil. Ziegler proclaimed it a study in sexual frustration, a howl of compressed desire.

Like many artists, Ziegler only rationalized images he barely understood. When Berthe looked at "The Young Widow," she saw something very different from frustrated desire. Even as Lothar

Engle bought the painting on the spot for 5,000 marks, she was ending her affair with him. She was ending a great many things.

That dark veil engulfing her face, focusing the viewer's eyes on a body that barely existed within the harsh lines of the formal figure, became a voice whispering wordless questions. In the dawn, when Lothar's tongue roved her body and she returned the compliment while he whispered *freedom, freedom*, Berthe was engulfed by a formless fear. It seemed to seep from the walls of Lothar's fashionable apartment off the Kurfurstendamm.

Essentially it was a fear of vanishing, like her mother, who had died of syphilis in a hotel room in Paris the previous year. She had contracted the disease from one of her lovers decades ago. For the last six months of her life she was blind and simple-minded. Her father had advised Berthe not to visit her. Better to remember *die Kleine Koenigen* (the Little Queen) as she was in her glory days, he wrote.

It had been easy to take his advice. Berthe had never been close to her mother, who was always kissing her goodbye as she departed for St. Moritz, Baden-Baden, Cannes. Governesses claimed far more of Berthe's affection. Even when she was posing naked for painters and playing advanced sexual games with Lothar Engle, once a month she visited her ancient Danish nurse in her tiny apartment near Alexanderplatz.

Now Berthe saw at least part of what had happened to her. If love was a joke as Lothar claimed and Germany was also a joke— which he also claimed—(though to give him credit, he said love was a good joke and Germany was a bad joke) what was to prevent a woman from vanishing? Even if she was the first female Schonberg to get a university degree. What did it matter, if tomorrow anarchy might boil up from Alexanderplatz or the Russians swarmed from the east with their mindless Bolshevism? "The Young Widow" triggered the search that led Berthe into the arms of Ernst von Hoffmann.

She had carefully concealed all this from everyone—above all from Lothar Engle, who would have combined Freudian analysis and Berlin cynicism to make a comedy of her fears.

The train raced through the forest of Grunewald while Berthe talked to Lothar in the almost empty car. Was she implicitly acknowledging he still had power over her? Was "The Young Widow" a kind of proof, a combination trophy and talisman? "I thought you married

Gertrude Netter and lived happily ever after," Berthe said.

"I divorced her two years ago. Everything was the right size—except her brain. I've never found anyone to replace you, Berthe. I still don't understand what you see in that sailor boy. Do you simply like to be in control? I'm sure he kisses your feet any time you demand it."

Vanishing. She suddenly wanted to explain it to Lothar, to someone. "It's much more complicated, darling."

"Why don't you come up to my apartment now and tell me all about it."

"That would be a mistake—for both of us!" she said, with a violence that only made him suspicious.

"Are you on your way to see someone else?"

"I'm going shopping at Wertheim's. My son, Georg, seems to grow an inch a month."

"How nauseatingly domestic."

At the train rolled into the Grune Strasse stop, she kissed him on the cheek. "Can't we just be fond of each other?"

"We can try," Lothar said. He seized her hand. "It's I who need to explain things, Berthe. You can't believe how badly I need someone I can talk honestly with."

On crowded Grune Strasse, Berthe walked swiftly toward the towering facade of Wertheim's, one of Berlin's biggest department stores. Waiting for a traffic light, she scanned the sidewalk behind her to make sure Lothar was not following her. There was no reason why he should—but Pastor Bruchmuller's remark about the Gestapo made her wary. In front of Wertheim's, she boarded a tram to complete her journey to the Siegessäule, the two-hundred-foot-high column that celebrated Germany's nineteenth-century victories over Austria and France. Nearby were immense statues of the architects of those fateful triumphs, which created modern Germany—bearlike Chancellor Otto Bismarck and diminutive Field Marshal Helmuth von Moltke.

The column and the statues overlooked the wide traffic circle known as Grosser Stern, in the center of the Tiergarten, Berlin's famous park. An icy wind howled across the asphalt expanse, causing pedestrians to clutch at hats and overcoats. Berthe thought of her husband facing similar blasts on the North Atlantic and was swept by a shuddering spasm of guilt. Was all of this a kind of madness?

Pastor Bruchmuller called to her from the terrace on top of the column and swiftly descended the 285 steps to join her. "No one is following you," he said. "A good sign."

They strolled through the winter-stripped Tiergarten to the Siegessallee on the northeast corner. The Victory Avenue was lined with huge statues of Germany's rulers, which Kaiser Wilhelm I had commissioned at the turn of the century. They were literally monuments to bad taste, from their excessive size to the discolored stone to the badly executed details. "I brought you here to say goodbye," Bruchmuller said. "I thought it was a good place to do it. Before these witnesses to Germany's grandiosity."

"Goodbye? What's happened? Where are you going?" Berthe asked. The word made her realize how much she depended on this man's serenity. It had become a kind of drug she imbibed at his church almost every Sunday.

"I've been dismissed as pastor of the church. The Brethern Council—the governing board of the Confessing churches—yielded to Heinrich Himmler's demand. He is, after all, Reich Commissar for the Consolidation of German Nationhood."

Bruchmuller's ironic use of Nazi titles was one of his most charming rhetorical devices. It reminded Berthe of Lothar Engle's fondness for puncturing egos in the Twenties the same way. He would take a title such as director of policy, which in German would often be a single word, *Politikinbezugaufdirektor*, and repeat it a dozen times in a single column, until it became ludicrous.

"What will you do?"

"I will imitate my friend Dietrich Bonhoeffer and become a wandering preacher. There are still a number of pastors courageous enough to invite me for a single Sunday. When the Gestapo assails them, they can claim ignorance—since the government has, of course, refused to publish our call for repentance."

Berthe struggled to control an impulse to weep. "I don't know what I'll do without you," she said.

"From the day we met I've sensed an inner struggle that you've tried to control with the will. But there are limits to that sort of existence."

Behind them, a company of twelve- or thirteen-year-old boys wearing brown Hitler Youth uniforms appeared at the head of the Siegesallee. They were led by a tall hulking man in the same brown uniform. He ordered them to surround the first statue on the right, the legendary Albert the Bear, the supposed founder of the Prussian state, and began lecturing them in an angry ranting style. "Here you see our warrior roots, the German hero who slew ten thousand Slavs in a single day. The Spree ran red with their blood—"

Several boys on the outer fringes of the group stared curiously at Berthe and Bruchmuller. "I think we may be better off in the woods," he said.

They retreated into the Tiergarten again. Only a few people were strolling along the curving paths beneath the gray sky. As they strolled, Bruchmuller began telling Berthe about a book that his friend Dietrich Bonhoeffer had written, *The Cost of Discipleship*. He had seen only part of it, but he thought it might be the greatest book ever written by a German.

"It may contain the answer to your dilemma," he said. "Bonhoeffer emphasizes that the act has priority over existence. Often, the act creates the kind of existence we seek."

"But a woman can't act. She can only exist. Once I vowed I wouldn't swallow such a fate. Yet here I am, trying to choke it down—with your help."

"Action is not impossible—but the cost could be very high. It might be more than you can ask yourself—or your husband and children—to pay."

They sat down on a bench overlooking the River Spree. A lone oarsman was in the middle of the winding stream, rowing with a methodical stroke, as if he were doomed to perform the task unto eternity. "I don't know what you're talking about," Berthe said.

"I need to know how much you oppose the regime. I know you dislike it. But millions of Germans feel that way. Are there deeper feelings?"

Berthe told him about the smell of burning offal in the Hoffmanns' living room the day after Kristallnacht. Bruchmuller seized her gloved hands and raised them to his lips. There was a sexual aura to the gesture. But it was not sensual. She did not feel an iota of physical desire stir in her body, although Friedrich Bruchmuller was a veritable Nordic god, with a rocklike jaw, a bold warrior's nose, deep blue eyes and blond hair. Siegfried incarnate, Berthe thought.

"I suspected, I hoped—" he said.

He began to talk in a compelling voice about the terrible truth she had encountered. Hitler's evil was deeper and darker than the anti-Semitic violence of Kristallnacht. In the concentration camps to which he had already deported thousands of German Jews and political enemies such as the Communists, there was a systematic program of starvation and physical abuse, aimed at nothing less than extermination. In conquered Poland, even worse atrocities were being perpetrated against the Jews and the Polish aristocracy, intelligentsia and priests. Russia faced the same fate—all part of the Nazis' determination to reduce inferior peoples to total subservience to the rule of a triumphant German superrace.

"It's the terrible working out of their doctrine of the primacy of the blood," Bruchmuller said. "They've proclaimed that blood alone matters, and only war, the supreme action of the blood, is noble. They hate us Christians as much as they hate the Jews. They see the cross as the symbol of the crucifixion of the body and its vital powers. Nazism is more than a transitory political phenomenon. It's a *faith*."

Berthe's eyes roved to the lone oarsman on the Spree. Was Bruchmuller right, when he included her as a Christian? In her university days she had shared the general conviction that Jesus was a prophet who no longer merited much honor. She had been more inclined to admire Helen Widerstand's favorite seer, Karl Marx.

In the same steady voice, Friedrich Bruchmuller began talking about the meaning of discipleship. A disciple must be prepared to pay the ultimate cost, to lay down his or her life for the master. That was almost in the category of a cliché, although an excruciating one, if and when the time came to confront it. But there was another side to discipleship that he and his friend Bonhoeffer had begun to perceive, the disciple's role when confronted by radical evil. "The disciple must be prepared to oppose the evil by any and all means. Everything is permitted."

"Everything?" Berthe said dazedly.

Friedrich Bruchmuller had no idea that those words had flung her back to her nights with Lothar Engle. On the wall dangled "The Young Widow," her face veiled in darkness, while Lothar whispered those same words: *Alles ist erlauben.*

"I'm talking, ultimately, about assassination. Bonhoeffer and I have concluded it will come to that, sooner or later. In the meantime, you must be prepared to lie, to dissemble in a hundred ways, to commit what Christians consider sinful acts, to prepare for the moment of redemption."

"Sinful acts?" Berthe said. "Where and how will I manage such things in my humdrum life?"

"Your humdrum life may soon be over. In a few days you'll meet a man I consider the most remarkable human being I've ever encountered. A man with a mind so subtle, it's impossible to grasp the moral shadings he perceives. He's part Faust, part Saint Augustine, part Bismarck. I can't guarantee you he's completely trustworthy. But he's our only hope."

"Who is he?"

"Admiral Wilhelm Canaris, the head of the Abwehr."

The Abwehr was the German secret service. The full name was *Amt Auslandsnachrichten und Abwehr*, Department of Foreign Intelligence and Counterintelligence. Berthe had occasionally heard her husband wonder why an admiral was head of this shadowy organization, whose chief business was the dishonorable profession of spying.

"I'm a member of the Abwehr," Bruchmuller said. "It's the main reason I haven't been arrested or conscripted into the army. Canaris has tried to protect people like Bonhoeffer and me. He sends us abroad, supposedly to set up clerical intelligence networks inside neutral countries such as Switzerland and Sweden. Actually we carry messages to the British secret service."

"What sort of messages?" Berthe asked. The whole conversation was growing more and more unreal. Was she dealing with a madman? Was insanity, a fantasy world, the explanation for Friedrich Bruchmuller's serenity?

"Only Admiral Canaris can reveal them to you. Even though I now believe we share the same faith, I don't completely trust you, Frau von Hoffmann. If you repeated this conversation to anyone, I would deny it."

A wan smile flitted across Bruchmuller's handsome face. "That may be the hardest part of the path we've chosen. The terrible necessity not to trust anyone, no matter how intensely faith urges it on us."

The solitary boatman had vanished around a bend in the Spree. This part of the Path lay through a dark wood. But she would continue to follow it. "I think I would like to meet the Admiral," Berthe said.

7

HOME IS THE SAILOR

Annie Talbot stood at the window of the art deco marine terminal in New York's La Guardia Field watching the white Pan American flying boat begin its descent to the black turgid waters of Flushing Bay. Tears streamed down her gamin face, wrecking her makeup. "Say something funny," she gasped to her brother Jack, who was standing beside her. "Zeke can't stand mushy women."

"I'm beginning to think you actually love this guy."

Annie confronted that rakish grin, which had broken her heart when, at the age of twelve, she had come out of her room wearing makeup and silk stockings for the first time and realized from the nonimpression she made that she would always be Jack's kid sister. As she watched the grin break several dozen other hearts in and around the U.S. Naval Academy and Washington, D.C., she also realized love was synonymous with fun and games in Jack's thesaurus. Sometimes she grieved for the victims but most of the time she ruefully admired Jack's prowess—and vowed she would never let any man treat her that way.

Suddenly Jack was introducing her to his Annapolis roommate, Jonathan Trumbull Talbot, surrounding Zeke's stiff earnest honesty with the aura of his effortless charm. What else explained why everyone she had ever dated instantly dwindled in comparison? It had to be the intuition that Jack wanted her to marry him, he was using her as a kind of bait to lure this quintessential American aristocrat into the Richman family.

And vice versa, of course, inserting the Richmans into the center of the Plymouth Rock crowd. In his cool, casual way, Jack was playing the assimilation game that their grandfather, Honest Abe, had begun by naming all his children after famous Americans, such as Ulysses S. Grant. Jack's Annapolis diploma was part of it and so was his stardom in the nation's press corps and his collection of inamoratas, who ranged from good ole Southern gals to precise articulators of Locust Valley lockjaw to delicious Daphne whose English sounded like one of Wordsworth's babbling brooks. So were the unspoken orders to the kid sister to prove she was worthy of their bloodline by making Jonathan Trumbull Talbot a happy husband.

Did that mean she had never loved the tall stubborn Yankee in that descending Pan American clipper? That was, as her Jewish grandmother used to say, as if to laugh. Large ideas like assimilation had nothing to do with the intimate discoveries of marriage. Zeke Talbot had been all the things she had imagined a husband should be in her girlish fantasies. Faithful, honest, courageous, considerate, tender. She could see him now in his clipper seat, legs braced, hands clenched against the claustrophobia that attacked him every time he flew because of his brother's death in that World War I training accident. She understood that wound and the far more serious traumas inflicted by his overpowering father. For ten of the past eleven years, her love had been a perfect mixture of forbearance and sympathy and admiration.

"The last reading I got from him, the poor sap was still your love slave," Jack said.

"Jack—it isn't funny anymore! I'm scared of what's happening to me and Zeke. To this whole crazy world."

She was trying to tell him how the old kidding about their opposite political and ethnic heritages had become exchanges edged with anger and ugly silences. But Jack had no interest in playing marriage counselor.

"Steady as you go, kid. He made it in one piece. He'll be kissing you in five minutes."

She shook her head, almost afraid to admit the whole truth, even to herself. "I felt so horribly guilty when they told me that he was dead. Is Roosevelt doing the right thing?"

Jack's grin became a scowl, as if a cold wind had struck his face.

"Yeah. We've got to stop Adolf and company. It doesn't matter how many rules we break."

She had an uneasy feeling Jack was breaking quite a few rules. When the Richmans rushed to Norfolk to console her, she overheard several tense exchanges between Jack and the Congressman. It had something to do with sneaking into foreign embassies to steal codes and how much hell was likely to erupt if the Irish-American branch of Sam's congressional district found out Jack was working with the British Secret Service.

"Including starting a war? That's what Zeke says we're doing."

"Including a war," Jack said.

It was enormously confusing. She had majored in modern European history at Trinity College. If pressed, she could still babble about the balance of power and the causes of the First World War. But after eleven years as a Navy wife, the farrago of dynasties and ethnic hatreds and national rivalries had become more and more unreal to her. She sometimes complained that her brain was turning to mush—and good-naturedly accused Zeke of not caring as long as other parts of her anatomy remained firm.

Then out of Germany had come this maniacal voice, spewing hatred at Jews, calling on the entire world to join him in mindless anti-Semitism—and backing up his evil crusade with legions of rumbling tanks and swarms of bombers. While millions of her fellow Americans, including her own husband, declared it was none of their business. That was worse than unreal, it was bizarre, disorienting, as if the world had fallen under the control of a Hollywood horror movie director. You looked at the honest, earnest face you had kissed and caressed and suddenly saw the flesh corrode, fangs protrude, the eyes glare with demented hostility.

No, it was not that bad. That was her lurid Irish-Jewish imagination, corrupted by too many double features with Estelle Cartwright and other wives at the local Bijou. A sad commentary on her college dreams of intellectual and artistic glory.

The thunder of the clipper's engines was filling the terminal as the big plane taxied to the debarkation ramp. "Come on, let's hail the conquered hero," Jack said, towing her into the crowd surging toward the arrival gate.

Annie found herself recoiling from this encounter. She half-knew what Zeke was going to say about losing his ship and crew to a German torpedo. Maybe he was right about Roosevelt, even if Jack did not think so. She was not at all sure she wanted to sacrifice her husband to save the British empire from Hitler's hordes. Not to mention the even less lovable Russians, from whose anti-Semitism the Reichman-Richmans had fled early in the nineteenth century.

"There he is."

The Jimmy Stewart jaw was jutting aggressively, the broad brow beneath the visored cap was furrowed earnestly, the proud mouth fixed resolutely in a nonsmile of disapproval. Oh Jesus, he was as angry as she had feared—at Roosevelt, at the country, at her. "Hey," Jack was yelling. "Hey, Zeke!"

His eyes found them and her fears temporarily vanished. His face came aglow with the most wonderful smile Annie had ever seen. He began wading through the crowd, parting people left and right with those long wrestler's arms. Annie pulled free of Jack's grasp and ran toward him, tears streaming again. She could not help it, Zeke was alive—after she had given him up to death, after she had knelt in the Norfolk base chapel and denounced herself for letting intellectual arrogance persuade her into a cold indifference to all religions, matching Zeke's bitter unfaith. He had been redeemed from the Atlantic's watery tomb, they were both redeemed, their love had been rescued by the mysterious workings of God's providence, she was absolutely sure of it.

Into his arms she hurtled to offer her mouth, her body, her self to him the way she had surrendered on their now almost mythical Hawaiian honeymoon eleven years ago. "Oh, oh, oh," she gasped, incapable of coherent speech. "Oh, Zeke."

"Glad to see you still remember my name," he said, pressing her against his chest with possessive intensity.

"They told me you were dead," Annie said, wiping her streaming eyes. "But I still prayed for you. I prayed day and night."

"The Navy's always at its most efficient when you least want it to be," he said.

He was unimpressed by, even disapproving of, her outburst of piety. A tremor of diminution passed through Annie's flesh. "Hey, Commander," Jack called. "You too far up the ladder to say hello to mere ex-ensigns these days?"

"Not when I'm in the right mood," Zeke said. Annie watched them mash each other's hands and exchange punches to the chest and arms that would have crippled her. Not for the first time she felt excluded by the mysterious camaraderie of men, with its undercurrent of competition and grudging respect, its intensity trebled, in Jack's and Zeke's case, by the even more mysterious bonding that four years in Annapolis created. "I've got a table reserved at the Rainbow Room, champagne on ice," Jack said.

"The Rainbow Room?" Zeke said. "I bet there's a Democratic fat cat at every table." He never let up on Jack for quitting the Navy to become a crusading liberal newspaperman with gold-plated Washington connections,

"They've got a few Republican Wall Street swindlers too," Jack said.

"Commander Talbot?" A large blue uniform loomed to their right. "I'm Dick Sweeney, from Cinclant. Admiral King sent me down here to escort you to Newport." He was about six feet four and as wide as a Sequoia tree. The face was incongruously boyish.

"He has no confidence in my ability to get there on my own?"

"Not exactly that, sir. He wants you there as soon as possible." He eyed Jack and nervously cleared his throat. "He—er—strictly instructed me not to let you talk to reporters."

"Don't worry, Lieutenant. I'm not working this beat," Jack said. "This guy's my brother-in-law."

Annie knew Zeke was supposed to report to Cinclant's headquarters. She had brought along his best blue uniform for him. She presumed the Navy simply wanted to hear all the grisly details on the sinking of the *Spencer Lewis*. Jack had assured her she was probably right—and then hinted she might be wrong.

"I was planning to report tomorrow," Zeke said. "But if that's an order—"

"It's definitely an order, Commander."

"Aw nuts," Jack said.

A short fat man with a gold watch chain across his paunch seized Zeke's arm as if it were a stanchion on a rolling destroyer. "My son told me how you saved his life from those Nazi swine, Commander!" he shouted. "I want you to know, anything you ever ask from Seymour Klein, anything, it's yours. My whole business, you can have it, when you come back from this war with Hitler's head. That's how I feel and that's what I say and may God strike me dead if I don't deliver on it!"

"We're not at war with Hitler, Mr. Klein—and I hope we never will be," Zeke said. "I have no more use for him than you do. But I don't think going to war with him makes any sense. Not all Germans are Nazis. The Commander of the U-boat who rescued us was a man I'd be happy to claim as a friend."

Seymour Klein looked baffled. "Well what I said—the gratitude of my whole family—stands just the same. Goodbye and God bless you."

Outside the terminal, Jack hailed a cab and said: "Zeke, if you get any more straight-arrow, your head's going to come to a point."

"I just told him the truth."

"How about letting me tell the Congressman the truth? He can get you a medal for saving that kid."

"No thanks."

Annie felt another tremor pass through her flesh, this time of dismay. Zeke was angry and Jack was trying to bribe him out of it and she was in the middle, trying to decide which one was right, as usual.

"Can I use the story for the column?"

"If you make me sound like a Democrat I'll sue you for slander."

"If I wrote anything that far from the truth I'd sue myself for malfeasance."

Two hours later, having parted company with Jack at Grand Central Station, they were on the New Haven and Hartford railroad to Newport. Lieutenant Sweeney dolefully informed Zeke that he was the only officer to survive the *Spencer Lewis*'s demise.

"Estelle Cartwright is coming apart," Annie said. "I almost felt guilty when I found out you were still alive."

Zeke told her the message the Pirate had given him as he began swimming to a life raft. Annie said she would call Estelle as soon as they reached Newport and pass it on to her.

"Don't you want to get out there and even the score with those guys, Commander?" Sweeney asked. "I'm starting to feel that way."

"The one person I want to even the score with is the so-called President of the United States," Zeke said. "He's responsible for Charlie Cartwright and all those other dead men. The more I think of it, the more I want to see the son of a bitch impeached."

Lieutenant Sweeney cleared his throat nervously and glanced around the crowded railroad car. Across the aisle, an overweight woman wearing a mink stole was absorbing every word of Zeke's tirade. "Commander," Sweeney said. "I've got orders to—er—prevent you from saying anything like that."

"Since when has the Navy decided to control the private opinions of its officers?" Zeke demanded.

"You're not in private now, Commander," Sweeney said, nodding toward the listener across the aisle.

"I agree with every word you just said, Commander," the woman declared in Locust Valley–ese that outlockjawed Jack's former girlfriend. "That man in the White House should have been impeached years ago. Half his cabinet are members of the Communist party! He's infiltrating traitors—and Jews—into the highest councils of our government!"

Not for the first time, Annie wondered about the wisdom of joining the Plymouth Rock crowd. So many of them had turned into spewers of hatred and craziness, like this woman, since Roosevelt led the Democrats to victory in 1932 and began trying to derrick the country out of the Depression. Their patent, raging selfishness stirred uneasy thoughts about America's so-called aristocracy. But for the moment, Annie almost welcomed the woman's intrusion because it forced Zeke to retract his wholesale condemnation of the President.

"I think that's going much too far, Madam," he said. "My disagreement with him is about the way he's trying to euchre us into an unnecessary war."

"Calm down, Zeke," Annie said. "You've been through an awful ordeal." She should have stopped there but the Plymouth Rock woman's arrogant stare added another explosive sentence. "I don't want to go to war any more than you do but I was hoping this thing changed your mind about the Germans."

"Why should it?" Zeke said. "There was no malice involved in Lieutenant Commander von Hoffmann's decision to torpedo the *Spencer Lewis*. He thought he was attacking an English destroyer. It was an act of war—and an act of courage. Submarines don't usually attack destroyers. If you miss with the first torpedo you can get sunk pretty quickly."

Annie was dismayed to see that Lieutenant Sweeney, in spite of his anxiety about keeping Zeke quiet, agreed with every word of that declaration. Men! They loved to measure themselves against an opposing male's courage. They secretly enjoyed trying to kill each other.

Zeke continued to orate: "We wouldn't have been out there on the North Atlantic if England and France hadn't rammed that phony war guilt clause down Germany's throat in 1919 and the great peacemaker Woodrow Wilson hadn't gone along with it. You've heard my father say that a hundred times. I heard it again on that submarine."

"When it came to political opinions, especially about Woodrow Wilson, your father is even less objective than you are."

This was absolutely the worst slur she could hurl at him and she knew it. If there was anything Jonathan Trumbull Talbot prided himself on, it was the objectivity of his opinions on everything, from religion to women to politics. He was also secondarily infuriated to hear her criticizing his father.

"When it comes to objectivity, I could make a few comments on your father and the Chicago party line, as promulgated by Boss Kelly," he snarled.

Annie's eyes filled with angry tears. Zeke knew she had no moral defense of her father's allegiance to one of the most corrupt political machines in the country. But she refused to lose her temper. She was still grateful for his resurrection, outrageous opinions and all. "As you can see, Lieutenant, he doesn't change his mind easily," she said.

"If you could persuade him to talk a little softer, I'd be awfully grateful, Mrs. Talbot," Sweeney said.

Annie asked Sweeney if he was married. He nodded eagerly and said he expected to be a father before the end of the year. They discussed children, football—Sweeney had been a mainstay of the Annapolis line—and life on various naval bases for the rest of the ride to Newport. There they checked into the Shamrock Cliff House, overlooking wind-whipped Narragansett Bay. Zeke put on the blue uniform she had brought from Norfolk. Annie sat on the bed, watching him, wishing he would kiss her, undress her, take her now. She hated the sense of his anger separating them. As he knotted his tie, she jumped up and flung her arms around him.

"I'm sorry I sounded off about your father," she said.

"I guess I deserved it. I didn't get much sleep on the plane. When you add that to a naturally rotten disposition—"

"I don't care I don't care I don't care!" she said, clinging to him. "I'm just so glad you're alive."

"How's Butch? Was he upset?"

"Horribly. He didn't eat for two days. I wish I could have brought him along but this summons from Admiral King—"

"I'll telephone him as soon as I get back."

She let him put on his coat. She brushed some lint off the sleeve. "Why do you think King wants to see you in such a hurry?"

"I have no idea."

"Jack said he thought it smelled like trouble."

"Jack could be right."

"Zeke—keep calm. Don't say something you'll regret."

"Such as?"

"The sort of stuff you were telling Sweeney on the train."

He loomed over her, suddenly solemn, even sullen. She felt difference slide between them like a steel wall. She tried to burst through it, kissing him fiercely, wildly. He returned it harshly, briefly. "I love you so much!" she cried.

"Ditto," he said.

From the hotel window, Annie watched him stride to the tan Navy car that had met them at the train station. The driver held the door for him. He vanished into the dark interior. Was it a paradigm of what was happening to their marriage? Something—call it history or destiny or fate—seemed to be consuming the confident heir to all things good and honorable she had married. Would this visit to Admiral King be the final gulp?

8

EYEBALL TO EYEBALL

Did women know how much they demoralized men? Jonathan Trumbull Talbot wondered as the car wound through Newport's narrow streets to the Navy base. There she stood in that hip-hugging green tweed suit, the matching green cloche revealing most of her midnight black hair, saying I love you with that oversize double bed in the background. Was this any way to calm down a man just back from three celibate months on the North Atlantic, on his way to a meeting with one of the more fearsome creatures in the upper ranks of the U.S. Navy?

In the Canary Islands, Talbot had pooh-poohed Consul Shaw Snyder's prediction that he was in deep shit. But this urgent summons to Newport had him fearing the worst. Even though all the officers from the *Spencer Lewis* were dead, some members of the bridge watch must have survived and reported their captain's negative comments on the President's policies. Nothing else explained Sweeney as an escort, with orders to keep him quiet. He was in danger of getting an official reprimand in his file—a fatal wound to a Navy career.

Sweeney led him past the flat-roofed administration building and assorted barracks to the boat dock. Admiral King was aboard his flagship, the cruiser *Augusta*, in the harbor. "He spends most of his time out there," Sweeney said. "Keeps the reporters at bay."

A launch ferried them out to the long sleek ship, with the odd break in the rear third of the superstructure to create a catapult site for her seaplanes. The usual salutes were exchanged with the tense lieutenant junior grade in charge of the quarterdeck. Officers of the Day aboard flagships were always jittery. Within minutes, Talbot was at the door of Admiral King's suite just below the bridge.

Sweeney shook hands. "Good luck, Commander," he said. "If I were you, I'd let your brother-in-law get you that medal. It could come in handy."

A marine in dress blues vanished into an inner compartment and returned to say Admiral King was busy. Talbot waited, brooding over Sweeney's remark. He was definitely deep in the stuff. Did Annie's plea to keep cool mean she knew it? Congressman Richman was in a position to pick up a lot of inside information. Numerous admirals devoted half their days to kissing his ass.

"Commander Talbot?"

Admiral Ernest J. King, Cinclant, was standing in the doorway of his stateroom. He looked the part of a fleet commander. The gaunt face seemed weathered by decades of sea winds. The nose was a prow, the chin an aggressive wedge, the eyes as hard and humorless as ball bearings.

"Yes sir," Talbot said, springing up, his hand half-extended for a shake. Cinclant did not reciprocate. On the contrary, he stepped back as if he was afraid a touch might lead to contamination. Something— perhaps his heart—started doing loops in Talbot's chest cavity.

In the Admiral's office, Talbot glimpsed bits and pieces of King's forty-two years in the Navy. A newsphoto of his efforts to raise the sunken American submarine *Squalus*, an official Navy photograph of him landing on a carrier—he had gotten his wings at the age of forty-five. King sat down behind a desk on which lay a single folder— Jonathan Trumbull Talbot's personnel file.

He did not ask Talbot to sit down. Instead, he extracted from the file a newspaper clipping. "Is any of this true?" he said.

It was from a German newspaper. An English translation was clipped beneath it—but Talbot read the German without difficulty.

A VOICE OF TRUTH

An interesting event in the North Atlantic has brought into sharp focus the American people's resistance to Franklin Roosevelt's determination to prosecute an undeclared war against the German Reich, financed by international Jewry. On November 9, the USS *Spencer Lewis*, on convoy duty off Iceland, was mistaken for a British destroyer and sunk by U-Boat 555, commanded by Kapitanleutnant Ernst von Hoffmann. The Kapitanleutnant rescued the captain of the destroyer, Lieutenant Commander Jonathan T. Talbot, and one of his crew, from the icy waters as a gesture of humanity, after they had been abandoned to death from exposure by their British comrades in arms. Talbot expressed his gratitude to Kapitanleutnant von Hoffmann— as well as his strong resentment of the sacrifice of his crew to Franklin Roosevelt's reckless policy, which threatens to embroil the United States in the coming British defeat. He told Kapitanleutnant von Hoffmann that many officers in the U.S. Navy, including some of flag rank, share this resentment. He suggested that if the American people knew the whole truth, they would demand Roosevelt's impeachment. To further demonstrate his pro-German feelings, Talbot joined Kapitanleutnant von Hoffmann on the bridge in a daring night attack on the convoy the *Spencer Lewis* had been escorting, and cheered his German rescuers when they sank three ships with their last three torpedoes, bringing U-boat 555's total for its cruise to 118,000 tons.

Talbot carefully returned the clipping to King's desk as if it were soaked in nitroglycerine and the slightest shock could trigger an explosion. "There's a great deal of exaggeration in that story, Admiral," he said.

"You didn't answer my question," King said, in a low but unmistakably murderous voice. "Is *any* of it true?"

"While I was having dinner with Kapitanleutnant von Hoffmann and his officers, I did express certain reservations toward the President's policy."

"Did you say other officers in the Navy, including some admirals, shared your opinion?"

"You know that's true, Admiral. You know it as well as I do."

King leaped to his feet, the prow of a jaw jutting. "I don't give a goddamn about what's true, Talbot. I am only concerned here with your appalling disloyalty to the U.S. Navy."

The bellow hit Talbot in the center of his body like a projectile from one of the *Augusta*'s eight-inch guns. For a moment his torso seemed to vanish. He floated there, a disembodied mind, in the sudden inferno engulfing Ernest J. King's stateroom.

"Disloyalty, Admiral?" he said, his voice sounding like a phonograph with a worn needle. "Is it disloyalty—or loyalty?"

"You call it loyalty to smear the reputation of the U.S. Navy for the benefit of those Nazi bastards?"

"There were no Nazis on that submarine, Admiral. Except perhaps one man. But I didn't talk to him. My exchange with Kapitanleutnant von Hoffmann was conversation between officers of the same rank—between two gentlemen."

Cinclant took a step back, either to avoid further contamination or to express astonishment. "I'm finding it hard to believe you're real, Talbot. Is this conversation actually taking place between two graduates of the U.S. Naval Academy with their country on the brink of war with Germany? What the fuck century are you living in?"

"I'm living in the twentieth century, Admiral. I've just spent a year at the Naval War College here in Newport studying the history of this century and earlier centuries. That's why I think Roosevelt's policy of putting almost half the fleet out there on the Atlantic to fight an undeclared war is unconstitutional and I think you know it as well as I do! It's also strategically unsound and you know that too!"

"Don't tell me what I know!" King bellowed. "I'll tell you what I know. Your career in this man's Navy is finished. I'm going to put a memorandum of this conversation in your file to make damn sure you don't advance one centimeter beyond your current rank."

Selfhood, manhood, was vanishing in this firestorm. Talbot clutched at shreds of his pride. "I'll tell you what I know, Admiral," he said. "I have the right to demand a court-martial to clear my name of these atrocious charges."

King rounded his desk and bore down on him like an aging battleship. "A court-martial. You'd love that, wouldn't you. You'd call in reporters from every anti-Roosevelt newspaper in the country. You'd turn it into a circus that would smear the Navy before the whole world."

He loomed over Talbot, now only an inch or two from his face. His breath had a distinct odor of stale whiskey. "You're not going to get any goddamn court-martial while I'm your commander, Talbot. Instead, you're going to deny these charges before they get picked up by the Washington *Times-Herald* or some other pro-German sheet. So far we've kept them at bay by maintaining you couldn't have said these things. You're going to call them a total fabrication. You're going to express your detestation of Nazi Germany for sinking your ship, killing three-fourths of your crew, and then attempting to ruin your reputation. You're going to do this for only one reason, aside from saving a few pieces of your miserable ass: because I'm ordering you to do it!"

It was Talbot's turn to step back, to put enough distance between himself and this four-striped monster to let him breathe—and perhaps think. "I'm not sure I can do that, Admiral," he said.

King went from amazement to disbelief to malice in a millisecond. "Talbot, either you do it, or you're going to find yourself court-martialed for a couple things I can barely bring myself to mention. Let's start with pederasty. Some of your surviving enlisted men will testify that you lured them to your cabin and tried to seduce them. Then we'll get into extortion and theft from the ship's payroll. Finally we'll drop the big one on you—treason. For a consideration from a German agent, you arranged to have your ship torpedoed so you could make these shocking statements to the world. How else can you explain why you were the only officer rescued? You think you can play dirty, Talbot? You don't even know the meaning of the word."

"Admiral," Talbot said. "I may not be the most obedient officer in the Navy. But I don't scare easily."

Everything inside him belied those words. His body felt like deliquescent mush. His brain seemed to be shattered fragments in his burning humming skull. He was not much different from the *Spencer Lewis* after the torpedo exploded.

King retreated behind his desk. "I'm not trying to scare you. I'm trying to make you think about what you're doing. Not just to your career—but to your wife and kid—and the rest of your family. Your father-in-law's a congressman. What do you think it'll do to his career to have a son-in-law accused of treason?"

The invocation of his father-in-law ignited such a blind fury in Talbot's chest, he could barely breathe. "I don't think it will bother him in the least, Admiral. You can always get elected in Chicago as long as you stay loyal to Ed Kelly and Franklin D. Roosevelt."

"Who or what are you loyal to, Talbot? That's what I can't figure out."

"The truth!"

"The truth," the Admiral said, rolling the word around his mouth as if it were a piece of two-hundred-year-old pork from the HMS

Bounty's ship's stores. "I swear to Christ, you tempt me to write a letter to the Superintendent of the goddamn Naval Academy, telling him not to admit anyone with an IQ over a hundred and ten. This fucking file says you're one of the brightest men to graduate in this century. You got some of the highest marks in the history of the War College. But do you know what I see in front of me? An asshole!"

King flipped Talbot's file closed. "I'll give you twenty-four hours to make that statement. Then I'm putting you under arrest while we prepare those charges against you. Now get the hell out of here."

Talbot stumbled down ladders to the quarterdeck, where the tense lieutenant junior grade summoned a motor whaleboat to get him back to Newport. He walked from the dock to the Shamrock Cliff House, hoping the cold air would extinguish some of the fury in his brain. The whole thing was unthinkable. No matter what they did to him, he was never going to tell those public lies.

In the Cliff House, Annie was sitting by the window, talking on the telephone. She had taken off her suitcoat. In silhouette, all Talbot could see at first was the outline of her breasts beneath her white nylon blouse. "Here's Zeke," she said. "Would you like to talk to him?" She put her hand over the mouthpiece. "It's Estelle Cartwright."

What could he say to this tormented woman? Her husband's life had just been wasted by an arrogant, blundering president? He had to summon oracular clichés about duty and courage, while she sobbed out her gratitude for the Pirate's farewell testament of love. The evasions only made Talbot more determined to tell the truth to someone, somewhere.

He hung up. "How did it go—with the Admiral?" Annie asked.

He told her in grisly detail. She listened, growing more and more pale. "Zeke, you've got to do it," she said. "You've got to deny it. He can destroy you. He can destroy Daddy."

"You and Daddy will have to take your chances with me," he snarled. "I'm going to let him court-martial me. I'll go public with my opinion of Roosevelt's unconstitutional war. I'll resign from the Navy and run for my father's old seat in Congress. I'll chase Roosevelt out of the goddamn White House."

"Zeke—when your father got elected to Congress, that district was ninety percent Republican. They've had a Democrat in that seat for the last eighteen years. It's not the same country. Nobody gives a damn for your great-great-grandfather's service in the Revolution or your great-grandfather's heroism at Gettysburg."

"I'll make them care. I'll sell myself as a man who'll tell them the truth about what's happening to this country."

"A guy who's lost his ship, his crew and his reputation isn't my idea of a winning candidate."

When it came to politics, Annie Richman Talbot had the instincts of a killer shark. What was happening to him? He felt engulfed by malevolence. Instead of pressing his lips against that soft troubled mouth and filling his hands with that silky black hair, Talbot was close to shouting curses at them. She was his enemy, his loving, beloved, desirable, detestable enemy. "I don't give a damn what you say. I'm going to do it," he raged.

Annie reached for the telephone. "I'm calling Daddy," she said. "And Jack."

9

A FATHERING VOICE

Three days after her meeting with Friedrich Bruchmuller, Berthe von Hoffmann received another phone call. "The Admiral will see you at three p.m.," said a stranger's voice.

The offices of Germany's secret service were in two gray stone townhouses on the Tirpitz Ufer, a quay overlooking a torpid, long unused canal. A few steps away was the wintry Tiergarten where she had talked with Bruchmuller. Around the corner was the huge frowning headquarters of the German Defense Ministry on the Bendlerstrasse. Just inside the low portico, a corporal directed her to an ancient elevator, which creaked to the fifth floor, where a secretary gestured her into a large office, dominated by a big nineteenth-century desk, bound in bronze.

On the desk was a model of a modern warship and a letterpress mounted with three brass monkeys, one with a tiny hand cupped to his ear, the second looking over his shoulder, the third with his hand over his mouth. Next to the monkeys stood a single book, which Berthe instantly recognized: *Frederick II*, Ernst Kantorwicz's epic biography of Germany's greatest medieval emperor. It was her favorite history book.

On the floor was a Persian carpet that had seen better days. On one wall behind the desk was a livid painting of Satan, surrounded by the flames of hell. Near it was a photograph of Adolf Hitler boarding a German battleship. On a cot in the corner, in a tangle of brown army blankets, perched a dachshund, who growled suspiciously.

"Frau von Hoffmann—I am Wilhelm Canaris."

The Admiral had entered the office through another door, behind Berthe. He took both her hands and made a little bow as he expressed his gratitude for this chance to talk with her. Short and slight, he was clearly a gentleman of the old regime. His personality had been formed in the strictly correct upper-class society of Berlin before the last war. His face was a formal mask, a model of Prussian repression—except for his piercing blue eyes, which combined a basilisk intensity with an unexpected glint of mockery.

"I had been hoping to meet the beautiful Berthe von Schonberg for a long time," he said, speaking with a slight lisp. "But as the fates that take delight in persecuting me would have it, when it finally occurs, I'm much too feeble to do anything about it."

"I'm also a married woman, Admiral," Berthe said, smiling.

"Married to a von Hoffmann—a noble house—and to the son who had the special courage to become a submariner. I was one myself in the last war. That alone would create a bond between us, far stronger than any erotic delights you might—in a moment of thoughtless generosity—offer me."

The ghost of a smile played across the Admiral's face, as if he did not entirely discount that possibility. But his lisp somehow contradicted the suggestion that she should take it seriously.

"There's another reason for this talk of a bond, which is perhaps even stronger, though it's now a part of history. Your father."

"My father? You knew him?"

"I was in charge of our undercover operations in Spain for the first years of the last war. Your father was one of my most dependable, most successful, most daring agents."

Berthe could not have been more astonished if the Admiral had told her Count Willi von Schonberg was a being from another planet. Her father, who specialized in self-mockery, who boasted that he had spent four comfortable years in Spain while German soldiers died by the hundreds of thousands on the Western and Eastern fronts and civilians starved on ersatz food on the home front? Who flaunted his Spanish mistress in his daughter's face? This man, who seemed to have a desire, a need, to be despised, was a secret hero?

"There are a hundred British ships at the bottom of the Mediter-

ranean thanks to information he obtained on his visits to Tangier,"
Canaris said. "It was he who discovered the British planned to assassinate me and helped me escape from Spain."

Berthe could only shake her head in bewilderment. Canaris
toyed with one of the monkeys on the letterpress. "Like you, he loved
Germany," the Admiral said.

The words stirred an enormous echoing dread in Berthe's heart.
Was that why she was here? Behind and beneath her admiration for
Pastor Bruchmuller lay a blind, blundering adoration of the father-
land? Was she no different from the massed millions who screamed
Heil Hitler at the Führer's rallies?

"Why—why didn't my father tell me, my mother, what he was
doing?"

"You and your mother were part of his disguise. It was important
for you to despise him. Undoubtedly this satisfied some obscure
need in his soul. You don't spend much time in espionage without
discovering almost everyone is acting out some secret inner drama."

"Yet you think—in spite of this—I love Germany?"

"Why else did you marry an obscure young sailor? I know the von
Hoffmanns. I know their dedication to the Germany that has somehow eluded our hopes."

She said nothing. But her silence was an assent. She had to admit
it. She had to face the Berthe von Schonberg of her student days, the
woman who had read Holderin and Goethe and Schiller and great
historians such as Kantorwicz and found her soul resonating with the
pride, the glory of Germany's rise from two hundred years of humiliation inflicted by foreign armies and French cultural imperialism.
She too had trembled at the beauty, the power of Johann Gottfried
Herder's invocation of the German *volk*, their simple virtues, their
sturdy unquestioning devotion to the fatherland, and grieved for the
fresh humiliations inflicted on them by the odious treaty of Versailles.
Lothar Engle had forced her to face the flaws, even the absurdity in
this emotion, ultimately to dismiss it as a childish thing. But it
remained a living memory, evoked now by this strange lisping man in
a shabby blue Navy coat. "I married Ernst to give my life some purpose, some meaning," Berthe said. "I also loved him."

"The purpose, the meaning—was Germany. He lives for it. He's
risking his life for it at this very moment off Iceland."

The Admiral paused and smiled reflectively, as if he was laughing at a certain tendency in himself. "No—I won't make speeches to you, Frau von Hoffmann. He has until quite recently risked his life off Iceland. At the moment he is safe and relatively happy in the Canary Islands, repairing damages from a depth charge attack by an American destroyer."

"Thank God," Berthe said.

"The attack did not stop him, I am equally happy to say, from getting three ships with his last three torpedoes. I predict you will soon welcome home a winner of the Knight's Cross."

"How happy we'll be—to see him. The children miss him terribly."

The Admiral contemplated her with his basilisk eyes. He undoubtedly noticed she said nothing about the Knight's Cross.

Was she telling him she no longer loved Germany? Perhaps. She did not care. Whatever the purpose of this visit, she resolved to tell this man nothing but the truth. "This love of Germany has its limitations, don't you think?" Canaris said. "The fatherland doesn't deserve contempt, in the style of the once-great critic of our shortcomings, Lothar Engle. But given the present situation, love hardly seems an appropriate word. Would you agree?"

"Pastor Bruchmuller told me certain things he learned from you about our conduct in Poland and Russia that apparently make it inappropriate."

Gloom consumed the Admiral's sensitive face. It was almost as if the black veil of "The Young Widow" had descended. "I've shared these reports with a few people. Perhaps you can help us share them more widely. But there is another, more difficult task I hope you'll undertake."

For some reason, Berthe shrank from the calm authority in the Admiral's voice. Was it the fathering voice she had never known? The voice of Germany?

"I wonder if you're ready to help defeat Germany in this war."

Again, the words were so astonishing, Berthe could say nothing, feel nothing. For a moment she had to remind herself she was sitting in the office of the director of the German secret service. A man wearing the blue coat and admiral's rank of the Navy in which her husband was risking his life and the lives of his crew in the name of victory.

"For Germany to lose this war will be a disaster. For her to win it will be a catastrophe," Admiral Canaris said. He toyed with the monkey who was covering his mouth and waited for Berthe to absorb the full impact of that remark. "If Pastor Bruchmuller has accurately reported to me his conversations with you, I think you understand and agree with those words."

Berthe shook her head dazedly. "I fear—I'm only beginning to understand."

"A Nazi victory will ensure the reign of evil for a hundred years. It will corrupt Germany's soul—and the soul of the world, over which I devoutly believe Germany has been designated to stand peculiar guard. Do you believe that?"

"I don't know! I'm not sure what I know or believe!"

"Knowledge is not as important as faith. Listen to me, now, while I explain what we're trying to do."

She sat there, as immobile as one of the statues in the Siegesallee, while Wilhelm Canaris told her he was the center of a conspiracy that included certain generals in the army and civilians in the government, the church and the diplomatic corps. They were trying to convince the army high command to stage a coup d'état against Hitler. They were also trying to convince the British to agree to a negotiated peace, in advance of the coup. Until they sent a clear signal of approval, the high command refused to act.

"It's an immensely difficult task," Canaris said. "Because the British naturally don't trust us. Above all, they don't trust me. My business is deception. Even while I'm sending them agents with secrets that can tip the balance of the war in their favor, I'm infiltrating other agents into their country—and other countries—to perform the usual business of this service. I have to produce information for the high command, or I become even more suspect than I already am."

"That's what you want me to be? One of those agents who carry secrets to them?"

"Yes. But not to the British. To the Americans. They're our best hope now. Perhaps our only hope."

"Why? They're not in the war."

"They will be soon. There are powerful forces at work in the United States, moving them inexorably toward war. Their President, Roosevelt, is at the center of it, after a long period of hesitation. The British have a gifted team of agents in the country, working tirelessly to disseminate anti-German propaganda. But the outbreak will probably come from the east—from our secretive ally, Japan."

He gestured to the painting of the devil on his wall. "My friend the Japanese ambassador gave me that as a sort of Faustian joke. He thinks our two countries are destined to rule the world. He doesn't seem to realize the Führer believes there is only room on the globe for one race of supermen."

"I thought I heard on the radio that the Japanese were negotiating a settlement with the Americans," Berthe said.

Canaris's smile had a chilling resemblance to the one Satan wore on the wall. "They were also negotiating with the Russians in 1903 when they attacked Port Arthur and wiped out their Pacific Fleet. As a student of duplicity, I admire their talents. The Americans, for reasons I can't quite divine, seem determined to provoke them. They've embargoed oil shipments to them since last June. In six weeks Japan will run out of oil. That would spell catastrophe for the million troops they have in China. They have to act."

"Will that bring the Americans into the war against Germany?"

"I hope so. That's when you'll begin your mission in Spain."

"Spain?"

Canaris nodded. "It's the best possible atmosphere in which you can meet Americans. The Abwehr has over three-hundred agents there, and another six-hundred part-time employees. We can guarantee your safety far better than in Switzerland or Portugal. Although I should add, guarantees in the Abwehr, as in all secret services, are written in invisible ink on paper that is soluble in water."

Berthe thought of the angel embracing the Ritterboot, the promise of sunlight, beauty, peace. She remembered the four years she had spent in Spain during the last war as peculiarly lacking these qualities. She had been a shy ten-year-old when the war began and a gawky adolescent when it ended. Even the sunlight, which had undoubtedly been bright, seemed dim in memory.

"Spain," she repeated.

"Where your father proved he loved Germany."

"But not me."

For a moment she felt nothing but a terrible rage. She wanted to scream obscenities in the Admiral's aristocratic face, echoes of the vile words her mother used to fling at smirking Count Willi von Schonberg.

"You were the only thing he loved. He told me that once."

"You're lying!"

She dimly realized a transformation, a metempsychosis, had occurred. She was talking to her father, that man with the permanent sneer on his rake's mouth, the eternal glass of champagne in his hand.

"I do quite a lot of lying in my business," Admiral Canaris said. "But I'm not lying now."

Berthe began to weep. Awful wracking sobs that threatened to become convulsions. "How can I do—such a thing? I can't leave—my children."

"You must. Here is how it will work. Your husband will be given an extended leave while his boat undergoes a complete overhaul. He himself needs a rest—his last medical report found him a candidate for a peptic ulcer. He'll be assigned to the Spanish Embassy as the naval attaché. Under no circumstances will you tell him anything about this conversation. But he'll be safe from wabos for at least three months. Meanwhile we'll see who the Americans send to Spain once they enter the war."

"It will be soon?"

Canaris glanced at his desk calendar. "It's now November fifteenth. My estimate is within a month's time, the Japanese will attack. I hope you and your husband will be in Spain by the first week in January."

He was no longer asking for her assent. He knew she belonged to him. The Satanic smile on the wall seemed somehow broader, more vulgar, more ominous. Canaris noticed her eyes on it and smiled in his polite ghostly way. "I keep that painting there to remind myself and the rest of the Abwehr that it is sometimes necessary to do evil to produce good."

Berthe heard Friedrich Bruchmuller telling her: *everything is permitted.* She began to understand why she had been selected for this mission to Spain. They expected Count Willi von Schonberg's daughter to share more than secrets with these magical Americans.

She listened numbly while Canaris told her that she must come to work here at Abwehr headquarters as soon as possible. She would serve as an analyst in the Foreign Countries Department—a natural assignment for someone with her knowledge of French and Spanish and Russian. It would make the transfer to Spain less noticeable, when it occurred. She could be described as a trusted employee, if the Gestapo objected to her because she had signed the call to repentance for Kristallnacht.

"That was my idea," Canaris said. "In due time I'll explain to the Gestapo that such gestures are necessary to give Bruchmuller the bona fides to deal with neutral churchmen. Meanwhile they'll be busy watching forty devout Christians who are utterly harmless, giving them less manpower to watch us."

Canaris was ready to enmesh anyone and everyone, even innocent believers, in his web of intrigue. Was it all part of the Path, Berthe wondered? Or was the Admiral in the service of a darker power?

10

TOTAL FABRICATIONS

"Zeke, what a hell of a mess," Congressman Sam Richman said.

An exhausted Annie Richman Talbot watched her father pace the hotel room overlooking Newport harbor, his six foot three bulk emanating political anxiety. His thinning gray hair was mussed, his usually well-pressed dark blue suit was rumpled. In a corner of the room, her brother Jack regarded Zeke with an unnerving mixture of affection and irritation. In another corner, her arms folded over her ample bosom, sat Annie's mother, Helen, glaring at both of them, a stiff black hat on her large red-haired head.

She was there to reinforce the message that in Chicago, politics was personal as well as public—and perhaps to remind Zeke that her husband seldom had a political thought without consulting the daughter of Big Mike Fitzmorris, alderman and leader of Chicago's storied Eleventh Ward from 1910 to 1930. The glare made Annie wonder if Helen was part of the reason she had married Zeke Talbot. Had her secret slogan been "Join the Navy—and get far far away from your mother"?

The Congressman had comandeered a Navy PBY to fly the Richmans from Washington. They had arrived in the dawn, making it clear that this imbroglio with Admiral King was very serious stuff. Their extreme concern had done a lot to change Zeke from raging maniac to subdued, sullen prisoner of war.

"I think I understand how you feel," her father said in his hoarse, heavy breathing way, puffing on his fifth or sixth cigarette since he arrived. "You ain't the only one who's sore at FDR for linin' up with Buckingham Palace. Half the micks in Chicago feel the same way. But the limeys are the only guys standin' up to Adolf—except the Russians, and no one in my district's rootin' for them, not even us Hebes, because they've treated us worse than the Germans ever did. Let's admit Hitler's gotta be stopped somehow. Is it really so bad, to stretch the Constitution a little to do it? Hell every president's pulled the same sort of stunts when he got in a tight spot. In her senior year at Trinity Annie did a paper on the Louisiana Purchase. It was all about how Hamilton and his pals screamed the buy was unconstitutional and Jefferson admitted it, for Crissakes. Lincoln violated the Constitution every second day durin' the Civil War—I don't know that for a fact—I ain't no legal scholar—but that's what Jack here tells me. He wrote a column on it last week."

The disdain in Zeke's eyes made Annie writhe. She knew he was comparing her father's bad grammar and slurred Chicago political wisdom to his own father's rolling periods à la Daniel Webster and observations from Montesquieu and Edmund Burke. In the past she too had mildly disdained her father's political style—or lack of it. Now every flaw mortified her.

The Congressman lit another cigarette and shifted gears. "You also can't ignore the way people feel about FDR. There's thirty million voters out there who think he's practically the Second Comin'. He's saved people from losin' their houses, their farms. He got them off bread lines. In Chicago, Catholics hang his picture in their front halls where they used to put a paintin' of Jesus. You got to think twice before you go up against a feelin' like that. Figuratively speakin', you'd be goin' into the ring against King Kong."

"And you'd be dragging Sam with you," Helen Richman said.

"That's the truth, Zeke," the Congressman said. "This wouldn't play too good in the Chicago *Tribune*, from my point of view. They've been after my head for years. They'd put everything you got to say against Roosevelt on the front page, next to my picture."

"You won't find ten Democratic congressmen who'll back you up," Jack Richman said.

Republicans were, of course, irrelevant. Annie winced as the implication registered on Zeke's face. Why couldn't Jack be more diplomatic? He seemed to be relishing this chance to remind his ex-roommate of the Talbots' political impotence.

"Lemme put it this way, Zeke," Sam Richman continued. "If we got a Republican president and your father was back up there in the State Department and Jack had somethin' on him—nothin' personal, you know but somethin' a guy on his staff did, I wouldn't want him to use it. I don't think he would use it, right, Jack?"

"Right," Jack said.

"But Roosevelt's getting us into the war—inch by inch!" Zeke said. "Isn't that important to you? Doesn't that make all this other stuff irrelevant?"

"You can't prove that, Zeke. All you can do is predict it. Personally, I think FDR's on the level when he says he hates war. When you're in this business for a while you know what comes from the gut."

Annie did not like the expression on Jack's face. Weary condescension would be the kindest way to describe it. A less kinder word would be contempt. Jack knew so much. He was deep inside the Roosevelt administration while her father and the rest of Congress were mostly spectators.

"Another thing you've got to remember," Jack said. "Roosevelt plays hardball. I could give you a long list of people who've had their phones tapped by the FBI, their income tax returns audited with malice aforethought, until they went to jail or cried uncle. He won't bat an eye if the Admiral goes to work on you."

And you, the fierce guardian of public morality when Republicans are in the wrong, will not say a word, of course. Annie could almost hear Zeke snarling this bitter comment in his head. She winced even more at the way the Congressman accepted Jack's description of Roosevelt's political ethics as casually as if it had been a remark on the weather. "Maybe it comes down to this, Zeke. You wanna stay in the Navy? Then you gotta let me cut a deal with King. Stop him from puttin' that memorandum in your file. Once that's in there, you're an instant has-been."

"You know that's how it works, Zeke," Jack said. To her surprise, Annie sensed defensiveness in these words. She suddenly remembered midnight conversations when Jack was still in the Navy, shortly after she had married Zeke. With a passion that had awed her, Zeke had lectured them on the Navy's mission—not merely to defend

America but to help fulfill her global destiny by projecting her power and influence throughout the world.

In those days, Zeke was the one who spoke in a proprietary way about the country. Now his attempt to do so had a forlorn eccentric quality. Maybe power was the only thing that counted. The Richmans had it and Talbots didn't and all the rest of this argument was sliced baloney.

"Whattya say, Zeke?" Sam Richman asked.

"I guess you better go see him," Zeke said. He looked so miserable, Annie almost switched sides. She was ready to urge her husband to tell Admiral King to go diddle himself and damn the consequences to everyone. How else could she ever convince this man she still loved him?

Forty-eight hours later, Lieutenant Commander Jonathan Trumbull Talbot stood before a half-dozen reporters in the press room of the U.S. Navy Department Building on Constitution Avenue and Seventeenth Street in Washington, D.C. In his hand was a statement that he read in a loud unreal voice, struggling through every sentence as if he were on the brink of aphasia.

"I wish to state categorically that recent attempts by the German government to conceal the true circumstances of the sinking of my ship, the USS *Spencer Lewis*, by smearing my character are untrue. The *Spencer Lewis* was torpedoed without warning on November ninth and most of its crew left to die in the North Atlantic. The submarine which picked up me and Fireman First Class Isidore Klein did so only to ascertain the name of the ship they had sunk. They treated us with minimal courtesy while on board. At no point did I ever express any disapproval of the American government's policy of escorting ships within the Atlantic defense zone designated by President Roosevelt. Nor did I ever suggest any approval of the German government or its leader, Adolf Hitler. Nor did I participate in an attack on ships in the convoy the *Spencer Lewis* had been escorting. These statements are total fabrications designed to conceal the German government's policy of murder on the high seas."

Sam Richman had gone to see Cinclant King, who was predictably polite to someone with the power to raise or lower the Navy's budget. There was no mention of a court-martial for pederasty and other imaginary sins. As soon as the Congressman assured him

Talbot would deny the German propaganda, the Admiral agreed to call the clash an unfortunate misunderstanding and promised not to put anything negative in Zeke's personnel file. They were soon on their way to Washington, where Zeke drew up this repudiation of Berlin's assertions, with Jack's help.

Annie, watching from the back of the briefing room, was demoralized. This press conference, the statement full of specific details, were Jack's ideas. He seemed determined to humiliate Zeke. On the plane back to Washington, D.C., Jack had told Annie in a curt, cold voice that it was time her husband learned a few lessons about politics. It was a side of her brother she had never seen before.

The reporters accepted copies of the printed statement from a lieutenant junior grade. There was no reason to get excited over it. The idea of an American naval officer joining the Germans in an attack was so absurd, it only proved the Nazis were the worst propagandists in the world. Most of the questions were attempts to extract some human interest from the story.

"How long did you stay aboard the submarine, Commander?"

"Four days," Zeke said.

"How would you describe the Germans' morale?"

"Excellent. They're thoroughly trained and dedicated to victory. If the sinking of the *Spencer Lewis* leads to war, we'd better be prepared for a tough fight."

Off to the right, the stage director of the charade, portly avuncular Admiral David C. Duncan, the Navy's Director of Public Information, cleared his throat nervously. "Commander Talbot is by no means implying the U.S. Navy isn't ready for that fight."

"Of course not," Zeke said. His eyes traveled down the room to ask Annie a wordless ironic question: Is this what America is all about? Forcing a man who had always tried to live up to the Naval Academy's code of honor to lie by the paragraph to conceal the bigger lie in which the Navy was collaborating with that prince of liars, the President of the United States?

But she still believed that same president had given hope to millions of Americans lost in the desolation of the Great Depression. His New Deal had expanded the reach of America's promises to include millions of others who had never felt included by them. His call for defiance of Nazism and fascism, his vision of a world organized around the Atlantic Charter's Four Freedoms, had exported hope to oppressed people around the globe. How did these noble goals get entangled in a web of lies?

Annie refused to accept Zeke's conclusion, that Roosevelt was endangering America's meaning and purpose with his amoral unconstitutional ruthlessness and his steadily accumulating power. There had to be some middle ground between glorification and condemnation but she did not know what it was.

The reporters shuffled out, showing no sign of shouting "Stop the presses!" There was a very good chance that no newspaper would print a word of Zeke's denial. Why get worked up about refuting a story that had never been published in America? But the Associated Press and United Press had already assured Admiral Duncan that the statement would go out over their wires to the rest of the world, where quite a few readers might be titillated by Lieutenant Commander Talbot's indignant rebuttal of Dr. Goebbels.

Upstairs in Admiral Duncan's office, Sam Richman slapped Zeke on the back. "They never laid a glove on you," he said.

"I've checked with personnel," Duncan said. "King didn't put anything in your file. But he's not exactly your number-one fan."

"Admiral King won't be around forever," Sam said. "He was one step from retirement when FDR gave him the Atlantic job." In his seventeen years in Congress, Sam had seen a lot of admirals come and go.

The expression on Admiral Duncan's face suggested Admiral King might be around long enough to do a lot of damage to Zeke's naval career. "I think you better lay low for a while," he said. "You haven't got a chance of getting another ship in the Atlantic. Nothing new is going to the Pacific. I'll see what I can do about finding you a slot here in Washington."

That night, after dinner with her mother and father, Annie and Zeke drove toward Norfolk. In the back seat, reading Albert Schweitzer's life of Jesus by flashlight, was their son, Butch. Annie had left him with her mother for the trip to Newport. He was currently studying all three religions in his heritage before deciding which one to accept.

"Are you satisfied with my performance?" Zeke asked. "Did I lie successfully enough to meet your exacting standards?"

"Zeke—there simply wasn't any other realistic alternative," Annie said.

"How about an idealistic alternative? Doesn't that interest you anymore?"

"Of course it does. But one man can't fight the entire U.S. government."

"I feel soiled by the whole thing. Don't you?"

"Yes," she said. "I loathed every minute of it."

Was she hoping this admission would repair the damage? "But you still feel it's better to go along to get along?" Zeke said.

Annie shook her head angrily. "I've never explicitly asked you do that and I never will!" she said. That was the literal truth but it left unexplored a vast subterranean cavern of implications. "Zeke—this was a crisis—created by your antipathy to FDR. I think it's time you rethought your attitude toward him."

He glared down the dark empty highway. "I have no intention of changing my mind about something that fundamental," he said.

"I don't get it," Butch said from the back seat. "Schweitzer is spending his whole life in Africa like a missionary. But he doesn't believe Jesus was God."

"It's very confusing," Annie said. "Like a lot of things in life."

"Do you think Jesus was God?"

"No," Annie said, twisting away from the spasm of guilt the admission cost her.

"How about you, Dad?"

"No, son. But he was a very good man. He believed in telling the truth, standing up for your ideals no matter what happened to you."

They spent the rest of the ride discussing whether to move to Washington, D.C. Annie's father had assured them he could find an apartment, in spite of the chronic shortage, and hinted he was eager to help them pay the rent, which would be two or three times what they were paying on their dead-end street on the outskirts of Norfolk. But Zeke had always refused to take a cent from the Congressman—or from his own father.

Zeke finally decided it would be best to stay in Norfolk. With the surge in defense spending, the price of everything was going up at an incredible pace and Washington would unquestionably break their budget. "I'll try to wangle a slot in some Bachelor Officers' Quarters—or rent a furnished room. I can mooch a dinner or two from my sister Ethel. We'll see each other on weekends."

"I hate that idea," Annie said, as they retreated to the living room after ordering Butch to bed.

"Which one—me seeing too much of Ethel—or you seeing me only on weekends?" he asked with a wry smile.

"Both," she said.

Zeke's sister Ethel was an elongated accumulation of New England arrogance, with an endless fund of putdowns and carping comments about how much her beloved baby brother needed tender loving care. Her husband, Ned Travis, was a rising star at the State Department.

"It doesn't make sense to uproot Butch for an assignment that won't last more than six months," Zeke said. "If it lasts any longer—"

"Let's worry about that if and when it happens," Annie said. She wrapped her arms around him and pressed her head against his chest. "We haven't seen each other for three months. All we've done is snarl and scream. What happened to that funny, clever guy I met in 1928, with his brand new Annapolis diploma and a starry look in his eyes that made me want to go around the world with him?"

"He's gotten older," Zeke said.

For a moment Annie almost despaired. She knew exactly what he was remembering—the Talbots' humiliating loss of power and influence. But there were days, weeks, months, whole years of their personal past that transcended this disappointment. There had to be a way of summing up the good memories. Almost as if some benevolent spirit was guiding her, Annie's eyes found a picture of her and Zeke on the beach at Waikiki, she in a white tanktop, he in navy blue trunks and flowered shirt. "If you live to be a hundred," she said. "I'll still remember the man I knew in Hawaii."

The gratitude on his face made her wonder if she had blundered into the only lesson they could share. "I love you so much. I hate the thought of anything, including Franklin D. Roosevelt and the U.S. Navy, getting in the way," Annie said.

"We won't let them," Zeke said. "Not as long as we can do this."

He began unbuttoning her blouse. Annie realized he wanted to make love on the couch, the way they had cavorted in that first magical year in Honolulu, when they had done it everywhere and anytime, four, sometimes five times a weekend in their bungalow overlooking Pearl Harbor.

The delight had been enlarged by a marvelous sense gift. She had been amazed by the totality of her surrender to him. He had struggled to match it with a giving, a tenderness, an adoration of his own. She vowed to somehow alter the way that gift had become possession, an assumption of ownership that he resented.

But Hawaii could not be transported across almost twelve years and six thousand miles to a rundown house on the outskirts of Norfolk, with an eleven-year-old gifted son sleeping—or more probably still reading by flashlight—in the back bedroom. "Zeke," Annie said, as he started to take off her blouse. "What if Butch wakes up? We better go in the bedroom."

He walked her into their bedroom, with its antique four poster bed, a gift of some Talbot great aunt. Kissing her neck, his hands cupped on her breasts, he kicked the door shut and began some serious undressing.

In seconds they were naked on the bed, his hands roving from her breasts to her pussy. Was this a lesson or an obliteration of a lesson? Annie wondered. Behind her closed eyes she ordered herself back to Hawaii. The trade wind was sighing through the windows, the Pacific's reaches billowed in the blue distance—instead of Norfolk's scruffy downtown. His tongue filled her mouth, his hands seized her rump and lifted her for the trip through what he used to call the tunnel of love. What had she called him? The sybaritic sandhog. They used to talk about how much they both wanted it, how stunned they were by the ecstasy of it. For both of them, it had been the first time, which somehow made it more precious.

"I love you so *much*," Annie whispered as he stroked her. "Doesn't that change everything?"

"I want it to, I wish it would," he whispered.

He was coming. It was too soon, she wasn't ready but she didn't care, they were together. Hawaii, the past, unqualified love was real again.

She opened her eyes and saw his face, divided by conflicting emotions. His eyes were searching for Hawaii, the trade wind, while his mouth was remembering *total fabrications to conceal*. What was happening to them? The ugly, angry present was invading the past. Duty honor country. *Total fabrications*. Coming!

"Oh, oh oh!" She was coming too, it was an event in its own right. She clung to him with all the strength in her short arms. "Oh Zeke! I—love—you!"

"I love you too. I really do. I'm sorry—"

That last word echoed eerily around the silent bedroom. He withdrew and cradled her in his arms, his lips against her throat. Annie switched on the bedside radio. "PLEASE GIVE ME SOMETHING TO REMEMBER YOU BY." Patti Page was warbling the year's hit song. Turning it down low, she snuggled against him. "The old sandhog is as sybaritic as ever," she murmured.

"Just as much fun in the tunnel," he said.

Was he ready for another trip? That would guarantee Hawaii's resurrection. Before she could suggest it, the telephone rang. Zeke shrugged on a bathrobe and strode to the front hall to catch it on the fourth jangle. "Oh—hello, Admiral. No. We made good time. Butch is already asleep. You have? That's fast work. Well—I guess I could do a lot worse. It'll be interesting work. Thanks a lot."

He trudged back to the bedroom. Annie could tell from his heavy footsteps that he was not bringing good news. "That was Duncan. Your father's got him hopping. He's found me a slot at ONI."

"Office of Naval Intelligence," Annie said. "It sounds impressive."

"To civilians."

There was no available answer to that one. After eleven years as a Navy wife, Annie knew ONI was a graveyard in which the living dead, those who had screwed up in any of a hundred possible ways in the tight-assed peacetime Navy—by ramming a flagship in fleet maneuvers, running aground in Pearl Harbor, offending an admiral's wife—drudged out their ruined careers. The division on Zeke's face was declining rapidly into the mouth that remembered only the total fabrications of the briefing room, the humiliation of succumbing to going along to get along.

Hawaii! Annie wanted to shout it. She wanted Zeke, maybe the whole miserable world, to realize how hard she had tried to get back to it. But she was left with the burdened, bitter man her husband had become, after twelve years of dwindling faith in the United States of America.

11

BEWARE THE GREEK

"The Abwehr?" Isolde von Hoffmann said, frowning at her daughter-in-law as if she had joined another subversive organization. "It's run by an admiral, isn't it? With an odd name?"

"Canaris," Berthe said, pinning her hair in the usual severe chignon.

"That's Greek, isn't it? How in the world did anyone from that despicable country get such a sensitive post?"

"His family has lived in Germany for over one hundred years."

"Isn't there a saying, beware the Greeks, bearing gifts?"

"It's from Virgil's *Aeneid*," Berthe said.

This won her only a malevolent glare from Frau Von Hoffmann. She disapproved of educated women in general and her daughter-in-law in particular. But she could not object to Berthe going to work for the Abwehr. It was patriotic. She was serving the Reich.

At the entrance to the Abwehr headquarters on the Tirpitz Ufer, Berthe met Admiral Canaris and a frowning man who looked almost like a caricature of the stiff, severe Prussian officer. Canaris introduced her to Colonel Hans Oster, his chief of staff. He clicked his heels, kissed her hand and said he was honored to meet a relative of the great general, Ulrich von Hoffmann. He had commanded a battery of field artillery under him on the Eastern front in the last war. With his usual wisp of a smile, Canaris told Berthe that Oster would assign her to her duties. She followed the Colonel to his office on the floor below Canaris. On his wall was a motto carved on wood in Bavarian script: *An eagle does not hunt flies.* "I'm assigning you to work with Count Helmuth von Moltke."

He paused to allow the name to have its expected impact. "He's the great-grandnephew of the general," he said. "He's one of us, heart and soul. I find it encouraging to think that the blood of the founder of the modern German Army is helping us rid the fatherland of the evil dwarfs who have taken possession of us."

Admiral Canaris expressed his disapproval of the regime with sly bemused regret. Colonel Oster's approach was pure ferocity. Berthe wondered uneasily if he talked this way to everyone.

She followed Oster to the second floor, where they found a thin fortyish man with fiercely intelligent dark eyes and a sensitive almost feminine mouth at a desk piled high with papers. He was wearing an old gray tweed jacket and rough country shirt. Oster introduced her to Count von Moltke. When he stood up to greet her, he revealed long legs. He towered over her and Oster. If there was a family resemblance to the statue of his ancestor near the Sieges Saule, it was in the bold, uncompromising gaze.

"I'm told you know Russian," Moltke said.

She nodded. "My father had a Russian mistress in Paris after the last war. I had to learn it in self-defense, to find out the atrocious things she said about me."

Count von Moltke's polite smile suggested he did not approve of Russian mistresses. "I fear you'll be reading equally atrocious words from the Eastern front," he said.

"The war is not going well?" Berthe said, frankly amazed. The newspapers and the radio reported nothing but victories.

"I wasn't referring to the military phase," Moltke said. "In spite of my name, I'm a mere civilian. You should ask Colonel Oster what he thinks of our chances for victory. I depend on his opinion absolutely in such matters."

His smile was gentle and immensely fond, as he deferred to the frowning Colonel. "Even if we get to Moscow, which I doubt," Oster said, his face as somber as his voice, "the war is lost. It's only a question of when everyone realizes it. Then will come the moment to dispose of the Führer incubus."

Again, Berthe was swept by a sense of unreality. These men were

talking about overthrowing Adolf Hitler, the leader who could summon a million Germans to worship him at torchlight rallies. Did they
know what they were doing?

Moltke, perhaps disturbed by the expression on her face, tried to
soften Oster's violent tone. "The Colonel is an ardent supporter of
assassination. Not all of us agree."

"You will, before long. Even the reverends agree!" Oster said.

"In the meantime, we must do what we can to mitigate the evil—
so Germany can face the world with at least a few shreds of honor on
her flag," Moltke said.

He assigned Berthe a desk and heaped a dozen files on it. They
had the names of towns and cities on the Eastern front on their
labels: Vilnius, Minsk, Smolensk. Each contained dispatches in Russian from Abwehr agents in the vicinity, often on torn pieces of wrapping paper. As Berthe deciphered the handwriting and the colloquial
Russian, a deeper sense of unreality began to pervade her.

Agent 666 wrote from Vilnius:

Today the Army withdrew from the city and handed over control to the SS.
They immediately began deporting Jews to railroad cars waiting in the
yards. Anyone who resisted was shot. Any Jew who belonged to the Communist party was handed over to a separate Kommando who marched them
to a field outside the city and machine gunned them. The bodies were
thrown in a ditch and covered with lime. The plight of the captured Russian
soldiers worsens each day. They are being systematically starved to death.
Today their ration was cut to a quarter of a pound of bread per man, plus
some greasy water they call soup. Typhus is rampant. The death rate is rising astronomically. This makes no sense, to alienate and/or destroy men
who would be eager to repay decent treatment by fighting in the ranks
against the Communists. Why can't the High Command grasp this fact?

Berthe typed out the translation, laid it on Moltke's desk and
began another report, from Riga. It was more of the same, with even
worse outrages against the Jews. In Riga the SS Commander decided
not to wait for railroad trains to transport them to concentration
camps. He began shooting them wholesale, men, women and children. Here, too, Russian prisoners were being starved, deprived of
medical treatment and otherwise abused by SS guards.

Moltke turned from files that he was studying to read Berthe's
translations. He groaned aloud. "More bestiality. We're inundated

with reports like these. It's almost inconceivable, isn't it? The German Army is permitting these murders to be committed. It's even worse in the Balkans. In a town in Serbia, seventeen hundred men and two hundred and forty women were executed for an attack on three German soldiers. I estimate we're murdering a thousand people a day."

"Can anything be done?"

Moltke's smile was even more ghostly than Canaris's. "I've dispatched a memorandum to General Keitel, the Chief of Staff, pointing out that the *Wehrmacht* is ultimately responsible for the conduct of everyone in the conquered territories and the SS abuses are violating international agreements on the treatment of prisoners of war and civilians. To my amazement, three generals have initialed it as it was passed up the chain of command."

For a moment Berthe was wreathed by an odd sense of glory, even of triumph. She felt flooded by gratitude that the Path had led her to this man. She understood the value of the name Moltke on such a memorandum. He was part of Canaris's plan—or hope—to arouse the latent morality in the German officer corps.

She also saw why Canaris had ordered her to come to work at Abwehr headquarters. It was not simply to give her a cover. It was to fill her mind and soul with the kind of knowledge she was translating in the dispatches from Vilnius and Minsk and Smolensk, to show her the appalling dimensions of the evil she had sensed in the Führer's raging rhetoric.

Also—to meet Helmuth von Moltke. Day by day, as they worked together, Berthe became more and more awed by the man. Never before had she encountered such committed idealism. He was a virtual personification of Immanuel Kant's great directive: *Act as if the maxim from which you act were to become through your will a universal law.* This principle, the categorical imperative, was the way a rational being achieved a clear conscience, an undefiled will. Moltke made Berthe wonder if her response to Ernst von Hoffmann's boyish devotion to the fatherland was only a first step on her spiritual journey.

Along with fighting the Nazi system in the courts (he was a trained lawyer) as well as in the councils of the army, Moltke was writing in hours stolen from sleep a comprehensive program to restore democracy to Germany after Hitler was deposed. On his estate in Silesia, he regularly gathered a dozen of Germany's best minds, who spent the weekend contributing their ideas to this document of rebirth.

Moltke soon had Berthe carrying urgent messages to judges and fellow lawyers in Berlin, trying to mitigate another ominous event— the deportation of the city's Jews to work camps in Poland. "The authorities want to spare us the sight of how they'll be left to perish from cold and hunger and so arrange this in Litzmannstadt and Auschwitz," he fumed, as he helped these unfortunate people to transfer property to relatives, to write wills and in numerous cases to protest the deportation with legal arguments—such as the denial that the deportee was of Jewish descent. Often, with the help of a certain printer who specialized in forgeries for the Abwehr, spurious birth certificates were created to outwit the SS.

But only a few could be helped this way. Each night at 9:15, when most of Berlin was on the way to bed, the SS rounded up another thousand Jews and detained them overnight in synagogues and then marched them to trains. On the way back from one of her errands, Berthe saw a column of these pathetic people being escorted to a railroad station. One old man collapsed. A compassionate woman passerby tried to help him. A policeman shoved her aside and kicked the old man into the gutter. He turned to the woman and said apologetically: "Those are our orders." The woman burst into tears.

When Berthe told Helmuth von Moltke the story, he amazed her by saying it was a sign of hope. "If that policeman is ashamed enough to apologize, it shows all is not lost. The categorical imperative still exists in the German soul. That is a fundamental part of my faith."

Mitigate the evil. All is not lost. The words haunted Berthe as she translated still more grisly accounts of massacres and prisoner abuse in Russia. An exclamation of disgust from Moltke interrupted her. He showed her the response to his memorandum of protest to General Keitel. The Chief of Staff had written on it: *These doubts correspond to military ideas from the wars of chivalry*.

"Put it in the file," Moltke said. "I think he'll live to regret those words."

Along with defeats, there were unexpected victories. One day Moltke rushed into the office and dumped a half-dozen sacks of mail on Berthe's desk. "Put on your postman's hat," he said. "We must work quickly."

The letters were from German prisoners of war in Russia. The Nazis had been claiming that the Russians took no prisoners and that justified their atrocious treatment of Russian POWs. They had forbidden the post office to deliver the letters, which proved them liars. A friend in the post office had sent them to the Abwehr, piously claiming he thought they might have information they could use. Berthe helped Moltke and several others dump the letters in nearby mail boxes. Two days later, he cheerfully informed her that the army was being inundated with requests to send food parcels to captured loved ones—and had agreed to let the Red Cross take charge of Russian prisoners.

Barbarities were not the only subject of the dispatches Berthe translated. Many dealt with the military situation on the Russian front, seen up close by the Abwehr's spies, who often crossed the battle lines by night. Far from being defeated, the Russians were taking full advantage of the onset of winter. They were rushing fresh troops from Siberia to the defense of Moscow. The German high command, presuming they were on their way to another lightning victory like the one in France, had made no preparation for fighting in below zero cold. Tanks were breaking down by the hundreds, flu and pneumonia were spreading through the ranks.

"You see how wise Colonel Oster is?" Moltke said, when Berthe handed these dispatches to him. His tone was sad—there was no hint of Oster's savage satisfaction in the coming debacle. Berthe suspected some ancestral loyalty to the German Army was speaking.

Moltke shoved back his chair and gazed out at the dark gloomy Tiergarten. "Are you a believing Christian, Frau von Hoffmann?" he asked.

"I wasn't until I met Pastor Bruchmuller. He's stirred a certain attraction to the old faith in me."

"More and more I begin to think there's no other answer to what's engulfing us but some sort of faith. We can't expect ordinary people to understand Kant's categorical imperative. But they can understand the Sermon on the Mount, the example of Jesus. What's surrounding us helps me appreciate religion more and more."

The Path, Berthe thought. This man is a lightbearer on the Path.

"I used to think the spark was called truth, but now I think faith is a better word. I find my thoughts crowded with Biblical images. The Deluge story. The Wise Men following the star from the east."

Suddenly Berthe found words on her lips. She did not know where they came from. "The Ark survives the waters. The Wise Men of the old civilization carry gifts through the desert to the Child of the new civilization."

They were together now, like themes in a Bach fugue. "Yes," Moltke said, mournful joy illuminating his angular face. "Yes. It's a blessing to be allowed to carry the spark, and a sacred duty. Beyond the desert, the Child is waiting for us."

"Then you believe in God's existence?" Berthe said.

Moltke nodded mournfully. "But I begin to think His nature is more hidden, more terrible, by our lights, than we have imagined. The salvation story utterly transcends human reason—and I fear we are destined to live it again and again. On that point, Nietzsche was right. Eternal recurrence is the true norm. Not this ridiculous faith in progress and world-transforming revolutions."

Nietzsche. Lothar Engle's favorite philosopher. He had done his utmost to make Berthe a follower of this great subversive, whose announcement of God's death still reverberated through Germany. Was this anguished drama in which she was entangled God's peculiar answer?

That night, as she trudged through whirling snowflakes to the underground, a man fell in step beside her. "I wish you'd told me you wanted to go to work. I would have found ample room for your talents in my office," Lothar Engle said. In his SS cloak, he was like a cleft of blackness in the gloomy November twilight.

"I felt so useless, sitting home exchanging glares with my mother-in-law," Berthe said.

"Why in the world have you gone to work for Canaris? Don't you know that lisping little queer is detested by everyone from Himmler to Goering?"

"I've barely met Admiral Canaris," Berthe said. "I had a mutual friend who knew Colonel Oster. He said they were looking for translators—"

"Let's have a drink. This is too important to talk about in the street."

Before she could protest, he swung her into a little café off the Bendlerstrasse, a dim empty place stale with tobacco fumes. They settled in a booth in the rear and Berthe ordered a raspberry and soda. Lothar asked for a double martini. His face was solemn.

"The Abwehr is not a place where the wife of a naval officer ought to be working, Berthe," he said.

"I like it," Berthe said. "The work is simple—the pace is slow. I don't want complicated responsibilities."

Lothar did not seem to be listening. "Have you heard of the Schwarze Kapelle?" he snapped.

The Black Orchestra? Berthe shook her head. "That's what the Gestapo calls them—conservatives like Oster, who are trying to foment a coup d'état against the Führer. Believe me, they're far more detested than the Rote Kapelle—about twenty Communist conspirators in the air ministry, who'll be arrested in a week or two. The Reds are simply spies for the other side. The Blacks pretend to speak for Germany—as if that were possible as long as Hitler is alive."

"Why doesn't Canaris do something about them?" she asked, trying to sound as innocent as possible.

"He finds them useful in his contacts with the West. Himmler, all of us in the SS are doing the same thing. We're trying to negotiate decent terms with the goddamn British so we can concentrate on the Russians, who are proving much more difficult than we expected. Eventually, Canaris will make a clean sweep of the Schwarze Kapelle and claim all the credit—making the Gestapo look like idiots. He and his friend Heydrich will divide up the power between them."

A half-dozen young staff officers from Army headquarters crowded into booths at the other end of the cafe and began talking in loud tones. Lothar dropped his voice to a murmur, which somehow made it even more unnerving. "I don't want you caught in this mess, Berthe."

Dazedly, she heard herself asking: "Canaris is a friend of Reinhard Heydrich's?" Everyone in Berlin knew this handsome playboy. The Nazi charmer, he was called. He was the head of the *Sicherheitdienst*, the Nazi party's foreign intelligence service. Heydrich was second only to Himmler in the SS.

"Canaris lives next door to him. His wife gives birthday parties for Heydrich's kids."

Lothar offered Berthe an English cigarette. She could not resist it. The vile ersatz tobacco in German cigarettes had forced her to give up smoking. "How do you still get them?" she asked, trying not to talk, much less think, about Canaris's friendship with Reinhard Heydrich.

"Through the Swedes. They're eager to satisfy our every need." Lothar inhaled the fragrant smoke and closed his eyes for a moment, his face aglow with pleasure. Berthe thought of Moltke, the different light she had seen on his face a few hours ago.

"You have two choices, to protect yourself," Lothar said. "One, quit your job immediately and come to work for me. Two, stay there and become an informer for us."

"I dislike both," Berthe said, amazed at the steadiness in her voice. Did she possibly have an inherited talent for espionage? Or was her need to keep this man at arm's length maximizing her survival instincts? "If I come to work for you, we'll be in bed within the week—and I can't do that to Ernst. You can't wound a man who needs steady nerves, a clear mind, to survive the kind of war he's fighting. As for informing—I don't think there's anything I could find—and I consider it morally repellent."

Lothar gulped his martini and inhaled another deep drag on the cigarette. "You're still that muddled idealist I rescued from the professors, aren't you? Marrying that stupid sailor was another outbreak of the disease. How can you still believe in anything when you see what's happened to Germany? Is there any morality in the triumph of National Socialism? As the lady who made the movie said, it's the triumph of the will."

He was talking about Leni Riefensthal's epic film of Hitler's ascendancy, a series of stunning images of the panoply of Nazi power. The massed parades, the banners, the torchlight processions, the impassioned speeches from swastika-draped platforms.

"Everything is still permitted, Berthe," Lothar said. "Everything."

She was assailed by an enormous echoing bewilderment. She saw not Lothar's sardonic sensual face, on which those words had once seemed to fit as perfectly as skin, but Friedrich Bruchmuller's saintly face. Did Bruchmuller know about Canaris's friendship with Reinhard Heydrich? Was that why the minister did not entirely trust him? Was she simply another pawn in the game Canaris was playing for Hitler?

The erotic intensity abruptly dwindled from Lothar's face, his eyes turned inward. "Things beyond both our imaginations are being permitted, Berthe. We were mere toddlers in the school of moral indifference, compared to these people."

For a moment she wanted to cry out in the name of their lost love, to rebuke this man, to ask him how he could join such a pack of murderers. But that love had almost destroyed her. It had been another triumph of the will—Lothar's will. For him, a woman had to be more than merely loved, she had to be owned, possessed in soul as well as body.

"They're doing terrible things to the Jews," Lothar said. "I never thought it would come to such barbarity. I really thought attacking them was a device, a useful if somewhat tawdry political gambit. But Himmler, Heydrich—the Führer himself—really mean it."

He began talking about Jewish Berliners they both knew— deported to camps where mere existence was barely sustainable, where there was one toilet for two thousand people—women and men.

"Can't you help any of them?" Berthe asked.

Lothar shook his head. "Not now, while the war in Russia is going badly. When we win—the mood may change. They may revive the scheme of deporting them to Madagascar—or even to Palestine. These brutes can be civilized, given time—and the removal of our external enemies."

Lothar seized her arm and reiterated his advice: either quit the Abwehr or inform on them. There was no other way he could guarantee her safety. Berthe rode home to Wannsee trying to measure Lothar Engle against Wilhelm Canaris.

The next day, Berthe asked to see the Admiral. Lothar Engle was not a phenomenon to discuss with Helmuth von Moltke. Canaris was amused by Lothar's proposition. He demanded a virtual recital of the entire conversation, including Lothar's bad conscience about the Jews. "The fellow is a very good actor," he said. "I know at least three Jews who came to him for help. A word to Himmler would have at least delayed their deportation. Engle refused to see them."

"But you are a friend of Reinhard Heydrich?" Berthe asked.

All amusement vanished from Canaris's face. Berthe saw—or feared she saw—a man who could remove her and her children from the face of the earth without a qualm.

"Yes," he said. "He served under me in the Navy. He was cashiered for fathering an illegitimate child. He's easily flattered."

The Admiral toyed with the monkey with a hand cupped to his ear. "Without his friendship, the Abwehr would have been absorbed by the Sicherheitdienst long ago. I think you should protect yourself—and us—by becoming an informer for Herr Engle."

"What shall I tell him?" Berthe said.

"I'll supply you with the information. Even a few documents. It will be another channel—I already have several—with which to confuse the SD. We'll have them scurrying from Ankara to Geneva to Paris to Madrid in search of treachery. And every time, we'll have a sound explanation for our activities. Finally—I'll go to the Führer and ask him to put an end to this nonsense—and throw them on the defensive for at least a year."

"Is there any news about the Americans and the Japanese?"

"They're getting closer to breaking off negotiations. But we don't know exactly what the little yellow fellows are going to do if that happens. We want them to attack the Russians in Siberia, of course. But I don't think they have the stomach for it. They fought a war with the Siberian Army in 1939 and took a terrible drubbing. I fear they'll go south for easier pickings in the Dutch East Indies and Singapore. The British will never be able to stop them."

"Will the Americans try?"

"That's the large unanswered question. Whether Roosevelt can persuade his Congress that American soldiers and sailors should die to preserve the Dutch and British empires. I fear not. Which leaves us with one somewhat forlorn hope."

"That they attack the Americans?"

Canaris nodded. "I've even selected the ideal place—their naval base at Pearl Harbor. With a little luck, they could do unto the American fleet what the British did to the Italians at Taranto in 1940. Of course the Japanese won't have the benefit of knowing the Italian naval code—which I arranged for the British to obtain through a double agent in Tangier."

Berthe felt her whole body stiffen with horror—and something else. Was it outrage? Could she tolerate this betrayal of victory? The Path suddenly vanished into a labyrinth of doubt. She was still Kapitanleutnant Ernst von Hoffmann's wife.

Satan leered over Canaris's shoulder. "I'm telling you almost everything," the Admiral said. "Only remember. To whom much is given, much will be expected."

12

A CHANCE TO CROW

Still brooding over his assignment to the Office of Naval Intelligence, Jonathan Talbot left his equally morose wife in Norfolk and took the Baltimore and Ohio Railroad to Washington to find a furnished room. Over breakfast Annie had made another try at persuading him to find an apartment and let her and Butch join him. But the ONI assignment had hardened his resentment against her and the Congressman and he persisted in playing Scrooge.

On the train his New England conscience gnawed. Two days at home had forced him to admit that in spite of their differences he still loved Annie. He even admitted that he appreciated Sam Richman's blundering attempt to rescue him and his torpedoed career. The Congressman and his wife were decent people, even if their political ethics were virtually nonexistent.

Talbot paged through the Washington *Times-Herald*, which seethed with war news. The Germans were stalled in front of Moscow but were still predicting they would celebrate Christmas in Red Square. The Luftwaffe was now smashing up British ports. Plymouth had been reduced to smoldering wreckage. The stone commemorating the departure of the *Mayflower* had been blown to bits. The U-boats had slaughtered another convoy in the North Atlantic.

The really hot news was the ongoing negotiations with the Japanese. They had a team of diplomats talking almost around the clock with Secretary of State Cordell Hull and his cohorts. The *Times-Herald* was accusing Roosevelt of trying to start a war with them by threatening a total cutoff of their oil supplies.

On an inside page, he found a one-column story about "Ex-Captain of the *Spencer Lewis*." It played up his statement that the Germans were thoroughly prepared for war. There was nothing about his denial of the slanders. When the man next to him finished reading the Washington *Post,* they switched papers. Lieutenant Commander Talbot was on the front page of the *Post,* "angrily" declaring his ship had been torpedoed without warning, exactly like the *Reuben James.* The *Times-Herald* was anti-Roosevelt and antiwar. The *Post* was pro-Roosevelt and pro-war. So much for the truth, as purveyed by the hawkeyed guardians of the fourth estate.

On a back page, he found himself the star of Jack Richman's column, "Behind the Headlines." Jack's Hollywood profile was displayed next to the title, guaranteeing him a steady supply of adoring women. At Annapolis, his nickname had been the Sultan. The column told its readers how an incident in the North Atlantic showed the world just how despicable the Nazis were. He then quoted liberally from Fireman First Class Klein, who avowed that the Germans wanted to feed him to the fishes and only the heroic opposition of his captain had saved his life.

"Typically," Jack continued, "Lieutenant Commander Talbot declined to take an iota of credit for this act of selflessness, saying he was only doing what every American naval officer would have done in the same circumstances." From there Jack described Klein's "hostile" reception aboard the Ritterboot, once the Germans found out he was Jewish. Whether Jack put the words in his mouth or was writing pure fiction, he had the fireman trembling for his life in the torpedo room, until his captain arrived and once more guaranteed his safety. "Can there be any doubt that President Roosevelt was right when he called on the free nations of the world to quarantine these beasts?" Jack asked in a fervid peroration.

The column more or less canceled Talbot's kind thoughts about the Richmans. He found himself remembering Annie's hostility whenever he disagreed with Jack. Big brother could do or say no wrong. Swallow it, Talbot told himself. It was part of the bitter lessons life seemed intent on teaching him.

In a day of scurrying around by trolley, bus and foot, Talbot located a furnished room in a comfortable house in Alexandria, just across the river from Washington. The landlady was the wife of an Army major who was on his way to the Philippines. She looked distraught as Talbot told her why he was in Washington, omitting his clash with Admiral King, of course. "Do you think we're going to war?" she said.

"I hope not. We're sure as hell not ready for it."

"That's what Bob says. He thinks we shouldn't even be trying to fight for the goddamn Philippines."

That night Talbot had dinner with his sister Ethel and her husband, Ned Travis, in their antique-filled house in northwest Washington. Sleek, assured, with iron gray hair, Travis was a Harvard graduate and he never let you forget it for more than five minutes. Annie had once won a bet with her husband about how many times Ned would mention Harvard at a dinner party. He hit seventeen, only three short of Annie's prediction of twenty. Talbot had estimated five.

Eight years older than her brother, Ethel was the perfect diplomat's wife—tall, dignified, with every artificial curl of her straight brown hair in a sort of permanent press on her narrow head. Over drinks, Talbot described his brawl with Admiral King. Ethel vibrated with sympathy and outrage. "Annie must be even more upset than I am," she said.

"She says I had it coming to me for daring to criticize Daddy's hero, FDR."

Ethel sighed. "I've always felt those people"—she meant the Richmans—"lacked a moral dimension," she said.

Talbot grimaced. "As Lincoln said about Mary, the only thing to do is squeeze a bad bargain all the harder."

Did he really mean that? Talbot wondered, remembering Annie in his arms two nights ago. Before he could modify the remark, Ned Travis returned from the kitchen with a fresh bottle of gin. Although the gloating agreement on Ethel's face made him wince, Talbot decided it was easier to change the subject. "Are we going to war in the Pacific, Ned?" he asked his brother-in-law.

Ned Travis surprised him by pooh-poohing that idea. He agreed with Stanley Hornbeck, the Chief of the Far Eastern desk at State, who insisted the Japs were bluffing. Stanley and Ned and Assistant Secretary of State Dean Acheson were a sort of "triumvirate" on the Japanese thing, Ned declared in his oratorical way. They were all convinced a strong stand would force Japan to get out of China and abandon their pretensions to dominating Asia. Since June, Acheson had refused to issue a single export license to ship so much as a gallon of oil to Japan. Result: the Japanese had come to Washington, hats in hand, to beg for mercy.

"Roosevelt is going along with this?" Talbot asked. He had not realized the United States had cut off all oil shipments to Japan. He would soon learn it was a well-kept unofficial secret.

"He was a bit uneasy when he found out about it in August," Travis said. "But he decided changing it would look as if we were backing down."

Talbot marveled at the similarity to his father's description of one of the causes of World War I—the backstage maneuvers the British Foreign Office had orchestrated, without saying a word to Parliament. Diplomats were a lot more dangerous than they looked—and in FDR's haphazard let's-try-anything administration, they were virtually immune to punishment. If the U.S. Navy found out a small clique of officers were making policy without consulting their superiors, they would be dismembered before sundown.

Ned Travis smoothly explained in diplomatese: "Foreign policy often outpaces public opinion, Zeke. Our attitude toward the Russians is another thing we've got to change. The stand the Red Army is making against Hitler is prima facie proof of communism's authenticity. It's the wave of the future in China, Japan, Germany—and Spain. It's time we came to terms with it if we ever hope to regain our national vitality."

Amazing stuff. But the State Department had a habit of cooking up grandiose political visions. Six months before Germany invaded Russia, Ned had been part of a negotiating team State had persuaded Roosevelt to send to Europe to see if they could cut a deal with Hitler that would have made the appeasement the British tried at Munich seem trivial. Talbot looked quizzically at his sister. "You agree with this sudden discovery of the virtues of Bolshevism?"

"It's not sudden, Zeke. Ned has been attending a discussion group organized by some Harvard friends at State. He's given it *very* serious thought. He feels communism's economic democracy is far more meaningful than our superficial political democracy. It's a lesson we've got to learn."

Ethel added a denunciation of the "dinosaurs"—the old European hands and the Russian specialists at State who were constantly trying to block a foreign policy based on this advanced point of view. Ned was risking his career to join the progressives under the banner of Undersecretary of State Sumner Welles.

"I trust you haven't mentioned any of this in Connecticut." He was talking about their parents.

Ethel shook her head. "I don't want to bring on another heart attack."

Talbot nodded, ruefully agreeing that the man who was once called the conscience of the Republican party was no longer a voice of authority, even in his own family. Age and powerlessness had reduced Roger Sherman Talbot to a bitter wraith.

On Monday morning, Talbot reported to the factorylike four-story stucco Navy building on Constitution Avenue, a few blocks from the White House. He was amazed to see a small army of protestors swarming down Seventeenth Street toward the Executive Mansion, waving placards listing the names of the men killed aboard the *Kearney*, the *Reuben James* and the *Spencer Lewis*. "Impeach Roosevelt!" they chanted. "He murdered these men!" Talbot was swept by a spasm of new resentment against his wife and her father. He should be marching with these people!

Instead, like a whipped schoolboy, he trudged into the rabbit warren of wings and stairways that housed the Navy's brain trust and was directed to the sixth wing of the second deck, where a small doleful-looking commander greeted him with a half-hearted hand-shake. "Art Jones. Everybody calls me Jonesy. I'm the Chief of Staff. The Director's upstairs getting his teeth kicked in by Admiral Turner. You're the guy who talked back to King. You're going to feel at home here."

In his offhand way, Jonesy explained the latest reason why any-one with a brain tried to avoid the Office of Naval Intelligence. ONI was being stepped on daily by the Director of War Plans, Admiral Richmond Kelly Turner. He was known even to his friends as "Terri-ble" in tribute to his capacity for raging oneupmanship. "He makes Ernie King look like Mary Poppins," Jonesy said.

To demonstrate his contempt for ONI, Terrible Turner had set up his own intelligence section inside War Plans. "We can send out facts to people in the field but all interpretations come from him," Jonesy explained.

"Because interpretations are what the CNO wants—and if you give him some good ones you're a comer?" Talbot said. The CNO was the Chief of Naval Operations, the Navy's top job.

Jonesy smiled bleakly. "You catch on fast. Turner doesn't want any comers around but him. That's why we just got our third DNI in twelve months." DNI stood for Director of Naval Intelligence.

He thumbed rapidly through Talbot's file. "You can help out in the European section," he said. "Good at languages and some brainpower to go with it, according to the Naval War College. Take a look at this while you're waiting for our new leader to reassemble his molars."

He flipped Talbot a stapled document that was sitting in a wire basket on his desk. It was stamped TOP SECRET. "We're supposed to refute this thing," Jonesy said. "If it becomes official policy, it turns Plan Orange into yesterday's newspaper."

Plan Orange was something every graduate of the Naval War College knew almost as well as his own name. It was the Navy's strategic bible for fighting the Japanese Combined Fleet for supremacy in the Pacific. Jonesy guided Talbot to an empty cubicle and he began reading the thick sheaf of mimeographed pages. Within minutes, his eyes were all but bulging out of his head.

Code-named Rainbow Five, this document was nothing less than the U.S. Army and Navy's plan for fighting a world war against Germany, Italy and Japan. It identified Germany as the main enemy and soberly examined what it would take to defeat her. At the minimum, America needed an army of 10 million men and vastly expanded naval and air forces. In 1943, Rainbow Five proposed an invasion of Europe by 5 million men! On the last page was a letter from Roosevelt, ordering the preparation of the plan. The president who promised he would never send an American boy to a foreign war was getting ready to send 5 million of them!

"Talbot?"

He sprang to his feet to shake hands with the DNI, chunky Rear Admiral Frederick S. "Bong" Jamison. Talbot had spent a year in China aboard the USS *Houston* under his command. He lit a cigarette and slumped in a chair beside Talbot's desk. "Glad to have you aboard. Don't worry about Ernie King. Anyone who talks back to that SOB is a friend of mine. I think we're nuts to be out there convoying for Hail Britannia and Company. I was on staff in London in the last war and I got to hate their arrogant guts."

Jamison was a devotee of Plan Orange. Aboard the *Houston* he had talked endlessly about the coming war with Japan. He was glad to see Jonesy had Talbot reading Rainbow Five. "Give me a critique of that damn thing as soon as possible in your best War College style. It's ninety percent an Army deal. Some major named Wedemeyer wrote it so naturally the Navy just wags along like the tail of a dog. Come up with a plan for something big in the Mediterranean, where a fleet will make a difference."

He added that Admiral Turner had ten men working on a revision upstairs in operations. "I want to show that SOB if he can invade my turf at will, I can return the compliment," Jamison said. The glint in his eyes recalled the fabled ensign who had gotten his nickname (and won a $50 bet) by sneaking into one of the most sacred temples in Peking in 1907 and whacking the gong that summoned the Emperor to his devotions. The Chinese had wanted to behead him and changed their minds only when a regiment of U.S. Marines surrounded the temple.

Talbot promised to get to work on his critique of Rainbow Five immediately. But he wondered if the mounting tension with the Japanese made the document, with its emphasis on a European war, almost irrelevant. Jamison shook his head. "The Army's flying a couple of hundred B-Seventeens to the Philippines. That puts them within bombing range of Japan. They're supposed to be the strategic deterrent that will keep the Japs quiet until we're ready to finish them off. I don't buy it, but it's official policy."

As Talbot went back to reading Rainbow Five, Admiral Jamison reappeared in the doorway of his cubicle. "I almost forgot. The guys in Communications Intelligence want to talk to you about your trip in that U-boat."

Following directions, Talbot found his way to another warren of offices on the fourth deck of the Navy building. A cheerful young lieutenant leaped out of his chair when he introduced himself. "You're the guy from the German submarine!" he said. Talbot found himself surrounded by a half-dozen officers with excited admiring smiles on their faces. He felt like a movie star.

"Did you by any chance see one of their Enigma machines?" asked the lieutenant, whose name was Morrison.

Talbot looked blank. Morrison explained that he was talking

about the Germans' cipher system. They called it Enigma, the Greek word for puzzle. "I saw some sort of machine in their radio shack," Talbot said.

The circle of admirers seemed to press closer. "Did you notice how many rotors it had?"

"What's a rotor?" Talbot asked.

Dismay on every face. Someone rushed into a cubicle and came back with a machine that looked exactly like the one Talbot had seen on the Ritterboot. Morrison pointed to one of three slots above the keyboard and pulled out a small circular drum. It looked a little like a typewriter ribbon spool. On its inner rim were the letters of the alphabet. "Three or four?" Morrison asked, anxiously pointing to the slots.

"Three, I think," Talbot said. "Where did you get this thing?"

"From the English. They've broken the code but the Germans keep beating them. We think they've added a slot for a fourth rotor."

Talbot asked for a quick explanation of how the Enigma worked. "A rotor is basically a wired codewheel," Morrison said, slipping the drum back into its slot. "It has twenty-six electrical contacts on it, one for each letter of the alphabet. When you send an electrical impulse into it by hitting A on the typing key, it comes out Q or whatever the particular cipher requires it to deliver. The more rotors you add, the more combinations of letters you have to play with. Unless you know the starting position of the rotors—the key—you can spend the rest of your life deciphering a single message."

Talbot was back in the Ritterboot, hearing Kapitanleutnant von Hoffmann confidently telling him: *it would take you the rest of your life to solve the codes this thing creates.* The Kapitanleutnant might not be quite as arrogant if he knew the British were using the same machine, grimly feeding ciphers into it to find the key that told them exactly where BDU was sending his submarines.

"We've had it a lot easier with the Japs," Morrison said. "Their Purple code uses a machine not nearly as complicated as this baby. We've built a dozen of them."

"We're reading the Japs' communications?"

"Hell yes," Morrison said. "We're up to our eyeballs in the stuff. We need a staff ten times bigger than we've got to decrypt and translate them."

"And a squad of Marines to make Admiral Turner and his fellow assholes in operations listen to our interpretations," said a swarthy saturnine lieutenant junior grade.

Morrison nodded dolefully. "Unless the President makes some fast moves on the diplomatic front, we're going to get our tails blown off in the Pacific before we ever get around to fighting the Germans. Sometimes I think that's exactly what he's hoping will happen."

"That presumes he knows what the hell he's doing in the first place," growled the saturnine lieutenant junior grade.

Talbot listened to this dialogue with an odd mixture of astonishment and hope. Maybe he would have the last laugh on the Roosevelt-worshipping Richmans. Maybe their Democratic hero was going to screw up on a global scale, giving a much-maligned lieutenant commander a chance to crow I told you so.

13

KNIGHT AT CROSS PURPOSES

On their way home at last! Kapitanleutnant Ernst von Hoffmann watched the green hills of the Canary Islands slide beneath the horizon. Now all they had to do was survive British patrol planes and ships off Gibraltar and in the Bay of Biscay, approaching France. The compartments of the Ritterboot resounded with the strains of "The Little Blue Boat," the traditional song every U-boat played as she began her homeward voyage. Below in the Zentrale, off-duty crew members were busy sewing pennants to be displayed from the periscope, one for each ship sunk. The Ritterboot would flaunt thirteen as they entered Lorient harbor.

During their two weeks in the Canaries, Hoffmann had arranged for the men to go ashore in small groups. The captain of the repair ship in the little fishing port had worked out an arrangement with the Spanish government. A certain number of women were bused to the village once a week for his men's entertainment. It was easy enough to arrange for a fresh contingent for the crews of the Ritterboot and the other submarine under repair.

Hoffmann had not joined the crew's carousing in the village. He had borrowed the repair ship captain's car and driven to Las Palmas, where the German consul entertained him with compliments and a very good dinner. Afterward, a Spaniard had driven him to a quiet house on the outskirts of the city, where a thick-bodied blond named

Sonia welcomed him. She was Russian, a refugee from the Communists, purportedly of noble blood. She said she was eager to reward one of the heroes of the Third Reich, whose brothers in arms were regaining her ancestral lands.

It was unexceptional sex, but several cuts above the purely animal stuff in the village. Hoffmann told himself he needed to discharge the accumulated tension and frustration of ten weeks of hunting and being hunted in the North Atlantic. He also felt, in a more obscure corner of his mind, that other women somehow protected him from his wife. He was still awed by Berthe von Schonberg, her knowledge of poetry, novels, art—none of which interested him. The awe stirred a sullen resentment in Hoffmann's mind. He had pursued Berthe at first to prove to himself that he could capture one of the best-known beauties in Berlin. He was still secretly astonished that the pursuit had turned into love, marriage, children.

First Officer Oskar Kurz joined Hoffmann on the bridge to take the watch. He was the only man who had not participated in the romps in the village. "How does it feel to be so superior to your sinful shipmates, Number One?" Hoffmann said.

"On the contrary, Herr Kaleu, their sarcasm—and yours—has deepened my humility."

"You feel you should be faithful to your wife, Number One?"

"I love her, Herr Kaleu," Kurz said.

"I love my wife too," Hoffmann said. "But a man can't let love be the dominant force in his life. That sort of thinking can turn your brain to mush, Number One."

"I will keep that in mind, Herr Kaleu."

Hoffmann felt a flush of irritation at the man. Not just for his fidelity, but for his religiosity. He had decided religion was a dead end. It got a man—or a country—nowhere. He remembered reading his oldest brother's letters from France in 1918. They were full of faith in God. *Gott mitt uns!* had been the battlecry of the Kaiser's army. Where had it gotten them?

In an angry tone, Hoffmann began telling Kurz there was only one worthwhile faith, the German volk. Wolfgang Griff joined them on the bridge and Hoffmann invited him into the conversation. "I was just telling Number One here his religious fanaticism is hopelessly outdated," Hoffmann said.

"I couldn't agree more, Herr Kaleu," Griff said. He began lectur-

ing them on the evils of Christianity. It was permeated by Jewish philosophy, Jewish corruption. It gave control of a man's conscience to a
pack of priests. It weakened a man's will, sapped his courage. "The
Jew, the Christian, live in the mind, in the pale sickly world of
thought. The German lives in the blood, in the will to power!"

"Any special orders to keep in mind during my watch, Herr
Kaleu?" Kurz said.

"Hold course three three zero. We don't want to come too close
to Gibraltar. Keep a very sharp watch for planes." He left Griff on the
bridge spouting more Nazi rhetoric at Kurz. It was exactly what Saint
Oskar deserved.

Descending the ladder, the Kapitanleutnant reproached himself.
What was wrong with him? Kurz was an excellent officer. His religion
was his own business. Maybe he shouldn't have screwed that white
Russian whore. She had put him in a rotten mood.

In the Zentrale, Chief Engineer Kleist was supervising the preparation of the pennants. Each one had the estimated tonnage of the
sunken ship on it, whenever they knew it. One pennant was red, signifying a warship—the *Spencer Lewis*. A red pennant was worth four
or five of the white ones that were used for merchant ships.

"We better not fly this one for the time being," Hoffmann said,
fingering the red pennant. "The Lion may not want to admit we sank
her."

"It'll just be among friends at Lorient, Herr Kaleu," Kleist said,
with his quizzical smile. "It was such a beautiful shot."

It had been a beautiful shot. The *Spencer Lewis* had just started
to zig-zag and the range, the angle of fire, had to be recomputed in a
split second. "All right," Hoffmann said.

"Herr Kaleu!" Rhule, the excitable red-haired radioman, was
standing in the door of the Zentrale with a yellow message in his
hand. His smile was so broad, Hoffmann wondered if he had just
heard that the panzers had reached Moscow.

He handed the message to Hoffmann as Wolfgang Griff
descended the ladder from the conning tower. Kleist read it over
Hoffmann's shoulder. "The fellow's right," Kleist said. "For once it is
wonderful news!" He maintained that almost everything they heard
from BDU led them straight to trouble.

"ADMIRAL KARL DÖNITZ AND THE STAFF OF THE
UBOOTWAFFE EXTEND THEIR CONGRATULATIONS TO

THE MEN OF UNTERSEEBOOT 555 ON THE FÜHRER'S DECISION TO AWARD THE KNIGHT'S CROSS FOR VALOR TO KAPITANLEUTNANT ERNST VON HOFFMANN."

Chief Engineer Kleist stepped back and saluted. "Herr Kaleu," he said. "On behalf of the crew of the Ritterboot, let me express our pride and pleasure." All the men in the Zentrale followed his example, coming to attention for a sustained salute.

Hoffmann almost burst into tears. Why did he value Kleist's admiration so much? "You see—there—who Admiral Dönitz is congratulating," he said, gesturing to the message. "The men—all of you—deserve to wear this decoration. I will always wear it with that in mind."

Wolfgang Griff's sharklike smile broke through the circle of beaming sailors crowding into the Zentrale as the news swept through the boat. "I think this is also a tribute to our astute handling of the American lieutenant commander and his Jew sailor, Herr Kaleu!"

Hoffmann did not entirely understand why, but the words stirred him to fury. Though they were probably correct. The Spanish newspapers in Las Palmas had carried front page versions of the story Griff had written, describing Talbot's endorsement of Germany's war. "It is a tribute to the bravery of this crew, Lieutenant Griff. Nothing else!" he said.

"It is nothing else but a tribute to the bravery, the daring, the seamanship of Kapitanleutnant von Hoffmann!" Kleist bellowed.

Griff dwindled into the crowd. Hoffmann felt his heart swell with wordless gratitude to this indomitable man. With him as his Chief Engineer, he would take the Ritterboot anywhere. Up the Thames to bombard the British Parliament!

ALARM! The bell clanged furiously. From the bridge, First Officer Kurz shouted: "Emergency dive. Two aircraft bearing one eight zero."

"Crew to the bow!" Hoffmann said. Griff and everyone but Kleist and the men on duty in the Zentrale stumbled down the narrow passageway to the forward torpedo room while the bridge hatch clanged and Kurz and the watch came crashing down the ladder. Hoffmann sprang up the ladder from the Zentrale to meet them in the conning tower. A furious Kurz had one of the watch, a seaman named Benz, by the collar. "This is going to be close, Herr Kaleu. This idiot went to sleep up there."

A spread of depth charges exploded with terrific violence. A giant hand seemed to seize the Ritterboot by the stern and whirl her off her axis. Tumbling, she spun down out of control, the needle on the depth gauge soaring past 100 meters with shocking speed. At 160 meters Kleist pulled her out, God only knew how.

Hoffmann was swept by a terrific loathing of this undersea life. What did a Knight's Cross mean when two minutes later they were plunging into the depths to be hunted like scurrying rodents? "Hard left rudder," he said.

Another spread of depth charges boomed harmlessly a hundred meters away. Kurz was still ferociously shaking Seaman Benz. Hoffmann calmed down the first officer and asked Benz if he had really fallen asleep. That was punishable by death, although as far as Hoffmann knew, no U-boat commander had ever invoked the regulation. No captain could retain the loyalty of his crew if he executed one of them. The crew was an organism more intensely linked than a family.

Benz, a skinny blond eighteen-year-old, shook his head. "I'm sick, Herr Kaleu," he said. "My head burns, my eyes keep watering, my stomach hurts. I couldn't concentrate on the horizon the way you trained us."

"Did you eat something in that Spanish village?" Hoffmann asked. He had ordered the crew to avoid food, for fear of a dysentery outbreak. BDU had issued a warning about it before they sailed. With only one toilet for fifty-two men, dysentery on a U-boat could became a sanitary disaster.

"My girl brought me some fresh fruit. I haven't had any fruit in such a long time, Herr Kaleu."

"Get some aspirin from the Chief Engineer and go to bed," Hoffmann said.

"I'm sorry, Herr Kaleu."

"It's all right. There'll be no punishment, Benz."

Benz's family was from the town of Posen, near the East Prussia border. Before the First War, it had been part of Germany; the Poles had claimed it in the peace settlement and most of the Germans became refugees. Benz had grown up in the Alexanderplatz section of Berlin, living mostly in the street. The Hoffmanns had been the ruling family of the Posen district for hundreds of years. The Kapitanleutnant suddenly wished his father could see him, dealing gently with one of the victims of their defeat, demonstrating that the Hoffmanns retained their ancient ability to rule men. His father had died in 1922, when Hoffmann was sixteen. He had never had a chance to win a word of approval from the silent, somber man, whose stupendous victories on the Eastern front had been wasted by Germany's defeat in the west.

Berthe, of course, would approve his compassion. But it had nothing to do with her mushy religious ideas. It was part of the psychology of leadership, to forgive a man after another officer had sufficiently terrorized him.

Three days later, the Ritterboot was in the Bay of Biscay, off the coast of Spain, where British Sunderlands were frequently thick as flies at a summer picnic. *Totenallee*, the sailors called it. "Death Alley." For the next nine days, Hoffmann joined most of the watches on the bridge to make sure the lookouts kept their eyes glued to their field glasses. They had to make three emergency dives to escape the tired bees but there was plenty of time to go deep. As dawn broke on the tenth day, they were close enough to the French coast to rely on air cover from the Luftwaffe. "Time to hoist our pennants, Herr Kaleu!" Chief Engineer Kleist said.

The thirteen flags, including the red one, were soon flapping briskly from halyards stretched from the attack periscope. Two hours later, the Ritterboot followed a stubby minesweeper known as an R-boat into the oily waters of Lorient harbor. The crew mustered on the deck as they passed the turreted chateau of Kernevel, the headquarters of Admiral Dönitz.

In another ten minutes, the Ritterboot approached the stubby pontoon ship *Isere* near the mouth of the Scorff River. An old wooden steamer that had once transported convicts to Devil's Island, the *Isere* now served as the arrival and departure headquarters for the Second U-boat Flotilla. On the deck, a crowd of welcomers cheered and clapped and a band struck up "Deutschland Uber Alles" as Hoffmann expertly reversed his engines and sidled the submarine alongside *Isere*'s mottled hull.

Fregattenkapitan Viktor Schutze, dour commander of the Second U-boat Flotilla, aappeared at the *Isere*'s rail as the deck force tied the lines. "Attention!" Hoffmann called to his crew. With their untrimmed beards and hair, their unpressed fatigues, they looked more like a mob of bandits than military men, but they snapped erect. "Heil, Five Five Five," Schutze said, with a brisk salute.

"Heil, Herr Fregattenkapitan," Hoffmann said, returning the salute. Schutze came aboard and climbed to the bridge to shake Hoffmann's hand. "Congratulations on a successful voyage—and your new neckware," he said, referring to the Knight's Cross. "Dönitz expects you tomorrow at nine o'clock German war time to discuss your KTB and other matters."

Hoffmann handed over the Kriegstagebuch, the war diary containing a precise account of each of the Ritterboot's kills and attempted kills, the depth charge attacks and all other events of consequence during the voyage. Meanwhile, nurses from the nearby military hospital streamed aboard with armloads of flowers and a kiss for every crewman.

"Herr Greiser!" Schutze called. For the first time Hoffmann noticed a big thick-necked man standing on the *Isere*'s deck. He wore the long brown double-breasted overcoat of a Nazi party political leader, complete with a red armband on which a swastika was emblazoned. He hauled himself up the ladder to the conning tower, where Schutze introduced him as Arthur Greiser, Gauleiter of the new province of Wartheland, in conquered Poland.

"When I learned of your winning the Knight's Cross, Herr Kapitanleutnant," Greiser said, "I decided on the spot that I would come here to give you a special greeting from the people of Posen. That's the capital of my province. We hope you'll visit us and help reestablish the name of Hoffmann and the rule of Germany."

"I'd be honored," Hoffmann said.

Schutze's expression suggested a certain unhappiness with the conversation. He asked Hoffmann if his men were ready to enjoy a good meal. "Why don't you ask them, Herr Fregattenkapitan," Hoffmann said.

Schutze repeated the question to the crew. The answer came back in a roar. "*Jawhol!*"

The nurses and other greeters returned to the *Isere* and the Ritterboot backed down the Scorff to the harbor. Within minutes they entered the huge steel reinforced pens that protected the U-boats from British bombers. Inside, beneath the glaring lights in the sixty-foot-high corrugated iron ceiling, they tied up at the damp gray stone of Bay Five. Behind them, immense steel shutters closed with a yawning roar, guaranteeing the Ritterboot's safety. Hoffmann felt a surge of pride at this prodigious piece of architecture, which had risen from the mud little more than six months after their conquest of France. Was there better proof of Germany's unique gifts?

The crew marched behind Hoffmann, Greiser and Schutze to one of the halls of the old French Naval Prefecture, where they were soon feasting on pâté, lobster and champagne. Before they sat down, Wolfgang Griff managed to insinuate himself into their circle and ostentatiously shake hands with Greiser. Drawing Hoffmann aside for a brief moment, he whispered that Greiser was a very important man, close to SS Chief Himmler.

Viktor Schutze and his staff demanded a narrative of their most spectacular kills, especially the final three-ship triumph against Convoy HX170. Greiser sat next to Hoffmann, adding toasts from the German "settlers" of Posen at the end of each story.

After the banquet, there was a ceremonial delivery of the mail, carefully stacked on the white tablecloth before each man. A hush fell over the room as everyone regained for a few minutes the family he had left behind in Germany. Oskar Kurz had by far the biggest pile. His wife must have written to him every day.

There were no letters from Berthe, a fact that seemed to disturb Greiser. "Aren't you married, Herr Kapitanleutnant?" he asked.

Hoffmann said he had explained to his wife that letters were not delivered until the end of the voyage, when they were so dated, they were meaningless. Greiser seemed unpersuaded by this practicality. "A good German wife would write anyway," he said. "She should want to pour out her admiration for your glorious services."

"You don't know Kapitanleutnant von Hoffmann's wife, Herr Gauleiter," Schutze said. "She's one of Berlin's great beauties. She's used to admiration going in the other direction."

"Beauty is no substitute for devotion to a soldier of the Reich. You should make that clear to her, Herr Kapitanleutnant."

The thought of lecturing Berthe almost made Hoffmann laugh. Greiser was a bit of a lout. Schutze obviously thought so. His repugnance was visible in his cold blue eyes. Fortunately they were rescued by the arrival of pitchers of German beer and an accordionist. The musician riffled his keys and they began singing old tavern songs. Greiser joined wholeheartedly in the choruses. After a half-hour of familiar melodies, he suddenly swung his head angrily toward Schutze and said: "Why not the Horst Wessel, Herr Fregattenkapitan? I thought you'd have sung it long ago."

"We don't sing Party songs in the Navy, Herr Gauleiter," Schutze said.

"You should!"

Schutze rose to his feet, signaled the accordionist and began singing in a nasal, offkey voice the hymn to Horst Wessel, the Nazi youth the Communists had killed in a street fight in 1933. The crew lurched to their feet and began singing it too. Everyone knew the song. The state radio played it a dozen times a week. Hoffmann nervously noticed that neither Oskar Kurz nor Chief Engineer Kleist opened their mouths.

Later, at the telegraph office, Hoffmann sent a wire to Berthe. SAFE AT LORIENT. SEE YOU SOON. In the officers' quarters of the old French naval complex, he found his uniforms unpacked and hanging in the closet. Next came the first bath in ten weeks, and a shave and haircut. For a moment, as the barber asked him if he wished to part with his entire beard, he hesitated, wondering if Berthe would like it. Unsure, he ordered it removed, thereby differing with Kleist and Kurz, who had decided to retain theirs. Hoffmann found himself wishing he had done the same thing. A beard was a kind of badge of the Ubootwaffe. Did Berthe prefer the beardless boy she had married?

A lance of pain speared Hoffmann's stomach. It swelled into a spray of smaller fragments of pain, as if a miniature torpedo had exploded in there. He had drunk quite a lot of the champagne and beer they had served at the celebration dinner. A man could not toast his crew with water. It looked as if that Navy doctor who had warned him to avoid alcohol was right. Where had he gotten this traitor stomach? Nothing seemed to help—milk, bicarbonate of soda, monosodium glutinate pills. For the rest of the night, he lay curled on his bed in agony.

At nine a.m., wearing his best blue uniform, Kapitanleutnant von Hoffmann stood before Admiral Karl Dönitz, the man everyone in the Ubootwaffe called the Lion. He was seated at his desk on the second floor of the turreted château he had made his headquarters. From the windows there were sweeping views of Lorient Harbor. Beside the desk was an immense globe of the world, symbol of the Kriegsmarine's ambition. The Wehrmacht seldom thought beyond dominating Europe.

"Heil, Herr Admiral," Hoffmann said, bringing his hand smartly to his forehead.

A smile broke across Dönitz's wide stern face. He walked around his desk and held out his hand. "How are you feeling, Hoffmann?" he said.

"Excellent, Herr Admiral," Hoffmann said, deeply stirred by hearing Dönitz address him using "du," the intimate word for you, normally reserved for family and close friends. Not all U-boat captains were accorded this privilege. The Lion did not feel as familiar with the more recent arrivals, who had been trained by other men. But commanders like Hoffmann, Prien, Hardegen, had been taught by Dönitz personally in the final years of peace. Each had spent nine exhausting months in the North Sea off Kiel convincing the Lion that he had the skills, the character, to command a U-boat.

"No more stomach problems?"

"Not even a twinge, Herr Admiral."

"I see nothing in your KTB to criticize. You had a good cruise, except for that mishap with the American destroyer."

"I deeply regret that mistake, Herr Admiral."

Dönitz pursed his lips. "Maybe it wasn't such a terrible mistake. Perhaps it will make the Führer realize we're at war with the Americans in all but name. I'm more concerned with your decision to pick up those two survivors. If there was one thing I thought I had communicated to my U-boat commanders, it was the necessity to be hard, to feel no pity for the enemy."

Carefully, while his stomach throbbed with pain, Hoffmann explained his attempt to mix diplomacy and war. Dönitz studied him with incredible intensity as he spoke. "It might have been better if you left them to die of hypothermia," the Lion said. "The captain issued a statement a few days ago, calling you a liar and smearing the Reich with typical British invective."

Slivers of pain darted into Hoffmann's chest. What detestable sons of bitches Americans were! "I'm deeply sorry to hear that, Herr Admiral."

"There's another matter that I must bring to your attention. Your wife seems to have signed some sort of church statement that disturbed some members of the Party. A criticism of Kristallnacht."

Kapitanleutnant von Hoffmann struggled to control himself. Was that the reason for this interrogation? Was the Admiral looking for signs of disloyalty? The mere idea almost made him explode. Dönitz assured him he did not think it was a serious matter. Everyone understood women were unpredictable emotional creatures. Still, it might be best if he made it clear to his wife that the last thing the Ubootwaffe wanted was a quarrel with the Party. They were having enough trouble getting the boats they needed to win the war.

"They promised me twenty boats a month. We'll be lucky to get six. Reichmarshal Goering insists on sequestering most of the aluminum for his aircraft. Not that he doesn't need replacements, after the beating the Luftwaffe took over England last year."

"You may be sure I'll speak to my wife, Herr Admiral," Hoffmann said.

Dönitz paced in front of the window for a moment. "Ah. There goes 667. Lenz," he said. He picked up a pair of field glasses on the windowsill and studied the U-boat as it followed an R-boat toward the harbor mouth, the dark water curling like a mustache around its snout. "I gave him one of the new long-range boats. He's going to the Cape of Good Hope."

The Admiral put down his glasses. "You don't look well to me, Hoffmann."

"I assure you, Herr Admiral—"

"I don't expect you to admit it. I remember how you performed in your Mutprobe."

Hoffmann smiled proudly. The *Mutprobe*, or test of courage, had been given when he was a midshipman. Each boy—they were only seventeen—had been placed in a room with a one-way mirror and ordered to lift a heavy metal bar. The testers sent surges of electricity through the bar to see who would hold onto it longest. Hoffmann had won, holding on twice as long as his nearest competitor.

"My old friend, Admiral Canaris, the head of the Abwehr, called me the other day," Dönitz continued. "He asked me to detach one of my best commanders for duty as an attaché in Spain. I've chosen you."

"Herr Admiral, I must respectfully protest! I wish to continue as a fighting man. How can I face my fellow commanders after such an assignment?"

"It's a very important assignment," Dönitz said sternly—though his eyes flashed with approval at Hoffmann's desire to keep fighting. "We're attempting to bring Spain into the war on our side. A man of your experience and reputation will be extremely useful there. You can also give valuable assistance to certain U-boat operations already in progress, with Spanish help."

Hoffmann said nothing. He still detested the whole idea. He was not a diplomat or a secret agent. "Canaris is one of us, you know. He sank fifteen ships in the Mediterranean in the last war," Dönitz said. "He appreciates the importance of the Ubootwaffe."

Hoffmann did not care if Canaris was the reincarnation of Otto von Bismarck and personally kissed every U-boat crewman in the fleet. He still detested the idea.

"Your wife of course will accompany you. Another reason to make sure she understands the importance of keeping her political opinions private."

Berthe! Hoffmann saw the whole thing. They were getting her out of the country to protect her from the Party. His mother had probably arranged it with Admiral Canaris. They had danced together at some stupid ball on the Kaiser's birthday in the old days.

Dönitz was telling him he needed a rest. It was going to be a long war. In three or four months he would be back at Lorient, ready to take charge of a new boat, with new technology, new weapons. The war was going well; even with the comparative handful of boats at sea, they were decimating the Atlantic convoys. If what they told him in Berlin was reliable, Germany would soon have another powerful ally: Japan. Tomorrow, at a ceremony in Lorient's town square, he would award him his Knight's Cross and distribute other medals to his crew. Kapitanleutnant von Hoffmann barely listened to the Admiral. He was absorbed in vowing to give Berthe von Schonberg the lecture of her life.

14

WAR STORY

"Annie, I tell you, Roosevelt's messing up on a scale beyond belief!"

Belief. It was fascinating, how often the word cropped up in her life, Annie thought. It was hard to believe the exultant wild man pacing up and down their Norfolk living room was the same morose husband she had kissed goodbye on his way to Washington, D.C., two weeks ago. That day, Jonathan Talbot had exhibited the enthusiasm of a man going to his own execution. Two or three days later, the midnight phone calls began, telling her how he was working on a top secret war plan called Rainbow Five and adding reams of equally secret stuff about the State Department's negotiations with the Japanese, all orchestrated around the theme song of overwhelming evidence that FDR was a liar and a charlatan of truly global proportions, who was blundering—or maneuvering—the country into an unnecessary war with Japan.

That was even harder to believe—but the one thing in her life Annie knew with absolute certainty was Jonathan Trumbull Talbot's inability to tell a lie. She listened as Zeke explained how the people in ONI's Communications Intelligence, led by an oddball genius named Laurence Safford, were reading every word the Japanese sent to their negotiators in Washington. Since the Japanese radioed Tokyo everything the Americans said to them, ONI also knew that the

United States was taking a recklessly uncompromising position in the talks.

"Today they told the Japanese they had to withdraw their entire army from China, before they got a drop of oil from us," Zeke said. "Do they really think Tokyo will swallow that kind of public humiliation?" At least as alarming was the response Tokyo had sent their diplomats: November 26 was the absolutely last day for reaching a settlement. After that, "things were going to automatically happen."

Exactly what that ominous phrase meant was the source of a raging debate between ONI and Admiral Richmond Kelly Turner in operations. ONI was convinced that the Japanese planned to attack U.S. and British bases in the Pacific while they drove south to seize the Dutch East Indies, guaranteeing them enough oil to fuel their war machine for a century. Turner maintained they were going to attack the Russians in Siberia to help the Germans finish off the Communists. Since Turner controlled all the interpretations sent out to the fleet in the Pacific, everyone in ONI was in a frenzy because in their opinion the commanders at Pearl Harbor and the Philippines were not getting a correct estimate of the situation.

The responsibility for the mess lay with the Chief of Naval Operations, Admiral Harold R. "Betty" Stark. "His nickname is a perfect summation of his character," Zeke said. "He's exactly what we heard about him in Newport—a weak-kneed yes-man." It was common Navy scuttlebutt that Stark was the only Admiral FDR could find to go along with his presidential order to station the Pacific fleet at Pearl Harbor to deter the Japanese from aggression. When the previous CNO, Admiral Paul O. Richardson, had protested strongly against exposing the ships to surprise attack, Roosevelt had fired him.

Unfortunately for the country, yes-men do not make good CNOs. Betty Stark could not stand up to any strong personality. People like Kelly Turner walked all over him, arrogating to themselves every square inch of turf they could grab. Ernie King was doing the same thing as Cinclant, demanding more and more ships, leaving the Navy badly outgunned by the Japanese in the Pacific.

Some of this could be dismissed as standard Navy infighting. It was Rainbow Five, the plan to invade Europe with five million men in 1943, that staggered Annie. How could the President violate his solemn promise to America's voters to stay out of foreign wars, unless the United States was attacked? Was the intransigent stance with the

Japanese intended to provoke an attack? Deception on such a scale, involving so many millions of young lives, was hardest of all to believe.

Everywhere Zeke went in search of information to give the Navy a bigger role in Rainbow Five, he found people reinforcing his low opinion of FDR. In the Munitions Building, down the street from the Navy building, he had located Major Albert Wedemeyer to ask how he had gathered information for his draft of the war plan. Wedemeyer was more than helpful, advising him to go to top people in the service bureaus, giving him names and phone numbers.

Suddenly Wedemeyer had become very serious. "Personally, I think we should stay home until they come after us. What do you think?" he asked Zeke.

By the time they parted, Zeke had learned there were a lot of generals who took a very dim view of Roosevelt's determination to fight Hitler in Europe. "With the French army gone, most of the manpower will have to be American and the casualties could be staggering," Zeke said.

Wedemeyer said the generals were particularly dismayed by Roosevelt's recent appearance before Congress waving a letter that he claimed was proof the Germans were planning to invade Brazil. Wedemeyer said the letter was a British forgery—and even if it were true, so what? In Brazil the Germans would be farther away from the United States than they were in Europe. As Zeke dilated on the way America was being drenched with British propaganda, Annie recalled Jack had devoted a column to that letter.

"Wedemeyer's joined America First," Zeke said. "Maybe I ought to do the same thing. At least I'd feel I was doing something to stop this craziness."

The Committee to Defend America First was the leading anti-war group. Its executive board was studded with retired generals and admirals and prominent business men. For a celebrity spokesman, it had none other than Charles A. Lindbergh.

"Zeke, I think that would be a mistake. It would only give King and his friends more ammunition against you when you come up for promotion next year."

"*If* I come up for promotion," he said. "There are guys who've been at ONI for five and six years without ever hearing from a promotion board."

"Dad won't let that happen. He's guaranteed me he'll get you out out of there in six months."

Zeke gave her his stoniest stare. It was not hard to connect this revelation to his remark that he had no intention of spending more than six months in ONI's purgatory before doing something drastic. "I thought it was more or less understood that you were never going to talk to your father about my career."

"It was—but I thought this situation called for a misunderstanding."

It was bizarre. She was defending herself for trying to keep him in the Navy—when more than once in the last eleven years she had come close to praying he would resign. In spite of its lofty talk about projecting America's power and influence around the world, the peacetime Navy seemed a ridiculous place for an intelligent man to waste his life. Until he got to be captain of a ship, Zeke spent most of his time worrying over trivial details such as how many sideboys a vice admiral merited when he appeared on a quarterdeck. But the thought of Zeke as a civilian troubled Annie even more. He was simply too honest, too honorable, too straight-arrow, to use her brother Jack's derogatory term, to prosper in politics or business.

"I don't want to be known as Congressman Richman's son-in-law," Zeke said. "I want to make it on my own or not at all. I told my own father to go to hell when he tried to push me into the State Department for the same reason."

Annie had to bite her lip to stop herself from telling him that defiance made perfect sense. If there was anything Jonathan Trumbull Talbot was less suited for, it was the double-talking world of diplomacy. The Navy was the right place for him, even if most of the time the jobs were trivial.

"Try looking at it this way," Annie said. "Congressman Richman's son-in-law is preferable to Admiral King's punching bag."

That temporarily shut him up. "Do you have a copy of Rainbow Five?" she asked. "I'd like to read it."

"It so happens I brought a copy along. I'm going to spend most of the weekend working on it."

"Even when I pry you out of Washington, I have to compete with Bong Jamison and Richmond Kelly Turner?"

"Yeah. But here you have a home team advantage they can't match."

That night they made what Annie privately called high-wire love. There were times when she wasn't in the mood to play the passionate surrenderer—when she felt or wanted to feel she was the equal of this brawny stubborn, confusing male. High-wire love was more sensual than surrender love, more artful, more daring. She made advances, suggested positions, she was more a courtesan, a mistress, than a wife, carefully controlling her reactions, making her own pleasure as important as his pleasure, almost shunting aside the deeper meanings of mutual gift, almost but not quite eliminating love.

It amused her to discover once more that Zeke liked this alternative wife in his bed. He sensed the game she was playing and tried to match her with a cool uncaring of his own, a teasing mixture of thrusts and withdrawals, of kisses in unexpected unconventional places, of wandering fingers and an exploring tongue. He found it as delicious as she did, an exhilarating combination of mockery and performance and gratification until—until—untilllllll—

That precious explosive moment when the wire snapped and they thudded laughing—yes laughing!—at the wonder of it, the blinding obliterating happiness of it, onto the Sealtest safety net beneath them.

In the morning Annie was ready to read Rainbow Five. She tackled it while Zeke spread a swarm of manuscripts, books and documents on the dining room's table and chairs and began adding the Navy's revisions to the war plan on their son's portable typewriter. (Butch was spending the day studying advanced calculus with a math teacher from one of the local high schools.) Rainbow's prose was straightforward and plain, with a minimum of government jargon. It described the world situation in the starkest imaginable terms. The German war machine was an awesome entity, which could only be defeated in head-on battle. It was quite possible that Britain or Russia or both might be forced to drop out of the war. In that case, the United States would have to be prepared to fight alone.

With the same brutal matter of factness, the plan discussed the appalling weakness of the current American army. There were potentially devastating shortages of tanks, cannon, machine guns and fighter planes. For eighteen months the United States would have to fight on the defensive. Not until the middle of 1943 could they hope to invade Europe. Annie did some rapid calculations on her fingers and concluded with some astonishment that the authors of the plan expected the war to start any moment—perhaps tomorrow! The presumptions, even the existence of this plan only made sense if everything Zeke said about the President somehow edging the United States into the war were true.

Tap tap tap. The typewriter clicked in the dining room. Each stroke was chipping away her confidence in Franklin Delano Roosevelt. It could only be retained if she agreed with her brother, Jack, that any and all rules should be broken to stop Adolf Hitler and his war machine. But she did not agree with Jack's offhand dismissal of morality as rules made by men, rules that could be changed to suit the convenience of other men. In her deepest self Annie responded to a vision of a moral world, where ideas such as trust and truth and justice meant something. She could tolerate Chicago's corruption in the name of family allegiance. But she wanted to believe the men in power at the summit of the nation, above all the President, were part of a moral order. She recoiled from losing this American faith, exposing her soul to the bitterness that had eroded so much of Zeke's good nature.

At lunch, Zeke wasted no time getting to the main point. "What do you think of our president now, after reading Rainbow Five?" he asked.

Tears ran down Annie's cheeks. At first she was not sure why. Was she weeping for her damaged faith in Franklin Roosevelt? The words she spoke were both an explanation and a defense. "I'm beginning to think you're right. We're going to have a war and I'm afraid you'll get killed!" she said. "That's ten times more important to me than what I think about FDR!"

"You can't get killed commanding a desk at ONI," Zeke said.

He began telling her her more about ONI's Japanese worries. The Communications Intelligence boys were also reading Tokyo's naval radio traffic, which was much harder to pick up and decipher than their diplomatic exchanges. A large part of their fleet, including a half-dozen carriers, had disappeared. On November 27, ONI had persuaded Admiral Turner to send a "war warning" to Pearl Harbor and the Philippines. But it was a vague statement that mostly rehashed old news and gave no specifics about possible targets except the obvious probability of an attack on the Philippines, in Nippon's backyard. Turner was still convinced the Japanese were going north, to Siberia.

In this atmosphere, Zeke said it was hard to concentrate on Rainbow Five, with its emphasis on a Europe-first strategy. But he had acquired reams of valuable information from the Navy's carrier mavens on their planes' ability to establish air supremacy for a landing in North Africa. More and more, he was shaping his revision into a plan for gradual conquest of the Mediterranean basin. After North Africa there would be amphibious assaults on Sicily, Italy and Greece.

Zeke worked until midnight on the invasion of North Africa. He told Annie about it as they got ready for bed. It would be an all-Navy show. They would deploy their four carriers and put 500 planes over the invading troops. "Most of the first wave will be Marines, of course," he told her as they went to bed. "You can't depend on the Army to do anything amphibious."

He was smiling contentedly as he turned off the light. Annie lay there wondering if planning to conquer half a continent made him happier than high-wire love or surrender love. If love was irrelevant in the lives of these infuriating demoralizing males. Maybe it was time she stopped worrying about all of them—husband, father, brother, son.

THUMP THUMP THUMP. Someone was knocking on the front door. It was barely dawn. The street lights were still glowing through the December gloom. Zeke slept on; nothing short of a sixteen-inch gun woke him up in the morning. His son was the same way. Annie shrugged into a bathrobe and rushed to the door. "Who is it?" she asked.

"Official U.S. Navy business!" boomed a voice.

She opened the door and stared into the white-belted chest of a Marine captain who was at least as big as Cinclant's Lieutenant Sweeney. Behind him stood two equally large corporals. All carried enormous pistols in white holsters on their hips. "Is this the home of Lieutenant Commander Jonathan Talbot?" the Captain asked.

Annie nodded. "I've got orders to put him under arrest and escort him to Washington, D.C.," the Captain said.

"What has he done?" Annie gasped, just managing to avoid adding "now."

The Captain held out his hand. One of the corporals slapped a rolled newspaper into it. The Captain unrolled it and held it up in front of Annie's horrified eyes.

The paper was the Washington *Times-Herald*. A giant headline screamed: FDR'S WAR PLANS! Underneath it, a subhead announced the 10-million-man army, the 5-million-man American Expeditionary Force. The text quoted from the Army's draft of Rainbow Five, discussing the equipment shortages, the possible collapse of England and Russia. It was unbelievable. How did they get it? Who would leak such a top secret document?

"Has Lieutenant Commander Talbot said anything to you about giving this information to this newspaper?" the Captain asked with the ferocity of a prosecuting attorney.

"Absolutely not!" Annie cried. "My husband is a man of honor. He wouldn't dream of doing such a thing."

It was close to the worst moment of Annie's life. She did not mean a word of that passionate protestation. She was all too ready to believe that Jonathan Trumbull Talbot, her heir of everything good and honorable, was guilty before he was even charged.

15

THIS IS NOT A DRILL

Escorted by the three marines, Jonathan Talbot arrived at the Navy building in a daze. In their car on the way from Norfolk, he had repeatedly denied leaking Rainbow Five to the *Times-Herald*. But he admitted discussing it with his wife and leaving his copy of the plan on the dining room table, where she or his son could easily have read it. The copy and all the other documents, a number of which were also stamped top secret, were in a suitcase that the Marine captain no doubt planned to deliver to Bong Jamison, along with presumption that Talbot was at the very least guilty of gross carelessness. The Captain was uninterested in his protests that people at ONI took top secret documents home all the time. The words were stamped on practically everything except the daily newspapers.

In ONI, everyone was standing around in small groups, talking in hushed tones. All eyes focused on him and the Marine escort and conversation ceased. Jonesy detached himself from one group and said: "Admiral Jamison wants to see you, Talbot."

Bong Jamison was not in a happy mood. He accepted the suitcase from the triumphant Marine captain and curtly told him to submit a written report. Disappointed by their failure to receive the Navy Cross if not the Medal of Honor, the corps withdrew, further con- vinced that sailors were a lower form of creation, only millimeters above soldiers and civilians.

"They want you—and me—upstairs," Jamison said. "Before we go, I want a straight answer. Did you leak this goddamn thing?"

"No."

Jamison only grunted. Why should he believe him? Lieutenant Commander Talbot was on record as a savage critic of FDR's war plans, with no less than Admiral Ernest J. King as a witness. Upstairs, Admiral Richmond Kelly Turner, a virtual King clone when it came to baleful eyes and a sneering mouth, made no attempt to conceal his glee. He was looking forward to a total annihilation of Jamison, Talbot and any lingering pockets of independence in ONI. "Admiral Stark is waiting," he said.

They ascended to the fourth deck and marched grimly down the hall. Talbot felt more and more like a spy on his way to a firing squad. People stood along the walls, giving him hostile stares. Doors opened and closed in swift succession and he found himself in a large office confronting a white-haired man with four gold stripes on his sleeves: Admiral Harold R. Stark. He looked like somebody's grandmother, dressed as a naval officer. "Talbot," he shrilled. "I just came from the Secretary of the Navy's office. Do you know what he said to me?"

"I have no idea, sir," Talbot said.

"'There's blood on the hands of the man who leaked this document!'"

Facing Ernie King, the dominant metaphor had been flame. Here it was ice. Admiral Stark lacked the personal force to create fire. The congealing sensation Talbot had noticed when he read the German newspaper story spread throughout his entire body, including his brain. Watching his naval career being destroyed by Betty Stark, he became a frozen crusader, someone who had wandered off course on the way to the promised land, an anachronism from another time, like the Siberian mammoths trapped by the ice age.

Stark was waving a Bible. "I want you to put your hand on this book and tell us the whole truth!"

"Sir! I don't need a Bible to make me tell the truth. I had nothing whatsoever to do with leaking Rainbow Five!" Talbot said. His voice boomed in his ears as if he were talking inside a knight's helmet with the visor closed.

"You swear to that on your honor as a graduate of the U.S. Naval Academy?"

"Jesus Christ, Betty, of course he does!" Jamison said. "Why the hell would he leak this thing? It makes the Navy look like a weak sister, a fucking afterthought."

"I just had a telephone call from Ernie King," Stark quavered. "A man whose judgment I respect. He says Talbot is his number-one suspect. He leaked it because he thinks he knows more than the President—because he's a goddamn Republican!"

"Admiral King said the same thing to me, earlier this morning," Turner said.

"Ernie King is in Newport, supposedly commanding the Atlantic fleet. It's none of his goddamn business," Jamison said.

Encased in his icy armor, Talbot listened to the quarreling admirals with the detachment of the dead. Whatever they decided was a matter of complete indifference to him. He was a frozen corpse, a metaphor of his expired dream of someday sitting in Admiral Stark's chair as Chief of Naval Operations.

"It may not be any of King's business, but it's sure as hell your business, Bong," Stark said. "This happened in your department. I expect you to make damn sure this man is not lying. The Navy's reputation is at stake in this thing. The President is having a shitfit. The isolationists are going to have a field day! What the hell do we do if Congress starts cutting the defense budget?"

Stark was telling Jamison his own career was on the line. "I believe Lieutenant Commander Talbot is telling the truth," Bong said.

"I don't," Admiral Turner said.

An aide appeared at the door to report the Secretary of the Navy was on the line. "Hello, Frank," Stark said, jamming the phone to his face like a man having convulsions. "All right, Frank. Of course we'll cooperate. I've got him here now. Of course."

He slammed down the phone. "The President's ordered the FBI to investigate the leak. I want our own people to do an independent investigation. Don't plan to go anywhere for a while, Commander Talbot."

"Yes sir," boomed the frozen crusader inside his helmet.

For the next two days, Pete Harrigan and Mike Casey, two FBI men with square Irish faces, interrogated Talbot for eight hours at a stretch, demanding an exact account of his every waking moment since he returned to Washington, D.C. Other agents interviewed his wife, his father-in-law, his landlady, Fireman Klein and other survivors of the *Spencer Lewis,* his fellow lieutenant commanders and their wives in nearby houses on their Norfolk street, fishing for evidence that Talbot was disloyal. Grim-lipped lieutenants from the B-section of Navy Intelligence were doing the same thing. His only consolation was the accidental discovery from a remark by one of his FBI interrogators that Major Albert Wedemeyer was the Army's suspect number one and was going through the same thing.

Talbot's father-in-law, his tearful wife, all asked the same sickening question. *Did you do it?* They did not seem to realize how vividly it revealed their real opinion of him. They apparently thought he was capable of violating his honor as a naval officer to play disgusting games with newspapermen.

At ONI, the pall of suspicion made Talbot a pariah. Jamison told him to forget about his revision of Rainbow Five. No one wanted to hear about it now. In Congress, isolationist Democrats and Republicans fulminated. Democratic Senator Burton K. Wheeler of Montana triumphantly declared Rainbow Five proved his prediction that Roosevelt would plow under every fourth American boy. A Republican congressman said the story was the biggest issue before the nation. Another Republican got the unanimous consent of the House to put the whole thing in the Congressional Record.

In "Behind The Headlines" Jack Richman, obviously desperate to defend FDR, boldly declared the leak was a plus, not a minus. Around the world, people living under the jackboots of the dictators knew that the United States was making mighty plans to rescue them. He quoted from British newspapers, which featured the leak in headlines brimming with exultation. Jack also reported the German Embassy had bought five hundred copies of the Washington *Times-Herald* and shipped them to Spain on Pan Am for rapid transmission to Berlin—proof, he said of how "scared" the Nazis were.

If he were a mere spectator, Talbot would have been jumping up and down in glee, calling his wife every ten minutes to extract another admission from her that she and her father and brother were wrong wrong wrong about Franklin D. Roosevelt and Jonathan Trumbull Talbot was right right right. As the centerpiece of the whole affair, he was too numb to care, much less gloat.

On Saturday he reported for duty at ONI as usual. He had no place else to go. The desks were fully manned. The ongoing crisis with the Japanese still had everyone in a frenzy. Talbot asked Jonesy if there was anything he could do on the European desk. The Chief of Staff glumly shook his head. "Bong says you can't even look at a piece of paper in here except maybe yesterday's *Times-Herald* until the FBI clears you."

Talbot nodded mournfully. He would do the same thing if he were Jamison. "What's the latest on the Japanese?"

Jonesy's eyes wandered to the doorway of his office to make sure no one was close enough to hear him telling secrets to a possible traitor. "We want to send a specific war warning to Pearl Harbor and the Philippines. Turner won't buy it."

Jonesy seized his arm. "Just between you and me, Talbot—did you do it?"

In the bilges of his sinking career, Jonesy dreamt of coming up with a pearl of triumph. Talbot shook his head and wandered back to his cubicle. The telephone rang and an operator told him his wife was calling. "Zeke," Annie said. "Can't you come home for the weekend? Yesterday some kid told Butch his father says you're a traitor. He's upset—and so am I."

Talbot called Mike Casey at the FBI and told him where he was going. "Make sure you're back here Monday morning. We got some more questions," he growled.

By nightfall Talbot was in Norfolk, assuring his son that he was not a traitor. He actually felt a few tremors of warmth, approximations of outrage, at being forced to say such a thing with his wife watching. Butch nodded, pretending to understand—but it was clear that he still felt some sort of earthquake had struck the family.

Later, Annie intimated she was ready for another trip through the tunnel of love. How could he explain to her that the sybaritic sandhog had vanished, possibly forever, and she was dealing with an icy corpse? For the first time in their marriage, he said he was not in the mood.

Annie's eyes filled with tears. "Zeke, I don't care what they do to you. I *love* you. This whole thing could be for the best. You haven't been happy in the Navy for a long time."

Here it comes, Talbot thought, how happier they would all be if he resigned and became a lobbyist for unions, corporations, everyone and anyone who saw the wisdom of having a powerful congressman's son-in-law represent them. That would be the final capitulation of the Talbots to the Richmans; he would become living, servile proof that power had changed hands.

But Annie made no such suggestion. Clinging to shreds of his humanity, Talbot lay beside his wife in their double bed, rigid, reminding himself that he still loved her. "Zeke," Annie whispered, moving against him. "*Did* you do it?"

"No," he said.

Annie went to sleep, which only stirred resentful thoughts. He envied her ability to sleep no matter what was happening. Like the time aboard the USS *Oklahoma* when the sailors in his division had neglected their shoeshines and the captain had chewed out Lieutenant Junior Grade Talbot in front of the entire wardroom. He had not slept for a week.

At breakfast Talbot tried to achieve a semblance of humanity, discussing Navy's football prospects for next year with Butch, debating whether to buy a new car with Annie. Later, he paged through the Sunday edition of the Washington *Times-Herald,* which bulged with speculation about the meaning of Rainbow Five and the ominous light it played on the negotiations with Japan.

"Hey, Dad, feel like giving the old arm a workout?" Butch asked. He stood in the middle of the living room, flipping the family football. They went out in the backyard and began lazily pitching the ball back and forth. Talbot wondered if Butch would turn out to be a bruiser like his older brother, who had been a football star at Yale along with graduating first in his class. Talbot had played football at the Choate School but lacked the weight to make the Annapolis team. No matter how smart Butch was, Talbot wanted him to be a normal American boy.

"Zeke!" Annie was standing at the back door. She had a skillet in her hand, a blue apron around her waist and a horrified expression on her face. "The radio—the Japanese are attacking Pearl Harbor!"

Ten seconds later, bells clanged, sirens whooped in the distance as ships in Norfolk Harbor went to general quarters. People ran onto their lawns along the street of stubby white stucco houses to stare at each other. Talbot raced into his house and frantically spun the radio's dial. He picked up nothing but occasional repetitions of the original news flash. Japanese planes were attacking American ships in Pearl Harbor. But that was all he needed to know—against the background of his previous weeks in ONI.

"It's war," Talbot said. "War in the Pacific."

Chunks of ice were falling off the frozen crusader. He was experiencing a miraculous resurrection. War in the Pacific, not the Atlantic. War that would leave Ernie King stranded as Cinclant, like the original beached whale. "War!" he whooped. "*War in the Pacific!*"

Annie was weeping. He tried to understand. He even felt, in his still semifrozen interior, a flush of sympathy for the men in Pearl, fighting off waves of torpedo and dive bombers. At the Naval War College, he had studied the 1940 British attack on the Italian fleet at Taranto. He knew how swiftly bombs came down, how brutally torpedoes smashed into hulls. He had friends, classmates in Pearl.

Annie was weeping for him—and for those friends dying out there in Roosevelt's war. He put his arms around her. "It's going to be okay," he said. He reached out and drew her and Butch against him. "They'll sink a few ships. But we'll even the score eventually."

For another moment, he was back on the North Atlantic mourning his dead aboard the sinking *Spencer Lewis*. Out of this remembered grief rose another man, the unrepentant crusader, the righteous truth-teller who had been vilified by Admirals Ernest J. King, Richmond Kelly Turner, and Harold Stark. That man was imagining an entirely different scene, with Butch elsewhere, while he exulted to Annie.

Don't you see what it means? It's the end of Rainbow Five, Roosevelt's Europe-first strategy. We're going to war in the Pacific! They'll fire Stark and Turner for blowing this thing! Who knows who'll be the new CNO? Maybe Bong Jamison. I'll get another ship, a destroyer—maybe a cruiser!

You'll get killed! Annie would sob, still stuck in her role of anxious wife.

Not a chance. This proves there's some justice in this world, after all.

Annie would continue to weep. Talbot reminded himself that a prophet was not always honored in his own country. He did not realize that in an unpredictable world, a prophet could also be very very wrong.

16

THE GERMAN WIFE

At their Wannsee villa on December 7, the Hoffmanns had just finished drinking their foul ersatz coffee and Berthe was helping the cook carry the dessert dishes to the kitchen, when Ernst turned on the radio to hear the nine o'clock bulletins. Protesting as usual, the children were being herded to bed by his mother. Berthe stopped clearing the table. The radio announcer's voice was shrill with compressed excitement.

Citizens of the Reich! I am happy to report an event of great significance. Today ships and planes of the Japanese Empire launched attacks on our British enemy in Malaya and the Dutch Islands of the East Indies, which had been placed under the protection of the British Far Eastern fleet. They have also attacked with great success the American fleet at Pearl Harbor in the islands of Hawaii and American planes and ships in the islands of the Philippines. Simultaneously the Japanese Foreign Office has declared a state of war now exists bewteen the empire of Japan and the Anglo-Saxon powers. In Pearl Harbor, Japanese torpedo planes and dive bombers have sunk seven American battleships, six cruisers and ten destroyers, effectively crippling the American Pacific fleet—

Ernst, in his old tweed hunting coat, bounded into the dining room. "Did you hear that?" he shouted. "They've caught the Americans napping. Exactly like the stupid Italians at Taranto!"

He rushed into the hall and shouted upstairs: "Mother! Bring the children down at once!"

They came tumbling down the stairs as the announcer continued to orate facts and figures of destroyed American ships and planes in the Philippines. "This is a great day, which you must share with us," Ernst said, placing both hands on Georg's small shoulders. "Last year, the Führer negotiated an alliance with the empire of Japan, on the other side of the world. Today they have declared war on the British and Americans and attacked them. They have won a great victory!"

"Heil the Japanese!" Georg shouted.

Isolde von Hoffmann clutched her ecstatic face. "God is good to Germany!" she cried.

"Will the Japanese kill all the Americans so you won't have to fight them, Father?" Greta said.

"Oh I may have to fight a few of them, my little darling," Ernst said, swooping her into his arms. "We'll write a special song to sing when I do. You can stay home here and sing it for me."

"An Amerikalied!" Georg cried.

He knew all the U-boat songs. His favorite was Englandlied, which his father had taught him. The U-boats always played it on their outward voyages.

We sail today against England
The enemy of our Reich.

Georg ran into the living room and found his toy submarine. He began marching around the dining room, singing Englandlied, substituting America for England. "That's enough!" Berthe said. "You have school tomorrow, good news—or bad news. It's already an hour past Greta's bedtime. She's developed terrible habits since her father came home."

She tried to sound jocular but the look Ernst gave her was not amused. "There is no bad news tonight," he said, and turned up the radio. The announcer reported fresh advances by the German armies in Russia. Once more he predicted they would celebrate Christmas in Moscow and Leningrad. The U-boats had demolished another convoy in the North Atlantic.

"I love you, Father, but I don't love Mother. She's a grouch!" Greta said. She gave her father a defiant kiss and scampered upstairs.

Georg followed her, clutching his submarine, still singing his Amerikalied. Berthe carefully stacked the rest of the dessert dishes and carried them out to the kitchen. For the time being she did not want to talk to her husband.

Without bothering to get a coat or sweater, she stepped out the back door into the frigid night to stare up at the glinting stars. For the last three days she had been waiting for the news. Ever since the leak of America's secret war plans to their newspapers, which the Abwehr agent at the German Embassy in Washington had cabled in its entirety to Admiral Canaris, everyone at headquarters on the Tirpitz Ufer knew war between Japan and America was inevitable. The great, the unknown question, was whether it would lead to war between Germany and America.

Since her primary mission was to make contact with the Americans, Berthe had been summoned to a special meeting with the Admiral and Colonel Oster soon after the revelations of Rainbow Five arrived in Berlin. She was given a copy to read and Canaris then began his interpretation.

"This is an enormously hopeful sign for the mission before you," he said. "It reveals that someone at the very top of the American government knows war with Japan is about to begin. But he recognizes that it is essentially a distraction from the foremost task the world faces—the defeat of Adolf Hitler. This document has been leaked for only one purpose. To stir the Führer to such a pitch of rage, he will declare war on the United States."

Berthe had asked why he was sure war between Japan and America was inevitable.

Canaris squinted, always a sign he was pleased. "Today, one of our agents in Moscow reported a flash from a Russian freighter bound for Vladivostok that sighted a Japanese task force steaming toward the American base at Pearl Harbor."

"Won't the Russians warn the Americans?" Berthe had asked, astonished once more at the world of espionage.

"Of course not. Stalin's only hope is America's entry into the war."

"Aren't we obligated to declare war on Japan's behalf by our treaty with them?" Berthe asked.

Canaris glumly shook his head, all pleasure draining from his face. He explained that the terms of the Tripartite Pact only required the partners to come to the assistance of each other if attacked by

hostile powers. There were no obligations if one of the partners was
the attacker. "You will note that the Japanese have not declared war
on Russia—and will probably never do so now. I fear the Führer may
be inclined to let them stew in their own juice, just as they're letting
us marinate in the snow before Moscow."

I'm telling you almost everything. Berthe was discovering the
Admiral always concealed potentially bad news. Desperately, Berthe
studied Canaris's worldly face for reassurance. Was he an apostle of
redemption—or was he part of the apparatus of evil? Lothar Engle
continued to pursue her, trying to convince her that Canaris was just
another player in the Nazi ring, shrewder, more subtle than the others. She had passed Lothar disinformation that Canaris had given her
about a disloyal Abwehr agent in Portugal.

The wind howled out of the east, carrying with it a foretaste of
snow. Clouds were thickening in the night sky, blurring the stars.
Berthe returned to the warm kitchen and helped the old cook, their
last servant, dry the dishes. The other servants had all left for better
paying jobs in the armament factories. Anything was preferable to
talking to her husband. But the last gold-rimmed dish was soon
stacked in the cabinets and conversation became unavoidable.

Ernst was pacing up and down the parlor, talking excitedly to his
mother. "I'm sure the Americans will come into the war now. We can
move against the shipping along their east coast. It will be the happiest hunting in the history of the Ubootwaffe. I've got to talk Dönitz
out of this ridiculous assignment to Spain."

Both Hoffmanns contemplated Berthe with undisguised dislike.
Discovering that his mother had nothing to do with his assignment to
Spain had only convinced Ernst that Berthe was the culprit. He had
combined this with a furious lecture on the role of the German wife,
which would have had her throwing things in another time and place.
While Isolde von Hoffmann nodded approval, Berthe had been told
that the German wife never made public statements about politics or
anything else without discovering first whether they coincided with
her husband's opinions. Even then, she usually maintained a discreet
silence and let him deal with such matters.

Berthe had the feeling Ernst had been wanting to reprimand her
for a long time. Perhaps not specifically in regard to the German wife
and politics, but in a wider context, to let her know he did not like
whole areas of her mind and soul. Berthe found the experience pro-

foundly disturbing—and she defended herself with vigor.

She had insisted that the Gestapo had never shown the slightest interest in the Kristallnacht petition. It had not been released to the newspapers. It was a private communication between Pastor Bruchmuller and the other signatories and the German government. The Reich chose to ignore it but there was not a sign that anyone thought it was worthy of punishment. They would never have allowed her to go to work for the Abwehr if she was considered untrustworthy. Millions of Germans, including his own mother, disapproved of the campaign against the Jews. Ernst had retreated, unconvinced, his rage at her undiminished.

Now he wheeled on her, even more determined to win the argument. "You've got to free me from this fellow Canaris," Ernst said.

"Husband dear," she said. "I'm in no position to persuade him to do anything."

"You don't want to persuade him," he said.

"That's true. I'll be much happier with you in Spain, rather than on the North Atlantic. There are no wabos in Madrid."

"There are worse things in this world than wabos!" Ernst said.

He looked so stern, so resolute, for a moment her will to deceive him, fueled by her anger since his obnoxious lecture, faltered. She remembered how simple, how fine their love had been, compared to Lothar Engle's perpetual mockery and interminable analysis. She almost hated Admiral Canaris.

"I have to go to work tomorrow. Good night," she said.

He was waiting on the bed in his undershorts when she emerged from her bath. They had made love twice since he came home. Both times it had bordered on the unpleasant. He had not attempted to soothe the bruises of his lecture. Now she was swept by another surge of regret, stronger than the emotion that had seized her downstairs. He looked simultaneously angry and hurt.

"I'm sorry for what's happening. I wish you could say that too," she said, sitting down beside him on the bed.

"I want to say it, but I can't," he said.

She kissed him softly on the lips. "I still love you," she said. "I'll always love you."

His answer was to lift the nightgown over her head and pull her down beside him. He toyed with the nipple of her left breast. "You're so beautiful," he said. "You think you can do anything."

"I don't."

"You talk to me the way you talk to Georg."

"I don't."

He slipped his hand between her thighs and inserted his finger in her vagina. "I'm not wearing my diaphragm," she said.

"I'll use a condom," he said.

Ernst pulled off his shorts, revealing a full erection. "Is this all you really love about me?" he said, taking her hand and wrapping it around his penis. It was warm, even hot.

"Of course not."

He slipped on the condom and entered her without another word. In a moment his muscular arms were crushing her lungs, his teeth were nibbling the flesh of her neck, then his tongue was deep in her mouth. *Making—love*. The words flared in Berthe's mind like a pair of eyes in the jungle. She almost heard a hyena laugh.

He began moving in her with deep deliberate strokes of possession, telling her in absolutely unquestionable terms that he—was—her—German—husband! In spite of the rage that was gathering in her mind, she felt the habit of surrender rising in her body. She willed it to cease but it kept rising, like chemicals in a beaker. Was he trying to prove that in a German marriage, there was no difference between love and loathing?

Stop! She wanted to scream the word, throw him off her but his tongue filled her mouth, his arms, his weight pinned her to the bed. *Stop! Stop!* Stop? From a scream the word had dwindled to a sigh. As the strokes continued, as the chemicals continued to rise, she wondered if it was exactly what she deserved for betraying him to Canaris, to Bruchmuller, to the Path. He was Siegfried, he was Manfred, he was Frederick II riding forth to certain death and what else should she do as a German woman but surrender to him?

Surrender was happening in her body, even if her mind refused it. This was a man in her arms, no doubt about that. She tried to remember other days, to establish some shadowy truce zone in which she could love him without reserve. Perhaps Spain was such a place—although she doubted it.

Oh. Oh. He was coming, his boyish face an odd frown of concentration. On what? His own pleasure? "Oh Berthe, Berthe," he whispered, "I love you in spite of everything. My heart belongs to you alone."

Dein ist mein herz allein. He was quoting from a saccharine Viennese operetta. But it did not matter. She came with a great shuddering gasp, melting in his arms. How could she explain it to anyone, Admiral Canaris, Lothar Engle, even herself?

The next morning, Berthe left her husband asleep with a smile on his face. He was probably dreaming of torpedoing an American· tanker in the mouth of New York Harbor—and would wake up with more sullen thoughts about his disloyal wife. At the Abwehr offices on the Tirpitz Ufer, she found the atmosphere loaded with tension. "We are about to witness a great secret battle," Colonel Oster told her, when she met him in the hall. "The Navy wants the Führer to declare war on America. The Army is moving heaven and earth to talk him out of it." Later in the day, Oster delivered another bulletin. "Roosevelt has spoken before the American Congress, denouncing Japan. There was no mention of Germany in his speech. You may not go to Spain after all."

At home that night, Berthe found Ernst saying goodbye to an unusual guest: a tall beefy man in the crisp brown uniform of a Nazi party leader. Ernst introduced him as Gauleiter Arthur Greiser. He kissed her hand with smarmy unctuousness and burbled about the fame of the beautiful Berthe von Schonberg. "Now I must thank the Führer's greatness for the privilege of meeting her in person."

"Gauleiter Greiser wishes us to come to Posen next weekend as his guests," Ernst said. "They want to stage a ceremony honoring my reception of the Knight's Cross."

"How nice," Berthe said, eyeing the hard, smooth flesh of Greiser's cheeks. So many Nazis had faces that emanated ruthlessness.

"We'll expect you on the noon train, Herr Kapitanleutnant," Greiser said. He slobbered over Berthe's hand again and drove away in a large black Mercedes Benz.

"I thought the Navy—and the Army—tried to have as little as possible to do with the Party," Berthe said.

"We do. But I talked it over with my brother Berthold and we agreed that given my current situation, it would be impolitic to refuse him."

"What current situation?" Berthe said.

"The one you've created with your crazy religious ideas," Ernst said.

"Berthold said that?" Berthe said.

Colonel Berthold von Hoffmann was on the general staff, serving at Army headquarters on the Bendlerstrasse. Five years older than Ernst, he always treated him—and Berthe—with a slight air of condescension. But he was a serious, intelligent man. Berthe was fond of both him and his wife. She valued their good opinion.

"No. I said it," Ernst snapped.

Nothing had changed between them. He was still angry. The next day, back at Abwehr headquarters, Berthe learned that Hitler had returned from the Russian front to plunge into intense discussions with Admiral Raeder, head of the German Navy, General Keitel, the Army commander, and Reichmarshal Goering, head of the Air Force, about the Japanese declaration of war and the significance of Rainbow Five. Abwehr friends in the Foreign Office reported Baron Oshima, the Japanese ambassador, was demanding an immediate declaration of war on America, but Germany's Foreign Minister, Joachim von Ribbentrop, had coolly informed him that the Reich had no obligation to do any such thing.

In the course of the day, others were summoned to the huge Reich chancellery overlooking the Siegesallee to offer their advice. Naturally, Admiral Canaris was one of the first. The knowledge of America's war-making potential was his province. He returned to tell Oster, who in turn told many others, including Berthe and Helmuth von Moltke, that the Admiral had advised the Führer to declare war immediately and unleash the U-boats. Canaris predicted they would be able to sink a thousand ships off the American East Coast before their Navy, caught in a two-ocean war, could organize an adequate defense.

In the evening, Berthe stopped for a drink with Lothar Engle, who now considered her his personal informant in the Abwehr. He wanted to know what Canaris was advising the Führer about war with America. Berthe saw no harm in telling him the truth. Lothar ground his teeth in impotent fury. "It's insanity. Himmler has been trying to reach Hitler all day to beg him to let Roosevelt stew in his Japanese juice. He's totally mishandled the situation with Japan and now he's stuck with fighting them while we clean up the Russians and the British. He couldn't get a declaration of war against Germany through the American Congress if he bribed every member. Can't Canaris see that?"

"Perhaps he's loyal to the Navy."

"That may be it. Which only proves he's totally unqualified for the job he holds. He's on a par with Dönitz, the Lion." Ice clicked against Lothar's teeth as he drained his martini. "Like the king of the beasts, he has a very small brain."

For twenty minutes Lothar chilled Berthe's flesh, telling her how fatal it would be if Hitler declared war on America. No armistice would rescue Germany this time. The British, backed by America's immense resources, would never negotiate peace. He quoted extensively from a recent series of broadcasts made by Robert Vansittart, Chief Diplomatic Advisor to the British Foreign Office. Eighty percent of the German people were the scum of the earth. The three leading traits of the German character were envy, self-pity and cruelty. For two thousand years, back to the days of the Romans, their hands had been drenched in innocent blood. "It will be a war of extermination, Berthe," Lothar said. "*Extermination.*"

In Wannsee, Hitler's silence on war with America had Ernst pacing the floor and calling friends in Navy headquarters. He could not understand what was wrong with the Führer. That night, when he turned on the radio for the nine o'clock bulletins, he found even more reason for exasperation. The announcer reported that Roosevelt had gone before Congress and made an insulting speech, accusing Germany of being in collusion with Japan in their surprise attack. The Foreign Ministry had issued a furious denial, accusing the President of attempting to lead the American people into a European war they did not want on behalf of British imperialism and international Jewish capitalism.

At Abwehr headquarters the next day, Berthe was summoned to Canaris's office at noon. The Admiral was in a cheerful mood. "Begin to brush up on your Spanish," he said. "The Führer has made his decision. Roosevelt has proven himself a master psychologist. His speech yesterday, on top of the leak of Rainbow Five, has so enraged the Führer, he has decided to declare war tomorrow. This day should go down in German history as the first day of our deliverance. Hitler's defeat is certain now."

"The Americans will go ahead with their plans to land five million men in Europe in 1943?"

Canaris nodded. "Hewing to Rainbow Five is the whole purpose of Roosevelt's maneuvers. It's also our best hope. If there's one principle on which the German General Staff has been resolved since nineteen-eighteen, it is to avoid a two-front war. Now we're faced with one. They'll be psychologically ready to remove Hitler—if England and America show a genuine readiness to make peace."

"What if they don't?" Berthe said.

"I try to be an optimist about such things. If I'm wrong—we'll have to turn to more radical solutions."

Berthe thought of that moment of surrender two nights ago in her husband's arms. Would it ever be possible again, now that she was committed to betraying Germany? Although Canaris tried to distinguish between Hitler and the nation, no one else—certainly not Ernst—would tolerate such subtleties. "I wish I could share your optimism, Herr Admiral," she said. "This whole thing seems more and more difficult—and awful for Germany."

"Remember what Nietzsche said: 'Man is a rope stretched over an abyss.'"

Nietzsche again. How his mocking nihilism haunted Germany. His disciple, Lothar Engle, had forced Berthe to stare into the Godless abyss—and she had recoiled into Ernst von Hoffmann's arms.

"I never really understood Nietzsche's talk of an abyss," Berthe said, deciding she had no obligation to tell the Admiral everything.

"I fear we may all soon understand it. But in the end, there is still, as our friend Moltke likes to believe, a star of hope."

Canaris said this with a flicker of a smile, which made Berthe suspect the Admiral was only reciting. He was too much the rationalist, the devious plotter, to rely on stars of hope. The next day, December 11, Hitler went before the Reichstag, the German Parliament, and declared war on the United States. He made one of his most rabble-rousing speeches, calling Roosevelt a hired tool of the Jews, a liar, a hypocrite. The Reichstag roared with laughter at his best sallies and voted unanimously to follow the Führer. Late that afternoon, Berthe received another call from Lothar Engle.

He sat in a booth in their usual cafe, downing martinis as if they were soda water. "Germany is doomed—Hitler is a madman," he said, over and over again. Then he seized her arm and made an impassioned plea for his boss, Heinrich Himmler. "Our only hope is a truce with the British and Americans. You can help us in Spain, Berthe. I can give you access to our people there. They can arrange things at the very highest level."

She thought of the Abwehr dispatches from Riga and Smolensk, describing Himmler's men massacring Jews and told him it was beyond her capacity to deceive her husband on such a fundamental matter.

"Perhaps I'll go myself," Lothar muttered.

The following day, Friday, Berthe and Ernst left for Posen to be entertained by Gauleiter Greiser. As she feared, Ernst was in a fury. His friends on the naval staff had told him six U-boats were being sent against the Americans immediately in an operation called *Pauchenschlag*—Drumbeat. They were to take up their stations and begin sinking ships on the same day, early in January.

In Posen (renamed from the Polish Poznan) a sixty-piece band was blaring the Horst Wessel march as the train pulled into the station. Gauleiter Greiser was there with a horde of brown uniformed underlings, cheering and clapping. Beside them, in pressed navy blue, was the entire crew of the Ritterboot, saluting their commander. Ernst was speechless with amazement and delight. It was an awesome display of Greiser's power in the Party.

They were driven in Mercedes Benz touring cars to the best hotel in the city, while thousands of people lined the streets, waving German flags, their right arms raised in the Hitler salute. Greiser's men returned it but Berthe noticed only Lieutenant Griff, the skinny naval correspondent, imitated them. The rest of the Ritterboot's crew waved politely instead.

At the brand new Hotel Ostland, the Hoffmanns' suite was full of flowers. Champagne cooled in a bucket on a table in the sitting room. Greiser and a half-dozen aides filled the room with guttural laughter as they displayed the hotel's amenities: radios built into the walls, a telephone in every room, even the bathroom, a refrigerated bar. "Were you pleased to see your crew?" Greiser roared. He seldom said anything below a bellow.

"Of course," Ernst said.

"Some of them wanted to stay home with their wives. They were told it was a duty to the Reich! Only one refused to come. Your first officer, Kurz. What's wrong with the fellow?"

"He's—what do you call it—slavishly devoted to his wife. What's the word, Berthe?"

"Uxorious."

"Yes. Uxorious. But he's a very good officer, otherwise."

"If I were you, I wouldn't let the fellow on my boat again," Greiser roared.

"He's religious," Lieutenant Griff said. He had inserted himself into the Gauleiter's entourage by virtue of his Party credentials. "Herr Kapitanleutnant von Hoffmann nicknamed him the Saint, which effectively neutralized his influence with the crew."

They all beamed at Ernst as if this was further proof of his genius as a U-boat commander. He stared at Berthe, as if he were daring her to say something critical.

That night, they attended a banquet for over 250 leading citizens of Posen in the hotel's blue-ceilinged ballroom. Giant swastikas hung on the glistening white walls. Ernst wore the black gold-edged Knight's Cross on a ribbon around his neck. He introduced Berthe to each of his crew. She was shocked by how young most of the sailors were. They were fighting the U-boat war with boys! She liked all the officers, especially Chief Engineer Kleist, who was thoroughly drunk before the party began. He told her now he knew why they had survived the wabos. She was the Ritterboot's guardian angel.

During dinner, Greiser talked—or better, orated—about the way they were restoring Posen and the surrounding countryside to Germany. Land, stolen from Germans after the last war, was being reclaimed, either by the original owners or by deserving Germans who were committed to an enlarged Reich.

Berthe asked how the Poles were accepting this policy. Greiser laughed harshly. "We haven't asked them," he said. "They know anyone who resists us will soon be under the ground." Berthe was about to bite into a piece of succulent pork. The meal had begun with pâté "direct from Paris," oysters from Norway's Skaggerag. She put down her knife and fork and listened as Greiser explained to Ernst his policy for restoring the province of Wartheland to Germany. "In the part of Poland we temporarily ceded to the Russians after our 1940 conquest, Stalin wiped out the entire ruling class—landlords, intellectuals, priests. They shot over fifteen thousand members of the officer corps. Can we let Communist scum outdo Germans acting in the name of the Führer's vision of a Thousand Year Reich?"

Suddenly the room was filled with the odor of burning offal. Why didn't anyone else notice it? Berthe wondered. The stench was setting her lungs, her brain on fire. But everyone, including her husband, continued to eat their pork and drink their Moselle wine, nodding polite approval of Greiser's murderous words.

Berthe fled into the lobby, struggling to control her nausea. She survived the elevator but she vomited just inside the front door of the suite, a slimy mess that the stocky, balding hall porter helped her clean up. As he muttered his sympathy, she realized he was Polish. Before her horrified eyes, the flesh peeled from his face and he was a grinning skull. "Oh!" she cried and stumbled into the bathroom to retch into the toilet bowl.

She returned to the ballroom in time for dessert, a huge slice of Linzer torte, which she left untouched on her plate. Greiser rose and hurled himself into a speech praising the courage and skill of the men of the Ritterboot, in particular, the heroism of her commanding officer. To demonstrate their gratitude, the German citizens of Posen had contributed voluntarily to a fund that would restore the Hoffmann manor house and estate on the outskirts of the city to pristine condition—and give it as a free gift to Kapitanleutnant von Hoffmann and his beautiful wife, in the hope that they would settle there as soon as possible.

It was a stunning gesture. The estate was at least 1,000 acres. The manor house, or *schloss*, was a vast, rambling stone pile, which Greiser said the Polish owners had used as a warehouse—proof, if any was needed, that Poles were incapable of civilization. While the audience cheered, Ernst rose to thank the Gauleiter for this generosity. His voice choked with emotion, he declared he was proud to represent the Hoffmanns in this restoration of the Reich. "I know I speak for my wife—and my children—when I say we will be honored to become citizens of Posen," he said.

He turned to Berthe, defiance mingling with pride on his handsome face. It was almost unbearable. The remnants of the stench still lingered in the blue and white ballroom. Berthe sat through the rest of the evening in a daze, trying not to listen to the rest of Greiser's speech, in which he repeated with increased ferocity his vision of a Poland without Poles. "We have made a good beginning of our program in Posen," he roared. "We'll do better in the months to come."

Upstairs in their suite, Ernst did not even try to restrain his jubilance. "I can't wait to tell Berthold!" he said, pouring himself a glass of champagne. "I remember him saying how stupid I was to join the Navy because sailors never got any tangible rewards. Whereas Army officers regularly acquired estates in conquered territories."

"How can you take anything from that man Greiser?" Berthe cried. "His hands are drenched in blood!"

Ernst froze with the champagne halfway to his mouth. An expression crept over his face that Berthe had never seen before. For a weird moment it reminded her of Lothar Engle. "What about me?" he said. "Aren't my hands drenched in blood too? Or do you think the salt water wipes them clean?"

"You're not massacring innocent people!"

"Really? Have you ever stopped to think about what a torpedo does inside a ship when it explodes? I've seen the pieces of bodies floating around the wreckage, my dear wife. Have you stopped to think about what happens to those who don't get dismembered? They freeze to death in the North Atlantic, slowly. It takes about an hour to die. The lucky few who get into lifeboats or onto rafts live a little longer. Maybe a day or two. They're all just as innocent as the Poles, Berthe, whatever that stupid word means. They have families, children, waiting for them at home. They're poor sailors, trying to eke out a living on the uncaring ocean. My torpedoes put an abrupt stop to their pathetic lives."

He took a long swallow of his champagne. "What Greiser is doing is hard, Berthe. But war is hard. The Poles tried to make war against us and lost. Now they have to pay the hard price. War is the way Germany rose to greatness and the way we'll continue to rise to even greater power and glory. I'm hard too, Berthe. I'm part of Germany's war machine. While you, my dear wife, are a mushy, sentimental fool."

Father, Father, is this the Germany you loved? Berthe wondered, watching her husband's face acquire a veneer of sleek malice. Was the Path taking her toward a heaven of salvation—or Nietzsche's livid stench-ridden abyss?

17

ESCAPE ARTIST

In Washington, D.C., Lieutenant Commander Jonathan Trumbull Talbot rode a roller coaster of historical proportions after Pearl Harbor. His FBI and B-section inquisitors grimly maintained he was still under suspicion for leaking Rainbow Five. But there was an air of make-believe in their bluster, as if even they did not believe it—or if they did, they realized it no longer mattered. As Talbot told one of them, Rainbow Five was as dead as the USS *Arizona*, whose pathetic capsized hulk was in every spread of pictures about Pearl.

For the first three days, everything seemed to be progressing as Talbot, in his Ezekiel mode, had predicted. Roosevelt went before Congress to declare Pearl Harbor a "day of infamy," while everyone in the Office of Naval Intelligence cursed and suggested alternative phrases, such as day of stupidity, day of hypocrisy, day of retribution. Stupidity won by a wide margin.

The President did not mention Germany in his brief speech and Congress voted resoundingly for war with Japan. So far so good. Talbot sent a cable to Admiral Dwight Herman, Deputy Chief of Staff to Hawaii's Commander, Admiral Husband Kimmel, begging him to request his transfer to the Pacific fleet. He had worked for Herman, a bright, talented comer, when he was chief of operations in Washington, D.C., three years ago and they had gotten along well.

The next day, December 9, Roosevelt went before Congress and made another speech, lambasting Hitler and Germany. He did not ask Congress to do anything on behalf of his vituperation. Everyone assumed he was trying to salvage some shreds of his Rainbow Five plan from the wreckage. In "Behind The Headlines" Jack Richman, demonstrating his superb White House connections, reported the President hoped he could preserve the American commitment to keep escorting British convoys out to MOMP. Jack added several paragraphs of dubious rumors from Europe that Hitler was the evil genius behind the Japanese attack.

Everyone in ONI bet against Roosevelt's chances. Public fury was focused totally on Japan. The top brass were exhuming musty copies of Homer Lea's pre–World War I classic, *The Valor of Ignorance*, in which this hunchbacked military genius had predicted the Japanese would conquer the Philippines with lightning speed—then mop up Hawaii and turn the Western states into provinces of Tokyo. In California they were rounding up everyone with a Japanese name and herding them into concentration camps well inland, in case an invasion fleet appeared off Los Angeles or San Francisco.

Like Talbot, the rest of ONI's denizens were more interested in the impact of the catastrophe at Pearl Harbor on the Navy's power structure—and their own futures. Everyone was gleefully certain Betty Stark and Richmond Kelly Turner would be consigned to some obscure installation on the edge of nowhere. The large unanswered question centered around the next Chief of Naval Operations. Would Roosevelt reappoint the Admiral who had predicted the Pearl Harbor disaster, James O. Richardson? That would be the act of a courageous patriot. J.O. was the most popular admiral in the Navy. It would unquestionably help restore morale. Jonesy was among the more vociferous backers of a Richardson reincarnation.

Others thought the victim of Pearl Harbor, Admiral Husband E. Kimmel, might rise to the top spot roaring threats of political retaliation. Who else could testify more graphically about the total failure of Betty Stark and Richmond Kelly Turner to send him the intelligence he needed to ward off the Japanese strike? Talbot thought Kimmel had a reasonable chance of pulling this off—which only made his telegram to Admiral Dwight Herman all the more plausible. If Kimmel came to Washington, Herman might rise to Cincpac, Commander-in-Chief of the Pacific Fleet.

Talbot was not above conferring with his father-in-law in these momentous days. Sam Richman predicted Congress would soon hold hearings that would roast Betty Stark and Terrible Turner over some very hot coals. Not a word was said about investigating the White House or the State Department but Talbot did not expect objectivity from the Congressman.

Only Annie persisted in dampening Talbot's ebullience with her fears for his survival. He had to admit she had a point, as the worst imaginable news continued to arrive from the Pacific. The backbone of the American battleship Navy had been smashed at Pearl Harbor. On Wednesday, December 10, they learned that HMS *Repulse* and *Prince of Wales,* two battleships dispatched by Churchill to defend Singapore, had been sunk by Japanese torpedo planes in the China Sea. In the Philippines, an immense Japanese army was landing on the shores of Lingayen Gulf, exactly as Homer Lea had predicted forty years ago, and MacArthur's puny forces could not hope to stop them. Most of the B-17s that were supposed to frighten the Japanese into passivity had been destroyed on the ground several hours after the Pearl Harbor attack.

Nevertheless, Talbot still sensed a renascence of the days when his father was a Washington titan and the CNO's job looked like the inevitable oyster of a man who had graduated first in his class at Annapolis. On Thursday morning, December 11, 1941, he strode into Main Navy with the swagger of a man who thought he was destiny's child.

Upstairs at ONI, Jonesy and a half-dozen other officers were sitting around the Chief of Staff's office shaking their heads morosely. "What's up?" Talbot said, assuming more bad news had arrived from the Pacific. "Are the Japs in Manila?"

"We just heard from some guys at State," Jonesy said. "Hitler's declared war on us."

Talbot sat down very slowly. He could not believe it. Why had Kapitanleutnant von Hoffmann gone to so much trouble to portray him as a secret ally of the Reich? Why had they refrained from sinking American warships, except for three cases of mistaken identity? Couldn't a child see they were playing into Roosevelt's hands? Hadn't they read Rainbow Five? "You're sure?" Talbot said.

Jonesy checked his watch and flipped on a radio on the windowsill. An announcer began reporting the news at the top of the hour. Adolf Hitler's denunciation of Roosevelt was the lead story.

Seconds later, with that gift of prescience that sent shudders through his bone structure, Talbot knew who was going to be the next Chief of Naval Operations: Admiral Ernest J. King.

Talbot did not know exactly why he knew it at first. But as he examined it, the intuition made rueful sense. King was the only admiral who had, in word and deed, endorsed Rainbow Five. He was also the only commander of a naval force that had not been defeated. At Pearl Harbor, Kimmel was a humiliated man. King was mean enough, tough enough—and ambitious enough—to play the game Roosevelt's way.

Maybe, now that Adolf Hitler had declared war, there was no other way to play it. A terrible thought, but within the revulsion and dismay that was engulfing him, Talbot's high caliber brain kept functioning.

He spent the rest of the day in another session with his two FBI interrogators. They went over the statements he had made, trying to find contradictions, omissions. By evening they were all exhausted. "I never thought you did it in the first place, Commander," Mike Casey said.

"Thanks. How about Wedemeyer? Have you cleared him too?"

"Yeah. We thought he was hot, with that German name," Casey said. "But his great-grandfather got here from Deutschland before the Civil War, for Christ's sake—and fought for the goddamn Confederacy!"

"It's over. They're blowin' the whistle," Pete Harrigan said.

"Who?"

"Somebody way up there," Harrigan said, pointing toward the sky. "I don't mean God."

Talbot was barely back in his furnished room in Alexandria when the telephone rang. "It's Congressman Richman," his landlady said, respect in her voice. She knew who was who in Washington.

"I got some bad news just now," the Congressman said.

"The new CNO?"

"It's Ernie King. He's gonna be more than CNO. Roosevelt's inventin' a new title for him: Cominch. He's gonna be commander in chief of everything that floats. The President called the chairman of the committee about an hour ago, linin' up support for him. Naturally I gotta go along. I'm sorry as hell, Zeke."

The Congressman's voice was thick with emotion. "I'll do what I can to protect you if he tries to pull anything really dirty. I don't care what it costs me. You and Annie and Butch mean more to me than this goddamn job."

For a moment Talbot felt ashamed of his low opinion of the Congressman. The man really cared about him. Sam Richman continued in the same lugubrious voice. "This whole thing makes me feel like goin' out and gettin' drunk for a month. I seen one big show. This one's gonna be a lot worse. These Germans ain't worn out like the guys we fought at St. Mihiel and the Argonne. And the Japs ain't exactly pushovers either, from what they left of the fleet at Pearl."

Talbot had forgotten the Congressman fought in World War I. He realized Richman was saying they might lose the war. For the first time Talbot admitted it was a very real possibility. The strategic side of his brain clicked into gear. He saw the enormous advantages the other side enjoyed, especially now that they had read Rainbow Five and knew the United States could not mount a major offensive until mid-1943. The Germans and the Japanese had eighteen months to make themselves masters of the world—and they had the war machines to do it.

"Go see my pal Admiral Duncan. Maybe he can do something," the Congressman said. "I'd move fast, before King gets a grip on things."

Talbot called Annie to tell her the bad news about King. As usual, her reaction was totally out of sync. "Zeke—he'll probably let you sit out the war in ONI. That's not so terrible. It's brainwork—what you're really good at."

Jesus Christ! Don't you have any appreciation of how a man feels and thinks? He managed to strangle that burst of rage and say: "That assumes King is capable of taking advice—which I doubt. I'm going to ask for a ship."

"If King's as mean as you say he is, he'll give you command of a minesweeper off Tierra del Fuego. I won't see you for the next five years."

Worse things could happen. Again, Talbot was shocked by the way the words burst into his mind. Was he beginning to think this woman was an albatross around his neck, bringing him nothing but bad luck? He hung up without even bothering to tell her when he might return to Norfolk.

The next morning, as he mounted the stairs in the Navy building,

Talbot found himself face-to-face with Admirals Richmond Kelly Turner and Ernest J. King. "Well well well," King said. "If it isn't the guy who knows more than the President. What do you think of the international situation these days, Commander?"

"I've learned a lot in the last few days, Admiral," Talbot said.

"You're in ONI?"

"Yes sir."

"When I want a book from the Library of Congress, I'll send you for it," King said. A dry sound rattled in Turner's throat, like the laughter of a corpse in a Hollywood horror movie.

"Admiral, I want another ship! I want to see action!"

A flicker of warmth in King's eyes suggested he approved of this sentiment. But a basic negation remained in place around the grim mouth. "I don't believe in giving a man a ship after he's lost one," he growled. "The crew would consider him a Jonah."

"I'll take anything, Admiral. Damage Control Officer, First Lieutenant. Supply Officer!"

"You're in the right place at ONI, Talbot."

"Where the B-section can keep an eye on you," Turner said.

The admirals left Talbot standing there with shit running down his face and climbed the stairs to the upper decks. He stumbled down the corridor of the second deck, his brain on fire with the realization that he and his fellow pariahs in ONI would not even have the satisfaction of seeing Richmond Kelly Turner hanged, drawn and quartered. No justice would be done in the matter of Pearl Harbor. King was going to protect his fellow son of a bitch.

When he issued this prophecy in ONI, everyone nodded glumly. They knew all about it. The two admirals had just paid them a visit to clean any evidence of official incompetence out of the files. Certain decrypts, such as the attack signal Tokyo had sent to their fleet, "East wind, rain," were headed for the nearest incinerator.

An hour later, Talbot was in Admiral Duncan's office, pleading for help. Duncan, a close student of the power curve, regarded him with something less than friendly ardor. Ernie King now had the authority to exile Duncan to Tierra del Fuego or other points south or north. He had absolute power to alter the lives of every man in the U.S. Navy. Duncan said he would see what could be done—but he was careful to promise nothing. From Admiral Herman in Pearl Harbor came only silence.

From elsewhere in the Pacific, the public news continued to arrive in avalanche proportions—all bad. The Japanese gobbled up Guam and the other islands in the Marianas and demolished a gallant Marine detachment on Wake Island after a fierce shootout. In the Philippines, MacArthur's thin battalions were in retreat. Talbot's landlady was in a frenzy about her husband's safety. The British were abandoning Malaya and falling back to their island fortress of Singapore. Jack Richman filled "Behind The Headlines" with frantic assurances that Roosevelt, like John Paul Jones, had not yet begun to fight.

Talbot's sister, Ethel, invited him to dinner. Ned Travis was working overtime at the State Department and Talbot had time to give Ethel a gloomy assessment of his entombment at ONI. She was enormously sympathetic. When Ned finally arrived, he confessed to being a little chastened by how badly his triumvirate had miscalculated the Japanese potential for belligerence—but not much. After all, no one in the State Department had gotten killed. Ned was soon cheerfully talking about the geopolitical implications of this century's second world war. "This time we're going to do it right!" he said.

He had no doubt whatsoever that the Allies would humble the Axis powers and the State Department would then have the delicious task of reordering the world according to proper priorities. He grandly predicted a first principle would be the elimination of capitalism, which would guarantee centuries of peaceful cooperation between the United States and the Soviet Union. The Soviet model would be the dominant style of government for Africa, Asia and most of South America, where things were too primitive to make political democracy useful for the time being.

Of immediate concern were Axis satellite countries, such as Spain. Fascism had scored one of its first triumphs there in 1939, when the Nationalists, backed by German and Italian planes and tanks, had defeated the Republicans, who were backed by Russian tanks and guns, while the United States maintained a feckless neutrality. "We're sending a whole new mission to Spain. A new ambassador, the works. Their number-one job will be to keep Franco from signing an alliance with Hitler. We expect the Germans to go all out in that direction now that we're in the war."

Ned sawed into his veal chop. "But the long-range goal of the mission will be the elimination of Franco. We'll need some people in the contingent who are capable of double-decker thinking. Particularly on the military side. Do you know—"

Ethel was looking at Ned in that special way wives communicate with husbands. Ned stopped sawing his veal chop; discomfort spread across his sly, somewhat dissolute face. "Zeke would be perfect for naval attaché!" Ethel said.

Ned now looked totally discomfited. He obviously wanted someone with better liberal credentials. Ethel met the problem Talbot style, head on. She argued the likelihood of finding a liberal in the upper ranks of the Navy was slight. Why not choose someone whose instincts were "basically liberal"—like hers. She was sure when Zeke got a look at Franco close up, he would become a firm advocate of overthrowing him. Moreover Zeke spoke Spanish and had spent a lot of time in Spain during their father's ambassadorship. He could make a contribution to keeping the Germans at bay.

"Are you interested, Zeke?" Ned asked, obviously hoping the answer was no.

Lieutenant Commander Diplomat? Talbot winced, thinking of the way he had defied his father's insistence on shoving him into the State Department. But helping to keep the Germans out of Spain might be one of the most important things anyone in the U.S. Navy would do for the next eighteen months. In his strategic mind's eye Talbot saw the Iberian peninsula jutting into the Atlantic like a great arm. If the Germans had access to that coast their planes and submarines could wreak awful havoc on convoys to England. At Gibraltar they could cut the lifeline to British troops in Egypt and India.

As for secretly working on the eventual ouster of General Franco—Talbot had no particular objections to that idea. His father had supported Franco, which was almost a reason in itself for Talbot to dislike him. From all reports he was unquestionably a ruthless dictator and Talbot, like any decent American, favored democracy over dictatorship.

Maybe, in spite of everything that had gone wrong, fate was conspiring to create this perfect job for him. It was a long way from commanding a fleet in an ultimate shootout with Imperial Japan—the kind of glory Talbot had dreamt of finding in his Annapolis days. It was a more obscure kind of glory. But it might be enough to satisfy him. It was certainly preferable to sitting in ONI writing intelligence estimates that Admiral Ernest J. King contemptuously consigned to the circular file.

"I'm interested," he said.

"I'll put your name into the hopper," Ned said.

"Olé!" cried Ethel, raising her wine glass. "We'll visit you and have a second honeymoon in the bargain." She and Ned had met in Spain, where he had been press attaché under Ambassador Roger Sherman Talbot.

"I'm afraid all overseas travel for wives is banned for the duration," Ned said with surprising curtness.

"You're a filthy liar!" Ethel hissed. Lips trembling, she lurched to her feet and fled the room. Another marriage on the rocks? Ned looked frightened. Did he expect Talbot to seize him by the throat and demand an explanation? He had nothing to worry about. Talbots never inquired into each other's private lives.

Ned muttered something about how hard it was to explain certain things to women. "I know exactly what you mean," Talbot said.

Ned's smile was grateful—if a bit snide. Talbot realized Ned probably shared Ethel's low opinion of Annie. Somehow that reinforced his desire to solve his career problems without any help from Congressman Richman. "I'm still interested in Spain," he said. "Very interested."

18

SMASH

Annie Talbot had just finished telling Butch he could stay overnight with his fourteen-year-old friend Fred, a fellow math whiz who was in his tutoring group. They were trying to solve some sort of problem in solid geometry that made her head spin. Suddenly a key was turning in the lock and Lieutenant Commander Jonathan Trumbull Talbot, the exonerated candidate for the traitor of the year award, was in the hall, hanging up his coat.

"I've escaped from ONI," he said triumphantly, after giving her a brief kiss.

"Marvelous. Where are you going?"

"Naval attaché in Madrid."

She was underwhelmed. More than once she had heard him dismiss an attaché's job as nothing more than a glorified bellboy or doorman. She only half-listened to his labored explanation of the importance of Spain, meanwhile convincing herself he was doing this for all the wrong reasons.

"Why run for cover so quickly, Zeke?" she said. "Why don't you stick it out at ONI for a while and see what happens in the war? King may fall on his face. It won't do you any good if you're three thousand miles away watching bullfights in Spain."

"Didn't you hear what I just said? I'll be doing a lot more than watching bullfights."

"You're not giving Dad a chance to help you."

"I've talked to him. He doesn't think he can do anything."

"Not right away. But give him time. He'll take you to parties, he'll introduce you to his friends in Congress, you'll meet all sorts of admirals and generals who'll be putting together staffs for big operations and looking for people with brains."

"I don't want to be exhibited as a favor the Congressman wants. I've had enough of going along to get along."

"Everybody does it, Zeke."

"I prefer Spain," he said.

"Because Ethel recommends it?"

"When are you going to stop dueling Ethel for influence over me? It's an entirely imaginary battle—with most of the dislike coming from your side."

"The hell you say."

"Can you at least concede that my sister has an honest interest in my welfare? It may be a lot more disinterested than yours. More and more I begin to think the way you see it, I'm only supposed to reflect glory on the Richmans."

"That's a rotten thing to say!"

She was so angry she started to cry, which only made her angrier. She fled into the bedroom with him in furious pursuit, demanding she concede him the right to run his own career. "All right, all right, all right!" she finally screamed, sounding like the prototype of the hysterical wife.

He was determined to get overseas as fast as possible. Was it primarily to get away from her? She had a dreadful suspicion that was the reason but she managed to refrain from saying it. There was nothing more she could do to stop him from going to Spain. All she could hope for was a flop on Ned Travis's part. Maybe they were opposed to nepotism at the State Department. She even considered calling her father to see if he could put in a negative fix, but that was much too vicious a thing to do to someone you were supposed to love.

Early in the following week, Zeke called from Washington to report that the State Department had examined his personnel file and given him the highest rating. For the rest of that week and the next week, Spain languished, while Bong Jamison put him to work on preparing an intelligence estimate of the danger German submarines

posed to American shipping along the East Coast. He traveled from
Maine to Florida, talking to admirals in charge of the various naval
districts—giving Annie no chance to diminish Spain with argument
and/or persuasion.

Zeke found the entire Atlantic coast in an appalling state of
strategic and tactical nudity. Not a single destroyer had been assigned
to the job of patrolling the 2,000-mile-long shoreline. There were no
plans for convoys. Everything, from tankers to transports, was sailing
unescorted, often with their cruising lights on, as if all they had to
worry about was a collision. Air reconnaissance was zero. The Navy
was locked in a nasty quarrel with the Army Air Force over who had
the right to control the nonexistent planes that would do the job.

From what he had seen of the Ubootwaffe's aggressive style in
the Ritterboot, Zeke had no doubt that Kapitanleutnant von Hoffmann and his friends would soon be operating along the East Coast.
He confirmed this opinion with a visit to Communication Intelligence, where they were getting weekly reports of British decrypts
from U-boats at sea. They had already pinpointed at least five boats
heading for the East Coast. Zeke wrote a blistering critique of the
Navy's total unpreparedness for this emergency, predicting that as
many as 200 ships a month could be sunk if something was not done
fast. Jamison sent it upstairs with his signature on it.

The next day, Admiral King's explosion almost took the roof off
the Navy building. When he found out Jonathan Talbot had written
the report, the detonation threatened to level downtown Washington.
He dragged Zeke upstairs for a half-hour of vituperation about his
insane desire to impugn the Navy's reputation. If he was caught mentioning his intelligence estimate to anyone, especially his brother-in-
law the newspaper columnist, King was going to have him committed
to St. Elizabeth's Hospital for psychiatric examination.

Annie heard all this on the telephone with mounting dismay and
apprehension. It made the idea of Zeke's staying at ONI or any place
else within range of King's claws intolerable. "I'm going to call Ned
Travis at the State Department and tell him now if ever is the time to
ask for Lieutenant Commander Talbot as the naval attaché to the
American Embassy in Madrid," Zeke said. He would see her for dinner with the final installment of their high-seas soap opera.

That night Zeke arrived in Norfolk on the B&O to exultantly
inform Annie of the denouement. "Ned got his hero, Undersecretary

of State Sumner Welles, to make the call. King said he was delighted to get rid of me."

All Annie could hear was the gloating tone. He had pulled off his own rescue without any help from Sam Richman—and was simultaneously declaring his independence from her advice.

Annie turned away without a word. "Where's Butch?" Zeke asked.

"Spending another night with his pal Fred, trying to square the circle."

He followed her into the kitchen, where she stirred a pot of soup on the stove. Minestrone, one of his favorites. She was wearing brown slacks and one of his old white shirts—an outfit she knew he disliked. He preferred her in skirts. "What the hell is wrong?" he said.

"You—a diplomat," she said.

The words spoke themselves. Annie instantly knew they were the greatest mistake of her life. After so many years of forbearance, sympathy, understanding, how could she commit such a blunder? Maybe for the same reason she had put on the slacks and dirty shirt. Because she felt like it.

"Jesus Jumping Christ!" Zeke roared. "That is the last condescending crack I'm going to take from you! I've had it with your goddamn superior attitude toward me just because Daddy's a congressman thanks to the Democrats' ability to steal votes by the thousands in Chicago and your brother is one of the best-known lying liberal columnists in the country!"

"You obnoxious son of a bitch!" Annie screamed. "You're the insufferable hypocrite in this thing, with your smarmy ideas about my country 'tis of thee and the idealism of all the Talbots back to 1776. Bullshit! They were all looking out for number one but they had a lot more brains than you. They knew how to make money and get connected to the right politicians. You're a goddamn walking anachronism and I wish to hell I never saw you!"

Eleven years of struggling to be the perfect wife were being vaporized in this explosion. So be it, Annie told herself, letting bitter fury fill her lungs. If morality was simply a word, as Jack maintained, and America was being run by a pack of murderous liars, as Zeke maintained, what was left besides money and power, neither of which she was ever going to see in this insufferable straight-arrow's company.

"I was an idiot to think you might actually appreciate honor and family tradition and devotion to this country," Zeke roared. "You don't appreciate anything but low, sneaking politics and whining supplication of everyone and anyone in power."

"Politics has nothing to do with this!" Annie shouted, refusing to concede anything, including half-truths, to him. "We're finally facing the way you've approached this marriage, with a sneer in your heart, looking down on me and my family from your ridiculous ancestral molehill. You're worse than the anti-Semites and the Ku-Kluxers. At least they don't conceal their opinions of Jews and Catholics. You came on with a smile and a thousand yards of bullshit about prejudice being un-American."

"This isn't prejudice," Zeke snarled. "It's postjudice. You remember enough Latin to get that idea, I hope. I've seen you up close and the sight is repulsive. I don't intend to put up with it any longer."

He stalked into the bedroom and began throwing clothes into an extra suitcase. Annie stayed in the kitchen dazedly telling herself this could not be happening, he would apologize, she would apologize, there would be a sweet, sad reconciliation in their antique four poster—until his footsteps thudded down the hall to the front door. She rushed out of the kitchen crying violently. "Zeke!" she sobbed. "At least wait until morning. Give us a chance to—"

Jonathan Trumbull Talbot slammed the door on those pleading words. He was through with the complications, the frustrations of married love. Annie knew exactly what he was thinking in his fevered masculine brain. He saw himself on his way to a rendezvous with history where he would prove how tough, how cold, how impersonal a man could be in his manipulation of people and events. Once and for all, he would insist on the icy authority of his analytic mind for guidance. Nothing else could impose meaning on a man's life.

It would be hard to imagine someone with a more mistaken grasp of his own character. But Annie no longer gave a damn about Jonathan Trumbull Talbot's delusions. "You rotten son of a bitch," she screamed. "I hope you fall on your face. Do you hear me? I hope you fall on your arrogant, condescending face! From now on I'm living my own life!"

Weeping, she wandered around the empty house for hours. She finally fell asleep on the couch with her clothes on, clutching the framed picture of her and Ensign Talbot smiling into a camera on Waikiki Beach in 1930. Awakening in the dawn, she flung the picture across the living room; it made a very satisfying smash against the far wall.

BOOK TWO

19

EACH OF US IS AS GOD MADE US—AND FREQUENTLY MUCH WORSE

From the window of the Paris-Madrid express, Berthe von Hoffmann gazed at the *mesata*, the endless barren plateau of central Spain. For some reason, the emptiness no longer troubled her. The luxury train was identical to the ones she had ridden twenty-five years ago as a girl: thick, burgundy velveteen drapes, red plush sofas, white lace window curtains. She was traveling back in time toward that difficult, no longer barren word, *father.*

In the distance burst a glimpse of white walls and cathedral spires. Avila, home of St. Teresa, Spain's famed woman mystic. Then came the foothills of the Guadamarra Mountains, with patches of snow glistening on them like fallen stars. Flocks of sheep munched grass beneath stumpy trees with dark green needles resting on their branches like immense birds' nests. Ernst asked what they were. "Umbrella pines," Berthe said.

It was the first time he had spoken since they left Paris. He had signed her into the Hotel Crillon and went down to Lorient to confer with Admiral Dönitz about his tasks in Spain. He returned in a vile mood and berated her for ruining his Navy career. Once more Berthe insisted she had nothing to do with his transfer to Spain—a lie that still stirred considerable guilt, in spite of what she had seen and heard in Posen.

While Ernst fumed, Berthe had continued her rounds of the couturiers. Admiral Canaris had given her an expense account of 50,000 marks. "I want you to be the best-dressed woman in Madrid," he said. The couturiers were all as obsequious as they had been in the days when the name Schonberg had produced visions of unlimited funds. But Berthe suspected her nationality had more to do with it than her Reichsmarks. On the majestic facade of the Palais Bourbon, home of France's National Assembly, hung a huge banner: DEUTSCHLAND SIEGT AM ALLEN FRONTEN—Germany triumphs on all fronts.

The head of the local Abwehr office called to ask if there was anything she needed. Another call was less offhand. "Frau von Hoffmann?" said a tense voice. "This is Elisabeth von Theismann. We met at the Greek ambassador's house in Berlin."

"Of course. I was hoping you'd call."

They agreed to meet at the Brasserie Lipp on the Boulevard St. Germain, but actually met at Bistro Solange, a small restaurant off the Place des Vosges, in an entirely different section of Paris. Admiral Canaris had supplied Berthe with a codebook containing alternative names of restaurants and hotels in Paris, Madrid, Barcelona and several other cities. "Remember, the SD love to tap telephones. It's one of their few skills," he said.

By this time Berthe understood the rivalry between the Abwehr and the Nazi *Sicherheitdienst.* In line with the Party's program to create a state within the state, the SD had a parallel structure to the Abwehr in Germany and in other countries around the world. It made her nervously aware that she could be under surveillance at any time.

Elisabeth von Theismann was the daughter of a German general who had resigned his commission rather than serve under Hitler. She was a short, rather stocky young woman with severely cut black hair and a somewhat plaintive manner. With her was a remarkably tall, handsome young man in a gray tweed suit that did not fit him very well—making Berthe suspect he was an Army officer. Elisabeth introduced him as Herr Paulus, an old friend. He burst out laughing and said in a voice loud enough to be heard on the other side of the wide Place des Vosges: "Oh for God's sake, I'm Colonel Claus von Stauffenberg. Either we trust each other or there's no point to any of this."

"But it's much better, if any of us are picked up—" Elisabeth von Theismann said.

Berthe saw she was hopelessly in love with this reckless giant. For the past year Elisabeth had been working for the Red Cross at Meaux, outside Paris. Her duties regularly took her inside the part of France controlled by the so-called Vichy government of Marshal Henri Pétain, the World War I hero who had surrendered France to the victorious Wehrmacht eighteen months ago. She had made some hopeful contacts inside the American embassy there—but she was not sure if they would continue, now that the Americans were at war with Germany. She gave Berthe an address in Meaux where she could mail her letters in a simple code supplied by Canaris. Everything coming out of Spain was read by German censors—an indication of how closely Franco was cooperating with the Reich. She would transmit the letters to Berlin in a Red Cross pouch, which was immune from SD inspection.

Stauffenberg, whom she had apparently brought along to examine Berthe for trustworthiness, interrupted impatiently. "I'm not sure if there's any point in all this pussyfooting with the Americans. They double-crossed us at Versailles in 1919. What makes you think they won't do it again?"

"We can't be sure of anything," Elisabeth von Theismann said. "But there's no point in clinging to past grievances. History has demonstrated again and again the pointlessness of such behavior."

Stauffenberg shook his head like a big dog who had just received a blow to teach him obedience. Berthe felt a rush of sympathy for Elisabeth von Theismann. It was so similar to her own experience with Ernst. "The more I think about it," Stauffenberg growled, "the more I wonder if women should be allowed into universities. It gives them delusions of grandeur. I intend to urge Count von Moltke to make that an essential part of his plan for a new Germany."

Berthe was not surprised to learn that Moltke was Stauffenberg's patron saint. He had met him through his younger brother, Carl Bernd von Moltke, who was an Army friend, and considered him the greatest living German. But Stauffenberg thought Moltke was much too inhibited by his Christian conscience. Like Colonel Oster, Stauffenberg was convinced that Germany's generals would never stage a revolt as long as Hitler was alive. Someone would have to kill the Führer.

Elisabeth vehemently disagreed with this idea. Not because it broke one of God's commandments, but because it was bad politics.

It would make Hitler a martyr and create a legacy of rage and frustration similar to the "stab in the back" myth of civilian or Jewish treachery that some people invoked to explain why Germany lost the last war. She agreed with Admiral Canaris—they had to wait until a major German defeat forced people to realize they could not win the war—and gave the generals an excuse to remove the Führer. Meanwhile, it was vital to prepare the Americans for the event. Berthe had listened, shuddering at what Ernst would think of the discussion.

Now the train window framed a distant view of the Escorial, the huge combination palace-monastery-mausoleum built by King Philip II at the height of Spain's imperial power. Ernst asked her about it and she gave him a swift summary of its creation and significance as a symbol of Spain's former grandeur. "Perhaps the Führer will build something like that after the war," Ernst said.

Finally, the golden dome of the Atocha, Madrid's northern railroad station, glistened dully beneath the gray winter sky. They found a sputtering taxi that looked as if it had been under artillery fire. One rear-door window was a mass of striated glass, the other window had been replaced by tape and cardboard. A horde of half-starved children pursued them, whining for pesetas. Everyone in the street looked shabby and sad. Numerous buildings still bore scars of the bombing and shelling that had preceded Madrid's capitulation, ending the Spanish Civil War, two years ago.

At the Ritz Hotel, the spacious lobby was full of Germans, not a few in uniform. Among the first to greet them was Wolfgang Griff, the little Nazi who had sailed on the Ritterboot. He had wangled himself a transfer to Spain to "rest his nerves" after a single venture beneath the Atlantic. Ernst was barely civil to him—which pleased Berthe immensely.

They were escorted to a suite by a troop of bellboys and found a half-dozen reporters eager to interview Ernst. An austere gray-haired man named Otto von Spaeth from the German embassy was on hand to translate, along with Hans Lazar, the bald, squat press attaché. Ernst talked confidently about the U-boat war while the newspapermen scribbled industriously.

"Do you think the American entry into the war will make a difference?" one asked.

"It will simplify matters. Now every ship in the convoys will be a target for our wolfpacks," Ernst said. "We're not worried about

America's Navy—they'll soon be fighting for survival against our new ally, Japan. In the opinion of the Ubootwaffe, Germany needs only one more ally to guarantee her victory in this war: Spain."

Ernst produced a map of the Atlantic and demonstrated how German planes and submarines operating from Spain would quickly cut the British supply line to Egypt and India. "Gibraltar would be handed over to Spain, making her the new arbiter of the Mediterranean. It would be a testament of the trust and friendship that already exists between Spain and Germany."

Berthe was fascinated by this bold, self-confident young man, issuing pronouncements on the course of the war and the future of Europe. The husband she usually saw displayed little of this commanding aura. At home he reverted to the sulky, defensive youngest brother. The journalists departed and Spaeth relaxed his stiff Prussian face to remark: "That was very well done, Herr Kapitanleutnant."

Griff and Lazar agreed—except for one thing. Ernst should have said the Führer was the genius behind the continental strategy of seizing Gibraltar. "I'll correct that in my next interview," Ernst said, loosening his tie. "I need a drink."

Berthe saw his collar was drenched with sweat. However well he performed, playing the public hero did not come naturally to him. They stopped for schnapps in the Ritz bar and toasted the Ubootwaffe. Ernst gulped down two drinks and asked Spaeth if he thought Spain might join the war. "I personally doubt it," he said. "The Führer himself conferred with General Franco on the Spanish border shortly before he launched his attack on Russia. Admiral Canaris, an old Franco friend, came along to contribute his best endeavors. The Caudillo put them off with a thousand excuses."

"It may be necessary to remove the General," Lazar said.

"I think that would be unwise," Spaeth said. "The country would collapse into anarchy."

Herr von Spaeth sipped his schnapps. His ultradignfied face, with a monocle fixed securely in the left eye, might have been peering from a news photograph taken at the Potsdam Palace in 1913. He was what Berthe's father called *eine Hohenzollernmumie*—a Hohenzollern mummy—one of the unbearably formal Prussians who had populated the Kaiser's court. Yet Admiral Canaris told Berthe that Spaeth was head of the Abwehr in Spain and one of the few people on the Madrid embassy staff she could trust.

A Mercedes wafted them to the embassy, a huge white-walled former palace on the Castellana, one of Madrid's most fashionable streets. Nearby, a squad of riot police were struggling with a crowd of several hundred Spaniards who were shouting insults and hurling stones over the walls of the building next door. Berthe asked Spaeth what was going on. "The Falange," he said offhandedly. "The Spanish Fascists. Protesting British support of the Soviets. That's the British embassy. They attack it at least once a month. We supply the money."

Inside the German embassy, Spaeth escorted them to the ambassador, a huge gaunt man named Eberhard von Stohrer. He was one of the tallest human beings Berthe had ever seen; she later learned he was six feet seven. He welcomed them with great cordiality, showering Ernst with compliments, then abruptly shifted to a more lugubrious tone. "Our situation in Spain is precarious. The English are fighting a ruthless war against us—not excluding assassination. I urge you to equip yourself with a pistol and be prepared to use it."

Ernst looked amazed—and pleased. The two expressions coalesced in that amoral hardness Berthe had found so repellent in Posen. "I appreciate the warning, Herr Ambassador."

That night, Ambassador von Stohrer gave a reception to welcome the new naval attaché and his wife to Madrid. A half-dozen officers from the Spanish Navy surrounded Ernst, listening admiringly to his kills and narrow escapes. Berthe found herself chatting with Counselor von Spaeth's wife, Maria, who was Spanish. A slim, austere gray-haired woman, she told Berthe she had a message from an old friend: the Marquesa de Montoya.

"Old friend?" Berthe said. "I have no doubt she's old but—" The Marquesa had been her father's mistress during his years in Madrid. As a girl, Berthe had hated the sight of her.

"She remembers you with great fondness—perhaps because of your father. I knew him. He was an irresistibly charming man."

You too? Berthe wanted to say. Was there any woman who didn't succumb to him? "She would love to see you," Maria von Spaeth continued. "She has powerful connections to the regime. She could be very useful in your mission here."

Berthe nodded, reminding herself that this woman was also in Admiral Canaris's immense spiderweb of intrigue. She let Maria von Spaeth lead her to her husband, who was standing in a corner, wearing an expensive gray suit that must have dated from 1910; tan spats peeked from beneath his trousers.

He greeted her with a certain avarice in his manner. "The Americans have not yet arrived in force. Their embassy is still manned by professional diplomats of the old school," he said. "But we're expecting their replacements in a week or two. In the meantime, enjoy yourself in Madrid. Add to your wardrobe. If there's anything you need in the way of money, let me know."

"Are we to continue living at the Ritz?" Berthe asked.

Spaeth shook his head. "It's much too easy to keep someone under surveillance there. The SD have all the phones tapped. We're selecting a comfortable apartment for you near the Retiro."

The Retiro was Madrid's Tiergarten. It stirred memories of walking through its green woods, rowing on its broad lake, with her father. "If anyone approaches you in my name, disregard him," Spaeth said, in ironic counterpoint. "He's almost certainly an SD agent. Any verbal communications from me will come with a reference to Avila. I met a friend of yours in Avila. I was thinking of you the other day when I was in Avila. That sort of thing."

"How will it all work?" Berthe said. "This—channel to the Americans. Admiral Canaris has told me very little."

"You'll seduce him, of course," Spaeth said, with more than a hint of impatience. "Once you have him securely in your power, and consider him safe, we can begin to deal with him. Always remember he can destroy us all with an indiscreet remark."

"Of course," she said. Did he think she came from a long line of spies? Perhaps her mother had also served the fatherland in the way these men so casually assumed for her. Behind Elisabeth von Theismann's plain face and governess's manner was there a Delilah who had bewitched the Nordic Samson, Count von Stauffenberg?

Meanwhile, there was more shopping, an apartment to decorate and turn into some sort of home. Berthe found the salon of Balenciaga, whose tubelike, long-sleeved wool dresses flattered the figure and also kept a woman warm in Madrid's largely unheated houses. The city's high society still lived as lavishly, if not quite as comfortably, as they had before the Civil War. Invitations cascaded in from hostesses eager to hear the story of the Ritterboot's triumphs from her heroic captain's lips. Among the first was one from the Marquesa de Montoya. Berthe had no trouble steering Ernst into a prompt acceptance. "I'm a performing monkey," he said. "It doesn't matter much where I dance."

He was in an even more vile mood, if possible, because every day the Spanish newspapers were full of headlines about the U-boats' *gran matanza* (great slaughter) of ships along the American East Coast. He ordered Berthe to translate every story down to the last comma, and speculated sullenly about which of the captains was making the most kills. Of course the sensational reports only made him more of a celebrity in Madrid. Everyone wanted to meet *El Capitan Submarino*.

On the morning of the day they were supposed to dine with the Marquesa de Montoya, a telephone call found Berthe reading another collection of *submarino matanzas* to Ernst. "My sweet girl," the Marquesa croaked in her gravelly voice. "The more I think of seeing you in a great crowd of people, the more it horrifies me. Could we have lunch?"

Berthe took a taxi to the Marquesa's palace on the Gran Via, another deluxe Madrid street. She expected to meet a woman who was of course much older but still as shamelessly seductive as the creature she had known as a girl. Instead she met a walking skeleton with an ascetic's mouth and eyes that were liquid pools of pain. They dined in her apartment on the upper floor of the palace. The food was simple but good: a clear soup, a plate of *angulas*, tiny eels caught in fresh water on the Atlantic Coast.

"I can't tell you how often I've dreamt of this day," the Marquesa said. "You're as beautiful as I always knew you'd be. I always thought of you as my daughter. Now you're the only living creature in my life on whom I can bestow the word child, however distantly."

"What's happened to your sons?"

"My oldest, Carlos, was a member of Parliament. He was assassinated by the Communists in nineteen-thirty-five. My middle son, Patricio, was killed in the siege of the Alcazar in thirty-eight. My youngest, Juan, was held as a hostage and shot as General Franco's advance guard entered Madrid. Some say it was the last bullet of the war."

"And your husband?"

"He lives in the country, mourning his sons. Most of the time he's quite mad. He was never a strong man."

Gazing into the lined, gaunt face, Berthe heard the triumphant implication: *but I am a strong woman*. Here was an ally. But could she ever escape that sense of outraged loathing her childhood enmity had woven around Elena de Montoya?

The Marquesa interrogated Berthe about her life. Was she happy with her husband and children? She decided to tell her the truth. "I adore the children. I was happy with Ernst until the war began."

"Ah. Is he a Nazi?"

"No! But he believes in the Führer the way you apparently believe in General Franco. Ignoring the blood on his hands."

A ghastly smile spread across the skull-like face, stretching the faded skin until Berthe thought it might rip. "Oh my dear, you still hate me, don't you. I don't blame you. I was very hateful in my youth. I try not to be so vicious in this sorrowful old age that God has so kindly bestowed on me. Though my nature still runs in that direction. Do you know the line from Cervantes, 'Each of us is as God made us, and frequently much worse'? My governess used to repeat it to me all the time. I never listened, of course."

"You don't believe in General Franco?"

"I believe in St. Teresa far more. I see no alternative to General Franco. You might take that message back to the people at your embassy who think they can accomplish something by removing him in a coup d'état."

"I'm afraid they're not interested in a woman's political opinions."

"Do you think the Spanish are any different? Tell them anyway." She sipped her wine and gestured to the maid to remove their luncheon plates. She had eaten almost nothing. When they were alone, she asked, in that low gravelly voice: "You don't believe in the Führer?"

Was this a trap? Berthe wondered. What if there was a recording device hidden behind the faded brocade draperies framing the double windows? She shook her head. "In what do you believe?" the Marquesa asked. "I always feel sorry for you poor Protestants, when you turn to that spiritual gruel the Reformation left for you to subsist on."

"Perhaps it's not so thin to us!" Berthe said, infuriated at her condescension. "Germans have a certain capacity for thought! The richness of the mind may be feast enough for us."

"Is it for you?" the Marquesa asked.

How could she tell her about the Path? She did not trust this woman on so many levels. "I've discovered something else which has given me great joy. Something you must know about," Berthe said. "My father's real role here in Spain during the last war."

The Marquesa looked utterly blank. "What was it?" she said.

Berthe told her without even trying to conceal her satisfaction. For the first time she felt superior to this woman, who had possessed her father so totally, yet knew nothing about his secret heroism.

"You got this from Canaris, no doubt," the Marquesa said.

"You know him?"

"I don't think anyone has ever really known Canaris. I was an acquaintance, like so many others, during his years here in the last war. I called him the Octopus. Just as you thought you were getting close to him, there was a cloud of black ink and he slithered away."

Just like you, Berthe thought. "Was he one of your lovers?"

"For a little while. Long enough for me to know I'd met my match," the Marquesa said. "He used me. He used everyone. Is he using you?"

"I'm not sure," Berthe said. "The last war was quite different from this one."

"Nonsense!" the Marquesa said. "It's all one war, my dear girl. Created by English greed and German arrogance. *Weltmacht!* How many times I heard that from Canaris. Your father was the only man I knew who had the good sense to ridicule it."

Weltmacht (world power) was the central idea of one of the University of Berlin's greatest historians, Heinrich von Treitschke. In the 1920s, Berthe had heard it preached with stubborn fury by his followers, who refused to accept the 1918 defeat. But that shopworn idea was not the essence of what Berthe was hearing from the Marquesa de Montoya. She was telling Berthe in her sly way that Canaris's story of Count Willi von Schonberg spying for the fatherland was fiction.

For a moment Berthe found it difficult to breathe.

"You don't think it's true—?" she cried.

"Let me say I doubt it. I doubt it so deeply I cannot believe it," she said.

Was Lothar Engle right, was Canaris simply playing Hitler's game more astutely than the clumsy thugs around Himmler and Heydrich? Was the declaration of war on America an immensely clever move on

Weltmacht's chessboard, a Knight's gambit that draws the overconfident enemy into a trap?

The Marquesa de Montoya was watching her through half-closed eyes—an old habit that had once been among her most seductive traits. "Do you believe in the Tarot cards?" she said.

"I know nothing about them," Berthe said.

"This is Spain, my dear, where the East and the West meet. Africa is just across the Straits of Gibraltar. My mother never did anything without reading the cards."

From a bureau drawer she drew cards twice the size of ordinary playing cards. They looked very old. "These have been in the family for a long time. They were supposedly a gift from a gypsy lover."

Berthe realized this was a very meaningful moment to Elena de Montoya. She was inducting her into one of her family's oldest rituals. The Marquesa briefly explained Tarot. There were seventy-eight cards; fifty-two roughly resembled a modern deck, divided into wands (clubs), cups (hearts), swords (spades) and pentacles (diamonds). There were twenty-two additional pictorial cards, full of allegorical meanings.

The Marquesa quickly shuffled and lay thirteen cards in the shape of a horseshoe on the cleared table. On the left was the King of Cups. "A fair-haired man will be your shadow—no matter how you try to elude him," she said.

On the other end of the horseshoe was a card that brought a grimace of dismay. A young man, carrying a white flower in one hand and a bundle on his shoulders, was gazing skyward, oblivious to the fact that he was about to walk off a cliff. "The Fool," the Marquesa said. "He signifies a new beginning. A new lover, not necessarily a happy affair."

"Why is he portrayed as a fool?" Berthe asked.

"Folly and expiation are two of the greatest themes of life," the Marquesa said.

Berthe began to wish she had never come to see this woman alone. She was stronger than she had ever imagined her. The Marquesa asked her to draw a card and lay it on the Fool. She drew the Knight of Swords (the Jack of Spades). The Marquesa clapped her hands with delight. "That means you can walk into danger and be rescued by the good stranger," she said.

She scanned the horseshoe of cards and said: "I see too many phallic symbols for a Protestant conscience. The future will not be easy for you."

She turned over the card at the apex of the horseshoe. It was the Queen of Swords (spades), a somber woman seated on a throne decorated with a winged angel and butterflies. "This is your significator, the card that sums up your role. She represents a woman who travels alone. She has loved and lost but will love again. She symbolizes will, determination, a woman who can bear whatever life presents her."

The Marquesa smiled mockingly. "The Queen of Swords is my significator too. It is a card of becoming. Painful becoming."

She turned over another card, in which two dogs bayed disconsolately at the moon, shining between two huge towers. "Sorrow awaits you in an ancient city. Probably not Madrid—it's not old enough. Beware when you go south to someplace like Granada."

"I have no intention of going to Granada!" Berthe said.

"If you're serious about seducing a man, you'll go to Granada," the Marquesa said. "I always took my lovers there."

Berthe struggled for calm. Did this woman know everything? The Marquesa asked Berthe to draw another card. It was a portrait of a juggler with a little table, knives and dice. "That could mean a happy end to your journey. Pagad the juggler is also a magician. You must draw one more card."

Berthe drew. The Marquesa looked unhappy and returned the card to the pack. "What was it?" Berthe asked.

With great reluctance, the Marquesa showed her a drawing of a young man hanging head down from a cross. "It's a card of transformation, at great cost. But Pagad makes me think you may escape the worst. Now I must take a nap in order to greet you and the other guests with my usual composure."

Berthe found herself out on the street, dazedly searching for a taxi. "Can I give you a lift?" said a familiar voice.

It was Ernst in a sleek white Bugatti roadster. "Where did you get this beautiful car?" Berthe asked.

"A gift of General Franco," he said insolently.

As they roared down the palm-lined Gran Via, Berthe glanced back and thought she saw a figure behind the curtains of the Marquesa's second-floor apartment. Was she watching her daughter meeting her shadow, the King of Cups?

Ernst was no longer king of her heart. No one was, if the Marquesa was right about her father. Her heart was as barren as the *mesata*, as animal as one of those sheep munching under the umbrella pines.

Was it all part of the Path? Or was fate, the Tarot, in charge? Ernst's blond hair blew in the wind.

20

HOPE IS THE DREGS IN THE
BOTTOM OF THE CUP

Once more, Jonathan Trumbull Talbot was sitting in a Pan American Clipper, his feet braced against the footrest, his stomach knotted, as the plane descended for a landing. But New York's towers did not soar skyward this time—nor was there any anticipation of a loving wife in the terminal. Instead, Lisbon sat stolidly on her seven terraced hills on the inner rim of the great harbor, with only church spires and cathedral buttresses rising above the muddle of medieval and modern buildings. Waiting for him was nothing more amorous than a bored, yawning customs inspector.

Beside Talbot sat the Madrid embassy's new financial officer, Harold C. Holcomb. A broad-shouldered truculent man in his fifties, Holcomb was a political science professor on leave from the University of California. He had spent several months in Madrid with Ernest Hemingway during the death throes of the Spanish Republic and talked of the experience with a mixture of grandiloquence and nostalgia. In his view, Franco's victory was a terrible wrong that had to be righted as soon as possible.

Holcomb was obviously part of the anti-Franco levy Ned Travis and his confreres at State were shipping to Madrid. He seemed disappointed when Talbot displayed no desire to argue with him. He consoled himself by persuading the stewardess to supply him with an endless stream of martinis.

In Talbot's pocket was a letter from Annie. He had read it several times during his fourteen-hour flight. He took it out and read it again. It was preferable to trying to talk to Holcomb. The drunker he got, the more his conversation became an extended monologue on the glories of socialism.

Annie's letter began with family business. She thanked him for getting Butch settled at the Choate School in Connecticut. He had easily qualified for the ninth grade and the school welcomed him warmly as the son of an alumnus. She was moving to Washington, where Jack was offering her a job on the staff of "Behind The Headlines." Then the tone shifted from matter-of-fact to glacial.

I have thought and thought about the terrible things you said to me in Norfolk. I've tried to tell myself that Adolf Hitler, Benito Mussolini and Emperor Hirohito are the real villains. But it hasn't worked very well. For Butch's sake, I think we should put off doing anything drastic for the time being. Admiral King and your brother-in-law Ned have arranged a separation which suits me just fine—and is definitely best for Butch. We don't have to explain anything to him or either sets of parents, who would go into spasms over the mere mention of the word divorce. If we decide it's over, after the war, it can be explained then in a less painful way. I'm sure a lot of marriages are going to collapse in the course of two- to three-year separations. Even though you've shaken my confidence in Roosevelt's methods, I haven't lost faith in the value of the cause for which he and my father and other Democrats have been fighting for the past nine years—a more decent America, with more justice, more equality, more opportunity for everyone, not just for your precious few with Plymouth Rock credentials. Now FDR's trying to do the same thing for the whole world in the face of the most malignant enemies we've ever confronted. Frankly, I can't imagine spending the rest of my life with a husband who dismisses these goals as mere rhetoric for popular consumption and sneers at me and my family because we believe in them. The man I married in 1930 was able to deal with political disagreements as honest but tolerable differences of opinion. Not so the raging maniac who returned from losing his ship off Iceland. I guess we've both got to decide which one is the real Zeke Talbot.

Annie

The letter stirred fury every time he read it. Which one is the real Zeke Talbot? Which one is the real Anna Richman? The tearful wife who was always mooing about how much she loved him? Or the snarling bitch who told him he was failure as a husband, a provider, a thinker, a man? Whatever happened to him in Spain could not be worse than swallowing that sort of abuse.

"Who's the letter from?" Holcomb asked.

"My wife," Talbot said, stuffing it back in his pocket.

"How long you been married?"

"Eleven years."

"Jesus. I've tried it twice. Never got past year five."

Talbot had spent another month in Washington after he walked out of his marriage. At the State Department he revived his almost moribund Spanish and heard lectures on the politics of the Spanish Civil War. He met the new ambassador, a genial Columbia University professor named Carleton Hayes. FDR had handpicked him for the job because he was a Catholic and a noted scholar of European history. The President's main concern seemed to be keeping Spain out of Hitler's grasp. It was not clear whether he shared the State Department's agenda beyond that immediate necessity.

The Navy Department wanted Talbot to do quite a lot of work. He was to scour Spain's ports for German submarines. He was also ordered to seek any and all information he could find about German naval codes. Off the East Coast, the debacle Talbot had predicted was gathering momentum. The U-boats were sinking two and three ships a day and the U.S. Navy was doing nothing but frantically trying to conceal it.

For a final fillip of preparation, Talbot had journeyed to Litchfield, Connecticut, to pay a duty call on his father. As an ex-ambassador to Spain, he might have some advice to offer him. Talbot found the situation in the wide-porched white house on the tree-lined main street unchanged. Roger Sherman Talbot was spending his days writing a book entitled *The Tragedy of the Twentieth Century,* in which he hoped to prove that Roosevelt, the New Deal State Department and the British Foreign Office had perpetrated an unholy stew of deceptions and blunders to plunge the world into this catastrophic conflict. Although he was so crippled by arthritis he was confined to a wheelchair, he worked at this task fourteen hours a day. Zeke's mother watched forlornly from the sidelines, once more replicating her lifelong sense of being dragged behind a runaway locomotive.

His father gave a tremendous guffaw when he heard about Talbot's assignment to Spain. His difficult younger son, who had scorned to become a diplomat in his footsteps, was now being forced into the part. He grew considerably more serious when he heard the plans Ned Travis and others at State had for Spain. "The sons of bitches," he said. "You've got to stop them."

He was appalled when Talbot told him he was going to make up his own mind about Franco. It was a replay of a dozen other clashes in which Jonathan Talbot refused to be his father's echo or imitator. The angry scenes that ensued always pained him—and simultaneously gave him intense satisfaction. This time a new element appeared in the drama: old age.

"I don't know one of the men around Franco," his father said. "The only person of any importance left from my days is the Marquesa de Montoya. Whatever's happening, she'll be in on it."

Talbot remembered the name. She and her pompous husband had been frequent visitors to the American embassy. Touched by his father's admission of helplessness, he was about to say something conciliatory when his mother cried: "I don't think he should go anywhere near that woman!"

"For the ten thousandth time, I never touched her," Roger Talbot said.

"For the ten thousandth and first time, I don't believe you," Grace Talbot said. He left his parents glaring at each other.

Once more the Pan Am clipper made light of Talbot's apprehensions and landed smoothly on the turgid water of Lisbon Harbor, brown with the silt of the Tagus River, whose wide mouth was just north of the city. Aboard the Lisbon-Madrid express train, Holcomb snored off his martinis. They rolled into the Spanish capital late in the afternoon. Outside the station, headlines shouted shocking news from street corner kiosks. SINGAPORE ABANDANO!

"Holy shit!" Harold Holcomb said, when Talbot told him it meant Singapore had surrendered to the Japanese. Talbot was almost as shocked. Singapore was supposed to be the strongest fortress in the world. There was no comfort in watching the eagerness with which Spaniards were buying papers and devouring the news of the British Empire's collapse in the Far East. Madrid looked almost as ravaged as Singapore. The scars of Franco's long siege lingered on many buildings—and on the hangdog expressions of the people shuffling along the streets. The women were mostly in black, the men in shabby unmatched suits and pants. Spain had not been a wealthy country for a long time but Madrid had always displayed a style and flair that befitted a national capital. "If these are the people who won the Civil War, I wonder what the losers look like," Talbot said.

"They are in jail, Señor. Only their guards can look at them," the taxi driver said.

"What do you think of General Franco?" Holcomb said.

"He is a great man. But I wish he had found another country to conquer."

"Lift up your heart, my friend. The day of jubilee is coming," Holcomb said. The American Civil War terminology was lost on the Spaniard.

The American embassy was in Madrid's most splendid private residence, the Palacio Montellano, which sprawled across an entire walled block in the wealthiest section of the city. The sight of its magnificent gardens and lofty windows sent a rush of pride through Talbot. As a diplomat's son, he was a strong believer in seeing his country put its best foot forward. Memory replaced sentiment as porters lugged their bags into the lofty entrance hall. Talbot found himself recalling how unhappy he had been in Madrid during his father's ambassadorship. His mother's sorrow for his older brother, dead in France, her crying fits when they dined alone, had been almost intolerable. He had often wondered if she wished it were he, not George Putnam Talbot, who was lying under a white cross in the Argonne cemetery at Montfaucon.

Ambassador Hayes had arrived a week ago. A tall balding man named Hamilton Boileau, the embassy's counselor—the second in command—escorted them into Hayes's office. The ambassador was more than a little downcast. "You've heard about Singapore?" he said.

Boileau said they would read something far worse in the papers tomorrow. General Franco had called on the Japanese ambassador to congratulate him for his country's victory.

"The Nazi son of a bitch!" Holcomb said.

"I shudder to think what the American newspapers will do with that one," Boileau said, ignoring Holcomb. "The press is terrorizing the State Department into mindless hostility to Spain."

"That depends on your point of view!" Holcomb said.

"You have a positive opinion of Franco?" Talbot asked.

Boileau stuck out a very stubborn jaw. "I don't travel with the

'Communism is the wave of the future' crowd. I've spent some time in our Moscow embassy."

"And learned nothing!" Holcomb said.

Speaking to Talbot as if Holcomb were invisible, Boileau explained that the State Department controlled the amount of oil and wheat the United States shipped to Spain. At the moment they were only permitting enough oil to keep the country comatose. Electricity regularly failed as the power companies ran out of fuel. Scarcely a Spaniard who owned a car or truck could afford to pay the astronomical gasoline prices created by the scarcity. As for wheat, people were starving in the streets of Madrid and other cities while American granaries bulged with reserves.

Boileau did not think this made any sense. Ambassador Hayes agreed with him. He talked anxiously about the way Spain seemed to be sliding into Hitler's arms. "Have you met Franco?" Talbot asked.

"Yes. We had a cordial conversation in which he expressed some polite sentiments for America. But he told me, quite candidly, that he thought Germany and Japan were going to win the war."

"My father was the ambassador in the Twenties," Talbot said. "They had a dictator then, too. His name was Primo Rivera. He liked Americans. But he had to be careful not to say it in public. I don't have to remind you, Mr. Ambassador—as a historian you know we beat hell out of these people in Teddy Roosevelt's splendid little war in 1898."

Hayes nodded glumly. Harold Holcomb said his father had gone up San Juan Hill with Teddy's Rough Riders. If any Spaniard made a crack about it, he was going to get a punch in the snoot. Boileau suggested Holcomb might feel better after a night's sleep. When the Californian departed, Boileau muttered something deprecatory to Hayes and invited Talbot to a reception for the new ambassador and his wife.

That evening, members of the diplomatic corps and Spaniards by the dozen swarmed into the embassy. Boileau introduced Talbot to the pint-sized, gray-haired British ambassador, Sir Samuel Hoare. With him was a spare man with aquiline, almost Mediterranean, features whom Hoare introduced as his old friend, Lord Robert Vansittart, until recently Chief Diplomatic Advisor to the British Foreign Office.

"Talbot?" Vansittart said. "I hope you're not related to Roger Talbot, the fellow who wrote *The Great Betrayal*."

Talbot admitted his father was the author of the book, which he had written in the early Twenties, attacking Wilson and the British and French for bungling the Treaty of Versailles.

"Have you inherited his inclination to favor the Huns?" Vansittart asked.

"My father tried not to favor anyone in that book," Talbot said. "But I certainly agree with his argument that it was foolish to blame the Germans for the war and turn them into permanent enemies. Hitler might never have come to power if we made a genuine peace the last time."

"Don't you think it's odd, Sir Samuel," Vansittart said to Hoare. "The Americans invented that admirable motto, 'the only good Indian is a dead Indian,' but they can't seem to apply it to a far worse scourge."

"Before long, I'm quite sure they'll be saying it about the Huns," Hoare growled.

The two Britons stalked away in search of more congenial company. Boileau glared after them. "Those two have an absolutely pathological hatred of the Germans. Vansittart makes speeches every week in the House of Lords, calling for their extermination. He's written a book, *The Black Record*, which preaches undiluted race hatred. It's been a bestseller in England. Sir Samuel helped it along by praising it extravagantly."

"What are you telling this fellow about my country?" The speaker was a dour stumpy man in the dress uniform of an officer of the British Navy, complete to a sword on his hip. He was standing in the doorway of a small hexagonal room where no less than six original Goyas were on display.

"I was telling him," Boileau said in his unflappable way, "that you were the only man in the British embassy I trusted."

He introduced Talbot to Captain Bernado Moorman, the English naval attaché, and left them on their own. "I've never met an Englishman named Bernado before," Talbot said.

"My mother was Spanish. A Catholic fanatic," Moorman said.

"You should be right at home in Spain."

"Anyone who's at home in this miserable country is either crazy or unconscious," he said. "It's been a bloody mess since the war of the Spanish Succession."

"That was—1703?" Talbot said.

"By Jove—you're the first American I've met who knew anything happened before bloody 1776," Moorman said.

His frown momentarily vanished, suggesting his contempt for Spain and the United States gave him obscure pleasure. Into the room strolled a squat young man in the uniform of the Spanish Navy. He had a wide, heavy jaw that gave him a truculent expression, which he reinforced by glaring at Moorman. "The question is, can anything be done to rescue Spain from its imbecility," the Englishman said. "Take Commander Sanchez here. Although he looks like Sancho Panza, he's actually a fairly intelligent fellow for a Spaniard. But he thinks the Germans are going to win the war."

Sanchez merely smiled. The furrows deepened on Moorman's forehead. "In 1588, he would have bet every cent in the family on King Philip's bloody Armada."

Sanchez bit his thick lower lip. "I have been told many times the English are insufferable but I never believed it until I met you, Captain Moorman."

Moorman seemed delighted by this compliment. "Jaime, old Sog, you don't know how to take a joke."

"When a man sees humor only in insults, it's hard to find him amusing," Sanchez said. He turned to Talbot and extended his hand. "I'm honored to meet you, Commander. I have no personal hostility to Americans, although my father lost his leg in battle with your fleet off Cuba in 1898. If there is anything we in the Navy Department can do to make your stay in Spain more pleasant, let me know."

"You might tell him where you're refueling and rearming German submarines, for starters," Moorman said.

"If you wish to have a friendly relationship with us, you must begin by ignoring Captain Moorman," Sanchez said. "I will leave you now, hoping that Goya's greatness will compensate for the company of this sour desperate man, who cannot bear to admit the hour of his country's doom has struck."

Talbot stared uneasily past Moorman at the Goyas, all portraits of the nobility of the painter's time. Their haughty stares seemed to permeate the room with condescension. He was uneasily aware that

Sanchez had driven a wedge between him and Moorman. They were allies in fact but not in spirit. Moorman seemed to sense it too. He glowered at the aristocratic Spanish faces on the walls and said: "I can be an awful bloody loudmouth at times, but I hope we can work together here in Spain. If we lose here—it's the end of England. You can always retreat to your continental redoubt. We'll become a German colony."

He exited as if someone had the point of a sword at his back. Talbot stood there, contemplating Goya's long-vanished aristocrats. History flared in his mind, a living presence. Perhaps he would fulfill his youthful dream of acting in great events even if he was not commanding a ship or a fleet.

"Is this Jonathan Trumbull Talbot?" said a throaty voice. Confronting him in an expensive English cut blue wool suit was a thin gray-haired, birdlike woman with small squinting eyes in a wrinkled face.

"Guilty as charged," he said.

"You don't recognize me! A sad commentary on the ravages of time. I'm Elena de Montoya."

The Marquesa herself, the woman his mother hated. She was looking incredibly old. But her voice, her eyes, were charged with energy. She asked him what his father was doing.

"He's spent the last nine years waiting for Franklin D. Roosevelt to lose an election," he said.

She sighed. "Such a brilliant man. But so opinionated. He thought politics involved moral principles. Are you the same way?"

"I'm afraid so," Talbot said.

She insisted that Talbot come to dinner tomorrow night. She wanted him to meet Spaniards who might be helpful to him and the United States. "The American entrance into the war may change a great many things in Spain," she said. "Few people can support the British, whom we feel betrayed us with their neutrality in the Civil War."

"We were neutral too," Talbot said.

"But you were far away." The Marquesa's eyes squinted, her smile became crafty. "Are you happily married, Jonathan? Madrid is full of attractive widows."

"My wife and I have separated," he said. "But I'm not quite in the market for a new one."

"You must tell me about it. Perhaps I can help. Though I have much to repent for in my life, I've acquired a certain amount of peasant wisdom in affairs of the heart."

The Marquesa stood on tiptoe to kiss Talbot on the cheek. "I want to help—in memory of many things," she whispered.

The next day Counselor Hamilton Boileau helped Talbot find a two-room apartment in the Calle de Echegaray, a narrow street lined with popular *tascas* (taverns). The apartment house was redolent with the nose-twisting odor of fried olive oil. "The national smell," Boileau called it.

With the apartment came Maria, a broad-bottomed, talkative woman who vowed to make his bed and tidy up after him for only twenty pesetas a month. Boileau offered her sixteen and she took it with alacrity. "Most of the Spanish pay eight," Boileau said. "Her husband's the sereno. A little extra may help keep out unwanted visitors."

The sereno was a Madrid institution—a combination concierge and auxiliary policeman, who guarded the city's apartments by night. Talbot wanted to know who the unwanted visitors might be. Boileau said that depended on the sort of work Talbot was going to do. If it involved undercover operations, the visitors might be extremely unwanted.

When Talbot declined to commit himself, Boileau sighed and said: "I hope, at the very least, you'll keep us informed. We won't interfere. But an embassy needs to know what everyone in the country is doing. Otherwise we can find ourselves looking like fools."

That night, Talbot taxied to the Marquesa de Montoya's palace on the Gran Via to find it as crowded as the American embassy yesterday. Among the first to greet him was Moorman, who merely nodded and muttered something about wishing he were elsewhere—and Commander Jaime Sanchez, who confided that the Marques de Montoya was his father's first cousin.

Jaime introduced Talbot to his older brother, Rafael Sanchez. The younger man's squat torso looked as if it had stepped out of a Goya painting. Rafael was a visitor from El Greco land. He had a narrow ascetic face and a spectrally thin body. "Rafael's going to inherit all this one day," Jaime said with patent envy. He explained that with the Marquesa's sons dead, Rafael was destined to be the next Marques de Montoya.

Rafael was in the foreign ministry. He expressed grave satisfaction in the new American ambassador, because he was a Catholic. "A Protestant is incapable of understanding Spain," he said.

Before Talbot could dispute that pronouncement, the Marquesa swept toward them in a flowing white dress with a fichu of diaphanous chiffon around her shoulders. "Ah, you're just in time for the gypsies," she said. They followed her into a ballroom, where a half-dozen swarthy men were strumming guitars and an exotic woman with inky black hair was dancing the fandango around a tall, dark-skinned caballero. Flinging the skirts of her black and white checked dress back and forth, smacking the palms of her hands to the beat, she exploded into the classic seductive dance of Spain. After two months of grim celibacy, Talbot felt his blood stir as she moved sinuously about the man. "Olé! Olé!" cried several admiring guests.

Fifteen minutes later, drenched with sweat, the dancers ended their performance in a storm of applause. The Marquesa took the floor to announce another performance—which would add a dimension to the city's culture. Berthe von Hoffmann, who had performed with several of the best quartets and quintets in Berlin, would sing a trio of songs by Gustav Mahler.

A tall, exquisitely beautiful blonde in a sheath of yellow silk emerged from the shadows on the other side of the room and stood beside a grand piano. A large jowly German riffled the keys and struck a plaintive chord. She began singing songs of muted melancholy, heavy with the double aura of fate and death. The contrast between the brazen fandango and this voice from the North made Talbot lightheaded. It was as if someone had opened a vein in his arm and injected a unique combination of philosophy and beauty.

"What a shame that we're fighting these people!" he said to Jaime Sanchez.

"*We* are not fighting them," Rafael Sanchez said.

Everyone followed the Marquesa de Montoya into a lofty dining room with huge sixteenth- and seventeenth-century chests along the wall beneath great cloth hangings depicting battles between the Christians and the Moors. Talbot found himself sitting on the Marquesa's right. Opposite him was Berthe von Hoffmann. Midway down the table on that side was a face that made Talbot feel the evening was a combination of good and bad dreams: Kapitanleutnant Ernst von Hoffmann in a dark blue uniform.

The Marquesa squinted; her smile was almost sublimely mischievous. "I believe you have not met Berthe von Hoffmann, Commander."

"Thank you for that wonderful music," he said in German.

She nodded nervously. "But I believe you have met Berthe's husband, Kapitanleutnant von Hoffmann," the Marquesa said.

"In much less comfortable surroundings," Talbot said. "How are you, Herr Kapitanleutnant? I thought you'd be off to New York by now, sinking everything in sight."

Hoffmann made a contemptuous noise and drank off an entire glass of champagne. Tension rippled around the table. Everyone seemed to be waiting for an eruption. "Come, come," the Marquesa said. "We're not fighting a war here. This is a house that has paid its debt to Mars. All we seek here is peace. Perhaps we should drink to that: an early peace?"

A few Spaniards lifted their glasses half-heartedly. But the idea did not receive a majority vote. Hoffmann continued to glare at Talbot. "Have I said something that offends you, Herr Kapitanleutnant?" Talbot said.

"You said it in your capital, Washington, D.C., two months ago. You called me a liar for claiming that you professed friendship for Germany after I rescued you from death in the North Atlantic. You denied sharing the bridge with me when we attacked the convoy you had been escorting until I sank your destroyer. Are you prepared to call me a liar again, to my face? Or will you admit, here and now, that you are the liar. Which is it, Commander?"

Talbot's brain started to congeal with shame. Why were the Furies pursuing him this way? Opposite him, Berthe von Hoffmann's deep blue eyes glowed with inexplicable sorrow—or was it sympathy? Somehow this steadied him. "I think, Herr Kapitanleutnant, that you were the first offender. What I said to you in the privacy of your cabin was an exchange between gentlemen, which was never intended to go beyond the confines of your U-boat. By revealing it to the world, you impugned my honor, my reputation as an officer of the U.S. Navy."

"Well said!" It was Moorman, seated at the bottom of the table. His cleft chin jutted, his face wore a glaze of antipathy.

"Our American guest has made a point," Rafael Sanchez said.

"The commander of a U-boat doesn't have a cabin!" Hoffmann snarled, ignoring Moorman and Sanchez. "You made your statement to me and my officers as we dined in the passageway. In public!"

"I don't think five officers on a submarine a hundred meters below the surface of the Atlantic constitute the public, Herr Kapitanleutnant."

"Well said again!" Moorman cried. Talbot was starting to enjoy this brawl. It was like finding your sea legs in a gale. Rafael Sanchez looked toward him as if he expected—or even hoped—he would continue his rebuttal.

"As for participating in the attack on the convoy—I accepted your invitation to join you on the bridge in the hope that I might learn something that would help me sink you the next time we met. Since we're meeting here on neutral ground, without our weapons, maybe we should just exchange apologies instead."

"I have no intention of apologizing for anything!" Hoffmann roared. "I'm calling you a liar to your face. Do you wish satisfaction? Or do you prefer to slink back to your embassy to get a new set of lies from your British masters here in Madrid—or your Jewish masters in Washington?"

"I take it you're asking me to fight a duel," Talbot said. "It's strictly forbidden by U.S. Navy regulations. I also find the idea morally repugnant."

"Save the big words!" Hoffmann snarled. "You're a coward!"

Although he spoke in German, most of the Spaniards at the table seemed to have no trouble understanding him—especially the last word: *Feigling*. Talbot saw covert agreement on the faces of most of the men. The German son of a bitch was winning the argument. Talbot's self-control vanished in a blaze of shame and anger. He was ready to lunge across the table and wrap his hands around the Kapitanleutnant's throat.

"If either of you say another word about a duel," the Marquesa de Montoya said, "I will report you to General Franco. You'll both be expelled from Spain within twenty-four hours. I never dreamt that such an exchange could take place at my table. If we cannot converse, we'll have music. Commander Sanchez, will you summon the gypsies?"

Jaime Sanchez hurried out and in a moment the gypsies filed into the rear of the dining room. The woman dancer began singing a flamenco song about a lover who had died in the bullring. The dinner, gazpacho followed by roast suckling pig, was swiftly served by a half-dozen young women under the stern eye of an ancient butler.

Wine flowed, the conversation resumed desultorily under the music. The gracious dark-haired woman sitting next to Talbot was the wife of General Vigon, one of Franco's closest associates. She talked charmingly of the days when American tourists flocked to Spain, many of them determined to follow the route Cervantes had given Don Quixote in his great novel. They were dismayed to discover La Mancha was one of the poorest parts of Spain and places such as El Toboso, which Cervantes had described as a great city, were really tiny villages of nine hundred souls, with nothing in them but a tasca and a church.

"Americans are droll, don't you think, Elena? They lack irony. Perhaps that is a gift that only comes with time."

"It's not a gift I'd wish for them," the Marquesa said.

"Germans lack irony too," Berthe von Hoffmann said. Her voice was exactly as Talbot had imagined it when he heard her sing. A soft musical sound, imbued with melancholy. "Perhaps it's a symptom of a certain naïveté—but also a certain capacity for hope."

"The Spanish lost that capacity a long time ago," the Marquesa said. "Instead we prefer the bitter proverb: 'Hope is the dregs in the bottom of the cup.'"

The words seemed to strike Berthe von Hoffmann like a slap. Her lips trembled and she bowed her head. Talbot felt a ballooning sensation of sympathy threaten to sunder his chest. Her choice of Mahler's songs was no accident. There was a genuine melancholy in this beautiful woman that he longed to explore. Who—or what—had disappointed her?

The gypsy woman was singing of an Arab girl who had been seduced by a Spanish soldier and left behind in Morocco. She was planning to throw herself into the sea in the hope that her body would wash up on Spain's shore and be a reproach to him.

Incredible, the swirling mixture of mood and music, wine and humiliation, anger and attraction. Talbot repeatedly lost the thread of the conversation as he gazed across the table at Berthe von Hoffmann. The contrast between her and Annie could not have been more complete. This woman was beauty chastened by time, thought, culture. He could not imagine her snapping and snarling at a man.

Back in the ballroom for coffee, another group of gypsies danced, this time as a group. Madame Vigon introduced Talbot to her husband, the General, who discussed the Abraham Lincoln Brigade, the American volunteers who had fought for the Communists. He said they had fought bravely. He had interrogated some of those who had been captured. "Sad deluded boys," he said. "They lived and died a Bolshevik lie."

Guests began leaving, car motors rumbled in the courtyard. In her sheath of yellow silk, Berthe von Hoffmann swayed before him. "Herr Talbot," she said, in that perfectly modulated voice. "I want to apologize for my husband's deplorable manners. I would never have come here if I thought such an exchange would take place. The Marquesa is an old and dear friend."

"Thank you," he said. "Perhaps you could tell him—I regret the whole thing. I really had no choice—"

"Your sentiments, your point about the public—were entirely correct," she said.

Twenty minutes later, Talbot walked down the dark Castellana with Moorman, listening to a savage lecture. "That German swine humiliated you in public, Commander," he said. "No Spaniard in the world would tolerate being called a coward to his face. You've only got one choice now. You've got to do something even more intolerable to him."

"What?" Talbot said, absorbed by Berthe von Hoffmann's melancholy beauty.

"Seduce his wife," Moorman said.

21

SO WILY ARE THE WAYS OF LOVE

The Marquesa lit a cigarette and inhaled it with a dry sucking sound. "He was only a boy when I knew him in the Twenties. But I could see even then he had a romantic nature. He was a dreamer, a visionary. His father was neither—a cold-eyed realist who spouted moralities in public and practiced the exact opposite in private. We spent some marvelous afternoons together."

"I'm not sure I want to know all this!" Berthe von Hoffmann cried.

"But you must, my dear. The more you understand a man, the more you can enjoy him. Men like Jonathan Talbot are the most adorable fools. They want to kill the bull, tilt at windmills. Cervantes has them exactly right. Seducing them can be a marvelous opportunity for amusement, mia hija. They're so easy to manipulate."

Hija. This woman was trying to make her a daughter. Berthe rejected the idea with a vehemence she struggled to conceal. "I had no idea Ernst would behave so monstrously. What if he finds out—and challenges Talbot to a duel again? Or kills him in some criminal way?"

"Ernst is an ambitious man. He won't jeopardize his career by doing anything outrageous."

Smoke wreathed the Marquesa's impudent nose. "Do you care if Ernst finds out? Other than this worry about a possible murder?

Where is he now—off with my nephew Sanchez, sampling the pleasures of Tangier."

Berthe thought of the man who had called her a sentimental fool in Posen. Yet she still preferred him to know nothing about her seduction of Jonathan Talbot.

"All you have to do, if he finds out, is tell him it's for the greater glory of Germany. I can't imagine a more ideal arrangement. When I think of the lies I had to invent to deceive my husband—"

Why was she hesitating? She had vowed to show the Marquesa that Berthe von Schonberg, the pathetic creature on whom she had once heaped condescending sympathy, could be as clever and uncaring in the intrigues of love as this female Doña Juan had been in her prime.

Was it the sincerity on Jonathan Talbot's face as he explained his repudiation of Ernst's propaganda? Was it something even more fundamental—the fact that Berthe von Hoffmann, the erstwhile queen of Berlin's cabaret set, had never seduced a man? She had been the seduced one, in the two brief affairs of her university years. With Lothar Engle and with Ernst the same pattern had prevailed.

"Aren't you attracted to him? He's handsome in that lean, craggy-faced American way. He looks like his father. But he has his mother's unstable temperament. She was destroyed by her older son's death. She took to sherry, pills, raged at her husband for sacrificing the boy to his political ambitions. As if he knew the future any more than she did!"

Berthe averted her eyes, afraid of what the Marquesa would see in them. The woman was a kind of monster, with her preternatural ability to control her feelings, her offhand dismissal of those unable to deal with fate's blows.

"Oh!" The Marquesa pressed both hands to her tiny face. In a flash Berthe could see her father, consumed with desire by the gesture. She could imagine that small, sensual body in Willi von Schonberg's arms, that supple mouth against his lips. Intolerable!

"I hope to God! But no—I have more confidence in you—" As usual, the Marquesa's voice dwindled to a croak when she was excited. "You're not going to fall in love with him!"

With no warning, Berthe was sitting in the Romanisches Cafe on Berlin's Tauentzienstrasse listening to frail, haunted Else Lasker-Schuler declaim her theory of poetry and love. Both poems and love were occurrences that simply happened in the poet, like apples or oranges grew upon a tree. The poet, especially if she were a woman, had no control whatsoever over either event.

> *Ich mochte nach am deinem Herzen lauschen*
> *Mit deiner fernsten Nahe mich verstauben*
> I want to listen closely at your heart
> In your remotest nearness find my counterpart

Lasker-Schuler had addressed those lines to God. But Berthe von Hoffmann was speaking them to someone or something else. Was it the pained honesty on Jonathan Talbot's face? Was she betraying that honesty by seducing him? In the Marquesa's philosophy, the very act of seduction was a betrayal, since she never had the slightest interest in a man for anything more than the pleasure he gave her, the uses to which she might put his influence.

"Here!" The Marquesa pulled from a drawer a thin book that she thrust into Berthe's hands. "I've given this to no more than a dozen other women. I collected it myself and had it privately printed. If you ever reveal me as its source, I'll be ruined."

"What is it?" Berthe asked.

"Spanish poetry written by women. I call it *Voices of Resistance*. It goes back to the earliest times, when women couldn't put their names on a book without fear of being burned at the stake. My favorite is Florencio Pinar, the first woman to sign a Spanish poem."

With her slyest smile, the Marquesa threw back her head and recited:

> Ell Amor ha tales manas
> Que quien no se guarda dellas.
> *So wily are the ways of love*
> *That one must always be on guard.*

The poem went on to explain that love entered the body without warning and lived violently in the *entranas*, the body's innermost parts, refusing to depart. Love was a *cancer de natura*, a cancer of nature, which consumed everything healthy with its quarrels and deceits.

Hija, Bertha thought. She could never be this Spanish woman's daughter. The Marquesa was too southern, too earthy for a German to begin to understand.

Yet she was her only link to that mocking enigmatic man Berthe called father. "What did you really think of my father?" she asked in a voice that was close to a snarl.

"Your father was the only man who understood me. The only man I came close to loving. Because he asked nothing of me," the Marquesa said.

Was there any consolation—or wisdom—in that? "What do you think of the war news?" Berthe asked, deliberately changing the subject.

"I think the Führer's failure to capture Moscow in December is a good sign. Hitler is not as great a strategist as Franco thinks."

"Does he really think that?"

"He'll heap praise on anyone who tries to destroy the Russians, after what they did to this country. I'm not far from him in that feeling." Something more than mere intrigue flickered in the Marquesa's haunted eyes.

Was that the zero-sum of Canaris's game? He too was ready to sacrifice anyone, lie to anyone and everyone, to help Hitler end once and for all the ancient German horror of the Slav hordes? Was the Admiral deceiving even Moltke and his friends, letting them speak for decency under his protection, when he cared about nothing but Germany, Germany, Germany? Sometimes Berthe wished she had never read history at the University of Berlin.

She had to trust Canaris—and somehow trust this incredibly intriguing woman who was either his ally or his dupe. For the moment it did not matter. Whatever Canaris had told the Marquesa, she was doing her utmost to help, for the time being. She had urged Berthe to select Jonathan Talbot as her target the moment she saw his name on the Spanish secret service list of new arrivals at the American embassy. His profile was promising—from a distinguished American family, with a father-in-law a prominent member of Congress. His encounter with Ernst in the North Atlantic somehow made it all seem *ordained*. The word rang in Berthe's mind whenever she thought about him.

What they had discovered since Talbot arrived—his separation from his wife, his coolness toward the British—only made him more promising. Berthe walked home to the apartment on the edge of the

Retiro Park thinking about Ernst. Was he in some Tangier brothel, sampling the exotic sex of North Africa? Several times, when they argued, he hinted that he enjoyed other women. But Berthe had told herself she could not expect total fidelity from a man who was separated from his wife for months at a time. She had married a sailor, not a saint.

She sat down by her American telephone—all Spain was wired by the ITT Corporation—but she did not call Jonathan Talbot. There had to be at least one more accidental meeting. Pursuit was too liable to arouse suspicion, contradiction.

The sereno arrived with her mail. There was a letter from Elisabeth von Theismann, telling about a trip to Cannes with Colonel von Stauffenberg and his wife, who was one of her closest friends. So much for clever Berthe's theory of seduction. She had been thinking like a Berliner, a bad habit she must break.

The second and third paragraphs, describing the weather in Cannes, a trip they took along the coast in a sailboat, was in code. Elisabeth reported failure with her contact at the American embassy in Vichy. As she feared, now that Germany and the United States were at war, the man, a State Department professional, declined to discuss anything but official business.

Another letter was from Helen Widerstand in Berlin. She had gone to Helmuth von Moltke to see if he could get money to Else Lasker-Schuler, who was in danger of starving in Jerusalem. Moltke said he would try to help her through the Abwehr agent in Damascus—and contributed five hundred marks out of his own pocket. Helen, who was inclined to dislike Prussian aristocrats—was enormously impressed by Moltke. She spent an hour discussing Germany's future with him and was amazed to discover how close his Christian socialism was to her Marxist version.

The telephone rang. "Frau von Hoffmann," a man's voice said. "This is Jonathan Talbot. I wonder if you and Kapitanleutnant von Hoffmann could have dinner with me tonight at Horcher's restaurant?"

"I'm afraid Herr von Hoffmann is in the south of Spain on naval business," she said.

"Would you consider dining alone with me? It might be the best way to make amends for what happened the other night. I could see it caused you a great deal of pain. More than it caused Herr von Hoffmann, I regret to say."

It was almost too good to be true. "What a lovely idea," Berthe said. "What time should I expect you?"

He arrived at her door in a wheezing taxi at nine-thirty—almost early for dinner in Madrid, where serious dining seldom started before ten. Berthe felt oddly girlish—and tried to conceal it by dressing in the highest style—a strapless black lace Balenciaga gown with a small bolero jacket.

The Madrid branch of Horcher's was as elegant as the Berlin original. Even the waiters wore white ties and tails. The plump headwaiter was agreeably surprised to find one of his old customers at his door. "Fräulein von Schonberg! What an honor this is!" he said, kissing her hand as he had often done when she arrived at the Berlin establishment on Lothar Engle's arm.

Berthe told him she was now Frau von Hoffmann and coolly introduced Talbot as the American naval attaché. "We are all neutrals here!" the headwaiter said. "Here we come only to feast the body and enrich the soul."

Drapes of green velvet, a carpet of deep crimson, amber light from silver candelabra—the atmosphere could not have been more romantic. Except for the stares of the diners—mostly German—as the headwaiter led them to a table in a corner.

Talbot, oblivious to the hostile looks, settled himself opposite Berthe and asked: "Where did you learn to sing so beautifully?"

"My mother was a singer in her youth. An opera star, in fact. She insisted it was my only hope of finding a husband. I was quite ugly as a girl."

"I find that hard to believe."

"I was unhappy. That makes you ugly."

"Why were you unhappy?"

"My father was a fool who gambled away most of his money before he died in a second-rate Paris hotel in nineteen-thirty."

Berthe was dismayed to discover this confession brought tears to her eyes. The Marquesa had advised her to play on this man's sympathy. But Berthe had no ability to conjure up convincing lies and was resorting to the truth—a mistake. Somehow this encounter had to be restructured around its central idea—deception.

"So that explains it," he said. "When I saw you at the Marquesa de Montoya's, I was struck by your melancholy. It touched something inside me. Maybe a similar feeling."

"Why are you melancholy?"

"Disappointment I suppose. I'm disappointed in a lot of things. My country, my career, my wife."

How alike we are, Berthe thought. But she could not say that. "Perhaps life is inherently disappointing. We start with unrealistic youthful expectations—"

"Are you disappointed in your country?" he asked.

Again, she had to remember the deceptive answer Canaris had given her. It would be a mistake to blurt out everything in the first meeting. The process had to be gradual, a careful mingling of the personal and the political. "I'm disappointed in Hitler," she said.

A waiter brought them champagne cocktails, courtesy of the house. The beaming headwaiter recited the recommendations of the evening—grilled whitefish with saffron rice, partridge in sour cream sauce. They accepted his advice, and let him choose the wine as well.

"Does Ernst believe in Hitler?" Talbot asked. "I'm not sure— from the conversation we had on the Ritterboot."

"I think he does," Berthe said. "I think he believes in him more and more each day."

Jonathan Talbot had no idea how these words resounded in Berthe's soul. They were redolent with regret and farewell. Around her, the rumble of German voices seemed to swell into an accusation.

"That must make it very difficult for you," Talbot said.

"It's another disappointment," she said, forcing a wry smile.

The fish arrived, fragrant and perfectly grilled. The wine steward poured a strong white wine from Galicia, called an Albarino. He pronounced it the equal of a good German Riesling. They ate and drank in silence for several minutes, broken only by agreeing on the excellence of the food and wine.

"Why are you disappointed with your wife?" she asked.

He shrugged. "I know she's disappointed with me. Maybe I just returned the compliment. We didn't agree on a lot of things that became pretty important. Politics. Religion."

He toyed with his fish. "Maybe marriage is like a plane ride that runs out of gas. The crash landing is nasty."

"You disagreed about your president, Roosevelt?" Berthe asked.

He nodded glumly. "I thought he was a great man at first. He rescued the country from collapse. But he's a liar. He lied us into this war."

"Your wife wasn't bothered by this?"

"Her ethics are more flexible than mine when it comes to that sort of thing. Her father's a politician with even more flexible ethics. She thinks I'm a fool for calling Roosevelt a liar in public. I've ruined my Navy career—just as she predicted I would."

His bitterness all but scalded her flesh. Berthe found herself shrinking from this task. Only the thought of the Marquesa mocking her squeamishness sustained her. "Another disappointment," she murmured.

"'My Country 'Tis of Thee.' Maybe that's our mistake," Talbot said.

"I don't understand," she said.

"It's one of our patriotic songs. The same tune as 'God Save the King.' Maybe patriotism is the fundamental blunder. But I can't quite believe that. If I cut myself off from my country—my life would lose a lot of its meaning. I don't see anything beyond it—do you?"

"You mean God?"

"Whatever you want to call him. I don't see much evidence of his interest in our affairs."

"Another disappointment?"

"You could call it that. Although for me, it goes back a long way."

He began telling her about his older brother's death in 1918. "I was out on the soccer field at the Choate School in Wallingford, Connecticut, when my father's chauffeur pulled up and said I had to come home right away. He told me the news as the car turned onto the highway to Litchfield. I couldn't believe it. Sometimes I still can't believe it. George was so much smarter, more talented, than me. He was going to be the family's great man. A senator at the very least. Maybe president."

He gulped some wine. "That's when I stopped believing in God. No God could let something like that happen. When you multiply it by the millions of others who died in the last war—God becomes even more of a joke."

How raw the wound still was, Berthe marveled. Now she was going to inflict another wound on this vulnerable man. Was Canaris turning her into a monster like Elena de Montoya? Berthe was assailed by a sudden inexplicable wish to share with this man the fragile faith she had discovered in Pastor Bruchmuller's church and on the twists and turns of the Path. But deception was the game here, not conversion.

She heard Bruchmuller saying: *everything is permitted*, while Lothar Engle repeated the words in a mocking falsetto in the background. Even this? she wondered. Was she permitted to hear a man reveal the deepest anguish of his soul and then use him like an enemy?

Enemy. The word momentarily steadied Berthe. She saw the U-boats prowling the American coasts, torpedoes smashing into hulls, burning oil fountaining toward the sky. The Afrika Corps roared toward Cairo in her blazing mind. The panzers fought Russia's hordes in the below zero winds and towering snowdrifts of her icy heart. *Enemy*.

The partridge arrived; it was even more delicious than the fish, with a velvety red Rioja wine from sunbaked Andulusia. They talked about films, books. He praised *All Quiet on the Western Front* but knew little else in German literature. All his favorite writers were American, with Hemingway leading the list.

She asked him why he liked someone whose ideas were so primitive. "He tells you how to be a man in a meaningless world," Talbot said.

There it was again, the extraordinary grieving emptiness in this enemy's soul. What will happen in your own soul if he says *I love you*? What will you feel when you see more disappointment on his face, inflicted by your cold German heart, in the fatherland's name? It could only end in pain, even if Canaris was trustworthy. Jonathan Talbot would instantly understand the central deception. He was too intelligent, too sensitive, not to see it.

Press attaché Hans Lazar and his new assistant, Wolfgang Griff, strolled toward the table, leering politely, inquisitively. "What have we here, Frau von Hoffmann?" Lazar said. "An attempt to persuade Commander Talbot of the justice of Germany's cause?"

"My husband was supposed to join us but he was called away to Barcelona," Berthe said. "Commander Talbot had the table reserved, the wine chosen—I thought it would be ungracious to let him dine alone."

"My intentions are strictly honorable," Talbot said, with a grin. "How could they be otherwise, considering what Kapitanleutnant Hoffmann did for me off Iceland?"

Full of longing, his eyes swung abruptly to meet Berthe's as he said this. She realized he meant it. He had no intention of seducing the wife of the man who had saved his life. She was dealing with old-fashioned honor as well as honesty.

"You repaid our kindness, Herr Commander, with slanders in your newspapers," Griff said.

"That's why I'm dining with Frau von Hoffmann," Talbot said. "To explain that statement—which has caused me some regret."

"I think it's become an entirely personal matter, Herr Griff," Berthe said. "There's nothing more passé than last month's newspapers."

"You're undoubtedly correct, my dear lady," Lazar said. He had the brains to see that he and his toady were stymied. He was probably also satisfied that they had made their point—Frau von Hoffmann knew she was being watched.

"I hope I haven't gotten you in trouble," Talbot said, as the two Nazis retreated.

Enemy, Berthe fiercely reminded herself. But compared to the enmity she felt for Lazar and Griff, did the word mean anything? "I think Ernst outranks them," she said.

Another wheezing taxi waited at Horcher's door. The headwaiter burbled good wishes. "If the world were run by restaurateurs, there would never be a war," Berthe said.

From the other side of the dark back seat, Talbot reached out for her. With amazing strength, he drew her against him and pressed his lips on her mouth. For a long, breathless moment he held her that way—and retreated into his dark corner again. "Forgive me," he said. "You're so beautiful."

What should she do or say? Tell him he was handsome, she wanted him? The idea appalled her. Inexplicably, there were a dozen reasons to say nothing. A sudden wish to remain faithful to Ernst. A dread of doing some irreparable harm to this man. She sat there, paralyzed, silent, letting him think she was shocked.

At her apartment, he jumped out and called for the sereno. "Voooey," was his answer, from somewhere up the shrouded block. *Coming.* In a few moments he was there, two dozen keys clanking around his fat belly, his mouth open for an enormous yawn.

It was hard to imagine a more total annihilator of romance. How did the Spanish manage their affairs? Berthe wondered, thinking of the nights when she and Lothar Engle had strolled home to his apartment off the Kurfurstendamm, untroubled by prying eyes.

"I'm glad Ernst was in Barcelona," Talbot said.

"I am too," she said.

Enemy. Don't listen to him, Berthe ordered her German heart. *Invite him up for a brandy*, whispered another voice. Was it the Marquesa, her patron saint of seduction? A third voice, a kind of silent presence, advised her against it.

"Meeting you makes me regret this war even more," Talbot said.

"You're a good man," she said, kissing him on the cheek and stumbling into the inky black stairwell after the sereno.

Upstairs, Berthe lit a candle and contemplated herself in her bedroom mirror. Coward? Fool? Patriot? the words flickered against the glass, which seemed to be sucking darkness from the room behind her. The Marquesa would undoubtedly choose the first two. As for Admiral Canaris, he would simply smile and say she had made a good start for a beginner in the spiderweb game. Only Helmuth von Moltke would understand the sadness flooding her soul as Berthe began to see where the Path was taking her.

22
BEHIND THE HEADLINES

The cold drizzle, the lowering clouds, were a perfect match for Annie Talbot's mood as she trudged up the long, curving drive to 1801 Foxhall Road, the latest mansion of Mrs. Marjorie Merriwether Post Close Hutton Davies. One of America's richest as well as most married women, she was now the wife of Joseph P. Davies, until recently the American Ambassador to the Soviet Union. They were giving a reception for the new Russian Ambassador to the United States, Maxim Litvinov.

Annie displayed her press card and invitation to the magisterial English butler at the door. "You can skip the reception line. The drinks are in the library," he said, with barely concealed contempt.

Annie gave him her sweetest smile and headed for the reception line in the Music Room. Litvinov, pudgy, balding, bespectacled, looked like a genial eager-to-please Chicago butcher embarrassed by his striped pants and cutaway. Beside him, his white-haired wife, in a floor-length dress of purple crepe, was infinitely more dignified.

"Mrs. Litvinov," Annie said, as she shook her hand. "I work for the column, 'Behind The Headlines.' We're extremely anxious to interview you about what women in the Soviet Union are doing to win the war."

"I'd be delighted. Call the embassy tomorrow morning," she replied in an upper-class English accent. This morning's Washington

Post had explained that she had met the ambassador in London when he was a fugitive from the Czar's secret police.

In the library, a half-dozen wives of Supreme Court justices took turns pouring tea from a golden pot into gold-rimmed cups once reserved for the lips of the Czar and his family. Behind them was a table piled with tiny sandwiches and petit fours in Mrs. Davies's favorite colors, green and pink. Through the windows echoed the beep of horns on Foxhall Road as a horde of VIPs tried to squirm their way through a half-mile-long traffic jam. Everyone who was anyone in Washington was rushing to be included in this newest and hottest social circle.

Nearby, in a silver frame surmounted by a lacquered red star, was an autographed photo of Josef Stalin. Annie paused to contemplate it and a man beside her said: "He must be laughing his head off."

"Why?" she asked.

"Watching the capitalists make fools of themselves."

"It all looks very dignified to me."

The man grunted contemptuously. His suit was shabby, his cuffs frayed. He was a bit overweight, balding, with knowing eyes and yellowing teeth in a heavy, rather haggard face. Annie felt a twinge of sympathy. She too was feeling haggard.

"Have you read this idiot's book, *Mission to Moscow*?" he said, gesturing to a framed picture of Davies in Red Square with the spires of the Kremlin behind him.

"No."

"I counted sixty-seven glaring errors of fact. The man is a total ass. I almost resigned from the service during that year in Moscow, watching him pollute the truth for personal publicity."

The man was obviously a State Department insider. She had come here hoping to meet someone like him. Every reporter had to develop her own sources. "I'm Annie Talbot," she said. "I've replaced Joe Turkow at 'Behind The Headlines.'"

"Roy Reeves," the man said. "What the hell's wrong with your boss? He's sounding more and more like FDR's Little Sir Echo. Especially when he writes about foreign policy."

Annie decided not to mention that her boss was also her brother—or to try to defend Jack's all-out support of the President. "You've got to read the column every day. It's a balancing act," she said.

A skeptical grunt.

"I'd like to hear more about those sixty-seven errors in *Mission to Moscow*," she said. Deflating the latest Washington celebrity had long been a "Behind The Headlines" specialty.

"Off the record?" he said.

"Deep background," she said.

"Call me at home," he said, slipping her his card.

"Annie Talbot! Why in the world are you wasting your time with this old reactionary!"

It was her brother-in-law, Ned Travis, looking suave in a gray Savile Row suit, complete with gold watch fob. Roy Reeves gazed at him with dyspeptic disapproval. "In my twenty years in the State Department, I've never heard that term directed at a fellow member of the service," he said.

"I heard the President directed it at you the other day, at the White House," Ned replied with a supercilious smile. He seized Annie's arm and led her across the room to meet the people who "really counted" at State. A half-dozen names flashed around a circle of youngish faces, all with the confident smiles and strong bone structure of the American elite. They began telling her how much they liked "Behind The Headlines" these days. Annie struggled to be grateful, simultaneously wishing she had been able to keep talking to gloomy Roy Reeves. Was it because his name rhymed with grieves?

Stop it, Annie told herself. Stop it once and for all. You are starting a new career, a new life. You do not have the slightest regret for the one that ended when Zeke Talbot slammed that door in your face. You have already worked your way past grief to mere disappointment, which will shortly become indifference—and after that comes happiness. An immense sun-swept beach of radiant happiness awaits you at the end of this cold, rain-soaked, tear-drenched winter.

"Saul," Ned Travis called. "Come over here and meet Annie Talbot."

Saul Randolph was over six feet, with gleaming dark hair, olive skin and hooded, probing eyes. It was a face Annie had seen in pictures of turn-of-the-century Jewish immigrants, redolent of difference, of a part of Europe that was truly foreign to America's Anglo-Saxon majority. The eyes had the same searching, skeptical quality of those refugees from Russian pogroms, but Randolph's mouth was different—tighter, more confident, even a bit disdainful, thanks to mastering this American world. "Saul's just switched from number four at the Treasury to number two at lend-lease. He's on the phone all the time asking State what to do next," Ned said in his arch, slightly condescending way.

Randolph smiled amiably. "You look too smart to believe these striped suiters," he said to Annie. "They still can't believe Harry Hopkins took the operation away from them."

"Shhhh," Ned said.

Cordell Hull, the white-haired Secretary of State, ambled past, nodding to them in an avuncular way. The circle muttered about the unlikelihood of his knowing a single one of their names. Insider jokes about Hull as a figurehead whizzed around. They abruptly ceased when Sumner Welles, the slim, patrician Undersecretary of State, wearing a suit that matched Ned Travis's down to the gold watch fob, towed no less a personage than Harry Hopkins into their midst.

Cynicism vanished, awe became transcendent in the presence of a man who, by way of ultimate proof that he was closer to Franklin D. Roosevelt than anyone else in Washington, D.C., had a bedroom on the second floor of the White House. Welles introduced Ned and his friends as his "Young Turks," who welcomed the help of people like Saul Randolph in their struggle to "capture" the State Department from "the Hooverites."

This was a rather astonishing remark in the ninth year of Roosevelt's presidency but no one challenged it. "Good, good," Hopkins said in a weary voice. "Maybe something will come of my dragging the Treasury into the foreign policy business." He gave Saul Randolph an insider's smile.

With his saffron skin and emaciated face, Hopkins looked much more haggard than Roy Reeves, making Annie wonder if the rumors about him having cancer were true. But the power he emanated made it difficult for her to feel any sympathy for him. Maybe Zeke was right: power was the only thing that mattered to her. Was it the elixir that transcended everything—health, happiness, the soul's salvation?

Hopkins began talking about the crucial importance of America's relationship to Russia—how vital it was to the President's foreign policy. Annie found herself flinging a ferocious rebuttal at Jonathan Trumbull Talbot. *You love power just as much as I do. You'd give a million dollars and almost any portion of your anatomy to be where I am right now.*

Then came the moment of benediction: Harry Hopkins's hand was on her arm, his tense smile flickered. "Jack tells me you're going to work for him. That's good news." He pecked her on the cheek. "Give my best to your father."

Eyes were revolving beneath the raised brows of the State Department's elite. Ned Travis looked as if he might have palpitations. Even Sumner Welles and Saul Randolph seemed impressed. Annie decided not to bother telling them that ten years ago, when Harry Hopkins ran the Works Progress Administration, he was constantly in and out of her father's apartment getting the latest line on how many more jobs the Democrats needed to carry Illinois. The WPA was the first but by no means the last application of Hopkins's famous New Deal dictum (which he of course denied saying): "We shall tax and tax, spend and spend, elect and elect."

A hubbub off to their left. Vice President Henry Wallace was getting up on one of Mrs. Davies's lime-green sofas, which was probably worth the price of an aircraft carrier. Annie noted he had at least removed his shoes. Pushing his Iowa cornhusker's haircut out of his eyes, he began telling them how much the President wished he could be here. "This is not merely the beginning of a new era in Soviet-American relations," he said. "It's the start of a new era in the history of the world. The two largest nations on earth, the only ones committed to the welfare of the common man, are joining forces to launch an age of fraternity and equality!"

"Isn't that the goddamnest bullshit you ever heard?" muttered a masculine voice behind Annie. She turned to find Andrew Jackson May, the stumpy Chairman of the House Military Affairs Committee, standing beside tall, austere John McCormack, the Speaker of the House. The Massachusetts Democrat nodded his frowning agreement with May's Kentucky-style sentiments as Wallace descended from the couch to embrace Ambassador Litvinov.

"That man is going to change the future of the world," Saul Randolph said, gazing at Wallace with unqualified admiration.

> Missed the Saturday dance,
> Would have gone but what for?
> Couldn't bear it without you,
> Don't get around much anymore.

The singer was shouting the words over the blaring swing band in the smoky Georgetown nightclub. Thanks to Mrs. Merriwether Post Hutton Close Davies and her husband, Annie was getting around very nicely tonight. She was doing a lively lindy at the end of Saul Randolph's arm. She only wished she could find a photographer somewhere to snap a picture to send to Lieutenant Commander Jonathan Trumbull Obnoxious Talbot at the American embassy in Madrid—in case he imagined his cowed wife was cringing in her parents' apartment bewailing her fate.

In the previous hour at the tiny nightclub table, she had learned a few things about Saul Randolph. His father had been a reporter for various New York newspapers. Saul had gone to Columbia University on a scholarship and acquired a Ph.D. in economics in 1932. After a stint on Wall Street with the Securities and Exchange Commission, he had come to Washington and within two years he had risen to Assistant Secretary of the Treasury.

"In charge of what?" Annie asked.

"Soaking the rich."

He talked exuberantly of his proposal to limit incomes to twenty-five thousand dollars a year for the duration of the war. He claimed Roosevelt was seriously considering it until Annie asked him how he hoped to get it through Congress. He switched to telling her how he was also running lend-lease, flying regularly to Moscow, dealing with the Russians. He was up to his hips in the Washington power game and enjoying every minute of it.

Back at the table, Ned Travis and his friends smiled drunken approval of her progress with Mr. Randolph. "Ned tells me you've broken up with your husband," he said.

"Not quite. But we parted on less than cordial terms."

"I broke up with my wife two years ago."

He was trying to be sympathetic but Annie's reaction was negative. No doubt Mrs. Randolph had failed to meet some sort of exacting male standard. "Tell me about the Russians," Annie said. "Do you think they can hold out?"

"Absolutely. They're pushing the Germans back right now." He heaped praise on General Philip Faymonville, head of the American military mission in Moscow. He was making enemies among his fellow generals because he endorsed Harry Hopkins's insistence on no-strings aid to the Soviets, overriding all attempts to hoard matériel for the American Army.

Faymonville was good stuff for a column on an unsung hero. "How do you get along with the Russians, personally?" Annie asked.

"They do a lot of yelling and screaming," Randolph said. "It's going to take a while for us to convince them that we really want to help them."

Ned Travis began assuring Annie that Randolph was exaggerating America's problems with the Russians. "You don't know what the hell you're talking about, Ned," Randolph said good-naturedly. "But I hope you're right in the long run. It's our only hope for a better world."

Although Annie maintained that Georgetown was perfectly safe at midnight, Randolph insisted on walking her home. She was living on the top floor of a row house only about three blocks from the nightclub. As they strolled through the continuing drizzle, Randolph wondered how she had vaulted from Navy wife into the top ranks of Washington journalism. She confessed Jack was her brother and she had done a previous stint with "Behind The Headlines" when Zeke spent a year in China in the mid-Thirties.

"Do you mind if I call you?" Randolph said, when they reached the doorway of the redbrick house. "Maybe the next time we can talk about something besides lend-lease."

He was telling her she had treated him more like a source than a friend. "I'm looking for someone who can share a sense of excitement, of mission, about American politics," he said.

Annie shivered in the drizzle. Upstairs was a big, empty double bed and an empty apartment. She had chosen it over urgent suggestions from her parents that she live with them like a forlorn, dutiful war bride. Could she fill that emptiness with a sense of mission about American politics? She thought of the angry defense of FDR she had flung at Zeke in her farewell letter. She gave Randolph her office phone number.

The next day at the morning story conference, Jack warmly approved General Faymonville as a lead for a column and ordered Annie and their skeletal chief researcher cum managing editor, Selma Shanley, to put together a dossier on him. Rotund Sidney Arnold, the other member of the invisible team who backed up Jack's reporting, had an equally juicy lead about skulduggery in the defense industries from the Senate Investigating Committee headed by Senator Harry S Truman. In an ebullient mood, Jack began telling them how the war was going to change the column from a Washington operation to a worldwide beat.

"I'm planning to spend a lot of time overseas getting shot at, something pantywaists like Pearson and Lippmann wouldn't do if they paid them by the bullet," he said.

Drew Pearson's "Washington Merry-Go-Round" regularly battled "Behind The Headlines" for the title of number-one column in American newspapers. Walter Lippmann's column, "Today And Tomorrow," ranked at the top in intellectual prestige.

"The old Navy man wants to see action," Sidney Arnold said. "Keep it under control, Jack. Don't let your guilty conscience get you killed."

"My conscience is absolutely untroubled," Jack said, defiantly lighting a cigarette. "That's why I haven't gone to confession in twenty years."

Annie sensed a secret that she was not being told and waited until Jack and Sidney Arnold departed before asking Selma Shanley why Jack was feeling guilty.

"My God," Selma said, flipping through the Washington *Times-Herald.* "Do you think they're going to ration Milky Ways?" Although she was so thin she looked as if she were constructed of cardboard, Selma ate like a boxer in training.

Annie repeated the question. Selma squirmed in her chair and hauled a West Point directory out of her research library to start checking out General Faymonville. "I haven't the faintest idea. In the news business, the less you remember and the more you forget about some things, the better off you are."

Annie called the Russian embassy and was told that Madame Litvinov would see her at four p.m. Madame served her tea from a samovar, along with genuine caviar on toast, meanwhile telling her about the emancipation of Russian women under communism. "I noticed yesterday," she said. "Most women were introduced to me as the wife of Mr. So-and-So. We don't have that in Russia. A Soviet woman is an individual first, standing on her own achievements, not a shadow of her husband's importance." For a half-hour she talked about Russian women who were flying planes, working in steel factories, serving as Army doctors.

The interview left Annie depressed for the next twenty-four hours. She did not know whether Madame Litvinov was telling the truth about Russian women, but she had spotted the central flaw in the lives of American women. Anna Richman Talbot was a perfect example. At thirty-three, she was operating for the first time in her life as a separate individual, sort of. Without her brother, she would undoubtedly be pounding a typewriter in some government agency for $1,600 a year or toiling in the lower ranks of the females who wrote the women's page in the nation's newspapers.

Rage rose in Annie's throat like foul fluid when she thought about her eleven years of devotion by day and surrender by night— which had produced nothing but revulsion in her husband's soul. What rotten bastards men were! Jack was not much better, with his endless affairs. He delivered the heartbreak on a faster schedule, that was all she could say for him.

It was not the stuff of dreams. After a mostly sleepless night, she called Roy Reeves at his home number. His deep baritone answered the telephone but inexplicably replied that Mr. Reeves was not at home. He took down her name and number and said the call would be returned. Five minutes later, he called back to tell her he was at a pay phone in a nearby drugstore. "Why in the world?" she asked.

"A lot of Washington phones are tapped. Mine is almost certainly one of them," he said.

"Tapped by whom?" Annie asked incredulously.

"Franklin Delano Roosevelt's FBI."

That made her wonder about Mr. Reeves. But she pressed on, telling him she was eager for that deep background talk about *Mission to Moscow*. She mentioned that she had interviewed Madame Litvinov yesterday and was filled with envy of the freedom and achievements of Soviet women. Reeves laughed so hard the receiver vibrated in Annie's hand. "Ivy Litvinov is full of shit," he said. "There are a few thousand women who are better off thanks to the revolution because they have fathers or uncles in the upper ranks of the Party. The rest are worse off than they were under the Czar. At least then they could pray to the Virgin Mary for consolation."

On that note of savage disillusion, she arranged to meet Reeves at noon in a neighborhood bar miles out on Connecticut Avenue. He wore the same shabby suit; his shirt cuffs were, if possible, even more frayed. He gave her a copy of *Mission to Moscow* with his criticisms scribbled in the margins. The mistakes ranged from lies about how well the Soviet system fed and clothed the average worker and his family to a portrait of Stalin as the protector of the proletariat that was, Reeves said, "the total opposite of the monster he is."

By now Annie was wondering if Reeves deserved the reactionary label Ned Travis had pinned on him. Still, if Selma Shanley confirmed even half of Reeves's facts, a mocking exposé of *Mission to Moscow* could make a juicy column.

"Why is Stalin a monster?" she asked. "Why don't we know the truth about the Soviet system? We've had reporters in Russia for a good decade—"

"Because American liberals think they can create a better world by closing their eyes and making a wish—and browbeating everyone else into believing it will come true," Reeves said. His voice bitter, he ticked off a list of apologists for Stalin's Russia, from Vice President Henry Wallace to Joseph Davies to Walter Duranty, the Moscow correspondent for the *New York Times*.

"I recognize the necessity to collaborate with the Russians to stop Hitler," Reeves said. "But it's an alliance that should be conducted with the greatest care—the total opposite of what our President and his impromptu New Deal diplomats like Harry Hopkins are doing. The problem confronting us is how to extricate Germany from Hitler's grasp—and from Stalin's grasp."

For a moment Annie was stunned by the precision with which Reeves stated this objective. It was her first exposure to the art of statecraft outside a history book. This overweight man in his shabby clothes thought like Bismarck and Disraeli and Metternich.

"How do you propose to do this?"

"I don't know. That's one of several reasons why diplomacy is a fascinating business. You never know what's going to turn up. There may be more opposition to Hitler inside Germany than we think. We know a fair number of his generals loathe him. They may depose him, now that he's gotten them into another two-front war. Stalin may die. Roosevelt may die. Running a war is an exhausting business." Reeves drained his third or fourth martini. "That's why I stay in the State Department. The stakes are worth the infighting, the lousy pay. We're arguing about the future of the world. Right now, State is putting together a committee to discuss what terms we'll offer the Germans when we defeat them. Not one person with any background in European history is on it. They're all pinhead New Dealers. But we've just begun to fight. That's why I'm talking to you."

Roy Reeves's calm confidence in his expertise shook Annie's assumption that she understood the world in which she was living. By the time Jack showed up from his usual two-hour liquid lunch, she had a report on her meeting with Reeves on his desk, attached to the copy of *Mission to Moscow*. The book was already on the best-seller list. *This has all the ingredients for an explosive column,* she wrote.

Jack read in silence for a half-hour, then called: "Annie!"

His voice had the hard, cold sound she had noticed during Zeke's imbroglio with Admiral King. He shuffled her papers together and let them flop on the desk. "Two years ago I would have published this thing and given you a bonus. Last year I might have considered it. Now it's strictly for the circular file."

"What's wrong with it?"

"It makes Roosevelt look bad."

"So what—if it's true?"

"Annie. Get that Catholic education out of your head once and for all. The truth is irrelevant in this brawl. Anything—I mean literally anything—goes if it contributes to victory. If it doesn't—if it creates disunity, antagonism to FDR—I don't want to hear about it."

"I don't buy that," she said.

"Either buy it or get the hell out of here," Jack said.

For a moment Jack vanished in a blur of angry tears. With a mighty effort Annie suppressed them. "I think the whole country ought to get a chance to discuss what Reeves said—about getting Germany away from Hitler—and keeping it away from Stalin," she said, hating the throb of emotion in her voice.

"By the time this war is over there won't be enough left of Germany to quarrel over," Jack said.

"Don't be ridiculous. There are seventy million Germans—"

"Don't give me the history major stuff! This column is a weapon—a weapon in an all-out war!"

"Jack—what's happening to you?"

For a moment she thought he was going to curse at her. Instead, he tapped a Lucky Strike into his hand and lit up. "I don't know. Maybe I'm trying to get beyond playing reporter, Annie. Stopping this guy Hitler, helping the President create a better postwar world, is probably the only thing I'll ever do that I can point to with pride."

There was that phrase again: a better world. Roy Reeves said it mockingly, Jack—and Saul Randolph—said it with disconcerting reverence. Who was right? "Why not be satisfied with being one of the best reporters in the country?"

"Ah—it's all unreal, Annie. The big stories, the exposés, the attacks, don't change zilch. The same dirty stuff goes on and on. Take Chicago. Do you think anything I'll ever write can change Chicago?"

"'Nothing but God can change Chicago.' I've heard the line," she said. It was one of their father's favorite cracks. "But aren't there other places a little more receptive to good reporting?"

Jack shook his head. Annie saw she was dealing with a state of soul—the opposite of Zeke Talbot's. He had a surfeit of righteousness, Jack had a surfeit of cynicism from growing up in the bosom of the nation's most corrupt political machine. She was in the middle as usual, expected to bow down to both of them and sigh: "I understand."

The hell of it was, she did understand, she sympathized. Did that mean she still loved both of these impossible male bastards? There was no hope of stopping them from treating her with condescension bordering on contempt? "Okay. Circular file the damn thing!" she said, and fled the office, tears streaming.

In wintry sunshine she walked for miles along the city's streets until the tears stopped and she found herself in Northeast Washington staring up at the domed chapel of her alma mater, Trinity College, with the red-roofed main building looming against the blue sky behind her. She pushed open the chapel's big double doors and walked into the silent vaulted interior. A half-dozen students knelt in the pews, praying to the presence behind the gold tabernacle on the white altar as she had done in her student days. She no longer believed anything was there. That thought stirred a bubble of anxiety in her soul. She decided it was time to stop flinching from it.

She sat down in a rear pew. This was a good place to think about her life, her future. With her son ensconced in prep school, writing cheerful letters about early admission to MIT, motherhood was no more than a bit part. Wifehood had blown up in her face. Jack had just made it clear that sister mostly meant cringing employee.

Maybe it was time to shuck all the males who had ruled her life. She was not doing this job to mark time until she reconciled with Zeke Talbot—a very unlikely event—or until she found another husband. Now or never, it was time to start building achievement into the center of her self—and there was only one way to do that. She had to become invulnerable to male disapproval.

She saw, not without a spear of regret, that she would even have to jettison Congressman Sam Richman, with his elastic ethics and his genial readiness to get along by going along. She hoped, in some way, shape or form she could continue to love him—and Jack—and even Zeke in distant rueful memory—but she was through kowtowing to them. Obeisance to maledom was herewith obliterated from her soul. Anna Richman Talbot was going to become a totally independent woman.

23

JOURNEY TO LA MANCHA

Captain Bernado Moorman seized the empty Sangria pitcher and shook it so hard, the ice cubes sounded like castanets. "You haven't called her again?" he said, glaring across the red-checked tablecloth at Talbot. They were eating dinner in a small restaurant near Talbot's apartment.

Talbot shook his head.

"You're a bloody fool, you know that? She admits she loathes Hitler, she lets you kiss her in the taxi, she kisses you on the cheek by way of goodnight—and you don't follow up! I wouldn't let you command a dinghy in my fleet, Commander. You don't know when to press home the attack."

No one could ever say that about Captain Moorman. Talbot kept wanting to ask him why he had never made admiral. He had been getting these insults for the past ten days, as he struggled to control his overwhelming desire to take Berthe von Hoffmann in his arms again.

Moorman shoved aside his half-finished paella and continued: "There's more here than saving face now, Talbot. Her bloody husband is traveling around Spain setting up all sorts of sly arrangements for the U-boats with his Falangist pal Sanchez."

"Deplorable. But I still can't seduce Berthe von Hoffmann."

"Talbot, I'm giving you a bloody order to do it! If you ignore it I'll get your bloody President to make things so hot for you over here you'll wish you were back in Washington emptying wastebaskets at ONI!"

Talbot found it hard to believe an obscure British naval attaché had access to the American White House. Moorman only grew more impassioned. "I know exactly how twits your age think, Talbot. You look at this old wreck and sneer why didn't he ever make admiral. I didn't make it because I've been on extended leave from the Navy for the past twenty bloody years. I'm head of British intelligence in Spain, and that means I can do things to you that you can't even imagine!"

"If I take any orders like that it'll be from American Naval Intelligence!" Talbot said, disliking this insufferable Englishman more and more.

"Naval Intelligence is only interested in bloody rot about torpedoes and engine speed," Moorman said. "I'm talking about spying and counterspying. You Americans don't have a clue about how to run that sort of ops. I hear you're puzzling together something called the OSS—the Office of Strategic Services. Meanwhile, Roosevelt's given us control of all intelligence operations in the Mediterranean."

Talbot knew nothing about the OSS. Was Moorman bluffing? It did not matter. He reiterated that he could not seduce a woman as vulnerable, as fine, as Berthe von Hoffmann. "Talbot," Moorman snarled. "She's the enemy. Forget that lofty expression in her Valkyrian blue eyes. She'll know a lot about what Ernst is doing in Tangier, Barcelona, Valencia, El Ferrol and God knows where bloody else."

"It's not just a question of ethics, Moorman. I'm being practical, too," Talbot protested. "How do you expect me to convince her I love her if ten seconds after I succeed I start asking her for stuff like that?"

Moorman put his head in his hands. "God almighty," he moaned. "I must have committed some terrible crimes in another life. Why else have I been condemned to spending two bloody wars in Spain and now I have to give love lessons to a bloody American idealist who seems to have grown up without discovering one thing about women!"

"I know a lot about women," Talbot said. "I'm telling you it can't be done."

"All right," Moorman said. "Here goes." He closed his eyes and sucked in his lips. "Darling Jonathan," he cooed in a makeshift German accent. "You're divine. How can I make you happier? You've made me so happy—"

Moorman ran both hands through his thinning hair until he looked like someone in immediate need of a straitjacket. "Darling Berthe," he gasped. "I've got a confession to make. I'm not in the Navy. I'm in American Intelligence. And I'm getting nowhere. The Spanish won't cooperate. If I don't turn in something soon, my career is kaput. I'm not asking you to betray anything serious. But what was Ernst doing last week in El Ferrol?"

"I still don't think it'll work."

"I'll give you another week. Then it's a cable to the bloody President recommending your immediate relief."

Furious—and a little unnerved—Talbot returned to the American embassy and sought out Counselor Hamilton Boileau. "This fellow Moorman," he said. "Is he more than just a naval attaché?"

Boileau's forehead wrinkled agreeably, as if he was pleased to discover Talbot had a few brain cells. "He runs their intelligence in Spain. He's got almost as many people working for him as the Abwehr, from what I hear. But I also hear at least half of them are working for Franco—which means for the Germans."

Back in his office, Talbot discovered a decrypted cable from the Office of Naval Intelligence.

URGENTLY NEED CHARTS OF COASTAL WATERS NORTH AFRICA MEDITERRANEAN AND ATLANTIC SHORES. USE UTMOST DISCRETION IN OBTAINING THEM. ALSO URGE MAXIMUM EFFORT RE GERMAN CODES. JAMISON

The charts could only mean one thing. Talbot pulled out a map of the Mediterranean and saw at a glance the precarious balance between the warring powers. General Erwin Rommel's Afrika Korps was poised on the Egyptian border for another attempt to take Cairo and the Suez Canal. For the past three months, the British had been trying to cut his supply line from Italy without much success. But an invasion of North Africa would put a force in the Afrika Korps' rear that no general could tolerate. Had they stolen the idea from his revision of Rainbow Five? It was a nice thought, even if he could never prove it.

Talbot decided it was time to pay another visit to the Marquesa de Montoya. She had been a firm friend of the United States during his father's ambassadorship. He remembered how often she had helped Roger Talbot cut his way through Spain's hostile bureaucracy to help American investors.

The Marquesa greeted him in her bedroom, wearing a flowing red silk gown. Her tiny wrinkled face, her squinting eyes, looked Chinese. The bedroom was furnished with extraordinary splendor. A rosered Aubusson rug covered the floor. A Goya, a portrait of an earlier Marquesa, hung on the wall. On the opposite wall was a painting of some saint being carried up to heaven in a burst of radiance. The bed was a huge four poster with particolored hanging drapes that made it resemble a gypsy caravan.

The Marquesa stretched herself on a chaise and gestured him to a chair. "I'm so glad you invited Berthe von Hoffmann to dinner," she said. "Though I fear it's caused her no end of trouble with her husband."

"I'm sorry to hear that," Talbot said.

"He's an insufferable young man. Swollen with his triumphs," she said. "He seems to think he has the right to order Berthe around. He doesn't realize the kind of woman he's married."

"You know her well?"

"Since she was a child of twelve or thirteen. A wan unhappy little thing."

Warmth, sympathy, flooded Talbot. "She told me she was unhappy. Her father was a gambler who lost everything."

"Count Willi was much worse than that," the Marquesa said. "He treated Berthe as if she didn't exist. His wife was the same way." The Marquesa lit a cigarette and exhaled a cloud of bluish gray smoke. "I tried to be a substitute mother but she was in rebellion against everyone from our generation—"

Talbot was remembering the kiss in the taxi. There had been no resistance. "Hard to believe she hasn't had a few lovers. Someone that beautiful—"

"She's an idealist. She's searching for a great love. Every woman has the desire—few the capacity."

"Men—more men than you'd think—want the same thing," Talbot said.

The Marquesa looked skeptical. Moorman said she had slept with half the crowned heads of Europe, which would inevitably induce a certain cynicism. It made Talbot wonder about his father's protestations that he had never touched her.

"Moorman—Captain Moorman—thinks I can persuade Berthe to tell us what Ernst is doing on his trips around Spain. I told him he was crazy."

"She's a woman of honor. The mere idea would appall her."

"Can you help me find out some other way? You told me there were Spaniards who sympathized with the United States. Maybe I could work with some of them. I'd like to put together a real dossier—and cram it down Moorman's throat!"

The Marquesa threw back her head and laughed softly. "You looked so much like your father when you said that. He could be extremely fierce when he got angry."

Talbot was immensely flattered. He had spent so much of his life trying to match his father's authoritative style. It did not come naturally to him. "Can you help?"

"My nephew Rafael Sanchez, perhaps. He's a permanent undersecretary in the foreign ministry. But it will be dangerous for you both. The Foreign Secretary, Serrano Suner, is the head of our fascists, the Falange. I'll arrange for you to meet Rafael at our ranch. We're planning a *tienta*—a testing of the heifers and a few bulls. It's our first since the Civil War ended."

The Marquesa strolled to the door with him. "Can you take one more piece of advice?"

"Of course."

"Cram things down Captain Moorman's throat. But continue to work with him. In spite of his awful personality, he's one of the bravest, most honest men in Spain."

The Spanish newspapers continued to reverberate with German and Japanese victories. The Philippines surrendered and the last remnants of resistance in the Dutch East Indies were mopped up. The American Far Eastern Fleet went down in slaughterous defeat in the Java Sea. In Russia the Germans launched a drive toward the Caucasus oil fields that stirred harrowing visions of a breakthrough that would give Hitler enough fuel to fight until the year 2000. General Franco raised a division of volunteers from the members of the Falange and dispatched it to the Russian front with maximum fanfare.

Talbot discovered Moorman was also invited to the weekend on the Montoya country estate. The Englishman offered to drive him down in a sporty little red Aston Martin. They roared along totally empty roads, with Moorman chanting a litany of pessimism and condemnation. Chief among his objects of scorn was Admiral Ernest J. King, who stubbornly refused to take any advice from the British Navy or British Intelligence to help him deal with the rampaging submarines off the American East Coast. "Why do you Yanks have chips on your shoulders?" Moorman complained.

Talbot was tempted to tell him British condescension put them there but he was slowly learning to be a diplomat. Besides, the deficiencies of Ernie King were hardly unpleasant music to his ears.

"I'm beginning to think we're going to lose this bloody war," Moorman said. "I thought it was settled in our favor when you fellows came in. But what good is all the muscle in the world if there's no brainpower to go with it?"

So it went for over two hours as they roared south through the arid landscape of La Mancha. The soil was as close to the color of bloodstains as land can get. Endless olive groves paraded along the sides of sloping ridges, their gray-green branches reaching up like supplicants to huge white windmills turning slowly in the cold April breeze. "Don't ever come here in the summer," Moorman said. "It's hotter than the Sahara."

They discussed the Marquesa, whom Moorman apparently knew well. "A remarkable woman," he said. "But never forget she's from Galicia, like her hero, Franco."

Galicia was the northernmost province of Spain. "The Spanish have a saying, when you meet someone from Galicia on a stairs, you never know whether they're going up or down."

"Were you in Spain during the Civil War?"

"I've been in and out since World War I," Moorman said. "I lost a ship to the U-boats, like you. In 1914. They wouldn't give me another one. The Jonah thing. So I quit the bloody Navy and went into this miserable racket."

"Were the Germans active here in World War I?"

Moorman nodded gloomily. "Swarming around exactly like they are now. Run by the slimiest, sneakiest little queer you've ever seen. Fellow named Canaris. He's head of their secret service these days, which proves, if anything does, the Nazis are swine. I hope he drops by here before we're through. I'd love another crack at him."

Moorman's face darkened, his voice dwindled to an obligatto snarl. "They beat our bloody socks off here in the last war. Of the thirteen million tons the U-boats put under, five million was in the Mediterranean and most of the information came from Canaris."

The Englishman shoved the accelerator to the floor, as if he hoped speed could somehow erase memory. "We got so desperate, we decided the only answer was to kill him. We had it all set up when a certain Spanish Army captain got him out of the country. Do you know who that was?"

Talbot shook his head.

"Francisco bloody Franco!"

At first, the red tiled roofs and white walls of the Montoya ranch loomed in the distance like a vision from the American southwest or the vast valleys of northern Mexico. On right and left in the pastures grazed herds of sleek black bulls. They gazed at the passing car with lordly disdain. "Don't worry," Moorman said. "They never attack when they're in a group. Only when they're alone and insecure. Maybe that's nature's way of teaching us the value of alliances."

The ranch was a small town unto itself, with stables, outbuildings, corrals, in which bulls snorted and gamboled, others in which stallions pranced. The Marquesa greeted them in the bare entrance hall of the main house wearing a sombrero and leather skirt. The ancient butler, the lord of the Madrid residence, escorted them down a long unheated second-floor corridor that still seemed to possess the chill of winter. Talbot's bedroom was surprisingly small, with only a single chest of drawers and a red damask canopied bed beneath a beamed ceiling.

Downstairs he found guests gathering in the cavernous living room before a roaring blaze in a huge stone fireplace. Everyone was drinking Scotch, "direct from the highlands," the Marquesa claimed, beaming at Moorman. The Marquesa casually led Talbot to her nephew, Rafael Sanchez. His younger brother Jaime was standing a few feet away assuring an attractive brunette that the Germans were going to win the war by the end of the year.

"How did Jaime get into the family?" Moorman said, joining them with a full glass of Scotch.

"A state secret," Rafael Sanchez said.

Jaime Sanchez overheard the remark and swung his truculent

head and heavy body in their direction. He gave his older brother a glare that was totally lacking in family affection. "Allow me to introduce Maria Bucholz, a living conjunction of Spain and Germany," he said, with a proprietary smile that made Talbot suspect he had sampled the union personally.

"Where does your loyalty lie, Señorita?" Rafael Sanchez asked.

"To the coming alliance between the two countries," Miss Bucholz said.

"But where does your allegiance lie?" Rafael insisted.

"I was born in Spain—but lately my soul has been wafted to Germany," Miss Sanchez said.

"El Capitan Submarino," Jaime said. "It makes me think I've gone into the wrong branch of the Navy."

"How much is Kapitanleutnant von Hoffmann paying her?" Moorman asked. "In Tangier I understand she gets as much as a hundred dollars a night."

"An Englishman could offer me five thousand!" Miss Bucholz said. "Still I would refuse him. You have no soul."

"Your manners are on a par with your morals, Captain Moorman," Jaime Sanchez said.

Berthe and Ernst von Hoffmann joined them before the fire. She was wearing a dark green suit with a skirt that displayed quite a lot of her magnificent legs. She gave Talbot a warm smile. Ernst barely said hello. Jaime Sanchez began describing how the Kapitanleutnant had joined the Tenth Italian Light Flotilla in a torpedo attack on Gibraltar two weeks ago which had sunk five ships in the anchorage. "For sheer daring, nothing in this or any other war equals the exploit," Sanchez said.

Spaniards crowded around to hear Ernst describe the unique sensation of piloting a torpedo underwater, attaching it to the hull of a British tanker and swimming to shore to watch the ship explode in a geyser of flaming oil. Moorman sizzled silently. Talbot found himself trying to identify the expression on Berthe von Hoffmann's face. Was it pride? He thought her smile was forced. But Ernst was her husband. How could a woman not admire such a daredevil?

The Marquesa invited everyone to dinner. In a huge dining room, warmed by another blazing fireplace, the table was set with ancient silver made from ore some early Marques de Montoya had personally brought home in his galleon from Peru or Mexico. At the head of the table sat the present Marques, staring into space. His blank eyes seemed swollen with nameless pain. The angular, shriveled face was so drained of life, it almost seemed mummified.

"My husband hasn't spoken since the Communists killed our last living son as they fled Madrid two years ago," the Marquesa said. "I always hope that in the company I assemble here, he'll find a face that will lure him back to humanity."

No one at the table seemed to have that magic component, in spite of the presence of generals, admirals, high-ranking officials from the Foreign Ministry and two young matadors, each from a famous family of *toreros*. The Marques continued to stare into his private emptiness, ignoring the food on his plate.

The war dominated the conversation. The British claimed they had bombed Cologne with a thousand planes two nights ago. The story made the Spaniards uneasy. Someone maintained the British did not have a thousand planes in their entire air force. Someone else reported that a friend in the Spanish embassy in London said the British were no longer eating white bread, and were rationing almost everything else, especially sugar.

Talbot was more interested in the whispers and smiles Ernst von Hoffmann devoted to Maria Bucholz, while Berthe watched from the other side of the table. Talbot asked her if she had returned to Horcher's since their visit. She said they could not afford the prices. Thereafter, one of the young matadors, Ordonez, who was seated on her right, absorbed most of her attention.

After dinner, Talbot strolled in the estate's gardens with Rafael Sanchez. The temperature had plunged and he was muffled in a black serape, which covered his shoulders and half his face. Like many Spaniards, he feared the night air. "Your brother told me your father lost a leg off Cuba in 1898," Talbot said. "That makes me a bit nervous about asking you for help."

"My father never held the slightest ill will against America for that unfortunate event," Rafael said. "On the contrary, it convinced him—and many others—that Spain had to change her ways and find common ground with the liberal spirit of the modern world."

"Is he still alive?"

"He was assassinated by the anarchists in Barcelona while visiting my mother's family, shortly before the Civil War began."

Talbot asked him if it would be possible to obtain the charts of the coastal waters Washington wanted so badly.

"Interesting," Sanchez said. "Yesterday Captain Moorman asked me the same thing—for the coastal waters of southern France—and Sicily. We refused him, of course. Our policy with the British is quite intransigent, at present. But we hope to persuade you Americans to give us more oil. In another two months, if a shipment doesn't arrive, our electricity will fail completely. We'll have to ground our commercial air lines."

Talbot brought up the question of German submarines being armed and serviced in Spanish ports. Sanchez's voice became even more hollow behind his serape. "Officially, Spain's posture in this war is neutral. But there are many people in Spain with different political opinions. We are a large, complex country. You had German sympathizers in your own country, did you not? The America First Committee? We cannot undertake to police every port in Spain. Our limited resources are committed to maintaining our fragile political unity. But if you can bring us evidence—photographs, eyewitness reports—of such activity, we'll act to stop it."

Sanchez excused himself and retreated to the nearest fireplace. It was a fairly safe bet that none of the pictures or eyewitness reports would come from the Spanish. Talbot would have to dig them up on his own.

Moorman bore down on him. "What the devil is the matter with you?" he snarled. "You barely looked at her all through dinner. How many times do I have to send you the message?"

"Go to hell," Talbot said, leaving his ally fuming in the cold dark courtyard.

Inside, most of the guests had gone to bed. Only Jaime Sanchez, Ernst von Hoffmann and Maria Bucholz were drinking before the moribund fire. On the other side of room, the young matador Ordonez was still conversing intensely with Berthe.

"Are you looking forward to the *tienta* tomorrow, Talbot?" Ernst asked in very loud German. "Matadors Ordonez and Rapela are going to give me some early morning lessons. Would you care to join us?"

Maria Bucholz gazed adoringly at her superman. The sneer on

Jaime Sanchez's porcine face implied German superiority was about to be demonstrated again. Talbot had let the Kapitanleutnant sink his destroyer. How could he presume to challenge him in the bullring? Berthe's beautiful face was expressionless but Talbot thought he saw concern in her eyes. "I can hardly wait," he said.

24

EL TORERO AMERICANO

Berthe von Hoffmann lay alone in her bed beside the open window. A new moon was peering from the starry sky, like a bewildered traveler in search of directions. Tomorrow she was going to watch Ernst try to humiliate Jonathan Talbot in the bullring. In her purse was a message from Admiral Canaris, urgently requesting a progress report.

Just before they left for La Mancha in Ernst's Bugatti, an Englishman had telephoned. "Do you know your husband has become infatuated with the most expensive whore in Tangier?" he said. "He's brought her to Madrid. Her name is Maria Bucholz."

Three hours later, Jaime Sanchez was introducing her to the woman, who looked neither expensive (her hair, her dress, were at least two years out of style) nor particularly whorish, although Berthe was unsure how whorishness looked in Spain. In Germany it was usually grotesquely blatant, in the style of an Expressionist painting. Ernst blandly informed her that Maria was a daring double agent who took money from the English and worked for Germany. She had obtained priceless information on the Gibraltar mine fields for them. During dinner, the looks, the whispers Ernst and Maria exchanged left no doubt that the English telephone caller had told the truth.

Ernst was probably in her bed even now, making love to her with the exultant knowledge that his sentimental fool of a wife was only a few doors away. Perhaps he was even confiding to giggling whorish Maria that his wife did not appreciate German hardness. While Maria exclaimed that she did. Ohhhh she did.

Berthe realized she and Ernst had begun playing the subjection game again. He had given no inkling of his sense of inferiority when he was the swaggering pursuer. The truculence, the sensitivity to real or imagined slights, had begun only after their marriage. He had resisted her politely, then stubbornly, then churlishly when she tried to persuade him to read Kantorowicz's *Frederick II,* Lasker-Schuler's poetry and her other favorite books. "I'm not your pupil!" he had raged. "I'm your husband!"

She had accepted it, she had even told herself it was typically German, which somehow soothed her anger into resignation. Germany's history for the past one hundred years could be explained by this morbid fear of subjection—and when she married Ernst she was also marrying Germany. It was perfectly clear. Lothar Engle had explained it to her in a scathing letter, hand-delivered on her wedding day.

Berthe stared up at the plaintive new moon. Should she make a wish? Instead she would listen to her body, to the anger and desire that were gathering there. Her hand slid slowly through her mound to the warm wet darkness between her thighs. Her finger found the little erectile tongue that spoke of love in a thousand swarming images behind her closed eyes. The black veil descended across her face, her buttocks tightened, her nipples hardened, she was the young widow before her Expressionist mirror again. She did not need Ernst, maybe she did not need any man, maybe all she needed was Germany and these waves of impersonal desire in order to fulfill Admiral Canaris's urgent command.

In the morning she awoke with Ernst snuffling beside her. She did not remember him coming to bed. A servant was knocking on the door, announcing that the *tienta* would begin in half an hour. Steaming mugs of coffee were on a tray beside the door to deal with the chill that permeated the room. Berthe further lowered the temperature by not saying a word to Ernst.

Outside, a harsh April sun cut through the layers of cold night air. The company assembled on the patio of the main house, the Marquesa chattering in her seemingly artless style, while two servants led the automaton who had been her husband, image of Spain's agony, toward a miniature bullring near the corrals. The young matador Ordonez, who had talked so intensely to her last night about love and death—ideas that in his feverish opinion linked Spain and Germany—accorded Berthe a special bow.

In the arena, the other young matador, Rapela, was giving lessons in handling the magenta and yellow cape to Ernst and Jonathan Talbot. The Marquesa sat with Moorman, discussing the bull. They agreed it was the noblest of nature's animals. The elephant was more majestic, the tiger more terrible. But none could match the bull's terrific courage. "When he's isolated, he'll attack anything that moves," Moorman said.

"Bulls have attacked autos, trains, airplanes, trucks. Often it is the machine that has lost," the Marquesa said in her most cheerful tone. "I love them. They're the male essence, blindly, gloriously brave. They alone in the animal kingdom have *pundonor.*"

Berthe asked what *pundonor* meant. The Marquesa said it was untranslatable. Literally, it was a contraction of *punta de honor*, point of honor. But in Spanish it meant something far more profound. "It's bravery without limits," she said. "It makes Spain the most terrible and beautiful country in the world."

"It's a form of insanity," Moorman growled. Everyone around him hurled imprecations on the English for their failure to appreciate the spiritual dimensions of life. But he refused to retract his opinion, even when someone began reciting Tennyson's "Charge of the Light Brigade."

While the men argued, the Marquesa explained a *tienta* to Berthe. She would see no bulls. The animals would be heifers, the future mothers of bulls. It was important to estimate their courage and stamina—because it was from the mother that the young bull derived these crucial qualities. She would not see a fight to the death. These animals were much too valuable to be killed.

The first heifer came hurtling out of the chute into the ring, a black snorting streak. Matador Rapela showed her the magenta side of his cloak and she rampaged toward it as if it were her only enemy on earth. With exquisite grace, Rapela sidestepped and spun on the balls of his feet like a ballet dancer as the heifer turned on her own length and charged again. After a half-dozen passes, in which the heifer's thin, sharp horns came within inches of the young matador's flesh, the spectators were shouting Olé! Into the ring cantered a picador, waving his cape, calling to attract the animal's attention. She charged him just as ferociously and as the horse danced away, the picador sank his long steel-tipped lance into her hump. The heifer wheeled and charged him again, unbothered by the pain.

"There's a brave one!" the Marquesa said, as the picador again scored with his lance and the heifer, blood streaming down her flanks, returned for a third charge.

Three of the next five heifers, who were fought alternately by Rapela and Ordonez, were equally brave. The other two were deficient. One quit, bellowing with pain, at the first thrust of the picador. The second was so peaceably inclined, she would not even charge Rapela. She ambled around the ring like a tourist out for exercise. "What will happen to her?" Berthe asked.

"You'll be dining on her at Horcher's before long," Moorman said.

Hardness, Berthe thought. Maybe Spain and Germany had a lot in common.

Ordonez fought the sixth heifer to complete the tienta. He had a showier style than Rapela, performing passes with his back turned, pretending to administer the death stroke when the heifer, winded from repeated charges, stood there, head down, eyeing him sullenly. That produced a last ferocious charge in which for an incredible moment animal and man seemed to blend within the flowing folds of the cape. The Marquesa told Berthe he was a member of a famous family of matadors. "One day that boy will achieve duende," she said.

Berthe asked her what *duende* meant. "Literally it means spirit," the Marquesa said. "But it's even more untranslatable than *pundonor*. We use it to designate an imperishable fragment of beauty that can only be achieved two or three times in a life."

It was Ernst's turn to perform. After a final conference with Rapela and a mock bow to the spectators, he strode to the center of the ring to encounter a heifer with only a modest amount of courage. She charged without much enthusiasm and had to be tempted to repeat the performance by numerous displays of the cape. Yet each time the animal attacked, Berthe felt a rush of panic, a blind appeal for her husband's survival. It was almost as bad as her night thoughts when he was at sea in the Ritterboot. Was he still winning the subjection game—in spite of everything he had said and done?

As the picador and ranch hands lured the heifer into the exit chute, a triumphant Ernst returned to the grandstand and handed the matador's cape to Jonathan Talbot. "It's like being on the wrong end of a torpedo attack, Commander," Ernst said. "I hope you have better luck this time."

Behind her, Berthe heard Moorman mutter: "Bastard!"

"Commander," Jaime Sanchez said, in a voice that was clearly intended to be heard by all the spectators. "Would you like to fight a real bull? You seem so confident of your ability—"

"Sure," Talbot said. "Bring him on."

A typical male, Berthe thought. He could not refuse the opportunity to outshine Ernst. As Talbot reached the center of the arena, out of the entrance chute hurtled a very real bull. Anger gleamed in his violent eyes, his inky black hide. With flesh and muscle packed on his flanks and haunches, he looked twice as big as the heifers. On his chest was a patch of white that resembled a bulging heart.

"Notice his right horn," Jaime Sanchez said. "We haven't been able to sell him because of it but in all other respects he's a very good bull."

The right horn, Berthe saw, had a crooked downward curl at the tip. "He could be badly hurt!" the Marquesa said.

Ernst was grinning at Maria Bucholz. He was part of the scheme. A wild almost uncontrollable anger swept Berthe as the bull lowered his head and charged Talbot's presentation of the cape. Ernst and his friend Sanchez were not simply trying to humiliate Talbot. They were hoping to maim him—even murder him.

"*Sinverguenza!*" murmured the Marquesa as the bull stormed past the barely withdrawn cape and wheeled for another charge. Berthe could only grasp the literal meaning of the exclamation—sin without shame. But she sensed it was an epithet aimed at Jaime Sanchez.

The bull pawed the earth, swinging his head from side to side, making it difficult to predict the angle of his next charge. Talbot fluttered the cape, a grim half-smile on his angular face. Did he realize he was confronting sudden death? If so, he did not show the slightest concern. Perhaps he was aware that his pundonor was being tested.

With a snort the bull charged again. As Talbot sidestepped, the bull swerved and for a flashing second the left horn, as sharp and deadly as a spear, seemed about to penetrate the American's groin. But Talbot sucked in his belly and it missed him by a fraction of an inch.

"Olé!" Moorman bellowed.

Talbot turned his head to give him a grateful grin. "Oh no," murmured the Marquesa. Berthe realized a matador never took his eyes off the bull. With a kind of sixth sense, the bull wheeled within his length and charged with incredible ferocity. He hit Talbot on the right hip, knocking him ten feet. The bull spun, head low for a goring. But Ordonez rushed into the arena from behind the barrier and flashed his cape just in time to distract him into a charge in his direction.

Talbot struggled to his feet and waved Ordonez back behind the barrier. "I'm all right," he said, flapping his cape. Ordonez retreated and the bull charged Talbot again. Dragging his left leg, he reeled back with only inches to spare. It was a grotesque parody of the grace displayed by Rapela and Ordonez but Talbot's stubborn refusal to quit was somehow poignant to Berthe.

"Pundonor!" It was the Marques de Montoya. He was standing up, pointing to Talbot. "Pundonor!"

For some reason the word galvanized the picador, who had been sitting on his horse behind the barrier, an impassive spectator. He pranced into the arena and the bull wheeled to assault this larger, more inviting target. The picador bloodied him, which only inspired an even more furious charge.

"That's enough. Get him out of there!" the Marquesa shouted.

The ranch hands waved capes around the exit chute. The bull charged them and vanished into the shadows. In the center of the arena, a swaying Talbot let his cape droop disconsolately around his feet and crumpled into the dust. Berthe swung herself over the grandstand railing and ran to him without thinking. She only wanted to find out if he was seriously hurt. "It's all right, he's gone!" she said, as she knelt beside him.

Talbot's eyes fluttered; he was in a daze. The Marquesa joined Berthe, babbling excitedly. Her husband had spoken! He had paid tribute to Talbot's courage. No, more than courage, to pundonor, the untranslatable attribute that every man must possess.

She and Berthe and a concerned Ordonez helped Talbot to his feet while the spectators gave him an Olé! "Too kind," he muttered. "Too kind. I made a fool of myself again."

"No you didn't," Berthe said.

Back at the main house, a doctor was summoned to examine the battered victim. He was pronounced badly bruised about the hip; his wrist was sprained and one or two ribs were probably broken, but he was otherwise sound. "A matador with such injuries would fight the next day," the doctor said.

"Sign me up!" Talbot said. "I'm ready for Madrid."

At lunch, everyone but Ernst and Jaime Sanchez was cheerful. Maria Bucholz was flattered by the intense attention of young Rapela, who had never been to Tangier. The Marques de Montoya sat at the head of the table, his eyes devouring their faces like a man who had awakened from a coma. He raised his wine glass and toasted Jonathan Talbot. "To the son of a noble house!" he said. "A man of courage like his father."

Talbot looked like he might explode with pride. How peculiar these Americans were, Berthe thought. Proud of their democracy, yet eager to worship their ancestors, like an aristocracy. But peculiarities, differences, were irrelevant. Her doubts had been resolved by that vicious drama in the bullring. The tienta had tested not only the heifers and the would-be matadors.

After lunch everyone retired to their rooms for the traditional siesta. Berthe offered to help Talbot up the stairs. "Do you realize what they tried to do?" she said, as he limped down the long bare hall, filled with spring sunshine.

"They gave me the wildest bull they could find, I know that much."

"They tried to kill you," she said.

He looked a little skeptical—as if getting run down by a raging bull failed to prove her point. "I want to protect you," she said. "Perhaps you can also protect me."

"There's nothing in this world that would give me more pleasure. But I don't want you to risk anything for me."

"Let me decide that," she said in the same low, unnatural voice. A glance over her shoulder found the hall empty. Would Ernst take his siesta with Maria Bucholz? Probably. But she did not particularly care whether he waited in vain for her in their room. The Path was unmistakably clear now.

They were in Talbot's room, beside a red-curtained bed. She closed the door and turned the heavy old-fashioned key in the lock and opened her arms to him. Somehow she liked the idea of loving him this first time in daylight. It was a lovely counterpoint to the dark veil of seduction and deception that she would have to weave around their love. She also liked the idea of loving him wounded, bruised, bandaged—the doctor had taped his broken ribs. She had to be gentle with him. The slightest pressure would cause him pain. That too was a consoling counterpoint for the brutal politics into which they would eventually plunge for Germany's sake.

"I love you," she said, as she unbuttoned his shirt. "Can you believe that?"

"No," he said. "It's too incredible."

"I haven't been happy with Ernst for a long time," she said.

The shirt was off. She ran her fingers over the adhesive on his ribs. "Are you in too much pain?" she said. The answer was a kiss as violent as the charge of the young bull. She let him unbutton her blouse, unhook her brassiere. The bravery, the ferocity, of those heifers had made no impression on him. He was a man, incapable of imagining love in any other way but as a conqueror. Did she want it any other way? No, she was ready and willing to abandon primary resentments, to grope toward some precarious authenticity that would perhaps only be visible to her.

His lips roved her neck, her breasts. Slowly, solemnly, their tongues greeting, exploring, they shed the rest of their clothes. She shivered in the room's cold, left over from the night. The sun was warming the other side of the house. Under the covers, she sought his warmth but all she felt at first was his cold hands on her back. He held her against him for a long time, his mouth in her hair.

"You're so beautiful you scare me," he whispered.

"I never think of myself as beautiful. I dislike the word," she said. "It separates me from the word woman. That's all I want to be. A woman. A woman who loves you."

"You'll have to kill me to stop me from thinking you're beautiful," he said, with that maddening honesty. "I'm going to love you for the rest of my life."

"Don't make such promises. They lead to heartbreak," Berthe said. "Let's only vow to love each other for as long as we're in Spain."

"I'll follow you to Germany. I'll follow you into the Reich chancellery, into Gestapo headquarters."

"No!" She suddenly glimpsed how terrible it could become. How she, not Ernst, could become his killer. "Let's make a promise now. Not to trade inflated words. Let's make everything we say as close to the truth as possible."

That was very good, Berthe. Knowing how far from the truth you are now. Admiral Canaris had chosen well. You are gifted in the art of deception after all. Perhaps you've finally found your metier.

He was kissing, caressing her breasts, his hand was roving her thighs, searching and finding her clitoris. Last night's desire swarmed against her eyes again, no longer impersonal, instead focused totally on this man, this stranger from beyond the ocean, with the blood of Englishmen and perhaps a dozen other races in his veins.

"Now?" he whispered and when she said yes oh yes he entered her. Now the beaker would begin to fill, to foam, there would be pleasure and release and murmured words of mutual satisfaction, then a sweet siesta in this warmest of beds.

"I love you," he whispered, moving slowly, tenderly, within her. "I love you."

Where was the beaker? Someone had misplaced or stolen it. Something was happening to beautiful Berthe, the Abwehr's best bet. There were no images behind her closed eyes, there was only a cloud of darkness, as if the young widow's veil had somehow been inserted under her skin. "I love you," he whispered, moving steadily now, but still with exquisite slowness. "I love you."

A cloud of darkness and behind or beneath it Else Lasker-Schuler whispering:

> I want to listen closely at your heart
> In your remotest nearness find my counterpart

No, it could not be happening. She groped frantically in the darkness for her lost beaker. She could not tolerate the pain, the confusion, the consequences of love. She almost prayed, she almost asked God not to let it happen but she recoiled from the blasphemy.

"I love you, I love you," he whispered. He was kissing her throat, her breasts, his tongue swarmed in her mouth. He moved against her clitoris and desire surged through her body. Then he was thrusting again and a dark voice whispered: *Ich kann nicht anders.*

Her breath had ceased to exist, she was absorbing air through some other medium. Her heart, her lungs, her flesh, began to dissolve. Only her skin remained over a cavern of bones, filled with white fire. "Now?" he said, stroking again with a fiercer more insistent rhythm. She saw the bull with the bulging heart on his breast lunging toward her, a heaving wall of darkness. "Now?"

Did she say yes? How could she with her tongue in his mouth, with her body bent like a bow against him? He was coming and she was coming and he was coming and she was coming and there was only one thing, a single presence in the red-curtained bed. "Oh, oh, oh!" Berthe cried, half a tribute to unknown depths and heights of honesty and mystery and hope, half a lament to the burden of the Marquesa de Montoya's favorite poem. She could hear her gleeful voice croaking the fateful words.

How wily are the ways of love.

25

IN THE COUNTRYSIDE OF THE STAR

"Old chap, it was all over both your faces when you came to dinner," Moorman said, as he and Talbot roared back to Madrid along the empty highway.

The raw bruise on Talbot's cheek burned as if someone had applied a blowtorch to it. Chips of pain throbbed in his battered hip, syncopating with savage slivers from his cracked ribs. He barely noticed these pangs. Gone too was Moorman's ability to intimidate and infuriate him. He did not care if the sky fell on him. He was in love with Berthe von Hoffmann.

"The expression on the Kapitanleutnant's face—" Moorman chortled.

Crammed into the tiny back seat was the young matador, Ordonez, who chanted Spanish hymns to Berthe's beauty. He begged Talbot to obtain a picture. Even a snapshot. He would wear it against his heart when he faced his first bull in Madrid.

"Do you think Hoffmann will do anything to her?" Talbot asked Moorman.

"He can hardly play the outraged husband with that tramp from Tangier on his arm," Moorman said.

"I hope you're right."

"Of course I'm right," Moorman said. "How did you do it, old boy? I insist on a complete recital."

"It's none of your goddamn business!" Talbot said. "It's not the business of the British government or the American government. It's a strictly private matter."

"There's no such thing in the middle of a war. Especially in the middle of this war," Moorman said. "Either you're useful to me, Talbot, or you're going home on the first rustbucket I can find departing Gibraltar for New Orleans by way of Madagascar. You'll be at sea so long your wife will have to shave off the barnacles to recognize you!"

"Angelical, a creature of the moon, a being from beyond the stars," moaned Ordonez in the back seat.

Talbot decided there was only one way to deal with Moorman: lie. He would pretend to be his faithful servant and put him off with endless evasions. No power on earth, not even a firing squad personally commanded by the Prime Minister of England or the President of the United States, was going to make him sacrifice Berthe von Hoffmann's love to their hungry pursuit of victory. In the first place he did not believe she had anything important to tell him. Even if she did, he was prepared to remain on the shadowy border of treachery to protect their love.

"I promise you I'll do my best to find out everything she knows," he said.

Too extravagant. Moorman squinted at him with those nasty, knowing eyes. But he said nothing for the moment. So it began.

At first Berthe came to his apartment as a solicitous nurse. The Madrid doctor who examined Talbot at Moorman's insistence ordered him to stay in bed for a week. She arrived with packages from the German embassy's kitchen, knockwurst and pastrami and a beer that was so yeasty and thick, it was like another course of food. They picnicked on his double bed. Afterward they made gentle, careful love and sat on the balcony, looking down on the teeming street life of the Calle de Echegaray.

Again and again, Talbot had to remind himself she was real. She was there, close enough to touch, kiss. Her skin was so white, so lustrous, the effect of sunlight on it was magical. It blended with her blond hair, her long blond eyelashes, the pale red of her lips to create an otherworldly effect. Ordonez was right. She was angelical, a creature of moonlight.

He told her about the boyish matador's infatuation, his desperate desire for a picture. He had already telephoned Talbot twice. "No,"

Berthe said. "I don't want to be part of that bestial business."

"I'm not an aficionado. But it's part of Spain," Talbot said, surprised by her vehemence. "Someday we'll visit the Caves of Altamira, where they've found paintings of bulls thousands of years old."

"I don't care!" Berthe said. There was a long pause. "But I would like to see Altamira."

"We'll go as soon as I can handle a car."

"It would be better if we met outside Madrid."

"Does Ernst know?"

"I think so. But he's saying nothing for the time being. Maria Bucholz is keeping him happy."

"Are you jealous of her?"

"I was angry at first. But that's not why I came to you."

He decided to match her honesty. "Moorman wants me to find out what Ernst is doing with Jaime Sanchez. I told him I'd try to persuade you to tell me. But it was a total absolute lie."

She smiled and lifted his hand to her mouth. "I've made you do something against your nature. Perhaps this whole thing is against your nature. You're being unfaithful to your wife."

"I told you she was out of my life. Now she's out forever."

"Don't take satisfaction in something so sad."

Pain throbbed in Talbot's chest. Was it his ribs or his conscience? He thought of Annie's anguished face in the kitchen doorway the night he left. "I love you so much—it obliterates her," he said.

For a moment he thought she was going to weep. Why did that passionate protestation trouble her? There was so much to understand, to learn, about this woman. Meanwhile, Moorman reminded him that they continued to lose the war. Almost every day he sent Talbot newspaper and intelligence reports of more sinkings by the U-boats in the Atlantic and on the East Coast, where the number of ships lost was, Moorman grimly reported, nearing 700. Rainbow Five's plan to invade Europe in 1943 was sinking in this rampage.

The only good news—and it was only semigood—came from the Pacific, where on May 7 an American fleet had clashed with a Japanese task force in the Coral Sea, north of Australia. It was a drawn battle, each side losing a carrier. That left the Americans with only three carriers, while the Japanese still had over a dozen. The Spanish newspapers trumpeted it as a Japanese victory, which did not raise morale at the American and British embassies.

Talbot tried to put the story out of his mind. It was too painful to think about classmates and friends fighting the battles he had dreamt about at Annapolis and the Naval War College. Berthe von Hoffmann became his consolation.

At first, because Talbot found driving with cracked ribs extremely painful, they kept their excursions short. They used a black 1940 Packard he borrowed from the embassy car pool. Counselor Hamilton Boileau had looked owlish when Talbot requested the car. He said joy riding was strictly forbidden because of the gasoline shortage. What was the purpose of this trip? "Espionage," Talbot said. "Captain Moorman at the British embassy will confirm it."

Boileau's diplomatic rigor relaxed. "It's all over Madrid," he said, with a playful leer. "Some people are born lucky."

Their first excursion was to Avila, only an hour from Madrid. The city was crammed with churches—and amazingly devoid of people. They walked the streets for an hour without encountering a single human being. It finally dawned on Talbot that most of the population had fled or been killed in the Civil War. In one of the churches, Berthe got into an endless conversation with an austere old nun about St. Teresa, the mystic who was Avila's patron saint. Talbot was bored and did not try to conceal it, coughing loudly and wandering off to stare at the statuary. Berthe apologized and tried to explain why Teresa interested her. She was a woman who seemed to have direct access to God in mystical prayer—and was apparently unbothered by the male-dominated world in which she had lived and worked.

Talbot scoffed at the notion of anyone having direct access to God. "Did any third parties monitor their conversations?" he said.

"In those days, God was not a subversive," Berthe said.

That night, when they made love, Berthe seemed to slip away from him down some secret alley in her self. There was none of their original sense of joyous encounter; in fact, very little joy. She knew it was happening. "I'm sorry," she said, as they drove back to Madrid. "We won't go there again."

"What was wrong? Was it my fault?"

"No. It was mine." No further explanation was forthcoming.

The following week, Talbot took Berthe to Segovia. Poised like a cruise ship between two rivers, its prow was the cream and gold Alcazar, soaring into the sky with the Guadamarra Mountains in the distance. They lunched in the shadow of a Roman aqueduct, with 165 lyrical arches, which Berthe counted with German exactitude, winning a bet from him. He told her about his prophetic nickname, which amused her. But she decided she preferred to call him Jonathan. She told him about her awful mother-in-law.

Still, Talbot was repeatedly jarred by abrupt dissonances. When they visited the tomb of Maria del Salto, a woman who had been unjustly accused of adultery and hurled from one of Segovia's many cliffs, Talbot scoffed at the legend that Maria had prayed to the Virgin and been rescued as she fell. "Don't ridicule such things!" Berthe said. "There are deep truths in them."

Talbot began to realize she was religious in a way he found very difficult to understand. As she explained it on the way back from Segovia, holiness was a primary human category, a fundamental experience that compelled respect. "Even if we're incapable of sharing it, we should revere it," she said.

"That's the kind of abstract German thinking my father used to laugh at," he said.

She gave him a look that seemed closer to hate than love. "I hope you don't despise everything German. I'm a German to the deepest depths of my soul."

In a flash of his prophetic self, Talbot heard pain, sorrow, personal defeat in those words. "What if Germany loses the war? Will you stop loving me?" he asked.

"Will you stop loving me, if they win it?"

"No. I've told you that already."

"Would you feel the same way if a German Army invaded America, smashed your cities to rubble, enslaved your people?"

"Yes."

"You know that will never happen. You're secure behind your oceans. That makes it easy to say yes."

She was right, of course. It pained him to realize how far he was from complete honesty with this woman. "Germany's total defeat, total destruction, is far more plausible. It's very, very difficult to love someone who wishes that fate for your country. Yet it's happened to me. I don't completely understand it."

There was something incomprehensible about her decision to love him. He felt blessed to a degree that induced bewilderment. But he was constantly shaken by bouts of uncertainty, doubt, even suspicion. Meanwhile Moorman relentlessly pursued him for information. Talbot began to wonder how much longer he could satisfy him with doubletalk about Berthe's delicate feelings.

The day after they returned from Segovia, Berthe sent Talbot a book, Ernst Kantorowicz's *Frederick II*. "This may help you understand what I—and others—feel about Germany," she wrote in a small, precise hand.

Talbot plunged into the book—and found himself mesmerized. Frederick was a medieval philosopher-king with enormous ambitions. At one point, in the middle of his fifty-six-year reign as Holy Roman Emperor, he ruled Germany, Italy, Sicily and the Kingdom of Jerusalem, wrested from the Moslems by the Crusaders. With some justification, he was called *"stupor mundi"*—wonder of the world. He surrounded himself with poets, painters and canny businessmen. His fleets traded with Spain and Egypt and Morocco. But in the end, beset by rivals, not the least of whom was the Pope, his empire collapsed and Germany's dream of ruling Europe vanished with him, to remain little more than a memory for the next six hundred years.

A few days after he finished *Frederick II*, Talbot received a phone call from Rafael Sanchez, asking him to come to the foreign ministry. It was Talbot's first visit to the elaborate building from which Spain conducted her international relations. It was not exactly reassuring to find black uniformed Falangist guards on the stairway, raising their arms in the Fascist salute. But Sanchez's comfortable office seemed to be a pro-American enclave. "Those charts you wish to obtain," he said in a carefully neutral voice. "They can be purchased from a man named Garcia in Coruna. They will cost you a thousand dollars. Here is his address." He apologized for dragging him to the foreign ministry, explaining he did not want to give him the information on the telephone, which was probably tapped.

As they strolled to the door, Sanchez said he hoped the Falangist guards had not troubled him. They would soon be gone. Franco was replacing the Foreign Minister, Serrano Suner, the head of the Falange, with a man named Jordana. Back in the American embassy, when Talbot told this to Counselor Boileau, he almost leaped out of his striped pants. "That's *very* important," he said. "It's the first evidence we've seen that Franco is tilting away from Hitler."

Coruna was in Galicia, Spain's northernmost province, only a few dozen miles from Spain's biggest naval base, El Ferrol—a logical place to purloin coastal charts. Talbot asked Berthe to join him, without mentioning the nature of his business in Coruna. On the way back they could visit the Caves of Altamira with their prehistoric bulls, on the coast south of Galicia.

They discussed Kantorowicz's *Frederick II* as they zoomed along the empty roads. Around them the fields sparkled in May sunshine but Berthe's voice was drenched in melancholy. "That book had more to do with Hitler's rise to power than anyone outside Germany realizes. To an incredible degree it aroused our yearning for a great leader—and the Nazis declared Hitler was the man. The yearning was so intense, so blinding, we didn't—or couldn't—look behind the image at the reality."

She was silent as they climbed into the forbidding mountains that separated Galicia from the rest of Spain. "The author of *Frederick II*—Kantorowicz—was Jewish. God has an odd sense of humor, don't you think?"

"What does God have to do with it?"

"I sense his presence in my life."

In a low, intense voice, she began telling him about the day she experienced the stench of evil in Hitler's words. Talbot was swept by a terrific dread. He sensed a force as powerful as a tornado in reverse, a fearful suction dragging Berthe away from him. He wanted to seize her with both hands and vow in the very face of the monster his perpetual resistance.

"Although I dread it—although the idea fills me with horror—I want to do everything I can to help defeat Hitler. I believe God has summoned me to join the attempt."

They were descending the barrier mountains to the rugged green landscape of Galicia as Berthe said these words. She writhed in the seat as she spoke them, as if some invisible force, independent of her will, was expelling them from her body. Again, Talbot was swept by a terrific premonition that if he welcomed her offer, he was exposing himself to loss, pain, defeat.

"Moorman chose well, didn't he," Berthe said. "Perhaps he's the one with supernatural powers."

"That obnoxious dried-up little son of a bitch? Not a chance."

He was trying to say he refused to work for Moorman, he did not care what she could tell him. But he could not manage it. They were fighting a war. Those drowning merchant sailors off the East Coast, the British soldiers waiting for Rommel's next thrust at Cairo, were real. If this woman could help him defeat Germany, he had to accept her offer.

Along the highway they noticed an unusual number of people trudging westward. Many had rucksacks on their backs. They carried primitive staffs, a kind of third leg to keep them going. A few rode mules. Almost all wore a silver or brass scallop shell clipped to their coats. Slowing for a curve, they saw a barrel-shaped woman propped against a boulder, weeping copiously. A morose nine- or ten-year-old boy sat beside her. "Stop!" Berthe said.

She sprang out and talked earnestly with the woman. In a moment she was picking up her rucksack and helping her and the boy into the car. Their body odor made Talbot's eyes water. "Her name is Teresa Santana and this is her son, Miguel. They're on pilgrimage to Santiago de Compostella. Her strength has given out and so has their food. She hasn't eaten in two days."

Talbot got out his road map. Santiago was the regional capital—and it was on the road to Coruna, more or less. "Why are you going to Santiago?" Berthe asked in Spanish.

"You mean you don't know?" said the woman in a voice that could easily smash mirrors. "It's the burying place of Saint James, the apostle who was the brother of Jesus. He converted Spain to the true faith, and his followers brought his body back to his favorite place on earth. Perhaps in heaven too, because he has returned so often to help us."

"*Santiago y cierre España!*" shouted the boy.

"That's what the knights cried out when they fought the Moors," Señora Santana bellowed. "Saint James and close ranks for Spain! They never lost a battle. Whenever the horsemen wavered or the bowmen lost their aim, Saint James appeared on his great horse with his fiery sword and they drove the infidels into the sea. Now people from all over the world come to Santiago to seek his help in other ways. They wear the humble scallop shell he used to drink from his gourd when he was here in the flesh."

"What sort of help are you seeking?" Berthe asked.

"I want Saint James to get my husband, Pablo, this boy's father, out of jail. The idiot fought for the Communists. I told him from the start Franco would win. Why not free him since he's spared his life? It makes no sense for him to lie in jail."

They stopped for lunch at a roadside *tasca*. Señora Santana wolfed down a huge plate of *percebes,* the ugly barnacles that attach themselves to the rocks along Galicia's coast, while the boy devoured ham with turnip tops. The señora asked them if they were married. When they said no, she nodded as if she had expected that answer.

In another hour they saw four brown towers in the distance. Teresa Santana excitedly told them that the towers belonged to the Cathedral of Saint James. The huge Romanesque building sat in the middle of an immense square. Teresa Santana led them to the main plaza, on the west. They entered the church through a small door and found themselves before a three-arched wall so dazzling in its profusion of beauty and humor and joy, Talbot was speechless.

This was the Portico de Gloria, Señora Santana told them triumphantly, as if she were personally responsible for it. Over a length of fifty feet and a height of sixty, a medieval sculptor had created a gallery of humanity, every face aglow with good cheer. Knaves, fools, heroes, frisky women, both beautiful and ugly, they were all here—as if Charles Dickens had translated his art into stone. Most remarkable of all was the pillar supporting the central arch. It was a Tree of Life, crammed with intricate interwoven carvings of humans and animals and vines soaring up to a joyful statue of Saint James.

Teresa Santana took Berthe's right hand and carefully placed the thumb and other fingers into five indentations in the writhing stone. "Pray," she said. "Pray to Saint James for strength to endure the worst and enjoy the best of life."

Berthe gazed up at the benevolent saint and turned to Talbot. "I'm too ashamed to pray," she said in German.

"That's a sign of intelligence," he said, also in German.

She withdrew her hand, looking hurt. Talbot let Señora Santana take his hand and place his fingers in the worn grooves. "For a thousand years, pilgrims have inserted their hands here," she shouted. "Perhaps it will bring you faith."

Where did this battleax get off telling him he had no faith? It stirred memories of conversations with Annie early in their marriage, when she had tried to make him a Catholic. He had no intention of believing in this glorification of myth and magic. Beautiful as it was, all this rigmarole about Jesus and Saint James belonged to a more credulous age.

Berthe was reading a guidebook she had bought in the square. She pointed to the tympanum above the Tree of Life pillar, where a figure of Jesus was surrounded by a man, a lion, a bull and an eagle. "That's from the first chapter of the book of Ezekiel," she said. "The prophet saw these figures emerge from a heavenly fire."

She asked Ezekiel Talbot what he thought they symbolized. "The lion is England, the bull is Germany, the eagle is America. The man is hoping he can persuade them to live together in peace and harmony so he can enjoy heaven with the bull's favorite daughter."

"I wish you took this more seriously," Berthe said. She was suddenly close to tears. Talbot could not understand it.

They walked through the vast, vaulted interior of the church to the high altar, where a stone statue of Saint James, attired in metal robes studded with diamonds, sat atop a blaze of gilt and candles. Berthe gazed up at it, looking more and more transported. Talbot began to feel threatened by her reaction to this place.

"I just realized what *Compostella* means," Berthe said. "It's a shortening of Campos de Estrella. The countryside where the star shone."

The imagery only meant more myth and magic to Talbot. He gruffly announced it was time to resume their trip to Coruna. He gave Señora Santana a one-hundred-peseta note to get her and the boy back to Barcelona. She kissed him, almost suffocating him with her body odor and said she would pray to Saint James for both of them. "May you be united in love and also in faith!" she cried.

The implication that they were united in neither irked Talbot. "Where the hell does that woman get the gall to give us advice?" he growled, as they headed out of town.

Berthe said nothing until they were on the highway, rolling past fields dotted with *horreos*, the rectangular Galician granaries, which sit on high stone legs to keep rats out of the grain. Suddenly she spoke in a low, intense voice. "There's a German submarine being repaired at the Spanish naval base in El Ferrol. Ernst is going there tomorrow to give the commander secret instructions for an attack on a Mediterranean-bound convoy. Then BDU is going to wire the boat a different set of instructions. It's a test to see if you or the British have broken their Enigma code."

Every nerve in Talbot's body went to general quarters. Was this an enormously subtle trap to find out if they had broken the code?

The Germans knew he had worked in naval intelligence. Moorman had told him the Abwehr had a dossier on everyone in the British and American embassies. "I'm afraid I don't even know what you're talking about," he said. "What's the Enigma code?"

He had to grip the wheel with both hands to keep the car on the road. Where had it gone, his commitment to love this woman with total honesty in spite of the war that raged around them? Was he a new kind of hypocrite, capable of fakery even with himself?

The lie hung in the warm spring air, as fetid as Señora Santana's body odor. "It's the code the U-boats use to communicate with their home base," Berthe said. "I've heard Ernst boast about how hard it would be to break. But apparently Admiral Dönitz is worried that some sort of break has occurred."

"I don't know anything about Enigma," he lied. "I was a mere destroyer captain until Ernst sank my ship. But it's very interesting to know there's a U-boat in El Ferrol. If I can figure out a way to see it, we can lodge a formal protest with the Spanish government."

At Coruna, stiff Atlantic winds buffeted them as Talbot drove to the Plaza de Maria Pita, a spacious square dominated by a city hall big enough for Paris. On a nearby narrow calle, he climbed four flights of stairs and knocked on an ancient sagging door. "Who is it?" growled a voice.

"A friend of Rafael Sanchez," Talbot said.

The door swung open and Talbot confronted a face that could have belonged to the old man of the sea. Drooping white mustaches, shaggy white hair, glaring eyes. "You want maps?" he said.

Talbot nodded and the man gestured him down a short hall into a room jammed with maps stuffed in cubby holes, dangling from walls. The old man pointed to a set in a leather case on a table. "They went to America with Columbus," he said. "My great-great-great-grandfather drew them. But you want something a bit more up to date, eh?"

"A bit," Talbot said.

"I've got you the official Spanish Navy stuff," he said. "It was expensive."

Talbot spread the charts on a table and found them models of clarity. The Mediterranean and Atlantic coasts of North Africa were spelled out down to the smallest bays and headlands. Shoal waters, reefs, were all lavishly visible. He paid the old man four thousand pesetas and asked him if he could use his telephone.

He called Moorman in Madrid. "I've picked up that wonderful objet d'art near Coruna that I told you about," he said. "I've found something else even more interesting. I hope you won't think it's too enigmatic. I'll tell you all about it when I get back. In the meantime, tell your patron not to do anything impulsive."

Moorman understood his phone was tapped and doubletalk was necessary. But would he get the allusion? Could he translate it into action—or, in this case—inaction? If the Germans found the British Navy hungrily circling where the U-boat was ordered to go by wireless—they would know Enigma had been broken—and enjoy the double play of smashing up the convoy in the bargain. "I can hardly wait to hear the whole story," Moorman said.

Talbot and Berthe roared on to El Ferrol, where Talbot bought a pair of field glasses in an optical store off the Plaza de España, which featured a huge statue of General Franco on horseback. He had been born and raised here, the son of a Navy clerk. They drove into the hills overlooking the wide, deep harbor; the naval base consumed a considerable chunk of the shoreline. Carefully scanning the ships in the anchorage, Talbot soon found a lone submarine, unmistakably a type VIIC, a twin of the Ritterboot, tied up at one of the more remote docks. As he watched, the U-boat's commander emerged on the bridge, wearing his white hat. The setting sun was sending long spectacular streaks of red across the Atlantic's horizon. They drove back to Coruna and ate in a seafood restaurant on the harbor's edge. In spite of the idyllic setting, Talbot felt melancholy pervading their conversation.

Berthe asked him what he would do about the submarine. "Protest," he said. "Violently. If the Spaniards want to keep eating American wheat, they better get rid of it."

Afterward they strolled the windswept harbor front holding hands. "Do you despise me for what I'm doing?" Berthe said, gazing at a stubby white fishing smack in the dusk.

"I don't completely understand it but I couldn't despise you. I love you."

"You love me in bed. But that's not me. I almost wish I was as old and ugly as the Marquesa de Montoya. Then we'd see how you really felt."

"I disagree. That is you in bed. You can't make me deny the most profound moment in my life. It was profound for you too."

She said nothing. But in the hotel room, they made strange half-hearted love. He felt her drifting away from him in a new, more alarming way, worse by far than the episodes in Avila. He sensed she was drifting away from herself as well. The lie he told her squatted on the bedpost leering at him, like a gargoyle. When he came her head was turned away, tears crept down her cheeks.

"Perhaps you're the one who's doing the despising," he said.

"I don't despise you. I admire you."

"I mean despising yourself."

Trust me. Tell me everything. They were the next logical words. But he could not say them. He had lied to her already. He could not ask her to trust him when he refused—or was unable—to trust her. Talbot lay awake for a long time, staring into the darkness. He sensed Berthe was also awake, beside him. There was a gulf as wide as El Ferrol's harbor between them.

26

MAXIMUM FEASIBLE MISUNDERSTANDING

The cold Atlantic wind hissed through the open window at the foot of the bed, making the white curtains dance in the gray dawn. Berthe von Hoffmann lay beside Jonathan Talbot, the loving witness of her treason. The loving sleeping witness, which seemed exactly right. She wanted him to sleep, even if she never closed her eyes again. She would be the sleepless sentinel of their love, ready to repel the accusing voices lurking out there on the Atlantic's heaving swells—or beneath them.

Was she incapable of adjusting her mind, her conscience, to Admiral Canaris's double standard? Or was it simply that the Admiral was not married to a submarine commander? But he had been one. He knew what it required in courage, commitment, self-sacrifice, to fight their kind of war. Yet he blandly, calmly, ordered her to begin betraying them.

Perhaps there was only one solution: tell Jonathan everything—about Canaris, the Schwarze Kapelle, Stauffenberg, Oster, Moltke. Risk the possibility of betrayal by holding out the larger hope that their love might play a part in defeating the evil that was engulfing Germany and the world. In return ask him in the name of the love he professed to sustain her faltering soul.

She would risk it. She shrugged out of her nightgown and waited for the vision to possess her. They would lie face-to-face, naked, scouring every deception, every evasion that was dividing them. It would do more than win his confidence, his loyalty. It would energize their love, lift it to a new dimension. It could never be holiness because of the vows they violated each time they kissed. But it could become brave, perhaps beautiful with the clarity of second sight.

"Jonathan," she whispered.

He muttered, snuffled, pawed at his eyes like a six-year-old. "Jonathan—"

Click. The door to the hall swung open and two figures thudded into the room, moving with almost supernatural speed. One of them wore a tan raincoat and fedora, the other wore black. The one in black, who was well over six feet, with an elongated, bony face, pressed the snout of a pistol against Berthe's cheek. "Don't make a sound," he said. He had an unmistakable American accent.

The other one jammed his gun against the side of Jonathan's head. "Don't move, Commander," he growled. He was short and stocky, with a square, pugnacious jaw.

"What the hell is going on?" Jonathan said, trying to sit up.

"Don't *move*," the stocky gunman said, shoving Jonathan back onto the bed. "We're going to take some pictures."

The tall gunman stepped back and pulled a small camera from his coat pocket. His companion also stepped back, giving him a clear shot of the bed. The camera clicked a half-dozen times and a flash attachment winked while Jonathan's temper visibly rose.

"Are you working for that son-of-a-bitch Ernie King?" he said. "Is he going to persecute me for the rest of my life?"

"We're OSS Counterintelligence, Commander," said the stocky gunman, keeping his pistol trained on Jonathan's head. "You're at the top of our suspects list. We've been tracking your little romance with Brunhilde here since it started."

"Who's your boss here in Spain? I'm going to have you both transferred to Antarctica," Jonathan said.

The gun wielder snickered contemptuously. "Hell, he's the guy who fingered you. He's been watching you ever since he landed in Lisbon in the seat next to you."

"Holcomb? That lush is in charge of American intelligence?" Jonathan said.

"He may drink hard but he knows a double agent when he sees one. You outtalked the FBI and the ONI in that Rainbow Five leak but you're not going to diddle the OSS. We play hardball."

"You're a goddamned idiot, do you know that?"

"Don't, Jonathan!" Berthe said, grabbing his arm. "I can't believe they're Americans. They're Sicherheitdienst. Nazis! They're looking for an excuse to kill you."

"They're Americans all right," Jonathan said, glaring at them. "Americans who've seen too many Hollywood B-movies. What the hell do you think you're accomplishing here?"

"We've been tailing you, Commander," the stocky gunman said. "We saw you go to that mapmaker here in town and then head for El Ferrol, where a German submarine was waiting."

"Oh my goodness. Then what did I do?"

"She bought a guidebook. Probably full of information from the local Abwehr agent. You passed it to that optical shop guy in El Ferrol. It's on the submarine by now."

"You're absolutely full of shit, do you know that?" Jonathan said, further terrifying Berthe. "You don't have a shred of evidence to prove any of this."

"We don't? What the hell do you think Al was just doing with his camera? We'll have a lot more dope from Miss Berlin before we leave this room."

Out of his coat pocket he drew a small wire recorder and flipped it onto the bed. "Brunhilde here's going to tell us all about your friendship, what you've been slipping her besides you know what— the works."

"Berthe," Jonathan said in German. "Ignore these morons."

"Dan—the son of a bitch speaks German," Al said. He had an incongruously thin, high-pitched voice.

"So do I," Dan said. "Tell her to talk, Commander. Or we'll persuade her to do it, our way."

"If you touch her," Jonathan said. "I'll kill both of you no matter how many bullets you put in me."

"Not if we start with a bullet in your brain," Dan said. He jammed his gun against Jonathan's head.

"Go to hell," Jonathan said. His voice was incredibly steady. Berthe realized he was welcoming this chance to dispel the distrust that had oozed between them yesterday. He was going to prove to her—and to himself—that he loved her, even if it killed him.

"I assure you, gentlemen," Berthe said in her halting accented

English. "I have nothing whatsoever to tell. What has occurred between me and Commander Talbot is a completely personal matter. I have no access to any war secrets."

"Don't say another word," Jonathan said in German. "I don't want you to plead with them."

"Go to work on her," Dan said.

Al looked nonplussed. He was clearly new at this job. "You want me to use the hose?" he said.

"I don't want you to give her a pair of goddamn silk stockings!" Dan said.

From his raincoat pocket Al reluctantly drew a length of rubber hose and wrapped one end around his big palm. Beside her Berthe felt Jonathan's body tense as Al approached the bed. Berthe tried to speak to Jonathan with her eyes. *I can bear it. I can bear it.* But she knew he was going to lunge at Al. He really did not care if Dan killed him.

"If you hit that woman, I will blow a hole in your head large enough to implant a brain where at present you have nothing but a malfunctioning gland!"

In the doorway stood Captain Bernado Moorman with a pistol in his hand. His unmistakable nationality paralyzed the two Americans.

"Who the hell are you?" Dan said.

"The director of British intelligence in Spain, which makes me your immediate commander, by order of President Franklin D. Roosevelt! Now put away that gun and get the hell out of here."

Dan reluctantly lowered his gun. In one marvelously fluid motion, Jonathan bounded out of bed and punched Dan in the face, sending him crashing over a chair. Al made a lunge to protect his partner but Moorman stepped in front of him, his gun leveled. "Pick him up and get going," he said.

"Leave the camera on the bed," Jonathan said. He had Dan's gun in his hand.

Cursing under his breath, Al surrendered the camera and dragged his groaning friend into the hall. Moorman slammed the door, threw his hat on the floor and unleashed a stream of expletives, most of which Berthe did not understand. "Rommel's captured Tobruk and half our ammo and food stocks in the Mediterranean yesterday, an absolute, total balls-up," he shouted. "The panzers have broken through in the Ukraine, They're halfway to the Baku oilfields.

Every German in Madrid is dancing in the streets in front of our embassy. Every Spaniard on our payroll is changing sides—and what do I get for reinforcements? A brigade of American twits from the so-called OSS."

As her terror subsided, Berthe began to tremble and weep. How could she trust these people? What was wrong with Canaris? Was he mad or simply the cleverest liar in existence? Jonathan was trying to put his American arms around her. She recoiled from his touch. She almost asked him if he had a rubber hose in his pocket to use at the right moment. She had betrayed herself to him and his murderous countrymen in her moonstruck search for her lost father, her strayed fatherland.

"We'll get those morons out of Spain. Tomorrow. I promise you," Jonathan said.

She thought of Saint James the Pilgrim. He was also known as Saint James Matamoros. Saint James the Moorslayer. Even the saints in this misbegotten country were killers. No wonder the Americans and the British were at home here. They were blood brothers in the business of killing Germans.

Wait. How did this mindless rage explain Jonathan's readiness to die the moment that rubber hose touched her flesh? She struggled for self-control but it eluded her. She wept, ashamed of herself but still weeping.

"I found out they were following you last night," Moorman said. "I smelled trouble and decided to come in person."

Jonathan got dressed and said he and Moorman would wait for Berthe in the hotel restaurant. When she joined them, they were having an intense conversation, which they broke off abruptly when they saw her. It was enough to stir angry suspicion all over again. But suspicion of what? Moorman excused himself to make a telephone call. Jonathan reached for her hand. "Are you feeling a little better?"

"Yes," she said, withdrawing her hand. She drank coffee and listened to him reiterate his fury at the OSS men. "Are there many Americans like Dan, eager to torture German women?" she asked.

"I hope not," Talbot said.

Berthe felt lost, bewildered, horrified. She wanted to go back to the Cathedral of Saint James and place her fingers in the Tree of Life again. This morning's nightmare had uprooted her. Or had it only defined her uprooted state?

Moorman rode back to Madrid with them, asleep in the back seat most of the time. He had driven half the night to reach Coruna in the dawn. One of his Spanish agents who had not yet defected would drive his Aston Martin back later in the day. The Englishman's presence inhibited all personal conversation, for which Berthe was grateful. She felt remote, almost sullen, as if she were a captive in the front seat of the racing American car. In a way she was.

In Madrid, the newspapers were black with headlines about the British collapse at Tobruk. At her apartment, a subdued Jonathan asked if he could call her. "I'll call you," she said.

Upstairs she began writing a letter to Canaris, telling him what had happened. Everything poured out, including her suspicion that he had lied to her about her father. *I don't know what I'm doing here. I've given myself to a man who doesn't trust me, a man from a country that can hardly wait to abuse Germany. I no longer trust you. I no longer trust myself.*

It took her another hour to translate it into code for forwarding to Elisabeth von Theismann in France. As she was finishing the task, Ernst walked into the apartment. He eyed her truculently and asked in his surliest tone if she was writing to the children. "No," she said. "To a friend in Berlin."

"Have you written to the children lately?"

"Last Sunday."

"You should write every day."

"Have you written to them?"

"At their age, that's a mother's job."

"I disagree. Georg adores you. So does Greta. They'd treasure a letter from you far more than from me. Your mother has taught them to despise me."

He chose to ignore this remark. Striding over to the window, he asked her if she had heard the news about Tobruk. "The British just collapsed. It could be the beginning of the end for them in Egypt."

She said nothing.

"Berthold has joined Army Group South. He's commanding a panzer brigade. He expects to spend the summer in Baku."

She asked if Berthold's wife and children were staying in Berlin. He said they had gone to her family's estate in Silesia. Berthold thought the British would begin bombing Berlin soon. He had been to Cologne. The thousand-plane raid had done tremendous damage.

"Don't you think bombing defenseless women and children is bestial?" he said.

"Yes," she said. "But I seem to recall the Luftwaffe did the same thing to the British—and you didn't say a word."

There was fury on his face. Fury and irresolution. "I never thought you'd do such a thing, Berthe!"

"What?"

"Go to bed with that American. Humiliate me in front of the entire German community here in Madrid. It's unforgivable."

"What you're doing with Maria—flaunting her in my face—isn't?"

"It's a man's—a sailor's—way of doing things."

A sullen tropical calm seemed to envelop Berthe's body. She felt almost serene. Invulnerable to him and all the other men who were determined to use her. He was part of a general conspiracy which transcended national borders.

"I forbid you to see him again!" Ernst rose on the balls of his feet as he said this, then fell back, exasperated at her indifference.

"You'll also stop seeing Maria?"

"I don't have the slightest intention of bargaining with you."

No, that would be another humiliation. His burly friend Jaime Sanchez would immediately divine that the Kapitanleutnant had been worsted, more or less, by his devious wife. "I have no intention of bargaining with you, either," she said.

Her voice thudded against the oozing walls of the apartment. By some trick they had sailed the entire building into the Equatorial Zone. "I'm not here in Madrid as your wife. I'm an agent of the Abwehr. Seducing Commander Talbot was part of my assignment. I'll probably go on seducing him, in the hope that he'll give me valuable information. I seem to recall you telling me we must be hard to win this war. I'm only applying your great principle to a sphere that suits me somewhat better than commanding a submarine."

He stood there, pain and bewilderment coursing his handsome face. Suddenly all she could remember was the first year of their marriage, when she thought she had discovered perfect happiness, perfect peace, in the arms of this marvelously physical man, who asked nothing from her mind but admiration. He was such a relief, after five years of Lothar Engle's endless analyses of her defects and failures.

Oh Ernst, Ernst, forgive me. Forgive me. The words trembled on her bitter lips. She was ready to confess everything to him, to betray Canaris, revile Jonathan Talbot and his American hoodlums. Ernst was Germany in its wounded innocence again, she was on the brink of recapturing the exaltation of her student days. But the boy-man she had married was no longer there. A crafty, ambitious, extremely angry stranger confronted her. "I don't believe a word of it," he said.

27

WARTIME PASSIONS

After three tries, Annie Talbot fought her way onto a jammed District of Columbia bus. A good half the passengers were men in uniform. The rest were government girls, as the newspapers called them. Annie winced at the fresh, eager faces. They were pouring into Washington by the thousands, to be housed in gigantic apartments across the Potomac in Alexandria, which was now called "Girl Town" or left to hunt for furnished rooms that they often wound up sharing with three or four other women in the same plight.

Annie had written a column about their frustrations. They were quitting in disgust and going home in droves, disillusioned with the way the government hired twice as many people as it needed for every job. Jack, in Hawaii for a voyage with the Pacific fleet, had called the column too negative and given her hell. Annie gave it right back to him in a fiery telegram that warned "Behind The Headlines" was getting out of touch with the way people felt about the sputtering American war effort—and Franklin D. Roosevelt's leadership. It was time to start criticizing the President for his own good.

Without bothering to consult Congress, FDR had created 156 government agencies ranging from the WPB (War Production Board) to the OWM (Office of War Mobilization) to SPAB (Supply Priority Allocation Board), each of them headed by an egotistic bureaucrat who fought furiously to defend his putative turf against other bureaucrats whose authority overlapped his bailiwick. Scarcely a week passed without a public feud erupting between the OPM (Office of Production Management) and the OPA (Office of Price Administration) or between the WLB (War Labor Board) and the WMC (War Manpower Commission). At times Vice President Henry Wallace, head of the BEW (Board of Economic Warfare) seemed to be feuding with everyone simultaneously. More than a few columnists and radio commentators were deriding the war effort as an "alphabet soup" muddle.

"Get off my foot, you Four-F bastard," said a tall astringent brunette.

"Sorry," said the balding youngish man clutching a pole beside her. He was the only male on the bus in civilian clothes.

Crammed against a window, Annie managed to elevate a folded copy of the Washington *Times-Herald* high enough to read a gossip column. An old Washingtonian lamented the decline of the capital's gentility. "Everybody's nerves are on edge. The ordinary courtesies seem to be vanishing. At dinner parties people start out talking abstractions and end up talking personalities. People want to be reasonable, rational, accessible. But wartime passions don't work that way."

Several soldiers started taunting the 4F with the clumsy feet. They speculated nastily on his problem and decided it was "no guts." The man grew so pale, his lips seemed bloodless. When he got off the bus in front of the Treasury Building, the astringent young woman snarled: "I think the yellow bastard broke my toe. Why don't one of you boys get even with him?"

A burly sailor shoved through the mass of bodies and jumped off yelling: "Hey buddy!" Everyone watched, without an iota of compassion on a single face. The 4F turned and the sailor flattened him with a punch in the mouth. The victor climbed back on the bus and asked the astringent young woman for her telephone number. She had already written it down for him.

Not for the first time, Annie was assailed by a dismaying intuition that most young Americans hated this war. They resented the way it had disrupted their lives, when it did not threaten to kill them. They were fighting it with sullen resignation and their anger was liable to erupt at anyone who, in their judgment, was escaping the nasty obligation. They were almost as surly toward the old men who had led them into the upheaval. Few people she interviewed had a good word to say for Franklin D. Roosevelt, who seemed to be hiding in the White House while defeat after defeat cascaded into the newspapers and over the radio.

Annie squirmed her way off the bus, which was waiting for several ancient trolleys to get through the intersection. She found the young man clutching a handkerchief to his lip, while a kindhearted older woman held his head in her lap. "I'm a reporter," Annie said. "Why are you Four-F?"

The man told her he had been beaten up by Mussolini's blackshirts on a trip to Italy in 1939. They had stomped and kicked him, injuring his back so badly he was unable to walk or stand for more than a half-hour at a time. A lawyer, he had come from Iowa at his own expense to make a contribution to the war effort. But he had decided he was wasting his time in Washington, even before he got his teeth loosened by the sailor. "It's a New Dealer's war," he said. "They won't give an honest Republican any job worth doing."

Annie took down his telephone number and said she would call him. It was a good story. But would Jack let her use it? She was growing more and more resentful of the pro-Roosevelt lockstep in which she was being forced to march. She had taken to calling Jack "Massa." Unfazed, he called her "Topsy." They were more than a match for each other.

She had yet to find out what was on his conscience. But she was working on it. Selma Shanley had hinted it had something to do with the leak of Rainbow Five.

At the office, she found Selma clattering away on her Underwood. "Saul Randolph called," she said.

"Aggressive, isn't he," Annie said.

"I hear it wins wars," Selma said.

It was the third time Mr. Randolph had telephoned since they met at Mrs. Davies's party for Maxim Litvinov. Twice, Annie had been unable to harmonize their schedules. With Jack away, she and Sidney Arnold were working overtime to keep the copy coming. Even Selma had deserted her desk for a few assignments. "Also that guy Reeves from State," Selma said. "He left one of his drugstore phone numbers, as usual."

"Promise not to mention it to our lord and master when he returns from the high seas."

Selma smiled in her spooky way. Sometimes Annie was tempted to ask her about her politics. She confined her political opinions to funny little poems that she dropped on Jack's desk or occasionally sent to other columnists, unsigned. Her latest was: *Why won't somebody tell the Pres / The war effort is a hell of a mes?*

Annie had continued to see Roy Reeves. He was simply too fascinating, too intelligent, to drop because Jack would not let her use what he was telling her about the U.S. State Department. The place was riven by a secret war between the realists, many of them Russian experts like Reeves, who saw the Soviet Union as a potential enemy, and liberal ideologues like Ned Travis who backed the White House policy of propitiating the Russians without restraint. Cordell Hull presided over the fray with a fuzzy indifference to who was winning the brawl.

"How are things at the riding academy?" Annie asked.

Across their narrow side street was the faded pink ten-story Albermarle Hotel. All day the windows offered a nonstop sex show that would have made Annie's mother faint and her father, who was on the congressional committee that ran the District of Columbia, call the chief of police.

"Slow start this morning. Only two busy windows," Selma said. "But it's always better after lunch."

The Albermarle made Annie wonder if her real problem in getting from grief through disappointment to happiness was celibacy. Nice girls were not supposed to want sex. But there were moments, alone in bed, when her body blazed with desire. More than one morning, she awoke with both arms clutched convulsively around her pillow. Maybe that meant she was not nice. Or maybe it just meant she was normal. Maybe it was part of her struggle to divorce herself once and for all from Zeke Talbot.

Annie returned Saul Randolph's call. He invited her to one of those intimate little dinners for twenty at the house of a capital power broker, Conrad Rumpleman. Something very big was up and Saul wanted her to be in on it. She deflated the presumptive favor by noting that Rumpleman was from Chicago and an old friend of her father's. But she accepted the invitation.

Annie called Roy Reeves at his drugstore and he was summoned to the phone. "I've got some very important news," he said. "Do you remember the committee I told you about—the one that was cooking up the terms we should offer the Germans and Japs when and if we beat them?"

"Of course," Annie said, although the memory was hazy. She was being bombarded with so many stories and potential stories, only Selma Shanley could keep track of them.

"It's being chaired by Norman Davis, one of FDR's favorite toadies. He helped Wilson commit our debacle at Versailles. Your brother-in-law Ned's the vice chairman—a title which incidentally is well chosen."

It was not the first time Reeves had taken a swipe at Ned's morals. "The committee asked for opinions from State's European and Far Eastern divisions. The consensus was for a moderate peace, as the best antidote to another war. Nazis and Japanese ultras guilty of war crimes like the Bataan Death March would, of course, be punished. Yesterday Davis got the word from the White House: unconditional surrender. Have you ever heard anything more idiotic in your life? Name me another war that ended that way, since the Romans obliterated Carthage."

"What's wrong with unconditional surrender?" Annie asked. She thought it had a decisive ring. Maybe Reeves was really just another anti-Roosevelt crank.

"It's too rigid. If the Germans see no political goal on our side except their annihilation, they'll fight until doomsday. A lot of Americans will die unnecessarily—Germany will end up a pile of rubble— and Stalin will be the master of Europe."

In the next room, the teletype began clattering. The hall door crashed open and Sidney Arnold began yelling at Selma Shanley to turn on the radio. "We won a big one," he whooped.

Annie got rid of Reeves and rushed into Selma's office. She was ripping pages off the teletype, her eyes wild. "It's big all right—and good old Jack was right there. Read this stuff."

Sidney passed the pages to Annie as fast as he could skim them. The Americans had fought a tremendous sea and air battle with the Japanese near the island of Midway, west of Hawaii. Jack had been aboard one of the American carriers. His story was an incredible beat. Jack passing ammunition to the antiaircraft gunners as Japanese divebombers whirled out of the sky. Jack talking to sweat-soaked American pilots just back from planting bombs that sank four Japanese carriers and a half-dozen other ships.

"Richman luck," Sidney Arnold said. "He's always there when the big stories break."

It was part luck and part the marvelous contacts and sources Jack had put together with help from his Annapolis classmates and his father the Congressman. But it made for great reporting. Putting on her managing editor's hat, Selma ordered Sidney and Annie to start shaping the raw wordage into columns. Meanwhile she got on the telephone to tell the Washington *Post* and other papers to hold space on their front pages.

When Saul Randolph picked her up that night, Annie was in a state of euphoria. Saul had heard about the victory, of course, but his reaction was considerably short of euphoric. "It's good news," he said. "Now maybe we can get the admirals to cooperate with the President and leave Japan on the back burner while we deal with Hitler."

As they rode out Massachusetts Avenue, Saul told her how German planes and submarines operating from bases in Norway had massacred recent convoys to Murmansk, crippling lend-lease aid to Russia. The losses in ships and men had risen so high, the British had recommended abandoning the effort until the American Navy reinforced them. The Russians were having paroxysms, accusing the capitalists of deserting them.

"I've been talking to people on Capitol Hill—and in the War Department—but no one seems to give a damn," Saul said. "You get the feeling some of them wouldn't mind if the Russians surrendered."

"Communism isn't exactly a popular ideology in this country," Annie said. "That's not going to change very soon."

"It's got to change—and it can change—if people like you decide to do something about it."

"Like me?" Annie said.

"'Behind The Headlines' has a lot of readers."

Annie had no enthusiasm for putting the column at the disposal of any party line. This one was particularly unappealing, after a half-dozen interviews with Roy Reeves. He had given her a gruesomely thorough briefing on Stalin's Russia, with its vast concentration camps, its perpetual secret police terror. She let silence signal her disagreement with Mr. Randolph.

"Have you heard from your husband lately?" Saul asked.

Annie shook her head, her euphoria abruptly dwindling. "He

writes to our son almost every week. From what Butch tells me I gather he likes Madrid."

"Are you planning to divorce him?"

"Not for the moment. I told him I'd wait until the end of the war to make a decision."

"My wife wants a divorce, now."

"I'm—sorry."

Randolph shrugged. "It was a mistake from the start. I imitated my father and married a nice Jewish girl. But mine was rich. She hated Washington from the day she got here. She wanted me to go back to New York and make a bundle on Wall Street working for her father."

Saul stared out at the mansions along Massachusetts Avenue, many of them foreign embassies. "She's having an affair—and she thinks she loves the guy."

Affair. The word made Annie shift uneasily in the seat. She had carefully avoided thinking about the possibility of Zeke having an affair. Yet she had to concede, on one level, it was more than probable. He was a vigorous man in his thirties who no longer loved his wife. But elsewhere in her mind, on a shadowy borderline where realism blurred into illusion, she wanted to believe he was still stubbornly, angrily, faithful to her.

"I might have stayed in New York—and wound up working for Daddy. But my college roommate went to Spain to fight in the Abraham Lincoln Brigade. He was killed in a German air raid on Madrid in 1939."

The taxi cruised to a stop before a three-story mansion, surrounded by blossoming cherry trees. "That's why I'm in Washington," Saul said. "You can do things here you can't do on Wall Street. In my mind they're a sort of memorial for Jeff."

Another male state of soul to understand. How many varieties could one woman juggle, Annie wondered, as they strolled up the winding walkway to Conrad Rumpleman's home away from home. In the foyer, Annie was nonplussed to discover her mother and father chatting with their host, a tall austere man with a blond, much younger second wife. Her mother's hostile glance obviously asked why Annie was arriving with Saul Randolph.

Annie finessed her embarrassment by introducing Saul and telling them about Jack's report from Midway—until she realized it was upsetting them. "Your mother had a dream the other night," her father said. "She saw Jack getting hurt. There was water all around him. She hasn't slept very well since. Neither have I."

The Congressman's face was a ghastly gray. Not for the first time, Annie felt secondary, almost irrelevant, compared to her parents' adoration of the family hero. Before she could commiserate, they were swept into the party. Drinks were poured, greetings exchanged with other politicians, such as Sol Bloom, the dandified diminutive Democratic Congressman from New York, and Herbert Lehman, the ultradignified Senator from that state, who launched into a monologue on the black market and its threat to the war effort. Sam Richman's eyes grew glazed; everyone in Chicago was doing business with "Mr. Black."

Annie nodded to Ned Travis, who was again traveling without Ethel, escorting Undersecretary of State Sumner Welles. They were in earnest conversation with the star of the evening, the morose, balding Secretary of the Treasury, Henry Morgenthau, Jr. Only Harry Hopkins was closer to the President. The Secretary had been a Roosevelt neighbor in the Hudson River Valley for over twenty years. He lunched with the President every Monday, alone.

Gradually it dawned on Annie that almost everyone on the guest list was Jewish, beginning, of course, with their host. Conrad Rumpleman had donated two million dollars to build the biggest synagogue in Chicago. There was a heavy delegation from the Treasury, but a half-dozen other government departments were also represented, from War to Justice to Labor, just below the cabinet level.

The conversation during the first part of the dinner was about the Midway battle and the chances of defeating the Japanese quickly. The man from the War Department quickly quashed that idea. Midway had been a defensive victory, which saved Hawaii from an invasion. The Japanese had a huge fleet. They were still threatening to cut the sea lanes to Australia.

"Nevertheless," Secretary Morgenthau said. "We've got to go all out to support the President's policy of defeating Hitler first. Saul Randolph tells me the Russians are accusing us of bad faith for suspending the Murmansk convoys. But there's an even better reason for Jewish-Americans to exert themselves. We've received word from sources in Europe that the Germans are massacring Jews in Poland, the Baltic States and Russia."

A collective shudder traveled around the table. The Secretary had gotten everyone's attention.

"It's a distinctly ominous development—and the best imaginable reason for us to unite behind the President. We've also got to renew our effort to get more Jewish refugees into this country by changing the immigration laws. Which brings us to the problem of the State Department."

Undersecretary of State Sumner Welles cleared his throat nervously. "There's still a lot of anti-Semitism in the upper reaches of State," he said. "We need help from our friends in the press and Congress to get rid of it."

"Wait a minute!" Sam Richman said. "Wait a goddamn minute! All the Chicago *Tribune*'s got to hear is Jews are acting as a pressure group in Washington and I'm out of office. Half the Democrats in Congress might be out of office. Don't you realize we got midterm elections coming up this November?"

The man from the War Department emphatically agreed and so did a half-dozen other voices around the table. A furious argument erupted, which soon descended to personalities. Sol Bloom called Annie's father a coward. Enraged, he asked Sol how many votes New York's scandal-crippled political machine, Tammany Hall, had contributed to Roosevelt's third term. "In Chicago we don't put Murphys ahead of Cohens or Cohens ahead of Blonskys. That's why we got an organization that can elect presidents!"

Morgenthau said Harry Hopkins would be very disappointed by the Congressman's attitude. "That's too bad," he snapped. "Harry ain't runnin' the WPA any more except for the one he's settin' up in Moscow."

The men did all the talking. Even Annie's mother, the one woman in the room who could have spoken with a political voice, did not say a word. But her eyes told Annie she agreed with everything her husband was saying. There was more than the realities of Chicago politics behind her father's attitude. He nodded in vigorous agreement with others who argued that Jews were still on trial in America. They had to be extremely careful not to offend anyone. Just beneath the surface of a lot of people's minds was the nasty idea that the Jews had gotten the United States into the war.

Secretary Morgenthau argued vehemently for going public with their point of view. Let the anti-Semites rant. It only revealed their essential ugliness. An all-out fight was, he added somewhat bitterly, the only way to get Roosevelt's attention. "You've got to prove to him that you have public support."

"Henry," Sam Richman said. "If you ever campaigned for office instead of ass-kissing your way to all your jobs, you'd know you're talkin' bullshit."

Morgenthau's face went blank with dismay at this insult. A multi-millionaire by inheritance, the Secretary had been appointed to all his public offices by FDR. He was not familiar with the rough democracy of the House of Representatives.

Sam Richman shoved back his chair. "I'm votin' with my feet on this thing. Let's go, Helen."

Wartime passions, Annie thought. The Congressman's wife joined him in a march toward the door. A half-dozen other couples rose to follow them. "Annie," her mother said. "Would you like a ride?"

"She came with me, Mrs. Richman. I'll take her home," Saul Randolph said. The tone was not polite. Was it also proprietary? Annie avoided her mother's reproachful glare.

The stay-behinds sat around lamenting and/or condemning the departees. Morgenthau kept reiterating his contention that you had to put pressure on Roosevelt to get anything done. Someone asked if Felix Frankfurter, who had the so-called Jewish seat on the Supreme Court, might be helpful.

Morgenthau shook his head, offended by the mere mention of the name. "He never tells FDR anything he doesn't want to hear. I don't know how anyone can call me an ass kisser when we've got him around."

It was appalling—and also fascinating. The Secretary was talking like a jealous courtier in the entourage of a powerful king. Was this what happened when a president stayed in office too long?

The attempt to create a united Jewish front was in ruins. Saul Randolph stubbornly suggested they should meet again in a few months, and meanwhile do their utmost to support Morgenthau's idea. The response was limp, and a general departure was soon underway.

At the door, Conrad Rumpleman murmured apologies to Annie. He had no idea the Congressman would react that way. He hoped he would not say anything to Boss Kelly in Chicago. "You know Sam too well to worry about that," Annie said.

In the taxi, Saul Randolph was silent for several blocks. "Do you agree with your father?" he finally said.

"He knows Chicago's politics a lot better than I do."

"Would you be offended if I said he lacked guts?"

"Not at all," Annie said with sudden scalding bitterness. "My husband used to tell me that all the time."

A long pause may—or may not—have been an apology. "Are you willing to cooperate with us—on attacking the State Department?"

"I can't speak for my brother. It depends on what you send me."

"Ned Travis has promised to get me some very good stuff about the anti-Semites in the Department."

There was another strategic pause. "Every time we see each other, politics seems to get in the way."

"People have been saying that in Washington for a long time. I bet John Adams said it to Abigail."

"Are you aware that you're a very attractive woman?"

"I'm aware that I'm a woman."

"Then why don't we begin the experiment?"

"I need a little more time to regroup my feelings."

"I think you need to get your mother off your back."

Annie was not thinking about her mother. She was measuring this man against the unqualified, absolutely personal way she and Zeke had been drawn to each other. She wanted that purity again but she ruefully conceded it was probably impossible. Maybe the purity had been a myth. Maybe in 1928 Zeke Talbot had represented power and influence, the real desires of her politicized Chicago heart. But Hawaii seemed to stand like a reproach barring the way to that cynical conclusion.

The taxi stopped in front of her apartment. Saul Randolph was drawing her across the back seat in an alarmingly purposeful way. The kiss was disconcertingly gentle. "I'll wait a while," he said.

The taxi dwindled into the night. She was barely in the apartment when the telephone rang. Her mother wanted to know why she was seeing Saul Randolph. "Jack told me you and Zeke have had a nasty quarrel," she said. "That hardly gives you carte blanche to start dating someone with Randolph's reputation."

"What sort of reputation does he have?"

"He's bedded half the women in Washington—and he doesn't care whether they're married or single."

Surely her mother knew her darling son Jack was one of the most active studs in the capital. His name was constantly in the gossip columns. But let even a hint of impropriety sully her daughter and she was on the warpath. "Mother, a little of your Irish puritanism goes a long way," Annie said.

"You're still Zeke's wife. Anything you do will reflect on him, on his career."

"I haven't done anything, Mother. But if I do, I'll be so discreet, not even you will find out about it."

Annie slept poorly. In her dreams she seemed to tour her childhood, holding her mother's impatient hand. She was on Chicago's Loop at Christmas time, she was at the White House meeting a president—always hanging back, being half-dragged along. In the dawn she lay there wondering if a daughter had been an unwanted appendage for Helen Fitzmorris Richman, who had grown up in a world where only men counted.

While she was eating breakfast, the telephone rang again. "Saul Randolph says you're receptive to some revelations from our files," Ned Travis said.

"I can't make any promises to use them," Annie said.

"We understand. Why aren't you being a little nicer to Saul? I could practically hear him panting when he called me last night."

"I'm a married woman, Ned."

"That isn't stopping Zeke in Spain. I'm on a liaison committee with the OSS. They tell me he's having a wonderful time with a beautiful German—the wife of a submarine captain. Zeke's a bit slow to grasp she's also an Abwehr agent but the OSS is working on that problem."

"Do you have documentation?"

"It'll be in your surprise package."

The ride downtown in the usual packed bus was dreamlike. She was isolated from the other lonely riders by the dimensions of her new loneliness. She was not angry; it was almost dismaying, how little anger she felt, now that it was definitely over. The new Annie, the woman who had resolved to be invulnerable to men, had progressed to the zone of mere disappointment. Could happiness be far away? For the moment, at least, it did not seem imminent.

At the office, her surprise package had just been delivered by a State Department messenger. On top was a photocopy of the OSS report from a man named Holcomb, telling how two of his counterintelligence agents had caught Lieutenant Commander Talbot in bed with a woman named Berthe von Hoffmann. There was much more about her identity and an altercation caused by the interference of a Captain Moorman of British Intelligence. Holcomb wanted the authority to arrest Zeke and ship him back to the United States under armed guard.

Underneath was another photocopy, this one of a letter from Warsaw in the spring of 1940, from a man named Hughes Rush, the counselor of the American embassy, addressed to Roy Reeves. It described the political situation in German-conquered Poland. There were reports of the liquidation of some "left-wing" Jews, but on the whole the Germans were behaving reasonably well. The "best people" in Poland seemed to think they might be able to live with their new masters. After all, the Poles had endured foreign domination for centuries, so they were used to it.

As for Poland's Jews, they were naturally unhappy and fearful. But Rush warned against the United States succumbing to a campaign by their "co-religionists" to let huge numbers of them into the country as refugees. There was absolutely nothing to justify such a radical "pollution" of the national gene pool. The Germans, of course, would be delighted to let them go. They were talking of shipping them all to Madagascar. At a recent dinner Rush told one of his friends in the German embassy that he thought the Belgian Congo might be a better choice.

There were a half-dozen letters from other diplomats in prewar Berlin, Hungary, Rumania, full of similar remarks. Three were addressed to Roy Reeves. You did not need Jewish blood to be revolted by this offal. But it helped.

Selma Shanley said Saul Randolph was on the telephone. Ma Bell's wires connected more than their voices. Annie told him how disgusted she was by Ned's revelations. He mournfully agreed. Ned had sent him copies of everything.

Including the OSS report on Zeke and Berthe von Hoffmann? Annie wondered. She decided she did not give a damn. "How about dinner tonight?" he said.

"We could have it at my place," Annie said. "If you contribute a few ration coupons."

"I'll do better than that," he said. "I'll bring a steak from my friend Mr. Black."

A little corruption. What better spice to stir her cynical Chicago heart? After dinner there might be something even more delicious than black market steak served in the bedroom. It would not, of course, be surrender love. That was forever barred from the new Annie's repertory. Instead there would be high-wire love of extremely daring dexterity. For a little while, Saul Randolph might be the happiest man in Washington, D.C.

28

THE PERDITION OF MEN

"A slut, that's what your friend the Admiral called you. In front of two of the highest ranking officials of the Reich. I had to sit there and hear my wife called a slut."

Berthe von Hoffmann watched her husband raging up and down their sparsely furnished living room. He had gone to Berlin to find out if she really was an agent of the Abwehr. Backed by his gauleiter friend, Greiser, he had persuaded the head of the rival *Sicherheitdienst* to challenge Canaris to his face for forcing the wife of a naval hero to commit adultery in the service of the Reich. Canaris had coolly informed them that he had put Frau von Hoffmann on the Abwehr payroll as a favor, to help meet expenses in Madrid. But he had not ordered her to seduce anyone. Her affair with Commander Talbot was a purely personal matter. The accusers had retreated in disarray—with Ernst by far the most humiliated.

The master spider on the Tirpitz Ufer left her no choice. She had to continue the deception. "I'm sorry I lied to you," Berthe said. "I'm attracted to Jonathan Talbot—and I'm no longer attracted to you. It's as simple as that."

Amazing, how secret agents could find comfort in half-truths. She was sorry she was lying to Ernst—sorry and simultaneously glad, every time she thought of Maria Bucholz. "I forbid you to see him again," Ernst said.

"I don't see how you can stop me. Any more than I can stop you from seeing that slut from Tangier."

"I'll stop that! I'll stop it, Berthe."

There was a disconcerting plea in his voice. He was becoming a boy again, the irresistible boy who loved Germany. The Path swerved down into deeper darkness. "It's much too late for such apologies," she said, knowing that she was abandoning Ernst, probably forever.

"You fucking bitch. Do you know what else I did when I went to see Greiser? I joined the Party. It's forbidden by naval regulations but I don't give a damn. I wanted to pledge my honor and my obedience to the Führer and his program to purify the Reich of your Jewish friends, of all and every kind of social disease—including unfaithful wives. I'm going to Dönitz to request sea duty immediately."

Berthe struggled to control her nausea, her grief. "When did you plan to tell me this loathsome news?" she said. "It doesn't exactly jibe with your plea for affection just now. Do you think I could ever tolerate a man who lives by their murderous creed?"

"Never mind when I intended to do anything," he snarled. "I'm ordering you to return to Germany—where you'll be under the constant surveillance of the Party."

"I don't think you can order me to go anywhere," Berthe said. "Our local Abwehr director thinks Talbot could be turned into a valuable double agent with a little more persuasion on my part."

"Persuasion."

She saw his right hand move, but the blow was too swift, too precise to dodge. The open palm cracked against her cheek like a rifle shot, jerking her head to the left so violently, she thought her neck was broken.

"Persuasion."

This time it was the left hand, jerking her head to the right. She felt blood trickle from the corner of her mouth. "Is this Party doctrine? Beating your wife?" she said.

"Persuasion."

The right hand this time. The room bulged with a reddish glow. She wiped away the blood with the back of her hand. *Ich kann nicht anders*, whispered the voice.

"I'm going back to Berlin and file for divorce," Ernst said. "I'm going to make sure you'll never see our children again."

Berthe found the throbbing pain in her face strangely satisfying.

There must be guilt involved in this business of betrayal. It was almost reassuring to think normal feelings were not entirely obliterated.

Ernst left the following day without speaking to her again. She stayed in the apartment for another three days until the swelling on her face went down. She wrote a letter to the children, telling them that she was going to remain in Madrid a while longer in the service of the Reich. *Father and I have had a quarrel*, she wrote. *No matter what he says, never doubt that I love you.* Would her mother-in-law read it to them? Unlikely. She could only hope a residue of humanity still existed in Isolde von Hoffmann's militarized heart.

The Marquesa thought it was time to tell Jonathan Talbot everything. Once more she urged Berthe to take him to Granada. "There's something about the south of Spain that empowers a woman. Go to the gypsy caves and listen to the flamencos. Remember it's a term of honor. The flamenco is not merely a singer but an artist who treasures freedom, spontaneity, delight."

But I'm none of those things. The Marquesa silenced her objection before it could be spoken. "Begin with your decision to stay in Spain for his sake. The rest should be easy—if you can become southern enough. The thing depends on you now. On your capacity as a woman." How those words, spoken with the Marquesa's usual amused squint, threatened her.

Granada. She only had to murmur the word and Jonathan Talbot was at her door. They drove south across the bare baking landscape of La Mancha in late July, Jonathan telling her about the way Holcomb and his OSS associates were throwing the American embassy into turmoil. They were assuring Basque separatists and underground Communists that Washington preferred them to Franco. The Spanish secret service knew every move they made and the Foreign Ministry was lodging a protest a day with the American ambassador. "Holcomb's trying to have me arrested. He claims you're an Abwehr agent," he said.

"How amusing," Berthe said.

"I'm helping the Ambassador put together a dossier on them that will get them transferred to Baffin Bay," he said.

That seemed an apt moment to tell him Ernst had gone back to Germany and she was staying in Spain. "It was easy to arrange," she lied. "Ambassador von Stohrer is an old friend of my father's. He's given me work at the embassy, decoding cables. He's a very under-standing man."

She almost laughed at her distance from the truth. Actually, Stohrer had summoned her to his office to give her a stern lecture. In his opinion, women should stay out of espionage. The damage they did to the nation's moral reputation was not worth the informa-tion they obtained.

"Ernst says he's going to divorce me," Berthe said.

"Do you care?"

"I care about the children."

"Butch—my son—troubles me too." He stared down the high-way, which emitted wavering lines of heat as it stretched across the vast sun-drenched plain toward the Sierra Nevada Mountains. "I haven't told my wife about you."

"You must never! Promise me."

"Why not? It seems the honest thing to do. You didn't try to hide me from Ernst."

"That's an entirely different matter. Ernst is not innocent." She waited for the next words, wondering how they would sound. "He's joined the Party."

Her voice sounded perfectly normal, as if she had made a remark on the weather. She wanted another reaction. Something as violent as the original stench. Perhaps it meant Ernst had not yet crossed the invisible border ruled by the Führer's evil will. Should she pray for him? She decided God was not interested in her prayers.

A hot wind battered her face, tore at her hair. South, Berthe thought, south of guilt and innocence, south of thought. That was where they were going. That was where she must learn to live. South to Andalusia, the land of passion and flamenco.

Three hours later, they crossed the last of the Vega, the fertile lowlands at the foot of the Sierra Nevadas, and saw Granada, sprawled on the foothills of the snowcapped mountains. They drove slowly through streets crowded with vivid Spanish faces. Berthe stud-ied the women, noting the careless swing of their hips, the way their hands spoke in syncopation with their flashing eyes. Hopeless, she thought. Those gifts were beyond her. They were not in her cold German blood.

They found a room in the Majestic Hotel, a rambling structure built in 1910. A strange wind poured through the wide windows of their high-ceilinged room, warm, but with a hint of the snowy Sierras at its core. Jonathan undressed her and they made love violently, swiftly, on the wide double bed and lay there in the sultry subtle wind.

South. The word stirred recklessness in Berthe's mind. The Marquesa's feline face smiled encouragement in the shadows along the wall. South. Could she become a different woman in this new country? Somewhere out on the street a guitar strummed—to be obliterated by the decidedly unromantic bray of a donkey. Don't be an ass, Berthe. Is that what the keeper of the Path was saying? She could almost hear Lothar Engle jeering the words.

No, she would deny that northern voice. That was Nietzsche and Schopenhauer, the sneer of German pessimism. She was with Goethe now, with Wilhelm Meister struggling for wisdom, with Iphigenia in Tauris, accepting yet transcending tragedy, with Margaret transforming Faust. She began telling Jonathan how stunned Goethe had been when he visited Rome and discovered love Italian-style. "Rome changed his life. Perhaps Granada will change mine."

"I never thought of myself as a sensualist," Jonathan said, toying with her left nipple.

"I abhorred the word. Love had to have a purpose, an ideal."

A shadow passed over his face. Was the wind blowing twilight into the room? No, this shadow came from within him. He wanted their love to have a noble purpose. Should she tell him now that the purpose awaited them in the not so distant future? She was swept by an almost uncontrollable love—yes it was unmistakably love—for this naive idealistic American, for his stubborn determination to seek spiritual altitudes—and share them with her, in defiance of the void in the center of his soul.

But first they needed, they deserved these hours of absolute freedom, of pure pleasure. Who told her that? The Marquesa again? Or was it her feminine self, breaking free at last from the oppressive weight of Hegel and history?

South. The guitar strummed. She wanted this man for his own sake, for the pleasure he gave her and she gave him. She wanted to possess him, to be the center of his universe, for the throb of pride, of joy, it stirred in her burgeoning heart. She wanted him to be the center of her world in a way that transcended the sentimental songs of adolescence. She wanted to love him without reservations, without hesitations, with the simple directness of the flesh, free of the mind's prying.

They began again, slower now, almost playful, exploring the possibility of duende. For the first time the meaning of that mysterious Spanish word became real for her. She saw how it blended time and eternity, flesh and passion and the risk, always the risk of failure. How the essence of its pathos was its bold embrace of time, of admitting the moment could never be regained, never duplicated and yet was worth seeking for its own sake.

There was nothing like it in German—nor, she suspected—in English. Perhaps a nation had to be very old, perhaps a people had to experience time in all its implacable irresistible reality, time and its losses, time and its deaths. Ultimately that was what duende became—the lover's, the flamenco singer's, the matador's defiance of death.

They came at last, came and came and came, impossibly, improbably together, with muffled wordless cries and a special cadence of heart and breath and blood. "I love you," Berthe said. "Always believe that, no matter what else you believe about me. Never stop believing that. I don't really understand it. I never expected it. The whole thing is as mysterious as this city, this country."

"I feel the same way," Jonathan said. "I don't understand it either."

In the last hours of the afternoon they drove across Granada to see its greatest treasure, the Alhambra Palace. They toiled up the steep path from the Plaza Nueva at the foot of the mountain and wandered through the gardens and courtyards and royal chambers where the Sultans of Granada had feasted with their wives and children. They breathed the incomparable scent of the boxwood trees and listened to the languorous songs of a thousand birds.

For Berthe the most beautiful space was the Courtyard of the Myrtles, with its long rectangular reflecting pool and the scallop shell of Saint James in the center as a decorative device. Never had she seen anything human come so close to capturing the idea of eternity. Just beyond it was the Courtyard of the Lions, with its wilderness of slim pillars supporting arches as delicate as rose petals around the fountain with the twelve crouching jungle beasts, who wore contented friendly smiles. Here, the artists seemed to be saying, was how beauty could tame nature to create heaven on earth.

That night they went to dinner in the gypsy caves above Granada. The wine was rough and the food was primitive but the guitars, the singers and dancers created the greatest flamenco in Spain. They quickly learned there were many kinds of flamencos. The *soleares* were songs of desolation and abandonment. Illuminated by a flickering torch, a swarthy gypsy of about twenty, slim, with haunted eyes, sang:

> Sometimes I would like
> To go mad and not feel
> For being mad takes away grief

In the deeper darkness of the cave's rear, a guitarist strummed *siguiryas*, another flamenco full of mourning. The song continued, a dialogue between chords and voice, exploring love and sorrow.

In another cave, finger snaps clicked, guitars twanged and dancers did the Grenadina, Granada's version of the fandango. They absorbed the tension between passion and control, the subtle interplay of mockery and surrender. They beat time on the tables and shouted olé! with the rest of the audience when the dancers and the music approached duende.

In a third cave they encountered a completely unexpected kind of flamenco, the *petenera*. It was sung by an older gypsy, gray-haired, with a lean scarred face. His voice was a wail of remembered desire.

> Where are you going, beautiful Jewess?
> All dressed up at such an hour?
> I am going to meet Rebeco
> Who is now in the synagogue.
>
> Whoever named you Petenera
> Didn't know how to name you.
> You should have been named
> The perdition of men.

There were many more verses, describing the despair, the murders, the suicides, Petenera's beauty caused in her small village. Afterward, Jonathan invited the singer to join them for a drink. Berthe asked what he knew about the origins of the peteneras. He said they were very old, he only knew his grandfather had sung them and he had learned them from his grandfather. They went back to the days when Jews lived in Andalusia, before the new world was discovered and Queen Isabella and King Ferdinand expelled them as killers of Christ, polluters of Spain's blood and faith.

Ich kann nicht anders, whispered the voice. For a moment Berthe was overwhelmed by the incomprehensible darkness of God. The whole thing made no sense. Beyond the rational borders of cause and effect lurked a universe of motives, a world of tragedies that defied the feeble light of reason.

They walked back to their hotel through Granada's silent, empty streets, subdued and sad. "Peteneras," Jonathan said. "I never heard them before. I guess I only went to the tourist flamencos when I came here in the Twenties."

Was he wondering if he too was involved with a Petenera—a woman who lured men to perdition? When Berthe thought about what she was doing to him and Ernst, she wondered the same thing.

Back in the hotel, the warm wind had absorbed more of the Sierras' snowy coolness. *South*, it seemed to whisper with increasing intensity. Berthe realized it was time to tell him. She could almost hear her Spanish mother, the Marquesa, whispering *now*.

"There's another reason why I've stayed in Spain."

In the shadowy room, illuminated only by one or two candles—like most of Spain, Granada turned off the electricity after midnight to save fuel—the words spilled out. "Admiral Canaris sent me here hoping to find someone like you. A man with an open mind. A man who didn't hate Germany."

It did not go well. The idea was so vast, so ambitious, she could easily imagine him deciding she was insane. Berthe von Hoffmann an emissary of the head of the German secret service who was in turn an emissary of certain members of the German general staff who were ready to lead a coup d'état against Adolf Hitler?

She watched disbelief batter his love. Perhaps he heard her own uncertainty, her anger at Canaris for lying about her father, her fear of Lothar Engle's ambiguities, her guilt over Ernst. She gathered herself like a flamenco singer for a final climactic cry. "It's the truth, Jonathan, the unbelievable truth! I know you want our love to have a purpose. Can you imagine a better one? Without your courage, your strength, I'll never do it. I'll creep back to Germany and await our fate—"

"I believe you!" The words were torn from his throat, a choked cry, like the chord of a siguirya. He held her while she wept with relief, with grief, with gratitude and kissed his mouth, his cheeks, his neck.

South, she was utterly south now, beyond the maps. She undressed him and stripped away her own clothes, the Balenciaga nonsense that concealed what had become fundamental. Not mere sex, not the flesh that entered and withdrew and entered again, not the act but the naked essence of the gift they were exchanging, the promise, the oath, the vow of trust.

She imagined it as a kind of wedding. With this kiss, I thee trust, with this touch, I thee trust, with this embrace, I thee trust forever and forever and forever. Was it possible? Was it all a trick of the wind, of warmth, of flamenco?

Duende, whispered the Marquesa. *You've achieved it, my daughter. I didn't think it was possible.*

Suddenly, unimaginably, warmth vanished. As Jonathan came and she struggled to meet him, the argument exploded in Berthe's mind. *But I'm still German.*

BOOK THREE

29

KNIGHT'S GAMBIT

"Old boy, I simply don't believe it. I can't believe you believe it. It's obvious what you were doing in Granada. Fucking your brains out."

It was quintessential Moorman. He sat in his office in the British embassy with a picture of his lost World War I destroyer on the wall, venting his hatred of Germany on Berthe von Hoffmann. His face was like a clenched fist, tight with malevolence.

"It makes perfect sense," Talbot said. "Every country in Europe has a resistance movement against Nazism. Why shouldn't the Germans have one?"

"If the story came from anyone but Canaris, I might possibly respond with wary interest. But that little queer is incapable of something this simple, this direct, this honorable."

Not for the first time, Talbot had the sensation of fighting two wars at the same time. "What's your explanation? Here's a woman who's abandoning her children, letting her husband divorce her for adultery, accepting loss and disgrace to bring us this message. Doesn't that prove something?"

"Yes. How bloody shrewd Canaris is. The slimy little bastard has an uncanny sixth sense about this business. He's always a step ahead on the chess board. Your Lorelei may believe every word of it. Canaris arranged that too, with the folderol of the heroic pastor—"

"And the spiritual experience? The stench of evil? Did Canaris pipe a sewer into her house? You're making this fellow sound more like Faust than a secret service director."

"So she's lying about that. So what?"

"I *know* she isn't lying."

He had him. Or almost had him. Moorman simply shifted his animus from Berthe to her gullible lover. "I simply can't believe you've become such a simpleton. I had hopes for you, Talbot. Compared to those OSS twits—"

Talbot retreated in a fury to Berthe's apartment. She was untroubled by Moorman's intransigence. "We'll have to wait for something to happen," she said. "We have to wait anyway. Canaris can do nothing until the Wehrmacht suffers a serious defeat. Perhaps the British too need a defeat. Your entrance into the war has made them overconfident."

She turned away from him and her voice acquired a tense uneasy tone. "Besides, we never had much hope of changing their minds. There's too much hate on both sides. What about your own country? Surely you're not going to let Moorman silence you?"

He sensed she was afraid he was going to start suspecting her again. Since Granada, they were linked in an uncanny, nearly metaphysical way. He could almost read her thoughts.

"I honestly don't know to whom I should go, here in Spain. I wouldn't dream of taking something like this to that OSS jerk, Holcomb. The Ambassador and his right-hand man, Boileau, only seem interested in keeping Franco neutral. I'm not sure I trust their discretion, anyway. If I identify you and they blab it to someone at the State Department, I could be signing your death warrant."

"That doesn't worry me," she said.

Once more he saw how guilty she felt. Guilty about betraying Ernst, abandoning her children—and even more guilty about betraying Germany. "It worries me," he said. "I now consider it my primary mission in life to prevent you from punishing yourself in some crazy way."

She smiled sadly and switched on the radio. They listened to Berlin's confident predictions that the panzers of the German Sixth Army, the conquerors of France, would soon seize Stalingrad, the immense industrial city that stretched for thirty miles along the Volga. Radio Berlin claimed the capture would wipe out half of Russia's remaining war production. The Volga, crucial for transporting food and war matériel north, would be cut, undermining resistance in front of Moscow and Leningrad.

"It's an epic," Berthe said, gazing at a map of Europe. "To have come so far—a thousand miles across the steppes."

"Should I start singing the Horst Wessel Lied?" Talbot said.

She looked as if she might weep. He held her until the spasm of German pride passed. The next day, Talbot dispatched a most secret cable to Admiral Jamison at the Office of Naval Intelligence.

HAVE DEVELOPED A CONTACT IN ABWEHR WHO CLAIMS TO REPRESENT DISSIDENT OFFICERS OF HIGH RANK IN THE GERMAN ARMY. THEY ARE READY TO STAGE A COUP D'ETAT AGAINST HITLER AT EARLIEST OPPORTUNITY. THEY WISH A PRELIMINARY STATEMENT OF CONDITIONS FOR A NEGOTIATED PEACE. PLEASE ADVISE COURSE TO PURSUE.

Two days later, Talbot received a reply from Jamison.

NO INTEREST WHATSOEVER IN SUCH NEGOTIATIONS. YOU ARE HEREBY ORDERED TO DISCONTINUE THE CONTACT IMMEDIATELY. THIS DIRECT FROM WHITE HOUSE.

When he showed it to Berthe, she could not believe it. She read it again and again. "No interest? None whatsoever?"

"We don't know who it went to at the White House. There's no reason to assume that's Roosevelt's decision. It might be my tormentor, Admiral King. He's perfectly capable of pretending he sent it to the White House. Or he could make sure it went to someone who would brush it off. The President is surrounded by layers of flunkies."

Berthe was still enormously discouraged. "I must report this to Canaris," she said.

Talbot told Moorman, who positively beamed at the news. In the murky world of intelligence, anyone who agreed with a man's opinion was welcomed as a friend—even if he was an American or some other callow colonial twit. "I see no reason not to continue to enjoy her," he said. "But I'd take that advice, as far as any negotiation is concerned."

Talbot started to tell Moorman he loved Berthe. But somewhere along the line, Moorman seemed to have dropped love out of his equation for living. Although he had no real confidence in the move, Talbot decided to try his brother-in-law Ned in the State Department. At least he could be depended on to be discreet, for Talbot's sake if for no other reason. He sent the cable and got an answer so quickly, it was impossible to believe Ned had discussed it with anyone.

STATE HAS ABSOLUTELY NO INTEREST IN SUCH NEGOTIATIONS. THEY RUN COUNTER TO PLANS BEING GENERATED AT THE HIGHEST LEVELS HERE FOR DEALING WITH POSTWAR GERMANY.

Talbot decided not to show this to Berthe. He showed it to Moorman, who did not like the sound of it. "It's what a lot of us have been worried about from the start. Just because you Americans are supplying most of the muscle, you're going to try to take over the thinking part of the war. That's a guarantee of disaster. You don't understand Europe and you never will."

By now, Talbot had grown so used to Moorman's condescension, he barely noticed it. He stuck to the main point. "Why sit there wringing your hands? Authorize me to negotiate with Canaris, through Berthe. Maybe we can outflank Washington."

"It's personal, dear boy. If there was someone else involved, besides Canaris, I might—note I said might—be interested, at least to the extent of passing it on to London to see how it plays. But not with that slimy Greek in the middle of it."

"I'm dismayed that you can be so petty."

Moorman virtually inflated with indignation. "Petty, petty? It's a moral judgment, dear fellow. Nothing in the least petty about it. I'm in favor of consigning that double-crossing little Greek to the lowest circle of Dante's inferno."

"What exactly did he do to you here in Spain during World War One?"

Moorman stared up at his lost destroyer. "He persuaded me to take a holiday in Tangier with him. It was in 1916. Half my friends had died on the Somme. I saw it as a sort of private truce in a war that had become a meaningless slaughter. He saw it as simple seduction. While we played at love in Tangier—he'd handed his business on to Count von Schonberg. Ships were being sunk, men were drowning."

Moorman's voice trailed off to a bitter growl. "I should have been court-martialed and shot."

Amazement and dismay must have been visible on Talbot's face. Moorman gave him a sardonic squint. "Don't worry. I won't make a bloody pass at you. I haven't touched a man or a woman's flesh since. Penitence. A very Spanish idea. I must have inherited it from my mother."

A dazed Talbot naturally told this story to Berthe. She flushed, trembled and her eyes filled with tears. "It's true, it's true," she said more to herself than to him. Haltingly, she tried to explain why Canaris's version of her father's role in Spain had been such a revelation to her—and how crushed she had been when the Marquesa debunked it.

Studying Berthe with the anxious eyes of love, Talbot suspected the Marquesa had known what she was doing. It would have been much better if Berthe were free of the temptations of patriotism. Now that word *Vaterland* had regained its capacity to demoralize her.

The next night, August 8, from Radio Berlin came a chorus of the Horst Wessel Lied, followed by an announcer's exultant voice.

"Today soldiers of the Reich repelled an attempted invasion of Europe at the French port of Dieppe. Units of the Wehrmacht met the enemy on the beaches with bayonet and bullet while the Luftwaffe pounded them and their ships without mercy. Within three hours of the first landing, not a single enemy soldier remained in action. They were all either dead or had surrendered. The enemy lost an estimated ten thousand men, four warships and perhaps forty landing craft."

The BBC told a different story, of course. Dieppe was a raid, a probe, to explore German defenses and experiment with tactics for the invasion that was soon to come. It was declared a success, in spite of "higher than expected" losses, because it demonstrated that the Germans could be taken by surprise. The next day, Talbot got the truth from a mortified Moorman. Dieppe was a fiasco from start to finish, a perfect example of how not to run anything, be it a raid or an invasion.

The troops had all been Canadians and their losses had been so heavy, there was grave concern in London that Canada might pull out of the war. "It's made everyone think twice about the bloody cross-channel invasion you Yanks wrote into your war plan, Rainbow Five. If this thing is a sample, and I'm afraid it is, an invasion could cost a half-million men. It could be the Somme all over again. England can't take another slaughter like that. There'll be a revolution."

He glared up at his lost destroyer. "Maybe you ought to see what your German beauty can turn up in the way of genuine negotiations. Make it clear it has to be somebody beyond—and preferably above—Canaris. I won't tolerate that lisping queer in the same country with me."

An ecstatic Berthe said she would fly to Berlin to deliver the message personally to Canaris. While she was gone, Holcomb of the OSS provided local entertainment. He imported several cases of Scotch, which he seemed bent on personally consuming. He and "Hem" each used to polish off a bottle a day during the siege of Madrid. Now, perhaps in tribute to a bigger war, he was aiming at two bottles. He reeled around the city, sneering at the British failure at Dieppe. What they needed was American know-how, American guts, he roared in various public places. He displayed the same loud-mouthed contempt for the Franco regime. Franco was a "pimple on the ass of history," he told Hamilton Boileau. The OSS was taking steps to see that he was surgically removed.

Berthe returned from Berlin to report Canaris would send an emissary to Madrid as soon as possible. She said the Admiral was dismayed by American indifference to his proposal. But he agreed with Talbot that it may not have reached the highest levels of the government. She also told them Canaris had learned that the Nazis had abandoned their prewar plan to exile Europe's Jews. Instead, at a secret conference in an SS-owned villa in Wannsee, they had decided to systematically destroy them in special concentration camps.

"Surely this can be used with your government and with the British," Berthe said. "Isn't rescuing these innocent people a good reason to negotiate with the despicable Germans?"

Talbot persuaded Moorman to pass on the tragic revelation to London. He sent lengthy cables to Ned Harris in the State Department and Admiral Jamison at Navy Intelligence. Ned replied first.

SIMILAR REPORTS FROM OTHER SOURCES. RECOLLEC-
TION OF BRITISH WORLD WAR I PROPAGANDA ABOUT
GERMANS EATING BELGIAN BABIES INCLINES EVERYONE
HERE TO INTENSE SKEPTICISM.

Jamison did not bother to debate the issue.

REPEAT ORDERS TO DISCONTINUE ALL GERMAN CON-
TACTS.

Admiral King obviously still considered Commander Talbot a
potential traitor.

Berthe also brought back some personal bad news from Berlin.
Ernst had filed for divorce and the court, perhaps influenced by Ernst's
friends in the Nazi party, had issued an immediate injunction, barring
Berthe from seeing her children. She had gone to the Hoffmann villa in
Wannsee and her mother-in-law had flourished the order in her face.
Isolde von Hoffmann had called Berthe a whore and refused to let her
in the house. "As I left, I looked up at Georg's bedroom window and
saw their faces pressed against the glass," Berthe said.

Talbot held her against him for a long time, trying to share her
pain.

They were distracted by more immediate problems. Wolfgang
Griff, the Nazi naval correspondent aboard the Ritterboot, was still
working in Spain. He made it his business to harass Berthe in various
ways. He formally complained to Ambassador von Stohrer about her
"liaison" with Talbot on the grounds that it made her a security risk.
After all, she was decoding cables from Berlin. Herr von Spaeth, the
Abwehr director, insisted that Berthe was in complete control of Talbot, and was obtaining valuable information from him.

Moorman decided it was time to leak a story to the Germans to
bolster Talbot's bona fides. "It also may get rid of that loudmouthed
OSS twit Holcomb and his entire band of bloody fools."

With help from Spanish Communist exiles, Holcomb and company had developed contacts with an underground group in Malaga
that had eluded the Spanish secret service. The OSS had begun
smuggling them thousands of rifles, machine guns, hand grenades
and other weaponry—enough to start a serious rebellion in the south

of Spain. Moorman's agents had been tracking the entire operation and he now proposed to blow it to the Germans, who would promptly inform Franco.

"It doesn't make much sense, does it," Talbot said. "Out on the Atlantic, people are dying to get weapons and food to the Communists in Russia. Here we're cutting them off at the knees."

"Everyone in the secret service thinks Churchill made one of the biggest mistakes of his mistake-studded career when he gave Stalin a bloody blank check the day after Hitler attacked him," Moorman said. "Those Bolshevik bastards are our enemies until death do us part. We're just starting hostilities here a bit ahead of schedule."

Talbot told Berthe about the Malaga operation and she passed it on to Abwehr chief Spaeth, who did exactly what Moorman expected—he notified the Spanish. Within a week, Madrid's newspapers were exploding with the story of a shootout in Malaga that left at least twenty dead and hundreds arrested. Holcomb came roaring into the embassy the next day on what looked like a permanent bender. He reeled into Talbot's office and bellowed: "You fucking son of a bitch. You did it. I don't know how but you did it. I'm going to have you court-martialed for treason."

The Spanish Foreign Ministry summoned Ambassador Hayes and Counselor Boileau for another tongue lashing about the OSS's antics. They returned vowing to get rid of Holcomb—and privately thanked Talbot and Moorman for blowing the operation. It was, Boileau raged, another instance of Roosevelt's indifference to letting his diplomatic right hand know what the left hand was doing.

From America came a very different response to Talbot's role in the Malaga shootout. It arrived in the form of a letter from his sister Ethel. She expressed husband Ned's "chagrin" at discovering he had "reverted" to his father's politics. Shifting effortlessly from the waspish to the malicious, Ethel told him Annie was "cutting a swath" among the numerous unattached males in wartime Washington. She had been seen dining out with a man on presidential assistant Harry Hopkins's lend-lease staff. If she heard more details (read dirt) Ethel promised to let him know immediately.

Talbot debated whether to show the letter to Berthe and decided against it. He was afraid it would only add to her guilt. When he saw her the following day, she was unexpectedly cheerful. "Helmuth von Moltke is coming tomorrow!" she said.

She looked girlish, dazzled. For a few minutes Talbot felt jealous. He demanded to know the secret of the Count's charm.

"Integrity," she said. "German integrity."

"That's better than American integrity?"

She gave him a defiant look. "I decline to answer that question."

She was so hopeful, Talbot could not bear to tell her how deeply he doubted their chances of success. More and more, as he pondered the negative replies he had received from Washington, he began to suspect their source was the President. No one would dare to deal with such a fundamental issue without making sure it had Roosevelt's approval.

They met Moltke in a house in Avila. Berthe drove him there in Ernst's Bugatti while Moorman brought Talbot in his Aston Martin. The white town on a hilltop, girdled by its medieval walls, seemed a good place to talk peace. To Berthe, who was still fascinated by St. Teresa, it was a symbol of hope. From the moment they met, Talbot was gripped by Moorman's metaphor of a chess game. Canaris had advanced his knight. Moltke's long-limbed frame, his dignified, angular face, might have stepped from an illustration in Kantorowicz's *Frederick II*. Perhaps influenced by his native respect for aristocracy, Moorman treated the Count with great courtesy. They talked for almost two hours, discussing the practical aspects of the coup against Hitler as well as the negotiated peace they hoped to achieve—essentially a return to the Europe of 1939.

Moltke insisted the German generals were ready to act. More than a few feared the worst from this drive on Stalingrad. With cool authoritative logic, Moltke dissected Hitler's strategy. The Sixth Army was creating a huge salient that could be attacked from three sides by the Russians. They were in serious danger of being trapped. If that happened, Moltke said, the generals would depose the Führer.

He listed the names of a half-dozen men—Beck, the former Chief of the General Staff; Stuelpnagel, the Commander in Paris; Kluge, the Commander on the Moscow front, who had agreed to support the conspiracy.

"What are you going to do with Hitler?" Moorman asked.

"At the moment, I and others, including Admiral Canaris, believe he should be seized along with the other Nazi leaders, and tried for crimes against humanity after peace is negotiated."

Moorman shook his head. There was a grim authority in the gesture. "You'll have to kill him."

"There are strong arguments against that policy. He's still extremely popular with large numbers of the German people. Only after they realize his crimes will they repudiate him. Assassination could turn him into a martyr and trigger a civil war."

Moorman retreated a step, a sign of how deeply Moltke impressed him. "Perhaps you're right. I'll make a full report of this offer to my government. In the meantime, I hope you'll make it clear that we'll require preliminary deeds as well as words, to convince us."

Moltke looked puzzled, but Berthe understood immediately. "He means information that will be useful to their military forces," she said.

"I see," Moltke said, his voice subsiding to a near whisper. He was unable to disguise how difficult he found the proposition.

"I knew it would fill you with loathing—as it does me," Berthe said. "But they require it. You can see why."

"I will speak to Admiral Canaris," Moltke said.

"Tell him this is what Moorman wants," the Englishman said, his bald head jutting forward like the thrust of a bull. "The fourth rotor of the Enigma machine. Nothing less."

Moorman snuffled triumphantly. "It isn't just a defeat on the battlefield that's needed. Until you start to lose the battle of the Atlantic, you'll never make peace."

The next day, Moltke flew back to Berlin, taking Berthe with him. A week later she returned and asked Talbot to meet her in the Retiro Park, where they could talk without fear of hidden microphones. She looked exhausted. She said she had encountered a man she disliked, Lothar Engle—a newspaperman who had joined the SS. He had pursued her around Berlin, demanding to know why she was staying in Spain, why Ernst was divorcing her.

She led him to a small grove of trees where they would be invisible to someone watching them through field glasses. "Here is your fourth rotor," she said. "Now you can win the U-boat war."

From her purse she took the small metal drum, similar to the ones Talbot had seen at the ONI in Washington, D.C.

"Admiral Canaris stressed I must give it to you, not Moorman. He hopes you will report it to your government as evidence of our good intentions. He urges you not to be discouraged by reprimands from your superiors. Good secret agents always receive such things."

Talbot nodded. "I'll send them the damnedest argument they've ever seen."

Later, he delivered the precious object to Moorman at the British embassy. He seized it with a gloating cry. "I didn't think they'd do it. Canaris, betraying the Ubootwaffe. It's almost enough to convince me he's serious."

All Talbot could see was the pain in Berthe's eyes. That night when he went to her apartment to tell her Moorman's reaction, he tried to love her in a new way. Not as the triumphant male conqueror, but as the consoler who shared her sorrow. He tried to focus his mind on this new dimension of himself, an unstable compound of shadows and wish.

She reached out for him with salty tears on her lips. Did she know, did she sense what he was trying to do? At first she seemed to be slipping away from him, the way he had lost her in their first weekend in Avila. But now he was following her into the darkness, groping down her mysterious Path. Gradually, he felt something new flowing between them, a deeper wordless trust that ended with sighs of gratitude.

"You're so dear to me," she whispered. "I wonder how I'll ever part with you."

"You never will," he insisted.

A moment later, he sensed ahead of them on the Path a creature that would make a mockery of that vow. A blend of darkness and disappointment and vengeance, it had no shape or substance yet. All he could do was fling in its blank face a desperate promise: "I'll never let you go."

30

THE SEA WOLF

Kapitanleutnant Ernst von Hoffmann stood on the steps of the Hotel Crillon, watching the elite Prussian Guards Regiment strut across the Place de la Concorde, rifles on their shoulders, helmets low on their frowning brows. Every day they marched from their quarters across the historic square, where Napoleon had once celebrated his victories, and down the Champs Élysées to the Arc de Triomphe. Ernst noticed that many Frenchmen turned their backs on the unbearable sight. It was living proof that the daily ritual was accomplishing its purpose: humiliation. For a man who had suffered another kind of humiliation in Spain, it was a very satisfying sight.

Upstairs in Ernst's room, eagerly awaiting his return, was a bleached blond French cabaret artist named Mimi. He had left a tearful Maria Bucholz in Madrid to entertain Wolfgang Griff, Jaime Sanchez and, no doubt, many others. He did not want to take any reminders of Spain with him to conquered France.

Hailing a taxi, he rode to the new headquarters of the Ubootwaffe, a modern apartment block on the Avenue Marechal Maunoury. After the Dieppe raid and a smaller strike at St. Nazaire by British commandos, Berlin had ordered Admiral Dönitz to retreat inland. Apparently the Führer found it hard to sleep nights, imagining the British swarming ashore at Lorient to capture the Lion, his staff and all their codes and plans.

In a half-hour, Ernst was standing at attention in Dönitz's inner office. He had a picture of the château at Lorient on the wall, perhaps a sign he had not abandoned that great house by the water willingly. He had brought with him the huge globe of the world, and on the wall was a map of the Atlantic, with red dots signifying U-boats on patrol. Ernst was gratified to see at least seventy-five or eighty of them.

The Lion was his usual cordial self, at first. He thanked Ernst for his efforts to acquire Spanish ports for the Ubootwaffe. He agreed with Ernst's written report on his mission, in which he condemned the Spanish as unreliable allies. Every time the British or Americans discovered a U-boat in a port, she was expelled with a bare minimum of foot-dragging. Several boats had been forced to put to sea without adequate fuel.

"In my opinion, Herr Admiral, Franco is playing a devious game with us," Ernst said. "Even the division he sent to Russia reeks of duplicity. It enabled him to get twenty thousand members of the Falange, our most ardent supporters, out of the country."

"I'll tell the Führer that the next time I see him," Dönitz said. He studied Ernst for another moment. "So you're ready to go back to sea."

"Yes, Herr Admiral."

"You've settled matters with your wife?"

"I'm divorcing her, Herr Admiral. I decided it was in the best interests of my children—and the Ubootwaffe."

Dönitz nodded, digesting the fact as impersonally as if Ernst had just told him he had gained weight. "As you know, I never interfere in the private lives of my commanders. It's beyond my sphere—and my competence. Having met your wife, I will only say it must have been a difficult decision."

The Lion glanced quickly at him, then looked away, a hint of an embarrassed smile on his face. He was talking as one man to another, telling Ernst how good he imagined Berthe must have been in bed. For a moment Ernst thought he would strangle with rage. "It was difficult, Herr Admiral."

Dönitz nodded, closing the subject. "The moment I received your request and decided there was nothing more for you to do in Spain, I notified operations to see if we could reconstitute your crew. You'll be pleased to hear a remarkable number of them have requested to serve under you again. Your First Officer, Kurz, your

Chief Engineer, Kleist. About twenty-five enlisted men. That's very good, considering how many of the others are probably at sea in other boats."

"I'm deeply pleased, Herr Admiral."

That was not exactly true. Ernst was not at all sure he wanted any of his old crew back. Above all Kurz and Kleist. He did not feel he was the same man who had commanded the Ritterboot. He had decided he could only find out the meaning, the dimension of the change, at sea. Losing Berthe had shaken him, enraged him—and, he hoped—ultimately hardened him. But only the shock of battle, the tension and joy of attack and evasion and more attacks could give him the certainty he wanted and needed.

"You're going to find a very different situation in the Atlantic," Dönitz said. "The enemy has designed a portable radar device that enables their planes to see submarines on the surface in the dark. We've had a number of boats lost or damaged in the Bay of Biscay in night air attacks that seemed to come from nowhere."

"Our scientists can't counter it?"

"We're equipping all boats with a French device that emits a warning signal when it picks up a radar beam. But its sensitivity is poor. The time lag is barely thirty seconds."

Again, Ernst was gripped by a near convulsion of rage at Berthe and Jonathan Talbot. He could almost hear Talbot exulting over the new radar, the Ubootwaffe losses. He vowed to wipe the sneer off his American face with the torpedoes of his new boat.

"There's another matter we must discuss—our object in the Atlantic war. Previously it was the ships. But the Americans are building freighters far faster than we can sink them. From now on our goal must be the destruction of the crews."

Ernst saw the policy made perfect sense. But he did not see how it could be implemented.

"In every convoy," Dönitz continued, "there's a rescue ship with special boats and hospital equipment. They drop behind the convoy to pick up survivors and often heave to while lowering boats. These should be your primary targets, whenever possible. Other measures will depend on circumstances—"

"I understand, Herr Admiral." Again he was far from speaking the truth. He would have to think long and hard about these orders.

"Herr Admiral—there's one other matter I feel I must mention to you. I've joined the National Socialist party. It was partly out of gratitude to Herr Gauleiter Greiser of Posen, who has restored my family's estate to me—"

"There's nothing in the Party's doctrine that contradicts the philosophy of the Ubootwaffe," Dönitz said. "They too preach hardness as the first prerequisite to victory. I visited the Führer only a week ago to discuss an incident in which British warships fired on German survivors of a minesweeper that was sunk off Norway. He urged us to practice total war. There's no other answer to an enemy who bombs defenseless women and children in our cities—"

Ernst was astonished. The Lion's face was flushed; he was close to losing his legendary composure. It was becoming extremely clear that he expected his commanders to display a hardness beyond all previous measurements of that quality. For a moment Ernst was bitterly grateful to Berthe. She had prepared him for this task. Perhaps he would send her a thank you note before he sailed.

A week later Ernst was in Kiel, the German Navy's main North Sea base, greeting his crew. He had no worries about the twenty-five veterans who had sailed with him before. But the other twenty enlisted men looked much too green. He was not pleased to learn that many of them had been drafted from the surface fleet, which the British had bottled up in Norwegian ports. One of the strengths of the Ubootwaffe had been the shared knowledge that every man aboard a boat was a volunteer.

Ernst marched the crew to U-boat 666 at her dock and led them aboard. She was another Class VIIC, an exact copy of the Ritterboot. He heard mutters of distress from the new men at the sardinelike living quarters. But the machinery gleamed, the fresh paint on the hull had a reassuring shine in the fall sunlight. The boat was brand new, direct from the shipyards. Ernst put the crew to work on loading her and invited Chief Engineer Kleist and First Officer Kurz to join him for a drink in the Lorelei, a favorite U-boat bar.

Kurz and Kleist agreed that the new men were a worry. But they thought the veterans would sell the newcomers on the virtues of the Old Man and all would be well.

"It looks like a good boat," Kurz said. "Except for the number."

"What's wrong with the number?" Ernst asked.

"It's the number of the beast that heralds the end of the world in the Book of Revelations," Kurz said.

"That's the last time I want you to mention that!" Ernst snapped. "On this voyage, keep your religion to yourself and your rosary in your pocket."

"As you say, Herr Kaleu," Kurz said, and listened politely while Ernst lectured him on the importance of communicating hardness to the crew—a quality that was incompatible with piety.

"We're putting a new symbol on our conning tower. A wolf's head. The era of the noble knight is over."

They thought he was paying tribute to Admiral Dönitz's *Rudeltaktic*, the wolf pack assaults on convoys by as many as a dozen U-boats. "A good idea," Kleist said. "The boat I was on got three ships in one of those attacks, even though the Commander was wetting his pants most of the time."

Kurz's wife had given birth to a baby girl. He showed Ernst her baptismal picture, complete with a smiling priest and beaming grandparents.

"Nobody's smiling like that in Cologne," Kleist said.

His brother-in-law had been killed in a recent air raid. "People are beginning to realize the Führer has sown the wind and we're about to reap a cyclone," he said.

"There'll be no more remarks like that on this voyage, Chief!" Ernst said. "This war is too serious, too desperate, to risk violating the führer principle with personal opinions!"

"Even among old comrades, Herr Kaleu?" Kleist said.

"Even among old comrades—because they're overheard and misunderstood by others."

They were finding out the Old Man had changed. Let them figure out how to deal with it. He had not invited them to sail with him. They had volunteered.

Two weeks later, Ernst had completed testing U-666 and honing his crew's skills on a ferocious crash schedule which had left them little time for sleep. On the conning tower Oskar Kurz had painted a white, larger than life-size wolf's head and Ernst told the crew they would be known as the Wolfseeboot. Sailing to Lorient, he received his sealed orders from Fregattenkapitan Viktor Schutze, still the commander of the Second U-boat Flotilla, and heard another lecture on the importance of destroying the enemy's crews. Ernst asked Schutze if he had any suggestions on how to achieve this goal. "We're leaving that to the ingenuity—and hardness—of individual commanders," Schutze said.

The news from the Wehrmacht's battlefronts was not good. The Russians were still fighting fiercely in the ruins of Stalingrad. The position of the Afrika Corps in Egypt was becoming more precarious every day. The British were building up supplies and men for a new offensive. Only the U-boats could stop them by carving up the convoys before they reached Gibraltar. Fregattenkapitan Schutze seemed to relish the Army's predicament. He was still locked in the traditional rivalry between the Kriegsmarine and the Wehrmacht. How difficult it was to change habits of mind from the old Germany! Perhaps the Nazi party, with its determination to cleanse and renew everything, was the harsh medicine they needed.

On October 1, 1942, the Wolfseeboot sortied from Lorient harbor in the dusk. A week later they were far out in the Bay of Biscay, off the Spanish coast. On the bridge was the Metox antiradar warning device that was supposed to protect them against enemy planes. Kleist said the thing was next to useless, which was hardly surprising—it was a French invention. Half the time it failed to provide even its promised thirty seconds warning.

Ernst met the challenge by demanding superhuman vigilance from his lookouts. He constantly appeared on the bridge to check them. Any man who did not have his field glasses jammed to his eyes, studying the horizon, sweeping nearby clouds, got a tongue lashing.

"Ship!" cried one of the lookouts as dawn broke on the seventh day of their voyage. Within five minutes, Ernst was on the bridge. Out of the gray haze emerged the strangest imaginable sight, a big three-masted schooner. Ernst clapped the lookout on the back; he was one of the new men and needed encouragement.

"It looks like the Flying Dutchman," said Kurz, who had the watch.

"She's French," Ernst said, reading the name on her bow through his glasses. "*Notre Dame de Chatelet*. What does it mean, Number One?"

"Our Lady of the Little Castle," Kurz said. "It's a fishing vessel, probably on the way to the Grand Banks off Newfoundland."

"They could also be out here radioing the position of every U-boat they see," Ernst said. "Get the gun crew up here."

The schooner was barely moving in the light wind. They closed to about a half-mile while the gun crew piled onto the deck and prepared the bow gun for firing. They shrugged into their life jackets and buckled on their lifelines. There was a moderate sea running. It was very easy to get washed off the bow of a U-boat.

Other men formed a human chain to pass the ammunition to the gunners. Kurz was puzzled and did not conceal it. "She hardly seems worth the trouble, Herr Kaleu," he said.

Ernst ignored him. "Clear for firing!" called the commander of the gun crew.

"Open fire!" Ernst said.

The cannon boomed. The first shot was short, the next one long. Ernst ordered Kurz to close the range. The third shot was a direct hit on the *Notre Dame de Chatelet*'s pilot house. Wood chips flew in all directions. It collapsed in a puff of smoke.

Men were pouring onto the schooner's decks. "Switch to incendiary shells!" Ernst ordered. "Open fire with the other guns."

Crewmen began firing the smaller 37 and 20 millimeter antiaircraft guns on the bridge. The next two bow gun's shells plowed into the hull. A gush of flame leaped amidships. Two more shells and the entire ship was ablaze. The sails, the masts, were burning. The frantic crew tried to get some lifeboats over the side but they too began to burn. Many of the sailors toppled to the deck in the rain of steel from the smaller guns.

The main gun suddenly ceased firing. Ernst was astonished to see it was unmanned. One of the new men had fallen overboard and the rest of the gun crew were hauling on his lifeline to rescue him. "What the hell are you doing?" Ernst shouted. "Keep shooting and let that dumb bastard swim!"

"Herr Kaleu. He's one of ours!" Kurz said.

"Say a prayer for him," Ernst said.

The gun crew returned to their task, pounding shell after shell into the schooner for another ten minutes while the overboard man gurgled on his lifeline. Finally the *Notre Dame de Chatelet* toppled onto her side and slid beneath the surface with a sizzling hiss. About a dozen surviving members of her crew were clustered in the water. The nearest land was at least two hundred miles away.

Ernst felt Kurz's eyes on him, wordlessly asking why they were not going to give the survivors a rubber raft or a few extra life preservers. They often made such noble gestures on their first cruises in 1940. "Full ahead," Ernst said. "We need to put some distance between us and all this smoke."

The burning schooner had sent a mile-high column into the sky. Ernst knew he had been issuing an open invitation to any and all enemy ships and planes in the vicinity. But he told himself it was more than worth it as the weary gun crew tied down the main gun and hauled the waterlogged overboard sailor onto the deck.

"I don't understand, Herr Kaleu," Kurz said in his mild but stubborn way. "She couldn't have been more than two hundred and fifty tons."

"I want them to get used to killing people," Ernst said.

31

LIFE ON THE HIGH WIRE

"How was Moscow?"

"Cold. A hell of a place to sleep alone. How was Washington?"

"Ditto to part two of your critique of Moscow."

"Can I see you tonight?"

"It will have to be late."

"Have I ever argued about late?"

"It's nice to know there's one thing we agree on."

"I think there's one other thing. How late?"

"Eleven."

"Eleven."

Annie put down the telephone and sat very still at her desk, waiting for the slow gathering of desire in her thighs, its swift spread to her breasts, her palms, the tips of her fingers. It happened almost every time she heard Saul Randolph's voice. He had spent the last ten days in Moscow. Now the matinees and evenings would begin again.

High above the gaping groundlings, Annie was performing a new kind of love, an exhilarating combination of the high wire and power. Every thrust, every caress, every kiss, was special because it was enlarged, intensified, by the awareness of this delicious mixture.

Almost as important was the knowledge that the exchange was more or less between equals. Usually a woman could offer only a shadowy semblance of power—influence through family or husband or friends or inherited money. Thanks to "Behind The Headlines," Annie had access to power that made men and buildings shake and sway in the American capital.

That was pretty much what she had done for a month after Saul and Ned Travis convinced her that anti-Semitism was rampant in the U.S. State Department. Twice a week Annie blasted prejudice, incompetence and hostility to the Four Freedoms among the "striped pantywaists." She blamed them for everything from the reluctance of the British empire to renounce its colonies to the awful possibility that the Russians might drop out of the war.

On Capitol Hill, liberal Democratic congressmen and senators reinforced the assault, which was extensively echoed in other columns, particularly Drew Pearson's "Washington Merry-Go-Round." FDR chimed in at several White House press conferences, remarking at one point that the State Department functioned as a kind of American Cliveden Set—the English aristocrats who had played a major role in the appeasement of Hitler.

It was exciting to receive scribbled notes from Harry Hopkins, telling her how much the President had enjoyed a recent column. Jack, back from the Pacific, patted her on the head and told her she was helping to win the war—and the peace. Saul Randolph was even more effusive. It had added an operatic fervor to the first months of their affair. Roy Reeves sent her a mournful note, regretting her capture by "the enemy." She sent him copies of the anti-Semitic letters Ned Travis had leaked to her and asked him to explain them, please. He admitted anti-Semitism lingered among some State Department blue bloods who could not tolerate the idea that Jews and Catholics were rising to positions of power in America. He mailed her a copy of a letter he had sent to the Warsaw embassy man, rebuking him for his prejudice. He pointed out that Congress, not the State Department, was responsible for the immigration laws and the Southern Democrats in control of both houses were adamantly opposed to changing them.

In several drugstore phone calls, Reeves maintained that Roosevelt and his New Dealers had something far more complex in mind when they attacked the State Department for anti-Semitism. That was a device to appease Jewish voters for their inability to get any action out of Congress—and simultaneously gain control of State for much larger, more ominous goals, connected to unconditional surrender and postwar peace plans.

Annie was growing weary of Reeves's conspiratorial approach to politics. "If Roosevelt wants control of the State Department, why can't he just fire Cordell Hull and appoint anyone he wants?" she asked.

"Because Hull is a former Senator and has enormous influence on Capitol Hill, where Roosevelt's popularity is declining to a nadir. He needs Hull to get a peace treaty through the Senate without a Woodrow Wilson–style fiasco."

By this time the striped pantywaists were a shredded target, no longer worth additional ink. She told Reeves she was extremely skeptical of his White House plot scenario, but she was glad to learn he at least was not among the anti-Semites. That left him on hold as a source while she went on to other matters, such as the wacky ideas of the OSS. She wrote a ferocious attack on a plan to attack Japan with swarms of bats with incendiary bombs strapped to their backs. When Jack refused to run it, she threatened to leak it to Drew Pearson and he grudgingly capitulated.

Tonight she was hoping to collect a dividend from remaining on good terms with Roy Reeves. He was taking her to dinner with an Army Air Force general who was an old friend. He had an inside story on the air war in Europe that Reeves described as "dynamite." Waiting for them in the same small bar several miles out on Connecticut Avenue was Harold Magnuson, a big ruddy-cheeked cigar-smoking Swede from Minnesota. He told her about another raging feud—this one between the British and American bomber commands in Europe. The British wanted the Americans to join them in "area bombing" German cities. The Americans were insisting on limiting their attacks to military targets.

"Area bombing is terror tactics pure and simple," Magnuson said in a surprisingly soft, husky voice. "The Brits think they can pound the Germans to their knees without invading the continent. We can't see killing women and children that way, no matter how noble the objective is. A lot of us don't think it will work in the first place."

"Has a decision been made?"

"It's been kicked upstairs to the White House."

"Where I predict Roosevelt will side with the British," Roy Reeves said.

"Why?" Annie said.

"Unconditional surrender," Reeves said. "The moment I heard that policy, I realized Roosevelt plans to destroy Germany as a nation." He gave Annie a grisly smile. "Another reason why he wants to purge the State Department."

"I don't know a thing about that side of it," General Magnuson said. "I think the President's a decent man who's under a lot of pressure to keep everybody happy. Coalition warfare is loaded with headaches for the guys at the top. We're hoping a little noise in the newspapers might help him do the right thing. Are you interested?"

"I'm interested, but I don't run the column," Annie said. "I'm just a working stiff."

"We'll send you some stuff anyway," Magnuson said. He clutched his drink and abruptly lost his calm, detached tone. "I've got a boy flying one of those Eighth Air Force bombers," he said. "I hate to think of him killing old people and little kids."

Back in her apartment, Annie took a long, hot bath and put on a black silk negligee that Saul Randolph had given her, after stuffing her blue wool college bathrobe in the backyard incinerator. She slipped into the double bed and tried not to think about the clean-cut American pilots in the recruiting posters dropping bombs on German children. She banished Roy Reeves and his struggle for the future of the world. For the two-hundredth time, she bid scornful farewell to Zeke Talbot and his patriotic posturing. They were all irrelevant for the next few hours.

As usual, Saul Randolph arrived carrying champagne and caviar direct from Moscow. He had made this minifeast a sort of signature of their meetings. He emerged from a quick shower wearing only a towel, his dark hair and skin gleaming in the lamplight, and they sat at opposite ends of the bed, sipping and nibbling, exchanging capital gossip.

Saul had heard Mrs. Merriwether Post Hutton Davies wanted a part in the movie Hollywood was making of *Mission to Moscow*. The Prime Minister of Canada was coming for a visit and Annie recited a lyric Selma Shanley had written about him.

William Lyon Mackenzie King
He never gives us a goddamn thing.

Saul had recently spent some time testifying on lend-lease before the Senate Finance Committee and had learned from Lister Hill of Alabama a formula for world peace. "Keep your head up, your tail over the dashboard and your face to the rising sun and the shadows will fall behind."

Laughing, Saul moved to Annie's end of the bed and his hand drifted beneath her negligee. His tongue was on her neck, her nipples; the towel and the negligee vanished into the shadows beyond the bed and darkness began to pulse in Annie's belly, her throat, her eyes. She had never wanted Zeke with such ravening intensity. That was obviously one of the defects of surrender love, the way it blurred the fine edge of desire. What a fool she had been, wasting eleven years on that Anglo-Saxon turkey.

"How did you get so good at this?" Saul said, as her tongue returned the compliments he had been giving her.

"It's all your fault," she said, mounting him. "If you clone yourself, it'll become an epidemic."

He placed his palms on her hardened nipples and Annie began sliding up and down that pulsing rod of flesh. "The FBI will of course investigate you," she murmured. "The war effort will have come to a complete stop between noon and three p.m. every day."

Spreading his legs, he began a series of slow exquisite thrusts. "The enemy will be at the gates," she whispered. "Panzers will be debarking—at Newport News—Japanese—paratroopers—will be descending—on Los Angeles. There will be only one thing—to do—one—magnificent gesture for you—and your fellow clones. It will solve—the meat shortage—for the rest of the year."

"Bitch," he snarled and rolled her over. Pinning her arms, he began stroking her in a totally dominant mode. She whimpered with pleasure, half-pretense, half-real. "If only you loved me—this would be—so much more meaningful—"

Darkness was gathering around his mouth. It oozed from his black hair, his olive skin, his vivid eyes. Annie bit his shoulder, his neck, she writhed beneath him, clawing his arms, his hairy thighs. "The snake woman dies—but she never—surrenders!"

She was eluding him as much or more as she was satisfying him. That was a vital part of high-wire love in Washington, D.C. At a height that was dizzying to contemplate, much less experience, surrender would be a fatal mistake. It could lead to a fall of terrifying proportions.

Darkness, Annie opened her mouth, her arms, her thighs to it, she let it penetrate her body through every orifice. It was the essence of the body's orgasm, the little death that the poets of love exalted, from Ovid to John Donne. It was release from the body's loneliness without abandoning the self's independence, a moment of mutual triumph that was both mythical and real.

"Now?" he said.

"No," she said. She always said no.

"*Now*," he insisted.

"No. I want it—to last—forever," she said.

"*Now!*" he said.

That was the signal for Annie to seek ultimate darkness behind her closed eyes. In this hiding place which refused even the possibility of light, it was dark darker darkest, an eruption of urtime, urplace, preceding the creation of the sun or moon, a reality that God had never penetrated with his effulgence. She let it crash through her, heavier than lava, as unpredictable as that bubbling boiling serpentine flow.

Where did he go in the ultimate moment? she wondered dazedly as he unwrapped his arms and swung his feet over the edge of the bed. In nonsurrender love didn't both parties have to hide somewhere?

Perhaps the question was superfluous. Saul did not need a hiding place. In fact, he did not seem to need an imagination. His mind was focused entirely on the present moment in the real world. He was puzzled—and finally bored—by Annie's interest in history.

In five minutes he was back, still naked, pouring the rest of the champagne. "The Russians are furious," he said, sitting beside her against the back of the bed. "Roosevelt made them a promise last June. A second front in 1942. He knew he couldn't deliver on it. But he was afraid they'd drop out of the war."

"So?"

"In August, Churchill flew to Moscow to tell Stalin we couldn't keep the promise. Stalin said that was the last straw. First canceling the Murmansk convoys, now this double-cross. A lot of Russians started telling me and other people they were ready to take any deal the Germans offered them. That's when Roosevelt decided we had to do something. So an invasion of North Africa is in the works, in spite of violent resistance by our Army and Navy."

Major news. Annie often picked up this sort of thing from Saul. It certified the mingling of power and pleasure that gave their affair its momentum. "North Africa's not Europe. Will it be enough to keep the Russians happy?" she asked.

Saul shook his head. "The President's got to make some gestures, some statements that will keep Stalin in the war. If all goes well in the invasion, there's going to be a conference at Casablanca that they hope Stalin will attend. Churchill and Roosevelt are going to give him a guarantee on the only terms they'll accept from Hitler."

"Unconditional surrender?" Annie said. She loved to be a step ahead of this man whenever possible. It was another way of equalizing their balance of power.

"Where did you hear about it?" Saul asked, slightly deflated.

"A source in the State Department."

"Don't you think it's a marvelous slogan? It would make a lot of sense, even if the Russians weren't in the equation. It's the only thing that will teach the Germans a lesson they'll never forget."

"Absolutely," Annie said, remembering—and dismissing—Roy Reeves's critique.

"It's top secret for the time being but you or Jack ought to be in Casablanca when FDR makes the announcement, so you can start giving it maximum support."

"I'll pass the word to my other lord and master."

"There's a lot of opposition to it inside the State Department. They think we should negotiate with those Nazi bastards."

"Revolting," she said, letting him think she might scorch the diplomats again. But the new Annie was in charge now, the wary independent woman.

At the office in the morning Annie told Jack about the North Africa invasion and he nodded cheerfully. "I've got it all lined up. I'm landing with the first wave."

Annie added the rest of it: unconditional surrender, the announcement at Casablanca. Jack thought the policy was brilliant. "FDR at his best!" he declared. He would cover the Casablanca meeting if the conquest of North Africa was completed by then. Otherwise she would have to handle it. Selma Shanley would get her the press credentials.

Jack was worried about the invasion. For one thing, the Allied force was relatively small, only 100,000 men. A lot depended on whether the French Army in North Africa, roughly the same size, resisted. In 1940 they had fought off a British-Free French attempt to seize Oran. From their capital in Vichy, the beaten French were trying to retain a few shreds of national glory under the leadership of the World War I hero, Marshal Henri Petain. No one was sure how they would react to this invasion of their African empire.

Annie told Jack about General Magnuson and the bombing controversy.

"Forget it," he said. "That's strictly for the circular file."

"Why not try to push Roosevelt in the right direction?" she asked, irked by this offhand dismissal. "Are you in favor of killing German women and children?"

"They killed a lot of British women and children," Jack said, starting to lose his temper. "I was over there. I saw it."

"But the Germans didn't kill any Americans," Annie said. "Anyway, isn't there something repulsive about that kind of revenge?"

"It's exactly what the bastards deserve!" Jack roared. "The more I listen to you, the more I wonder about letting women anywhere near a war. You win wars by being tough, cruel, relentless! Get that through your pretty head once and for all!"

A week later, Jack vanished, along with a number of Annie's Army and Navy contacts in the War Department. For two weeks Washington seethed with wild rumors. A lot of people predicted an attack on Spain, others said it was Dieppe again, to make up for the British bungle. At dinner parties and lunches, Annie and Saul Randolph exchanged insider smiles. Sharing a big secret was a marvelous stimulant to a Washington affair.

On November 8, black headlines, tense voices on the radio, announced that allied troops were storming ashore at Oran, Algiers and other exotic ports of call. Eight hours later, the teletype clicked out a hair-raising dispatch from Jack. There had been strong French resistance around Port Lyautey, and a fierce battle erupted between Vichy and American tanks, with the Americans in trouble from the start because their radios had been ruined by exposure to damp sea air on the voyage from the states. In prose studded with vivid imagery, Jack told how a fifty-year-old reserve colonel named Paul Stapleton walked from tank to tank in his battalion, ignoring blizzards

324 ==== THOMAS FLEMING

of machine gun and cannon fire, to direct the American defense.

"You can smell the gunpowder," Sidney Arnold said.

"I'm smelling too damn much of it," Selma Shanley said. "Somebody better tell our hero bullets go through newspapermen too."

Before Annie could start worrying about Jack, they were swamped by the diplomatic side of the North African story. Instead of fighting the French Army, the Americans under General Dwight D. Eisenhower negotiated a cease fire with the Vichy official in command of the region, Admiral Jean Darlan. A State Department professional, Robert D. Murphy, played a key role in the secret negotiations that persuaded Darlan to order his men to lay down their weapons. Jack covered it as a breaking story, getting interviews with Eisenhower and Murphy within hours of the announcement. His tone was exultant. The invasion's success seemed guaranteed.

That night, Annie went to dinner with Saul Randolph at the mansion of society hostess Evalyn Walsh McClean. She was looking forward to a celebratory evening and a very good dinner. The aging Mrs. McClean was a somewhat faded ghost from the 1920s when she had boasted First Ladies such as Florence Harding as best friends. But she always had an interesting mix of people from Congress, the courts and the executive branch.

"Isn't that wonderful news from North Africa?" she said to Saul in the taxi.

"How in God's name can you say that?" he said. "I've been sick to my stomach all day over it."

Totally bewildered, Annie listened to him denounce Eisenhower, Robert Murphy and the State Department. Secretary Morgenthau had gone to the White House this afternoon and told FDR he and everyone in the Treasury Department were appalled and disgusted by the deal with Darlan. "The Secretary told me he's thinking of resigning. I told him I felt the same way," Saul said.

"But it saved American lives."

"It besmirched American honor! That bastard Darlan is a French Nazi. He applied Hitler's Nuremberg laws in North Africa. Jews were barred from holding office, forbidden to vote."

"I'm beginning to wonder which of us is the romantic, which the realist," Annie said. "As we say in Chicago, you've got to give a little to get a little. We call it dealing, the State Department calls it diplomacy."

"Chicago disgusts me almost as much as Vichy France, if you want to know the truth," Saul said. "Are you in favor of exporting Chicago's politics to the rest of the world? Is that what you think Americans should die for? This war is either a crusade that will change the future of the world—or it's a brainless slaughter that means nothing—like World War One."

"The people who went to France in World War One—my father was one of them—thought they were going to change the future of the world. Doesn't that tell you something?"

"Yes. This time we've got to do it right! That's why I keep asking you to give the Soviet Union more coverage in 'Behind The Headlines.' Cooperation—and eventual convergence with their system—is crucial to the future of the world."

> Soviet Union hits the spot
> Twelve million soldiers that's a lot
> Timoshenko and Stalin too
> Soviet Union is Red White and Blue

It was another Selma Shanley lyric, making fun of the way the ad men in the Office of War Information tried to sell the Russians to the American people. The words were on Annie's lips but she chose not to say them. By now it had become very clear to her that Saul Randolph had a vision of the future that she found hard to share. It involved social engineering of the boldest kind—the use of government power to redistribute America's wealth, not only within the United States but around the world. It presumed that poverty was mankind's essential problem and once that was removed, we would be on our way to heaven on earth.

Whenever Saul talked this way, Annie started reciting: *pride, covetousness, lust, anger, gluttony, envy and sloth*. She found it hard if not impossible to believe that the eradication of poverty would change mankind's predilection for the seven deadly sins. In an occasional daydream she pointed out to Saul how often he and his fellow liberals committed some of them, notably pride, lust, envy and anger. But she never voiced such abrasive thoughts. She told herself she had learned a lesson from Zeke Talbot. She would sheathe her wicked tongue, even if it sometimes almost choked her.

At Evalyn Walsh McClean's splendid mansion, they sat opposite chunky Senator Burton K. Wheeler of Montana. Although he was a Democrat, he had opposed Roosevelt's unneutral prewar foreign policy and he was still a leader of the growing anti-Roosevelt bloc in the Senate. Annie tried to keep the conversation light by asking him what he considered the administration's least serious fault.

"Failing to put a muzzle on Henry Wallace," Wheeler said. "If I hear one more speech about exporting the New Deal to the rest of the world, I'm going to throw up."

Someone else urged him to admit that occasionally Roosevelt did something right. Wheeler grudgingly conceded the deal with Admiral Darlan was one of the President's few good moves.

"Senator," Saul Randolph said. "I always thought you were a Nazi at heart. Now I know you're one."

Dismay spread from face to face around the table. Aside from the general desire to avoid a nasty argument, it was not customary to speak so bluntly to a U.S. Senator. Wheeler replied with a blast at lend-lease and the entire Treasury Department, which he said was honeycombed with Communists. The whole table was soon in a wild shouting match that left their aging hostess, Mrs. McClean, in tears. A congressman tried to soothe matters by suggesting a vote on the deal with Darlan. The pro-Darlanists won by a two to one margin. Saul flung down his napkin and invited Annie to join him at the nearest White Tower. "I'd rather eat with ordinary people who believe in democracy and decency," he roared.

They dined in silence on hamburgers the size of half-dollars. Annie ate six of them. In Georgetown Saul paid the taxi and followed Annie up the stairs to her apartment, where he opened a split of champagne from the refrigerator and slumped back on the couch, morosely sipping it.

"Saul, that was a mistake," Annie said. "You had no right to ruin poor old Evalyn's dinner party."

"It wasn't a mistake," he said. "It's important to resist these fascist bastards. Otherwise we're never going to get the stupid blundering past off our backs. We're never going to cleanse this world."

"Hail, Rabbi," Annie said, raising her glass.

"What the hell does that mean?"

"That's what they said to Jesus when he started acting like the Messiah."

"I sometimes think you're too smart for your own good. Or mine."

She saw, she understood, what was wrong. Tonight he wanted more than high-wire love. The betrayal of his political ideals in distant Algiers had wounded the whole enterprise that had brought him to Washington. His martyred roommate's ghost hovered reproachfully above them. For a moment sympathy stirred in Annie's throat. But it did not descend to the rest of her body. It did not penetrate her heart. It would take more than wounded idealism to tempt her into surrender love again.

She suddenly wanted to give Saul a lecture on the idea of progress, possibly the most important concept that the French Enlightenment had unleashed on the modern world. It had spurred science, democracy and created the political vision of men like Thomas Jefferson. It had also spawned men like Robespierre, Napoleon and Lenin and piled up mountains of corpses in their wake. Anna Richman had written a brilliant paper on the ambiguities of progress in her senior year at Trinity College.

Before she could speak, Saul's lips were on her throat. "Can't you see how much I need you?" he whispered. "What have I got to do, crawl on my knees?"

The plea was so at variance with her perception of their affair, she almost fell off the wire. She recovered by pretending an ardor that she did not feel. She let him undress her and lead her into the bedroom. "I love the way you do this," she whispered as he entered her. "I only wish it could fix everything in this crazy world."

"When I'm with you like this, I can pretend it does."

Sweetness, the sympathetic cousin of surrender, was surging through her flesh. She twisted her head away, avoiding another kiss. "I want to pretend. I want to pretend with you," she said. Was that the truth or part of a performance? Somehow Annie managed to cling to the wire, telling herself the gift remained qualified for the time being. It was not, it could never be, a substitute for her lecture on the idea of progress, an alternative to his admitting she had a mind.

When the sighs subsided, there was more champagne—and the authority returned to Saul's voice. "Now that you've softened them up, it's time to make another move on the State Department. The Russians have a list of people they want out of there."

Her mind, where had it gone? Annie groped for it in the engulf-ing sweetness. "Stalin is purging the U.S. State Department?" she said.

"The President's given it his full approval," Saul said.

From a confusing distance, Annie heard Roy Reeves telling her that Roosevelt had devious reasons of his own for attacking the State Department.

"A lot of them are the anti-Semites you gunned down two months ago," Saul said.

"That's my privilege. I wasn't doing it for Stalin. Or Roosevelt."

"Haven't you read *Mission to Moscow?*" Saul said. "Surely you don't still believe the Vatican's version of the Soviet Union?"

The slow ebb of pleasure, its replacement by the elixir of power, the sweet mingling of these two sensualities, vanished from Annie's mind and body. "*Mission to Moscow* is absolute bullshit, " she said. "I've got a memorandum in my files from my source at the State Department listing sixty-seven errors of fact!"

She might as well have talked to a hatrack. Saul padded to the closet and drew a folded paper from his coat pocket. "Here's the list," he said. "Anything you can get on these guys will help ease them out."

Roy Reeves's name was at the head of the list. "He's target num-ber one as far as Litvinov is concerned," Saul said. "They had a lot of collisions in Moscow when Max was Foreign Minister."

"I know him," Annie said. "He's always struck me as a patriot."

"He's considered the Vatican's man at State. He goes to church or Mass or whatever the hell you call it every day."

Was that the source of Roy Reeves's integrity? "Being a Catholic has nothing to do with it," Annie said. "The man deals in facts. There's a stench of evil around Stalin."

"You're being ridiculous. He's tough, brutal—but evil? I don't know what the word means."

One of the oddities about the idea of progress is its annihilation of traditional ideas like evil. Progress has many of the characteristics of the shark. It is a predator idea. That was vintage Annie Richman circa 1927 but Saul Randolph was obviously uninterested in hearing the lecture. He was too busy giving her his standard spiel on the Soviet Union. It was a society with serious defects, such as concentra-tion camps. But how could Americans criticize them when we had ten million blacks living in segregated semislavery in the South? Progressive Russians were trying to change their system just like progressive Americans were trying to change the United States.

In a way, Annie was almost grateful for the spiel. She was ready for the peroration. "I want Roy Reeves to be number one on your hit list. I promised Litvinov we'd deliver."

"I'm sorry," Annie said. "The answer is no."

As angry disappointment distorted Saul's handsome face, Annie saw everything that was wrong with the way men thought and felt about sex and love. She also saw everything that was wrong with the way women usually thought and felt about it. For both it was a kind of war in which the conqueror and the conquered presumed surrender on one front meant surrender on all fronts. The logic of it was enormously difficult to resist. But she was going to try, no matter how much it complicated life on the high wire.

32

VISITOR FROM THE ABYSS

AFRICANO INVASION screamed the headlines in Madrid's newspapers as Berthe von Hoffmann walked from her apartment to the German embassy on November 9. A huge allied fleet had appeared off the North African coast yesterday. Thousands of American and British troops were swarming ashore to seize French Morocco, Algeria and Tunisia.

The news was, at best, a consolation in the fog of gloom that was engulfing her. Its root cause was the failure of the British and Americans to respond to the Schwarze Kapelle's peace overtures. The immediate cause was the calamitous rout the British had inflicted on the Afrika Korps at El Alamein in the Egyptian desert two weeks ago. For the first time she had to confront the reality of German defeat—and its impact had been agonizing.

At the embassy, she poured out her discouragement in a letter to Canaris, inserted, as usual, in a chatty note to Elisabeth von Theismann, who was still in France, acting as her conduit to Berlin.

When news of the North African invasion came over the radio, Jonathan Talbot told me about the diplomatic maneuvers here in Madrid to insure Spain's neutrality. The British ambassador, Hoare, favored a coup d'état to oust Franco. It would be led by ten generals whom he had bribed by depositing a million pounds in a Swiss bank. The Americans opposed this

plan and with the help of the Marquesa de Montoya extracted a promise
from the Caudillo that his 150,000 troops in Spanish Morocco would do
nothing. He was undoubtedly influenced by the defeat the British inflicted
on the Afrika Korps at El Alamein two weeks ago. What effect, if any, these
events will have on our hopes remains obscure. Herr von Spaeth thinks
Africa is a mere sideshow and will have no impact on the high command's
reluctance to cooperate with us. Jonathan Talbot's efforts to use your revelations about the Jews have met with almost complete indifference in America. The BBC, as you probably know, has begun broadcasting some information but it is regarded here as propaganda. For the past month, Talbot and
Moorman have been too involved with the preparations for the invasion to
give our concerns much thought. They are both in Tangier at the moment,
no doubt making sure Franco keeps his promise. More and more, I wonder
what I can accomplish here. I begin to think the Americans and the British
are playing with us, hoping to extract more information from you, without
the slightest interest in reciprocating. I exempt Jonathan Talbot from this
conclusion; he personally remains committed to us. But what can he accomplish in the face of such massive indifference?

She mailed the letter at the embassy, hoping it would receive no
more than a passing glance from the censor, who was a Sicherheitdienst man. Previously, the Abwehr had censored the mail. But the SD
had convinced someone in the Foreign Office that they should handle the job in Spain. It was one more sign of how closely the Nazis
were watching Canaris—how much they were all under suspicion—
and how Canaris was being forced to give ground.

Always, beneath this obvious anxiety, was Lothar Engle's warning
that the process was not a surrender but a merger, the absorption of
the SD by the Abwehr or vice versa, with Canaris the slippery amoral
confidence man who was deceiving everyone—including his own
agents. Berthe repeatedly tried to dismiss this possibility, but at times
it was like the young widow's veil, suffocating her.

The pasty-faced clerk in the embassy mail room wordlessly
handed her a letter. It was from Ernst. He thought she would like to
know he was sailing in U-Boat 666—with a wolf's head on the conning tower. All day, as she decoded routine messages, she thought
about him and his crew on the Atlantic. Would the British, with the
fourth rotor for the Enigma in their hands, know his every move, and
wait for him with wabos and air bombs? She could not bear the
thought that she would be the cause of his death. How could she

ever face her children again? They would hate her, no matter what she told them about the Führer's crimes.

The next morning her telephone rang as she was departing for work. A voice said: "This is your friend from Avila. Could you join me for a walk in the Retiro? I'll meet you by the boat lake."

In the bright November sunshine, the Abwehr chief in Spain, Otto von Spaeth, formal to his spats as usual, was strolling up and down beside the placid water. "I have alarming news from Berlin," he said in his usual monotone. "Your friend Elisabeth von Theismann has been arrested. If she confesses under torture, I might be required to order you home for questioning."

From his coat pocket he took a small vial. "This is a cyanide capsule. If the situation warrants it, you might consider taking it. Death is almost instantaneous. Many agents carry one."

Death. To walk from this world of sunshine and greenery into its gray blankness. Never to hold Jonathan Talbot in her arms again. Never to see her children again. Yet Berthe soberly put the vial in her purse and thanked Herr von Spaeth as if he were a doctor or a minister who had given her the best possible advice for her condition.

For the next two days, all she could see was Elisabeth von Theismann's face streaming blood. When Jonathan returned from Tangier, she told him what had happened—and showed him the cyanide capsule. "Give me that damn thing," he said.

She was shocked by his presumption. "Why?" she said.

"You're never going to take cyanide as long as I'm around."

"You're not all-powerful. You must know that."

"I won't let you keep it!"

"Are you afraid I'll use it on impulse some day? You think it's the sort of thing a woman might do?"

"I don't know what I think," he said, walking toward her, his hand out. "I only know I want to get rid of it."

She shook her head. "I'm afraid I must keep it," she said. "I don't know how brave I am when it comes to pain."

When they made love later that night, death was a spectral third in the bed. He oozed from the cyanide capsule in her purse like a special effect in a surrealist film. Staring through his grinning mouth and empty eye sockets into Jonathan's face gave every touch, every kiss, a strange new resonance. Dark chords in a minor key, played by a swelling, oddly sweet cello, resounded through her flesh. Jonathan's face became unutterably dear to her. She loved his angry determination to banish death for her sake. She trusted him with an absolute gift that reached out for the eternal. An amazing sweetness permeated her surrender.

Afterward, as she dozed in his arms, a verse from Johann Gottlieb Fichte's *Addresses to the German People* spoke in her mind.

And thus you are to act,
As though the destiny of German life
Hung solely from your deeds and you
And you alone were responsible.

Jonathan pressed his lips against her throat and said: "Give me that capsule."

"No," she said, all sweetness vanishing. On the very deepest level, he still did not trust her. That made her angry—and finally, sad.

None of this got Elisabeth von Theismann out of the Gestapo's clutches. But Berthe soon became as distracted as Jonathan by what transpired as the Americans fought their way inland against unexpectedly stiff resistance from the French army—and reached a hasty agreement with the French Admiral Jean Darlan that persuaded French troops to stop fighting.

"Darlan is Hitler's greatest admirer in France," Berthe said. "Why are you Americans willing to negotiate with him—but not with anti-Nazi Germans?"

Jonathan could only shake his head and confess his embarrassment. A week later, her "friend from Avila" called again to invite her for another walk in the Retiro park. This time Herr von Spaeth met her at the entrance and hailed a taxi that took them into the winding streets of the old Moorish section of Madrid. Nervously scanning the passersby, he hurried her into the dim interior of a small parish church. In the front pew before the white altar sat a man in the uniform of a Spanish naval officer. Closer, Berthe realized it was Admiral Canaris.

"I always come here when I visit Madrid," Canaris said. "It's where Queen Isabella prayed for the success of Columbus's voyage. Think of the history those prayers encompassed!"

"We're still trying to catch up to it," Herr von Spaeth said, with a wry smile.

"I'm here incognito," Canaris said to Berthe. "I hope you haven't become so enamored of your American lover that you'll betray me to Moorman's untender mercies."

"Never!" Berthe said.

"I'm on my way to Tangier to repair the havoc Moorman has wreaked among our agents there. The Führer is determined to seize Tunisia and fight it out for North Africa. He's prepared to throw 300,000 first-line troops into the battle—when he needs them desperately to reinforce the Sixth Army at Stalingrad. It's megalomania but it may inflict a stunning defeat on the British and Americans— when we can least afford one. If the Russians win at Stalingrad and the Anglo-Saxons lose in Tunisia—we may be forced to negotiate with the Russians. Generals tend to be impressed by force majeure."

All this in his dry melancholy voice. The man was evil. Why didn't he stir nausea in her flesh? Her revulsion only seemed to infest her mind. For some reason it stopped at the border of her body. Was it because they were in a sacred place?

"You must pass this information to your friend Talbot immediately. If the Anglo-Americans seize Tunis with an amphibious force or a paratrooper division, they could easily block the entire operation."

Berthe gazed at Herr Spaeth's graven Hohenzollernmumie face. There was no expression on it. Yet he was listening to high treason— with a cyanide capsule in his pocket.

She wanted to ask Canaris if the story about his tryst with Moorman in Tangier was true. But she already believed it. In the Admiral's mind, morals were as interchangeable as identities—or secret agents. "How is Elisabeth von Theismann?" she asked with barely concealed anger.

"She's still under interrogation," Canaris said. "Himmler forced me to surrender control of the police in France. This gave the SD access to certain information that aroused their suspicion of her. But I doubt if it's serious enough to cause her any harm."

"How is Count von Moltke?" she asked, as if she needed to invoke some sort of moral voice between them.

"He's well," Canaris said gravely. "Working indefatigably for our cause. As I am, dear Frau von Hoffmann. I know you don't believe it, but I am."

He was gone, gliding into the quarter's crowded streets with

Spaeth, leaving Berthe alone with her confusion and dismay. She gave the usual signal to Jonathan on the telephone and they met at her apartment. She told him about her meeting with Canaris and his warning of a major German response in Tunisia. "Please don't tell this to Moorman," she said.

"I have to tell Moorman. He's still in charge of intelligence around here."

"He'll seize Canaris—and ruin everything! Why can't you communicate this directly to your government? You Americans are the ones we want to negotiate with."

He gave her a look that was so weighted with suspicion, it was almost unloving. "I'm afraid you've got to negotiate with both countries," he said.

Moorman took the warning of Hitler's North African counteroffensive so seriously, he arranged for a trip to Avila, where he debriefed Berthe for an hour in the British safe house. A camera whirred in a projection booth while she repeated the warning and the rest of the conversation. "Why am I being filmed?" she asked, unable to contain her loathing of Moorman. "To make sure I'm thoroughly trapped?"

"The film will be sent to England so psychologists can study you for signs of possible pathology," Moorman said.

"I hope they know the difference between pathology and simple detestation," she said.

Jonathan sat in a corner of the room, his jaw clenched, looking like a Hollywood cowboy on his way to the OK Corral. On the way back to Madrid, Berthe asked Moorman if he planned to harass Canaris while he was in Tangier. "I intend to kidnap him," he said. "I've had a long-standing plan on tap with the intelligence director at Gibraltar."

"Can't you stop him?" Berthe cried to Jonathan.

"If I let him go, will you promise me another present, even better than the fourth rotor?" Moorman said.

"Yes. Anything!" Berthe said. Was the loathsome little toad going to ask her to go to bed with him?

"The rockets," Moorman said. "Where are they building them?"

"I've never heard of any rockets."

"Canaris knows about them. Long-range flying bombs. I suspect that's why Hitler's playing fast and loose with the German Army. He

thinks a few defeats may be good for the generals. It will destroy
their prestige and reduce them to slavish obedience. Then he'll rescue them and Germany with the rockets. Blow London and Moscow
off the map."

"Why can't you simply say you'll negotiate?" Berthe said.

"Because we don't trust you yet—and we haven't been able to
talk the Americans into it. This affair with Darlan has raised absolute
hell in their newspapers. Personally I'm not surprised. They have a
predilection for moral crusades. Making the world safe for democracy and that sort of rot."

Moorman was lolling in the rear seat of the car, his legs crossed,
staring out at the stark landscape of Castile. The casual posture
seemed to redouble the smug pleasure of his words. At the wheel,
Jonathan stared morosely down the highway, not even trying to disagree with him. Why not seize the wheel, smash the car into the first
boulder she saw? That would settle everything. She would die like a
good German, destroying two enemies.

To her bewilderment, she felt Jonathan's hand on her arm. Did
he know what she was thinking? She choked out the words of submission. "I will try to find out what I can—about the rockets."

Back in her apartment, she clung to Jonathan, weeping fiercely.
"He wants to humiliate every German he meets. That's all he cares
about!" she said.

"It's just a bad English habit," Jonathan said. "He tries to humiliate me too. Remember how much Canaris humiliated him the last
time around."

He poured her a brandy. "Better yet, remember what we felt in
Granada when we heard Petenera."

How could she forget that? How could she forget Kristallnacht,
the stench of evil, those reports of mass murder Moltke showed her?
Was it this exposure to other countries, their perversities and blind
passions that made her begin to yearn secretly for a German victory
in spite of everything? Did this wilderness of deception ultimately
lead to self-deception?

"Don't stop loving me no matter what I become," she said.

"Don't *worry*," he said, an American expression that frequently
baffled her.

In the next two weeks, Jonathan's reassurance acquired an ironic
ring. Both she and his British and American confreres found them-

selves worrying a great deal. The high command in London and Washington ignored Canaris's warning about Hitler's determination to fight a major battle in North Africa. They made no attempt to seize Tunis. The British did not even bother to reinforce their fleet or air force at Gibraltar. The Allies were stunned when the Luftwaffe and the Italian Navy combined to fling a bridge of ships from southern France to Tunis and pour in over 350,000 men.

Jonathan claimed to be pleased. He said it might persuade Moorman to lay off Canaris. He avoided her eyes in an uncharacteristic way as he said this.

"What does that mean?" she said. "I thought he agreed to let the Admiral go back to Berlin unmolested."

"He did—but—"

Halfheartedly, he confessed to a new dimension of deception. Off the Spanish coast as the North African invasion fleet approached was a U-boat wolfpack. Thanks to the acquisition of the fourth rotor of the Enigma machine and some creative work by British cryptanalysts in London, they knew exactly where the submarines were from eavesdropping on their radio traffic. The U-boats posed a serious threat to the invasion—until they were decoyed into pursuing a convoy of twenty-six empty ships heading out of Gibraltar. "On orders from Moorman, I've been telling my Spanish contacts we got the information about the wolfpack from Canaris personally," Jonathan said.

"That's absolutely despicable!" Berthe said.

"It's a cover to make sure the U-boat high command doesn't start changing the codes."

"I don't care!"

Jonathan took her hands. "Yes you do. I promised you—and myself—that I'd trust you absolutely. That's why I'm telling you this. Moorman would have me shot if he found out about it. All you have to do is send a message to Canaris—or to Admiral Dönitz—and we're blown. But I know you won't do it."

"There's still such a thing as conscience in this business. Some degree of moral responsibility."

"Between us. Only between us."

"No. Between us and the world. The rotten beastly world."

Suddenly all the news was coming from Radio Berlin, accompanied by funereal music. The great Sixth Army was no longer conquering Stalingrad. Exactly as Count Moltke had predicted, two slashing Russian thrusts on either side of the salient had cut them off from the rest of the German Army. They were trapped, starving, supplied only by a trickle of supplies delivered from the air through the freezing rain and snow and fog of the oncoming Russian winter. Her brother-in-law, Berthold von Hoffmann, was among them. Berthe thought of his wife and their two children listening to the same funereal music—while she rejoiced.

Or pretended to rejoice. The smiles of hope, the kisses of conspiratorial affection she gave Jonathan were just genuine enough to satisfy his exultant inattention. It was the great defeat for which they had been waiting and praying and scheming. Where was authentic joy, unquestioning hope? She did not know. She only knew that she began to dread Jonathan's visits, to wonder how much longer she could continue to deceive him.

Perhaps it was the oncoming Christmas season, which naturally stirred nostalgia and regret in her German soul. There would be no rejoicing anywhere in the Reich this Christmas. For a present, the Berlin Superior Court mailed her a divorce decree, formally severing her from Kapitanleutnant Ernst von Hoffmann, the cause adultery, the charge uncontested. She did not show the letter to Jonathan—a bad sign.

On the day before Christmas, she returned to her apartment through the biting cold of the Madrid night air, which according to legend, could snuff out a candle—or a life—with equal savagery. Jonathan was planning to take her to dinner to celebrate the season and their rising hopes. She was not at all sure she could bear it.

When she opened the door of her apartment, she saw the back of a man's head in one of the wing chairs in the living room, outlined against the twilit windows. He was listening to Radio Berlin, which was reporting a new attempt by the Sixth Army to break out of the Stalingrad trap. Berthe felt her whole body recoil at the thought of another night spent discussing the debacle and its meaning.

"Oh turn that off!" she said. "Surely tonight of all nights we can talk about something else—"

The man in the wing chair stood up and strolled to the door of the living room. His face remained in shadow. Berthe had not turned on the light in the dining room. She flipped the switch and Lothar Engle smiled mockingly at her in the black uniform of an SS Oberführer. "How prescient of you, dear Berthe. That's exactly what I want to do. Talk to you about something else—which may help us redeem our faltering fatherland."

"I can't imagine what that would be," she said.

Lothar strolled toward her, the mocking smile still in place. It was not dissimilar to his usual smile. But his eyes exuded something very different from their old warmth. "Let's start with Elisabeth von Theismann," he said, crowding her back against the door. "She died like a classic heroine, without telling us a thing. She was really extraordinary. Can you imagine what they did to her, Berthe?"

She shook her head, nausea flooding her body. She was breathing evil. The stench was seeping from his pores.

"They inserted an electrified rod into a very personal part of her body and turned the current up to full. It caused unspeakable convulsions. I would hate to see anyone insert something like that into you, darling Berthe."

"Why should they? I only knew Elisabeth slightly—through mutual friends."

"You wrote her a great many letters for such a slight acquaintance. She had them all listed in an odd little book she kept. She got a great many letters from people in France but you were the only one who wrote from Spain."

From an inner pocket he took a letter wrapped in oilskin. "Of course, you didn't sign your real name—an oddity in itself. No one in the SD knew who Helene—or any of the others were—which no doubt induced them to turn up the juice in that obscene device higher and higher. When Elisabeth finally died they sent all the documents to Berlin where they landed on the desk of the one man who could recognize Helene's handwriting."

She remained standing with her back against the door. Lothar reached past her and put on the chain. "It's all so coincidental, Berthe. Here you are, freshly divorced, completely available—and I'm the only one who suspects what you're doing. It's enough to make even an atheist wonder if someone has arranged our reunion in accordance with a marvelous plan."

He pulled out a dining room chair and sat down in it, legs crossed nonchalantly, exactly like Moorman in the back of the car. "You can make it all perfectly easy, dear darling Berthe, by telling me everything. Exactly what you've been doing here in Spain at the behest of Admiral Canaris. Exactly what's in the rather labored prose of this letter, which I would never imagine you had written, if it wasn't for the handwriting."

"There's nothing to tell," she said. "I'm not working for Admiral Canaris. The letter to Elisabeth Theismann deals with an affair I've been having with an American here in Spain."

"Ohhh. You're going to be difficult."

Lothar's cruel smile remained in place. Berthe thought of the cheerful smiles on the faces of the sculptures in the Portico Gloria of the cathedral in Santiago de Compostella. Saint James in the Field of the Star. Did it mean anything? Was the Star, the Path, mere scraps of a lost faith? Was she some sort of hysteric, easily explained by Freud and his friends?

"Here's what we'll do. We'll drive south for the holidays. To Granada or Seville or some other romantic place. I'll insert something into that private place of yours which used to make you very talkative. Don't you remember, dear Berthe? How you used to confess all your secret fears and worries and longings to me? By the time the holidays are over, it will be exactly the same. You'll be ready to go back to Berlin with me and tell Herr Himmler and others—perhaps even the Führer—everything you know about the treacherous head of our secret service. I'll protect you from punishment. I'll convince them you were a double agent all the time, working for me. They'll be so pleased they may make me the head of the new combined intelligence service."

"Lothar—I have nothing to tell."

He sprang up and grabbed a fistful of her hair. She thought for a moment he was going to rip it out of her head. "Berthe—if I love anything in this world, it's you. Do you believe that?"

She tried to say yes. But she was too terrified.

"That won't stop me from turning you over to the interrogators. We've gone much too far. We can't let personal emotions get in the way."

She saw he had accepted everything—the annihilation of the Jews, the justification of every kind of terror and brutality. He had become one of them.

"Go in that bedroom and pack a bag. We're leaving immediately on our southern honeymoon."

He shoved her into the bedroom. She could hear him pacing up and down the dining room. She flung underclothes, an extra dress into a suitcase. What else could she do?

Jonathan was coming here later tonight. He had a key. When she did not answer his knock he would almost certainly come in and search the apartment. Quickly she grabbed a piece of writing paper from her dresser and scribbled: *My SS friend Lothar Engle has taken me south to Granada or Seville. He knows everything. You must follow us and somehow kill him.*

33

MURDER MOST FOUL

Kill him? Jonathan Talbot stood in the middle of Berthe's disordered bedroom, the note clutched in his hand. *Kill him?*

Had Berthe gone crazy? He was not an assassin by trade. Annapolis had only trained him to kill people at long ranges—a mile, two miles, ten miles, depending on the size of the guns a ship carried. He tore across moonlit Madrid to Moorman's apartment and persuaded the sereno to let him pound on the door until the little Englishman opened it in his pajamas, cursing violently.

He read the message and said: "Let's first find out if Engle's genuine."

"I know he's genuine. She's told me about him."

Moorman merely snorted and got dressed, lecturing him on not believing anything he heard from the lips of Germans. They drove to the British embassy and a sleepy radio operator raised London. Messages crackled and sputtered and a snub-nosed young code clerk toiled to translate them while Moorman muttered about his incompetence, laziness and insubordination.

"Lothar Engle. Former journalist. Risen rather high and fast in the SS. Director of their propaganda department," Moorman said, reading from Engle's London file as they strolled to his office. "You shouldn't have any difficulty killing him."

The words caused another upheaval in Talbot's nervous system. "How?" he said.

"That's what we've got to decide, old chap. Once we discover where they've gone, which should be fairly simple. I'll alert our agents in Granada and Seville. Your Lorelei will be easy to spot. Spain has a distinct shortage of beautiful blondes. Meanwhile we can select a method. It will have to be quiet and quick. Poison won't do. You can't get close enough to him. Trying to bribe a Spaniard to do the job could be a balls-up. You never know where their loyalty lies."

"What's wrong with a gun?" Talbot said.

"Noise and mess. We don't want the Spanish police involved in this. Even with a silencer, you've got blood. You might accidentally shoot her. Or he might shoot you. We've got to presume he's armed."

Moorman gazed at a painting of the Taj Mahal on the wall, not far from his lost destroyer. He had spent ten years in India between the wars, running agents who disrupted Mohandas Ghandi's independence movement. "Thuggee," he said. "That could be the answer."

"What?" Talbot said.

"Haven't you seen the bloody movie, *The Lives of the Bengal Lancers*? The Thugs were a thriving Indian sect until we more or less wiped them out. They specialized in ritual murder with a silk cord around the throat. Blamed it all on their bloodthirsty goddess, Kali. It's makes for a clean, noiseless death."

"Where do I get the cord? And the training?"

Moorman grinned in his macabre way and took a strand of silk from his desk drawer. "This is the real thing," he said fondly. "I bought it from the grandson of an authentic Thug in Mysore."

He tied knots at each end of it, pulled hard on them, and sprang out of his chair with amazing agility for a man his age. In a flash he had the silk around Talbot's throat, pulling it tight. In ten seconds Talbot's eyes bulged, life began draining from his body. "Rather good, don't you think?" Moorman said, letting him breathe again.

"Wonderful," Talbot gasped. "How do I get close enough to use it? Invite him to my bedroom for tea?"

"I rather think you'll have to invite yourself to his bedroom."

Suddenly all traces of amusement—which was, he realized, a form of panic—vanished from Talbot's mind and body. For the first time he realized why Engle was taking Berthe south to Andalusia.

South was romance—with a twisted Nazi sneer in the middle of the word. Maybe it would not be so hard to kill him, after all.

After a few hours of fitful sleep, Talbot spent most of the next day practicing the fine art of Thuggee murder. As a former wrestler, he had more than enough forearm strength. Moorman pronounced him a first-class candidate for membership in the cult of Kali.

"What exactly does she represent?" Talbot said.

"The dark face of God," Moorman said. "She's the consort of Shiva, the god of death, disease and desolation. The Hindus believe good and evil are both divine. Some of them have decided it makes sense to worship the evil gods. They're the ones who can do you real damage. They may have a point, don't you think?"

Talbot was flooded by a new sense of the unimaginable nakedness of a universe where everything—anything—was permitted. He did not need any special foresight to imagine what Lothar Engle might be doing to Berthe. Or what she might do in response—take that cyanide capsule.

Around noon, one of Moorman's Spanish agents called from Granada. A blond German woman and a dark-haired officer in an SS uniform had checked into the Majestic Hotel late last night. Talbot and Moorman were soon heading south in his Aston Martin at top speed.

As dusk shrouded the highway, Grenada's red-roofed houses appeared in the distance, surmounted by the Alhambra on its commanding hill. The burnt Sienna rock and dark green vegetation of the hill were swallowed in shadows, making the ancient turrets and ramparts seem suspended in space. Moorman pulled off the road into a nearby olive grove and lifted a pickax out of the car's trunk. "What the hell's that?" Talbot asked.

"It's part of the ritual. The Goddess expects you to dig the victim's grave before you do the deed."

"Have you gone completely nuts?" Talbot growled.

"Dig," Moorman said. "That's an order."

In forty minutes, with Talbot hacking in the soft earth and Moorman shoveling out the loose clods, they had excavated a grave. With every stroke of the pickax, Talbot began to accept the reality of the task he was about to perform. He was going to murder a man at close range. He was going to listen to him choke for breath. He was going to see life vanish, agonizing death invade his tormented body. What-

ever else the worshippers of Kali had in mind, the ritual grave-dig-
ging made primitive psychological sense.

Moorman decided to avoid the Majestic Hotel. Although Engle
had no specific reason to suspect he was being followed, he was
probably on the alert for strangers—and by now he might know an
American around Talbot's age was Berthe's lover. Moorman chose a
smaller hotel a few blocks away and left Talbot in his room while he
conferred with his local Spanish agent—one of the few he trusted.
"He lost one son fighting for the Reds, the other for Franco," he
said.

An hour later he returned with the agent, Victor Cruz, a small
man with the face of a sorrowful chipmunk. He had kept Berthe and
Engle under surveillance, he said. They had stayed in the room most
of the day. The chambermaid heard sounds of weeping, cries of pain.
At dinner, the señorita's eyes were red-rimmed, her manner morose.
The señor talked of visiting the Alhambra Palace tomorrow. "That's
where you're going to kill him," Moorman said.

"You're crazy!" Talbot said.

"Not at all. I've looked over their hotel. The place is falling apart.
Every door squeaks, the floorboards creak like a Hollywood haunted
house. You couldn't get into his room without risking a bullet in the
head."

"I'll try it anyway. I can't stand the thought of her spending
another night with him."

Moorman refused to alter his battle plan. "You'll go to the
Alhambra as a fellow German tourist. There won't be any other
bloody tourists around. Just in case, we'll bribe the gatekeeper to say
the place is closed for the day after you follow them in. Strike up a
conversation with them. You're working for the German economic
mission, buying metals for the Reich's war machine. There's a big
bauxite mine not far from here. At the first opportunity, you slip the
silk around his throat. We'll hide the body in the gardens and get it
out to the grave after dark."

"Can't we smuggle a message to Berthe—through the chambermaid—a waiter—telling here I'm here?"

"Too risky. She'll have to keep the faith, or however they say it in
German."

Ich kann nicht anders. Would that be Berthe's final plea to God's
shrouded face—as she reached for the cyanide capsule? Talbot did

not sleep five minutes in the entire night. In the other bed, Moorman snored blissfully.

In the morning they took a taxi to the foot of the hill on which the Alhambra Palace sprawled. They drank coffee in a tasca off the Plaza Nueva for a half-hour while Victor Cruz hovered in the doorway, watching the street. Finally he labored over to them to announce in his lugubrious way that Berthe and Engle had arrived. "They are mounting the hill," he said. "No one else has entered the palace. You will be alone with them."

Talbot felt in his pocket for his Thuggee silk cord and toiled up the hill in the bright sunshine. Would his German be good enough to fool Engle? He had only spoken it to Berthe since he came to Spain. He worried even more about the cut of his white linen suit, which he had bought in Washington, D.C. Every nation had its own distinctive tailoring.

There was no sign of them in the Court of the Myrtles, with its marvelous reflecting pool, or in the Court of the Lions, next door. They must have wandered into the gardens. He doubled back and found them strolling along the tan pebbled paths. Engle was like a dark angel in his black SS uniform; he had his arm around Berthe's waist. At first glance they might have been lovers—until the tense arc of Berthe's shoulders made it clear she was a reluctant partner in the embrace.

"Guten Tag, meine Freunden (Good day, my friends)," Talbot said. "What a pleasant surprise to meet fellow Germans here."

Berthe's whole body went rigid with shock. Did Engle notice it? He returned the greeting with minimal pleasure, which was understandable under any circumstances. Talbot introduced himself as Gustav Vogler, the new agent for the German Economic Mission in Andalusia. Engle's crafty mouth wavered between friendliness and suspicion—and finally chose politeness.

They shook hands and Engle introduced Berthe as Fräulein von Schonberg. Talbot-Vogler clicked his heels and kissed her hand. "Charmed and delighted, Fräulein. Have you visited this wonderful palace before?"

"Many times," Berthe said.

"Ah, perhaps you'll consent to be our guide. The human voice is so much more refreshing than a book."

"I'd be delighted," Berthe said. "It's Oberführer Engle's first visit too."

Berthe led them into the palace, talking smoothly about the symbolism of Saint James's scallop shell in the reflecting pool of the Hall of the Myrtles. "It's almost as if the Moslems had foreseen their own expulsion," she said.

"Their tolerance was their undoing," Engle said. "Empires require hardness. The sultans grew too soft, surrounded by all this beauty." He was even more contemptuous of the Court of the Lions, dismissing it as sentimental. Talbot-Vogler warmly agreed with him, while he watched for the moment when he could produce his murderous silk cord. Moorman had urged him to wait until some degree of friendship had been established. That was the way the Thugs operated in their heyday.

On one of the palace's upper floors, they found a plaque on the wall: *In these quarters Washington Irving wrote his* Tales of the Alhambra *in the year 1829.* Engle asked Talbot-Vogler if he had ever read the book. He said no and Engle assured him he had missed nothing. "More sentimental rubbish," he said. "He sides with the Moors and portrays the Spanish as cruel and brutal. A typical American inability to recognize what constitutes imperial greatness. That's why America will never achieve world power."

Weltmacht. Engle's lips caressed the word. "Undoubtedly, Herr Oberführer," Talbot-Vogler said.

"In fact," Engle said, "there's only one work of art I want to see here in Granada. It's not in this papier-mâché Moslem gaucherie— it's in the royal palace of Charles V."

"I've always been so offended by the ugliness of that building, I've never gone into it," Berthe said.

"More sentimentality," Engle said. "Or shall we simply call it a feminine reaction to masculine architecture?" Guidebook in hand, he strode ahead of them into the gardens where they soon gazed up at the stark bulky fortress Emperor Charles V had built in the middle of the Alhambra to let the world know, if anyone doubted it, that Spain had conquered the Moslems. It was nothing less than a cube of raw rock, with some of the ugliest, most over-ornamented windows Talbot had ever seen.

"It looks like it belongs on a cliff above the Rhine," Berthe said.

"There may be hope for you in the new Germany after all, Fräulein von Schonberg," Engle said.

On the second floor, Engle hurried ahead of them into another bare cavernous hall. On the wall was an immense painting of a huge column of figures plodding into the distance. Surmounting them were King Ferdinand and Queen Isabella. To their right and left were two cardinals, one in red, the other in black. The black cardinal was pointing his finger at the retreating figures, his whole being a virtual declaration of banishment.

"It's the Expulsion of the Jews by Emilio Sala," Lothar Engle said. "It won a prize at the Berlin Exposition of 1891. Before I leave Madrid I hope to persuade General Franco to let me take it to Berlin, where we plan to hang it in the Reich chancellery."

He stood with his arms folded across his chest, his head tilted back to get the full effect of the immense canvas. "What do you think of it, Fräulein von Schonberg?"

Now. Moorman's voice hissed in Talbot's head. Out of his pocket came the Thug's ribbon of silk. Without a sound, he whipped it around Engle's exposed throat and pulled it tight. The German gave a strangling cry of terror and instinctively clutched at the cord. He realized he could never loosen it and pulled a gun from beneath his coat.

This maneuver was not included in the Thugs' book of tactics, which had been written in the thirteenth century. Twisting both ends of the silk cord in the fingers of one hand, Talbot chopped ferociously at Engle's wrist as he tried to turn his body and get off a shot. The gun clattered to the floor while Engle continued to emit the strangling cry.

Die, you son of a bitch, die, Talbot demanded. In that horrendous instant, the Thug's cord broke. So much for the English penchant for tradition. Later, Talbot would learn the last Thug had been eliminated from India by 1840. The silk was at least a hundred years old.

Engle staggered away, clutching his throat. Talbot sprang after him and replaced silk with fingers. He threw the Oberführer to the floor and began choking him to death. He had never done it before and did not know the best grip. But it seemed to be working until Engle somehow slipped his long arms inside Talbot's elbows and gouged his eyes.

The pain was incredible. Talbot had to let go of Engle's throat and tear away those hands or risk blindness. They rolled across the room, a cursing, snarling tangle while Talbot tried to regain his grip on the German's throat, which he could barely see through a fog of tears and blood. With a near maniacal burst of strength, Engle broke free and stumbled to his feet. As Talbot rose to go after him, the German kicked him in the stomach.

Talbot toppled to the floor in agony. Why had he listened to Moorman? Why hadn't he brought along a pistol? He was screwing up again, finally and fatally this time.

"The gun, where is the gun?" Engle screamed at Berthe.

"Here," Berthe said.

Three shots in swift succession shattered the silence of the empty palace. Peering through the bloody haze in his eyes, Talbot saw Berthe holding the gun in both hands, aiming it at Engle's chest.

"Berthe! No!" Engle cried. "I love you!"

Two more shots boomed around the figures of the banished Jews and the denunciatory cardinals and the sovereign monarchs. Blood gushed from Engle's mouth and he toppled backward onto the floor. "I—loved—you," he groaned one more time.

Berthe remained frozen, arms extended, staring at the gun as if it were a foreign object some alien presence had placed in her unwilling hands. "Oh," she sobbed. "Oh my God."

Talbot stumbled to his feet and put his arms around her. "It's all right," he said. "He's dead."

"I loved him," Berthe said. "I loved him once. How could I kill him? What have we become?"

34

THE EMPEROR SPEAKS

"It's like a meeting of two emperors of the later period of the Roman empire," Annie Talbot said, as she and Saul Randolph prepared for the final day of the Casablanca Conference. "Churchill is the emperor of the East, Roosevelt of the West."

"It'll be the last period of the British Empire if I have anything to say about it," Saul growled.

They were not in the raffish French-Arab city for which the conference had been named. They were in Anfa, an idyllic resort about five miles from Casablanca, on a knoll overlooking the dark blue Atlantic. Palm trees rustled in the balmy sea breezes; around the white villas the air was thick with the lavender scent of bougainvillea. It was quite a contrast to the fetid air and spectacular stenches in the winding alleys of Casablanca.

It was an even starker contrast to the weather the German Sixth Army was enduring in the freezing ruins of Stalingrad. Each day the triumphant bulletins from Moscow were circulated as part of the daily diet of war news for the emperors and their staffs. Annie got her copy from Ned Travis, who was part of a State Department task force at the conference. An exultant Saul Randolph used the news to argue violently for a redoubled effort to give the Russians even more lend-lease guns, tanks and planes—a proposal the British resisted.

Jack Richman was with the American and British soldiers who

were fighting German and Italian troops in neighboring Tunisia. Annie was here to cover the announcement of the policy of unconditional surrender. It had now become more than a gesture to keep the Russians in the war—although Stalin's refusal to come to Casablanca had intensified that worry. The political fallout of Roosevelt's embrace of Admiral Darlan had continued to ravage the President's standing among America's liberals. Worse, in the midterm elections, which took place a week before the North African invasion, disgruntled voters had let the White House know how unhappy they were with the floundering American war effort. The Democrats had come within eight votes of losing control of the House of Representatives.

Unconditional surrender—still a closely held secret—had now become a resurrection of moral purpose, a restoration of fervor to Roosevelt's shaken coalition. Annie still saw nothing wrong with the idea—and a great many things right about it. Her enthusiasm may have acquired an extra edge by way of apologizing to Saul Randolph for her absolute refusal to target Roy Reeves for expulsion from the State Department, at Stalin's request. Saul had accepted her defiance with good grace—which prompted her to summon new fervor for their high-wire performances in her bedroom.

The two emperors and their staffs were arguing about what the next step in the war should be. To the dismay of impatient Americans like Saul, the Eastern emperor, Churchill, had a plan, while their Western emperor, Roosevelt, had only a few vague ideas. The British had also brought along a 6,000-ton ship crammed with staff studies, teleprinters and radio equipment that enabled them to draw on even more voluminous files in London. Churchill literally overwhelmed the flabbergasted Roosevelt with data that demolished any hope of launching a second front in 1943, in accordance with the Rainbow Five war plan. Instead, the British argued irresistibly for continuing the war in the Mediterranean for another year, invading Sicily, Italy and possibly Greece.

Around noon, Annie stood among a swarm of fellow reporters in the sunny courtyard of the Roosevelt villa as the President, in a dark gray suit and black tie, his lifeless legs jauntily crossed, flashed his famous smile and reported that the Casablanca conference was ending with complete unanimity between the British and Americans. This was a blatant lie. Annie had spent the previous week listening to the seething animosities between the two sides. Last night Saul Randolph told her General George Marshall, the Army's chief of staff, was so infuriated by the British capture of Roosevelt's mind that he was threatening to join Admiral King in a recommendation to switch the main American war effort to Japan.

But it was the sort of lie that someone from Chicago had grown up hearing from City Hall every day. Annie was unbothered by it as FDR, leaning back in his chair, declared he no longer had the slightest doubt that the Nazi and Japanese regimes were doomed. Earlier in the day, Moscow had reported that the last remnants of the Stalingrad pocket had surrendered. "Not only are we going to win, Mr. Churchill and I have agreed we are going to do it in a way that guarantees the future peace of the world."

Paper rustled as reporters reached for pads and pencils. The President waved his cigarette holder as if it were a magic wand. "We're going to apply an old American idea to the twentieth century. Some of you Britishers know we had a general called U. S. Grant. In my and the Prime Minister's younger days, he was known as Unconditional Surrender Grant, because he insisted on those terms when Lee surrendered at Appomattox Courthouse. That is going to be the only peace terms we'll accept—the unconditional surrender of the German, Japanese and Italian military forces and governments."

So much for a gentleman's C at Harvard, Annie thought, gazing at the complacent smile on the President's face. Roosevelt did not have the facts straight on one of the primary events in American history. Ulysses Simpson Grant got his nickname because he insisted on unconditional surrender when he besieged a small Confederate Army in Fort Donelson on the Ohio River in 1862—a perfectly appropriate reaction to the enemy general's attempt to negotiate his way out of the trap. When Robert E. Lee surrendered the main Southern Army at Appomattox, effectively ending the Civil War, Grant had given him generous terms.

Suddenly Annie heard Roy Reeves scathingly denouncing unconditional surrender. Had Roosevelt's thinking about it been as superficial as his knowledge of its role in American history?

For an odd moment Winston Churchill, replete with homburg, dark blue suit and vest and unlit cigar, stared at his American colleague as if the announcement had taken him by surprise. He quickly recovered and said he shared the President's "unconquerable will" to obtain the unconditional surrender "of the criminal forces who have plunged the world into storm and ruin."

While other reporters scribbled frantically, Annie, hearing little she had not expected, let her mind and eyes wander. On the tip of the half-moon–shaped crowd around the President she saw a frowning Zeke Talbot in his Navy whites, beside a diminutive British Navy officer with a face like a clenched fist.

Saul Randolph was standing with a cluster of his lend-lease staffers on the opposite tip of the semicircle. He was gazing at Roosevelt with voracious intensity. This was the man who had given meaning to his life, a purpose beyond the pursuit of profits on Wall Street. She was in the middle as usual. What was Zeke doing here? Had he been summoned by Admiral King to be excoriated for sleeping with a German spy? Maybe she should tell the Admiral that Congressman Richman no longer gave a damn what the Navy did to Lieutenant Commander Talbot.

In a few minutes the press briefing ended with Roosevelt urging reporters to call Casablanca "the unconditional surrender conference." The crowd began drifting out of the courtyard. Annie eased her way through the strollers until she was side by side with Zeke and his English friend. "You meet the damnedest people in North Africa," she said.

"Annie!" Zeke was speechless with shock—or was it embarrassment? Did he have his fräulein stashed somewhere in the vicinity? She might have pretended to defect into his arms. All the clichés of the spy novel whirled through Annie's head while Zeke introduced her to Captain Bernado Moorman.

"How do you do," he said, shaking her hand. His manner suggested he knew what an unwelcome sight she was and wanted to have no part of a possible public shouting match. "I'm sure you two have a great deal you want to talk about. I see some old friends on Winston's staff—"

He slithered into the crowd, leaving them alone—if the word had any meaning with some two hundred people swirling around them. Annie decided it had a great deal of meaning. This was a dream come true. Here she was with her lover only a few dozen feet away, ready to be displayed on demand. She was wearing white, which always went well with her inky black hair, which she had cut and curled only last night. She could not be looking or feeling better.

"How's Butch?" Zeke said.

"He stayed with me during the Christmas holidays. He's doing fabulously at Choate. Straight A's in everything. He's grown two inches and gained fifteen pounds."

"Did he get my Christmas present?"

"The bullfighter's cape? He loved it."

Zeke nodded nostalgically. "My father gave me one when I was at Choate. I used to practice with the damn thing by the hour."

There was a long pause in which Annie made it clear she had no further desire to discuss parenthood or his boyhood memories. "So," she said. "How's Spain?"

"A mess," he said. "That's why I'm here. We're trying to get the goddamn OSS kicked out of the country before they put Franco in Hitler's lap. I've got a memorandum a yard long from the Ambassador listing the idiotic things they're doing."

"Get me a copy," she said. "Maybe we can use it in a column."

"After what I just heard in that courtyard, I'm not sure if it matters. Can you imagine a more idiotic policy? Unconditional surrender?"

Annie's temper started to simmer. Why was she really surprised? she asked herself. Retrograde minds thought alike. Maybe her suspicion that Roy Reeves was a reactionary was sound after all. Why had she bothered to protect him? She had a sentimental streak—her worst weakness.

"I think it's an absolutely brilliant policy," she said. "It solves a great many political problems with one shining stroke. You're thinking like someone stuck in a backwater of the war, Commander. In Washington we get a more realistic estimate of the situation. We're at the center of things."

Was that crushing enough? She hoped so. As usual, Lieutenant Commander Talbot, the self-styled Conscience of the Country, refused to admit he was squashed, if his ego even permitted him to notice it. He shook his head and said: "It's going to ruin so many things! A chance to end the war with no more bloodshed. It makes me look like a fool but that's irrelevant compared to what's being destroyed."

"I hate to say it in public like this, Commander," she said. "But you're babbling even more than you were the last time I saw you."

"Annie?" Saul Randolph was hovering in the middle distance. She introduced him to Zeke as one of her closest Washington friends. "When do you want to pull out?" he asked.

"Whenever you're ready," she said. "Two o'clock?"

"Do you have time for lunch?" Zeke said. "I'm not babbling. Maybe if I told you the whole story—"

"I know quite a bit of the story," Annie said. "Including why you think it's a terrible mistake to hammer the Germans into the rubble until they beg for mercy. I saw an OSS memo that described exactly why you were *persuaded* to take such a benevolent view of our enemies. It has something—or everything—to do with a certain Berthe von Hoffmann. I hope they put the memo in your personnel file as proof of your high moral character—and your stupidity."

Did *that* squash him enough? It seemed to have some sort of impact. He could not look into her eyes. "I was going to tell you the whole story," he said in a low, almost inarticulate voice. "Including her."

He was unbelievable. Who else but Zeke Talbot would expect his almost–ex-wife to change her mind about one of the most fundamental decisions of the war by prefacing his argument with a confession of adultery? "I am not in the least troubled by her," Annie raged. "I've found a man who offers me a lot more than you ever did with your perpetual putdowns and whining complaints about your superior officers and commander-in-chief."

"I hope you love him as much as I love Berthe," he said.

The words came at her with the transparent honesty and simplicity that were Zeke Talbot's trademark—honesty and simplicity that had dwindled over their married years into brutal bluntness yet somehow retained in its maddening essence the original purity that had won her love. Tears were choking her throat; the white villas, the palm trees, wavered in the searing sunlight. "Oh God!" Annie cried, appealing to the only entity with the power to prevent the desolation inside her from becoming collapse. "Don't you know—yet—that she's a German agent? She works for the Abwehr!"

"That's a formality," he said. "She's really an envoy from the German resistance movement."

"The—German—resistance—movement?"

She spaced the words to maximize her disbelief. She had heard of the French, the Belgian, the Dutch, the Norwegian, the Danish, the Czech, the Yugoslav, the Greek resistance movements. She had written columns about some of them from information supplied by the OSS. How could a German resistance movement exist without

Annie Talbot, the ultimate Washington insider, knowing about it?

"There are generals, colonels, some of the top people in the Abwehr and the diplomatic corps in it. They want to overthrow Hitler and negotiate a peace. Berthe's their agent in Spain. They've got other people trying to make contact with us in Switzerland, Turkey, Sweden. I've written to the Navy, the State Department about it—and run into a stone wall. Now I know why. Unconditional surrender! How can you ask generals in command of two or three million men to buy that? They'll say if Germany's going to be destroyed, we might as well go down fighting! Die like men instead of wimps."

He was making horrendous sense but Annie could not admit it. "They don't deserve anything better. Do you know what they're doing to the Jews? Has Fräulein von Hoffmann told you that?"

"It's Frau von Hoffmann," Zeke said. "She's wrecked her marriage, abandoned her kids to get this message to me—or through me. The Jews are one of the reasons she's doing this. Maybe the primary reason. What the hell will unconditional surrender do for them? It could prolong the war two or three years, giving the Nazis that much more time to exterminate them."

He was making even more horrendous, intolerable sense—if there was such a thing as a German resistance movement. That was the question he was finessing, with the help of his Aryan Mata Hari. "You're going to have to show me a lot more than love letters from Frau von Hoffmann to convince me—or anyone else in Washington."

"I know that," he said, his head drooping. "I'm on the losing side, as usual. But this time I know it's the right side." He looked wearily around them. They were alone in the center of the complex of villas. Everyone was inside packing. "Sometimes I think Berthe is right. The whole thing is out of our hands. It's as mysterious as the Spanish idea of God."

Annie struggled with wildly conflicting emotions. Zeke Talbot talking about God without the usual edge of bitterness and contempt in his voice? Abandoning an argument without a trace of his usual righteous arrogance? What sort of woman was this Berthe von Hoffmann? Did she have magical powers? How does any woman penetrate a man's soul deep enough to change him? These were very threatening thoughts to a specialist in high-wire love, Washington, D.C., division.

Annie almost preferred the husband she knew, boiling with determination, conviction, energy, even if it was totally wrongheaded. "If you really believe it," she said, "act like a reporter. Dig up more evidence. Put together a dossier."

"I've put one together. I sent it to Ned Travis. Are you interested? I'll send you a copy."

"Go ahead. Throw in a photograph of Frau von Hoffmann to guarantee my persuasion."

"Annie—I'm sorry as hell," he said. "It just happened."

"I'm not sorry," she all but hissed, new rage flooding her. It was infinitely preferable to thinking about unconditional surrender. "I'm positively overjoyed by it. She eliminates the possibility of my feeling the slightest shred of guilt for my departure from the cowlike fidelity you undoubtedly expected."

"I didn't expect anything. I wasn't thinking when I left Washington. I didn't start again until I met Berthe. I knew I was losing you. But I thought that had already happened—"

"You were right about that."

She could not stand this humble resignation, this hangdog guilt. She began to feel as if she were punching a stuffed dummy. "I have to pack," she said. "Saul and I are driving to Marrakesh for a few days. Have you and Frau von Hoffmann been there, by any chance? I hear it's incredibly beautiful. They call it the Paris of North Africa."

"Annie!" he said, seizing her arm. "Hate me all you want. I deserve it. I was a rotten lousy husband for the last couple of years. But do something about this thing. The future of the world is at stake!"

The words shredded her nervous system. Maybe Roy Reeves was a magician, God's eunuch pursuing her with spells and scary phrases. But Annie was too angry, too wounded, to regain her self-control. "It may be the future of your world," she said. "But it isn't mine."

"It is!" Zeke said, as she strode down the palm-tree-shaded path. "It's everybody's world!"

She left him there, as stranded as Don Quixote in the middle of La Mancha, and twice as futile, and drove across the desert to devote three days to high-wire love with Saul Randolph in romantic Marrakesh.

35

INCONDICIONAL ABANDANO

"No, no," Berthe von Hoffmann said, turning her head away when Jonathan Talbot tried to kiss her the night before he left for Casablanca. "No!"

On the radio, Berlin was broadcasting the last dirges for the Sixth Army in Stalingrad. They had finally surrendered. Three hundred and fifty thousand men. The newspapers were full of their haggard beaten faces. The BBC gloated day and night. The great defeat for which the Schwarze Kapelle had been hoping had occurred—and no one was to blame but Adolf Hitler. The moment for the generals' revolt had arrived. She should be rejoicing. Instead she was filled with self-loathing, horror, sadness. Night after night she lay awake, thinking about the cyanide capsule in her purse.

It was not simply the violent end of her trip to Granada with Lothar Engle. It was not her tormented regret for pulling the trigger of the pistol that had killed him. She had pulled it five times to make sure he was dead. It was not the gruesome business of hiding his body in the Alhambra's gardens, scouring his blood from the floor, returning that night to bury him in the olive grove, like a scene from a lost tragedy by Aeschylus. It was what had happened during those two days and nights before Jonathan Talbot came to Granada.

Again and again, Lothar walked toward her across the dim hotel room. He was naked. He had grown fat. His body sagged in inappropriate places. *Now, Berthe,* he said. *Now you'll do all the things every man in Berlin imagined the young widow was ready to do for him for the right price. Then we'll begin our study of one of my favorite authors, the Marquis de Sade.*

For days now, she had tried to explain it to the one person in Madrid who might understand, the Marquesa de Montoya. "I wanted Lothar to defile me. I did everything he asked. Nothing was too obscene."

"But you didn't tell him anything," the Marquesa pointed out, her eyes brimming with sympathy.

"I would have told him everything if it had lasted another day. First I had to become totally defiled. He knew that. He knew so much about me. He knew exactly how to mock my ridiculous spiritual pretensions."

"We all think our spiritual pretensions are ridiculous in moments of brutal honesty," the Marquesa said. "Look at me, pretending to be a penitente—when I really regret nothing. I'm doing it for my husband's sake. He blames me for the loss of our sons. Oh how he loathes me. You can't imagine what he says to me when we're alone."

Not even the Marquesa's abasement meant anything. It was only more humiliation, more regret. "Once I wished you the worst possible fate," Berthe said. "Now that it's come it only makes me despise myself even more."

She would not let Jonathan Talbot touch her. "I don't deserve you," she said. "I don't deserve even the smallest shred of happiness."

To the Marquesa she said much more. "Sexual love is a lie," she raged. "It means everything—and nothing. I'll never let any man touch me again. Not even Jonathan, even though I still love him."

"You want to make him as miserable as yourself, is that it?" the Marquesa said.

"No. I want to make sure I'm not tricked into happiness again."

"How wily are the ways of love," the Marquesa said, reciting from her favorite poem. "You can't expel love from your body any more than you can expel it from your mind."

"I'll be the first," Berthe vowed.

The Marquesa produced her Cheshire smile. "You must make a pilgrimage to the shrine of the Virgin in Extramadura. The Virgin of Guadalupe, we call her. Only she can heal your wounds. They're beyond my powers."

Jonathan was hoping to wangle an interview with President Roosevelt at Casablanca. He was hoping a personal plea might be more effective than his letters and cables. A clever agent would have sent him off with kisses and caresses. She was a failure at everything, even the crudest levels of the espionage business. "It's okay, I understand," he said. "I really do understand."

"You're so good. I almost hate you for it!" she cried.

"I'll let you do or say anything to me—if you give me that cyanide capsule."

"No," she said.

He stalked out, muttering. She knew he went straight to the Marquesa de Montoya. Within the hour she was on the telephone arranging to pick her up for the trip to the shrine of the Virgin of Guadalupe. It was better than listening to the dirges of Stalingrad, the burbles of triumph from Casablanca. Berthe allowed herself to be collected like a piece of baggage and inserted into the back of the Marquesa's ancient yellow Hispano-Suiza. They rumbled west into the barren wasteland of Extramadura, the poorest part of Spain, penned between barrier mountains and the Portuguese border.

They passed village after village of clustered white houses where, the Marquesa remarked, nothing had changed for eight hundred years. The road had as many as ten right-angle turns to the half-mile. The chauffeur, who was almost as old as the Marquesa, said his arms were wearing out. The Marquesa ordered him to stop so she could vomit into the ditch. "I get sick every time I make this awful trip," she said.

Berthe was feeling somewhat ashamed of herself when they finally reached Guadalupe. Part of the shrine's fascination, apparently, was its proximity to nothing in Spain that could possibly be construed as important. "The Virgin knows what it takes to humble Spanish pride," the Marquesa said.

Was she hoping the formula would also work for German pride? If so she was being ridiculous. Berthe von Hoffmann had no pride left. She had been humiliated by everything that had happened to her in Spain until the whole idea of pride was a sick joke. Her self-respect had been stripped away, shred by shred, until there was nothing left for her raw flesh to embrace but soothing cyanidal darkness.

The Marquesa, oblivious to her frown, explained how the Virgin had come to Guadalupe. Tradition claimed the statue had been carved from life by Saint Luke, the author of the third Gospel, and carried to Spain in the sixth century. It was buried to escape possible desecration by the Moslem hordes and rediscovered by a wandering shepherd seven hundred years later. In the next several centuries, nobles, kings and popes had bestowed wealth on the shrine and its guardian monastery.

After glancing at the illuminated manuscripts and jeweled chalices, they mounted a red marble staircase to the *camarin*, the heart of the shrine. At first Berthe saw nothing but a lot of expensive robes and jewels on some sort of pedestal in a gold-lined niche. The Marquesa signaled to two young priests and they slowly turned the pedestal until the Virgin faced them. She was wearing a gown of brilliant yellow and a halo of precious stones. Her face was scarred a dark brown from her long slumber in the earth. On her right arm she carried a small infant Jesus, also dark brown from long burial.

The oval shape of the face, the tapered chin, the staring solemnity of the expression, reminded Berthe of the angel in her dream of the death of the Ritterboot. This figure also had no nationality. She was beyond the human—yet she embraced a child. "Think of what she means. Think of what she brings to earth," the Marquesa murmured. "The power of women."

"What power do we have," Berthe said. "Except the power to submit."

"That can be the first step to other powers," the Marquesa said.

"Stupid," Berthe said, as they returned to the car. "A perfect example of what's wrong with Catholicism. Spending millions to put golden robes on a statue while half of Spain is starving. Martin Luther was right."

"I was afraid you'd say that," the Marquesa replied. "We'll try another one. Spain has many Virgins."

They took to the road again, this time heading north to the town of Estella, near the French border. Here they contemplated the Virgin of El Puy. She too had been buried to escape Moorish desecration and discovered by two shepherds who followed a curious conjunction of two stars to a place on the wild plateau of El Puy in the year 1085. Berthe felt vaguely stirred by the story of the star but otherwise disdained this Virgin, who wore a very Spanish smile on her altar in an ultramodern church full of slim pillars and fanciful arches. "On to Pontevedra," the Marquesa sighed.

This time they drove halfway across Spain, the Marquesa talking complacently, brilliantly, about her many lovers, analyzing each one with devastating exactitude, until there was a perfect balance of his virtues and defects. Winding through the mountains they reached Pontevedra, a small town not far from Santiago de Compostella in the province of Galicia.

In a little gingerbread sanctuary in the form of a combined cross and a scallop shell stood a pilgrim Virgin. Dressed in the stiff brocade of the eighteenth century, she was unmistakably German, and she carried on her arm a fat, contented Jesus who looked exactly like Georg as a baby.

A shudder, a near convulsion of sorrow passed through Berthe's body. For the first time she saw, she felt, the universality of the word woman. How it transcended every boundary of nation and race and blood. But she saw no power in it. The purpose of this pilgrimage still eluded her.

"Hold me, please hold me," she whispered to the Marquesa.

"You're too big for me to hold," she said, but she tried to wrap her small arms around her.

Tears poured down Berthe's cheeks. "Good, good," the Marquesa said. "I've been hoping you'd cry. You have to learn to cry and cry and cry. That may be the most important part of being a woman."

In her Spanish mother's arms, Berthe wept all the way back to Madrid. Gradually she felt better. It was as if her tears were cleansing the memory of Lothar Engle's power over her, and the ugly opinions he preached about Germany. Did finding a mother somehow release a dimension of womanhood that had lain unborn in her soul? She wondered if it would change her feeling for Jonathan.

As they reached the business section of Madrid, Berthe saw strange words on the newsstand placards. *Incondicional Abandono*. Unconditional surrender. "What in the world does that mean?" the Marquesa said.

They bought a newspaper and Berthe read it aloud as they rode to the Marquesa's palace on the Gran Via. "'Today Roosevelt and Churchill enunciated a new policy for the prosecution of the war. They declared they would accept no terms from Germany except unconditional surrender. The authorities in Germany reacted to this announcement with predictable severity. Dr. Joseph Goebbels, the Reich's Minister of Propaganda, said it only proved what Hitler had

foreseen from the first—this was a war to the death with international Jewry. Unconditional surrender would mean the annihilation
of Germany, the enslavement of her people—'"

"They must be insane," the Marquesa said. "Even in our Civil
War, we gave the Communists terms. We allowed their leaders to
escape abroad in their own aircraft. We allowed thousands to go into
exile in France."

"It plays directly into Hitler's hands," Berthe said. "The generals
will never revolt now."

"Perhaps this is why we've made our journey," the Marquesa
said.

"What do you mean?" Berthe said. She had been shocked back to
the world of politics. She had almost forgotten the Virgin of Pontevedra.

"You must help them bear it," the Marquesa said. "You're ready
to do that now."

Bear what? Berthe wondered. She was not at all sure what had
happened to her at Pontevedra. Why did a fit of weeping prepare her
for this unspecified task? She parted from her Spanish mother coldly,
not even returning her fervent kiss. "I'll pray and pray for you," the
Marquesa said.

"To whom?" Berthe asked curtly.

"The Virgin of Guadalupe, of course."

The next morning Berthe reported for duty at the embassy.
Ambassador von Stohrer met her in the lobby. He looked as if he had
aged ten years since she last saw him. "You've heard the news, no
doubt," he said. "Now we know where the Führer is leading us. To
the abyss."

In the hall to her office, she encountered Wolfgang Griff. He
waved a copy of the *Volkischer Beobachter*, the official Nazi paper, at
her. It carried a huge headline: TOTALKRIEG! (Total War!). "Do you
subscribe to this proposition, Frau von Hoffmann?" he asked, thrusting the paper in her face. "It's the Reich's response to Roosevelt's
unconditional surrender."

"Of course," she said.

His laugh had a slightly hysterical trill. "I talked to my father on the
telephone last night. He said Dr. Goebbels is delighted with Roosevelt's announcement. He considers it world-historical tomfoolery of
the first order. He would never have been able to think up so rousing a

slogan. How can a German do anything but fight to the finish, now?"

"All in all then, this is a day of rejoicing?" Berthe said.

"Not entirely. I urged my father to call for an investigation of your conduct—the conduct of the entire Abwehr here in Spain. Your marvelous American contact, Herr Talbot, told us nothing about the invasion of North Africa."

"Commander Talbot remains a valuable source of information—which you may be ruining, Herr Griff, by discussing him in loud tones in a public corridor," Berthe said.

"We're in the German embassy!" Griff shouted. "There are no traitors here. If there are, the SD will soon root them out."

A door burst open. Otto von Spaeth, the Abwehr chief, grabbed Griff by the collar. "Frau von Hoffmann is absolutely correct, Herr Griff. The conduct of the Abwehr is none of your business. Go tell your stupid lies to the Spanish reporters."

"We'll soon see who's telling lies," Griff said and retreated down the corridor, waving the rolled up *Volkischer Beobachter* in his hand like a club.

Spaeth gestured Berthe into his office. "I have a message of the greatest urgency from Admiral Canaris. He needs to know as much as you can find out about the background and intent of this unconditional surrender policy. Must we take it literally, or are there unstated terms? Is it a complete surrender to Lord Vansittart and his ilk?"

Spaeth's skin was chalky, his tie was loose, his vest unbuttoned. He had even forgotten to put on his spats. "Forgive my appearance," he said. "I haven't slept since I heard about it."

"Talbot is in Casablanca now, attempting to find a friendly ear for our project," she said. "I'm sure he'll do his utmost to answer the Admiral's questions when he returns."

Spaeth sank into his desk chair. "I lived through one German defeat," he said. "I don't think I want to survive another one—on such terms."

He tried to light a cigarette. His hand was shaking so badly the match burned his fingers instead. "Griff's threats are not idle ones, I fear. The British are telling people that the Abwehr is responsible for the enemy's knowledge of a certain submarine force that might have inflicted heavy damage on the amphibious landing in North Africa—but were decoyed away. I hope you haven't kept a diary. Destroy everything—deny everything."

The man's pain was palpable, like an open wound. "I've sent my wife to Portugal. She'll be safe there. Excuse me. There are certain files I must remove."

That night, as Berthe listened to Radio Berlin broadcasting defiance of unconditional surrender, the Marquesa telephoned. She had received a message from Jonathan Talbot. He was returning to Madrid tomorrow. Berthe telephoned Spaeth to let him know they might soon have more information. There was no answer. She called three more times, the last call at midnight. Still no answer.

An icy intuition sent her into the street in search of a taxi. She rode swiftly to the calle off the Gran Via, only a few steps from the Marquesa's palace, and persuaded the sereno to let her into the apartment by telling him she feared Herr von Spaeth was ill. She found him sitting in a chair in the living room. In another room, Radio Berlin announced that Hitler had ordered the Army in Tunisia to fight to the death in imitation of the defenders of Stalingrad.

Herr von Spaeth was no longer interested in such heroics. The cyanide vial was gripped in his left fist. His usually impassive face was twisted in a grimace of pain, which was probably a reaction to the cyanide, but could be interpreted as a final expression of disgust with a treacherous world. Berthe extracted the vial from the stiffened fingers and flushed it down the toilet. She told the wide-eyed sereno to call the German embassy and report the news of Herr von Spaeth's unexpected death. Then she walked through the bitterly cold Madrid night to the Marquesa's palace. The sleepy maid who answered the front bell was outraged, but the Marquesa did not seem in the least disturbed—or even surprised—by her visit. She said she seldom went to sleep before dawn.

Berthe told her where she had been, what was happening at the German embassy. "I'm not going to bear it," she said. "Someday, perhaps. But not now. For now I reject any and all forms of submission or acceptance. I'll play any part, tell any lie, perform any act to rescue Germany from this obscenity."

"You're my daughter after all," the Marquesa said, patting her hand. "The German Virgin of Pontevedra would be dismayed. The Spanish Virgin of El Puy would be horrified. But the Virgin of Guadalupe will simply nod and bide her time."

Berthe was sick of Virgins, sick of Spain, sick of mothers, fathers, lovers, sick! At her apartment, she found Jonathan waiting for her, an artificial smile on his face. She returned it. She wanted to announce the anguished woman he had left in Madrid after the bloody shootout with Lothar Engle had vanished. She had been replaced by a stranger who kissed him too voraciously. "How contented you look," she said. "It must have been a very successful meeting."

"We've gotten the OSS off our backs," he said.

"And the rest? I hope you can tell me something useful about this new policy of unconditional surrender. The SD is pressing Canaris rather hard."

"I'm sorry to hear that. It's a hell of a mess. I had no idea—"

"I asked you to think, dear Jonathan, not lament." The peremptory tone was all wrong. She did not care. She wanted it to be wrong. "I'll let you debrief me in the bedroom," he said.

"Why not," she said.

A half-hour later, he lay beside her, feeling he had made love to a stranger. Exactly what Berthe wanted him to feel. "What's wrong?"

"Nothing's wrong," she said.

"I thought you'd be upset by the announcement of unconditional surrender."

"Why should I be? I found it rather liberating. Now we're equal. Your country is just as despicable as mine."

The words exploded from her throat with the involuntary force of bullets pulled by a blind trigger finger. Total war was now part of their love and it had already become the stronger force.

"You've joined the Vansittarts, the Moormans. You want to destroy us all. Maybe some of us deserve destruction. But not the German nation. Not my daughter and my son."

"I love you," he said. "I want you to love me in spite of what's happening."

"Give me some information. Then we'll see about loving."

"Don't do this, Berthe. We mean something to each other no matter what our countries do. We're separate from them."

"We can never be separate from them," she said.

"We can! We will be!"

She turned her face away from him. "Give me the information. Haven't I given you what you wanted?"

They were a long way from Granada.

36

OH CAPTAIN, MY CAPTAIN

"Alarm!"

The bells clanged, the lookout watch came crashing into the Zentrale, First Officer Kurz bringing up the rear, losing his grip on the wet ladder and falling on top of one of the seamen. "Crew to the bow!" roared Kapitanleutnant von Hoffmann.

The Wolfseeboot slanted down into the North Atlantic's depths as the crew rushed to obey their commander. Only Kurz and his groaning victim ignored the order. "My ribs, Herr Kaleu, I think they're broken," he whined. It was Benz, the seaman who had fallen asleep on watch during the last voyage of the Ritterboot. He was a chronic complainer.

Kurz helped him to his feet, babbling apologies. "To the bow!" Ernst said. "That includes you, Number One."

Stupendous explosions sent the Wolfseeboot tilting to port so radically, Ernst thought they had taken a fatal hit. Kurz and Benz slid across the deck in a thrashing tangle. "On your feet. To the bow!" Ernst roared, hanging onto the periscope. They pulled themselves erect as Chief Kleist performed another of his routine miracles to regain control of the dive. More wabos boomed above them at a less menacing distance as Kurz and Benz stumbled out of the Zentrale.

Pain prowled Ernst's stomach. A huge convoy was only a few miles away and the eight U-boats of Wolf Pack Sturmer were in rake position to launch a classic assault. But the enemy had introduced something new to the war-fighting equation in this swath of the mid-Atlantic known to both sides as the Gap—because it was beyond the range of landbased planes. Small "jeep" carriers were now roaming the once-happy hunting ground, escorted by destroyers. Their planes kept the U-boats down—where their slow underwater speed could not keep pace with the convoys.

This was the Wolfseeboot's fifth emergency dive in twenty-four hours. Day or night, it made no difference to the planes, which were equipped with ever more sophisticated radar to pick up a boat on the surface miles away. The Metox device on the conning tower, with its thirty- or forty-second warning signal, was the U-boats' only protection. Ernst had drilled the bridge watches until they could get under in twenty-five seconds—but each dive was still a terrifying experience.

Ernst could see courage ebbing in the faces of his crew as the narrow escapes multiplied—and there were fewer and fewer kills to show for it. He preached vigorous sermons over the loudspeakers to restore their commitment. Kurz jestingly told him he had a future in the ministry after the war. But Ernst did not preach faith in God. Faith in the führer principle was his message, the Führer who united the German volk with links of steel resolve.

For the Ubootwaffe, the year 1942 had ended on a stupendously satisfying note. They had sunk 7,850,000 tons of enemy shipping. The year 1943 began even more auspiciously. They had gone over a million tons in each of the first three months. But their losses had also leaped ominously. In March, a staggering fifteen boats had failed to return. There were alarming signs that in April the toll might be higher.

The Wolfseeboot had been in the middle of these struggles. Three times they had returned to Lorient with pennants worth over 100,000 tons flying from the conning tower. The Führer had added oak leaves to Ernst's Knight's Cross. The newspapers had run pictures, Radio Berlin had trumpeted his heroism. Admiral Dönitz had signed his KBT—his war diary—with a chorus of superlatives.

Every time Ernst saw his picture in the newspaper or heard his name on the radio, he was filled with savage satisfaction. *Are you listening, Berthe?* he asked across the distance to Spain. Twice, on his return from a cruise, he had written her a letter, describing how he had trained his men to sink ships with shellfire to inflict maximum damage on the crews. He also told her how he had made a point of sinking the rescue ships in a convoy. He wanted Berthe to know just how hard he had become.

Admiral Dönitz had congratulated him for carrying out the new orders he had given him in Paris—which were reiterated by Flotilla Commander Viktor Schutze before each cruise began. Sinking a convoy's rescue ship meant there was no one to pick up survivors from the icy Atlantic. Convoy escorts were usually forbidden to do it—they were precious assets that could not be risked for a few men—and no merchant ship in the convoy was permitted to drop out of line for any reason. As the news of the new tactic spread through the enemy's merchant marine, it was bound to have an impact on recruiting crews for the new ships the Americans kept building.

The U-boats were supplying the German people with the only good news in the war. Ernst still found it hard to believe that his brother Berthold was gone—vanished into Russia's frozen vastness with his comrades in the Sixth Army. Almost as dismaying was the mounting evidence of General Rommel's imminent defeat in North Africa. The Wolfseeboot had spent its first cruise off Gibraltar, vainly trying to rescue that situation.

Worst of all was the news from the home front. American and British bombers were inflicting horrendous damage on Germany's cities. The military situation could be obscured with vague phrases and promises of future offensives, but the havoc wreaked by the bombers was impossible to deny. At least half the crew had lost relatives in the rain of death from the skies. Last month in Hamburg, a thousand British planes had created a firestorm of 800 degrees centigrade that had sucked all the oxygen out of the air, asphyxiating forty thousand people in their basement shelters and melting their bodies into greasy black masses.

"Approaching one hundred and fifty meters, Herr Kaleu," said Chief Kleist in the Zentrale.

"Level off and proceed north-northeast," Ernst said.

"Herr Kaleu," said the radioman, Ruhle. "An order from BDU."

WOLF PACK STURMER MUST ATTACK CONVOY HC130 REGARDLESS OF CONSEQUENCES. BEGIN IMMEDIATE ASSAULT. CONTINUE DAY AND NIGHT WITHOUT RESPITE. DÖNITZ.

A grim sign that the tonnage figures for April were down. Ernst ordered Kleist to periscope depth. A gale had arisen, one of those unpredictable whirlwinds of rain and wind that swept down from the Arctic. It was a good time to attack. The U-boats' worst enemy, the planes, would be confined to their carriers by such weather.

Minutes after they surfaced and Ernst led the watch to the conning tower, a lookout reported another submarine off the port bow. It was the U-850, commanded by Rudolf Eckmann. Ernst did not think much of this pudgy Silesian. Transferred from a minesweeper six months ago, he was on his second cruise. On his first sortie he had sunk nothing and his timidity had earned him a reprimand from Dönitz. Chief Kleist was probably right when he said Eckmann had been born too far from salt water. He was ominous proof that the Ubootwaffe had been forced to lower standards for its commanders.

Ernst called a signalman to the rainswept bridge. Have—you—received—attack—order? Ernst asked, through the flapping flags.

Yes—but—doubt—it—is—practical—in—this—weather, Eckmann replied.

Order—leaves—no—room—for—such—judgment, Ernst replied.

They headed north northeast through the heaving sea. Again and again icy water deluged the bridge, filling their boots, sloshing down the necks of their sou'westers. Why hadn't the Berlin bureaucrats who bought this foul weather gear been forced to wear it on a U-boat bridge before they signed the purchase contract? Eckmann stayed abreast of the Wolfseeboot at a distance of about a half-mile.

The Metox suddenly emitted its warning whine. Ernst kept his eyes focused on the horizon, looking for signs of the convoy. "Alarm, Herr Kaleu?" asked Kurz.

Ernst shook his head. He was gambling that the Metox was picking up radar from a surface ship, invisible in the gale. On the surface their new diesels could outrun most British and American escorts in this weather. "U-eight-five-two submerging, Herr Kaleu," called another lookout.

Ernst turned his head in time to see the conning tower vanish beneath the waves. So much for Eckmann's courage. They plowed on through the breakers and no planes appeared to shower them with bombs. The gale mounted in force. Again and again foaming mountains buried the entire bridge, sending more sluices of freezing water under their rain gear.

Hard, Ernst told himself, as his shirt congealed against his flesh in the howling arctic wind. We'll show these bastards how hard Germans can be. A wild roll flung everyone up against the steel sides of the conning tower. "My ribs, Herr Kaleu!" It was Seaman Benz, whining again.

"Send him below!" Ernst shouted at Kurz. "How can you tolerate such a weakling on your watch, Number One?"

"I think he's really hurt, Herr Kaleu."

"Nonsense!"

"Ship!"

"Ship!"

Through the howling spray a ten-thousand-ton tanker loomed dead ahead. Five thousand meters beyond it lay another ship, almost as big, wallowing in the trough of the running sea. The convoy must have zigged back in their direction.

"Prepare tubes one and two for firing," Ernst said. "Stand by to dive. Clear the bridge."

It would be impossible to fire torpedoes on the surface in this wild sea. They went crashing into the tower as the Wolfseeboot submerged. "Keep her at periscope depth, Chief!" Ernst shouted.

"Boat balanced," Kleist reported.

The radioman, Ruhle, now acting as the sound man, reported: "Propeller noise at two hundred and twenty degrees—sound bearing steady. Quite loud. No other noise."

Ernst had the tanker in the periscope lens. The ship beyond it was also visible. If only Eckmann were with him! They could take both of them. "Range three thousand meters. Go to zero! Half-speed ahead," Ernst said.

He spun the periscope to see if there were any destroyers in sight. Nothing but the boiling sea. "Tube one, fire! Tube two, fire!"

"Both torpedoes on their way!" Ruhle shouted. Ernst could feel exultance surge through the boat.

"Blow tanks, take her up, Chief. Watch to the bridge!" Ernst said.

He led the way up the ladders to the bridge. They got there in time to see the torpedoes complete their run. Both hit home, beautiful shots sending water and oil cascading six hundred feet into the raging gale. Flames engulfed the tanker from bow to stern. Burning oil gushed from the torn hull into the churning sea. There was no need to worry about the crew surviving this one.

"Full ahead. Let's see if we can get his partner before the escorts get here."

They drove through the flaming sea as the tanker's crew tried to lower boats. The other ship fired rockets and began zigzagging erratically. Suddenly she lurched like a prizefighter hit by a roundhouse right. Water and pieces of the superstructure cascaded into the sky. Out of the depths rose another U-boat.

"It's eight-eight-nine, Herr Kaleu," Kurz reported with the help of his glasses. Kapitanleutnant Werner Ulbricht, another veteran. Ernst had gone through cadet school with him. Weaklings like Eckmann may have fallen behind but Wolf Pack Sturmer was still carrying the fight to the enemy.

The gale lost force almost as abruptly as it began—typical of the Arctic winds. Ulbricht emerged on his bridge and they exchanged congratulations via their signal flags. Ulbricht said the main body of the convoy was a good ten miles north. They had picked off two stragglers who must have been disoriented by the gale or developed engine trouble.

"Alarm!"

Kurz was pointing aft. A huge plane was roaring toward them at attack altitude. It was an American B-24 Liberator, based in Iceland. Flotilla Commander Schutze had reported a rumor that a substantial number of these long-range bombers had been shifted there. They could fly twice as far as the old British Sunderlands, the "tired bees" they usually dodged with no trouble in the first three years of the war. The Liberator had picked them up on his radar and dropped through the low overcast for his bomb run. Ernst cursed the French-made Metox in Kleist's name. It had yet to make a sound.

"Hard right rudder," Ernst shouted. There was no time to dive. "Shoot him down."

Ulbricht ordered hard left rudder and the two boats veered in opposite directions. Two of the bridge watch tore the tarpaulin off the 20- and 37-millimeter guns and opened up on the Liberator as it roared toward them at no more than 1,000 feet. The plane's gunners fired back and bullets clanged off the Wolfseeboot's hull. The pilot veered away, deciding Ulbricht was a safer target. He had cleared his bridge and was trying to dive.

For a terrible moment Ernst was paralyzed, unable to take his eyes off U-889. Out of the Liberator's open bomb bays hurtled three five-hundred-pound bombs. They exploded around U-889 with a stupendous crash; the submarine vanished in an enormous column of spray. U-889 emerged from the shroud of mist and smoke with her conning tower split open, listing fatally to port. Beside him Ernst heard Kurz praying. "Holy Mary Mother of God have mercy on them in the hour of their deaths."

The words galvanized Ernst into rage—and action. "Fuck your prayers, Number One. Let's get this boat under. Alarm!"

As he waited for the others to go down the hatch, Ernst watched the Liberator make a lumbering turn about a mile away and head back for another bomb run. "Crew to the bow!" Ernst roared as he slammed the hatch.

They headed down as fast as Kleist could flood his tanks. Radioman Ruhle clamped on his sound gear as distant explosions swept through the Wolfseeboot. They were bombing 889 again. The Liberator pilot preferred a sure thing to a long shot, as Ernst suspected he would. "U-889 is breaking up," the radioman said.

"Hard right rudder," Ernst said. "Motors ahead full."

He wanted to put some distance between him and the place where he had dove.

The diving gauge soon showed 100 meters. "Level her out, Chief," Ernst said.

"Boat in balance," Kleist said. Thunderous explosions resounded off the stern, to port. The Liberator had dropped a cluster of bombs comfortably wide of the mark. But their worries were not over. The radioman reported a destroyer approaching. For another two hours she prowled the area, her sonar pinging, dropping spread after spread of wabos. Ernst zigged and zagged, staying a step ahead of the enemy captain every time. "The bastards must have an endless supply of the goddamn things," Kleist said, after the fourteenth or fifteenth explosion.

The air turned foul. "We'll have our revenge," Ernst said. He doubled back to the area where 889 had gone down, hoping her debris might inspire the destroyer captain to decide he had won the game. The trick worked. Radioman Ruhle reported: "He's leaving."

"Take me up to periscope depth," Ernst said.

Five minutes later, in his lens rocked exactly what he had been hoping to see: the convoy's rescue ship, combing the area for possible survivors. She had boats swung out, ready to lower away. "Take a look, Saint Oskar!" Ernst said.

"Another rescuer," Kurz said. "They're hardly worth the trouble, Herr Kaleu. Barely fifteen hundred tons."

"I'm not interested in your goddamn opinion!" Ernst said, catching the implied criticism in his First Officer's remark. He rapped out orders to load tubes three and four and maneuvered the Wolfseeboot into position for a perfect shot. The first torpedo hit dead amidships. Ernst ordered the tanks blown and they surfaced as the rescuer began listing drastically to port.

"Gun crews to action stations!" Ernst roared and the sailors raced up the ladder. By the time he reached the bridge, the loader had removed the waterproof tampion from the muzzle of the bow gun and the aimer had slipped the optical sight into the L-shaped bracket on the port side of the gun. Three other men were passing the heavy ammunition to the loader. They had been trained to have the gun ready to fire within 120 seconds of the Commander's order.

First Officer Kurz had followed Ernst to the bridge. "She's going down nicely, Herr Kaleu," he said.

"Not fast enough," Ernst said. "Open fire!"

It was fascinating, the way the human mind worked, Ernst thought, as the bow gun boomed. No one objected to shelling a ship, because that was within the legitimate rules of sea warfare. It did not seem to occur to them that the shells were killing men aboard the target. As the incendiary shells smashed into the listing rescuer, she began burning fiercely. The frantic crew cut away lifeboats and leaped into the sea.

In five minutes the ship was lying on her port side, ready for her death dive. The water was full of men clinging to rafts and pieces of wreckage. Ernst ordered the helmsman to head toward one of the lifeboats. It had about twenty men in it; a dozen others clung to the sides.

"What ship was that?" he called to the lifeboat.

"The rescue ship *Martin de Porres,*" replied a man in the bow. "What do you care, you Nazi son of a bitch?" His accent was unmistakably American.

"Who was Martin de Porres, Number One?"

"A Spanish saint, Herr Kaleu," Kurz said. "Famous for his works of mercy."

Hard, Ernst thought. He was going to show everyone how hard a German could be. "Bring four machine guns to the bridge," he said, handing Seaman Benz the key to the Wolfseeboot's armory. In five minutes the guns were on the bridge. He handed one to Kurz, another to Benz, a third to a petty officer.

"Open fire on them when I give the order," he said. He trained his gun on the American in the bow of the lifeboat and shouted: "Fire!"

Ernst pulled the trigger and the man toppled back into the crowded boat, his chest spurting blood. Ernst poured bullets into the rest of the boat while men cried out in anguish and rage and crumpled with blood pouring from dozens of wounds. Some jumped overboard, where they were shot by Benz and the petty officer.

"Herr Kaleu!" It was Oskar Kurz. Tears were streaming down his bearded cheeks. "I cannot fire this gun. I cannot obey your order. Shoot me, I beg you. Shoot me."

"You may go below, Number One," Ernst said. "Send the Second Officer up here in your place."

The Second Officer arrived along with Chief Kleist. Ernst handed Kurz's gun to the Second Officer and ordered him to shoot the men on rafts. "They're killing our women and children in our cities. They deserve no mercy!" he said.

"Jesus Christ! What does that matter?" Kleist shouted. "We're sailors. These men are sailors too."

"Go below, Chief. You have no business up here. Your job is to keep the boat running," Ernst said.

He aimed his gun at a man who was desperately trying to swim away from the Wolfseeboot as it approached him. He pulled the trigger and the man screamed and rolled over on his back. Ernst poured another volley into him. An enormous exultance swept through him. He imagined Berthe watching it all, wringing her hands, tears of disapproval streaming down her beautiful face. "We must kill them all," he said. "We want no witnesses."

For another ten minutes they cruised up and down, firing methodically at swimmers until there were no living men in sight. They crisscrossed the area again, firing into rafts and the riddled lifeboat to make sure no one escaped. Finally Ernst decided he was risking the Wolfseeboot. The *Martin de Porres* still lay on her side, flames and smoke gushing from her portholes, stubbornly refusing to sink. They headed north in pursuit of the convoy.

Within fifteen minutes, planes from a carrier drove them under. They dove to 150 fathoms and took a terrific pounding. In the Zentrale, Chief Kleist and his men studiously avoided Ernst's eyes. Their disapproval swirled around him like a noxious gas. Even the radioman, Ruhle, who had been with Ernst since the first voyage in the Ritterboot, spoke in a strained, guarded voice as he reported messages from other members of Wolf Pack Sturmer.

The messages were not encouraging. Carrier aircraft filled the skies over Convoy HC130. Two other boats had been damaged by air attacks and were limping for home. Silence from four others suggested they may have joined Werner Ulbricht for an eternal sleep in the depths.

"Herr Kaleu!" Kleist whirled in his seat to all but fling the words at him. "On behalf of the crew I must report to you that many men are seriously concerned over what just transpired with the convoy rescue ship. They feel such tactics expose them to a similar fate if we're forced to abandon our boat."

"Nonsense," Ernst said. "We left no witnesses. We're fighting a total war, Chief. You heard what Roosevelt and Churchill said at Casablanca. Unconditional surrender! That means the enslavement, even the annihilation of the German people."

"Admittedly, the enemy's tactics are despicable. But do two wrongs make a right, Herr Kaleu? If we do things that the men feel dishonor us as Germans—"

"Herr Kaleu!" Oskar Kurz swayed in the passageway to the officers' quarters. "Shooting men in lifeboats is also, if I remember correctly, forbidden by a general order issued last year."

"The Führer has given us permission to dispense with honor, and ignore general orders. He has called on us to be men of iron. As strong, as hard, as heartless as this boat." For a moment Ernst felt dazed. He was talking to Kleist and Kurz as if they were strangers, enemies. So be it, he told himself. Hardness included everyone. "I will regard any further disagreement on this matter as treason to the Reich. Heil Hitler!"

There was a long empty pause. "Heil Hitler, Herr Kaleu," said Chief Kleist in a voice that seemed to come from the gray depths outside the boat. He turned away to stare at his dials.

"Heil Hitler," said Oskar Kurz in an equally lifeless voice.

"Another message from BDU, Herr Kaleu," said radioman Ruhle. "To all boats in Pack Sturmer."

BREAK OFF ATTACK ON CONVOY HC130. CONCENTRATION OF ENEMY AIRCRAFT AND SURFACE PROTECTION PRO-HIBITIVE. RETURN TO BASE. MAKE NO FURTHER ATTACKS UNLESS TARGET OF OPPORTUNITY PRESENTS MINIMUM DANGER TO BOAT.

It was unbelievable. The Lion was retreating.

Ernst ordered the navigator to set a course for Lorient. The transit of the Bay of Biscay was a nightmare. Six times they dived to escape low altitude aircraft attacks which racked the Wolfseeboot with depth charges. They limped into Lorient with a malfunctioning rudder and one diesel barely breathing.

No band greeted them, no smiling nurses with their arms full of flowers, even though 60,000 tons of victory pennants fluttered from their conning tower. Lorient was a dismal place, these days. The area around the waterfront had been smashed by Allied bombers, still trying to destroy the great concrete shelters. The pontoon ship *Isere* had been abandoned. Army troops, nurses, everyone but the most essential personnel had fled into the countryside.

Only their grim-faced flotilla commander, Viktor Schutze, recently promoted to Kapitan zur See, watched them tie up beside the concrete pier. In his office, Ernst learned that the Wolfseeboot was one of the lucky ones. A staggering thirty-seven boats had been lost in April. Schutze recited a litany of the dead, many of them Ernst's friends and classmates.

"The Lion has decided he can no longer risk men like you in battle. He needs you *Halschmerzen* types to inspire the newcomers," Schutze said.

Literally, *Halschmerzen* meant "afflicted with throat trouble." It was used by the cynics in the Ubootwaffe to describe the winners of the Knight's Cross, which was worn at the throat. It implied that such commanders were likely to risk their crews and boats to win the coveted prize.

"Herr Kapitan, I assure I never gave a moment's thought to my throat when I was at sea. Or on land, for that matter," Ernst said.

"I'm only joking," Schutze said. "Anyway, you're going on the beach like me. But your luck continues to hold. Dönitz wants you in Berlin to show you off to the Führer and his assorted buffoons. At least you can see your wife—and you don't have to send *Draufgangers* out week after week, knowing they won't come back."

Draufganger meant daredevil, another term of opprobrium in the Ubootwaffe. They too had a bad habit of getting themselves and their crews killed. "I divorced my wife six months ago," Ernst said.

"So Berlin will be twice as much fun."

Schutze barely glanced at his Kriegstagebuch. "The Lion will go over it. He likes to read good news. He doesn't get much of it these days."

That meant another week before Ernst could report what he had done to the survivors of the *Martin de Porres*. He had not mentioned it in the war diary, of course. But he felt an acute need to report it to someone. He decided he was glad Kapitan zur See Schutze would not be the man. Somehow the Lion himself was the only person he wanted to tell.

"Would you recommend any of your officers for command?" Schutze asked.

"Oskar Kurz," Ernst said. "He's—a very good man."

He could not quite believe he had said it. Was it a way of admitting a certain regret for the *Martin de Porres*? Or was it simply a fact? Compared to the cowards and second-raters they were getting as commanders these days, Kurz was an excellent choice.

Before Ernst left for Berlin, he said goodbye to Kurz, Chief Kleist and the other officers and wished them luck. He did not tell Kurz he had recommended him for command. Kleist, already well into getting drunk, sighed and said: "There goes our *Lebensversicherung*." It was the ultimate compliment old-timers in the Ubootwaffe paid to a commander. The word meant life insurance.

In Berlin, Ernst was shocked by the air-raid damage. Whole sections of the inner city had been leveled. The Siegesallee, with its heroic statues of Germany's past leaders, had been smashed to bits. He reported to naval headquarters in the imposing Hotel am Steinplatz in Charlottenberg and presented his Kriegstagebuch to a solemn Dönitz.

Promoted to Grossadmiral (Grand Admiral), the Lion was running both the Ubootwaffe and the entire Kriegsmarine, with thousands of miles of coastline and hundreds of surface ships under his command. So he only had time to skim the war diary. But his eye fell on two items that pleased him. "Two more rescue ships," he said. "That's good shooting."

Ernst took a deep breath and told him about the other shooting. The Lion listened without so much as a flicker of emotion on his face. "I approve what you have done completely. I only wish other commanders could match your hardness," he said. "But because we are confronting enemies who are doing their utmost to smear the Reich and the Führer before the whole world, while their bombers commit crimes infinitely more bestial against our women and children in our cities, you must never mention this to another person. If there is any complaint from the enemy, I will of course deny all knowledge and dismiss it as propaganda."

"I understand, Herr Grossadmiral."

Dönitz put his hand on Ernst's shoulder and gave him a fierce squeeze. "This makes me even more convinced of the correctness of my decision to withdraw you from sea duty. For the time being, we have lost the battle of the Atlantic."

The incredible words demolished Ernst's elation. He felt as deflated, as two dimensional, as the rug under his feet.

"But we shall return to the battle," Dönitz continued in the same relentless voice. "We shall develop new weapons for the boats, new boats that will equal the enemy's weapons. This is a temporary defeat. You will help us develop these weapons, Hoffmann. You will inspire the new crews with the story of your exploits, your hardness."

"Yes, Herr Grossadmiral."

"The U-boat arm is the only offensive weapon Germany has left. We cannot concede the Atlantic to the enemy. If we do, Germany is defeated."

"Yes, Herr Grossadmiral."

In his throat, his chest, his belly, Ernst felt a swelling sensation, as if he were a U-boat that had gone too deep and the implosion, the collapse of seams, the upward gush of tormented air was about to occur. What was it? He had to name the feeling.

The word floated into his mind, whispered by Berthe's mocking voice: *doubt.*

BOOK FOUR

37

THE VOICE IN THE NIGHT

Berthe von Hoffmann sat in her apartment overlooking the Retiro Park in Madrid, listening to Radio Berlin play dirges for the German Army in Tunisia. After winning some minor victories, Hitler's attempt to inflict a stunning defeat on the Anglo-Americans had collapsed when the enemy's overwhelming sea and air power cut off the Wehrmacht's gasoline supply. On the Russian front, stupendous battles raged, with German armies in retreat everywhere.

Each day hopelessness thickened in Berthe's flesh. She had lost interest in her appearance. Her unwashed hair streeled; without makeup, her skin was sallow, rough. Around her she saw nothing but hatred for Germany. General Franco had recently issued a call for a peace conference. The Pope had seconded the proposal. The Americans dismissed the idea with a sneer. In England, the Labor Party voted enthusiastic approval of Lord Robert Vansittart's demand that the German people be held as responsible as the Nazi party for the crimes of the war.

Yesterday, at the embassy, Berthe had gone to a screening of a film of Joseph Goebbel's Total War rally in the Sportspalast Stadium in Berlin. A hundred thousand Party members had roared defiance and hysterical resolve in the teeth of Franklin Roosevelt's unconditional surrender declaration. In the cables from Berlin she decoded later in the day, a new word appeared. *Bombenbrandschrumpfle-*

ichen. It meant incendiary bomb–shrunken bodies. Berthe's hope-lessness oozed into despair.

Last week she had flown to Berlin to see Admiral Canaris. She also tried to see her children. Her mother-in-law was unrelenting. She waved the court decree in her face again and said she would not allow Berthe to contaminate them. At Abwehr headquarters, Berthe told Canaris what Moorman and Talbot were doing in Spain—accusing him to cover their signal intelligence successes in breaking the Enigma code. He shrugged and said he would do the same thing if he were in their place.

"Is there any hope?" Berthe said.

"There's always hope," Canaris said. "Depending on what we hope for. The longer I live, the more convinced I become that we can do very little to alter the course of history. The more violent the attempt, the more violent the frustration."

He was talking about his opposition to assassinating Hitler. Colonel Oster, the chief proponent of this solution, had been interro-gated by the Gestapo and confined to his home under informal arrest. He had made a habit of propositioning high-ranking officers to join him in the attempt. One of them must have betrayed him. The generals remained in disarray because of the announcement of unconditional surrender. They were hoping for a victory in the East or the West that would give them at least a chance of changing those humiliating terms.

"You don't agree with this policy?" Berthe asked.

"I think eventually we'll have to accept unconditional surrender. We'll have to accept the full consequences of our crimes."

Never, Berthe vowed. She was one with the generals, in spite of being trapped in this universal spider's web of intrigue. "If your enemy is despicable, it frees you from such obligations."

Canaris soothingly admitted she might be right. He said he was hanging on to the control of the Abwehr by a thread. Another unpleasant surprise such as unconditional surrender might finish him with the Führer. That was why it was important for her and others to continue to supply him with information. It did not matter if it was tainted. As long as it had the appearance of authenticity, he would look like he was doing his job. She would retain her cover to probe the Americans for an opening to negotiations.

"I begin to think you're wrong about the Americans," Berthe said.

"Except for a few extremists like Vansittart, the British are far less fanatic. But Moorman stands like an ugly little ogre before their door, demanding information. For instance, he wants to know if Germany is building secret rocket weapons that would alter the course of the war."

"That would be a very large gift. Ask him what he'll offer in exchange. It will have to be substantial."

Loathsome. They were selling off their fatherland, piece by piece. She carefully avoided meeting Helmuth von Moltke at the Abwehr offices. He was the only man with the power to challenge her disgust. Instead she spent most of her brief stay in Berlin with Helen Widerstand, who breathed detestation of Hitler and the generals and the British and the Americans. Only the Russians received a cautious blessing from Helen, because she hoped they would help German Marxists create a socialist society.

Almost casually, at the end of her meeting with Canaris, Berthe inquired about Colonel Claus von Stauffenberg, the outspoken giant she had met with Elisabeth von Theismann in Paris.

"A sad tale," Canaris said. "He was badly wounded when a plane strafed his staff car in Tunisia. He's recuperating in a hospital in Munich."

As she rose to leave, Canaris twisted in his chair. For a moment she thought he was in pain. "Peenemünde. The island in the Baltic. That's where they're developing the rockets. But don't give it to Moorman without some sort of quid pro quo."

The Admiral too found betrayal difficult at the deeper levels. Berthe asked him to be more specific about what she should demand.

"I've heard from one of our few surviving agents in London that Eisenhower is opposed to unconditional surrender. An approach to him might be worth the price—"

Berthe flew to Munich and found Stauffenberg prone in a bed, swathed in bandages. He had lost his right arm and his left eye, and all but two fingers on his surviving hand. He greeted her listlessly.

"I haven't come to offer you sympathy," she said. "But to tell you what they did to Elisabeth von Theismann."

"She was one of my wife's closest friends. We've tried to find out more about her since she was arrested—"

She told him how Elisabeth had died. "Kill him. Kill Hitler for all our sakes. For Germany's sake," she whispered.

Berthe saw herself enveloping him in her demonic arms like the angel had embraced the Ritterboot—but for an utterly opposite reason. She was not a messenger of mercy. She was an agent of death and destruction. Back in Madrid, she told the story to the Marquesa with passionate satisfaction.

"You're in the final stages," the Marquesa said.

"Of what?"

"Of refusing to accept the situation. I was the same way until my last son was killed on the last day of the Civil War. Then it all became perfectly clear to me."

"What became clear?" Berthe snarled. "The absurdity of believing in God?"

"It isn't a question of believing in Him or not. He comes to you— or He doesn't—in His own good time. Haven't you noticed how in Spain we never say 'God go with you'? Instead we say 'Go with God.'"

"I don't even know what you're talking about!" Berthe said.

"You will—soon."

She was as loathsome as the rest of them, with her pseudoreligious wisdom and her crafty smile. Berthe let her read the Tarot cards for the third or fourth time that month. She had begun consulting them almost religiously since they visited the shrines of the Virgin. The Fool always remained near the center of the horseshoe of cards, reaffirming the Marquesa's conviction that folly and expiation were the essence of Berthe's spiritual journey. The frequent appearance of Pagad the Juggler renewed her faith in the Good Stranger. "Possibly, he and the Fool are the same person," she said, with her mortuary smile. But the final card was almost always the man hanging upside down from the cross, the symbol of the transformation in which Berthe no longer believed.

Switching off Radio Berlin, Berthe sat in the fading light of her second spring in Madrid, waiting for Jonathan Talbot. He would do one of two things. Reaffirm his dogged devotion to her—or give her more false information to pass on to Berlin to further confuse the High Command. Possibly both. But he would not ask her to make love. That had ceased since the day she revealed that she only loved one thing: Germany.

Perhaps she had killed the wrong man in Granada. She should have let Lothar Engle drag her back to Berlin. She should have told him and his slimy SS friends everything. Why not? She could no longer distinguish between one side or the other. She was living in a daze of moral and spiritual revulsion.

She took out Ernst's last two letters, about sinking the rescue ships in a convoy. Was she responsible for the hatred and evil that was invading his soul? He seemed to think so. The letters were an accusation, a torture device. She began thinking about the cyanide capsule in her purse. Gradually, as darkness thickened in the Retiro, she realized Jonathan Talbot was not coming. Had she finally succeeded in driving him away?

There was a knock on the door. She opened it to find herself confronting a pale young man in the gray-green uniform of a German infantry officer. "Frau von Hoffmann? I'm Captain Axel von dem Herzner. Admiral Canaris has sent me to you."

She gestured him into the room. He walked with a heavy limp. "Forgive my awkwardness," he said. "I'm still getting used to my artificial leg."

She told him to sit down and made some coffee. He thanked her with abnormal ardor. "The Admiral tells me that you've tried to communicate something of the crimes the SS are committing against the Jews. But without success."

"Yes."

"He thought an eyewitness account might be helpful. He said you would have a recording device. But I was not to use my real name."

She got out a small machine on which she had made a number of recordings of Jonathan's conversations with her to bolster her claim to being a successful agent. Captain von dem Herzner began telling her how his colonel had sent him to a recently captured military airfield in the Ukraine last year in search of vodka left behind by the fleeing Russians.

On the other side of the field, about a quarter of a mile away, he saw a line of naked people being herded along by several dozen SS men. He drove across the field to find out more about this strange sight. "I was told they were Jews," Herzner said. "I asked where they were taking them."

"'To the pit,' replied one of the SS men." The line of naked men, women and children was almost a half-mile long. "I particularly remember a beautiful young girl. As she passed me, she held up her hands and pointed to her fingers. 'Twenty-three years old,' she said."

Captain von dem Herzner gulped down the last of his coffee and asked Berthe if she had some brandy. "I followed the line of march as it left the airport and disappeared into a small wood. I got out of my car and walked through the wood. On the other side of it I saw a great ditch. It must have stretched for a quarter of a mile. As the Jews reached the edge of the ditch, they were told to lie down. An SS man walked along the line, shooting each of them in the back of the neck. They were then flung into the ditch."

In Spain we never say "God go with you." It's always "Go with God." Was this the word of God being spoken to her paralyzed mind and body? Was this the next part of the Path?

Captain von dem Herzner continued his story. "I asked the SS man in command, a Sturmbannführer, if he was acting under orders. We had the same rank and he answered me with great insolence. Of course, he said. He told me to get the hell out of there and attend to my own business, which was killing Russians. His business was killing Jews."

Herzner gulped his brandy. "I reported to my colonel what I had seen. I suggested we march the regiment to the airport and disperse the SS men at gunpoint, then notify the division and Army staff of what was happening. I could not believe this was being done with the approval of the high command. The colonel drove to the airport and talked to the SS Standartenführer who was in overall command. He came back and told me there was nothing we could do. The SS had more heavy weapons than we did. They were acting under orders that came straight from Berlin."

Tears streamed down Captain von dem Herzner's face. "Every night when I try to sleep I think of that girl who told me she was twenty-three years old. The same age I am. I've thought and thought about what I should have said or done to stop it. I didn't have an answer—until I lost my leg in the retreat and I was posted to the Abwehr and met Helmuth von Moltke who told me of his efforts to stop such terrible deeds. Then I suddenly realized—with no prompting from him—what I should have done. I should have stripped off my uniform and lay down naked beside those Jews. I should have asked the SS to shoot a German officer. I think it might have stopped them for a while."

Now Captain von dem Herzner was stripping himself naked

before the whole world. Berthe turned off the recorder and gave him more brandy. "How could this evil get loose in the German soul, Frau von Hoffmann? Do you have an answer?" he asked.

"No."

Her voice was cold, almost uncaring. This wounded soldier was searching for sympathy, healing. But she had no compassion to offer him. All she could urge him to do was commit murder in return as she had told the mutilated Stauffenberg. Dimly, Berthe saw this might be a mistake. Maybe Canaris's way, the slow cunning cultivation of eventual defeat, was not only safer, it was spiritually superior. But this possibility came and went in a glimpse.

"I'll try to get your statement circulated in London and Washington."

Captain von dem Herzner trudged into the Madrid night. The telephone rang. It was Jonathan Talbot, apologizing for being so late. He had been conferring with the new OSS chief for Spain. Twenty minutes later, he arrived looking wary. He frequently approached her as if she might detonate in his face. She rewound the recorder and played Captain von dem Herzner's statement for him.

"Make a copy and give it to me," he said. "Along with a translation. The new OSS guy is a really decent, intelligent man. I'll try using him as a channel. Donovan, the head of the OSS, is a Republican. My father knew him slightly in the Twenties."

There was very little hope in his voice. It was becoming more and more apparent that the slaughter of the Jews was making no impression on the Western leaders as an argument for an early peace. If anything, they were inclined to see it as another reason for redoubling their determination to insist on unconditional surrender. Were the German generals the wise men—in their groping for a chance to inflict a defeat before they acted to overthrow Hitler?

"I've got some new disinformation for you," Jonathan said. "It's about the Metox radar warning device on the U-boats. We want you to tell Berlin the British have developed a radar gun that homes in on the damn thing, turning it into a giveaway of every U-boat's position, the moment one of them surfaces."

"They'll take them off the U-boats, leaving them totally exposed to air attacks?"

"Exactly. Moorman says they're leaking it to Berlin through three or four channels. It's a beautiful double play, don't you think?"

This business was corrupting him too. From a man who prided himself on telling the truth he had become a connoisseur of clever lies. "I refuse to cooperate on this matter," Berthe said.

Ever since unconditional surrender had been proclaimed at Casablanca, she had felt free to pick and choose among the lies they proposed to her. Those that seemed relatively trivial or vague, such as a report that the Americans were diverting most of their available manpower to the war in the Pacific, she sent to Berlin. Those that might inflict actual harm on the German war effort she coolly rejected.

Jonathan paced the room. "On this one you have no choice," he said. "It's a direct order to me from Moorman. He wants it in Berlin as soon as possible. He hates to threaten you but—"

"But you let him. My protector grows less heroic by the day."

"Less patient, maybe. I never claimed to be heroic."

"Is this a sign of desperation? Are the U-boats still winning the Atlantic war?"

"As a matter of fact, no. We sank forty-one boats in the last four weeks. That's why this Metox thing can hit them hard. They'll be groping for an explanation. They'll grab this and shut down the only eyes they've got left."

Berthe writhed, thinking of Ernst. Was the Wolfseeboot one of the forty-one that lay at the bottom of the Atlantic, gashed by wabos, crushed by the pressure of the depths? No. Somehow she was sure she would know when that happened. He would come to her in sleep or daydream to say goodbye. Instead, she was being asked by her American lover to multiply his humiliation and defeat.

"Tell Moorman he can go to hell—or to Vansittart. Did you hear about the Labor Party's approval of his resolution?"

"Yes, but they're not in power. Moorman says Churchill's not going to buy mass vengeance. It's against British tradition."

She said nothing. But the question asked itself. Then why unconditional surrender?

"I'm as appalled by the stupidity of unconditional surrender as you are," he said. "How many times do I have to tell you that?"

He was suffering. She was inflicting pain on him. But the knowledge only seemed to increase her determination to go on doing it. He paced the room again, probably fuming at the inconsistencies and stupidities of women.

"I wasn't going to show you this," he said. "I know it'll upset you. But maybe it's the only way to make you cooperate."

He pulled a folded yellow paper out of the inside pocket of his coat and handed it to her.

FROM: COMMANDER, CONVOY HC130

TO: COMMANDER, WESTERN APPROACHES

AT APPROXIMATELY 1300 HOURS, HMS *ASPERITY*, ONE OF THE ESCORTS IN CONVOY HC130, RESPONDED TO A DISTRESS SIGNAL FROM RESCUE SHIP SS *MARTIN DE PORRES*. RESPONSE WAS DELAYED BY ORDERS TO ATTACK U-BOAT IN ITS VICINITY, IDENTIFIED BY AIRCRAFT FROM CARRIER HMS *HERMES*. WHEN HMS *ASPERITY* REACHED SCENE OF SS *MARTIN DE PORRES* DISTRESS CALL SHE DISCOVERED THE SHIP HAD BEEN SUNK. THE SURFACE OF THE SEA WAS LITTERED WITH WRECKAGE AND CORPSES. ALL THE BODIES HAD DIED OF MACHINE GUN FIRE. MANY WERE RIDDLED BEYOND RECOGNITION. HMS *ASPERITY* LOWERED BOATS AND ROWED TO RAFTS AND A DRIFTING SHIP'S BOAT. ALL IN BOAT WERE DEAD EXCEPT ONE MAN, WHO WAS BADLY WOUNDED. TAKEN ABOARD *ASPERITY*, THE MAN, GIDEON JONES, A NEGRO COOK, SAID THEY HAD BEEN TORPEDOED AND SUNK BY A U-BOAT WHICH THEN SURFACED AND MACHINE GUNNED SURVIVORS. THE U-BOAT'S NUMBER WAS CLEARLY VISIBLE ON ITS CONNING TOWER: 666. ABOVE IT WAS A DRAWING OF A WOLF'S HEAD. STRONGLY URGE A PROTEST AGAINST THIS BARBARITY TO THE HIGHEST LEVELS OF THE ALLIED AND GERMAN COMMANDS AS WELL AS TO THE INTERNATIONAL RED CROSS.

The Path, Berthe thought. How could this obscenity be on the Path? How could she be responsible for turning the Ritterboot into the Wolfseeboot? "This isn't made up? It's not another one of Moorman's tricks?" Berthe said.

"Do you really think I wouldn't tell you the truth, if it was?"

"Get out of here!" she screamed. "I can't bear your smirking,

scaly honesty anymore. It's almost as disgusting as Moorman's dis-
honesty."

He grabbed her by the arms and dragged her out of the chair.
"Once and for all, we've got to stop thinking of each other as people
from two different countries. We're together in this thing. Together
in our love—and in our desire to save the lives of millions of innocent
people."

She tried to twist free but he held her in a wrestler's grip. She
turned her head away as if he was loathsome to look at—and he was.
She loathed this love that was taking Germany away from her—the
Germany her soul adored—the Germany that she had loved in
Ernst's arms. She thought of Captain von dem Herzner, his tormented boyish face, the pride with which he said the words "German
officer." He was exactly like Ernst, as if Ernst had managed to repeal
the last four nightmare years and returned to her with the innocence
and pride and honor of their wedding night miraculously restored.

"I'll send the Metox story to Berlin. Isn't that all you really want?"

"You know damn well what I really want!"

"You can't have it. I can't stop loving Germany. Why don't you ask
me to tear out my eyes, cut off my breasts? It's part of me."

"Why can't you love me—and Germany?"

"That's—impossible."

She watched his shoulders slump, his head droop. Was this what
she wanted? Her own private victory in the desert of defeat? A victory that left her barren of every kind of affection? Perhaps.

"What will they do to Ernst?"

"After the war they'll put him on trial—and hang him."

"You ask me to cooperate with this idea? You expect me to face
my children with their father's blood on my hands?"

"You're not responsible for him! You're not responsible for any of
them."

"They're part of me. Part of my blood!"

For the first time she saw the crucial difference between Germans and Americans. They were not bound by blood, by the mystical
tribal sense of the volk.

"You can't stop loving Germany?" he said. "After listening to
Captain von dem Herzner's story? After reading this production by
Kapitanleutnant von Hoffmann? What the hell's the matter with you?

I've stopped loving the United States. They haven't committed mass murder. They've just elected an arrogant lying son of a bitch as president. We're both free to step back and say: 'I divorce myself from this country. I didn't choose it. I was born into it and taught to love it as a child. But now I can put off childish things—'"

His words were stripping away skin, his rage was like scalding water. "Jonathan, I want to but I can't I can't I can't!"

He drew her into his arms. "You can—and you will. I have—faith that you will."

She heard the falter before the word *faith*. This was a journey down a path for him, too. He kissed her gently on the cheek and left her. She almost called him back, almost offered herself to him as a forlorn apology for her failure.

Exhausted, she lay on the bed and emptied her mind of thought, her body of feeling. The cyanide capsule floated like a space ship in the stillness just above her head. All she had to do was reach up and seize it. Perhaps she only had to open her lips and it would glide down her grateful throat.

In a dark night.

Who whispered those words? She was suddenly as tense as a rabbit or a squirrel, hunted by a falcon. Someone was pursuing her in this darkness. Someone she wanted to evade, avoid, deny.

In a dark night.

The same words. Who said them? They were spoken without sound. They opened in her mind like a flower in the dawn. Was this another twist of the Path? Suddenly she wanted to pray. For the first time since she was a child and her nurse made her pray for her father and her mother. But it was a strange prayer. It was a plea for everything and nothing. A wordless explosion of her mind toward the night sky, the upward thrust of a rocket that catapulted her spirit from bed, body, the earth itself.

In a dark night.
With anxious love inflamed.

Suddenly she knew with a certainty that swiftly became terror that this was no ordinary voice. She stumbled from the bed to a little book the Marquesa had given her about Spanish mysticism. There were the words, where she had stopped reading with the sullen conclusion that no Spaniard could have anything to say to the German soul. There, on the printed page, by the light of a wavering candle, exactly as they might have looked five centuries ago, was the next stage of the Path.

Not the most easy but the most difficult
Not the most savory but the most insipid
Not that which pleases but that which displeases
Not to desire the greatest but the least.
Not to desire anything but to desire nothing.

The next day, when she told the Marquesa, she embraced her with tears in her eyes. "I knew it was coming," she said. "I knew it."

"What? What am I becoming?"

"Germany. Defeated, desolate Germany. It's so difficult. Only a woman can do it. I struggled against it for so long. I told so many lies to myself about Spain. But at last I accepted it, the reality of our defeat. There's happiness in it. A terrible dark happiness."

Berthe shrank from this woman who claimed to be her mother. What kind of gift was this to offer a daughter? "Trust me," the Marquesa said. "Trust the Virgin of Guadalupe. The woman who stands outside time—beside God."

A virtual convulsion shook Berthe's body. "You want me to throw away my mind!"

"No. I want you to fill it with love. For all of them. For Jonathan. For Ernst. Even for Moorman. For America. For Germany. For Spain."

"I can't do it," Berthe sobbed. She suddenly was a little girl, wailing into her nurse's apron when her mother called to say she was staying in Paris for another month. "I love nothing, no one, not even you—except Germany."

"That will change. The moment of transformation will come. The Virgin won't let you fail."

"Mutter," Berthe sobbed. "Mutter." The word she had never been able to speak without pain. She clung to the Marquesa, a fellow woman in a world at war with love.

Gently, firmly, the Marquesa disengaged herself. "Now," she said. "We're ready for a new beginning."

38

THE REAL WAR

"The German resistance movement? There's no such thing," Ned
Travis said.

"Zeke told me he sent you a long report on it," Annie said.

"I would say Zeke's unreliability has been certified by his behavior at Casablanca. He tried to get to see the President! He wanted to
sell him some moonshine about negotiating peace with the Germans.
I'm beginning to think he may be mentally ill. Megalomania. Or adolescent infatuation with Berthe von what's-her-name. The head of
ONI, Admiral Jamison, gave him hell and sent him back to Spain. It's
a good thing Admiral King didn't hear about it."

Who was lying? Annie bet on Ned, who had always worn subterfuge on his foxy face. Zeke Talbot was incapable of inventing a
fantasy intended to deceive his country. She had resisted calling Ned
or anyone else at the State Department for two months, hoping Zeke
would send her his dossier on his supposedly peace-loving Germans,
in spite of her scathing contempt for the idea. Evidently he and Frau
von Hoffmann had jointly decided she was not worth the postage.

Ned could afford to lie with casual arrogance. He was riding the
crest of the unconditional surrender euphoria that was sweeping
Washington. Saul Randolph had called it exactly right. The Casablanca
declaration had won rave reviews in the newspapers and on the radio.
Gone were the mutterings about malaise in the editorial pages and

columns. The President had been transformed from sly diplomatic fixer to a warrior high priest, leading a crusade that would settle for nothing less than total victory.

Saul Randolph and Annie were also enjoying a private euphoria, which he called Marrakesh madness. Annie could not deny the rapture, whirling dervishes of it, suffused with a sweetness that often bordered alarmingly on surrender. He was falling in love with her, a process that the new Annie, between bouts of ardor, watched with bemused interest from her high wire.

She soon saw it tilted the balance of power between them in her favor. Saul found it harder and harder to reproach her when she coolly deviated from him politically. She absolutely refused to join the drive to purge the State Department of everyone with negative ideas about the Russians. In the wake of Casablanca, this campaign had been renewed with fresh confidence in imminent victory by everyone from FDR to Saul's boss, Morgenthau, to Drew Pearson to Walter Lippmann. One of the most outspoken Russian specialists found himself exiled to the Mideast as Ambassador to Iraq. Others were deported to equally obscure embassies in South America. But Roy Reeves, the man Ambassador Litvinov wanted eliminated above everyone else, managed to survive—to Saul's exasperation.

He was even more unhappy when Annie began digging beneath the apparently universal endorsement of unconditional surrender. Reeves prompted this quest when he told her that Secretary of State Cordell Hull loathed the idea. In the War Department, she discovered a stunning lack of enthusiasm for the slogan, from Secretary of War Henry Stimson to the lowliest staff captain. But no one was willing to speak on the record and incur the President's wrath. Annie began interviewing historians at the capital's numerous universities, and found a majority of them thought it was a very bad idea.

This historical hegira inevitably brought Annie to her alma mater, Trinity College, to interview Sister Agatha Clare, the head of the history department. A large, horse-faced woman with a doctorate from the Sorbonne, Sister Agatha found it difficult to voice her opinion of unconditional surrender at first. She adored Franklin D. Roosevelt. In an essay on him in *Commonweal* magazine, she had declared him that rarest of creatures, a natural politician, with an inborn talent for crystallizing what his fellow citizens were thinking in a dim, inarticulate way.

Sister Agatha finally admitted she disliked unconditional surrender. She felt sure it had been foisted on the President by some of his advisors. "It's so inflexible—it's un-Rooseveltian," she said. "But he's a man—a crippled man, alas—maybe he thought it was necessary to impress his fellow males with his toughness. I've also heard he's been troubled all his life by his failure to see action in World War One. He sat it out in Washington, D.C., while his cousins, Theodore Roosevelt's sons, were in the thick of the fighting. I gather Uncle Theodore wrote him a rather stinging rebuke about it. That would be another reason for this masculine overcompensation."

Sister Agatha smiled briefly and nibbled one of the chocolate mints she kept in her desk. She loved to explore the psychological dimensions of history. Annie had noted in her student days that the foibles explored were almost always male.

"I predict FDR will modify unconditional surrender—perhaps even dump it—at the appropriate moment," she continued. "That would be very Rooseveltian. He's a marvelous chameleon—which is exactly what a politician should be."

Sister Agatha said unconditional surrender sounded as if the Allies intended to destroy Germany. If that was their intention, idiocy was being compounded with stupidity. "Germany is the economic heart of Europe," she said. "You can't have peace—which presupposes prosperity—in Europe without Germany any more than you can expect a body without a heart to be anything but a rotting corpse."

For some reason, *a body without a heart* produced an alarming tremor in the former Anna Richman's nervous system. Maybe it had something to do with the aura created by Sister Agatha's black robes or the way her white wimple emphasized the luminous intelligence of her homely face.

"Do you by any chance know a man at the State Department named Roy Reeves?" Annie asked. It was a foolish question, which could only lead to more tremors.

"We're old friends," Sister Agatha said. "When State organized their group of Russian specialists fifteen years ago, I asked them if I might be given access, confidentially, of course, to information they gathered about the Soviet regime. Mr. Reeves was one of several people they sent out here to brief me. The things they told me! I'm afraid there's a reign of evil in Moscow comparable only to Rome under Nero. Worse, the system doesn't *work*. I think Mr. Reeves was even more disappointed than I was about that."

Sister Agatha nibbled another mint. "He's one of those old-line Americans who's lost his original family faith. It dwindled away into Unitarianism, then into various religions of progress, including, I suspect, communism. When he returned from his latest tour in Moscow, he became a Catholic. I can't claim any direct influence. He preferred to deal with the Jesuits in Georgetown. But I had been praying for him—"

Annie was gripping her pencil so hard she was sure it was going to snap. Is that enough punishment? Is the next step self-flagellation?

"How is that handsome husband of yours?" Sister Agatha asked. "I can still remember your wedding. In those Navy whites, he was unquestionably the best-looking groom I've ever seen."

The simple, sensible thing to say was obviously a cliché such as "Fine." Instead Annie muttered: "I'm afraid we've broken up."

"Oh my dear," Sister Agatha said. "How terrible. What happened?"

"We had an argument—about politics. He said awful things to me—unforgivable."

Sister Agatha's pale eyebrows rose almost imperceptibly. Annie knew exactly what she was thinking: Jesus said we should forgive and forgive—seventy times seven. Annie wanted to tell Sister Agatha she no longer believed in Jesus, as a historian she had concluded that he was one of a hundred messiahs who had roamed Israel in his day and gotten himself crucified by the Romans. She wanted to accuse her obnoxious faithless husband of inspiring her to investigate the evidence and reach this dismaying conclusion, which therefore *exonerated* her from any obligation to fidelity. She wanted to tell Sister Agatha just how far from fidelity she had emigrated, with what headlong reckless arrogance she had become a *sinner* and was proud of it. Do you hear me, Sister, proud of it! Because that was what a woman had to do in this miserable male world to become a person. Unless she chose to sequester herself from men in the first place by taking a vow of chastity.

Not a word of this was spoken, of course. Annie sat there, her pencil poised over her reporter's pad, watching Sister Agatha's eyebrows recede to their normal position. "I'll pray for you," she said.

Five minutes later, Annie fled down Michigan Avenue in the

April sunshine clutching her purse and notebook, a fugitive from the green lawns and echoing halls where she had once strolled, carelessly confidently certain that for a woman there was nothing complicated about life, you just found a husband and loved him unto death and transfiguration.

Back in the office, still trembling, she called Saul Randolph. "I feel like a matinee," she said. It was the first time she had ever asked him to come to her, by daylight or darkness. Would he dislike it?

"I'm seeing Litvinov," he said.

"Not even wham-bam thank you, ma'am?" she said.

"Tonight. A lot more than that tonight."

Tonight might be too late. But how do you explain to your liberal, agnostic lover that you are in danger of collapsing into the arms of Holy Mother Church?

She hung up and read Jack's latest column in the Washington *Post*. It was an eye-opening description of a fifty-six-ton German Tiger tank captured intact in Tunisia. Its firepower, its armor, its gunsight, were immensely superior to anything the Americans could put on the battlefield. If the Navy had not cut off the panzers' fuel supply, they would have massacred the second-rate tanks in which Americans were dying, while the War Production Board and all the other alphabet soup agencies churned out self-congratulatory statistics. Jack's exposure to the battlefield was changing him from an all-out Roosevelt supporter to an often vehement critic of the war effort.

The telephone rang. "It's your father," Selma Shanley said.

"Can you come up to the Hill? I'll be on the floor. Send in a page for me," the Congressman said.

"What's up?"

"Dirty business."

Annie caught a taxi that got her to the Capitol in minutes. A red-haired, red-cheeked page about Butch's age hastened to summon Sam Richman from the floor of the House, which was in its usual tumultuous chaos. In his familiar office, with pictures and mementos of Chicago everywhere, she felt almost safe. Sister Agatha could not reach her here. But a new alarm jangled her nerves. The Congressman looked terrible. He seemed to have aged five years in the last six months. He had become the party whip, the man responsible for lining up votes on key issues—a miserable task in a House of Representatives where the Democrats had only an eight-vote majority.

"Are you feeling okay?" she said.

"Sure, sure," he said, lighting the inevitable cigarette. "This whip thing's a bitch, that's all. The goddamn Southerners hate FDR's guts. They're in bed with the Republicans, always lookin' for a chance to embarrass him. This brawl in the State Department's just handed them a lulu. They're circulatin' stuff about the New Dealer's hero, Sumner Welles—and your sister-in-law's husband, Ned Travis."

"What sort of stuff?"

The Congressman suddenly became her father. He looked vastly uncomfortable. "They're homosexual. You know what that means?"

"Of course I know what it means. I spent eleven years in the U.S. Navy. They have a scandal a month about it."

"Okay," Sam said, relieved enough to relapse into his usual vocabulary. "They're queer as Chinese currency. Ned's a regular in some bar near the Mayflower. Welles seems to have a taste for black Pullman porters."

The Chairman of the House Foreign Affairs committee, a Southerner, was threatening to hold hearings. Someone had leaked him reports from FBI files. Several Republican senators had copies. "We're tryin' to work out a deal. Let 'em resign and keep the stuff quiet. You know Ned Travis?"

She nodded, repelled by how ugly the power game could become. "Who leaked it?" she asked. "Off the record."

"Hull himself, I'd bet on it. He had one of his favorite fixers, a fat guy named Roy Reeves, up here all last week talkin' to people. FDR's got no one to blame but himself. He let Harry Hopkins go too far. He was pushin' Welles to become Secretary of State, for Crissake."

The Congressman gave her a weary, semi-apologetic smile. "Remember, I used to say only God could change Chicago? I begin to think He couldn't change Washington, no matter how hard He tried. The stakes are too high around here."

"What am I supposed to do?"

"Sumner Welles is loaded with dough and doesn't have to give a damn. Ned's like Zeke, his family lost everything in the Crash and he's tryin' to bluff his way through. Go see him and tell him it can't be done. Here's copies of some of the FBI stuff. Show it to him if you have to. Pretend you got it as a leak. That ought to scare the shit out of him. Tell him you won't use it but someone else sure as hell will. Work fast—these guys are impatient."

In the taxi to the State Department, Annie read the methodical FBI prose. A dozen, two dozen nights of Ned getting drunk in a bar called the Jewel Box and leaving with a different young man each evening. Lurid details of his flirtatious ways, his wittily obscene remarks. Occasionally the FBI followed Ned to the assignations at a small hotel. They even included a photo of the register with his signature. For a final laugh he sometimes signed William Howard Taft.

At State, a receptionist told her Ned had left for the day. She took another taxi to Northwest Washington, where the Travises lived. Sitting back on a green lawn beneath an old oak tree, their white Cape Cod house had a storybook tranquillity. Ethel Travis answered the bell and the storybook vanished. Her haunted eyes, her drawn face belonged to a woman living in hell.

"You want to see Ned?" she asked.

"It's important."

"He's upstairs packing. He's going to Florida with one of his friends."

"Can I come in?"

Ethel continued to bar the door. "I suppose you're going to print the whole disgusting story. There's nothing I can do to stop you. Where did you get it? From that vile reactionary, Roy Reeves?"

"From my father."

"That's even better."

Ethel's bitterness was absolute. She had lost even the semblance of hope. "We have a son in prep school, just like you. Would it do any good to appeal to you in his name?"

"I'm not going to print it, Ethel. No one is, if we can get Ned to listen to reason."

"Reason," she said. She began to sob. "You don't know how hard I've tried. How I've pleaded with him. Begged him to see a doctor, a minister. Anyone. But he wouldn't—he couldn't—stop it."

She swayed and clung to the brass door handle. Teenagers rode past on bicycles. Women walked dogs in the benevolent spring sunshine. Ethel spoke over Annie's head, not to the passersby but to some invisible figure far away. "I never really loved him. I married him to please Papa. I thought he wanted me to marry a diplomat. Then I realized nothing I did pleased him—or displeased him. He didn't give a damn what I did. There I was, stuck with this freak, who married me for only one reason—to get promoted as fast as possible."

She whirled and ran into the house. Annie found her at the bottom of the stairs, screaming: "Did you hear what I just told my sister-in-law? I'm married to a hypocritical freak!"

Ned appeared in the dim upstairs hall. All vestiges of the foxy-faced master of subterfuge were gone. "Ned," Annie said. "I've got something I want you to read. Something you can't run away from."

He slowly descended the stairs and she handed him the FBI reports. He walked into the living room and sat on the couch, flipping them, reading only a line or two on each page. "Call my father," Annie said. "Tell him you'll resign. Welles has already resigned."

"He's had his career," Ned cried. "I've spent twenty years waiting for mine to begin—"

What should she say to Ned? Give him a lecture on Washington power plays? Or tell him he was being sacrificed in the name of the future of the world? Instead Annie spoke to Ethel.

"I'm sorry for all the rotten thoughts I've had about you. It was just stupid envy. I thought Zeke listened to you more than to me."

She was trying to say she wanted to be Ethel's friend, especially now that they shared failed marriages.

"Thank you for coming all the way out here," Ethel said, tumbling the words together until they became little more than a mumble. Then she somehow managed to speak in an almost normal voice. "He'll call your father. I'll see to it."

Annie went back to the office but she found it impossible to think, much less write. In her Georgetown apartment, she turned on the radio and got the Office of War Information's DRB (Domestic Radio Bureau). They were yakking about women's role in the war effort.

Announcer: Woman power!

Woman: Woman power! The power to create and sustain life. The power to inspire men to bravery, to give security to little children. A limitless, ever-flowing source of moral and spiritual energy— working for victory! That is woman power!

Annie sat there, brooding about Ethel Travis, about the things women did for men. Where did they get this insane desire to please fathers, brothers, husbands? Men were just the opposite. They seemed to have an equally insane need to defy everyone, especially mothers and wives. Zeke Talbot was a perfect example. Maybe the war between the sexes was the real war.

Outside a taxi door slammed, masculine footsteps thudded up the stairs. It was Saul Randolph. She had totally forgotten she had invited him to a matinee, which he had postponed to an evening performance. The front door opened and there he was with the champagne and caviar, not exactly delighted to find his Marrakesh houri still in her sweaty working clothes. On the night after they returned from North Africa, she had met him wearing nothing but Chanel No. 5.

Something about the way he clunked the champagne on the mantelpiece of her fake fireplace suggested there was more to his displeasure than her inadequate welcome. "Have you heard about Welles and Travis?" he snarled.

"Yes," she said.

Usually they did not discuss serious politics until after they had made love. Ardor was primary here. Politics, power, acquired a special tang, a subtler sense of privilege only in the afterglow of ardor. It was important to pretend, for a little while, that the assemblage of hair, eyes, breasts, thighs, known as Annie Talbot, was more important than Harry Hopkins's or Henry Morgenthau's current status in the White House pantheon, the President's latest decision or nondecision about the Jews, the War Department's newest power play in the Europe versus Pacific strategy argument.

"The striped-pants sons of bitches," Saul said. "They're announcing a reorganization but absolutely nothing's going to change. Your friend Reeves is actually moving *up*. They've put him in charge of the European desk. One of the most important jobs in the goddamn department. He'll control all the cable traffic from England, Spain, Portugal—"

Hurrah. The small silent cheer tinkled like the key of a harpsichord in Annie's mind as she kissed him. "Calm down. Let's take a shower together."

They had done that one night at Marrakesh. The results had been sensational slithery love, slammed against the wet tiles, his hand clutching a fistful of her streaming hair, a new chapter in high-wire wildness.

"Take a bath," he said. "I just heard about this thing. Morgenthau called when I was halfway out the door."

She bathed but without benefit of erotic daydreams. Saul kept talking about the debacle through the half-open door. How they were planning to mount a counterattack with Drew Pearson as the leading edge, how they might try to block State's reorganization in Congress, how they hoped the President would stick with them.

Annie almost told him to shut up, he was sounding sillier and sillier. Congress, with its coalition of Roosevelt-hating Southerners and Republicans, was already rejoicing at the New Dealers' humiliation and FDR would do everything in his power to disassociate himself from such a fiasco.

"Where did they get the information, that's what I want to know," Saul said.

"The FBI," Annie said. "My father showed me the reports this afternoon."

This triggered a denunciation of J. Edgar Hoover as another fascist menace. What a wonderful way to stir the glands, Annie thought, as visions of the Federal Bureau of Investigation Director's porky profile wafted through her imagination.

On the bed in her negligee while Saul showered, Annie felt as if she were lying on a mattress stuffed with ice cubes. He emerged, moisture gleaming on the dark hairs of his broad chest and hope revived. He was a hunk of man, every bit as appealing as the one she had discarded. "Relax, calm *down*," she said, stripping the towel from his hips. She fell back on the bed, the negligee half-opened from top to bottom, an invitation to the waltz—or the mazurka—or the foxtrot—or the lindy.

The more Annie thought about it, the more definitely it became the lindy, to a boogie-woogie beat. She wanted, she needed, some wildness, even a lot of wildness to scour Sister Agatha and Ethel Travis from her brain.

Instead she got wham-bam thank you, ma'am. *Vidi, vici, veni,* was that what old Julius said to his wife as he hopped off her and headed back to the Capitoline Hill? She tried to tell herself it was not Saul's fault. He simply could not stop thinking about his defeat. Even as he stroked her, Annie could see obscure arguments raging behind his frown of concentration. Suddenly, terribly, Annie wondered if this was nothing more significant than a workout. Could he get almost the same effect from a visit to the Army-Navy Club exercise room? A reduction in tension, if not in rage, with the help of a friendly attendant?

"Oh, oh, Saul," she cried, for the benefit of Zeke Talbot, Ethel Travis, and Berthe von Hoffmann, who were all waiting to see her topple from the high wire. She would perform, she was a trouper, the show had to go on because if it stopped the whole world might do the same thing and that would be disastrous, wouldn't it? People, cars, trains, buildings, tanks, trucks flying into outer space, deprived of the vital ingredient that kept everyone's feet (or wheels or tires or treads) on the ground: gravity.

The word also meant taking things seriously, which Anna Richman Talbot was trying desperately not to do because if she succumbed to that imperative, she might conceivably or inconceivably face an array of truths she was trying very hard to avoid. So she squirmed and sighed and cried: "Saul, Saul. Oh! Oh!" and told herself the performance was really quite amusing.

There. He was almost smiling as he withdrew. He thought it was amusing or satisfying or something other than disgustingly hypocritical and cowardly. He went into the bathroom and wiped himself and came out and poured the champagne and opened the caviar. The champagne had gotten warm and ditto the caviar, which made it so salty Annie could barely get it down her throat.

Wasn't there something in the Bible about the salt losing its savor? So far so good. She would be a pillar of salt like old Lot's wife if she ate any more of this stuff. Mrs. Lot's mistake, of course, had been looking back, but after two or three thousand years women had learned not to do that, at least. Never never never look back because you'll see what's gaining on you.

Saul slumped against the headboard and gulped his warm champagne. "If you'd done your part of the job, maybe this wouldn't have happened," he said.

"What part?"

"Attacking Reeves. Blasting the whole goddamn setup."

He was blaming her because his brilliant boss Morgenthau and his friend Harry Hopkins and all the other astute males of the White House brain trust had bet their wads on the wrong horse. He was treating her like a wife.

By a sheer act of will, Annie clung to the high wire. But for the first time she began to wonder how much longer the performance would last before she screamed into this man's face words of ultimate gravity: *the future of the world*. The weight of those words would almost certainly snap the wire and send them spinning down into God knows where.

39

ENEMY COUNTRY

"I'm doing this against my better judgment!" Bernado Moorman said as the decrepit Iberian Airlines plane labored toward London. "I don't fancy taking orders from a bloody woman. And a German in the bargain!"

"It's the fortunes of war, old boy," Jonathan Talbot said.

After months of alternating rage and icy hostility, Berthe von Hoffmann had undergone a startling transformation a few days after Talbot told her about Ernst's high seas murder rampage. She agreed to send the Metox disinformation to Berlin to further demoralize the Ubootwaffe. She said she was ready to reveal the site of the secret German rocket plant—if he and Moorman were willing to repay her with a renewed effort on behalf of Canaris and the German resistance.

She also claimed she was ready to return to Talbot's arms "as a penitent." But she was not the same woman who had embraced him in Granada. She was closer to the elusive creature he had tried to grasp in Avila and Coruna, a being whose spirit was elsewhere. For Talbot it was only discouraging proof that her love for him had never been more than a performance on behalf of Germany. But the nobility of her motive made it impossible for him to reproach her. On the contrary, he felt even more committed to that promise of absolute devotion he had made on the Montoya ranch in La Mancha. He was determined to show her that his love, at least, had been real.

When Talbot put Berthe's proposition to Moorman, the diminutive Englishman had snarled that he was much too busy to worry about minor matters for the time being. He was deep in disinformation and information collecting for the invasion of Sicily. In one of their most elaborate hoaxes, British intelligence dropped a dead body into the water off the southern coast of Spain, clad in an officer's uniform, with a briefcase attached to his wrist containing plans for invasions of Sardinia and Greece. The Spanish immediately passed the information on to the Germans.

There was only one thing wrong with this marvelous deception. It did not work. When the Americans and British landed in Sicily on the morning of July 10, 1943, they were greeted on the beaches by the fifty-six-ton Tiger tanks of the Herman Goering Panzer Division and for a few hours came perilously close to being driven into the sea. Only point-blank fire from the naval guns of the escorting fleet rescued the situation. Jack Richman told Jonathan about it in a letter from Tunis, where the doctors were picking shrapnel out of his left leg. *The Navy saved the Army's ass, take my word for it*, he wrote, still loyal to old Annapolis.

Most of the 150,000 Italian soldiers on Sicily surrendered, but the outnumbered Germans retreated pugnaciously to Messina and evacuated everyone and everything—men, tanks, guns, trucks, even some Italians who wanted to keep fighting—across the straits to the mainland. Unfortunately, no one saw much significance in this feat.

Meanwhile, Berlin, Munich, Cologne, Bremen were hammered by thousand-plane fleets dropping a new bomb, weighing a thousand pounds. The British called it the blockbuster. The American Eighth Air Force bombed by day, the Royal Air Force Bomber Command by night. British and American newspapers were full of predictions that the Nazi regime was on the brink of collapse. Berthe, reading the cable traffic informing various members of the embassy that they had lost wives, sons, daughters, parents, told Talbot the newspapers might be right—if it were not for unconditional surrender.

Moorman scoffed and pointed to a Madrid suddenly vibrant with pro-Americanism. Over a thousand people showed up at the American embassy for a party celebrating the capture of Sicily. General Franco conferred with Ambassador Hayes about withdrawing the Spanish division from the Russian front. Moorman grew even more scornful in his refusal to negotiate with Berthe about the secret rocket site.

One day in August Berthe slipped Talbot a copy of a cable from Berlin that obliterated most of Moorman's arrogance. A "National Committee to Free Germany" had broadcast an appeal to the German people for an early peace. Talbot rushed a copy to Washington and a surly Moorman did likewise to London. The leader of the committee was one of the Sixth Army generals who had surrendered at Stalingrad. Several other captured German generals endorsed his plea, which was, of course, broadcast from Moscow. There was not a word in the proposal about unconditional surrender or Vansittart-like demands to punish every German on earth. On the contrary, the Committee assured the German people that the Soviet Union held no grudge against them. They only wanted to defeat Hitler and his war machine.

Berlin instructed Ambassador von Stohrer to assure General Franco that the German people had nothing but contempt for the proposal. The mere fact that the Nazis felt compelled to send this reassurance suggested how rattled they were by the Russian offer.

The Spaniards were almost as unnerved. The Marquesa de Montoya upbraided Talbot at one of her dinner parties with uncharacteristic fury. She said General Franco saw Bolshevism advancing into the heart of Europe on the Free Germany Committee's Trojan horse. Rafael Sanchez added diplomatic gravity to the ordeal. "If you were a German, which would you choose—Stalin's offer or unconditional surrender from the enemy who is incinerating your cities?" he asked.

Talbot's ability to reply to these accusations was further undermined by developments in Italy. On July 26, 1943, Mussolini resigned and King Victor Emmanuel replaced him with Field Marshal Pietro Badoglio, who immediately ordered the Spanish Ambassador to Rome to send out peace feelers. When Roosevelt insisted on unconditional surrender, the Italians angrily broke off the negotiations. Meanwhile Communist-led mobs swarmed into the streets of Italy's cities, giving the already suspicious Germans a perfect excuse to rush dozens of divisions into the country to help restore order.

After telling the American people in a fireside chat on July 28 that the United States would "have no truck" with fascism, Roosevelt yielded to British pressure and resumed secret negotiations with Badoglio in August. An angry Moorman pointed out that Badoglio still had a formidable fleet, some loyal Italian Army divisions—and 74,000 British soldiers, captured in the Middle East, whom he could hand over to the Germans. The American refusal to negotiate was idiocy. After more weeks of haggling, the Italians agreed to sign an unconditional surrender statement that was a mere formula, with guarantees of favorable treatment later. The moment it was announced, an acerbic Berthe von Hoffmann asked Talbot why Roosevelt was willing to negotiate with an Italian general, but not with a German one.

A week later, on September 9, 1943, the Anglo-American Army that had captured Sicily invaded Italy. The British landed at Reggio di Calabria, on the toe of the boot, while the Americans splashed ashore at the Bay of Salerno, south of Naples. Everyone talked about being in Rome in a month. But the Allies quickly discovered that the weeks wasted wrangling over unconditional surrender had given the Germans time to impose a drastically different schedule on the campaign.

In a letter to Talbot, Jack Richman described Salerno as the most terrifying five days of his life. The Herman Goering Division was back in action, along with several other panzer divisions. This time not even point-blank naval gunfire stopped the Tiger tanks. Only an airlift of the elite Eighty-second Airborne Division from Sicily saved the Americans from being driven into the sea. "Unconditional surrender!" said an appalled Moorman. "The goddamn slogan's being written in blood!"

The Germans retreated in the same murderous style they had displayed in Sicily to bristling fortifications called the Gustav Line in the mountains north of Naples. Freezing rain and snow began to fall as British and American soldiers took horrendous casualties struggling to gain a few yards up muddy slopes. Among the early victims was Jack Richman, badly wounded by German shellfire. Rome was still a hundred miles away and the rest of Italy was unquestionably part of Hitler's *Festung Europa* (Fortress Europe).

In Madrid, Moorman began to resemble the man who had been shaken to the soles of his shoes by Dieppe. He admitted there might be something to be said for negotiating with the Schwarze Kapelle. What exactly did Frau von Hoffmann expect in return for her revelation of the location of the German rocket center?

Three months ago, a snarling Valkyrie would have confronted the obnoxious little Englishman. The new Berthe coolly pointed out that the British had the most to gain from the destruction of the rocket site. She therefore wanted Moorman to go to London and personally urge his superiors to press the Americans to alter the unconditional surrender policy.

"Jonathan will go with you to make sure you don't spend most of your time sampling the Athenaeum Club's vintage port," she said. "While he's at it he might try to locate one or two Americans who see some point in rescuing Germany from Hitler."

"If they exist, I'll find them," Talbot said.

"I suggest you start with General Eisenhower," she said, letting Talbot presume this was sarcasm.

After eighteen months in Madrid, with its broad boulevards and spacious squares, its brilliant sunlight, its baking summers and frigid winters, London was a shock. Beneath perpetually gray, drizzling skies, the city's sheer mass, concentrated by the narrow streets, reiterated by the surging crowds, seemed overwhelming. Moorman claimed to hate the place. "As my favorite writer, Evelyn Waugh said, it's a city ruled by Lilliputians and exploited by Yahoos," he growled.

But Talbot found the size and vitality of the city reassuring. This was unquestionably a world capital. The scent of power was in the air. Around Mayfair, the streets were full of uniformed Americans on a dozen different staffs, all working on plans for the great cross-channel invasion. Talbot knew a lot of the Navy men and they introduced him to the Army men, many of whom listened with astonishment and intense interest to his story of a plot within the German Army to overthrow Hitler. They led him to his acquaintance from the Rainbow Five imbroglio, Albert Wedemeyer, now a major general. "Ike's got to hear about this," he said.

Talbot had presumed that Eisenhower, recently appointed Supreme Commander of the Allied Forces in Europe, was a political echo of FDR. Wedemeyer shook his head. "He detested the idea of unconditional surrender from the minute he heard it at Casablanca. Right after Roosevelt announced it at that press conference, Ike said to me: 'If a soldier's offered the choice of swinging on a gallows or charging twenty bayonets, he'll charge the bayonets.'"

Wedemeyer added his own detestation of the slogan, based on the two years he spent as an exchange student at the War College in Berlin in the late Thirties. "I saw how many people in the German officer corps despised the Nazis," he said. "Instead of trying to widen the breach, Roosevelt's welded them together."

Within twenty-four hours, Wedemeyer escorted Talbot into a red-brick apartment building on Grosvenor Square that served as American headquarters in London. A kitchen in the basement filled the halls with the smell of boiled cabbage and Brussels sprouts, two staples of everyone's diet in wartime England. Eisenhower did not look up from the documents he was reading until Talbot reached his desk. When he met his gaze, Talbot was struck by the energy he emanated. It seemed to pour from the high forehead, the fiercely intelligent eyes.

He gestured Talbot to a seat and listened intently to his description of the Schwarze Kapelle. "Have you met a German general who can vouch for the seriousness of this thing?" he asked.

"No."

"I think you ought to make that your first priority." He turned to Wedemeyer. "Get Commander Talbot here in touch with the OSS and find out what they can do about inserting him into Germany as soon as possible."

Talbot felt the hair on the back of his neck rise significantly. This was a man who cut through details to essentials. For a moment he considered trying to convince Ike that Berthe von Hoffmann and Helmuth von Moltke were more than enough reassurance. But he realized the hair-raising assignment was an oblique compliment. Eisenhower had sized him up and decided he had the nerve and judgment to do the job.

"I've tried to communicate all this to Washington," he said. "I got nowhere."

"I'll handle Washington if this turns out to be as good as you say it is," Eisenhower said. "Jesus Christ! This could save the lives of a half-million British and American soldiers."

Talbot all but floated out of Eisenhower's headquarters. General Wedemeyer brought him abruptly down to earth. "I don't think it's going to be nearly as easy as Ike thinks it will be, no matter what you bring back. Ike's not a politician."

At the Athenaeum Club, over some of Moorman's favorite port, the two compared notes, while Wedemeyer listened. "I got all the way up to Winston's private secretary," Moorman said. "He assures me Winnie's never believed in unconditional surrender in the first place. But he's been leery of Stalin's reaction if they found out we're seriously negotiating with the Huns. Now he thinks this Free Germany Committee may be a perfect excuse to tell the bloody Bolshies to go to hell."

Eisenhower's embrace of unconditional surrender almost catapulted Moorman into optimism. But he regained his pessimistic high ground when he heard the proposal to parachute Talbot into Berlin to talk to a German general. "Too risky," he said. "We've lost a dozen good men in air drops into Germany."

Albert Wedemeyer's derisive snort revealed a little of his anti-English prejudices. "Wait till you see what the OSS can put together here in London. They've got a complete setup, from tailors to forgers to printers, every one of them German."

Talbot urged Moorman to go back to Spain and ask Berthe to cooperate. "Tell her it's coming from the very top—Eisenhower himself. If she makes the right arrangements, I'll meet her in Berlin."

"Do you have an unnatural desire to die before a firing squad?" Moorman asked. Talbot realized the Englishman was genuinely worried about him. Was there a human heart concealed beneath those layers of imperious crust?

Still muttering about firing squads, Moorman departed for Madrid and Wedemeyer escorted Talbot to 72 Grosvenor Street to meet a lanky young Irish-American named William Casey, who wore a cocky grin and talked with machine-gun speed. He was in charge of OSS's Secret Intelligence Section and was delighted at the chance to parachute Talbot into Germany. "We've put a half-dozen people into the Ruhr," he said. "You'll be the first into Berlin. We could learn a lot from the experience."

"How many of the people you've put into the Ruhr have gotten back?" Talbot asked.

"None. They tried to get out through Switzerland. Too many land mines and SS patrols. We'll try to come up with a better escape route for you."

Talbot found himself wishing for less improvisation and more experience. But it was too late to crawl back to Moorman and beg him to let the British handle his delivery. American honor was now at stake, along with his existence.

Casey was fascinated by Talbot's description of the mission. He told him Allen Dulles, the OSS station chief in Switzerland, had also been in touch with the Canaris circle. He too bemoaned Washington's indifference to it.

Two days later, a cable arrived from Moorman, using a prearranged code.

THE LADY HAS AGREED TO WALTZ. WE HAVE EXCHANGED PRESENTS. DETAILS OF THE DANCE WILL FOLLOW AS SOON AS POSSIBLE. STRIKE UP THE BAND.

Exchanging presents meant Berthe had told him the location of the German rocket research center. In London, the band was already hard at work. Casey and his team had selected a German identity for Talbot. He was going to be a toolmaker named Kurt Eisen. They gave him a two-page biography that he was required to memorize and repeat back to one of Casey's assistants. A print shop hidden in the basement of 72 Grosvenor Street produced a *Kenncarte* from the Berlin Labor Office, a *Wehrpassbuch,* certifying Kurt Eisen's exemption from military service, and a Nazi party membership card. A shop manned by a German refugee tailor named Schlepper created a set of shabby workingman's clothes.

All this took a week—time enough for Berthe to arrange to meet him in Berlin on the day before Christmas. In spite of Talbot's doubts about getting out of Germany alive, he grew friendly with Casey. It was hard to resist his Irish enthusiasm. He sought Casey's advice when he received a cable from Hamilton Boileau, the Madrid embassy's second in command, warning him that letters from Washington were piling up on his desk. Talbot told Casey about Ernie King and how he had become a naval attaché.

A lawyer in civilian life, Casey immediately adopted Talbot as his client. "What you need to do is get the hell out of the Navy. Join the OSS. Then King can't touch you and you can push this Schwarze Kapelle idea for all its worth."

Time unreeled. Talbot was back seventeen years arguing desperately with his father about his choice of a Navy career. While his father denigrated the military mind and his mother stood in the doorway behind her husband shaking her head, silently saying no, not for my sake. Go your own way. So many strands of memory and desire woven into that word *Navy.* A dream of escape from his father's glowering oversight, of exploring the globe, a dream of selfless service, a dream of fame. Franklin D. Roosevelt, Ernest J. King and his stubborn refusal to get along by going along had obliterated those dreams. Reluctantly, ruefully, Talbot decided Casey was right.

They parted agreeing that while Talbot was risking his neck in Berlin, Casey would urge General William Donovan, the commander of the OSS, to liberate him from the clutches of Admiral King. A handshake later that day and Talbot was on his way to an airfield in the west of England. Fog and rain swept in from the channel, perfect weather for their flight, the baby-faced pilot of the two-engined all-wood plane told him.

They took off into the rainy night without mishap and were soon hurtling east across the shrouded English Channel. The navigator, who did not look much older than Talbot's son, Butch, hunched over his maps, giving the pilot new headings every half-hour. Talbot fought airsickness and his fundamental fear of flying.

The London shops had been full of Christmas decorations. He thought of his son, in Washington, D.C., celebrating the holiday with his in-laws, his bitter wife in the arms of some White House insider. He had made a hell of a mess of his life so far, trying to be a patriot. Gazing up at the night sky, he wondered if Berthe was right, if an immense presence brooded over the world, leading individuals and nations toward mysterious destinies.

He could not believe it. But for the first time he found himself wanting to believe it, not only because he knew it would please Berthe—but for his own sake. It would help him sustain the purity of the love he still felt for her, even if she was unable to return it. If he survived this war, it might help him make amends in some way for the wounds he had inflicted on Annie. What a lousy husband he had been! Maybe there was something to that religious idea of penitence. He felt a need for some of that old medicine. Maybe that was Berthe's real role in his life.

Another two hours and the pilot advised Talbot to get into his parachute. He had been given a one-day lesson in how to land without breaking his legs. As they climbed for a little more altitude, in the distance the sky began to glow with lurid white and red flashes. On the ground, a witches' sabbath of yellow and red flames soon leaped wildly. "Berlin," the pilot drawled. "The Brits are givin' it the thousand-plane treatment. That's why we picked tonight for your visit. The poor old Luftwaffe's goin' to be too busy to bother with this crate."

In ten more minutes, the navigator announced they were over the landing site—a swath of farmland west of the German capital. Talbot leaped into the night, counted to five to make sure he was beyond the plane's tail surfaces and pulled his ripcord. He hurtled to earth at what seemed to him twice the promised rate and crunched into a wheat field.

To his amazement, nothing was broken or dislocated. He buried his parachute and started walking toward Berlin, which burned briskly on the horizon for most of the night. In the morning he was on the outskirts of the city—which did not mean much, he knew. Berlin was forty-four miles wide. It was like being on the outskirts of Los Angeles.

Eventually, he found the Schnellbahn, the inner-city railroad and tried to buy a ticket to the Tiergarten. A sad-faced clerk with the mustache of a Prussian general informed him that the trains were only running to Alexanderplatz. The bombers had smashed the line beyond that point. "The Führer will find an answer to them, don't worry, my friend," Talbot said. "Heil Hitler."

"Heil Hitler," the clerk said with an absolute minimum of enthusiasm.

From the railway, Talbot could see fire trucks still spraying water on blocks of shattered flats and houses. Ambulances beeped their way through crowds of dazed men and women, many weeping hysterically. Some pawed pathetically at ruins where loved ones were probably buried. By the time he reached the Tirpitz Ufer with its stately townhouses beside the stagnant canal, he was wondering if his mission was a waste of time. Could men talk reasonably about peace when their country was being obliterated all around them?

In the adjacent Tiergarten, Berthe, hatless, wearing a green cloth coat, was walking up and down the path to keep warm in the wintry air. "Oh!" she cried, flinging her arms around him. "I didn't sleep all night."

"I thought you had faith."

"I try to rely on it. But it guarantees nothing."

She led him into Abwehr headquarters. In five minutes he was shaking hands with Admiral Wilhelm Canaris. Never had Talbot seen a subtler, craftier face. Canaris eyed his shabby clothes and asked for his forged identity papers. "Not bad," he said, "except for your clothes. They're much too ragged for a well-paid toolmaker. If the police stopped you, I'm afraid you'd be in trouble."

He grew solemn. "As an officer and a man of honor, I need not remind you that I'm putting my life in your hands. The men whom you will soon meet will also be risking their lives and reputations. I must ask you never to use their names or mine in a written document to anyone."

"I understand."

"Now we must get you out of those inappropriate clothes."

Summoning an aide, Canaris told him to find a uniform for "Captain von Bulow," who had been on detached service for the Abwehr in Belgrade. Within a half-hour, Talbot was outfitted as a German infantry captain. Briskly, Canaris told him to go home with Berthe and get some sleep. They would travel to their rendezvous after dark.

A nervous Berthe drove him to a row house in the Schonberg section of Berlin where Talbot slept for three hours and had dinner with Berthe's Amazonian friend, Helen Widerstand. She lectured him on unconditional surrender as a typical piece of capitalist stupidity and pointed to the Russian offer of decent terms as proof that communism was Germany's best hope. Talbot wondered if Berthe enjoyed watching him encounter a woman who made her look like a model of sweetness and light.

At about eight o'clock, Canaris joined them and with Berthe at the wheel they began their journey through blacked-out Berlin. The Abwehr chief used the half-hour ride to brief Talbot extensively on the men he was about to meet. They finally reached a row of substantial stone houses, set back on modest lawns. Inside, Canaris led them into a book-lined study. Near the door, Count Helmuth von Moltke was standing beside an Army officer of about the same extraordinary height, scanning the titles. Moltke greeted Talbot with a smile and a handshake and Canaris introduced the Army officer. He had a patch over one eye, and the right sleeve of his jacket was empty. "This is Colonel Count Claus Schenk von Stauffenberg," Canaris said.

"And I am ex-General Ludwig Beck," said a deep voice from the other side of the room. Talbot hastened to shake hands with this strong-jawed, gray-haired man in a tweed jacket. Canaris had made it clear that he was the central figure in the conspiracy. Beck had been chief of the Army's general staff when Hitler invaded Czechoslovakia in 1939, in violation of the Munich agreement. Beck had resigned in protest, creating an instant focus of resistance to Nazism within the

German Army. Thousands of officers admired him in secret and were ready to obey him.

"And I am General Friedrich Olbricht," said a man who had walked in the door behind them. Tall, with a wary, oblique mouth and close-set eyes, he struck Talbot as unsure of himself. But he was a crucial figure in the apparatus the Schwarze Kapelle had constructed, because he was in command of the police in Berlin and knew exactly where Goebbels and other powerful Nazis could be found at any hour of the day or night.

"These three officers are representative of the military members of our movement," Admiral Canaris said. "You've met Count von Moltke, who is perhaps our best civilian spokesman."

Beck took charge of the meeting. He told Talbot they had already enlisted over 400 officers in their plan to overthrow the Nazi regime. Many of them were in key positions. Major General Henning von Tresckow, for instance, was chief of staff of Army Group Center on the Eastern front. Field Marshal Guenther von Kluge, the commander of that million-man force, had promised his support the moment Hitler's death released him from his oath of obedience to him. The code name for the coup d'état was *Valkyrie*. It had been designated as an emergency signal for the *Ersatzwehr*, the Reich's Home Army, a half-million-man force composed of trainees, recuperating wounded, officers in schools and divisions in rest areas.

When *Valkyrie* appeared on the *Ersatzwehr*'s teleprinters, they were to go into action to suppress a possible revolt by the millions of foreigners toiling as slave laborers in the Reich's factories. Colonel von Stauffenberg was chief of staff of the Home Army. Its commander, General Friedrich Fromm, had agreed to cooperate with them.

"Our plan is to put Valkyrie into effect the moment Hitler is killed," General Beck said. "We'll have the men and guns to disarm the Gestapo, the SS, and other Nazis here in Berlin and in key cities across the country. At the same time, General von Kluge has promised General von Tresckow that he will detach a number of divisions to prevent units from Army Group North or South from coming to the Nazis' assistance. We seriously doubt that bloodshed will be necessary to prevent such a movement. The moment Hitler's death is announced, we're certain nine-tenths of the Army's high command will join us."

"We plan to arrest Goering, Goebbels, Himmler and other leading figures of the Party immediately," Olbricht said. "If they resist, they will be shot dead on the spot."

There was a pause. Colonel von Stauffenberg cleared his throat and asked Talbot if he had any questions thus far. He shook his head and said he was impressed by the size of the forces they hoped to command. Stauffenberg smiled wryly. "Like everything in war, their success is somewhat unpredictable. We therefore propose to coordinate our plans with your forces if possible. Within twenty-four hours of Valkyrie, it would be extremely helpful if perhaps three divisions could be landed near Hamburg, and additional forces in Holland, that could move quickly into the Ruhr Valley. The Army commanders of both districts have pledged their cooperation."

"What about your army in France?" Talbot said, uneasy at the thought of inserting this relatively small force into the middle of 70 million Germans. "You're got forty or fifty divisions there. They could eat all of you—and those Anglo-American reinforcements—alive."

"The commander in Paris, General von Stuelpnagel, has agreed to block all railroad traffic in and out of the city. This will make it impossible for most of the troops, who are west of Paris, to move."

Talbot shook his head. "I don't think you'll ever get any American or British general to agree to exposing their troops to possible annihilation," he said. "If you're going to do this thing, you'll have to manage the shooting part of it on your own."

"I predicted this reaction," Admiral Canaris said mournfully. "I've warned these gentlemen we must be satisfied with your political support."

"I agree," Count von Moltke said in an even more mournful voice.

Olbricht glared at Canaris. "I think you're surrendering the point too easily, Herr Admiral!" he said. "You should make it clear that if these gentlemen decline to deal with us, we're prepared to negotiate with the Russians."

"I for one am not prepared to do any such thing," General Beck said. "Surely the fifteen-thousand Polish officers Stalin massacred in 1940 should make clear to you what the fate of the German officer corps would be. Add to this the conversation the Abwehr reports Stalin had with Roosevelt at their recent meeting in Teheran—"

"I know nothing about that," Talbot said.

"One of our Moscow agents reports that Stalin proposed executing fifty thousand German officers," Canaris said. "Churchill objected and Roosevelt suggested as a compromise shooting only forty-nine thousand. Do you think he was joking?"

"I'm sure he was," Talbot said.

"I'm sure Stalin wasn't," Beck said.

"What do you mean by political support?" Talbot asked Canaris.

"A statement that in some way modifies the terms of unconditional surrender. So the average soldier—and the general officer—can feel that if he gives up the fight, he's not betraying his nation to slavery and humiliation. Something along the lines Stalin has already issued through this Free Germany Committee," Canaris said. "But with more sincerity."

"I think—hope—that's possible."

"We would also like an unspoken promise that you're prepared to deal with us as honorable men who wish to join with you in putting Hitler and his crew on trial for their crimes," Olbricht said.

"I thought you were going to kill Hitler," Talbot said.

"I'm one of those who would prefer to seize him," General Olbricht said.

"Impossible!" Stauffenberg said. "He must be killed. It's the only way to free the Army from their oath of loyalty to him."

"I have reluctantly come to the same conclusion," General Beck said.

"So—even more reluctantly—have I," Count von Moltke said.

Canaris smiled thinly. "As you can see, Commander Talbot, there are certain things not yet finally decided. Which makes a gesture of support from your side all the more important."

"Assuming I get out of your country alive, I'll do my best to report this conversation to the highest levels of the British and American governments," Talbot said.

"You need have no worries about your safe return, Commander," Canaris said. He seemed offended by the implication that he could not—or would not—protect him.

"Ultimately it comes down to trust on both sides," Berthe said.

Talbot sensed she was telling him his promise was too vague, too formal, to give these men the reassurance, the unity, they desperately needed. She was asking him for words of unqualified support, for her sake—and for Germany's sake.

One more time, Talbot looked from Stauffenberg to Beck to

Olbricht to Moltke. Stauffenberg and Moltke were unquestionably idealists, driven by moral fervor. The older Beck was made of heavier, graver, more cautious material, as befitted a commanding general. Olbricht was a skeptic, a natural attitude for a policeman. Canaris remained an enigma—but in the company of these other men, above all, of Moltke—the Admiral too acquired an aura of moral force. These were honorable men, brave men. "If necessary," Talbot said, "I'll go to Washington and personally urge President Roosevelt to renounce unconditional surrender."

40

A PAGE OF GLORY

We have lost the battle of the Atlantic.

The voice rumbled through Ernst von Hoffmann's head like the croak of a foghorn off Kiel, first unbearably loud, then dwindling to a whisper as the klaxon turned on its base to broadcast its warning to other points of the compass. He swung his feet over the edge of the bed on the second floor of the Hoffmann villa in Wannsee and peered at the clock. Five a.m. Staff officers of Grossadmiral Dönitz seldom slept much later.

Ernst pulled on a bathrobe, lit a cigarette and trudged into the study. Flicking on a light, he stared blearily at a report on the Metox radar warning device, which the Abwehr had reported the British had compromised. They supposedly had a radar gun which homed in on it, changing it from a savior to an exterminator. The best radar experts in Germany had studied the problem and concluded the Abwehr report was probably true.

We have lost the battle of the Atlantic. Four months had passed since those numbing words resounded in Ernst's ears. Almost every day, he relived the stunning moment—and waited for the new weapons Germany's scientists were supposed to be producing to reverse the temporary defeat. The weapons did not seem to be forthcoming. Instead there were only improvisations, such as putting extra anti-aircraft guns on the bridges of existing U-boats, on the harebrained theory that four guns could do a better job of fighting off a plane than two.

Ernst had gone to work as a staff officer with the Grossadmiral's grim determination driving him. He adjusted his life to Dönitz's habit of calling people at six a.m. and becoming more than a little irked if they were still asleep. That meant a minimum of late nights in search of Berlin's pleasures—which were dwindling fast anyway, because of the air raids. At first he picked up prostitutes at random on the Unter den Linden or Kurfurstendamm, but in September he found one he particularly liked. Margaret was small, shapely and lively—and she responded passionately when he told her he was a U-boat officer.

"What makes you partial to U-boat men?" he asked, as he paid her.

"I have a brother in the Ubootwaffe," she said.

"What's his name?"

"Benz—as in Mercedes," she said.

When Ernst told her Benz was part of his old crew, an odd semi-affection sprang between them. She promised to wait for him each Tuesday night at ten underneath the lamppost on the Bendlerstrasse, opposite Army headquarters. "Just like Lili Marlene," she said, referring to the heroine of the Ubootwaffe's favorite song. She claimed it would amuse her to tell the junior general staff officers she was reserved by the Navy. He began keeping the date.

His mother urged him to marry again. She had a laundry list of available women, all widows of men killed on the Russian front. Ernst told her this was more than he was prepared to do in the service of the Reich. She was not amused. Not for the first time, Ernst wished this humorless woman had not married his father.

Once the General had confided to him, in an uncharacteristic intimacy not long before he died, that he had been in love with another woman, who had refused him. "A party girl," he said. "A sparkler." That chance conversation had been a powerful influence in Ernst's pursuit of Berthe von Hoffmann.

Now he was a father, thrown into uncomfortable intimacy with his son and daughter. He had no time to give them—only enough to make them wonder why they saw so little of him. Anyway, all Georg wanted to talk about was the U-boat war, which he still envisioned in totally heroic terms.

Ernst lit another cigarette and plowed to the end of his final draft of the report on the Metox system—which promised an early replacement, modified and improved to pick up even the shortest radar wave lengths. That would give the U-boat counteroffensive unimpeachable protection. By now he had learned that the Grossadmiral always wanted a report, however negative, to end on an optimistic note.

This report was especially important. It was not going to Konteradmiral Godt, the Ubootwaffe commander, or into a file at naval headquarters. It was going to the Führer—and Ernst von Hoffmann, newly promoted to fregattenkapitan zur see (commander) was going with it. Yesterday he had been summoned to the Grossadmiral's office, with the great globe of the world beside the desk, and told that tomorrow he would accompany him to the Wolfschanze (Wolf's Lair), the Führer's headquarters. "Wear your Knight's Cross," Dönitz said.

The realization that he was about to meet Adolf Hitler left Ernst in a daze for the rest of the day. When he confided it to his mother and the children at supper, Georg's face became wreathed in near ecstasy. "Oh Father," he said. "Please, will you say Heil! to him, for me?"

"I promise," he said. Georg had leaped from his seat, run around the table and kissed him.

Ernst and Dönitz traveled to the Wolfschanze, which was deep in a forest in East Prussia, in the Grossadmiral's private train. It was a working trip. Dönitz devoured report after report, condensing them into four- or five-line memorandums dictated to a secretary and typed for ready reference.

The Wolfschanze was surrounded by three rings of blockhouses and an electrified barbed-wire fence. In the two outer rings, SS troops in armored vehicles patrolled the dank, dark woods. At a checkpoint, more SS men inspected their passes and their commander, an oberführer, abruptly asked the Grossadmiral if he vouched for Ernst's reliability. Although Dönitz replied with a curt *"Jawohl!"* the Oberführer insisted on going through Ernst's briefcase.

Finally they descended into a deep, brightly lit underground bunker. Ahead of them in a doorway was Adolf Hitler, smiling at them. "Heil, my Führer," Dönitz said and raised his right arm. Ernst echoed him and repeated the gesture.

"Heil, Herr Grossadmiral," Hitler said, barely flapping his arm in response. He was wearing a loose green Army jacket with no trace of rank or decorations and floppy black trousers. His shoes needed a shine. On his head he wore a heavy cap with flaps that covered his ears. Ernst would later learn the cap was lined with steel to repel a possible assassin's bullet.

"My Führer," Dönitz said. "I would like you to meet Fregat- tenkapitan von Hoffmann, one of my finest U-boat commanders. He has become an invaluable member of my staff."

The Führer shook hands in his most cordial style. It should have been one of the most inspiring moment of Ernst's life. But the man within inches of his eyes was not the electrifying figure he had watched from a distance in mass rallies at the Sportspalast in Berlin. That man had been a virile god, surrounded by blazing torches, hurl- ing defiance of Germany's foes into the night air.

This man was pudgy and stooped, with pale, pouchy skin and flecks of gray in his hair and mustache. Even more shocking were his dulled, oddly wistful eyes. When he withdrew his handshake, Ernst realized the Führer's left arm had a violent tremor. He quickly thrust it behind his back and seized it with his right hand to control it. For the first time Ernst understood the reason for the pictures that so frequently showed Hitler in this posture. As the Führer led them into the simply furnished conference room, his left leg dragged noticeably with every step. Although Ernst tried to resist what his eyes were telling him, the truth was undeniable. This was a sick, anx- ious, aging man. There was something almost pathetic in the way he told Dönitz he had been looking forward to the meeting.

"Only the Navy brings me good news these days," he said. "From the Army's generals come only whines and excuses. As for the Luft- waffe, there's only one word to describe the conduct of Goering and his pilots—cowardly."

With Ernst handing him the reports, the Grossadmiral pro- ceeded to give the Führer nothing but bad news. The battle of the Atlantic continued to go poorly. Neither the surface fleet, mostly based in Norway, nor the U-boats could stop the convoys to Mur- mansk, which were now protected by jeep carriers and a vastly rein- forced escort fleet. Operations in the Mediterranean had been aban- doned. Nevertheless, almost magically, Dönitz's loyalty and optimism managed to transform these announcements into a positive program.

U-boats were now available to operate along the African coast and in the Indian Ocean. The discovery that the Metox radar device had been responsible for much of their losses meant they could soon resume operations in the Atlantic. The boats were being fitted with air breathing devices that would enable them to cruise underwater indefinitely.

The Führer nodded, exclaimed with pleasure, his eyes glowing. Whereupon the Grossadmiral proceeded to extract from Hitler promises to expand the U-boat construction program, although it would require an extra 30,000 tons of steel a month and another 150,000 skilled workers. Ernst industriously took notes of everything. The future shape of Germany's war effort, certainly the future shape of the Navy, was being altered here.

"Now my Führer," Dönitz said, his normally harsh voice a purr of satisfaction, "I wish you to hear something else, for your ears only, from Fregattenkapitan von Hoffmann. How we are making war on the enemy's merchant crews. Tell the Führer the fate of the survivors of the SS *Martin de Porres,* Hoffmann."

It was both a dream and a nightmare. For a moment Ernst felt as if he were still on the bridge of the Wolfseeboot, machine gun in his hands, after the last riddled body had floated away. This was another Mutprobe, he told himself, another test of his courage and strength. But the exhortation did not seem to work. When he had told the story to the Grossadmiral, he had felt relieved of a heavy weight. Why wasn't the same thing happening with the Führer?

Yet he told the story well, with dignity and resolution. He had become an excellent speaker, thanks to numerous appearances at Kiel to address new U-boat crews. He had never explicitly mentioned the *Martin de Porres*, but it had remained in the forefront of his mind as he urged on the raw young faces the necessity to make war not only on the enemy's ships but on his crews. Ernst could not understand why it was so difficult to tell the whole story to the Führer. Every word was causing him pain—but he continued to speak in a calm, steady voice.

It was amazingly similar to the way he had clung to the electrified iron bar in his cadet days. Every detail tore through his body with the same brutality. But he bore it like a man, a German officer, until it ended with the death of the last frantic swimmer.

Arms wide, a delighted smile on his face, the Führer walked toward Ernst, still dragging his left leg. "You have done *well*, Herr Fregattenkapitan!" Hitler said. "You have let them know how *hard* Germans can become. I'm particularly glad you showed it to the

Americans. Of all our enemies, they're the ones I hate the most."

The Führer did a little dance as he turned to Dönitz. He lifted his good leg as he pirouetted on his bad leg. "I think the Fregattenkapitan deserves more than oak leaves on his Knight's Cross. Do you agree, Herr Grossadmiral?"

"I agree most heartily, my Führer," Dönitz said.

"I hereby award you the Knight's Cross with Oak Leaves, Swords and Diamonds," Hitler said.

This was the highest military award in the Reich. Only a half-dozen soldiers of the Wehrmacht and one officer of the Ubootwaffe had received it. For an incredible moment Ernst wanted to shout an angry objection, to protest that he and his crew deserved the award for a thousand other moments of courage in the North Atlantic. He strangled the impulse and choked: "Thank you, my Führer."

"Now I can *enjoy* my lunch," Hitler said. "You always bring the best news, Herr Grossadmiral."

They followed the Führer to the dining room of the bunker, where they sat down to lunch with stolid Colonel General Alfred Jodl, Hitler's personal chief of staff; beefy, glowering Martin Bormann, his secretary; slim, prim-lipped Heinrich Himmler, the head of the SS; and Oberführer Julius Rattenhuber, the surly, hulking security chief of the Wolfschanze.

The Führer gave them a buoyant version of Dönitz's promise that the U-boats would soon be back in action. This led to a much less buoyant lecture to Jodl on the failures of the Army. If the Wehrmacht did its job and smashed the next Russian offensive while the U-boats cut off the men and weapons needed for an invasion of France, he predicted the long-awaited rupture between the Russians and the Anglo-Americans would occur.

"From that viewpoint, my Führer," Himmler said, "I don't think we're doing enough on the diplomatic front to tempt the Anglo-Americans into an offer. That's the key to the whole enterprise—to persuade one or the other that great advantages can be gained from a separate peace. Once again I urge you to get rid of Foreign Minister von Ribbentrop, my Führer. Appoint a man with some brains. "

"Whom do you suggest?" the Führer asked, as he shoveled down an odd-looking lunch. It was mostly cereal, with a salad and some cooked vegetables in other dishes. Ernst and the others were eating excellent pork chops.

"Canaris, perhaps."

"Come come, Reichsführer," Martin Bormann said, wiping his thick lips. "That's almost too obvious. So the SS would then take over the Abwehr?"

"That would make a great deal of sense, as I've said more than once," Himmler snapped, not even trying to conceal his dislike of the secretary.

"Such power plays are unseemly when the future of the Reich is at a critical stage," Bormann said. His face was now livid with unmistakable hatred of the Reichsführer.

Himmler remained unruffled. "The Führer knows I'm only thinking of his welfare. Putting the Abwehr under my control would remove a burden from his mind. Canaris could be placed in a position where he might do us a great deal of good."

"From what I hear, he would do us more good under the ground," Bormann said. "I can't understand your tolerant attitude toward a man many suspect is a traitor, Herr Reichsführer."

"Now, now, Bormann," the Führer said. "Enough of this bickering. Himmler is here to give us a report on the Jewish program. What are the latest figures, Reichsführer?"

"The program is progressing on schedule, my Führer," Himmler said. "By the end of the coming year, 1944, we shall have eliminated all but a few productive Jews, who can still serve the Reich through labor. By the end of the following year, the extermination will be complete. There will not be a living Jew in Europe."

"You see, Jodl, you see why this talk of making a stand on the East Prussia border must cease?" Hitler said. "All our extermination camps are in Poland. If we give them up, the greatest single purpose of my life would have to be abandoned!"

"I understand, my Führer," the general said. Ernst heard no enthusiasm whatsoever in the words.

Bormann began querying Himmler on the extermination program. He wanted to know when they were going to rid Germany of the "Iron Cross Jews"—the men who had won decorations in the last war and had been exempted from deportation. Himmler replied that he had exempted them because many were highly regarded by their fellow Germans and he did not want to disrupt civilian morale any more than necessary.

For a moment all Ernst could see was the moon face of the Hoffmann family doctor, Wilhelm Einstein, hovering over his bed after he fell into the Grosser Wannsee from his sailboat in the middle of November and almost died from exposure. Dr. Einstein had won an Iron Cross fighting under General von Hoffmann on the Eastern front. He had always been ready to respond to an emergency at any hour of the day or night. He had still been practicing medicine when Georg was a baby. He had come at four a.m. when Georg was two or three and started running a high fever from a strep throat. Berthe and Ernst's mother had been frantic until the old doctor swabbed Georg's throat and prescribed some medicine that banished the fever in twenty-four hours. Einstein had died the following year.

Bormann and Himmler were arguing violently over how to deal with the Iron Cross Jews. The Führer abruptly decided the dispute. "As a man who won the Iron Cross first-class, I can assure you, Himmler, that any Jew who won a decoration did it through fraud and bribery."

"We will bend to the task, my Führer," Himmler said, ignoring Bormann's triumphant sneer.

"Enough bickering!" the Führer said. "We have with us today an authentic German hero in the person of Fregattenkapitan von Hoffmann, who has put four hundred thousand tons of enemy shipping on the Atlantic bottom. Better than that, on his last voyage he performed an exploit that I think you will all enjoy. Tell them what happened to the American crewmen of the SS *Martin de Porres* who survived your torpedoes, Herr Fregattenkapitan."

Again, the mixture of dream and nightmare consumed Ernst. His eyes roved the faces around the table as he spoke. Bormann licked his wolfish lips; Himmler listened with his head slightly to one side, eyes emotionless behind his pince-nez; General Jodl wore a disapproving frown; Oberführer Rattenhuber acquired a delighted smile on his fleshy face. "Wonderful!" he roared, as Ernst finished. "Were any of them Jews?"

"I didn't think it was necessary to inquire, Herr Oberführer," Ernst said. "We killed them all."

Suddenly he was back on the bridge of the Ritterboot, hearing Wolfgang Griff urge him to poison Jonathan Talbot and his Jewish fireman, remembering his scornful reply, the flash of pleasure as he imagined Berthe's approval.

Berthe! She stood in the far corner of the dining room, gazing at him with sad reproachful eyes. *Go to hell*, he told her. *Maybe that's where we're all going but I want you to go first.* My God how he hated that woman! Infinitely more than he hated any Jew or American.

"You see what can be accomplished with a little hardness, gentlemen," the Führer said. "I hope you tell this story to your fellow generals, Jodl. Maybe it will inspire the Wehrmacht to show as much devotion to my principles as the Kriegsmarine."

Suddenly the Führer bent double in his seat, gripped by a tremendous rage. "To think that I, a soldier of the German Army, a winner of the Iron Cross, first-class, am forced to say such a thing!"

For five full minutes the Führer hurled expletives and curses at Jodl and his fellow generals. Finally he slumped in his chair, whimpering. No one in the room said a word for another full minute.

"I think your point has been made and well made, my Führer," Bormann said in a soothing voice. "Now it's time for your nap. You must be careful not to exhaust yourself. Too much depends on your guidance."

"I could not agree more, my Führer," Grossadmiral Dönitz said. The others murmured agreement, even Jodl. Only Ernst was silent, feeling his assent was superfluous.

Nodding wearily, the Führer allowed Bormann to lead him from the room. As the door closed, Himmler sighed loudly. "The drugs are taking their toll," he said.

Outside, as they waited for the car that would take them back to their train, Reichsführer Himmler emerged from the bunker looking vexed. "My damned plane has engine trouble," he said. "Could I hitch a ride back to Berlin with you, Herr Grossadmiral? I must be there by nightfall."

Dönitz was delighted to give one of the most powerful men in the Reich a ride. As they cruised through the gray afternoon, Himmler talked freely about the war and their prospects for victory. He was counting heavily on the rupture of the enemy alliance. Churchill loathed Stalin and vice versa. There were strong voices in the United States, such as the millionaire Democratic politician, Joseph P. Kennedy, who saw no point in making the world safe for communism.

All they needed was time. He was profoundly encouraged by the Grossadmiral's optimism about renewing the U-boat offensive. He was also hopeful about the new rocket weapons they were developing—although a recent British air raid on the development site, the Baltic island of Peenemünde, had set things back at least six months.

"You don't know how much I envy you military men, Herr Grossadmiral," Himmler said. "I'm left with mostly boring, dirty jobs. This Jewish business, for instance. It's something for which me and my men can never claim any credit. We can't talk about it in public. If it's so much as mentioned, seventy million worthy Germans rise up—and each one of them has a decent Jew he wants to spare. Of course the others are vermin but this one is an A-1 Jew."

The Reichsführer nibbled his narrow mustache. He was feeling extremely sorry for himself. "Not one of them has seen a hundred or five hundred or a thousand corpses lying side by side. I tell you, what my men have been facing in the East is a page of glory in its own right. To have stuck it out through three million executions—and still remained decent men. That's what has made us hard. It's a page of glory that will never be written. We accept that. But sometimes we wish sycophants like that snake Martin Bormann did not prevent the Führer from expressing some appreciation to us."

"I'm sure the Führer appreciates it," Dönitz said. "Don't you agree, Hoffmann?"

"What? Oh—of course, Herr Grossadmiral."

Berthe. Berthe was sitting at the other end of the car, listening to this conversation. Making Fregattenkapitan von Hoffmann listen to the words, listen and understand them. Three—million—executions. While he confronted the memory of his own decent Jew, Dr. Wilhelm Einstein.

"Your men are not alone in their hard tasks, Herr Reichsführer," Dönitz said. "You heard Fregattenkapitan von Hoffmann's story today. That was as hard as anything your SS has done. To turn against the ancient code of the sea, which makes every shipwrecked man a brother! That's the kind of hardness I'm asking my captains to embrace. Their glory will never be written either."

"Excuse me, Herr Grossadmiral. The fellow Bormann upsets me," Himmler said.

"Our colleague Goering has the same effect on me," Dönitz said. "In private we Kriegsmariners call him the gravedigger of the Reich."

"A by no means unjustified title," Himmler said.

Ernst felt bewilderment swell into anxiety in his belly. How could this hatred and contempt be swirling around the Führer? The

Grossadmiral seemed to accept it as a fact of life. In another half-hour they were in Berlin. Reichsführer Himmler was met by a squadron of saluting SS men and driven away in a cavalcade of limousines.

"Hard," Dönitz said, as they rode to naval headquarters in their own limousine. "That fellow doesn't know the meaning of the word. Can you imagine him in a U-boat? Let's hope someday we can tell the true story of this war, Hoffmann."

"I would be honored to help you write it, Herr Grossadmiral."

Ernst was stunned to realize he did not mean a word of that reply. It was the first lie he had ever told Karl Dönitz. Did it mean he no longer admired him? He labored until nine o'clock on his notes of the conference with the Führer. As he left naval headquarters, the words of "Lili Marlene" crooned in his head. It was Tuesday. Would Margaret be waiting? He wanted someone, something to separate him from the memory of the day.

He took the subway to the Bendlerstrasse and was chagrined to discover no sign of her near the familiar lamppost. He decided to wait a few minutes and paced up and down in the cold. Through a rear door in a townhouse facing the Tirpitz Ufer someone hurried into the night. In spite of the blackout, Ernst recognized the blond hair, the striding walk. Berthe!

"What brings you to Berlin?" he said.

She recognized his voice. "I'm reporting to Canaris," she said.

"Devoted to your pimp, like all whores."

Up the block behind him, Margaret began whistling "Lili Marlene." Ernst was grateful for the darkness that concealed her dirty tan raincoat, her unkempt hair, her grinning slattern's mouth. "I'm waiting for her," he said, gesturing toward the sound. "I guess I have a weakness for sluts. That must explain why I married you."

"Ernst—I'm going back to Spain in a few days. Can I see the children before I go?"

"No."

"Ernst, please—I beg you. It's Christmas time."

"Will you come to the Hotel Adlon with me tonight? Along with her?"

"No."

Margaret's whistle was wearing thin. "It's the only way you'll see the children."

"No."

He had a terrific desire to smash that perfect face once and for all. But he controlled it. How could he explain it to the Grossadmiral if he was arrested in front of Army headquarters for beating up his ex-wife? He left her standing forlornly in the night and strolled up the Bendlerstrasse to Margaret.

"Who's the blonde?" she asked.

"A high-priced whore I used to know," Ernst said.

He got home to Wannsee around 11:30, feeling dismal. Nothing Margaret tried really aroused him, although he came several times. It was almost as unsatisfying as masturbation.

As he opened the front door, a small figure darted toward him: Georg. "Father! I couldn't sleep. I wanted to hear about the Führer. What was he like?"

"He was exactly as I'd always imagined," Ernst said. "Strong, kind, wise. He has a brilliant plan for winning the war."

"Did he ask you about the Ubootwaffe? What did you tell him?"

Suddenly Ernst was engulfed by a bewildering overwhelming nausea. It broke over him like a wave, filling his throat with a terrible urge to vomit. "I—I told him many things."

"What, Father? I want to know exactly what you said."

"It's much too late for that! Go to bed now!"

"Please, Father!"

"Go to bed! That's an order."

Georg retreated a few steps. "Father! Mother was here today. She stood on the lawn. Grandmother wouldn't let her come in. Greta and I felt very sad. Why can't we talk to her?"

"I said go to bed!"

In the bathroom, Ernst gulped down several monosodium glutinate tablets. His traitor stomach had not bothered him since he went on Dönitz's staff. He heard someone saying *a page of glory that can never be written*. Was it Dönitz—or Himmler, the whining, self-pitying exterminator of the Jews?

Ernst stared out at the moonlit lawn where Berthe had stood earlier in the day. The voice whispered in his mind again. *A page of glory that can never be written*. It was Berthe. This time he knew what she was really saying.

A page of glory he could never mention to his own son.

BOOK FIVE

41

THE MIDNIGHT VISITOR

"Jack!"

Annie almost flew into his arms—until she realized she might knock him down. Her brother was teetering on a cane. He looked as if he had lost about thirty pounds. But the reckless grin was intact and so was his *joie de vivre*. He let Annie and Selma Shanley kiss him and help him to a chair, where he regaled them with stories of moonlit romance in the American Army Hospital in Cairo. His favorite nurse had gotten herself transferred back to Washington to continue to console him.

"It's *Farewell to Arms* plus Henry Miller," Selma said.

"What about Daphne?" Annie asked.

"She's back in England, waiting for me," Jack said. "I may give her a ring."

"How many carats?" Annie asked. She had met Daphne at a British embassy party. The poor woman was hopelessly in love with this incurable skirtlifter.

"Listen to her," Jack said. "She's joined forces with my mother. Thank God for you, Selma. You're the only dame in Washington who doesn't think I should get married."

"That's because I plan to catch you just before you collapse into your wheelchair," Selma said.

"For a while in Italy, I thought I was there already," Jack said. A

German 88 millimeter shell had burst in front of the car in which Jack had been riding with three other correspondents. The two in the front seat had been killed instantly. One had been decapitated. Jack and the man in the back had been riddled with shell fragments. Annie knew the gory details because Jack had written an unforgettable column about it. A dozen GIs risked their lives to drag him and the other survivor from the smoking wreckage, as more shells burst around them.

It had been a difficult time for "Behind The Headlines." Sidney Arnold had flown overseas to take up the war-zone slack while Jack recuperated from his multiple wounds, and Annie and Selma had worked overtime in Washington to keep the copy flowing to the newspapers three times a week. Lately Annie had begun to feel she could use a little time in a wheelchair herself. They left Selma typing up a juicy column on the recent conference between Roosevelt, Churchill and Stalin in Teheran. Annie had gotten a very inside account from Saul Randolph, who had been there collecting kudos from Stalin for lend-lease's delivery of the 750,000th vehicle to Murmansk.

Annie and Jack taxied to the familiar Connecticut Avenue apartment for a joyful reunion with the Congressman and Helen. As usual, Annie winced at the intensity of her parents' adoration of Jack. Her mother did everything short of giving him a physical examination to make sure he was intact. The Congressman told funny stories about Hinky Dink Kenna and Bathhouse John Coughlin and other legendary Chicago pols with a gusto he never displayed to her. But Annie could not get angry at them—they were both looking too old and haggard.

Jack insisted on escorting Annie home to Georgetown as if she were sixteen and surprised her by accepting an invitation to come up for a drink. Watching him mount the stairs was heartbreaking. A shell fragment had raised havoc with his left knee. "I think you should stay right here in Washington for the next twelve months!" she said, as she handed him a brandy.

"Can't," he said. "Gotta catch the big one."

"What big one?"

"The invasion of France. It's going to be the biggest thing in history. Eisenhower's promised me a clearance for the first wave. After that, maybe I'll head for the wheelchair. Maybe marry Daphne, if I can talk her into divorcing her cluck of a husband."

"How can you get around a battlefield on a cane?" she cried.

"I'll have a car and driver. I'm a big deal, kiddo. Generals fight to get into the old column."

He belted down his brandy and demanded another one. "That was a damn good column on Teheran. Where did you get that stuff about Roosevelt treating Churchill like his valet?"

"Saul Randolph, the number two man at lend-lease. He was there."

"He's been here, too, I gather."

"Has Selma been writing you weekly reports on me? I wouldn't put it past either of you."

"Never mind who told me. Is it really over between you and Zeke?"

"I've gotten zero letters from him in two years. When I saw him in Casablanca he told me he was in love with a German woman he met in Madrid. I'd call that over and out."

"Maybe."

"Don't start an advice to the lovelorn column. You've got the wrong background for it."

He acknowledged the direct hit with a grin. "I just happen to love you, kiddo. I'm entitled."

To do what? Annie wondered. Mess up her life on a catastrophic scale? Yet she could not deny the melting sensation in her solar plexus at that damnable word, *kiddo*. For twenty years she had adored the way he said that to her. Maybe Sister Agatha had the right idea: the convent. That would insulate you from men. Nothing else seemed to work.

Jack surprised her by not saying another word about Zeke or Saul Randolph. Instead they talked business for the next half-hour. Sidney Arnold was doing a good job in Italy and wanted to stay in the war zone. Jack told her to hire another reporter for Washington. Annie wanted to know where they stood on some of the major issues. Jack's test of a story's value, did it help win the war, was no longer adequate. The war was heading toward a climax and political divisions in Washington were taking on larger and larger importance.

She told him about Roosevelt's defeat in the brawl over the State Department, which was still reverberating in the columns. An even bigger explosion had taken place in Congress last month. Roosevelt had tried to veto the tax bill for the coming fiscal year, calling it, among other things, a bill that catered to the greedy rather than the needy. The House and Senate had reacted with incredible fury, overriding the veto by overwhelming margins in both houses.

"Half the Democrats in Congress are starting to hate Roosevelt," Annie said. "They can't stand the way he's running the country with executive orders and alphabet soup agencies. Some people, including a certain Congressman from Chicago, are calling that veto message Roosevelt's farewell address."

Once more Jack surprised her. "I'm going to let you decide the Washington stuff," he said. "Just remember one thing: as far as I'm concerned, the only people who count are the guys who are doing the dying. Anything that helps them, that holds down their casualties, that helps to end the dying as soon as possible is what we should go after. Any and every kind of Washington asininity. I don't care who or what it is or who gets sore at us, if it helps those kids—"

There were tears on Jack's face. "I'm thinking of Salerno," he said. "I've never seen anything like the bravery. The Germans had the beach zeroed in. The shells came in like raindrops but those kids—"

He gulped the rest of his brandy and sat there, sobbing. Annie could not believe it. Nothing, absolutely nothing, ever ruffled Jack. It was one of her life's primary axioms. Since girlhood she had struggled to achieve his unshakable coolness, only to relapse again and again into her usual emotional spasticity. She flung herself down beside him on the couch and wrapped her arms around him.

Annie had begun to suspect the quality of your life depended on your ability to exchange love. Zeke Talbot had largely destroyed that capacity in her. Maybe it was a hopeful sign that he had not ruined what existed and would always exist between her and Jack. Maybe there would come a moment with Saul Randolph when sweetness became a new, a different kind of surrender, that did not require submission on other fronts.

"Let me give you some orders, Boss," Annie said when Jack finally stopped weeping. "Don't you dare get killed in this invasion. I need someone in this world I can confess my sins to."

"How about Saul?"

"He doesn't believe in sin."

"Sounds like my kind of guy."

"He is and he isn't."

"Do you love him?"

"I like him. He takes me inside things the way Daphne got you inside certain embassies. But I'm never going to love anybody again the way I loved Zeke. You can only be that dumb once in a lifetime."

"What bullshit."

They left it that way. She introduced Jack to Saul Randolph and they got on beautifully. Jack featured him in a column as "The Man Who Makes Lend-Lease Work"—something that had never occurred to Annie, although she did not object when Jack claimed she had suggested it. Poor Saul had no idea he was getting a political rub-down, Chicago-style. Meanwhile the invalid let his nurse console him until he talked his doctors into discharging him from the hospital. The next day he kissed everybody goodbye and flew back to Europe on Pan Am.

At eleven the next morning, Saul Randolph was on the tele-phone. "I'm in a matinee mood," he said.

"I can't, possibly," Annie said. "I'm having lunch with a Congress-woman."

"Cancel it! Tell her you have an impassioned lover on your hands."

"Tonight," she said firmly, although the word *lover* made her pulse flutter. It was the first time Saul had used it.

"What time?"

"I'm having dinner with one of Senator Truman's staffers at the Carlton House. We're thinking of hiring him for the column. Why don't you reserve a room upstairs and save yourself a trip to George-town? We'll split the price."

"What *time?*"

"Nine."

His starring role in "Behind The Headlines" had banished the last of Saul's grumpiness over her failure to help him disembowel the State Department. New euphoria had also helped to heal those wounds. At Teheran, so the story went—and Saul was by no means alone in telling it—Roosevelt and Harry Hopkins had executed an end run on the State Department, Congress—and Winston Churchill. All three of these obstacles to American-Soviet wartime communion and postwar bliss had been circumvented by the Presi-dent's political wizardry. FDR had charmed Stalin.

Of course he had been forced to give away a few things, such as the independence of Lithuania, Estonia, Latvia and probably Poland, Bulgaria and Rumania. But how could anyone carp at such minor concessions in the light of a future aglow with Soviet-American friendship? Everyone from Henry Wallace to Cordell Hull rejoiced. The long-predicted new era of perpetual peace seemed just over the horizon—if they could dispose of a few million heavily armed Germans and Japanese.

The normally restrained *Atlantic Monthly* reported that Americans had returned from Teheran "with the impression that Stalin is both a military genius and a man of his word." The *New Republic* called anti-Stalinists like Roy Reeves the "Hang-Back Boys" and urged its readers to trust the "democratic leadership" of the First Secretary of the Communist Party. The *Nation* assured its readers that the coming Soviet dominance of Eastern Europe was not imperialistic but derived from the "tremendous popularity which the USSR enjoyed among large sections of Balkan peoples, especially peasants and workers." The head of a major New York publishing house proposed that all books critical of Russia be taken off the shelves of the nation's libraries and bookstores for the duration of the war.

This incredible unanimity may have been one reason why Annie had arranged a lunch with the nation's newest Congresswoman, Clare Booth Luce. Playwright, actress and wife of *Time* magazine's panjandrum Henry Luce, she had been briskly attacking the Roosevelt administration since she arrived in Washington with the Republican minilandslide of 1942. They met in a secluded corner of the Carlton House dining room. Mrs. Luce was wearing a sky blue business suit and a cloche that perfectly matched her azure eyes. On her lapel was a diamond brooch that was probably worth Annie's yearly salary.

Up close she was so tiny she was almost doll-like, with skin the color of blanc de chine. She seemed surprisingly demure—until they started to converse. "I suppose you have orders to dismember me," she said in an arch, rather affected voice.

"Why?"

She peered at a card on her table. "You're sleeping with Saul Randolph, who has been described as Henry Morgenthau's left and Harry Hopkins's right testicle." She sipped her iced tea and delivered her most devastating smile. "It must make for a crowded bed."

"Good staff work," Annie said. "I've heard you make your lovers genuflect first. Is that true?"

"No, but it's a wonderful idea."

Mrs. Luce's smile suggested she was enjoying herself. "Then there's your father, the voice of Chicago in our midst. He gives me terrible glares every time I open my mouth on the floor of the House."

"That's because you keep making his friends look silly."

"Do you really think so? I get the most awful vibrations of animosity when I speak. It comes in waves from both sides of the aisle. I always sit down feeling lonely. "

"They can't bear to think you have a mind."

Mrs. Luce perceptibly relaxed. She admired the natural wave in Annie's hair, confessing that she had to spend hours creating one. They exchanged data on Washington hairdressers and dress shops. In five minutes they were ready for some frank politics.

"What do you think of the current love feast with Russia?"

"Globaloney," Mrs. Luce said. "If Henry Wallace likes it, there's got to be something wrong with it."

"Everyone seems to like it."

"It's the doggy thing. Haven't you noticed it? It comes with being male. They love to run in packs."

Mrs. Luce was definitely enjoying herself. "Men are happiest in groups, where they can give each other a warm bath of mutual agreement and constant congratulation."

"Women don't group?"

"Have you ever seen a pack of cats? No, women are much better at sitting on the sidelines watching the canines mess things up. If one of them comes too close to Pussy—zap! Out came the claws."

"You think that's our role in life?"

The supple mouth curved maliciously. "It's one of our roles, darling. Every woman is an actress, playing a number of parts. It takes time to perfect them all. Incidentally, everything I've said so far, except the globaloney stuff, is off the record."

Mrs. Luce spent the rest of the lunch predicting that Roosevelt would not run in 1944. She cited a *Fortune* magazine poll which reported that 59.7 percent of the American people would not vote for him if the war ended before the election. This amounted to "emotional repudiation," she maintained. He should step down and let the Republican–Conservative Democratic majority in Congress take charge of the peace. If Woodrow Wilson had done that, this second world war would never have happened.

"Liberals are good at waging wars," Mrs. Luce said. "Their moral fervor is useful. But they're terrible at making peace. Moralism inevitably breeds delusions of righteousness and demands for punishment—emotions that have to be barred from serious peacemaking."

"You don't agree with the policy of unconditional surrender?"

"Absolute idiocy."

Was all this wisdom or the flutters of a brilliant butterfly? Annie did not really care. It was going to make a very good column. Selma Shanley gave it one of her rare raves when Annie handed it in at five p.m.

Usually, once a story was written, its details sank out of Annie's mind. But the off-the-record part of Mrs. Luce's observations would not go away. *Doggy.* The word scampered back and forth in Annie's consciousness as she toured a cocktail party at the Mayflower Hotel for Henry Wallace, who was about to leave on a fact-finding tour of the world for the President. One of the Vice President's long simmering feuds with other alphabet soup agency czars had exploded with potentially fatal political results. The opponent had an army of friends on Capitol Hill who were panting to investigate Henry down to his toenail clippings. FDR was getting him out of town one jump ahead of the posse. Nevertheless, around and around went the same opinions from the mouths of hundreds of confident males. The war—and the peace—were as good as won thanks to the dawn of an era of Soviet-American friendship. Roosevelt was the genius of the age—and Wallace was his heir apparent.

To break the monotony Annie headed for a couple of generals she knew from the War Department. They were both about her father's age and treated her with cheerful paternalism. Unfortunately what they told her was anything but cheerful. Their opinions—and jaws—were grimly set against the prevailing euphoria. They were both deeply worried about the coming invasion of Europe.

One, an Army Air Force man, talked about how hard it was to bomb an entrenched enemy who had had two years to dig deep. The other general, a specialist in amphibious warfare, thought the casualties could be as high as 50 percent.

"How many in the first wave?" Annie asked.

"Eighty, maybe ninety percent," the General said.

A terrible, formless fear began to swell in Annie's body. Jack could die in this invasion and for some reason she did not understand, he seemed to almost welcome the chance. Did he still feel guilty over quitting the Navy? Was that Zeke Talbot's fault, with his endless harping on "My Country 'Tis of Thee"?

Dinner at the Carlton House with the Truman Committee investigator was a respite of sorts. He knew where dozens of smelly bodies were buried inside and outside Washington, D.C. He had worked as a congressional aide and was on first-name terms with dozens of people on the Hill. Annie hired him on the spot for twice his government salary and sauntered to the hotel desk to introduce herself as Mrs. Black. The clerk said her husband had called and would be a few minutes late. He gave her the key to room 377 and up she went to bathe and await Saul Randolph between deliciously cool flowered sheets.

The moment Annie put her head on the pillow, she realized how tired she was. By the time Saul arrived she was dozing, not exactly the best preparation for a performance on the high wire. Maybe they could do it in slow motion? Desire stirred when he emerged gleaming from the shower, but she was still far from prepared when he slipped under the covers and pressed her against him.

"Hold up your left hand," he said. "I've got something I want to put on it."

A second later, a diamond as big as the Carlton House—Washington, D.C.'s Ritz—gleamed on her fourth finger. "It doesn't mean anything unless you want it to mean something," he said.

"Saul," Annie said. "There's a question that goes with this and an answer I can't—"

"I don't want an answer now. I just want you," he said.

Sweetness. Her drowsy state made it especially difficult to control. The kisses, the touches, accumulated a terrific yearning that somehow combined with a ravaging sadness that left her feeling almost frightened at first, then vaguely, guiltily angry as she struggled to stay on the high wire. By the time it ended she was thoroughly awake and full of mournful wonder. She heard Clare Booth Luce telling her a woman had to learn to play a number of roles. Was this a new one, the almost wife? She let the sweetness speak as he came: "Oh Saul, Saul!" But she stayed on the high wire.

Afterward she insisted the ring's appearances would be limited to the bedroom for the time being. Saul merely smiled and called room service for some champagne and caviar. While they waited for it he began talking about Teheran again. He described the way FDR had dangled the invasion of France before Stalin, while Churchill wet his knickers at the thought of what the casualties might do to his majority in Parliament.

"Maybe Churchill had a point," Annie said. "I just talked to a couple of generals who told me the casualties on the first day might be ninety percent."

The champagne arrived and Saul filled the glasses. "You shouldn't print that," he said. "You shouldn't print a single line that weakens Roosevelt at this point. If this invasion fails we could have something close to a class war between the liberals and conservatives in this country. Have you read the Conant article in the *Atlantic Monthly*? He thinks we'll have one in ten years if we don't do something drastic."

He began quoting from an essay by the President of Harvard, urging a program to achieve equality by a massive redistribution of wealth once a generation.

"The earth belongs to the living," Annie said.

Saul looked blank.

"It's an old idea cooked up by one of the extremists in the French Revolution. Jefferson proposed it to Madison in a letter from Paris. Madison annihilated it by return mail and Jefferson never mentioned it again."

Doggy. Saul looked as if he might howl—or even whine—with exasperation. "I bet you graduated cum laude," he said.

"Summa cum laude," Annie said.

He could not understand why Annie would not run with the New Deal group-thinkers in their alphabet soup offices woofing about the nobility of the common man and radical solutions to his problems. They never mentioned the common woman. It never seemed to occur to them that she might have some ideas of her own.

Stop stop STOP! Where did this eruption of cynicism come from? Annie stared dazedly at the ring on her finger. It was Saul's attempt to make her part of this better world he devoutly believed was coming from the wedding of American democracy and Russian communism that he and his fellow liberals were determined to solemnize with Franklin D. Roosevelt's help. Maybe it was possible. Maybe she should somehow abolish her mind. Maybe they should do it doggy-style from now on.

Saul refilled her champagne glass and Annie downed it in a single defiant swallow. "I've told you before—I'll print what I please," she said. "But I'll lay off FDR. I don't kick a man when he's down."

Back to her lonely Georgetown apartment went Anna Richman Talbot, tough-talking girl reporter with an almost-engagement ring in her purse and too much champagne in her belly. Groping up the dark stairs, thinking of Jack and D-Day, wondering if she could dare pray for him, telling herself to forget it, maybe she could hire Sister Agatha for so much per rosary but she would do it for nothing. Not like former summa cum laude history major, Anna Richman, who did it to arf-arf with the power woofers.

Her head whirled. Why had she finished that bottle? Was she going to get sick? Crash slam into the living room and down the hall to the john. Some spectacular retching but nothing came up. Clammy with perspiration, she stumbled back to the living room and switched on the light.

"Hello, Annie."

Zeke Talbot sat on the couch in a brown tweed English suit, looking older and, for some reason, slightly wiser. She realized it was the same morose expression he had worn at Casablanca. "How did you get in here?" she gasped.

"I told the landlady I was your husband, just back from overseas."

"What the hell do you want?"

"Your help," he said. "I want to get into the White House and convince the President to negotiate with the German resistance movement."

"The State Department says there's no such thing."

"Annie, I've been to Berlin. I've met them. They're for real. Look at this."

He pulled a snapshot out of his pocket. An extremely tall man in a worn gray tweed jacket stood beside Zeke in front of a round tower. "That's Count Helmuth von Moltke. The building in the background is the Sieges Saule, the victory monument the Germans put up after they won the Franco-Prussian War."

From a briefcase he dragged the report he had sent the State Department. He piled other documents on top of it. A description of his mission to Berlin on Eisenhower's orders. A blow-by-blow of his conversations with various generals and colonels and an admiral named Canaris, whom he described as the plot's mastermind.

"Ike sent the whole thing to Roosevelt with a recommendation that we modify the unconditional surrender policy and see what happens. He was told politics was not his job—and if he didn't want to command the invasion they'd find someone else. That's when I decided I had to make good on a promise I made in Berlin—that I'd take this to Roosevelt personally."

It was the greatest story of the war. In his infuriating straight-arrow way, Zeke said she could not publish it! The merest mention of the Schwarze Kapelle could lead to their extinction.

"You haven't lost your talent for driving me crazy!" she cried.

"Annie—these men are ready to lead a revolt that will make the invasion unnecessary. But Roosevelt refuses to even admit they exist. We can save a million lives if we change his mind. We can keep the Russians out of the heart of Europe. We can change the future of the world."

That fateful phrase again. Along with Jack's voice, telling her to give priority to whatever saved the lives of those soldiers with whom he had fallen in love. "I'll do everything I can," she said. "But first I've got to get some sleep."

"I called Ethel but she wasn't home. I'll try one of the hotels."

She told him why Ethel was not home. His jaw sagged with disbelief. "As for a hotel room, you can't get one in Washington without maximum clout. People are sleeping on lobby floors and the tops of dining room tables."

For a vicious moment she almost told him about the room she had just vacated and why it might be available. But he was such an easy target, with that sad, stubborn honesty his only shield from her cruelty, she dropped the idea. "You better stay here—on the couch," she said.

It was the weirdest, scariest moment of her life—leaving him there and plodding down the short hall to the bedroom. She wanted to take a bath that would last for hours. She wanted to emerge sanitized—and savoring the knowledge that he had been lying there, imagining the water flowing over her naked skin. But she was too tired for such nonsense. She was even too tired to be angry at her adulterous husband—or savor the triumph of having him crawl to her for help.

"By the way," she said, with her hand on the bedroom door knob. "Why aren't you in uniform?"

"I've finally taken your advice," he said. "I've quit the Navy. I've joined the OSS."

"Zeke!" she said, too tired to stifle the impulse. "That's the best news I've heard in a year."

For an odd confusing moment, they were man and wife again. "I'm not that happy about it," he growled. "But it became a necessity."

They were back in the web of loving advice and stubborn resentment that had led to the Great Explosion. Oh Zeke, Annie wanted to cry. Is it possible that somewhere sometime somehow we could love each other again?

But he was not here for love. He was here, and so was she, for only one purpose now, a purpose that had nothing to do with such trivialities as individual happiness or the soul's salvation. The future of the world was the impersonal game they were playing. So she simply snarled: "Good night!"

42

BLIND HATRED

"Harry," said Congressman Richman, "I don't give a damn how sick he is. I want this. I want my son-in-law to tell the President what he found in Berlin. My daughter will be there to make sure he's treated right."

There were faint squawking noises on the other end of the phone, which Jonathan Talbot could not decipher, but he gathered they were a final protest from Harry Hopkins.

"Harry," the Congressman said. "I've been playin' his game, sittin' on the Polacks in my district. They're sore as hell about the way he's sellin' Poland to Stalin for a handshake. One wink from me and you'll have a hundred thousand of them outside the White House wavin' signs and screamin' 'Down with Rooseveltski.'"

Yesterday, before Annie launched the campaign to get him into the White House, she gave Talbot a lecture on how to conduct himself. Indignation and vituperation were out. So was what she called his "righteousness act." Instead it was "Roosevelt admiration time." He was going to tell everyone, including FDR, how much the anti-Hitler Germans admired him, trusted him, placed their hopes in him.

Annie also made it clear that she was not doing this for him, although if he pulled it off, he would probably become semifamous because she would be forced to write a column about him. Several columns, in fact. She was doing it a, because it was news; b, because it might save soldiers' lives; and c, because it might save Jack's life. Zeke Talbot's role meant absolutely nothing to her, although she confessed a grudging admiration for his having the nerve to parachute into Berlin.

Now Annie sat on the other side of the Congressman's office in a trim blue suit, her black hair fluffed and gleaming, a black briefcase on her lap. Talbot was amazed by how beautiful she looked. He had seen too much of her in sloppy slacks and his discarded shirts, without a trace of makeup. With eyeshadow, lipstick and the other ingredients of a career woman's warpaint, she was incredibly attractive— and hard. That part surprised and disappointed him because Annie had always been the opposite of hard; if anything too tender, too quick to dissolve into tears when they argued. He did not like hard women. But her inner life was no longer any of his business.

She obviously hated him but that did not surprise Talbot either. For a man whose intentions were always good, he seemed to have a strange capacity for inspiring hatred in women. He suspected Berthe was close to hating him too, though there was nothing personal in her feelings. He was simply a weak link in her campaign to rescue her beloved Germany from catastrophe.

The Congressman slammed down the telephone. "He'll see you tonight at six in his upstairs study. A half-hour max. He's got a dinner with King Constantine of Greece. Get there at five-forty-five. You may get a couple of extra minutes out of him."

Talbot spent the day boiling the Germans' proposals down to a single page, under Annie's editorial direction. She made him rewrite it a dozen times, striking out words that were "unappealing" or "fuzzy." On the twelfth rejection he revolted and accused her of torturing him. She read it over again and decided it was "passable."

At 5:40 they arrived at the front portico of the executive mansion. A black butler led them to an elevator that took them up to the second floor. There, another black butler led them down a long, dark hall lined with bookcases, on top of which were numerous silver-framed autographed portraits of crowned heads. Eventually they reached a door on the south side of the hall, where the butler made a murmured introduction. "Come in, come in!" boomed an unmistakably Rooseveltian voice.

Wearing a dark blue cloak around his shoulders, Franklin Roosevelt sat in his wheelchair a few feet behind the desk in his oval study. On the walls were a scattering of old naval prints and pictures of his wife, his mother and John Paul Jones. The President had a magnifying glass in his hand through which he was studying a page from a portfolio on his lap. It took Talbot a moment to realize it was his famous stamp collection. Somehow this fact confirmed that he was face-to-face with "That Man in the White House," his father's nemesis, the commander in chief of eight million American soldiers and sailors, the most powerful politician in the world.

Still studying the page of stamps, Roosevelt said: "This has been billed to me as the most important piece of news I'm likely to hear this year. Direct from Berlin, no less. Is that why you're along, Annie?"

"I've got a strong personal interest in this story, Mr. President," she said. Talbot could see she was flattered by the use of her first name. The fabled Roosevelt charm was in good working order.

"You and Jack are doing a wonderful job with that column. It's brought the reality of the war home to a lot of people. I'm not always as enthused about some of the Washington stories. But at least you check your facts, unlike Drew Pearson."

"I hope you're enthused about this story, Mr. President," Annie said.

The President laughed in a mirthless way. "I have to confess I'm glad we're talking off the record. I know your father, Mr. Talbot. One of those Old Guard Republicans who think the whole world should revolve around their fixed ideas. I gather you're pretty much the same way."

"My father doesn't think so, Mr. President. To hear him talk, I've never taken his advice on anything."

FDR grimaced half-humorously. "I could multiply that paternal complaint times four," he said. "I remember one of my boys—I think it was Jimmy—informing me I could tell him nothing about how to succeed because I'd never held a job."

So far the conversation had been conducted between FDR and the page full of stamps, with them as spectators. He obviously had no enthusiasm for this meeting.

"So!" FDR said, clicking the page back in the portfolio. "I hear you've got a scheme to end the war overnight by negotiating with some Germans who've somehow escaped the notice of the State Department. Tell me about it."

He flipped the stamp portfolio shut and pulled on the right wheel of his wheelchair so it spun in a half-circle. A single shove rolled him to the desk. In profile, he did not look much different from the pictures in the newspapers. Face-to-face, his skin was a grayish tan over sunken cheeks, his neck was droopy with loose flesh. Dark blue circles turned his eyes into hooded caverns. The bloodless lips flecked away from his gums in a parody of a smile. This was an exhausted man.

Swiftly, Talbot recapitulated his encounter with Berthe in Spain, omitting the sexual side of it, and his growing involvement with the Schwarze Kapelle, climaxed by his trip to Berlin. Describing his meeting with the chief plotters, he put particular stress on Helmuth von Moltke in the hope that he could convince Roosevelt there were estimable civilians as well as generals involved. The President's lips curled from a parody of a smile to an authentic sneer.

"Do you seriously expect me to negotiate with a man named von Moltke? He's got to be the ultimate Prussian aristocrat. Does he wear a monocle?"

"No, Mr. President. He isn't the only spokesman—"

"Probably stuck it in his pocket to make you think he was a Democrat. These bastards killed ten million people in World War One and now they think they can pull Hitler's chestnuts out of the fire? This only proves I made the right decision when I told those milksop Eighth Air Force flyboys to do it the British way—pick a city and flatten it and the hell with how many young, old and middle-aged Germans we kill. I know Germany. I visited it regularly with my mother when I was a boy. I toured the Western front in the last war. When they start whining for peace it only proves we've got them on the ropes. I remember Cousin Theodore damning Wilson for not fighting until we got an unconditional surrender from the Kaiser and his pals. I thought he was wrong but Versailles—and Hitler— changed my mind. We made a colossal mistake, letting the British and French talk us into that armistice. Wilson thought he could handle the goddamn Europeans at the Peace Conference but they made a fool out of him. They're not going to do that to me. By the time this war is over, Germany will be rubble and the British Empire will be kaput. The French Empire is already kaput. I'm going to see they all stay that way. We're going to police our part of the world and let Stalin police his part—"

This astonishing monologue came at Talbot and Annie like a breaking wave, a rising crescendo of fury. Talbot's hopes, never very high, plunged toward bottomless fathoms.

"Mr. President!" he said. "I can only tell you by every standard I know, as a graduate of the Naval Academy, as a reader of history, these Germans are honorable men. They despise Hitler as much as you do."

"Then why did they put him in power?" FDR snarled. "Why did they put me and the rest of the world through this ordeal? They forced me into taking this country to war, the one thing I vowed I'd never do. I saw how it destroyed Wilson. You can see how it's destroying me. You think I don't bleed when men die? You think I don't gag when I think of the lies I've had to tell, the stunts I've had to pull, to get us into the war before Hitler sewed up Europe?"

FDR's breath was coming in shallow gasps. It was a paroxysm of rage left over from Belleau Wood and the Argonne and the frustrations festering since Wilson failed at Versailles. Like Moorman, this man was fighting the last war as much as he was fighting this one. It was all one war, one stupendous explosion of violence—and hatred.

"Mr. President," Talbot said. "As you may know, I was critical of the way you got us into this war. But what I've seen and heard in Madrid and Berlin has convinced me I was wrong. We should have joined the British and French in fighting the Nazis from the day the war began. But I think you're wrong when you blame every living German for Nazism. Negotiating with the Schwarze Kapelle could eliminate the need for an invasion of Europe. It could save thousands of American lives. It could also save the lives of millions of Jews facing extermination."

The President hunched in his wheelchair, as if he were bored or offended. "Are you finally getting to the point?"

"The point, Mr. President?"

"The Jews. I'm sure Sam Richman's as upset about them as Henry Morgenthau and Saul Randolph and a lot of other good Democrats." The President's face darkened. "If I went out and told the reporters tomorrow I was going to alter the unconditional surrender policy on the off chance it might save some Jews in German concentration camps, I wouldn't get reelected this November. I'd be buried by ten million votes. Do I make myself clear?"

Was the President telling them that the United States of America was as anti-Semitic under its democratic surface as Nazi Germany? Or was he telling them that only he understood how fragile the American commitment to the war was, how deep the antagonism to it ran—and he could not afford to tamper with it? Maybe he was only revealing the toll that the virulence of the anti-Roosevelt opposition—and his recent defeats in Congress—had taken on him.

"Then there's the Russians. Until I got into the picture and injected a little trust into the equation, Churchill and Stalin were like a couple of Marmeluke sultans, each afraid to taste the food first for fear it was poisoned. Stalin was convinced—he's still half-convinced—that the British were going to stall on the second front until he and Hitler had bled each other to death. Can you imagine what he'd do if he caught me negotiating with Helmuth von Moltke?"

Roosevelt added a metallic ripple of contempt to his pronouncement of von Moltke. Talbot considered pointing out that the Russians were offering the Germans peace without a word about unconditional surrender. But he decided there was no hope of fighting this man's detestation of the German aristocracy. He fell back to his last argument.

"A proclamation from General Eisenhower, softening the unconditional surrender policy, might be almost as effective. It would encourage a lot of generals—and a lot of lower ranks—to get rid of Hitler."

Roosevelt tried to light a cigarette. His hand trembled so violently, Talbot took the lighter and held it for him. "A proclamation," he muttered. He was slumped in his wheelchair now, his head lolling to one side. The emotional intensity of his monologues seemed to have drained the last iota of energy out of him. "Proc'mation," he said, slurring the word.

"Explaining unconditional surrender," Talbot said. "Telling the Germans it doesn't mean their extermination. Or their enslavement."

"Procl'mazun," the President muttered. "You think it might work? Trick the bastards into surrendering?"

He grinned rakishly and half sat up, energized by the thought. "Might be a good idea. Might save lives. Of course, once we get our hands on their gizzards, that's when we tell them what we've really got ready for them. We're going to make sure the von Moltkes and von Schlieffens and von Hohenzollerns never start another war. We're going to let Joe Stalin shoot fifty thousand of them—and turn the whole damn country into Kansas and Nebraska. Morgenthau's working on a plan to absolutely eviscerate their heavy industry—"

What should he say or do? Talbot wondered. Should he acquiesce in a deception and salvage a proclamation? He let the words in the forefront of his mind, his instinctive reaction, speak. "Mr. President," he said. "I don't think that would be honorable."

FDR's mouth sagged. It seemed to take a long time for the idea to seep into his exhausted mind. "You're a throwback," he said, the ghost of a grin playing across his mouth. "A throwback to Cousin Theodore—or maybe to old George and his cherry tree."

Five minutes later they were out on Pennsylvania Avenue. Annie had a strange expression on her face. The hardness had vanished. She had the dazed look of a victim of an explosion.

"Do you think we might get a proclamation in spite of what I said about turning it into a double cross not being honorable?" Talbot asked. "I expected a kick in the shins from you for that one."

"It was the right thing to say. The only thing to say!" Annie cried.

"A proclamation won't stop the invasion. Eisenhower could only issue it after they're ashore. He can't send them a signal that practically says ready or not here we come."

Annie did not seem to be listening. "Blind hatred," she said. "It's nothing but blind hatred."

"He's a very sick man. Maybe we shouldn't judge him too harshly," Talbot said. He was trying to be as unindignant as possible; it was not difficult because he did not feel indignant at all. Mild disappointment was the most he could summon for the moment. Was it because the whole exchange reminded him of an argument with his father? Maybe he never really believed there was any hope of changing Roosevelt's mind.

Annie rubbed her eyes and Talbot realized she was fighting back tears. What was wrong with her? Maybe she was not quite as hard as she looked. He wanted to put his arms around her—not in any hope of reclaiming her but simply to say he was sorry she was so upset. But touching was forbidden.

"Thanks for your help," he said. "Please thank your father too."

Head down, Annie rushed away from him along the uneven sidewalk in front of the White House, past white-helmeted soldiers at the entrance gates. "Are you all right?" he said, striding after her. "Where are you going? What are you going to do?"

"Maybe join the convent!" Annie said. "It may be my only hope of sanity."

Talbot flew back to London the next day, puzzling over that bizarre remark. Women were incomprehensible creatures. The boredom of the long flight eventually eroded the temporary comfort of that smug observation. Somewhere over the mid-Atlantic, Talbot was forced to ask himself what he really thought and felt about his half hour in the White House. He could not answer the question. His brain, his emotions, congealed. It was easier to spend the last five hours in the air rereading yesterday's newspapers.

In the British capital, he sent a coded message to Moorman, asking him to break the bad news to Berthe as gently as possible. On Grosvenor Street, he reported his presidential interview to Bill Casey who looked grave and wangled him another appointment with Eisenhower. The Supreme Commander was even more disturbed by Talbot's account, at first. Talbot watched him struggle to keep the full implication at arm's length. "You got him at a bad time. His health has been terrible for the last couple of months. It's good to know he'll at least consider a proclamation."

Eisenhower thought even a vague statement might weaken the German will to resist once he got his Army ashore. He was convinced that the German generals were still betting they had a chance to throw them back into the sea. "That's what I'd try to do if I were in their shoes," he said, with a wry grin. "If they pull it off, they'll have something to negotiate."

"What about Churchill? Any chance of changing his mind about unconditional surrender?"

"I talked to him before FDR stepped on me. He didn't seem inclined to rock the boat over it."

On the way out of Ike's headquarters, Talbot ran into his friend General Albert Wedemeyer. Talbot confided his dwindling hopes to him. "Pay a visit to Parliament tomorrow," he said. "Churchill's making a report on the war to the House of Commons. I hear there's going to be some questions about unconditional surrender."

Wedemeyer got Talbot into the House galleries for Churchill's appearance. After the Prime Minister reported optimistically on the progress of the war, a fierce debate erupted over unconditional surrender. Speaker after speaker attacked it as an utterly idiotic idea. They demanded to know why the Prime Minister had not tried to change Roosevelt's mind. As they drew closer to the decision to invade Europe, the policy seemed more and more foolish.

Churchill's famous aplomb almost faltered. He claimed that he had not heard about the idea until Roosevelt floated it at Casablanca. Now "international complexities" made it extremely difficult to revise.

"And indeed, why should it be revised?" boomed a voice from the government's benches. A bulky, red-faced member proceeded to read to the House selections from a recent speech by Lord Robert Vansittart, calling for the "total destruction" of Germany. Anthony Eden, the British Foreign Secretary, rose to second the idea, declaring England would be "soiled" by negotiating with a nation that had produced a political movement as loathsome as Nazism.

Blind hatred was also loose in the House of Commons—and Churchill, whatever his personal feelings, obviously did not have the political strength to oppose it. Talbot stumbled back to Grosvenor Street and listened to William Casey explain the whole mess as proof of the inexorable operation of Murphy's Law. "It wouldn't bother you if you were Irish, Talbot. You'd know if something can go wrong, it always will."

Casey put Talbot back to work for the OSS on a more practical level. The invasion of Europe was now a certainty within a month or two. It was time to start befuddling the Germans in every possible way about the landing site. Casey handed Talbot a sheaf of documents that suggested it was going to consist of a feint on the French coast and a landing in Holland, code-named Stuyvesant Square.

"Give that to your friendly Brunhilde for transmission to Berlin," he said.

Talbot flew back to Madrid, where he found Berthe von Hoffmann near despair. The Gestapo had arrested Helmuth von Moltke. He had attended a party at which several people had made indiscreet remarks about the Führer. Himmler had arrested the entire guest list—and gone to Hitler with a demand for Canaris's head. The Führer had dismissed Canaris—but he did not arrest him. Instead Hitler put him in charge of the home front war effort. Through Abwehr loyalists, Canaris sent Berthe assurances he was still in touch with all the branches of the conspiracy.

Meanwhile, Hitler had survived no less than three attempts to assassinate him. Stauffenberg and his friends put a bomb in his

plane, concealed in a brandy bottle. The plane flew at an unexpectedly high altitude and the detonator, which depended on an acid
solution, froze and failed to explode. A young lieutenant volunteered
to kill him (and himself) while demonstrating a new greatcoat, under
which a bomb would be concealed. Allied planes destroyed the coat
the day before the demonstration. A bomb timed to go off fifteen
minutes after Hitler arrived at an exhibition honoring German war
dead missed when the Führer cut his visit to ten minutes, skipping a
planned speech.

"It makes me wonder if God is trying to tell us something. Is
Canaris right? Should the evil be endured until the bitter end?"

Her mention of God irritated Talbot. It seemed to underscore his
futility. With brutal bluntness—as if his failures were her fault—he
told her the grisly details of his visit to the White House and threw in
the Vansittart outburst in the House of Commons. It was crazy. In
spite of those moments when he groped toward faith, he still
resented this presence that had taken Berthe away from him.

He only succeeded in arousing her German loyalties. "It makes
me almost hope your invasion fails."

He pulled out the papers for the imaginary Stuyvesant Square
operation and thrust them at her. "Here's some more lies to send to
Berlin."

She stared numbly at the top page. "You don't love me anymore,
do you?" she said.

Suddenly all Talbot could see was FDR's exhausted mouth spewing hatred of Germans. For a moment he wondered if hatred was a
communicable disease and he had become contaminated. He was
instantly assailed by the memory of Granada, of that unforgettable
moment of love and truth. "It's the other way around and you know
it," he said with unconcealed bitterness.

She did not even try to answer him.

43

IMMORTAL HONOR

They were like a divorced couple, Berthe thought. Former lovers who had worn each other out with too many demands, too much caring. Fools who had tried to ignore the world's indifference in the childish belief that their love had some magical power to change everything. Now they inhabited the ashes, trying not to blame each other.

"I'm sorry I was so rotten to you the other day," Jonathan said, staring gloomily out at sunny Madrid.

"I got even," Berthe said. "I told Berlin I persuaded you to admit that stuff you gave me about invading the Netherlands was all disinformation. The new head of the Abwehr, Walter Schellenberg, commended me for it. I'm a heroine of the Reich."

"I don't blame you," Jonathan said, still staring out at Madrid.

"Branding it as false might be the very thing that will make the high command suspect it's true."

Jonathan said nothing. She could not decide whether he was mourning the death of their love or his failed meeting with Roosevelt. The Marquesa, as usual, had her own interpretation. Jonathan's love was moving in the classic pattern described by the ancients from eros to agape, from the selfish love of desire to the selfless love of the spirit. This was relatively common among women but extremely rare for a man. "You see it only among a few idealists," she said, carefully balancing mockery and admiration in the style of her hero, Cervantes.

The idea had stirred a sullen wish to compete with him in Berthe's soul. But Germany stood like a Minotaur barring the path. Germany, nothing but Germany mattered now. Personal love was irrelevant, an excrescence on the face of history.

Moorman arrived, giving Berthe his usual disapproving squint. They were going to the bullfights as guests of the Marquesa. Ordonez, the young bullfighter who worshipped a mythical Berthe von Hoffmann, was making his debut as a full-fledged matador and he had asked the Marquesa to bring her.

Moorman had just returned from London, where he had heard the story of what he called Canaris's last throw. Through a French resistance contact, the Admiral had written directly to Stewart Menzies, the head of British Intelligence, offering an immediate truce in the West if the British recognized the Schwarze Kapelle as the legitimate government of Germany. Menzies had forwarded the proposal to the Foreign Office, where it had been rejected without qualifiers.

The only piece of good news was from Eisenhower via Jonathan's OSS friend, Bill Casey. The General was working on a proclamation to broadcast to the Germans the minute he got his Army ashore in France or Belgium or the Netherlands. It was not going to prevent the invasion. That was ordained, now. But it would call on the Wehrmacht to surrender and assure them that the Allies did not intend to exterminate or enslave the German people. Eisenhower had sent a copy of the proposed broadcast to the White House and had heard no objections to it.

Moorman could not stop talking about the invasion. On May 15, there had been a secret meeting at one of the English public schools, attended by the King, Churchill, Eden, Menzies, all the top generals. They had described the force that was being thrown at the Germans: 11,000 planes, 5,000 ships, 1 million men. The overwhelming numbers had erased British fears of a World War I–size slaughter on the beaches. The smell of victory was in the air and Moorman, a perfect barometer of his country's mood as usual, pontificated in his most obnoxious vein.

"On the whole, I think the Foreign Office did the right thing with Canaris. I still suspect the little queer of trying to split the alliance," he said. Berthe gritted her teeth and said nothing, while Jonathan halfheartedly disagreed with him.

A horn beeped outside and they descended to find the Marquesa waiting for them in her Hispano-Suiza. It was a beautiful day, redolent with thick, warm May sunshine. Las Ventas, Madrid's *plaza de toros*, was jammed with cheerful Spaniards, swigging wine, munching bread, calling to friends and relations. The Marquesa's seats were in a box only a few feet away from one reserved for General Franco. A few minutes before the first bull, the Caudillo himself appeared. The crowd cheered somewhat halfheartedly, Berthe thought, when he rose to wave to them.

"A bullfight is the one place in Spain where politics is irrelevant," the Marquesa explained.

"I still don't understand why you insisted I come," Berthe said. "You know I hate this so-called sport."

"A beautiful woman has a responsibility to those who love her," the Marquesa said. "Especially when the love is as pure and disinterested as this boy's. Ordonez may well die out there today. Many *novilleros* die on the day they attempt to become matadors. They feel compelled to dare too much."

The corrida began with the usual magnificent procession, led by two senior matadors and Ordonez in their brocaded coats, their elaborate parade capes slung over their shoulders. They were followed by the *bandilleros* and the picadors—the traditional members of the *cuadrilla* (crew). The first two bulls were dispatched by the senior matadors with calm, almost casual efficiency. Finally it was Ordonez's turn—the man the crowd had come to see, hoping he would surpass his uncle and brothers and cousins. As the body of the second bull was dragged from the ring, the arena underwent a vast stirring. People stood up and milled in the aisles.

Behind them, a soft voice said: "May an old admirer pay his respects to the Marquesa de Montoya?" It was the Caudillo, flanked by two large, nervous bodyguards. Close up there was a startling solidity to the man. His utterly plain but impeccably neat brown uniform seemed sculpted onto his bulky body.

He entered the box and kissed the Marquesa's hand. He paid Berthe a similar compliment when the Marquesa introduced her and shook hands briefly with Jonathan Talbot and Bernado Moorman. "Do your spies tell you unconditional victory is near, Captain Moorman?" Franco said, in a conversational tone.

"Hopes are rising, Caudillo."

"You're a fool," Franco said. "You and your whole country are fools. You had the opportunity to disarm Germany and you threw it away when you turned your back on Canaris. You'll pay for that in blood, Moorman. The Germans aren't going to collapse the moment you land your army in France. They'll fight you on the Seine, in the Ardennes, on the Rhine. They'll fight with the desperation of the cornered man. The stupidity of this unconditional surrender demand appalls me. It will leave Europe in ruins, prey to a century of Bolshevism. A new dark age."

A woman tried to press past the bodyguards to present the Caudillo with a wreath of flowers. "For my sons. For my lost sons!" she cried.

Franco gestured to the bodyguards. They let the woman into the box to present the wreath. She fell on her knees before the General and kissed his hand. "No, no, you mustn't," he said. The bodyguards led her gently back to the aisle.

Franco handed the flowers to the Marquesa. He was still absorbed in his argument. "As for the Americans, their behavior is totally incomprehensible to me. British hatred of Germany is understandable. Rather like Spain's hatred of Bolshevism. It's natural to hate an enemy who has caused you great pain. But the United States has not suffered much at Germany's hands."

"I'm afraid President Roosevelt hates the Germans just as much you hate the Russians, General," Jonathan said.

"Let me tell you something you both might want to pass up the line," Franco said. "In 1940, when France was prostrate and England tottering, Hitler came to the Spanish border at Hendaye. I went to see him with my heart in my throat. I expected an immediate demand to permit his panzers to assault Gibraltar, his submarines to operate from our ports. An invitation, in short, to join the Axis powers. I thought Spain was in no position to refuse it."

The Caudillo looked out at the bullring. Young Ordonez was beginning the *alternativa*, the ceremony of elevation. Accompanied by the senior matador, he was walking around the arena, accepting polite applause from the crowd.

"Canaris came with Hitler," Franco continued. "He visited me the night before the conference and advised me to refuse everything. To make outrageous demands in return for our cooperation, demands that Hitler could never meet—such as the absorption of French

Morocco, a million tons of wheat a year, oil for our civilian and military needs. He assured me Hitler would retreat rather than overrun Spain by force. The Führer was superstitiously determined to avoid Napoleon's mistakes."

In the arena, the rite was in progress. The senior matador bowed to the box where he thought the Caudillo was watching. He realized his mistake and bowed to the Marquesa's box. Franco acknowledged him with a wave. The matador advanced to the center of the arena, where he gave Ordonez his muleta, the red flannel cloth, smaller than a cape, and his sword. As the crowd applauded, the matador embraced him and Ordonez held aloft his montera, the bullfighter's soft black cap, whirled it in a slow circle and left it in the center of the arena, as a sign that he was dedicating his first bull to the people of Madrid. The senior matador escorted him to the barrier, just below their box, to await the bull.

"Where would the British Empire be now, Captain Moorman— even with America on her side—if I had permitted Hitler to take Gibraltar?" Franco said, his eyes on Ordonez. "Ask your superiors in the Foreign Office that question—and then ask them how they can disregard Canaris. Ask the same question of your State Department, Mr. Talbot."

Moorman's lips worked spasmodically, but if he said anything, it was swallowed by the roar of the crowd as the bull rocketed from the pen. Ordonez calmly emerged from the barrier and advanced to the center of the arena to challenge him. The Caudillo kissed the Marquesa's hand again and returned to his box, leaving Talbot and Moorman with dazed expressions on their faces.

"Do you recognize that immense creature, Jonathan?" the Marquesa said. "It's a younger brother of the bull that almost killed you."

He was as huge and ferocious as his crooked horned sibling. He had the same white patch on his chest that so strangely resembled a human heart—or an outline map of Germany. As the bull made his first charge, Ordonez caped him beautifully. His feet were planted firmly, only the cloth moved. "Six hundred and seventy-five kilos," the Marquesa said. "Over fourteen hundred pounds."

Again and again, Ordonez brought the bull by him in a series of passes known as veronicas. Sometimes the flowing union of beast and cape and man seemed to take place in slow motion. With the final corner of the cloth Ordonez turned the bull so smoothly, the creature seemed completely under his control.

After a half-dozen veronicas, Ordonez and his subalterns were satisfied that the bull was charging the cape well and had no murderous eccentricities. The trumpets blared and two picadors cantered into the ring on their padded horses. They waved their long steel-tipped lances at the bull and he wheeled on these new much more appealing targets. He charged the first picador so ferociously, he got under his lance and sent horse and rider flying. The terrified horse bolted and the picador ran for his life while the crowd hooted delightedly and Ordonez rescued his assistant with a *quite*, a wave of the cape, that drew the bull into a pass at the matador.

After another veronica, the second picador rode to the attack, ready for the worst now. He cantered sideways as the bull rushed and sank his lance into the hump.

"This is called pegging him," the Marquesa said. "They have to do to it several times to weaken him."

Blood streamed down the bull's flanks. Berthe turned her head away. Why was the Marquesa inflicting this on her? Linking it with Franco's visit, which Berthe was sure was not by chance. What was her enigmatic Spanish mother trying to tell her?

After two more encounters with the picador, the bull's great horns were hanging heavily. Ordonez lured him into a tauntingly slow veronica and then retreated to the side of the arena as the first banderillo advanced with his pointed sticks. "He's placing them *al cuartero*," the Marquesa explained. "Watch how he circles past the horns in a sharper arc than the bull can follow."

In a gesture of seeming recklessness, each of the three bandilleros leaped on tiptoe within inches of the bull's horns and plunged his two sticks into the hump. The crowd gave them a strong ovation. "You don't often see that!" the Marquesa said. "They're all placed perfectly, far back on the *morillo*, centered and very close together."

The Marquesa ordered Berthe to watch closely now. "The bull has taken heart from the bandilleros. They're only minor wounds and he thinks he almost got each of the bandilleros. He's sure that he'll get the matador this time. It's so beautiful—and so sad. To capture the inner meaning of the corrida you must give your heart to the bull."

Ordonez was striding across the arena toward their box. Directly in front of it, he raised his montera to Berthe, offering her his *brindis*, his toast to the death of the bull.

"Stand up and bow!" the Marquesa ordered. Berthe obeyed, feeling more and more trapped in a ritual she did not like or understand. Ordonez returned her bow and wheeled to begin the faena, the climax of the contest. With his muleta stretched over his sword, he tested the bull with a series of passes, ending with a *pase por alto*, whipping the cape so high the bull reared after it, both forefeet off the ground.

"Now the right-hand passes begin," the Marquesa said. "They're both doing beautifully!"

It took Berthe a moment to realize she meant Ordonez and the bull. Why should she give her heart to this poor doomed beast? He was incredibly, blindly brave and he proved it with his ferocious attacks on the muleta. Ordonez led the bull through a series of breathtaking passes, beginning with the bull's head so low the horns were almost scraping the ground and ending with the *pase de pecho*, in which the horn brushed Ordonez's chest.

The crowd went wild. This was the Ordonez tradition. They flung seat cushions, handkerchiefs, even hats and shoes into the arena. In the middle of the oval, Ordonez shifted the muleta to his left hand and began another series of passes, traditionally more dangerous, called naturals, in which he held the sword behind his back and the drooping cloth brought the bull to within a fraction of an inch of his body again and again. Each drew thunderous olés from the crowd.

Tail switching, blood oozing, the bull was beaten but still dangerous. He glowered at Ordonez with malevolent eyes and pawed the sandy earth.

"Isn't he magnificent? The way he faces death unafraid," the Marquesa said.

Again, she was talking about the bull. Suddenly Berthe understood what the Marquesa was telling her. The bull was Germany. Bleeding from a dozen wounds, exhausted from defiantly slashing at every foe, he waited for the matador's final thrust, still hoping to inflict a deadly wound.

Sword raised to chest level, Ordonez measured his adversary. The bull lunged, the matador flicked the muleta to the left, drawing the horn just far enough from his body to escape death while he plunged the sword to the hilt in the precise spot where it avoided bone and muscle and penetrated the bull's chest cavity.

Ordonez released the sword and stepped away from the bull. The animal stood there motionless, not even his tail moving, blood gushing from his mouth and nose. But he refused to die. "He'll have to use the *descabello*," the Marquesa said.

A murmur of protest swept around them. It had been a perfect bullfight. This final thrust with a short sword, which was extremely difficult, might go wrong. Berthe could feel the silent crowd urging Ordonez to let the bull bleed to death rather than risk his—and their—duende. But Berthe wanted him to end it. Her heart was with the bull. Was it simple obedience to the Marquesa? No, it was genuine admiration for the bull's brute bravery—the same thing she secretly admired in defiant, desperate Germany.

Ordonez was back with the descabello. He wafted the muleta under the bull's drooping nostrils and plunged the short sword into the precise spot at the back of the skull that brought instantaneous death. For another moment the bull stood there, defying gravity. Ordonez flicked his muleta to the left one more time and the bull toppled in that direction to lie in the sand, bloody tongue protruding.

Germany, Berthe thought. My beloved Germany. This is how you are going to die. Your Spanish mother is rehearsing your sorrow. She is showing you with terrible clarity the future of the Path. She is telling you to practice grief, not to flinch from it.

"What a wonderful bull!" the Marquesa said. "You'll have to wait ten years to see a corrida like that again."

The crowd was showering Ordonez with flowers, shawls, wine bags. Olés resounded into the blue sky. He was achieving his dream. For fifteen minutes here, for another quarter of an hour ten years from now in Seville or Malaga or Barcelona, he would blend his country's fascination with courage and death into his nerves and muscles and will and in the presence of a perfect bull he would become Spain.

A terrible wish grew in Berthe's soul. She wanted to do the same thing. She wanted to become Germany. Was that the destiny awaiting her on the Path?

Back at the Marquesa's palace, Rafael Sanchez paced the entrance hall. He did not waste any time getting to the point. "I presume you spoke with the Caudillo," he said.

"He was explicit," the Marquesa said.

"I trust you will communicate his sentiments to your governments?"

"Explicitly," Moorman said, with a sour grimace. "But I don't think there's any hope of changing anyone's mind now."

"Nevertheless, Admiral Canaris wishes to meet with you and Mr. Talbot tomorrow at Hendaye."

Moorman shook his head. "The Foreign Office has directed us to break off all contacts with the Schwarze Kapelle."

"Bernado," the Marquesa said. "Since when have you ever obeyed the Foreign Office?"

"This may be the first time," Moorman admitted. "But I happen to think the prohibition has merit. I still don't trust Canaris. I don't care what he did for General Franco. The only thing he really loves in this world is Germany and whatever the game he's playing now—that's at the heart of it."

"Jonathan, you must go!" Berthe said.

"I'll go," he said. "But I agree with Moorman. It won't do any good."

"He wishes you to come too, Frau von Hoffmann," Rafael Sanchez said. "May I urge you not to let your hopes rise too high?" His normal solemnity verged into mournful concern as he said this. Had the Marquesa told him about her travails?

Before she could thank him, Ordonez arrived with a retinue of followers. Bowing before his Madonna, he presented Berthe with the bull's ear. She thanked him gravely and allowed him to kiss her hand. "You have won a place of immortal honor in my life," she said, while the Marquesa beamed approval.

This time the new matador knelt as he kissed her hand. For some bizarre reason Berthe liked it. Returning from the arena in the car Moorman had discoursed in his cynical way about what a racket bullfighting was. The matadors were regularly cheated of their fees by scheming promoters, they had to pay off venal newspaper critics, the bulls most of them fought were preselected for timidity and small size. Yet here was this nineteen-year-old, creating a life of honor and adoration in her name.

The next morning, the Marquesa's Hispano-Suiza was at Berthe's apartment to take them to Hendaye. The Marquesa was in the back seat "for the ride," she claimed. Rafael Sanchez rode beside the chauffeur. They drove through a landscape abloom with spring wild-flowers. Entire meadows were blood red with poppies, others cerulean with sun-spangled bluebells.

In the little border town of Hendaye, Rafael Sanchez hurried into the Hotel Splendide, which was anything but splendid, and dis-covered a Mr. Candaules was awaiting them in his room. "An inter-esting name," Rafael said, as they went up in the creaking elevator. "Candaules was king of ancient Lydia. He exposed his wife to a rival, Gyges, hoping to buy him off. Instead, Gyges combined forces with the outraged wife and put Candaules to death."

"Germany is the Admiral's wife," Berthe said. "He's never loved anything or anyone else. It's his way of telling us what he's risking."

In his small room, with tired wallpaper drooping from the walls, Canaris looked weary and harassed. "Captain Moorman could not come?" he asked.

"His government forbade him," Rafael Sanchez said.

"A pity, " Canaris said. "I have very important news to impart. Possibly decisive. General Rommel has joined our ranks."

Canaris did not need to tell them the creator of the Afrika Korps was the most popular general in the German Army. "He's in com-mand of the Army in France. A single encouraging signal from Lon-don or Washington is all he requires to order his troops to lay down their guns and open the coast to an unopposed landing of the Anglo-American Army."

"I'll communicate this to General Eisenhower and my superiors in Washington as soon as possible," Jonathan said.

"Frau von Hoffmann reported the failure of your meeting with Roosevelt, Commander," Canaris said. "Could you tell me about it in more detail?"

Jonathan flushed, floundered, but eventually revealed the awful depth of Roosevelt's hatred of Germany. Canaris was staggered beyond words. He could not reply to Jonathan. He spoke instead to Rafael Sanchez. "How strange history is. It bestows immense gifts on a man—and then adds a defect which threatens the whole purpose and meaning of them."

Berthe wondered if he was thinking of Hitler as well as Roo-sevelt. Or was he back in the mists of history, thinking of their *stupor mundi*, the Emperor Frederick II? It did not matter. The Path was growing clearer and clearer to her unwilling eyes.

From a briefcase Canaris drew a thick bundle of documents and handed them to Jonathan. "My last peace offering," he said. "At the very least it will shorten the war."

Jonathan's eyes widened as he glanced at the papers. They were unquestionably important. "I wish I could be more hopeful, Admiral," he said.

"I have always valued candor," Canaris said.

"Will the others go ahead with the Valkyrie plan?" Berthe asked.

"Colonel von Stauffenberg has taken personal charge of the operation. I must confess I fear the worst. Hitler has a charmed life. If they fail—it will truly be *finis Germaniae*. The Nazis will wipe us out to the last man."

"The Marquesa de Montoya is waiting in her car," Rafael Sanchez said. "She wondered if she might say a few words to you of a personal nature."

"It will be a pleasure to renew her acquaintance."

Canaris descended in the creaking elevator with them and they waited in the Hotel Splendide's moldy lobby while he spoke with the Marquesa in the car. Jonathan fingered the documents in his lap.

"This is the order of battle for the German Army in France," he said to Rafael Sanchez. "Would you call the Madrid airport and reserve a seat for me on the first available plane to London?"

Canaris returned while Sanchez was on the telephone. "An amazing woman," he said. "If a man married purely from predilection, I would have proposed twenty-five years ago."

Sanchez returned to tell Jonathan he had gotten him on a six p.m. flight from Barcelona, only a short drive from Hendaye. When they reached the airport the plane was on the runway, its propellers whirling. Jonathan kissed Berthe and said: "I'll see you in Madrid."

She shook her head. "I'm going back to Berlin. I can't stay here in safety while the others are risking so much."

"Berthe! You heard what Canaris said. If it doesn't work—"

His face was full of anxious pain and possessive anger. She felt love renew itself in her mind and body. Jonathan whirled to the Marquesa. "Don't let her do it!"

"How can I stop her?" the Marquesa said.

"You could if you wanted to!" Jonathan snarled.

An airport official was waving frantically to them. The plane's motors thundered. A stewardess stood impatiently in the open door in the center of the fuselage. "Then I'll see you in Berlin!" Jonathan said.

He raced for the plane. The stewardess lowered a ladder. He scrambled up, the door closed and the plane roared down the runway. They watched until it became a speck in the sky.

"Don't let him come," Berthe said. "Germans—and Germans alone—must do this thing."

"Don't worry about it. His government won't let him go," Rafael Sanchez said with bitter contempt.

"He'll come anyway. But by the time he gets there it will be over, one way or the other," Berthe said.

"I think Canaris is right. It would be better not to kill Hitler," the Marquesa said.

"No," Berthe said. "Germany's honor requires another attempt."

"Pundonor. How Spanish you've become," the Marquesa said.

44

DEATH MAKES A SELECTION

In London, Jonathan Talbot's delivery of Canaris's final gift made him a momentary hero. Knowing an enemy's order of battle was as close as a general can come to being able to read the opposing commander's mind. Talbot's fame was brief because everyone from Supreme Commander Eisenhower to OSS officers like Bill Casey were totally absorbed in the stupendous preparations for D-Day.

Eisenhower, probably the world's busiest human being at that point, somehow found time to call Talbot to his headquarters to thank him. Without much hope, Talbot asked Ike if he thought Rommel's offer might change Roosevelt's mind about unconditional surrender. The Supreme Commander curtly shook his head. "It's been made very clear to me that the President refuses to negotiate with *any* German," he said.

Talbot asked him for orders to return to Berlin to participate in the plot to depose Hitler. Eisenhower shook his head again, his luminous intelligence fusing with his instinct for command. "I don't think there should be any Americans connected to that thing," he said. "It's got to be something the Germans do on their own. Besides, I want your input on my proclamation to the German Army. That's still on the agenda."

Like everything else in the U.S. Army (and U.S. Navy) the proclamation was written by a committee. Talbot handed in suggestions that disappeared into the labyrinth of supreme headquarters. Bill Casey, a passionate supporter of the idea, tried to monitor its progress without much success. Talbot's inside contacts at headquarters were virtually nil. His friend, General Wedemeyer, had left London to take command of American forces in China several months ago.

Again and again frustration swelled in Talbot's chest when he thought of the million British and American young men who were going to assault Hitler's fortress in a week or two. The German Army's order of battle revealed that the Wehrmacht had at least forty divisions, including a half-dozen panzer divisions, in France. Casey and other intelligence gurus thought a lot of them were understrength but that still left close to a half-million soldiers ready to throw the invasion back into the sea. "It's going to be bloody," Casey said. He bemoaned the OSS's lack of influence with Roosevelt—and almost everyone else in the military power structure.

One night, as Talbot emerged from OSS headquarters, a hand seized his arm. Jack Richman growled: "I'm taking you into custody. I know a spook when I see one."

They headed for the Cross and Crown, a favorite American pub off Piccadilly. Jack had come up to London from Cornwall, where he had been schmoozing with the American Fourth Division, which was slated to land on a piece of the French coast designated as Utah Beach. He had gotten to know Theodore Roosevelt, Jr., the late president's son, one of the division's brigadier generals.

"He reminds me of you," Jack said. "He takes this patriotism bullshit seriously. The guy's fifty-six years old. He got shot up twice in the last war and walks with a cane. But he's going to be one step ahead of everybody else when we hit the beach."

"I heard you were operating on a cane until quite recently," Talbot said. "Has it ever occurred to you that you might have used up your luck?"

"Impossible," Jack said. "My Irish mother lined my diaper with shamrocks."

"Sounds like a lot of shit to me," Talbot said.

He had spent enough midnight hours arguing with Jack to know that this cynicism was part of his Chicago style. As the night went on, they got down to more serious conversation. "Three strikes are supposed to be out in the first wave game," Jack said. "I'm the only reporter still on his feet from the first wavers in the Mediterranean shows. The rest are either dead, in the hospital or on the booze. In case, here's some letters I'd like you to deliver."

One was addressed to his father and mother, a second to Annie and a third to an English woman named Daphne Soames. He talked about his father more frankly than Talbot had ever heard him. "I know you don't approve of him," he said. "He's a rough diamond. But you've got to remember where he started—in one of the worst slums in Chicago—without a cent in his pocket. His first job was rushing the growler—getting beer—for a local brothel. From there he graduated to running slips for the local numbers boss. For a guy with that background, he's stayed reasonably honest. He's a pretty good congressman."

"I got to know him a lot better last month," Talbot said. He told him what the Congressman—and Annie—had done to get him into the White House. He managed to tell the story without the slightest indignation. Annie would have been proud of him.

Somberly, Jack admitted that Moltke, Canaris and their friends sounded like honorable men. "Don't hold it against FDR, Zeke. He's still a great president. He's giving it his best shot. He's putting his life on the line with the rest of us—"

"He's as sick as he looks?"

"Worse. Admiral Leahy—his chief of staff—told me, his heart is barely functioning and his blood pressure is off the chart. It's a miracle he's still alive."

Talbot remembered the hatred choking the President's voice—and that strangled cry: *Do you think I don't bleed when men die?* Maybe—a bizarre thought—Roosevelt's refusal to negotiate with the Germans was a death sentence for his exhausted body. A lot of men would be dying on French beaches very soon.

Talbot looked around him at the cheerful Americans in Army and Navy uniforms. They were sloshing down beer and Scotch, singing the hit songs of the year to their British girlfriends—"Green Eyes," "I'd Like to Get You on a Slow Boat to China" and "Mairzy Doats" a nonsense number that was everyone's favorite. Ignoring death, the hooded figure in the corner, as he made his selections.

"When one of these shows explodes all around you, it makes you pretty humble," Jack said. "You realize you're involved with something a thousand times bigger than you are. Your life is completely in God's hands."

"I can't believe it. The original skeptic's been converted?" Talbot said.

"Seeing what these kids do for each other under fire—it's the closest thing to holiness I'll ever encounter, Zeke. When you realize they're dying for this idea called America—it changes a lot of things inside your head. Suddenly you're beyond politics—into the goddamn meaning of life."

"What is it? Tell me in words of one syllable."

"The best thing I've heard is from a West Pointer I met—let's just call him Charlie. He rates all his Army assignments the same way—whether they give him a chance to make a contribution. After North Africa, he was offered a nice safe staff job in Washington. Instead he waded ashore in Sicily and Salerno—because he thought he could make a bigger contribution there."

"I'm going to remember that one," Talbot said.

Next came a question that had obviously been on Jack's mind for a long time. "What the hell's wrong between you and Annie?"

Talbot told him about the eruption in Norfolk, taking most of the blame. "I was a bastard," he said. But he could not resist adding a reproach. "Things were going sour long before that. She even thought I'd leaked Rainbow Five."

"Zeke," Jack said, pointing to his jaw. "You've got my permission to hit me once after you hear what I'm about to tell you."

Jack ordered another round and chugalugged it. "I leaked Rainbow Five."

"You son of a bitch! Why?"

"Orders from the White House. Roosevelt knew the Japs were going to start a war somewhere. He wanted to make sure Hitler joined them so we could finish him off first. The leak was a kind of 'up yours, Adolf.' A declaration that we were coming after him as soon as possible. Just the sort of thing that would goad an egomaniac like Hitler into declaring war on us."

Talbot was not angry. It was much too late for anger. He saw why Jack had headed for the war zone and insisted on joining the first wave in every invasion. Far more literally than FDR, he was putting his life on the line to justify that deception.

"My biggest regret is what it did to you and Annie, Zeke," Jack said. "I couldn't say anything then. You were so worked up you'd have turned in your old buddy."

He ordered another drink. "Annie took it pretty hard. But I think she still loves you. This guy she's seeing is one of those New York intellectuals—all brains and no balls. Maybe that's why she picked him out. Women do the damnedest things to tell you what they're thinking. It's like reading code."

Talbot considered telling Jack about Berthe and decided against it. When the pub closed they wobbled drunkenly through London's empty blacked-out streets to Talbot's billet in a third-rate hotel, reminiscing about Annapolis days. As Jack recalled some of their late-night antics in Bancroft Hall, the huge midshipmen's dormitory, Talbot realized why his ex-roommate and brother-in-law had come up to London. He expected to die on Utah Beach and he was looking back over his life, savoring youth and friendship and sonship and brotherhood one last time.

Finally they swayed at the entrance of Talbot's hotel. "It's been a good life, Zeke. No matter what the hell happens the day after tomorrow."

He laughed drunkenly and put his finger to his lips. "That's a secret. A very big secret."

He gave Talbot a left hook that paralyzed his shoulder. "You've been one of the best parts of it, Zeke. Getting to meet a real hundred-percent American. We should have put it in headlines. Jewish-Irishman from Chicago meets American from Connecticut—and likes him! That's the most incredible part of it."

"American from Connecticut meets Jewish-Irishman from Chicago—and discovers he's really an American! That's even more incredible."

Jack threw his arms around him for a fierce embrace. "So long, Zeke. Straighten out that thing with Annie if you can. She's a piece of my heart. I wish she was still a piece of yours."

The next day, as Talbot sat in his cubicle at OSS headquarters with yet another draft of Eisenhower's proclamation in front of him, Bill Casey wandered in with gloom all over his long sharp-featured Irish face. The date on Talbot's desk calendar was June 5. "You can stop working on that thing," he said. "It's kaput."

"What? How—why?" Talbot said.

"My guy at Supreme Headquarters says Churchill visited Ike yesterday and tore his ass off about it. He called it silly, stupid, he claimed it made us look as if we were afraid of the Germans and were trying to talk them out of fighting."

"That's absolute bullshit!" Talbot said.

"I suspect Churchill knows it too. The inside dope is, Winnie was doing a favor for FDR. He never intended to let Ike issue this thing in the first place. But he waited until the perfect moment—and got the PM to wield the knife."

Talbot stared at the earnest words assuring German soldiers America and Great Britain would not destroy their nation if they abandoned Hitler and Nazism. With a groan he crumpled the proclamation into a ball and implored Casey to insert him into Germany as soon as possible with or without Ike's permission.

Casey glumly shook his head. "Everything's committed to France," he said.

"Tonight's the night?" Talbot asked. Casey nodded.

For the next twenty-four hours, Talbot, Casey and everyone else at OSS and at every other American headquarters in London existed on coffee and sleep snatched in chairs and on desktops as they listened to and read the often horrendous reports pouring in from D-Day's beaches. Compared to Omaha Beach, where nothing went right, men drowned by the hundreds and tanks sank by the dozen, Utah Beach seemed relatively easy. Everyone talked about how Theodore Roosevelt, Jr., had stood in the center of the beach, directing traffic, while shrapnel and bullets whizzed around him. Only Talbot heard the story with a sinking heart. There was no mention of "Behind The Headlines" as its source.

The next day, Talbot received a phone call from a 1928 classmate who was in charge of naval communications at Supreme Headquarters. "Jack Richman gave me your number," he said. "I think he had a feeling he was running out of luck. A machine gun got him ten seconds after he hit the beach."

The following day, exhaustion mingling with depression in his mind and body, Talbot stood on a quay in Plymouth's bomb-battered harbor, watching a gray LST rumble toward the dock with the first dead of the invasion in its steel belly. The clumsy, squarish boat seemed perfectly suited for a hearse.

On the quay, Talbot walked along the rows of bodies, reading the name tags. There were at least two hundred of them, tied into canvas bags. As he found Jack at the end of the third row, a squadron of fighter bombers roared over the harbor en route to attack the Germans in France. He untied the bag and pondered Jack's face. There was no blood, no visible wound. He looked peaceful, even contented—as if he had proved something to himself. What was it? He really was an American? Or a real Annapolis man? Those years as a reporter, pursuing hot stories and the great American dollar, could not compare to this moment of authenticity?

That night, back in London, Talbot mailed Jack's letters to Annie with a letter of his own. He told her how he had escorted Jack's body to a nearby graveyard, where he was temporarily buried.

As I stood beside Jack's grave, I wondered if I was to blame, if those portentous midnight sermons about the meaning of America I preached to him at Annapolis had anything to do with his readiness to tackle one of the most dangerous jobs in the war. I could almost hear him saying: "Zeke, you're full of it as usual." I realized he never needed me to tell him how to love his country. It was as natural to him as breathing—like his courage.

On our last night in London together, Jack and I talked about you and our breakup. I made him a promise that I'd do my best to see if we could somehow repair the damage, when and if this war ever ends—and if I survive it. In a few weeks I hope to go back to Germany to try to do what I can to help the resistance movement overthrow Hitler. I have no idea what I can contribute. But I feel compelled to do it in Jack's name—and in the name of Berthe von Hoffmann, who's risking her life there right now. Before I go I want to affirm the reality of the love I felt for you for almost all the years of our marriage. It is one of the things I treasure most and no matter what happens to me in Germany or between us afterward if I survive, I want you to know how I feel now.

Please give your mother and father my deepest sympathy.

Zeke

The next day, Talbot went to see Bill Casey and begged him to write a set of orders sending him back to Germany as soon as possible to reestablish contact with the Schwarze Kapelle. Casey clearly yearned to say yes, so the OSS could claim they ended the war without any help from the Army, Navy or Air Force. But he turned him down.

"What the hell can you do besides get yourself killed?" he said. "I agree with Ike. We should stay out of the thing until when and if the Germans pull it off. If they manage it, you'll be on a plane before you can say parachute."

"You don't sound optimistic about their chances."

"Let's put it this way," Casey said. "If they were a horse I wouldn't bet anything on them I couldn't afford to lose."

45

THE LOST WAR

U-BOAT MEN! THE LONG-AWAITED ENEMY INVASION OF
FRANCE HAS BEGUN. YOU ARE HEREBY ORDERED TO
ATTACK THE ENEMY FLEET REGARDLESS OF LOSSES.
THIS IS THE GREAT HOUR OF TESTING FOR THE REICH.
THE UBOOTWAFFE MUST NOT FAIL TO PLAY ITS PART.
EVERY ENEMY VESSEL TAKING PART IN THE LANDING,
EVEN IF IT ONLY CARRIES HALF A HUNDRED SOLDIERS
OR A TANK, IS A TARGET WHICH DEMANDS THE FULL MIS-
SION OF THE U-BOAT. IT IS TO BE ATTACKED EVEN IF THIS
CARRIES THE RISK OF THE LOSS OF ONE'S OWN BOAT.

In the communications room at naval headquarters in Berlin,
Fregattenkapitan Ernst von Hoffmann broadcast this ridiculous
order to the submarine fleet. He knew it made no sense. There was
nothing the Ubootwaffe could do to stop the immense armada that
was swarming off the coast of Normandy. The troop transports were
protected by thousands of planes, hundreds of destroyers and light
patrol boats. Grossadmiral Dönitz was sending U-boat crews to certain death. Ernst could only hope that most of the commanders had
the sense to ignore the order.

How could he think such thoughts? How could nine months on
the Grossadmiral's staff, nine months at the heart of the Reich's war

effort, give birth to such defeatism? Once more Ernst exhorted himself to hardness, resolution, hope. He was rising steadily in Dönitz's
esteem; he had become his favorite escort for his periodic trips to the
Wolfschanze to report to the Führer.

Wolfgang Griff rushed into the communication room, his lips
twitching, his eyes bloodshot. He too had been up all night. "They
have a hundred thousand men ashore. The Wehrmacht's doing nothing. I smell treachery!"

Ernst shrugged. Having a father high in the Gestapo created a
paranoid fear of traitors in Griff's feverish imagination. Ernst
declined to believe that German Army officers would ever plot
against the Führer. They had taken an oath of loyalty to him, like the
rest of the Reich's soldiers and sailors and airmen.

The less he saw of Griff the better. He reminded Ernst of
Spain—and Berthe. He had told him Berthe was back in Berlin.
She—and Griff—had been expelled from Madrid along with approximately half the swollen staff of the German embassy as part of General Franco's shift toward pro–Anglo-Saxon neutrality. Ernst had
expected more pleas to see the children but he had not heard a word
from her. Griff said she was working for Walter Schellenberg, the
new director of the combined Abwehr-Sicherheitdienst, living alone
in a basement flat in Charlottenberg, only a few blocks from naval
headquarters.

Thinking of her had stirred fantasies of a midnight visit. Not for
sex but to find out if she was still a critic of the Führer—now that the
British and Americans had announced plans to enslave Germany
after they surrendered unconditionally. He had never made the visit.
He was still afraid she would somehow talk him down—and he
would lose his temper and hit her again.

Ernst still found it hard to believe he had struck her. Sometimes,
when he awoke at dawn, he relived the moment and took her in his
arms and kissed her bruised, beautiful face and begged her forgiveness. Fully awake, he would reproach himself. Love turned a man to
mush.

"We have to announce a victory for the Kriegsmarine, Herr Fregattenkapitan," Griff said. "Are there battleships in this invasion
fleet?"

"Undoubtedly."

"We'll report the destruction of two battleships and a cruiser.

That's well within the scope of a successful U-boat attack, wouldn't you say?"

"Of course."

It was nauseating to think the Ubootwaffe had been reduced to telling such blatant lies. Ernst trudged back to his small office, where he kept track of the figures on the new U-boat construction the Grossadmiral had persuaded the Führer to order—and the progress being made on new models and devices to resume the offensive in the Atlantic. They now had twice as many boats as they sent to sea in 1942—but the new weapons to enable them to survive the enemy's radar and omnipresent air power still had not materialized.

So far the only encouraging device was the schnorkel, named for its Dutch inventor. It breathed air through a tube at the tip of the periscope, enabling the U-boat to remain underwater indefinitely running on its diesels. But it was a far from perfect solution. Whenever a wave broke over the schnorkel, the diesels devoured all the air in the submerged boat, threatening the crew with asphyxiation. When the schnorkel reemerged from the wave, the abrupt shift in pressure all but ruptured a crew's eardrums.

Headquarters was soon swarming with staff officers routed from their beds by the emergency. Maybe this was a good time to visit Berthe. No one would miss him for a while. Ernst strolled through the predawn darkness to the address Griff had given him. Several houses on the street had been reduced to rubble. It was remarkable, the way bombs blew up a single house, leaving those on either side of it relatively intact.

Berthe's flat had an outside door. As he knocked, he heard a typewriter clicking. "Who is it?" she asked.

She flung open the door at the sound of his voice. "What do you want?" she said. She was extraordinarily alarmed—and extraordinarily attractive in a blue nightrobe, with large buttons down the front. Her blond hair was loose, streaming, a sight that had always aroused him.

"Can't a man visit his ex-wife on impulse?"

"I'm terribly busy," she said.

"At six in the morning?" he said. "Surely you can make me a cup of coffee. I want to talk about the children."

The word made her waver.

"All right. If you'll wait a moment." She disappeared down a short hall. He sauntered after her. He was damned if he was going to be left standing in the street like a messenger. In the doorway to a combination study and sitting room, Berthe was frantically collecting papers she had spread around the desk, on chairs, on the floor. "I've never known you to be such a hausfrau," he said.

She whirled, clutching the papers to her breasts. Her loose hair gave her a slightly berserk appearance. For some reason, she seemed afraid of him. "What do you *want*?" she said.

"I really have no idea. I just felt like seeing you."

"The court made it very clear that we're no longer man and wife. Which means you have no such privilege. Please go!"

Ernst leaned against the door jamb and lit a cigarette. "The invasion has succeeded. Are you happy to hear it?"

"I'm a mere woman. What do you care what I think?" she said, stuffing the papers into a desk drawer.

"Why didn't you defect to your American hero? Have you changed your mind about the war?"

"Only to this extent. I can now honestly say to God, a plague on both their houses."

He wanted her. He had never found a woman like her. So beautiful, so subtly defiant. The combination made every surrender a special event, a conquest.

Was that the reason for the extraordinary words that were swirling in his throat? In the flashing second between their realization and their expression, Ernst managed to explain them as seduction. But the moment he spoke them, he knew they were much more serious. "I've changed my mind too, Berthe. It's a hopeless mess. The war is lost."

She drew a deep shuddering breath. "How terrible for you to know that."

"Terrible?"

"After what you've done."

"What have I done?"

"Machine-gunned those helpless men in the water."

The shock of those words was unbelievable. It was as if a British blockbuster had exploded in the street, rupturing the lungs of everyone within several hundred yards. Ernst heard himself shouting words that seemed to tear out pieces of his ruined lungs with every breath.

"That never happened! It's vicious English propaganda! We received a complaint about it from the Red Cross and Grossadmiral Dönitz repudiated it!"

"One of them survived, Ernst. A black man in the lifeboat. Talbot showed me the official report. U-boat six-six-six. The Wolfseeboot."

"English lies!" he shouted in her beautiful face.

Beautiful? It was the ugliest face he had ever seen. This time he was going to smash it for good. But before he could raise his fist, tears streamed down those curving cheeks, the sensuous mouth curled into grief. "They're going to hang you, Ernst. After the war they'll come looking for you. They'll convict you of murder and hang you. When I think of what that will mean to Georg and Greta I almost pray for a German victory."

"English lies!" he roared.

A shoe pounded on the floor. The landlady angrily reminded them it was six a.m. People were trying to sleep.

"English lies," Ernst gasped, struggling for breath. Maybe he should smash her face anyway.

From the dark doorway behind Berthe emerged an incredibly tall Wehrmacht officer. A colonel. He had a patch over one eye and numerous scars on his handsome face. One sleeve of his uniform was empty. Three fingers were missing on his other hand. "Herr Fregattenkapitan," he said. "I think you better go quietly. Otherwise I'll have you arrested."

"Who the hell are you?" Ernst snarled.

"Claus Schenk von Stauffenberg is the name. I can be reached at the headquarters of the Home Army on the Bendlerstrasse if you want to do something ridiculous, like sending me a challenge."

"I learn something new about my wife every day," Ernst said.

"May I remind you, Herr Fregattenkapitan, she's not your wife anymore?" Stauffenberg said.

Berthe said nothing. Her face remained wet with grieving tears.

"Now you know why I'm going to fight to the death," Ernst said and stumbled into the street.

Back at naval headquarters the atmosphere grew more and more frenzied. Dönitz reiterated his attack order to all forces. Four destroyers sortied from Brest and were wiped out almost instantly by a British destroyer flotilla. Motor torpedo boats from Le Havre and other channel ports made equally futile but heroic attacks on the flanks of the Anglo-Saxon armada, sinking one destroyer and a half-dozen smaller craft—but they were soon annihilated by a ferocious sea and air counterattack. Those not sunk in the English Channel were destroyed at their docks by the swarming planes.

Only a few of the U-boats were equipped with schnorkels. That meant most were forced to creep along underwater on batteries, making only 30 or 40 miles a day. The majority were destroyed or crippled by air attacks the moment they surfaced to recharge their batteries. Not until nine days after the invasion did one boat finally get in position for an attack—which sank a troop landing craft. The equivalent of using a cannon to kill a flea.

Only at the end of June did the gloom and embarrassment suffusing headquarters lift a little. One of the radiomen from the communications room rushed into Ernst's office while he was on night watch and flung a transmission on his desk. "Herr Fregattenkapitan. Your old boat, the six-six-six, has done something to redeem the Kriegsmarine's honor."

Ernst snatched up the transmission.

FOUR SHIPS SUNK. COASTAL CONVOY. KURZ.

They had made the Saint the commander of the Wolfseeboot. Ernst was swept by a terrific wish to be in his place, fighting and perhaps dying as a man of honor in defense of the Reich. When Dönitz made his usual six a.m. appearance at headquarters, Ernst showed him the report. "Herr Grossadmiral," he said. "Would you give me permission to go to sea again? I feel my talents are not suited to staff work."

"Out of the question, Hoffmann," Dönitz said, his voice clanging like metal in Ernst's ears. "You've become a vital part of our headquarters team. When you talk to those liars at the shipyards with the Knight's Cross at your throat, they tell you the truth about their production—or lack of it. Your speeches to the new crews have become a glorious part of the Ubootwaffe's tradition."

Soon, Dönitz told Ernst, new weapons would be unleashed on the enemy. The first was a pilotless plane designated the V-1. Each would carry a 1,000-pound bomb into British cities without costing the Reich a man. Next was a rocket that would soar 90 miles high and come down at a speed of 3,500 miles an hour. No amount of antiaircraft or radar weaponry could stop the V-2.

Ernst felt light-headed. The Führer was going to rescue them after all. "Are they in mass production, Herr Grossadmiral?"

"Unfortunately no. Their numbers will be rather limited. But the enemy won't know that. One or both may well persuade them to talk peace."

A few days later, Ernst conferred with Albert Speer, the suave civilian who had replaced Goering as head of the Reich's war production. With him was Admiral Canaris, who as head of economic warfare was responsible for marshaling the needed manpower for the tasks assigned to the industrial machine. Speer reported new U-boat construction was continuing at record levels, thanks to a temporary slowdown in the bombing of Kiel and other shipyards while the Anglo-Saxon air fleet concentrated on the Normandy beachhead.

"Are we making similar progress on the new rocket weapons?" Ernst asked.

Speer shook his head. "As Admiral Canaris here has pointed out more than once, those things make no sense. They take as many man hours to build as a bomber—and they deliver a paltry half ton of bombs."

"While a bomber," Canaris said, "an American or British bomber, at any rate, can deliver ten tons on the Reich. In such a contest there can only be one winner."

At the end of the conference, Canaris asked Ernst for a ride to the airport in his staff car. The Admiral's headquarters was now in Bavaria, outside Munich. "Have you seen your wife since she returned to Berlin?" he asked as they drove down the capital's bomb-blasted streets.

"Once or twice," Ernst said. "I gather she's having an affair with a fellow named Stauffenberg."

The news seemed to shock the Admiral. "I think you misunderstand her relationship to Stauffenberg. Likewise her liaison with the American, Talbot. I regret urging it on her as a duty to the Reich. We got very little from the fellow."

He pinched the bridge of his nose as if he was trying to extinguish a painful thought. "I was hoping you and she might reach a new understanding. I knew your father. I assure you he would have the same reaction to the Führer as your wife. It is the reaction every honorable German must have eventually."

They were at the airport. Ernst was too astonished to speak. Was this man a traitor? Or was he only voicing the disillusionment with the Führer that was spreading everywhere? He was tempted to give him a lecture on the vital importance of sustaining the führer principle. But Fregattenkapitans did not lecture admirals.

Canaris labored toward the terminal, a stooped, enigmatic figure. Ernst decided the Admiral had been trying to heal a wound he thought he had inflicted on him and Berthe in Spain. But all Spain had done was reveal the hollowness of their marriage. He drove back to naval headquarters, struggling with an overwhelming sense of futility.

The next day, the V-1 pilotless planes were flung at British cities. The enemy bellowed hypocrisy about attacking defenseless civilians—a sure sign they were being hurt. The stubby-winged creatures, which Goebbels called Retribution Weapon I, buoyed morale throughout the Reich. Dönitz ordered their achievements broadcast to all the U-boats at sea. New hope of victory enabled naval headquarters to swallow the appalling loss of sixty-six boats fighting the invasion. But Ernst was unable to share the chortles of Griff and other fervid optimists. Not even Dönitz's unbending faith in final victory could erase the memory of Canaris's pessimism. Especially after a 2,000-plane British raid devastated central Berlin.

On the nineteenth of July, Ernst journeyed to Kiel to speak to another group of U-boat school graduates. They all looked so incredibly young! Ten-year-old Georg would be at home in their ranks. He proclaimed the Ubootwaffe's doctrine of relentless attack and assured them that the enemy, distracted by the victory weapons, would present them with tempting targets. Nausea swelled in his stomach as he spoke. For a berserk second he imagined himself shouting: *This is all bullshit. The war is lost!* But he blundered to the end of his speech.

As he left the auditorium, he almost collided with a staggering Chief Kleist. The Wolfseeboot was in Kiel for repairs. Shortly after they sank the four ships in the coastal convoy, they had taken a terrific pounding from an air attack that left them without diesel power. They had crept back on batteries. Kleist dragged him to a bar where Kurz and two other officers were drinking schnapps. They stayed there until two a.m. Toward the end of the evening, a thoroughly drunk Kurz told a little story. When they returned to Lorient from their last Atlantic sortie, every man in the crew had been offered a chance to select a new watch from a chest full of them on the dock.

"I forbade the men to touch them, Herr Fregattenkapitan," Kurz said. "They were all used, all made in Poland. I told the men they were drenched in innocent blood. If a single one of these things came aboard our boat, we would be on our way to our last voyage."

The words seemed to blunder in Ernst's face like bats. "You did exactly the right thing, Herr Kaleu," he mumbled. "I would have done exactly the same thing."

"Herr Fregattenkapitan," Kleist said. "Tell us the truth. Is the war lost?"

Lost? asked a crafty echo in Ernst's head. Who said that? Tell them the war is lost, Ernst, and you know what they'll do? They'll figure out how to survive. If they manage it, they'll be around to testify at your trial. Don't tell them any such thing. Exhort them to attack, strike, sink, like wolves of the sea!

Instead, incomprehensibly, Ernst told them the truth. Saying it to Berthe somehow made it easier to say to these men, his comrades, his crew. "It's lost. Barring a miracle."

"So we must draw our own conclusions," Kurz said in his deep, mournful voice.

The next day Ernst returned to Berlin with an agonizing hangover. He dimly remembered confessing the war was lost. But he managed to doubt he had really said it. He convinced himself it was more a wish than a fact. Why would he be so stupid as to cooperate in preserving witnesses for the prosecution?

He sat in his little office, staring at the meaningless U-boat production figures. The VIIC model was an obsolete weapon, yet they continued to produce it, stick a schnorkel on it and tell men to die in it. Jesus!

"Hoffmann!" It was the Grossadmiral himself in the doorway, looking more agitated than Ernst had ever seen him. "You must come with me immediately. I'm leaving for the Wolfschanze. There's been an attempt on the Führer's life."

Two hours later, they were circling the forest at Rastenburg in Dönitz's private plane. A car driven by a naval staff officer assigned as liaison to the Wolfschanze was waiting for them on the tarmac. They roared along the winding road through the gloomy woods, slowing down only for the checkpoints, while the staff officer gave them a rapid summary of what had happened. Someone had smuggled a

powerful bomb into the Führer's daily staff conference. It had
exploded at 12:45, killing several officers, but miraculously sparing
Hitler.

SS troops and vehicles swarmed in the forest. Planes droned
overhead. In minutes they reached the Wolfschanze's center. A full
company of heavily armed SS guarded the entrance to the concrete
bunker. Nearby was the still-smoking ruins of the timber hut in
which the bomb had exploded. It was the warm weather that had
saved the Führer's life, the staff officer babbled. They had moved the
conference to the hut to escape the stifling bunker. If they had met
in the bunker, the blast would have been contained by the concrete
walls and killed everyone in the room.

In the bunker, the first person they encountered was their old
traveling companion, Reichsführer Heinrich Himmler. His eyes glistened like slivers of ice behind his pince-nez. "I'm happy to see you,
Herr Grossadmiral. Never before has the Führer needed loyal supporters so badly," he said.

"What do you mean? Is there is a widespread revolt?" Dönitz
asked. The idea seemed to flabbergast him.

"How widespread it is hard to say at the moment. But we know
its center—from the man who planted the bomb: Colonel Claus
Schenk von Stauffenberg. The plot originates from the headquarters
of the Home Army on the Bendlerstrasse. I fear we shall find other
members of the Wehrmacht's high command are deeply involved."

The name Stauffenberg seemed to separate Ernst's scalp from
the rest of his throbbing head. He felt as if his brain was exposed to
bolts of electricity. Stauffenberg—the man he had met in Berthe's
apartment at six a.m. a month ago. The reason why she was so agitated by his visit became clear.

The next few hours at the Wolfschanze would have been dreamlike, even without this stunning realization. In about a half-hour, they
were ushered into the Führer's presence—to find him drinking tea
with Mussolini, the deposed dictator of Italy. Hitler struggled to his
feet and grasped Dönitz by both hands like a drowning man seizing a
lifeline. "Grossadmiral," he croaked. "I knew you'd come. I knew you
would not desert me."

"How could you think otherwise, my Führer?" Dönitz said.

"You see, Duce, the loyalty of my Navy?" Hitler said to Mussolini. The back of his left hand was black and blue. The hair on the

back of his head was singed. Wads of cotton stuck out of both ears, emergency treatment for ruptured eardrums.

Mussolini was a shrunken parody of the barrel-chested, jut-jawed man whose picture Ernst had seen in a hundred newspapers. German paratroopers had snatched him from the hands of his no longer loyal subjects and Hitler had made him head of a puppet regime in northern Italy. The ex-Duce hunched slavishly over his teacup and muttered: "No doubt of it. This was a sign from heaven."

"Look at this, Herr Grossadmiral. Look at the uniform I was wearing!" Hitler said. From a nearby table the Führer snatched up his jacket, which had a square hole ripped out of the back. The seat of the trousers was in shreds.

"Providence has protected you, my Führer," Dönitz said.

"Can there be a more definite sign that my mission is destined to end gloriously?" Hitler cried. He seemed to be glaring at Ernst as he said this. Before Ernst could think of an answer, Reichmarshal Goering, Reichsführer Himmler, Foreign Minister von Ribbentrop and General Keitel, the Army chief of staff, entered the room. Each paid elaborate tribute to the Führer's charmed life. He seemed bored with their effusions. No one paid the slightest attention to Mussolini.

With uncharacteristic fury, Grossadmiral Dönitz attacked General Keitel and the entire general staff. How could the Army tolerate such treachery? Goering delightedly joined in sneering at the Army's loyalty—until Dönitz turned on him too, scornfully blaming the Luftwaffe for the failure to stop the invasion of France and the loss of so many U-boats from enemy air attack. The Grossadmiral seemed bent on elevating the Navy to the top of the military hierarchy. While the commanders snarled insults at each other, white-uniformed SS servants served everyone tea.

"Enough!" Hitler's eyes were bulging, his mouth twitching. "Enough! The Reich must be purged of these traitors! I want them tortured until they name every conspirator and then I want them exterminated like vermin—and their families too. Fathers, mothers, brothers, children! We shall act with the ferocity of the Germans of old. We shall invoke the law of Sippenhaft! I demand the most ruthless, the most extensive blood purge in German history."

Sippenhaft. The word filled Ernst's mind with horror. Berthe had explained it once, when they were discussing the old Teutonic sagas.

The tribes believed in the preeminence of blood. When a man proved disloyal, they considered his blood—and the blood of all his relations—tainted. The entire family was marked for extermination. It was unbelievable to hear this primitive custom being invoked by the ruler of modern Germany. Especially when, if Berthe was connected to the conspiracy, it could mean the death of their children.

Foam flecking his lips, Hitler raged on for a full hour. A telephone call from Berlin finally interrupted him. It was from Goebbels, who connected Hitler to the commander of a battalion of Prussian Guards that had sealed off the Bendlerstrasse when they received the Code Valkyrie signal. Colonel von Stauffenberg, General Olbricht and General Beck had told him Hitler was dead and Beck had become Army commander. The moment the officer heard the Führer's voice, he vowed to arrest the conspirators as soon as possible.

Hitler slumped into a chair, utterly spent, and wondered if the German people deserved the sacrifices he had made for them. Dönitz, Goering and the others rushed to assure him of their loyalty—and the devotion of the volk. Finally Dönitz judged it was safe to withdraw. For the next two hours, Ernst helped the Grossadmiral prepare a radio address which he broadcast at eight o'clock.

MEN OF THE NAVY! THE TREACHEROUS ATTEMPT ON THE LIFE OF THE FÜHRER FILLS EACH AND EVERY ONE OF US WITH HOLY WRATH AND BITTER RAGE TOWARD OUR CRIMINAL ENEMIES AND THEIR HIRELINGS. PROVIDENCE SPARED THE GERMAN PEOPLE AND ARMED FORCES THIS INCONCEIVABLE MISFORTUNE. IN THE MIRACULOUS ESCAPE OF OUR FÜHRER WE SEE ADDITIONAL PROOF OF THE RIGHTEOUSNESS OF OUR CAUSE.

The Grossadmiral all but ate the microphone, pouring passion into every word. Ernst listened in hungover agony, wishing it were true. He wanted that foam-flecked madman they called the Führer to somehow still embody the justice of Germany's cause. Didn't justice persist, in spite of terrible crimes committed in its name? He groped for the hardness that had once been his pride, before he was exposed to the Wolfschanze—and Berthe.

Yes, Berthe. For the first time he connected the two causes of his disillusion. But Berthe had gone beyond destroying his faith in Germany's war. She was threatening the lives of their children—and his own life. In the whirlwind of the Führer's hysterical Sippenhaft, even an ex-husband of a traitor would not be safe. Maybe it was time to show her just how hard he could be. Maybe it was time to kill her.

46

LABYRINTHINE WAYS

GERMAN RACIAL COMRADES. IF I SPEAK TO YOU TODAY, I DO SO ONLY FOR TWO REASONS: FIRST, SO THAT YOU CAN HEAR MY VOICE AND KNOW THAT I MYSELF AM UNINJURED AND WELL. SECONDLY, SO THAT YOU MAY ALSO LEARN THE DETAILS ABOUT A CRIME THAT HAS NOT ITS LIKE IN GERMAN HISTORY.

Berthe von Hoffmann sat in her darkened flat, numbly listening to Hitler describe the attempt to kill him and name Colonel von Stauffenberg as the perpetrator. She heard him dismiss the other conspirators as a very small coterie of criminal elements who would now be mercilessly extirpated. As the Führer proclaimed his escape an "assignment from Providence," she realized with mounting despair that the failed attempt would have exactly that impression on most Germans. They would all believe in Hitler for a little while longer.

Canaris was right. It would have been better to continue to betray military secrets, to give ruinously bad advice whenever possible, to spread disillusion and defeatism, to allow history's inevitability to consume the Nazi nightmare.

Canaris was wrong. They had shown the world, even if no one listened, that there were Germans who cared enough about honor and truth to die for it.

Right or wrong, it was irrelevant now. She was doomed. A knock on the door. Were they coming already? She opened it and Ernst shoved his way into the room. His movements were rough, angry. Was he drunk? He pushed her back down the hall into the sitting room and lit a candle.

"So, Berthe," he said.

"So, Ernst," she said.

"They shot your friend Stauffenberg against the wall of the Bendlerblock three hours ago. He died crying: 'Long live holy Germany.' Did he whisper that to you when he visited here at six a.m.?"

"He never touched me, Ernst. He called me Frau von Hoffmann. He was a very correct, very religious man."

"What did you do for him?"

"I helped type up the proclamation he intended to make tonight. He was going to proclaim a republic and announce who would be head of state, commander of the Army. It went through many drafts."

"Do you have any of them around here?"

"No. Each draft was systematically burned as soon as a new one was approved."

"The Gestapo found the last one in Stauffenberg's office. What did you do with the typewriter?"

"It's dismantled and buried."

"Where?"

"I have no idea. Stauffenberg took the pieces away with him."

"Did anyone else know you were doing this?"

"I'm not sure. Perhaps General Beck or General Olbricht."

"They're both dead. Beck shot himself. Olbricht died beside Stauffenberg."

"How do you know so much? Have you joined the Gestapo?"

His face seemed hooded by darkness in the flickering candlelight. She saw hardness spread across it like a mask. "I've been to the Wolfschanze and back today with Dönitz. I'm trying to decide whether I should kill you, Berthe. The Führer has proclaimed a Sippenhaft. Our children's lives may be at stake."

"It won't be necessary to kill me. I have a cyanide capsule. Do you think I should take it?"

He was silent for a long time. His face seemed to dissolve into fragments and reform into the implacable mask. "Yes," he said.

She went into her bedroom and got the capsule and returned

with a glass of water. She put the deadly pink object on the table between them. "Do you still love me in any way?"

"I still desire you. I suppose that's a kind of love. But you've destroyed too much, Berthe. In some ways you were always a destroyer, even when you pretended to love me. You never loved Ernst von Hoffmann. You loved some meaning of me in your head."

"That's not true. I loved both. But they got farther and farther apart."

"If it had been real love you would have gone on loving me no matter what I did."

"Perhaps you're right. Promise me you won't tell the children how I died or why."

"Do you really think I'm such a fool? It'll be hard enough to lie to them about you—with the memory of what I'm about to see—"

He began to weep. Were they genuine tears? Or drunken self-pity?

"Ernst—"

"Take it. Don't make me cram it down your throat!"

The mask had shattered. He was looking away from her into the dark corner. This was one Mutprobe too many. Berthe picked up the capsule. It felt as light as a flower petal in her hand. So this was where the Path had taken her. It seemed more like defeat than victory, oblivion rather than transcendence. She thought of Jesus, the man of sorrows, and tried one last time to accept God's incomprehensible mystery as she raised the capsule to her lips.

A fist pounded on the door.

"Don't!" Ernst said and knocked the cyanide capsule flying. "Is there another way out?"

She shook her head. "The landlady keeps the back door bolted from the outside. She doesn't permit me to use the garden."

The fist pounded again. Berthe went down the hall and answered the door. A black uniformed figure flicked a slitted flashlight in her face. "Frau von Hoffmann?" he said.

"Yes."

"Brigadeführer Schellenberg wishes to see you immediately."

"Am I being arrested?"

"I have no idea. Get in the car."

"May I get my coat?" The night air was unusually cold for July.

The SS man grunted an assent. In the sitting room, Ernst seized her arm. "For God's sake, don't tell them I was here," he whispered.

It was probably the last time they would see each other. But Berthe could summon no emotion. She felt detached from what was happening. Perhaps she considered herself already dead. She had been so close to death, minutes before.

In a half-hour she was in Brigadeführer Walter Schellenberg's office in the Berkaerstrasse. She had met Canaris's successor for no more than five minutes when she returned from Spain, her name on the list of the expelled, courtesy of Rafael Sanchez. A smooth, wily looking charmer, Schellenberg had blandly congratulated her for her efforts in Madrid. Since the Reich was now on the defensive everywhere, he had no place else to send her, abroad. So he assigned her to the decoding room and apparently forgot about her.

"Sit down, Frau von Hoffmann," he said, lighting a cigarette. He offered her one, which she politely declined. He took a long drag and said: "No doubt you're deeply disappointed by the events of the day."

"On the contrary. The Führer has escaped unharmed."

"There's no need to dissemble. Your landlady is on the Gestapo payroll. She reported every visit Colonel von Stauffenberg made to you. She noted the industrious clicking of your typewriter in the small hours of the night."

"So you know everything."

"We know a lot, my dear lady. In fact, you could easily say we know too much. You and your aristocratic friends are by no means the only people in Berlin who were disappointed by the failure of Count von Stauffenberg's bomb. Even now, in Gestapo headquarters certain files are being destroyed. Reichsführer Himmler has been forced to defer his dreams of ascent."

Berthe's detachment vanished. She was swept by horror, loathing. "Canaris," she said. "Was he—is he—on your side?"

"Not exactly," Schellenberg said. "But we occasionally nodded to each other in the labyrinth. We too saw that negotiation with the West was our only hope. Now the Admiral will be arrested. A great many people will be arrested. A great many people will be persuaded to tell us all they know in the Gestapo's cellars below PrinzAlbrechtstrasse."

Schellenberg had no idea how deeply those words consoled Berthe. It would have been unbearable to die thinking she had been a dupe and her love for Jonathan Talbot a grotesque charade. "I would like to see my children before I die," she said.

"You aren't going to die for a while. Your testimony may prove useful in the prosecution of certain leaders of the conspiracy, such as Helmuth von Moltke. In the meantime you're going to take a vacation at our expense at a concentration camp not far from Berlin."

Berthe spent the rest of the night in a cubicle near Schellenberg's office. The hall resounded with tramping feet, anxious voices. Names were shouted, often with a curse attached. She recognized a few of them. Her old mentor, Bruchmuller, was one. He was apparently in Sweden. She heard them discussing the best way to force him to come home. They decided it would be simplest to threaten to hand his mother over to the Gestapo.

In the dawn, the same hulking SS man who had taken Berthe from her flat drove her to a railroad station on the north side of Berlin where a freight train stood on a siding, the engine huffing steam. SS men in summer uniforms, shorts and knee-high stockings, lounged beside beside it.

"An additional prisoner for Ravensbruck," her escort said. He handed the SS commander a document.

"Everyone on this train is French," the commander said. "I don't think they'll be very nice to her."

Her escort shrugged. "It's a short ride." He gave Berthe a mocking bow. "Auf Wiedersehen, meine frau," he said.

"Auf Wiedersehen," Berthe said, though she did not have the slightest desire to see him again. He had a striking resemblance to a Neanderthal man.

The July sun was beginning to beat down with unusual intensity. One of the SS men unlocked the sliding door of the nearest box car and two others hoisted Berthe into it. She found herself confronting about forty women, all glaring suspiciously at her. The stench in the car was unbelievable. The only toilet was a battered tin can in one corner, which was full to overflowing.

"Hello," she said, in awkward French. "My name is Berthe von Hoffmann."

"*Von* Hoffmann," sneered a short fat woman with a harelip. "What the hell are you doing under arrest?"

"I—I offended the authorities by cooperating in a plot to—to overthrow Hitler."

"Do you expect us to believe that?" screamed the harelip. "You're a fucking Gestapo spy."

"If that were true, wouldn't they have given the job to someone who could speak better French?" Berthe said.

The harelip smashed her across the face with the back of her hand. "You're a fucking German. That's enough for me."

As she drew back her hand for another blow, a thin, elegantly dressed red-haired woman seized her arm. "Let her alone. I doubt if even the Gestapo could find someone to climb into this pigsty. What's she going to learn from us, anyhow?"

"A lot of us have done more than write political junk about Joan of Arc, Countess," snarled the harelip. "We've tried to defend the workers, advance the class struggle."

The red-haired woman, who was about Berthe's age, regarded the harelip with undisguised loathing. "It's people like you who undermined France," she said. "There'll be guillotines waiting for you in the Place de la Concorde after General de Gaulle rescues us."

"Fuck General de Gaulle," shouted the harelip. "You'll be the one with your tits in a guillotine. All the rotten exploiters will go!"

The train lurched into motion. The harelip continued to glare menacingly at Berthe while the Countess introduced herself. She had been arrested for writing for an underground newspaper in Paris and spent three months in city prisons there. She and almost everyone else except certain *canaille* (dogs) like the harelip had been treated quite well. Her family had been permitted to send her regular packages of food. The prisoners had been shipped to Germany because the Anglo-Americans would soon break out of their Normandy beachhead and the city was certain to fall to them in a few weeks. So far, the SS train guards had treated them decently. "They tell us Ravensbruck is a good camp. We'll be happy there," she said. "Is that true?"

She was disappointed when Berthe said she knew nothing about Ravensbruck. She had never even heard of it. In about two hours the train pulled into Furstenburg, about 40 kilometers north of Berlin. The SS train guards shouted orders and everyone jumped down from the boxcars. About 300 women wearing every imaginable style of clothing assembled in rough ranks beside the train. The SS were now in full uniform and they seemed to have regained their customary ruthlessness. "Anyone who tries to escape on the march will be shot without mercy!" roared their commander.

Five to a rank, they trudged down a hot, dusty road through a wood of massive pine trees. They passed small, comfortable looking homes, with children and adults standing outside watching the procession. Along the edge of the road Berthe noticed a number of leaflets of the sort dropped by British and American planes. When the guards were distracted by a woman who fainted, she was able to scoop one up.

Germans—have you heard the latest news? Some of your generals have tried to kill your Führer. No doubt they thought they could fight the war more efficiently. But it does not matter who's running Germany, you're heading for defeat. This quarrel among the ruling clique of gangsters proves it. The best thing you can do is quit working at your factory job and go on strike against Hitler, the generals, everybody. You're beaten and this bomb attack on the Führer proves it.

This was their reward for the years of agonized planning and discussion and sacrifice: the enemy's mockery. For a moment Berthe was tempted to curse God—to denounce Him in the name of the dead, Elisabeth von Theismann and Otto von Spaeth and Claus von Stauffenberg, as well as the living, Canaris, Moltke and the other members of the Schwarze Kapelle who would now die terrible deaths. Yes and in the name of the slaughtered Jews and the hundreds of thousands of young men on both sides who would now die by machine-gun bullets and shellfire and bombs in France and Russia. Where was His compassion, His mercy?

She heard the Marquesa telling her Germany was the doomed bull whom only a few aficionados could love in secret. But it was no consolation. It only seemed to intensify her bitterness.

Ahead of them loomed a wide green gate, guarded by a half-dozen SS men. As they passed through it, they saw rows of bottle-green barracks with alleys between them covered with black coal dust. From the barracks swarmed gnomelike women, many with shaved heads, all dressed in blue and gray striped skirts and jackets, with heavy wooden-soled galoshes on their feet. Almost all had festering sores on their arms and legs. "Food!" they screamed. "Have you got any food?"

Many of the new arrivals, including the Countess, had suitcases full of canned meat and vegetables. The Countess gave a few items to the imploring creatures, but most of the newcomers clung to their treasures, realizing there was no hope of satisfying the beseechers. Berthe, who had nothing to offer, watched the melee without illusions. She had not been sent to Ravensbruck by chance.

Ich kann nicht anders whispered the keeper of the Path. There was a pleading, strangely weary timbre to the words, as if the being who spoke them had almost lost hope that anyone would understand Him. Was it her own voice, faltering as she saw the ultimate cost of discipleship? Or was it God himself, asking her to comprehend the darkest dimension of His being, the secret essence of His relationship with humankind?

47

IN SEARCH OF PURITY

For a month Jack's death left Annie in a surreal world of grief and work. She wept with and for her parents, who were totally devastated. She wept with and for Selma Shanley, who obviously loved Jack in some deep, furtive way which might or might not have involved a brief affair long ago. She wept for herself, because she loved him too. Simultaneously she had to take charge of "Behind The Headlines"—and rescue it from annihilation.

That meant she spent the month of June traveling by plane and train and bus to visit the fifty major papers who took the column, persuading them to let her keep it alive under her byline. In airports and train stations and hotel rooms she talked on the telephone to the managing editors of the other 550 papers, making the same pitch. All it required was brain surgery to alter the calcified conviction of the aging bozos in charge of America's fourth estate that no woman could report hard news—especially war news.

Selma Shanley backed her up by mailing packets of her columns, which included some of the biggest beats of the year, such as the inside story of the Teheran conference. But the crucial endorsement came from Jack: in his farewell letter, he had urged her to keep the column going to help win the war—and added she had the talent to do it.

The combined effort managed to hold on to 350 papers, a more than respectable number, although Annie knew in her heart at least half of them were doing it as a favor to Jack. When the war ended, they would terminate her faster than Congress planned to scuttle lend-lease.

She told herself the struggle helped her deal, if that was a permissible word, with her grief for Jack. But nothing seemed to fill the void in her soul created by her encounter with Franklin D. Roosevelt. The President's mindless hatred of Germany and equally mindless embrace of Stalin's Russia had emptied all moral content from her vision of America.

She managed to find time to visit Trinity and pour out her anguish to Sister Agatha, who mournfully confessed she was not surprised. On a scale even more grandiose than Wilson in 1917, Roosevelt had made a covenant with power, ignoring the fateful ways that power corrupts a man's fragile control of his passions. Annie's mistake was putting too much faith and hope for the future in a man.

With her usual maddening skill, Sister Agatha managed to make this both a feminist message and a sad commentary on the former Anna Richman's loss of faith in God. Both applied, of course, but Annie sullenly vowed to show her and anyone else who was watching that she was tough enough to get along without either enthusiasm. Zeke's letter, announcing his determination to risk his life in Germany for Berthe von Hoffmann's sake, contributed to this bitter resolution. She barely noticed the mushy stuff about treasuring the memory of their love.

Her resolve was buoyed by the undoubted fact that Jack's death had made her important in a much more public way. There she was with her little snub nose poised above dramatic revelations and startling opinions of Washington and world politics three times a week in 350 cities in 48 states and Alaska. That had to be why Assistant Secretary of the Treasury Saul Randolph on loan as Assistant Chief Administrator of Lend-Lease continued to pursue her. Annie found it hard to believe her leaden performances in the bedroom had anything to do with it. Lately her libido's decline was making the Crash of 1929 look like a down escalator running at half-speed.

Wait wait WAIT! Annie told herself as she crawled into a cab outside the office. A heat wave was wrapping Washington in a gigantic wool blanket making breathing and thinking almost equally difficult. She was being rotten to Saul again. He was exhibiting the patience of a saint—or a lover. The diamond ring still spent most of its time in the silk-lined box in her purse. But he repeatedly insisted he understood, he did not expect a decision until the war was over and a semblance of sanity returned to their lives.

At the Carlton House, Saul was early as usual. Champagne was cooling in a silver bucket, ditto the caviar in a silver bowl up to its edges in crushed ice. He greeted her with a kiss and got into the politics before Annie could unbutton her blouse.

"It's all over!" he chortled. "The President's given Wallace a letter, saying he's his personal choice for the ticket."

"Wonderful!" Annie said, stepping into the shower. As the hot water beat on her weary flesh, her tired brain began to function. How could a man who had spent seven years in Washington believe Franklin D. Roosevelt meant what he said? Maybe everybody, not just Catholics and other true believers, lived on faith.

For the past two weeks, the Democratic party had been in a frenzy, trying to decide whom to choose as Franklin D. Roosevelt's running mate in the upcoming presidential election. For Saul and his boss Henry Morgenthau and the rest of the New Dealers, there was only one possible choice: Henry Wallace. Not only was he the incumbent Vice President, which gave him talking rights to the job, he was the only Democrat on the horizon with a genuine commitment to Roosevelt's liberal legacy.

As she toweled herself, Saul stood in the doorway, talking excitedly about the upcoming convention. The CIO and the AFL were shipping a small Army of Wallace supporters to Chicago. A Gallup poll gave him a 65 percent approval rating among Democratic rank and file.

Wrapped in her towel, Annie sipped champagne and murmured apparent approval.

"I hope you'll get behind him," Saul said. A modest concession to her new importance. Once upon a time Mr. Randolph had used *want* to express his political desires. Now he confined it to his sexual desires. "Everything could be riding on this," Saul said. "Roosevelt's a very sick man. Morgenthau says we're probably nominating the next president. The other guys are talking about Truman."

"What's wrong with Truman?"

"He's not one of us. When Hitler attacked Stalin, he said we should let them bleed each other white." Saul took an angry gulp of champagne. "A liberal from Missouri is a contradiction in terms, any-way."

Arf-arf, woof-woof, he was running with his male pack again. She was still fascinated by this masculine habit of brutal exclusion, of splitting into us and the other guys. The Truman staffer she had hired had told Annie a lot about the Senator from Missouri. Most of it was positive. He was tough, blunt, honest. He made an interesting distinction between liberals and professional liberals. He maintained most Americans were liberals, even in Missouri—but professional liberals were another matter. Truman despised them. He thought they were all arrogant elitists at heart, no matter how much they talked about democracy and the common man.

"Get me an interview with Henry," Annie said. "In the mean-time—"

The champagne was fuzzing everything nicely. Saul peeled away the towel and there was sweet Annie, prone on her high wire. She managed to summon a fair amount of enthusiasm for the perfor-mance. Was it because she already intended to double-cross Saul and eviscerate Henry Wallace? Her Irish-Jewish Chicago conscience insisted on some sort of payoff?

No, no no, Annie vowed, as sweetness surged and she reminded herself that she genuinely admired Saul's idealism, his wishes and hopes for a better world for the common man, a phrase she had unfortunately begun to dislike. She did not exactly have an open mind on Henry Wallace, but she was not ready to demolish him. Not yet, not now, when Saul was asking her when she was going to admit she loved him; he was not Zeke Talbot's clone, he wanted to let her be her own woman everywhere but in the bedroom. There she belonged she belonged—she *belonged*—to him.

And she almost did. She almost, almost wished she did. There was something wonderfully noble, sweet and ultimately sad about his desire to save the world. But she stayed on the high wire.

The next day, when Saul sent her a copy of Roosevelt's letter, sweetness, the flutters of love's possibilities had long subsided. She read the letter with bewilderment. How could Saul consider it an endorsement? Anyone with even a modicum of political smarts could see it was the kiss of Judas. FDR called Wallace his "personal choice" for Vice President—but carefully stated he had no desire to dictate to the convention. This was tantamount to old Julius sending a Christian into the Colosseum, claiming he wanted him to survive in spite of some problems he might have with the lions.

Around noon her father asked her to come to his office. He looked so old, so sad, so tired, she almost wept. But he was still in the political game, in spite of his grief for Jack. "It's Truman," he said. "I want you behind him in the column. We're lining up support from here to Spokane and back."

The big city bosses, including Chicago's own, Ed Kelly, had gone to Roosevelt and told him Wallace was an albatross who would cost the party a dozen states. The Great Chameleon had asked them who they wanted and their answer was Truman. FDR had capitulated and given the Democratic party chairman a letter, endorsing him.

A protest crowded into Annie's throat. Shouldn't she tell this man he did not own her any more than Saul Randolph did? The Congressman stopped her before she could organize the first sentence.

"This is not fun and games, Babe. The future of the goddamn country's at stake. Maybe of the world. FDR's a dyin' man and Henry Wallace is an absolute total asshole who doesn't know the difference between a Communist and a Hottentot. After the way FDR's sold out the Polacks, I doubt if he does either. I'm callin' you on this one and I don't care what it does to your love life."

"Aye-aye, sir," Annie said. To her amazement, she felt a flush of warmth, of pride. He was talking to her like a man. As if she were an equal member of their Chicago tribe. She was still discovering what was primary, what was secondary in the new Annie's soul.

Saul Randolph arranged an interview with the Vice President. Annie went vowing to be fair. She was underwhelmed from the moment they shook hands. Wallace had a shy way of looking at you, ducking his head way down and peering out from under the shock of silver-gray hair that swept to the right on his head like a great shaggy arc. His laugh was too quick and too frequent—"Whuh-whuh-whuh!"—while a certain tenseness never left his lips.

The tension was not entirely surprising. In Washington Wallace was surrounded by a hatred so ferocious it sometimes verged on the appalling. Ever since Roosevelt rammed him down the Democratic party's throat as his Vice President in 1940, he had been the butt of savage jokes and vicious invective. Instead of trying to charm or at least soothe his opponents, he had attacked them in grandiloquent speeches and confrontational press releases. He stuck to this losing game plan in the interview, dismissing his critics as mental midgets, styling himself as the only Democrat with FDR's "vision."

Henry Wallace looks like a hayseed, talks like a prophet and acts like an embarrassed schoolboy. That was the opening sentence he deserved, but it would have given away the game. Instead, only an expert could detect the sabotage in the column—the way Annie lured the Vice President into declaring his admiration for Stalin, and into insisting that if the New Deal was dead, the Democratic party was dead. Liberals would read it with tears in their eyes, but the other guys would regard it as ammunition.

Annie's support of Truman was even more covert. She published a column recapitulating some of the more spectacular revelations of his investigating committee and ended by wondering if the American people wanted a "district attorney type" for president. (The answer, since every voter assumed Washington, D.C., was hopelessly corrupt, was yes.) She ran another column entitled: "Truman: the Bosses' Friend?" which concluded that he was not their friend. He was too honest. A third one leaked the existence of FDR's letter endorsing the Senator and piously concluded the President wanted an "open convention" to decide between Truman and Wallace.

On the plane to Chicago, Saul Randolph complained about how much ink she was giving Truman. She murmured double-talk about keeping her editors happy and he was soon filling her ears with the machinations of the Wallacemen, who were planning to pack the galleries and put their man over on the first ballot. Annie duly reported this to her father, who passed it on to Ed Kelly, and the other guys adjusted their strategy accordingly. She was sure they got the same information from a dozen other people but she enjoyed contributing her mite to the massacre.

On July 19, with the temperature outside over one hundred degrees, Annie made sweaty love with Saul on the seventh floor of the Stevens Hotel. Saul was so confident, so excited, about the coming Wallace victory, he did not notice that she left the almost-engagement ring in her purse.

The next day, July 20, saw Roosevelt renominated and in the evening the all-out push for Wallace began. The CIO-packed galleries roared for his immediate nomination. The organist played "Iowa, That's Where the Tall Corn Grows" so many times, to remind everyone that Wallace was from America's heartland, it was a miracle her fingers did not fall off. Then the other guys went to work. The organist was ordered to change her repertoire or a man with an ax was going to amputate her amplifiers. Someone else flung open the convention hall doors, letting hundreds of nondelegates pour into the arena, where the temperature was around 120 degrees. People began collapsing from lack of oxygen, and Ed Kelly rushed to the platform and screamed about a fire hazard. The chairman gaveled the convention into recess and the Wallace stampede was over.

Annie spent the night wandering the halls of the Stevens and other hotels with her father, watching delegates being whipped into line for Truman with copies of Roosevelt's endorsement letter. She returned to her room in the dawn to find Saul slumped on the bed drinking beer. "It's all over," he said.

He was so sad, she stripped off her clothes and consoled him. For a little while, they almost regained some of the sweetness of Marrakesh. He had no way of knowing it was synthetic, a compound of pity and guilt for her betrayal of his liberal dreams.

"Wild news on the radio, did you hear it?" Saul said, as Annie drifted down into an exhausted sleep.

"What?"

"Someone tried to kill Hitler. Some Army officers, apparently. They put a bomb in his headquarters. But he survived."

Annie was wide awake, staring into the Chicago dawn. "Were any Americans involved?" she asked.

"I have no idea. It was just a news flash."

Somehow Annie knew that these were Zeke's people. Was Berthe von Hoffmann there, risking her beautiful German neck? Was Zeke with her, on the run now from Hitler's Gestapo? Heroically sacrificing their lives for an ideal while she played dirty politics and made lying love to a man she had double-crossed?

In the name of what? Her bitter determination to be a woman in her own right, with the power of screwing or not screwing men, in all the meanings of that phrase, as she chose? All the July humidity in Chicago suddenly seemed to concentrate in the room. Struggling for breath, Annie found herself desperately wishing, wanting something more than that. Something that lifted up her heart, that made her proud of herself and her country.

The next night, after another flurry for Wallace, Truman was nominated in a landslide. Annie spent the day as close to a radio as possible, listening to the garbled contradictory accounts of the attempt to kill Hitler. By the time Truman and his wife and daughter were being mobbed by wild-eyed supporters in the Chicago Convention Hall, official Washington seemed to have concluded the assassination attempt was probably the act of a lone sorehead, who had taken a dislike to Hitler for some personal reason. From Roosevelt came not a word. He was on the high seas, en route to an inspection of Hawaii to shore up his support among the Pacific-firsters.

On the way back to Washington Annie shared a compartment on the Baltimore and Ohio's elegant Capitol Limited with a morose Saul Randolph. They had dinner with his boss, Henry Morgenthau, Jr., who was equally dismayed by the convention's results. The Secretary of the Treasury descanted on the way the big city machines and the Southern conservatives had seized control of the Democratic party. The White House was rapidly becoming a liberal island in a sea of know-nothings, he moaned, obviously assuming Annie shared Saul's politics.

"We can still win the peace, Henry," Saul said.

"How is the draft coming along?" Morgenthau said.

"You'll have it by the end of the week."

Morgenthau smiled arcanely at Annie. "A little top secret business," he said.

The Secretary launched into a jeremiad against high-ranking Democrats, apparently quite numerous, who had tried to persuade Roosevelt not to run for a fourth term. They had wanted him to resign in favor of Gen. George C. Marshall, who would have been nominated for president on a "win the war" platform. That would have destroyed the last vestiges of liberalism in the Democratic party. Morgenthau said he had compiled a list of the defectors and he planned to show it to the President when the time was ripe.

Annie tsk-tsked and Saul Randolph all but volunteered to set up the guillotines on Pennsylvania Avenue, while she thought, not for the first time, that FDR had been in office too long. With Morgenthau, the king-and-courtier syndrome was in full flower.

Back in their compartment, columnist Anna Richman went to work on finding out more about the top secret draft Saul was writing to win the peace. He proudly informed her it was a plan to make sure Germany never started another war. "Roosevelt's given it the green light," Saul said.

Annie was back in the White House with Zeke, staring at FDR's death-haunted face while the magical voice gushed hate: *"We're going to let Joe Stalin shoot fifty thousand of them—and turn the whole damn country into Kansas and Nebraska. Morgenthau's working on a plan to absolutely eviscerate their heavy industry."* Then came a gap in the tape until Zeke said: *"Mr. President, that wouldn't be honorable."*

"There's a conference with Churchill scheduled for Quebec in early September. The President needs a final draft to show him up there. He wants Winston's approval before we go ahead."

"It sounds marvelous," Annie said. Saul beamed agreeably. He could not imagine anyone disagreeing with the plan, which, he told her proudly, was mostly his idea. Arf-arf, yap-yap, Annie thought.

Back in Washington, the plot to kill Hitler vanished from the news. But it coalesced with heavy fighting in Normandy to create rising expectations of an early end to the war. All the Americans and British had to do was break out of the beachhead and the German Army would collapse, the inside dopesters said. That added urgency— and pungency—to what was soon being called the Morgenthau Plan. Everyone had heard rumors but no one knew anything about it— except columnist Anna Richman. Saul Randolph had described it to her in exultant detail before he and Morgenthau accompanied Roosevelt to Canada for the conference with Churchill.

The plan called for the complete demolition of Germany's heavy industry. They were even going to flood the coal mines of the Ruhr and Saar valleys. The Germans would not be permitted to manufacture anything larger than bottlecaps. Using data dug out of the Library of Congress by Selma Shanley, Annie estimated the plan would leave 40 million Germans with no visible means of support— making them prime candidates for Communist party membership.

Annie asked Saul if he worried that without a strong Germany, Stalin would be the master of Europe. Saul sighed wearily, making it clear he had written off her negative attitude toward communism as a hangover from her unfortunate Catholic education. "Roosevelt approves the plan one hundred percent," he said.

Arf-arf, yap-yap, Annie thought.

By the time the FDR met Churchill in Quebec, the British and Americans had broken out of the Normandy beachhead and liberated Paris. But the Germans showed no signs of collapsing. On the contrary, they had massacred an attempt to break into Germany from the north, at Arnhem. More dismaying, at least to politicians from Chicago, was Stalin's cruel double-cross of the Polish underground, which had risen in revolt in Warsaw as the Red Army approached the capital. Stalin slammed the brakes on his war machine and waited until the Germans had slaughtered two hundred thousand non-Communist Poles before he returned to the offensive. Sam Richman was deluged with telegrams from outraged Polish Democrats who no longer had much interest in voting for Rooseveltski—or a congressman who supported him.

But the news from Quebec, as Saul Randolph reported it, was glorious. Churchill had swallowed hard and agreed to the Morgenthau Plan. "At first he loathed it," Saul said. "He said it would make Stalin the real winner of the war. But he came around when we told him that unless he agreed he was never going to see the six point five billion dollars in postwar lend-lease he's asking for."

The War Department and the State Department were both opposed to the plan, Saul added triumphantly. But it was an accomplished fact. Stalin had accepted it in principle, though he grumbled about not getting all the reparations he wanted from German industry. He agreed to it because it would guarantee world peace for generations. That was all the Russians wanted: peace and prosperity.

Yap-yap, arf-arf, Annie thought, while Warsaw was knee-deep in the corpses of Polish patriots. Saul was telling her all this in their room in the Carlton House, after which they made their usual champagne-soaked love. For Annie the performance was etched in elegy. It was the finale of *Swan Lake*, the closing moments of *Lohengrin*. Zeke Talbot's voice floated through her head: *Mr. President, I don't think that would be honorable*. Zeke, the man she *hated*, infesting her soul like a virus while Saul Randolph stroked away, muttering incoherences about love. The worst of it was a fleeting taste of remembered sweetness.

Earlier in the day she had mailed her notes on the Morgenthau Plan to rival columnist Drew Pearson. It was the only way she could prove to herself that she was betraying Saul for a principle, not a story. It also shielded her father from Roosevelt's wrath.

Taking a leaf from Roy Reeves's stylebook, she arranged for Drew to interview her on a drugstore pay phone the following day, refusing to give her name. She said that she was leaking this sensational beat to him as his reward for supporting the forces of progress and peace and justice over the years. Drew swallowed this malarkey like a baby sucking on a honey-dipped pacifier. Two days later his column was devoted to a breathless account of Roosevelt's determination to annihilate Germany's heavy industry and feed the Germans "three bowls of soup a day with nothing in them."

Other reporters rushed to consult their sources and soon the *New York Times,* the *Wall Street Journal* and the Washington *Evening Star* published comprehensive accounts of the Morgenthau Plan's development and the maneuvering that led to its apparent approval at Quebec. These stories expressed grave concern about the way FDR had cavalierly ignored protests from the State and War departments and had not mentioned a word about this stupendous foreign policy departure to a single member of Congress.

Almost immediately, political aftershocks began rolling through the capital. Secretary of War Henry Stimson, the personification of the old-line Protestant establishment, went public with his opposition to the plan as a clear violation of the Atlantic Charter's Four Freedoms, which guaranteed equal rights and economic opportunity to both the winners and the losers of the war. An astonishing majority of newspapers across the country assailed the plan. *Time* magazine called it a "policy of hate." Joseph Goebbels seized on it as final proof that the Allies intended to enslave the German people. The Republican candidate for president, Thomas E. Dewey, excoriated it, saying it was costing American lives by making the Germans fight with renewed desperation.

Finally, from the Great Chameleon in the White House came an announcement that the plan was nothing more than a suggestion—it definitely did not have the President's endorsement. Privately, Roosevelt was telling his inner circle that Morgenthau and his friends had "pulled a boner."

From the Treasury Department came a howl of rage that echoed across Washington. Secretary Morgenthau launched a furious investigation to find out who had leaked the plan. From Saul Randolph there was only silence for another long unnerving week. Then came a call at three a.m. one hot, humid September night.

"Hello, you fucking bitch," said the thick drunken voice. "I just want to tell you what I think of you."

"You just did," Annie said.

"I thought it was you from the start. Yesterday we got one of Pearson's big-mouthed flunkies soused and he told us the leaker was a woman. That cinched it. I should have known you can take the girl out of Chicago but you can't take Chicago out of the girl."

"Probably not," Annie said.

He had a perfect right to revile her. She had an obligation to endure it. She could not possibly explain why she did it. How a sentence spoken to the President of the United States by an Annapolis man she abhorred had somehow created a chemical imbalance in her brain and forced her to jettison a life with a man she liked and might eventually have loved. Plus a chance to savor with him the wonderful feeling of Doing Good. For all she knew the Morgenthau Plan might have been a great idea, though in the name of those 200,000 slaughtered Poles in Warsaw, she doubted it. But any attempt to explain all this would only further convince Saul that women should be manacled, confined and lobotomized whenever possible.

"It's my last night in Washington. Morgenthau thinks I leaked it to you. It doesn't matter how often I deny it. He'll go on thinking it. I didn't bother to tell him I *trusted* you. I didn't bother to tell him anything. It would only make me look like a bigger jerk."

She knew exactly what he meant. Morgenthau probably believed he did not leak the plan. He just wanted to know how Saul let things go so wrong.

"Why did you do it? Is it because you graduated summa cum laude from that fucking one-lung Catholic girls' school? Has that given you permanent delusions of grandeur?"

She was tempted to say arf-arf, yap-yap, but she tried to be rational. "I happen to think the American people have a right to make up their own minds about the future of the world instead of trusting everything to Franklin Delano Roosevelt and his little group of friends."

"The people," he said. "The *people*? The slobs your old man and Ed Kelly march to the polls in Chicago? The pea brains on the farms in Ohio? The retards in the South? You trust the people to decide anything important?"

There it was, the professional liberal's fundamental disdain for the people he was trying to save. Of course, she did not trust the people any more than Saul did. How could she, growing up in Chicago and Washington, D.C.? "Maybe," she said, bitter tears flooding her throat. "I just don't trust *men*."

Annie slammed down the telephone and sat there sobbing until the September dawn swept a chilly wind through the apartment. She stumbled into the office feeling like Dracula's daughter with a stake in her heart. "Call the guys in the War Department," she told Selma Shanley. "Tell them I want to go to France."

"Why?" Selma said.

"The column needs a jolt of electricity."

"You need a month's vacation a lot more," Selma said.

"Don't argue with me!" Annie said. "I want to prove a woman can cover a real war just as well as she can cover the phony wars here in Washington."

"Just because Jack got himself killed doesn't mean you've got an obligation to do it too," Selma said.

Annie did not want Jack's death, she wanted the life he had experienced before it, the caring, the exaltation that had cleansed Chicago's cynicism from his soul. She wanted to weep genuine tears, not the crocodile variety that everyone shed in Washington, D.C. She wanted to rediscover nobility and courage in the word *American*. It was her only hope of saving her battered soul.

"Call them," she said. "I want to leave as soon as possible."

48

TRANSFORMATIONS

The groaning tram, with half its windows gone, swayed past the ruined buildings on the Kurfurstendamm, where Berliners once enjoyed a cornucopia of cabarets, beer halls and cafés. Jonathan Talbot hunched in his seat as two policemen approached him. Wordlessly, he produced his Kenncarte, certifying his identity as Hans Blucher, a printer at Ullstein Publishing Company, and his Wehrpassbuch, proving his exemption from military service because of a weak heart. It was a random check, more to remind Berliners that the regime was watching them than for any hope or desire to catch spies or saboteurs.

Still, tension sent sweat oozing down Talbot's chest. Between his legs was a shortwave radio that would guarantee his immediate arrest and execution if the policemen were inquisitive enough to open the suitcase. But they passed on to other expressionless passengers, who may have had worries of their own about changed identities or names on wanted lists.

As darkness fell, Talbot stumbled down a littered street in Charlottenburg and let himself into a small house. The first thing he heard was a plaintive voice saying: "I'm going to have to sweep the streets. They told me there are no other jobs available for people like me."

Ursula Fleischman swayed in the center of Helen Widerstand's living room, which was lined with sandbags. About twenty-five, she was a wisp of a woman with a bad cough and unhealthy red spots in her cheeks. A typist at Helen's publishing house, she had been fired in obedience to an SS decree barring "half-breeds"—children of Christian-Jewish marriages—from all but the most menial jobs.

"You'll have to do it," Helen Widerstand said. She towered over the girl like a giantess from a fable. "Just goof off as much as possible. We can't take another U-boat. The house is bulging at the walls."

U-boat was Berlin underground slang for a person trying to live without papers, subsisting on forged or stolen ration cards or the generosity of friends. Already, there were eight U-boats in Helen's house. They included Frank, a witty Jewish doctor who had been on the run since 1941, and Karl, a mournful major who had unilaterally quit the war when his regiment was ordered to fight the Americans. Every time someone unexpected knocked on the front door, there was a stampede to the cellar.

"Can't we print up a new identity for her?" Talbot asked, after Ursula departed into the cold Berlin night. He was thinking of his part-Jewish son, the outrageous injustice of persecuting someone for an accident of birth.

"We can only ask a printer to risk his life for the most desperate cases," Helen said. "Pushing a broom for a few months won't kill her—I hope."

Helen had become the queen of the Berlin underground. She was also its nerve center, its brains. Through her associates at Ullstein's, which published one of Berlin's biggest newspapers, she was in touch with almost everything that was happening in the Reich as the war rumbled toward a climax. She even had a secret sympathizer inside the Gestapo who leaked information to her. Again and again she flashed warnings to groups such as the Iron Cross Jews, enabling them to go underground before the SS rounded them up for deportation. Through a network of doctors, she arranged for fake medical certificates, which exempted men from service in the newly organized *Volksturm*, the people's Army, which was drafting everyone from sixteen to sixty. Through her contacts with printers, she created false identities for others on the run.

But Berthe von Hoffmann, the person she and Talbot wanted to help more than anyone else, remained out of their reach in the Ravensbruck concentration camp. Helen had heard through her

Gestapo contact that Berthe had refused to testify against Helmuth von Moltke or any of the other members of the Schwarze Kapelle and had therefore been left on the starvation rations of the French women with whom she had arrived at the camp. Otherwise they had no news of Prisoner 66688.

Talbot had been living in Helen's house for almost two months now, moving around Berlin and its environs using a half-dozen different disguises supplied by his mentor, William Casey, the OSS Secret Intelligence Chief in London. With Irish ebullience, Casey had equipped Talbot with every weapon and alias in his possession, and wrote out an elaborate assignment to justify using such precious goods on a mission to rescue Berthe—a German national who was in danger of death for an operation that the President of the United States had forbidden everyone, generals, diplomats, and secret agents, to countenance. Casey even gave him papers and a silver warrant identity disk that certified him as a member of the Gestapo.

Talbot's orders required him to report on the morale of the Berlin civilian population and garrison to help evaluate the forces required to capture the city. When he arrived in the capital, the Allied high command was predicting the war would be over by Christmas. Everyone was feeling euphoric over the liberation of Paris in mid-August. But the Wehrmacht's resistance had stiffened so dramatically, Casey had just told Talbot over his SSTR-1 shortwave radio that Washington and London now estimated the struggle might last another year!

Berthe would never survive that long in Ravensbruck. Talbot joined Helen Widerstand as a Berlin couple bicycling the countryside for food, something thousands were doing daily. With the help of her Gestapo ally, Helen approached a hulking SS woman guard at the camp and implored her to smuggle a package to Berthe. Helen sweetened the plea with a bundle of Reichsmarks and an appeal to German solidarity, plus a tearful assurance that Berthe was innocent. The woman agreed with a minimum of fuss. They gave her sausages, bread and a cake bought from a nearby farmer, and Talbot asked her to tell Berthe it was a token of the friendship they had begun in Spain.

The following week they returned with another basket of food. The SS woman angrily refused to accept it. "Your friend is crazy," she said. "She gave away the first basket to those goddamn French bitches, down to the last morsel."

For the next few weeks, Helmuth von Moltke's trial absorbed most of Helen's time and attention. Talbot had been in Berlin for the trials of the generals and colonels who had been part of the Schwarze Kapelle. He had seen the films Propaganda Minister Goebbels had released—in which these proud, dignified men wearing prison clothes that were ludicrously too big or too small—to make them look like clowns—calmly defended their decision to assassinate the Führer. The judge, an oafish loudmouth named Freisler, and a courtroom packed with Party members, sneered and cursed at them. Although Goebbels synchronized the trials with propaganda blasts about "the Jew Morgenthau's" plan to destroy Germany, the films had been abruptly withdrawn when the regime discovered they were having a negative impact on the public.

Moltke's trial was conducted in secret. Only about twenty carefully selected Party members constituted the audience. But they leaked enough information for Helen Widerstand to give the underground a vivid reconstruction of the proceedings.

Moltke handled his own defense. With unwavering courage and impeccable logic, he demolished all the Reich's accusations. None of the conspirators had talked under Gestapo torture—a terrible testimony to their courage. The prosecutors had no evidence Moltke had ever recommended the use of force against Hitler or anyone else. They could only prove he had discussed with friends his objections to the Nazi regime's murderous policies. But this was enough to condemn him.

"Count Moltke," Freisler said, as he pronounced the death sentence. "Christianity and National Socialism have one thing in common: they both demand the whole man."

"Judge," Moltke replied, "if I must hang, I am in favor of dying on this issue."

Helen Widerstand organized a desperate effort to save Moltke, using her Gestapo ally and a half-dozen other contacts inside the SS to try to persuade Himmler to pardon him. But no one had the courage to intervene on Moltke's behalf. Finally it came down to the desperate chance that Himmler's adjutant, who was an old police friend of Helen's Gestapo ally, might put in a pleading word with the Reichsführer when and if he found him in the right mood.

Alas, the adjutant had gotten drunk on New Year's Eve and badly burned his feet dancing on a hot stove. The burns became infected and he was unable to get out of bed. While they waited for him to recover, the chaplain at Moltke's prison telephoned to tell Helen Widerstand he was dead. They had hanged him, pastors Bonhoeffer and Bruchmuller and several others on only a few hours notice.

"Is that how Berthe's God works?" Helen mused wryly. "The greatest German of this century dies because some drunken fool danced on a hot stove?"

Helen received an answer of sorts that night, when Moltke's wife, Freya, visited to thank them for their attempt to save her husband. Her chiseled features blazed with grief and affirmation as she told them that success or failure was not as important as bearing witness to the spark of faith in the human soul. "As long as we do that, everything, even dying, takes on meaning."

Talbot tried to refocus Helen's attention on Berthe, who might be the next victim of Stauffenberg's bomb. "We've got to reach her," he said. "Maybe we can persuade her to be reasonable and eat some smuggled food."

They bicycled to Ravensbruck again and found the compliant SS woman guard. Helen handed her another bundle of Reichsmarks and assured her that she and her "husband" were in complete agreement about Berthe's perverse determination to starve herself. "Perhaps if you let us correspond with her, we could persuade her to be more reasonable—more *German*."

The SS woman did not think it would do any good. But the Reichsmarks were persuasive. She said she would get Berthe a pen and some paper and would act as a mail carrier. She had a boyfriend in the Sicherheitdienst and frequently came to Berlin to see him.

They gave the guard a letter telling Berthe about Moltke's death—phrasing it in the negative, of course, pretending to be appalled by his defiance of Nazism. They closed with an urgent plea for Berthe to profit from Moltke's example—and be more cooperative. Otherwise their "spark of hope" for her would be extinguished.

Within a week, Talbot was reading a letter from Berthe.

Dearest J:
How wonderful of you to know that what I wanted to do more than anything else in this world is speak to you. I wish you had been able to continue to send me food. I can't tell you how good it made me feel, to share it with my fellow women, ignoring who was French, who was Polish,

who was Russian. But I have to confess, to my shame, it made me proud to be German—and share it. Please contrive some way to send me another basket, to see if I can finally overcome this obnoxious trait. I have tried to do penance by giving half my daily piece of bread to whomever sits next to me at supper. But I could never have done any of this if I had not learned you were in Berlin. The thought that you were risking so much for my sake was proof that God exists in our hearts even when we try to deny Him. I simply don't believe any merely human motive would drive a man to do such a thing for a woman who had treated him so badly. How I regret that wound I inflicted on you. My one wish now is that God will fill the void in your soul with faith.

Let me share a terrible truth about God that I have acquired here in Ravensbruck: His helplessness. The idea began as a whisper in my soul and slowly grew as I watched so many innocent women die of starvation and overwork. Nothing else explains history's agony. God too is groping toward the light with which His stupendous journey into time began. The Bible abounds with evidence for this heartrending conclusion. Job, the just man, reduced to despair on his dunghill, the innocents slaughtered by King Herod, Jesus, who proclaimed himself God's son, abandoned to a humiliating death.

Oh my dearest, the key to the mystery is the word *love*. Consider our own painful example. You offered me a perfect love that renounced control and ultimately even desire, a love that I, enmeshed in my blind worship of Germany, could not return. Yet you persisted in loving me. God does the same thing with men and women—and much more. Just as your perfect love for me and my broken-winged love for you enabled us to become one being for a little while in Granada, so God, a perfect spirit, has entered into His creatures, has *become* them. He grieves our griefs, weeps our tears, mourns our blunders, exactly as you watched over me, with infinite forbearance. He wishes the same happiness and joy for all mankind you wish for me but we are trapped in the prison of history, unable to believe in our terrible freedom, His primary gift, only feebly, dimly, aware of His presence, too often mistaking his forbearance for indifference. When Martin Luther cried: *Ich kann nicht anders,* he was speaking with God's own voice! God is suffering here in Ravensbruck and in the Jewish death camps in Poland as He suffered with Job and with Jesus on the cross! Do you see how this transforms everything?

The letter demoralized Talbot. He felt he had lost Berthe in a new and final way, she had abandoned him for union with her inscrutable God. He showed it to Helen Widerstand, expecting a similar reaction. "There's only one thing left to do," Helen said. "Pray for her."

"I thought you were a Marxist. An atheist!" Talbot said.

"I'm a Marxist who's met Helmuth von Moltke and Berthe von Hoffmann," Helen said. "Do you know how to pray? I haven't the faintest idea how to go about it."

Talbot curtly admitted he had never prayed as an adult. Helen assembled the eight U-boats and Ursula Fleischman, who slept at the house, and Helen asked them if they had any idea how to pray for Berthe. The answer was a series of embarrassed coughs. A few had tattered tags of formal prayers in their heads from Jewish, Protestant and Catholic rituals. Helen ruled them out. "This prayer has to have personal emotion in it," she said. "Spiritual energy."

"I think, as a first step, we should get down on our knees," Major Karl said.

"I second that motion," said the Jewish doctor, Frank. "Even though it's the first time I've ever done it."

They all knelt in the sandbagged living room.

"Now what?" Helen said.

"Maybe something will come to us," Talbot said. "That's how the Quakers do it." He was being sarcastic, but everyone took him literally. Doctor Frank had read about the Quakers. He gave them a little lecture on their faith in the inner light.

"You're turning this into a university course!" Ursula Fleischman cried. "Stop being so *German!*"

A moment later, the sirens wailed and a tremendous air raid began. The house shuddered and shook as blockbusters crashed around them. A direct hit would obliterate them all.

"Should we stay here, or head for the cellar?" Helen asked.

"I think we should stay here, " Major Karl said. "The first principle of praying should be trust."

"I think they call it faith," Doctor Frank said.

"Talbot," Helen said. "Read Berthe's letter."

By the light of a flickering candle, he read Berthe's affirmation of God's baffled love, while the roar of 1,000 bombers, the crash of 2,000 antiaircraft guns and the explosions of twice that many bombs shattered the night.

"A fascinating idea," Doctor Frank said. "I'm not sure I agree with it—"

"She's not asking us to agree with it!" Helen snapped. "Prophets—saints—aren't interested in logic. They just send messages—"

"What's the point in praying to a helpless God?" Talbot said, stubbornly clinging to his rationalism.

"It's a mystery!" Ursula Fleischman cried. Her arms were extended to form a cross. "Love is a mystery, hate is a mystery, life is a mystery. Why can't God be a mystery?"

"Maybe the Quakers are on to something," Major Karl said.

"We appoint you our spokeswoman, Ursula," Helen said.

The candle caught an eerie radiance on Ursula's face. The unhealthy red spots on her cheeks seemed to glow with a ghastly effulgence. Talbot wondered if she were dying of tuberculosis.

"God," she said. "If you are worthy of the name father, you will listen to eleven people who have no faith in you. We ask you to surround Berthe von Hoffmann with your care. We have no idea how you can do it. But we join this American, Jonathan Talbot, in lifting up our hearts in admiration and, yes, love, for her. None of us have the courage to pay the full price of discipleship, as she is doing. If you respond to this prayer, we can only offer you the promise that all of us will attempt to become disciples in her name!"

Again and again, explosions all but obliterated Ursula's voice. Flames flickered around the edges of the blackout curtains. The floor, the walls, continued to tremble. But no one moved except Helen Widerstand, who also stretched out her arms to form a cross.

"Does everyone agree with that?" Helen shouted above the blasts. "Will everyone make that pledge?"

There was a general mutter of assent in which Talbot more or less joined. But in his heart he was rejecting Ursula's prayer. He was never going to be anyone's disciple. First last and always, he was an independent operator. Only independent American ingenuity—and *action*—were going to save Berthe.

A tremendous blast blew in a window. Helen struggled to her feet and said: "That's enough faith for one night. Let's get down in the goddamn cellar."

49

VENGEANCE IS MINE, SAITH THE LORD

In London, columnist Anna Richman listened politely while Supreme Commander Dwight D. Eisenhower took five minutes from running the war to welcome her to Europe. She knew it was not a tribute to her reputation as a journalist, though having 350 papers behind her did not hurt. To the U.S. Army she was a congressman's daughter and across her forehead the desk warriors in Washington had virtually emblazoned: *postwar appropriations.*

After saying some nice things about Jack and expressing off-the-record regret that Zeke's attempts to alter unconditional surrender had failed, Ike shipped her to bespectacled Omar Bradley, his ground commander in France, who lectured her on the dangers of getting too close to the front. People kept getting killed up there by bullets and shell bursts. Annie said all the appropriate things about being careful and not being afraid and wanting to prove a woman could be as brave as a man, while the General listened with polite incredulity.

Bradley forwarded her to a balding, intense Army group commander named Matthew Ridgway, who issued the same warnings even more emphatically. At that point, she went over to the offensive and demanded a car and driver. Ridgway, who had just told her he could remember the names of 7,000 regulars from his twenty-five years in the Army, decided he had the perfect escort in his own headquarters. "In a pinch, he could hold off an entire German division," he said, reaching for a telephone.

Five minutes later, Master Sergeant Nathan Bedford Forrest Homewood loomed over them. He was six feet tall and almost six feet wide. Ridgway said he had been in the Army for thirty-two years and had lost his entire company on Omaha Beach at D-Day. He was "helping out" at headquarters while he "settled down."

"Homewood," Ridgway said in his crisp way, "the safety of this young woman is very important to the Army. You can't do anything more important for the Army than making sure she gets home in one piece. The Army—"

And so forth. Ridgway must have used "Army" twenty times in his lecture, while Homewood muttered: "Yes, General, sure, General." Annie began to suspect Ridgway had something more complicated in mind than her mere protection.

"Excuse me, Ma'am," Homewood snarled, as they headed down the road in a jeep. "But at the front—where you gonna pee?"

"In the bushes," Annie snapped. "While you stand guard to make sure nobody peeks."

The Sergeant drove in glowering silence, resisting all of Annie's attempts at conversation, until paranoia threatened her precarious equilibrium. Would this Neanderthal be eager to snarl "I told you so" over her riddled corpse, within minutes of getting to the front? They stopped for the night at a village inn and Homewood drank three bottles of *vin ordinaire,* which made him talkative. He told her about his boyhood in an Alabama sharecropper's shack with nine brothers and sisters and a father who was usually drunk. Then he started talking about his lost company—how hard they had trained, how much he had taught them—all wasted when their landing craft was hit by a half-dozen German .88 shells.

Annie realized the Sergeant was having the Army equivalent of a nervous breakdown. Ridgway's rhetoric was an attempt to convince Homewood that he still had a contribution to make, even if he was not in mental shape to lead a company. She decided there was a column here, even though D-Day was no longer hot copy. She got Homewood to tell her names, hometowns, anecdotes and by morning it was written. She showed it to the Sergeant at breakfast. He asked her to read it to him; he could not read "worth shit," he admitted.

Homewood was mesmerized. He stared at the typewritten pages and muttered: "People are gonna read this. It won't all be forgot. They'll know I done my damnedest." He asked if the column was published in Alabama.

"In five papers," Annie said.

Homewood stopped drinking more than a bottle of wine each night and began talking almost eagerly about escorting her to the front. He grew impatient when Annie spent their first two weeks together visiting prisoner of war camps, where she interviewed captured officers who had been stationed in Paris when the bomb exploded in Hitler's headquarters. From Zeke she knew the Paris commander, Gen. Karl Heinrich von Stuelpnagel, had been a key player in the plot. He had committed suicide rather than allow Hitler to get his hands on him. She found one of his aides, a slim hatchet-faced captain named Kurz, who told her that even with Hitler alive, the plot almost succeeded in France. General von Stuelpnagel had locked up all the Nazis in the Paris garrison. But he could not persuade the city's regular Army units to join him and eventually found himself with no loyalists but his immediate staff.

"Why wouldn't the regulars go along?" Annie asked.

"The oath of loyalty to the Führer—and that damnable insistence on unconditional surrender," Kurz said. With maximum bitterness he added: "Now that I've heard about the Morgenthau Plan for Germany, I regret to say they were right. If I were a free man, you would find me facing you in battle."

Confirming the story with a half-dozen other interviews, Annie wrote a blazing column excoriating unconditional surrender and calling on Roosevelt to modify it. She handed it to the Army censors at press headquarters in a big building in Versailles and retired to her hotel feeling savagely triumphant. If she went home a corpse, this story would be her legacy. It would show all the condescending male editors who had canceled "Behind The Headlines" what a woman reporter could accomplish.

If her queasy intimations of violent death came true, it might even make Zeke Talbot shed a regretful tear and give Berthe von Hoffmann uncomfortable thoughts. That presumed, of course, they were not lying in some shallow grave reserved for the Gestapo's victims. Or buried under tons of rubble in bomb-shattered Berlin.

The next morning Annie rushed to Versailles expecting an excited cable from Selma congratulating her for the column. Instead she found a message in her mailbox that the chief censor wanted to see her. A tired-looking colonel with a lantern jaw, he sat behind a desk in an ornate room out of the reign of Louis XIV. "Uh, Miss Richman, uh," he said. "We can't send this."

He handed her the story. Across the top, in red pencil, someone had written: *This subject has been barred from transmission by direct order of the President.* In Washington the press was free. Overseas, the news was under the control of the commander in chief. "If it makes you feel any better," the Colonel said. "I think it's a hell of an important story."

The Colonel fiddled with a paper clip. "He got reelected yesterday. Twenty-five million for, twenty-two million against. Not a landslide, but a win is a win. He's still in charge."

Annie had almost forgotten about the election. Roosevelt's mastery of power was incontestable. Why was she trying to challenge it? Fighting back bitter tears, she stumbled into the street, where Sergeant Homewood was waiting in their jeep. "I'm ready to go to the front," she said.

They arrived at the headquarters of the First Army in the flat plain beyond Aachen, the first German city to fall, in time for an offensive that everyone in the lower ranks hoped would end the war by Christmas. Homewood's friends—he knew old Army types everywhere—confided that it was an all-out push, aimed at breaching the Rhine and capturing the Ruhr, Germany's industrial heartland. Every infantry regiment had received a full quota of replacements; behind the front lines, artillery pieces stood hub to hub.

On November 2, after a thunderous barrage, Pennsylvanians of the Twenty-eighth Division attacked into the towering fir trees of the Hurtgen Forest south of Aachen. Annie followed them. It was impossible to see more than ten or twenty feet in any direction. Machine guns spat, rifle bullets whined everywhere. Artillery shells exploded in the treetops scattering metal fragments and jagged chunks of wood that shredded bodies.

Sergeant Homewood revealed an uncanny instinct for anticipating imminent death. Again and again, he blasted German snipers out of trees with his Garand rifle or mashed Annie into the mud seconds before a shell exploded. Between close calls he kept urging her to visit some less lethal part of the front. She ignored him and huddled in muddy foxholes talking about the war with stubble-bearded men whose lips twitched and hands shook in the perpetual presence of sudden death. She watched them go forward into the deadly cough of machine guns, the murderous whine of incoming mortars, she held plasma bottles over blood-soaked bodies while cursing medics injected morphine. Ten days later, as the Twenty-eighth Division stumbled out of the forest with 6,000 men dead and wounded, the rest staring zombies, Annie wrote a series of vivid columns, celebrating their agony.

But beneath the admiration, she had to deal with a growing bewilderment. The heroism, the caring these men displayed had no political vision. Most of them had no animosity against the Germans. The whole thing was a dirty job that history had handed them and manhood required them to meet it with courage and determination. Gradually she began to understand why Jack had been so tormented by their bleeding and dying. He had helped to start this war for reasons that had seemed vivid and vital to the future of the world from the vantage point of Washington, D.C. But it was hard, if not impossible, to glimpse a better future in the murderous gloom of the Hurtgen Forest.

Outside the forest, the rest of the First Army, and the Ninth Army just north of it, were not doing much better than the Pennsylvanians. The American high command called up a massive air assault code-named Operation Queen. Ten thousand tons of bombs descended on the Germans inside and outside the forest. When the American infantry and tanks went forward, they found the enemy very much alive in dugouts and pillboxes.

Across a landscape slashed by the raw scars of strip mines, dotted with ugly fields of stock beets and dozens of drab, stoutly built villages that became instant fortresses, the battle raged for a month. Homewood loved every minute of it. Attaching them to an infantry company, the Sergeant would use Annie as an excuse to demand maximum performance. "She's gonna make you famous," he would insist. "She done it for me and all I did was get my goddamn ass blown off at Omaha Beach."

When the foot soldiers advanced a bitter bloody quarter of a mile, Homewood would be right behind them, roaring advice to the officers and sergeants. "Dig in, dig in, these bastards will counterattack you inside an hour. They always do that." Meanwhile he would be excavating a foxhole as deep as a mineshaft for himself and Annie and squashing her into it. She would protest furiously that she wanted to see what was happening and crouch beside him taking notes, while the Germans doggedly counterattacked through the rain or sleet, exactly as Homewood had predicted.

"Why can't they see they're beaten?" Annie asked.

"Because they're tough sons of bitches!" the Sergeant roared. His Garand crashed in her ears, and another German toppled writhing into the mud.

Watching and listening to Homewood, Annie entered the ethos of the professional soldier. Homewood admired the Germans. They were "very, very good," he said. War, in Homewood's view, was a blood sport in which the lucky survived. The lucky and the brave. A vision of a better world was as irrelevant to him as it would have been to one of Julius Caesar's centurions.

By mid-December, American casualties had reached 57,000 men, plus another 70,000 down from pneumonia, trench foot and combat fatigue. The victory offensive petered out with the Allied Army nowhere near the Rhine, much less across it. Annie sought wisdom at Ninth Army headquarters. She asked the Ninth's elongated commander, Gen. William "Big Bill" Simpson, what was wrong.

Except for a kind crinkle at the corner of Simpson's shrewd eyes, his sharp-featured face might have matched the stereotype of the Prussian officer. "I just saw Eisenhower," he said. "He told me he's cabled Washington urging them to find a solution to reducing the German will to resist."

"By changing the policy of unconditional surrender?" Annie asked.

"Are we off the record?" Simpson asked.

"Sure."

"That would be the most obvious thing to do. I've got a colonel on my staff who's been interrogating prisoners. Seventy percent of them say they would have surrendered six months ago if it wasn't for unconditional surrender."

Three days later, Annie asked Simpson if Washington had responded. The General sighed and shook his head. "Roosevelt wouldn't budge but he let Ike ask Churchill to make a statement. Winnie said it was too late in the war to admit a mistake that big. He told us to imitate General Grant, and fight it out on this line if it takes all summer—or in our case—all winter."

In mid-December, a few days after the Americans fell back to a sullen, weary defensive, 1,000 German tanks and 250,000 men came slashing out of the forest of the Ardennes in a daring thrust aimed at seizing Antwerp, the Allies' chief supply port, and stranding their armies in the field without food or gasoline. Annie and Homewood were in the middle of the sleety chaos of retreating GIs and rampaging panzers. She attached herself to General Ridgway's headquarters and told her readers how the crisis transformed him into a veritable god of war, ruthlessly relieving fellow generals when they crumbled under pressure, grimly ordering exhausted men to hold to the death at bomb-pitted crossroads and in shell-smashed villages. Several times she watched Sergeant Homewood take charge of a demoralized company in one of these godforsaken places and organize a defense.

For Annie the climax of the battle was not the relief of the trapped paratroopers of the 101st Airborne in the surrounded city of Bastogne. It was a trip through a snowbound landscape to Malmedy, on the Belgian border. Homewood had heard from an old fellow sergeant at Ridgway's headquarters that in the fields outside the little village there was a story waiting to be told. Two hours later Annie sat in their jeep, staring at the bodies of 101 Americans lying in frozen agony, where they had been machine-gunned after they surrendered.

Homewood's attitude toward the Germans underwent a radical change. "The sons of bitches," he muttered under his breath. "The goddamn sons of bitches."

In a nearby prisoner of war camp, Annie found 800 survivors of *Kampfgruppe Pieper*—the battle group that had committed the massacre. Several officers told her they had received orders from Hitler that the American front "was to be broken by terror." She talked to Josef Pieper, the squat German colonel who had been in command at the scene. He was missing several teeth and his face was a mass of bruises. The Americans had persuaded him to confess the way Chicago police extracted guilty pleas from uncooperative criminals.

Annie wrote a series of columns describing the Malmedy massacre. With bitter sarcasm she told how the Germans had tried to explain Malmedy as *Blutrausch,* an intoxication of the blood that seizes troops in battle. "The Germans are marvelous at finding phrases which anesthetize the conscience," she wrote, not realizing that she was co-opting some of Zeke Talbot's prophetic gift.

The Battle of the Bulge, as the Ardennes offensive came to be called, killed and wounded another 81,000 Americans. As the Germans retreated an immense Allied host began a drive to the Rhine: 4 million men in three Army groups, 21 corps, 73 divisions. A confident American intelligence officer on the Ninth Army staff told Annie that each German battalion of 1,000 men now faced a 15,000-man American division.

Still the Wehrmacht fought on, bitter clashes exploding without warning in isolated towns while American tank columns rolled unopposed through other villages. Homewood led Annie to the hot spots, proclaiming his eagerness to kill as many Germans as possible to pay for Malmedy.

In a village only seven miles from the Rhine, fifty German paratroopers blasted advancing Americans with rocket grenades and machine-gun fire. Defeating them involved a Gettysburg-style assault over open ground and a house-to-house fight with grenades and bayonets. Only two Germans surrendered. At least one hundred Americans from the Eighty-fourth Division lay dead in the ruins beside the rest of them.

Homewood ruefully shook his head. "They may be sons of bitches but they're awful *good* sons of bitches."

In early February, as the Americans and British cleared pockets of Germans from the west bank of the Rhine, Roosevelt and Churchill met with Stalin at the Russian Black Sea resort of Yalta. Now, if ever, would be the moment to alter unconditional surrender. Virtually everyone in the American Army agreed that the Germans needed only a nudge to begin an avalanche of capitulation. Instead, the policy was reaffirmed, along with a lot of globaloney about the sanctity of borders and everyone's right to elect the government of his choice.

The Wehrmacht fought on, doggedly retreating to the east bank of the Rhine, blowing up bridge after bridge. The rumor mills predicted it would take a D-Day–size bloodbath to cross the deep swift river that had protected Germany for centuries. But luck—and some defective demolition fuses—enabled the Americans to seize a huge bridge at Remagen on March 7. By mid-March the Allies were surging into the heart of Germany. From north and south, armored columns closed a vise around the Ruhr, trapping more than 400,000 German soldiers.

As Annie and Homewood rode with a company of the Second Armored Division into the picture-postcard town of Hamelin, where the Pied Piper had once played, *panzerfausts*—German bazookas—erupted from rooftops ahead of them. The tank just in front of their jeep exploded into a fireball. A man rolled out of the turret, burning like a matchstick and lay twitching on the cobblestones. Three other tanks were hit; their crews scrambled out, dragging wounded men to safety, and the burly captain in command hastily withdrew the company to a hill outside the town.

"Call in a TOT," Homewood said. "Don't waste another man on that goddamn town."

A TOT was a time-on-target bombardment, which called in fire from every artillery battalion within range. "Look, someone's trying to surrender," Annie said. Below them on the main street, an old man was waving part of a sheet nailed to a broomstick.

"Call in a TOT," Homewood said.

The captain got on his radio. "There's ten battalions within range," he said. He pulled out a map and began reading coordinates to his headquarters. Fifteen minutes later, a huge whine vibrated in the sky above them. From north, south and west, a deluge of artillery shells descended on Hamelin. Gingerbread houses collapsed, fires erupted everywhere. In a half-hour the town was a smoldering wreck.

Once more the tanks rumbled up the cobblestoned main street. The old man, his face smeared with dirt and dust, staggered from a cellar. "Children!" he cried. "They're nothing but children."

Homewood peered past him into the smoke and roared: "Get down!"

Annie dove for the floor of the jeep as Homewood's forty-five boomed. When she looked up, two blond-haired boys in Hitler youth uniforms were sprawled in the street, blood gushing from chest wounds. Long-handled potato masher grenades lay on the cobblestones beside them. The old man wept helplessly.

"Jesus!" Homewood said. "They can't be more than twelve years old."

In 1945, the Pied Piper of Hamelin was Adolf Hitler. They found the bodies of a hundred heavily armed twelve- and thirteen-year-olds in the smoking rubble.

Annie began making notes for a book on the last two years of the war. It would tell the story of a president who allowed his blind hatred and ignorance and arrogance to compound the madness and hatred of Nazism. If Zeke was dead, it would be a memorial to his stubborn honesty, to the tragedy of the German resistance movement. Above all, it would be a denunciation of the murderous idea of total war and total victory—and the malevolent folly of unconditional surrender.

The next day, Homewood returned from an early morning visit to Second Armored headquarters as Annie finished writing a column on the destruction of Hamelin. "Nordhausen," he said. "There's somethin' hot there."

It was April 11, 1945—a date Annie would remember for the rest of her life. They rode with two armored task forces, named for their colonels—Wellborn and Lovelady—to the small city at the foot of the looming Harz Mountains. Beyond the neat rows of civilian houses lay a sprawling complex of buildings ringed by barbed wire. Entering the gates, Annie was almost overwhelmed by the stench. "This place must be a goddamned slaughterhouse!" Homewood said.

Moments later the inmates of Nordhausen tottered toward them, pipestem arms flapping inside striped coats, ghastly smiles on their death's-head faces. An American captain reeled out of one of the buildings and vomited against the wall. Annie and Homewood went inside to stare at rows upon rows of skin-covered skeletons lying in their own feces. A naked teenage girl lay in the middle of the floor where she had fallen, her body rotted with gangrene.

An American stumbled up the stairs, a handkerchief to his face and mumbled, "The cellar's worse. My God!" Her reporter's code required Annie to go down and Homewood followed to protect her. The stench of death was indescribable. The living lay in bunks beside the dead, their eyes focused on nothing. Beneath the stairs lay seventy-five bodies stacked like cordwood. In the dimness she found a major from the medical corps. "There's nothing we can do," he said. "Half of them will be dead in the next twenty-four hours."

"Sons of sons of sons of sons of bitches!" Homewood said.

The world had discovered Germany's concentration camps. On the same day, other American Army units liberated Ohrdruf and Buchenwald. Before nightfall correspondents were swarming through all three camps. Annie's story and their stories blazed a message of horror to an aghast world. They detailed the beatings, the

starvation, the casual executions by SS guards, the smoking cremato-
riums where the bodies vanished. First Jews, then slave laborers
from other European countries had been consumed in Nordhausen's
holocaust. Nearby, in vast tunnels beneath the Harz Mountains, they
had toiled on the V-2 rockets that had devastated London. Each day,
at least 150 died from malnutrition or physical abuse.

As she wrote the story, Annie realized she was saying farewell to
her book on the tragedy of the German resistance movement. The
hatred unleashed by these revelations would make Roosevelt's insistence on unconditional surrender seem like wisdom. Maybe it was
wisdom. She felt nothing but hatred in her soul now. She exulted as
Homewood told her that the GIs had found one of the German
rocket scientists hiding in the underground factory and had beaten
him to a senseless pulp. She all but cheered as the cowed citizens of
Nordhausen were dragged from their neat houses and forced to see
the bestialities that had been committed on their doorsteps. She felt
no pity when several went home and hanged themselves.

The next day, General Eisenhower arrived to see Nordhausen for
himself. His face convulsed in atypical fury, he issued orders to bring
every American unit in the vicinity to the place. "People complain
that American soldiers don't know what they're fighting for. Here
they can at least find out what they're fighting *against,*" he said.

"General," Annie said. "Does this mean you'll drive as rapidly as
possible on Berlin? Perhaps you can capture Hitler and make him
pay for these crimes."

"Nothing would please me more," Eisenhower said. "But President Roosevelt agreed at the Yalta Conference to let the Russians
capture Berlin. Our forces have been ordered to halt on the River
Elbe."

Unhappiness on several faces in Eisenhower's entourage alerted
Annie to a story. She mingled with the majors and colonels while the
Supreme Commander had lunch in Nordhausen. From the lower
ranks she learned that Churchill had visited Eisenhower two days ago
and begged him to advance as rapidly as possible on Berlin. The Russians were already breaking all the promises they had made at Yalta
to tolerate non-Communist politicians in Poland and the other
nations of Eastern Europe. Churchill wanted to rescue Eastern Germany from Stalin. A violent argument had ensued among the Americans and the British, with numerous American generals on the prime

minister's side. The decision had finally been referred to the White House—and Roosevelt had ruled against Churchill.

The President's policy was still anchored in his blind hatred of Germany and his amoral attempt to placate Stalin. But after Nordhausen, who could say it was wrong? Zeke Talbot's heroism, Annie's betrayal of Saul Randolph in the name of the future of the world, were all for nothing. They were mere ripplets on history's brutal current, ridiculously meaningless gestures.

Roosevelt, the master of power, had prevailed. Annie shuddered at what he would do to Germany now, with the horrors of the concentration camps in his speechwriters' hands. The Morgenthau Plan would be revived, with even more vengeful details. America would be embroiled in Europe's hatreds as never before—with communism adding class hatred to the murderous stew.

Eisenhower offered a glimpse of what was coming as he left Nordhausen. The General returned the salute of the boyish sentry at the gate of the camp and asked: "Still find it hard to hate them?"

"No sir!" the soldier replied.

Annie wrestled with these bitter thoughts as they drove east toward the Elbe. Homewood had picked up some more hot news. The commander of the Second Armored Division had a plan for a lightning thrust to Berlin. Maybe he would do it without asking Ike's okay. "Imagine bein' in on capturin' Adolf?" he chortled. "It'd be the story of the century!"

Annie barely listened. The news, that precursor of history, was turning to ashes in her mouth. On the night of April 12, they found the Second Armored Division's headquarters in a neat little German village a few miles from the banks of the Elbe. Walking into the operations center, Annie thought the atmosphere was oddly subdued. She had expected an array of exultant young American faces, eager to tell her how they had advanced 75 miles in a single day to reach this historic point.

Homewood was puzzled too. "What the hell's wrong with you guys?" he asked.

"Haven't you heard about it?" a cherubic choked-up captain said. "The President's dead. A heart attack or stroke or some damned thing."

Several enlisted men were sobbing. "I feel as if I lost my best friend," one said.

The master of power had discovered his limits—on the brink of a victory that would have made him virtually omnipotent. Annie trembled from head to foot. Men did not control history any more than women did. They were all ultimately helpless in its unforeseeable twists and turns. Was it possible that above and beyond the febrile plans and policies and solutions of presidents and generals, prime ministers and dictators, kings and commissars, an inscrutable God brooded over the future of the world?

50

BEYOND HISTORY

A morose Jonathan Talbot paced the living room of Helen Wider-stand's house, while their resident physician, Dr. Frank, gave injections to a half-dozen men from the neighborhood. The drugs would induce a rapid heartbeat and other symptoms of coronary disease and exempt them from service in the Volksturm.

Night and day, Berlin shuddered under the impact of thousands of tons of bombs. The Third Reich was dying in a cataclysm of flame and explosions. But the Germans fought on. Every block was scoured again and again for Volksturm fugitives. On the Eastern and Western fronts, their disintegrating armies continued a desperate resistance.

Through the front door crashed Helen Widerstand with an armful of groceries—and some electrifying news. "The Americans are on the Elbe! That's only fifty miles away!"

Hope crowding his throat, Talbot bicycled into the countryside with his radio and contacted William Casey in London to make another report on the situation in the capital. (He changed locations each time to make sure German monitors did not catch up to him.) Once more he assured Casey that everyone in Berlin except the most fanatical Nazis was praying that the Americans would arrive before the Russians.

UNLIKELY NOW BERLIN CONCEDED TO RUSSIAN SPHERE, clicked the signal from London. CONCEDED BY

WHOM. WHEN? WHERE? Talbot asked. ROOSEVELT. YALTA CONFERENCE, was the reply.

Radio Berlin had reported Churchill, Roosevelt and Stalin had met at Yalta in the Crimea to decide postwar policy. Hitler's propaganda expert, Joseph Goebbels, tried to paint Stalin as the master manipulator who was seducing the two Westerners into an unholy pact with Bolshevism. It began to look as if for once the Nazis were not far wrong.

The disappointment was par for Jonathan Trumbull Talbot's course. From a man who had once presumed everything in his life was going exactly the way he wanted it, he had descended to total pessimism—nothing in his life went right. He was condemned to perpetual futility, if not an early death. Berthe von Hoffmann remained out of reach in Ravensbruck, welcoming the fate her helpless God was inflicting on her. This news from Casey unquestionably sealed her doom.

On the way back to Helen Widerstand's house, Talbot got caught in a daylight air raid. The bombs came down in terrifying numbers and he was right in the middle of them. He leaped off his bike and raced for the doorway of a big, solid looking building, lugging his twenty-pound radio. A blast knocked him down a flight of stairs. He crawled down a hall into a shelter filled with screaming, sobbing women as more bombs blasted the top floors of the building. Miraculously, the basement floor held up under six stories of rubble. It took nine hours for firemen to break through a wall and rescue them.

At Helen Widerstand's house, he found her and the eight U-boats listening anxiously to Radio Berlin. "Roosevelt's dead," Helen said. "A cerebral hemorrhage. What do you think it means?"

It was stunning news—but Talbot saw it would do little to change their situation. He told them about the decision to let the Russians capture Berlin. "The vice president—an ex-senator named Truman—will become president. He won't make any policy changes. Roosevelt was too popular. He'll just play caretaker."

"We all better start praying extra hard to get Berthe out of Ravensbruck," Helen said. "The Russians aren't more than thirty miles away from it."

That night they could hear the thud of artillery in the east. The sky glowed with fiery explosions. On the radio, Goebbels frantically tried to convert the news of Roosevelt's death into a sign from providence that their Führer, still alive in spite of traitorous attempts to kill him, was destined to triumph. From his bunker under the ruined chancellery, Hitler announced Berlin would be defended to the last man, woman and child.

The U-boats could not understand why Talbot did not get out of Berlin while there was still time to escape. Even Helen intimated there was no sensible reason for him to stay. But he stubbornly rejected this cautionary advice. The promise he had made to Berthe in La Mancha was still paramount, even if it no longer had anything to do with romance.

Two days later, Helen came crashing into the house with truly electrifying news. Berthe had been transferred from Ravensbruck to the Lehrterstrasse Prison, the Gestapo's preferred Berlin jail. Everyone even vaguely connected to the Schwarze Kapelle conspiracy was being gathered there for purposes that could only be construed as ominous.

At least they could communicate with Berthe again. The prison chaplain was a resister who had smuggled letters to and from Moltke and other victims of Hitler's Sippenhaft. They were also able to send Berthe food and warm blankets. Like almost everything else in Berlin, the Lehrterstrasse's heating system had expired. The huge, red brick jail was like a giant refrigerator.

Berthe's first letter was not reassuring.

Dearest J:

Thank you for the food, which I could barely eat. My stomach seems to have shriveled to the size of a four-year-old's. But that is the least of my woes. Before they dispatched me from Ravensbruck, they cut off my hair! It was a filthy mess, I know, surely an offense against the Gestapo's pristine standards. But it affected me terribly. To think, in spite of the wreck I've become, I could still harbor this last shred of female vanity! It shows God is by no means making a mistake, sending me this ordeal. When it comes to holiness, I am a very difficult case. Of course, you could have told Him that long ago. It pains me to think how much I failed to love you—and Ernst— and so many others as they should have been loved—for themselves, without demands or questions. I can only hope my jailers won't prolong the agony much longer. I heard from the Ravensbruck commander as I was being transferred that they've recently hanged Admiral Canaris, Colonel

Oster and several others. He said Canaris spent his last night on earth reading Kantorowicz's biography of Frederick II. I find that wonderfully ennobling—and sad. Pray that when the moment comes, I can meet it with similar courage.

"I've had it up to here with this holiness bullshit," Talbot raged at Helen Widerstand. "Let's try to get her out of there. Get your printer to work on forging some papers. Talk your Gestapo pal into telling us what to say."

Helen's Gestapo ally had abandoned any and all sentimental attachments to the regime. He was more than willing to help arrange Berthe's rescue. But smuggling the papers out of Gestapo headquarters on PrinzAlbrechtstrasse and struggling across Berlin's bomb-cratered distances took maddening amounts of time. The first print shop in which the transfer orders were to be fabricated was demolished by a bomb. The papers had to be stolen all over again while Helen found another printer—not easy, because it was the sort of work for which a man and his entire family would be executed without trial.

By the time the papers were finally ready, Russian shells were exploding in Berlin's suburbs. The city was all but sealed off except for a narrow passage to the west when Talbot slipped his silver warrant identity disk over his head and equipped himself with a Walther pistol and his papers certifying him as Gerhard Bonfils of the Gestapo. With his suitcase radio strapped on the back of his bicycle, he navigated along the littered streets to the Lehrterstrasse. Helen Widerstand rode a half-block behind him and Karl, the runaway major, a half-block behind her. On several street corners, corpses of Volksturm deserters swung from lampposts, with TRAITOR scrawled on cards around their necks.

In front of the huge star-shaped prison clustered a pathetic group of elderly men and women, still loyally sending in food and blankets and letters to their loved ones. Most of them had the straight backs and stiff features of the old Prussian nobility. "The new meeting place for the elite," Helen said as they rode past.

A block and a half away, Talbot stashed his bike and radio in the dark hallway of a wrecked building, with Helen and Major Karl as their guardians. Helen had clothes and a hat for Berthe in a suitcase strapped to her bike. Their plan was to take Berthe back to Helen's house, where Dr. Frank could care for her for a few days. Meanwhile Talbot would pedal into the countryside and ask William Casey for a plane.

As Talbot walked past acres of rubble toward the prison, he knew that if anyone challenged the order transferring Berthe to PrinzAl-brechtstrasse, he was in trouble. The possibility of meeting another Gestapo agent in the prison was also large. He had no small talk to exchange with him. Helen's Gestapo ally said only a squad of totally trustworthy agents were dealing with the Schwarze Kapelle survivors.

If it came to a challenge, Talbot planned to rely on his OSS weaponry. In a shoulder holster he was carrying a Bigot, a .45 pistol that fired a dart with terrific force, killing instantly and silently. He hoped noiseless murder would give them time to run for cover in the surrounding ruins. U-boater Major Karl had two Walther pistols under his coat and promised to do some shooting to slow down the pursuit.

Talbot was about a hundred yards from the entrance to the build-ing when a gray military car turned the corner, coming from the direction of the Reich chancellery. He could see two men in visored hats in the front seat. Talbot stared at the ground and walked a little faster.

The car screeched to a stop. The driver flung open the front door and sprang into the dusty street. He was wearing a dark blue naval officer's uniform. "Talbot!" shouted Wolfgang Griff. "Aren't you Tal-bot?" He had a gun in his hand.

The passenger got out on the other side. He too was in a Navy uniform. "Of course he's Talbot," Ernst von Hoffmann said. "What the hell are you doing in Berlin, Commander?"

"I'm afraid you're mistaken," Talbot said. "I'm Gerhard Bonfils of the Gestapo. Here are my papers."

"His German is as perfect as ever," Ernst said.

Griff's tongue darted across his lips in his snakelike way. "Shall I shoot him, Herr Fregattenkapitan? There's no time for formalities."

Talbot ignored him. "I still don't know what you're talking about. I'm Gerhard Bonfils and I have papers here ordering me to transfer Berthe von Hoffmann from the Lehrterstrasse Prison to PrinzAl-brechtstrasse." He pulled out the papers and handed them to Ernst.

"Bullshit," Griff snarled. "What's my father's rank in the Gestapo? What's his function?"

"I was transferred from the Ruhr only last month. I don't know many people at PrinzAlbrechtstrasse."

"Everyone knows my father. He's in charge of interrogating prisoners."

Talbot could only stare helplessly at the pistol. So this was how it was going to end. God was displaying his divine indifference to human hopes once more. Berthe had tried to explain the tiny light she had glimpsed at the heart of the mystery, the possibility of God's helplessness. All Talbot could taste in his soul was his old familiar bitterness, scalding his mind and heart with ultimate intensity.

"Berthe is in the Lehrterstrasse?" Ernst said, glancing at the papers.

"They've gathered all the survivors of the Schwarze Kapelle for a final slaughter," Talbot said, abandoning his Gestapo pretenses.

"Shall I shoot him, Herr Fregattenkapitan?" Griff asked. "There's no time to waste if we want to get out of this city."

"Put him in the car. I want to find out from Berthe what this fellow's been doing in Berlin. It—it could be important."

"I don't see how—" Griff whined.

"Put him in the car!" Ernst said.

Griff prodded Talbot into the back seat and slithered after him, his gun still trained on him. Ernst disappeared into the prison. "I suppose he wants to hand you both over to the Gestapo," Griff said. "You and darling traitorous Berthe can be my father's last customers. They'll begin with the glove. They put your hand into it and slowly turn a screw that drives spikes into your fingertips. Then they'll use the iron pants. That's a pair of tubes lined with spikes. They screw them tighter and tighter, driving them in all the way to the bone. They usually put your head inside a metal hood and cover it with a blanket to muffle the screams. But they won't bother doing that with you. Then they stretch you on a rack until you can hear your ligaments begin to crack like whips. Then you're trussed up and clubbed so that each time you fall forward on your face with your full weight. By that time you'll tell them anything. You'll confess every detail of how often you fucked Berthe. You'll tell them the names of every person who helped you in Berlin. If you balk, they'll hang you upside down and go to work on Berthe. I'm almost tempted to stay around to watch the fun—"

Ich kann nicht anders. The voice growled in Talbot's head with a ferocity that paralyzed him. Was it merely a personal lamentation, testifying to the central truth in his journey down Berthe's shrouded Path? Or was it also the strangled cry of God, confessing His vast tormented helplessness? For a stunning moment Talbot felt lifted up by a presence that defied terror and pain. He met this Nazi howl from the abyss with a faith that his death and Berthe's death would have meaning beyond and above the power of any country, king, Führer or president. A fantastic sense of triumph suffused him. Love had carried him beyond history to the shore of the eternal.

51

ANOTHER PAGE OF GLORY

Berthe in Berlin. It was too bizarre, Ernst thought, as he strode into the Lehrterstrasse Prison. But everything was bizarre these days. He had just come from the Führer bunker beside the ruined Reich chancellery, where he had met Adolf Hitler for the last time. Ranting, whining, the Führer had explained why Fregattenkapitan von Hoffmann had been summoned to Berlin. He was to convey a personal order to Grossadmiral Dönitz, an order that the Führer did not wish to send through Army headquarters, which handled all the bunker's incoming and outgoing radio messages.

The hysterical words still reverberated in Ernst's skull. "Because the Grossadmiral has repeatedly proven himself to be the most faithful of my followers, I hereby authorize him to assume the power and authority of Führer when he receives an appropriate message from Party Minister Bormann. It will inform him that I have committed suicide, in company with Dr. Goebbels and others in the bunker with whom I have made a solemn pact. As Führer, I enjoin on the Grossadmiral as his first task the capture and execution of Reichs-führer Himmler! We have discovered through interceptions of enemy broadcasts that he is attempting to negotiate a truce with the Western powers. Destroy the traitor! That is my last order!"

Heil, Hitler, Ernst thought with bitter irony as he entered the courtyard of the prison. Two sullen SS guards raised their arms in the

Party salute. Ernst returned it. "I want to see the prisoner, Berthe von Hoffmann. I believe she's being held here under investigation for treason," Ernst said.

One of the guards led him down a corridor to a huge, canary yellow iron door. On the left was a small window behind which sat another SS man, with a round, fat suspicious face. Ernst repeated his request; the doorkeeper paged through an alphabetical list and found Berthe's name and cell number. He summoned an internal guard, who was not an SS man. He led Ernst up corrugated iron stairs and along an upper platform past cell doors that did not reach the ceiling, as in a cheap lavatory. The place was very noisy, with guards clanking around in heavy boots, whistling and shouting to each other.

Why did he want to see Berthe? Ernst wondered. To thank her for not betraying him? The Gestapo had not tortured her. They had parked her in Ravensbruck, one of the milder concentration camps, where she could meditate on her sins and perhaps decide to make a full confession. Apparently, they knew little or nothing of her involvement with Stauffenberg. The Schwarze Kapelle had covered their tracks well.

Was he thinking of using Talbot's papers to take her out of this jail and hand them both over to the Gestapo? That would hardly make sense. In revenge she might tell enough lies to land him in the cellars of PrinzAlbrechtstrasse or wherever the Gestapo might set up shop in the crumbling fortress of the Reich. On the other hand, if he was a true follower of the Führer, it was important to find out if there were other Americans in Berlin besides Talbot. They might pose a security threat.

That too was laughable. The main security threat was only a few miles away—some five or six thousand Russian tanks and several hundred thousand infantrymen. No, he simply wanted to see Berthe again for no particular reason—except perhaps to tell her he expected to die soon after the SS executed her.

Seven days ago, they had evacuated naval headquarters and fled to Plon, north of Berlin. The Army's high command had set up a headquarters not far away, in Neu Roofen. It was soon apparent that resistance was collapsing everywhere. The roads were clogged with refugees fleeing west. Local Army commanders were making on the spot decisions about whether to surrender, retreat or fight.

Grossadmiral Dönitz was one of the few who refused to waver.

Only yesterday he had sent 3,000 naval cadets armed with panzer-fausts and World War I–vintage rifles north to stop Russian tanks. "The Kriegsmarine will fight to the end!" he declared. He told Ernst and his other aides that on the final day, he would surrender the Navy and seek death in battle. He obviously expected them to imitate his example.

Yes, Ernst thought. He wanted to tell that to Berthe. Perhaps it would console her to know he would not be dragged in front of a British court and hanged for machine gunning the survivors of the *Martin de Porres.* Perhaps she would also want to know the children were safe. He had evacuated them from Berlin months ago and sent them south to Bavaria, where his mother had relatives.

The guard stopped before Cell 98, unlocked the heavy steel door, and stepped back to permit Ernst to enter. There were no windows. Light glared from a powerful lamp in the ceiling. Berthe lay on a cot, curled in a fetal position, her face to the wall. She rolled over, blinking against the glaring overhead light like an animal in a zoo.

Ernst had expected proud Berthe, her golden hair gleaming, defiantly invoking her strange God and His mysterious consolation. This creature in front him was shaved virtually bald. Her face was a mass of sores. More ugly pustules oozed on her pipestem arms and legs and neck. Her skin was a dirty yellow. Beneath her thin, soiled dress there was barely a sign of a body. She had shrunk to a ruined toy.

"Berthe! My God—what's happened to you?" Ernst said, as the guard's footsteps retreated down the corridor.

"Ernst?" She trembled and moved away from him like a trapped rodent. "Have you come to mock the ruins?"

"I had no idea. I swear to God, Berthe, I had no idea!"

"Why bother to lie now, Ernst? It's almost over."

"I swear to God, Berthe, I thought you were being treated reasonably well."

A faint smile twisted her mouth. "Now you know the truth, Ernst."

Somewhere in Ernst's mind huge structures collapsed, massive statues toppled into Berlin's rubble. Once this woman had been his Germany. Her voice had sung its songs to him, her lips had recited its poetry. Her beauty had been a glow of triumph in his arms, a sense of northern treasure. In her mind lived centuries of German history that she had shared with him, a thick-headed sailor who could never have graduated from a university. The love she had offered him with her lips, her breasts, her thighs had been his page of glory.

Everything tumbled into the rubble: *führer, volk, vaterland.* The words became treachery, betrayal, monstrous lies fed to him and the rest of the German people in the name of insane revenge on other races and nations. Hardness vanished too, another myth propagated by that shambling, whining coward in the führerbunker. Finally crashed the figure of the Lion, the Grossadmiral with his blind faith in obsolete U-boats and the führer principle. A wintry wind from beyond the stars howled through the ruins of Ernst von Hoffmann's world.

Suddenly he knew exactly what he was going to do. "You must pull yourself together, Berthe, and come with me. No harm will befall you, I swear it on our love, on the faces of our children. You must find the strength to walk out of here beside me. This must look like an ordinary transfer. If I have to carry you, the guards may suspect I've succumbed to pity and I'm trying to rescue you."

She looked at him with total disbelief.

"Berthe. You must do it, for Georg and Greta's sake. Not for my sake or your own sake. Do you want to leave them at the mercy of my mother and her relatives for the rest of their lives? Get up! Get on your feet!"

She struggled to a sitting position. He lifted her erect and she collapsed into his arms. He picked her up. She could not weigh more than ninety pounds.

"Oh my love," he whispered. "If only I'd listened to you. If only I'd managed to save honor from the wreck." He kissed the running sores around her mouth. "You must walk," he said. "You have to look strong enough for a Gestapo interrogation."

Past whistling, indifferent interior guards Berthe hobbled, clinging to his arm. Her feet were swollen to twice their normal size. Every step was agony. At the yellow door Ernst presented Talbot's transfer orders to the fat SS guardian. "Lieutenant Wolfgang Griff and I just captured one of her accomplices in the plot against the Führer. We're taking them both to PrinzAlbrechtstrasse," he said.

"Is she related to you, Herr Fregattenkapitan?" the man asked, scanning the papers.

"She's my ex-wife. I divorced her years ago. I guess I smelled disloyalty."

"You can still smell it," the guard said, wrinkling his nose. Berthe's body odor was rank.

Berthe hobbled beside him to the car. He thrust her into the backseat beside Griff, who emitted a squawk of revulsion. "What a piece of offal she's become, Herr Fregattenkapitan," he said.

Talbot could only stare at Berthe in disbelieving horror.

She shrank into the corner of the backseat, mortified by his presence. "Ernst, how could you lie to me this way?" she cried. "Did you want him to see me before you killed him? Did you want us both to die with disgust in our hearts?"

"We won't die that way," Talbot said. "Nothing they do to us can change the way we've loved each other—and what we've tried to do in the name of that love—to carry a spark of faith through time."

Exaltation transformed Berthe's shrunken face. "Oh, Jonathan," she said. "Now I can bear anything."

So that was how he seduced her, Ernst thought. He pretended to believe in her incomprehensible God. For a moment Ernst almost ordered Griff to shoot the double-talking American on the spot. But he was an essential part of his plan to save Berthe. "You drive," he said to Griff. "I'll get in the back with her."

Ernst ordered Talbot into the front seat, took Griff's pistol and got in beside Berthe. Griff slid behind the wheel. "Where to, Prinz Albrechtstrasse?" he asked.

Russian shells began exploding in the rubble only a few blocks away. "I don't think we have time," Ernst said. "Unless we want to join the Führer in his Götterdämmerung. Head out of the city. We'll dispose of these two at some convenient spot."

"I hope you'll let me pull the trigger, Herr Fregattenkapitan," Griff said. "I'll give it to them in the back of the neck, the way we kill Jews."

"You can shoot Berthe. I reserve the pleasure of shooting Talbot," Ernst said.

"Let him go, Ernst. He's innocent. He only came here because he loved me," Berthe said.

He pressed her hand trying to tell her he was playacting for Griff's benefit. They crunched past burned-out blocks of apartment houses, threaded around anti-tank barricades manned by fifteen- and sixteen-year-olds in the Volksturm, beeped through crowds of refugees heading west pushing bicycles or baby carriages loaded with a few pathetic possessions. Here and there people stood in lines before food shops while Russian guns thundered in the distance.

Finally they reached the forest of Grunewald, where the crowds of refugees thinned because most of them were taking a more direct route west. Having driven to the city that day, Griff knew the only way out lay along this route to Potsdam. Soon they were deep in the Grunewald, which was beginning to bud. The air was rich with the scent of spring.

"I think this will do for our place of execution," Ernst said.

Griff slowed the car and pulled off the road into a grassy glade. Huge pine trees loomed against the blue sky. Ernst put the pistol against the back of Griff's neck and pulled the trigger. The little Nazi unleashed an aborted scream and slumped over the wheel.

"What happens now?" Talbot said, eyeing the pistol. He probably thought Ernst intended to kill him and Berthe too and had eliminated Griff because he did not want a witness.

"You're going to take off his uniform and help me put it on Berthe," Ernst said. "Then you're going to put on my uniform and drive west until you reach the Elbe. The American Ninth Army has a beachhead on the east bank. All you have to worry about are some remnants of the Wehrmacht pretending to oppose them."

They dragged Griff's body deeper into the forest and swiftly exchanged clothes. Talbot was almost exactly Ernst's size, so they had no problem. Griff's uniform fit Berthe's shrunken body fairly well.

"If you're stopped by any German roadblocks, tell them you're evacuating this officer by order of Grossadmiral Dönitz. She certainly looks sick enough to qualify for emergency transportation. Tell them you're taking her to a clinic in Magdeburg, which is still in our hands. Here are my papers, certifying you as a member of the Grossadmiral's staff. And Griff's."

He handed the two wallets to Talbot. "What are you going to do?" Talbot asked.

"Don't worry about me," Ernst said. "I'm letting you go for two reasons. Berthe needs you—and you may be able to talk your Americans into pushing a tank column into this side of Berlin and save some of the city from the Russians."

"I'll try," Talbot said.

"I'll always love you," Berthe said, tears streaming down her ruined face. "I never really stopped."

"Promise me you won't tell the children the whole truth about me for twenty-five—even fifty years. So when they hear it they'll be adults, with enough maturity to bear the blow."

"I promise. On the memory of our love."

He kissed her sad, ugly mouth again. "Take care of her, Talbot. If you fail, my ghost will haunt you."

"I'll do my best," Talbot said. For some reason he looked downcast. Ernst wondered if Berthe's farewell words had given him a small victory in the personal war he had waged with this infuriating American since they met aboard the Ritterboot.

He watched them drive west and then walked back through the Grunewald to the main highway. Using Talbot's Silver Warranty Gestapo disk, he hitched a ride on an Army truck to the center of Berlin. The men in the truck were all overage members of the Volksturm. Assuming he was on Gestapo assignment to check up on their performance, they glared sullenly at him until some SS police waved the truck to a stop and ordered everyone to disembark at an anti-tank barricade on the Bendlerstrasse, not far from the Tiergarten. The streets up ahead were under Russian artillery fire. There were Russian tanks not more than a mile away.

Ernst left them conferring with the SS Sturmbahnführer in charge of the barricade and walked past the blasted hulk of Army headquarters and the courtyard where Stauffenberg and the other leaders of the Schwarze Kapelle had died eight months ago. A few blocks away he found about forty Volksturm kids armed with old rifles and a half-dozen gasoline bombs manning another anti-tank barrier.

A low-slung Russian T-34 tank rounded the corner and advanced on the barrier, its cannon leveled. The first shot was high. The second shot hit the barrier, killed a half-dozen kids and sent the rest into wild flight. Alone, Ernst seized one of the gasoline bombs, lit the fuse with his cigarette lighter, and leaped through the hole in the barrier.

He came at the tank on the dead run, the bomb hefted in his right hand, the fuse sizzling fiercely. Attack! Strike! Sink! He was performing once more in the best tradition of the Ubootwaffe. The tank braked to a stop as if the commander could not believe the sight of a single civilian attacking his armored monster. He waggled his cannon at him but Ernst was much too small a target for the big gun. The commander switched to his machine gun seconds too late.

"Long live holy Germany!" Ernst shouted and flung the gasoline bomb as the machine gun opened fire. He was not among the men of honor but he could at least die in the doorway of their temple of fame. Somehow he was sure Berthe would eventually find his hand in the darkness and drag him inside. As a dozen bullets riddled Ernst's chest, the tank exploded into a fountain of blue and yellow flame.

It was another page of glory that would never be written.

52

A SPECIAL PROVIDENCE

Annie Talbot watched the single engine Piper Cub bump to a landing in an open field a few hundred yards from the Elbe River. Out of the tiny plane crawled Gen. William "Big Bill" Simpson, the commander of the Ninth Army. Annie joined a half-dozen other reporters who rushed to ask the question of the hour: "Any luck, General? Are we on our way to Berlin?"

Simpson shook his head. "I did my damnedest, boys. Ike said no."

Roosevelt's death had encouraged General Simpson to fly to Omar Bradley's headquarters with a plan of attack that would have put the Ninth Army in Berlin in twenty-four hours. Glumly he told them Bradley had called Eisenhower and tried to change his mind. But Ike's answer was still no, exactly as Annie had expected. It was too soon to alter the arrangements Franklin Roosevelt had made, no matter what Eisenhower and the new president, Harry Truman, thought of them. America was still undergoing a paroxysm of grief as millions mourned the man whose charismatic leadership had been a part of their lives for over a dozen years.

Annie trudged back to the room Sergeant Homewood had wangled for her in the nearby village, listening to other reporters curse Ike for blowing the last big story of the war. In her pocket was another cable from Saul Randolph. They had started arriving the day after Roosevelt's death. The first one read:

NORDHAUSEN. WHAT DO YOU THINK NOW, MISS SUMMA CUM LOUSY?

The next one read:

DACHAU. WHAT DO YOU THINK NOW, MISS SUMMA CUM LOUSIER?

The latest one read:

BUCHENWALD. WHAT DO YOU THINK NOW, MISS SUMMA CUM LOUSIEST?

At the head of the village's main street was a small church, little more than a rectangular slant-roofed box with a weathered steeple. Not for the first time, Annie walked in and sat down in a rear pew. For some reason she responded to the stark simplicity of the interior. The walls were whitewashed, the only decoration was a bare cross above the altar. It was the total opposite of Trinity College's elegant chapel, with its marble floors and stained-glass windows and gold tabernacle.

This church seemed a better place to deal with essentials. God, faith, love, marriage, politics, history, men, women. She wanted to go back to the roots of her life and rethink everything. But she did not get very far. A strange numbness dulled her body and an even stranger blankness paralyzed her mind.

She brooded about the decision to abandon Berlin to the Russians. Did it matter? If Zeke Talbot was still alive in the besieged city, he could be killed by an American tank just as easily as by a Russian tank. He was not a part of her future. He had chosen to risk his life for beautiful Berthe. He was not the reason she had wasted a week in this miserable village.

A cough. An officer was sitting across the aisle from her. A big bear of a man with a round, good-natured face. A major's gold leaves gleamed on his solid shoulders.

"I don't belong here," she said, trying to forestall a religious conversation. "I'm a fallen away Catholic."

"Neither do I," he said with a quick smile. "I'm Jewish."

She shook hands with Rabbi Abraham Weiss. "I saw you at Nordhausen," he said. "Is that why you're here?"

"Maybe," she said. "Is it why you're here?"

He nodded. "I need someplace to think about God. I sense His presence here. People have prayed to Him here."

"You still believe in Him? After Nordhausen, Orhdruf, Buchen-wald, Dachau?" She could have added a dozen other names to the list of German death camps that were now public knowledge.

"For the time being I can't communicate with Him," Rabbi Weiss said, his voice thick with mourning tones. "I'm like Job on his dungheap—or worse. But I intend to go on believing, in the hope that some light will break through. It may take a long time. Mean-while, maybe I can help others."

"'Oh, Lord, I believe, help thou my unbelief,'" Annie said. "The centurion said that to Jesus. I never understood what it meant."

"For some reason I've been thinking of two very different things," Rabbi Weiss said. "The first is a book I read recently about Lincoln's religion. In the White House he came to believe in a God that presided over history. Again and again he sensed His presence when he made decisions without completely understanding why, without all the information he needed. It's a biblical idea. The Puritans used to look for those kinds of signs. They called them special providences."

Rabbi Weiss was silent for a long time as if he was hoping this piece of America's history would somehow become light in their darkness. Ultimately that hope seemed to dwindle. Annie could almost feel the renewal of his grief. "What's the other thing you were thinking about?" she finally asked.

"A story out of the Hasidic tradition. About a rabbi who's travel-ing in a desolate countryside. As night falls, he takes refuge from the cold in a barn. He hears some movement in the back of the building and he strikes a match. He finds a very old man slumped against the wall and realizes it's God. 'What are you doing here?' he asks.

"God turns His head away and says: 'I am weary, Rabbi, weary unto death.'"

Another long silence that was finally broken by the crash of artillery along the Elbe. As Rabbi Weiss rose to leave, Annie stepped into the aisle and caught his arm. "I hope you'll go on believing, Rabbi," she said.

For a moment they embraced and Annie felt part of something again. She was not a detached individual drifting helplessly in his-tory's blind, brutal current. Although she did not believe, she was filled with an inexplicable hope that somehow, somewhere, she might find help for her unbelief.

The artillery fire intensified. Annie emerged from the church to find Sergeant Homewood cursing the Germans. He told her Ninth Army engineers had tried to build a pontoon bridge over the 500-foot-wide Elbe River. A hurricane of .88 millimeter shells from batteries in the nearby fortress city of Magdeburg had swept men and matériel into the sluggish stream.

The next day she and the Sergeant crossed the Elbe in a DUKW, an amphibious vehicle aptly called a Duck; the peculiar spelling stood for the factory in which it was built, Detroit United Kaiser Works. Annie wanted to visit three battalions of the Second Armored Division infantry who were dug in there, waiting for the engineers to try for another bridge that would get them some tanks and heavier weapons to defend themselves.

As they hiked from company to company, collecting opinions on why they should head for Berlin and the hell with Ike, out of a nearby forest debouched a swarm of German tanks and self-propelled guns determined to drive the Americans back across the Elbe. A furious battle erupted, with the lightly armed infantrymen getting the worst of it.

Annie sat on the edge of a foxhole watching Sergeant Homewood seize a bazooka from a dead infantryman and fire it at an oncoming tank. The rocket barely scratched the monster's paint. The turret swiveled angrily from left to right, the long snout of the main gun primed to spew death. Was this the solution to her muddled life? Annie decided the answer was no and dove for the bottom of the foxhole seconds before a shell hissed through the space she had been occupying.

Other bazookamen took the tank under fire and Sergeant Homewood roared, "Let's get the hell out of here" and slung Annie over his shoulder and raced for the riverbank with machine gun and shellfire shredding the landscape all around them. The surviving American infantrymen joined them in headlong flight, some swimming, others piling into DUKWs and anything else that could float, in a miniature replay of the British escape from Dunkirk in 1940.

Furious at being lugged out of the fight like a two-year-old, Annie defied Homewood and waded into the river to help drag wounded and dying men to safety. She discovered Rabbi Weiss doing the same thing. "Do you see what I mean?" he said. "There's still a lot we can do."

A distraught captain vowed he was going to get Annie a medal. She barely heard him. Behind Rabbi Weiss dead Americans drifted face down in the Elbe's turgid current. Suddenly all she could see were the Americans she had failed to save—from Jack to the haunted men in the Hurtgen Forest to the twisted bodies in the snow at Malmedy. Back in her room, she stripped off her blood-soaked clothes and lay on the bed sobbing.

Around nightfall, Homewood slipped another cable from Saul Randolph under the door. This one read: AUSCHWITZ. ETC., ETC., ETC.

"Are you okay?" Homewood asked.

"I'm fine," she said.

Annie did not come out of her room for the next two days. She spent the time writing and rewriting a letter to Saul Randolph, explaining why she no longer believed that vicious thing she had said to him about not trusting men. The world, history, was too cruel, too blundering, for men and women to make war on each other. They had to somehow collaborate in trust—and in forgiveness. In the end she decided it was a waste of time and ripped it up.

An alarmed Sergeant Homewood tried to talk to her about combat fatigue. It had nothing to do with courage. He had seen it happen to some of the bravest men he knew in World War I and in this war. "You got more guts than any ten infantrymen I ever seen," the Sergeant declared. "It's okay to feel shaky and maybe even cry a little. I seen guys a lot bigger and tougher than me do it. I did it after D-Day."

With the lecture Homewood delivered another cable—this one from Selma Shanley.

TEN CANCELLATIONS IN YESTERDAY'S MAIL. BOZOS CONSIDER WAR OVER. NO MORE INTEREST IN COMBAT COPY. URGE IMMEDIATE RETURN TO WASHINGTON. NEW PRESIDENT BIG STORY NOW.

While Annie read this infuriating news, Homewood was telling her that a few miles to the south the Eighty-third Infantry Division had established another bridgehead over the Elbe, complete with a pontoon bridge, which was beyond the range of Magdeburg's guns. They had named it the Harry S Truman bridge. The Germans, now identified as the Twelfth Army, had attacked them but these Americans had tanks and artillery in abundance thanks to the pontoon bridge and had easily beaten them off. "Whattya say we take a look at it?" the Sergeant said.

Annie realized this behemoth was doing his best to lure her back to work. Selma's cable added urgency to that idea. They drove to the Harry S Truman bridge, which the Eighty-third Division had stubbornly subtitled "Gateway to Berlin." Everyone in the Ninth Army was still furious at being denied the privilege of conquering Hitler's capital.

At an outpost manned by a company of tanks, there was no sign of a German. To the east, broad meadows stretched on either side of a highway that presumably went straight to Berlin. Byroads ran off it to Magdeburg and other destinations. "All quiet on the western front?" Annie asked.

The tankers nodded glumly. Homewood wandered off to schmooze with another old regular whom he had discovered in the Eighty-third Division's ranks. "Any Germans left up there, do you think?" Annie asked, gesturing to the Twelfth Army's defense line.

"Hell, yes," one of the tankers said. He handed her a pair of binoculars and told her where to look. About two miles up the highway, a line of entrenchments snaked into some woods. Behind the dirt and log wall she could see the turrets of several tanks.

"I bet there's nothing between them and Berlin," she said. Homewood had told her Ninth Army intelligence had established that the Twelfth Army consisted of no more than 5,000 men and a few dozen tanks.

"Probably not," said the tanker, a lean young captain who had no doubt been briefed on the Twelfth Army's pathetic size.

"Berlin's the only story left," Annie said. "I'd love to get there for the surrender. According to Radio Moscow, there are only a few pockets of resistance left."

The Captain's expression reminded Annie of Zeke Talbot when a strong desire to tell her she was crazy clashed with his training to be polite to women. He looked a little like Zeke. The same blond hair, proud, purposeful blue eyes and confident mouth.

"If you shot them up a little bit, I bet I could whiz right past them," she said.

"Can't do that without getting court-martialed, Ma'am," the Captain said. "Orders are only to shoot if we get shot at."

Annie raised the binoculars to her eyes again. A gray car with two people in the front seat pulled into the checkpoint and an officer emerged from the entrenchments to speak to the driver. The officer turned away and studied some documents the driver gave him, then disappeared behind the entrenchments. The car lurched away from the checkpoint and roared down the highway toward them. Machine-gun fire from one of the tanks pursued it, striking sparks on the concrete. The officer leveled a pistol and added his bullets to the fusillade.

"Why are they shooting at that car?" Annie said.

"Don't know," the Captain said, retrieving his field glasses. The staff car had developed a very bad wobble. A rear tire had been hit. One of the German tanks backed away from the entrenchments and headed for the highway to finish it off.

"Can't you help them?" Annie said.

The Captain got on the telephone to regimental headquarters. He gave someone a terse description of what was happening and slammed down the phone in disgust. "No," he said.

The car continued to wobble toward them. The tank was on the highway by now, turning slowly to pursue it. Machine gun fire continued to skip down the highway and the car suddenly slewed off the road as one of its front tires went flat. The German tank began rumbling toward the hapless fugitives. "Well, I'm going to help them!" Annie said.

She slammed the jeep into gear and went lurching across the field onto the highway. The possibility of getting killed by the tank or other German gunfire was high. But so were the chances of saving a life or two—and getting one more very good story. Maybe the two people in the car were fugitives from Berlin, with white hot eyewitness tales to tell.

Up ahead, the driver had leaped out of the car. He ran around it and dragged his companion from the passenger side of the front seat and began loping down the highway, carrying him in his arms. They both wore the dark blue uniforms of German naval officers. The German tank rumbled toward them, its machine gun flickering. But the range was much too great for that inaccurate weapon.

The car had been halfway to the American lines when it went off the road. This gave Annie's jeep, which could hit sixty miles an hour, an advantage over the tank, whose top speed was about twenty-five. As she bore down on the fugitives, the tank commander recognized this and opened up on her with his main gun. A shell screamed over Annie's head to explode somewhere behind her.

The shell was almost instantly answered with a round from the American lines. It tore up mud and dirt only a few yards from the German tank. Glancing over her shoulder, Annie saw a half-dozen American tanks heading her way, with Sergeant Homewood in the turret of one of them.

The runner was starting to tire. His lope had become a stagger as Annie roared up to him. "*Schnell! Schnell!*" she shouted. Hurry up! Another shell screamed over her head to add urgency to her words. All six American tanks were now firing at the Germans and the Germans had opened up on them with every gun in their lines. Explosions tore up the muddy fields all around them.

The man stumbled toward her, still stubbornly lugging his friend. Shrapnel clanged off the jeep's fenders. Annie barely noticed it. She was staring dazedly at Zeke Talbot—and he had stopped to stare even more incomprehensibly at her. "Jesus Christ!" he gasped. "What the hell are you doing here?"

"You better get in. I'll explain later," Annie shouted.

She had trouble recognizing as human the creature Zeke was carrying in his arms. The way the neck flopped, the arms and legs dangled, it might have been an oversized stuffed doll. The officer's cap had fallen off revealing a bald head and a shrunken face of an old man. From the sleeves protruded wrists that were mere skin-covered bones.

"Who—or what—is that?" Annie said as Zeke thrust the creature into the front seat of the jeep and they headed for the American lines with more shells bursting around them.

"Berthe von Hoffmann," Zeke said.

Gazing into the glazed eyes of the woman whose name had desolated her heart, Annie was overwhelmed by confusion. Instead of beauty she could never equal, here was suffering she could not possibly match. "Who did this to her?" she cried.

"The Nazis."

For a dazed moment, Annie sensed an opening in the blankness that had been engulfing her. Had this woman's agony been revealed to her as a special providence, a prelude to healing? Her emergence from the ruins of the thousand-year Reich in Zeke's arms had to be a kind of statement, a witness to the inexplicable ways history flung meaning from the depths of its upheavals. Perhaps her story was the heart of the book she had thought of writing about the war—a book that began resurrecting itself with new depth and breadth, no longer a political tirade but a human journey across a landscape of visible evil and invisible good.

Excited GIs swarmed around their jeep as they reached the safety of the American lines. Within minutes, Berthe was being rushed to a field hospital in an Army ambulance. Annie and Zeke followed them in the jeep.

"How did you rescue her?" Annie said. "She must have been in a concentration camp—"

"I didn't rescue her. God did. I don't know how or even why. But He did it, Annie." As he told her the story, new certainty swelled in Annie's soul. It might take fifty years for people to accept this woman's journey as part of Europe's agony, America's agony—above all, the Jews' agony. She would wait, she would write it and rewrite it until the book included everyone's story, even her own corrupted journey. Though her woman's hopes and wishes no longer seemed transcendentally important.

Beyond the Elbe the cannonading ceased. They watched as the ambulance driver called for help and agitated doctors and nurses carried Berthe von Hoffmann into the field hospital.

"I suppose you love her more than ever," Annie said.

"Maybe," Zeke said. "But she doesn't love me. She just told her husband she never stopped loving him—and Germany."

Annie clutched the wheel with both hands, looking straight ahead at the huge red cross on the field hospital's side flap, refusing to allow even the possibility of forgiveness into her heart. Ruefully, she simultaneously admitted she had no control over that mysterious organ.

"I guess that convinces you once and for all that I'm a damn fool," Zeke said.

"I don't know what I think!" Annie said. "Maybe I'll just stop thinking for a while."

53

ON PILGRIMAGE

In the edenic forest of Grunewald, with Russian and German guns thudding in the distance, Berthe von Hoffmann foresaw Ernst's fiery death. She virtually participated in it. "Let me go with him. I want to die with him," she sobbed.

Jonathan Talbot ignored her. He shoved the car into gear and headed for the Elbe. The resolution on his craggy American face slowly restored Berthe to a semblance of reality. Love—his love— was a kind of lifeline, slowly, stubbornly dragging her out of the abyss. She was too weak, too overwhelmed by her encounter with Ernst, by the last nightmare months in Ravensbruck, to be more than a spectator to this enormous fact.

As they drove, she gradually discerned the pain on Jonathan's face. Those farewell words to Ernst had inflicted another wound on his love for her. She wondered if she had destroyed the spark of faith that God, in spite of all her blunders, had created in his soul. She wanted to tell him that she had recovered her love for him. In Ravensbruck she had paid her debt to Germany. Those farewell words to Ernst were the final installment of the liability that history and her forlorn love for her lost father had inflicted on her soul.

As they drove, Jonathan took from his inside coat pocket an ugly looking pistol with a steel dart in its muzzle. He told her it would kill instantly and silently. He planned to use it if they were stopped at a

German Army checkpoint. It might give them a few seconds head start by causing terror and confusion.

They saw no German soldiers on the fifty-mile drive to the Elbe, except a few hundred deserters heading west like them, trying to surrender to the Americans. Only when they were within sight of their river of salvation did they encounter a checkpoint, bolstered by tanks and other weapons. A handsome young captain who reminded Berthe of Ernst ten years ago listened politely as Jonathan explained that he wanted to take his seriously ill passenger to nearby Magdeburg for treatment.

The Captain looked skeptical and peremptorily ordered them to wait while he conferred with higher authority. As he turned away, Jonathan drew the dart gun from beneath his coat. He was going to shoot him in the back. Unquestionably, they would have gained several seconds—perhaps several dozen—during which the others at the checkpoint would have been thrown into disarray by the Captain's sudden silent collapse. But Berthe could not bear the thought of witnessing another death. "Don't, please," she begged Jonathan.

So they roared away from the checkpoint without the slightest advantage and gunfire soon crippled their car, convincing Berthe that she was fated to be a Petenera, the perdition of men. But Jonathan never said a word of reproach. He was like one of those knights Cervantes ridiculed in *Don Quixote*, committed to enduring every imaginable form of danger and doom for his beloved. He was the Fool and the Good Stranger, united in the same man, exactly as the Marquesa had predicted from the Tarot cards.

When the car careened off the road, he dragged her out of the seat and began running through the gunfire for the American lines, ignoring her pleas to abandon her—until the stunning moment when he shoved her into the front seat of another vehicle, and she found herself face to face with a dark-haired woman whom she instantly knew was Jonathan's wife.

Here was another proof of the Path, of God's incomprehensible love defying coincidence. But Berthe could find no consolation, much less joy in it. All she could see in the woman's eyes was hatred so bitter, so fierce, it seemed capable of inflicting death.

As they drove at top speed to an American field hospital, Berthe felt life guttering out in her mind and body. She almost told the gentle, smiling doctors and nurses who thrust intravenous feeding tubes into her arms not to bother, to let her escape this final tangle of folly and antipathy.

She sank into a blank darkness and found herself back in the Madrid arena watching Germany, the doomed bull with blood drooling from his nostrils, topple into the dust. Matador Ordonez turned to ask her approval. Her heart swelled with a last spasm of refusal and revulsion. Then she heard her voice booming over a loudspeaker: YOU HAVE WON A PLACE OF IMMORTAL HONOR IN MY LIFE.

She was speaking from the topmost rim of the bullring, where she hung from a cross, upside down. Jonathan hung beside her in the same position, like the figure of transformation on the Marquesa's Tarot cards. Berthe reached out to him but her hand fell short of touching him. A strange resentment seemed to be convulsing his face. Berthe wondered if he was grieving because he thought she still loved Germany more than she loved him. She tried to tell him this was no longer true. *Ich liebe dich, Ich liebe dich*, she said. But he did not seem to understand her. She wondered if he was disgusted by all things German, including her. Or was abandoning her love a necessary part of his transformation?

Berthe looked out over Madrid, seeing the great city, Spain and all Europe upside down, forever strange and alien. She saw the Path she had followed, twisting from Berlin across Germany and France to Madrid and beyond it to the shrine of the Virgin in Extramadura and the spires of the cathedral of Santiago de Compostella in Galicia. A great wind filled the Path, as if Boreas himself had come down from Olympus to create the ultimate cyclone. Out of its dark whirling funnel emerged the angel who had embraced the Ritterboot. His immense face filled the arena with glowing compassion as he gathered the dead bull to his breast.

Somewhere in Madrid's streets, a mournful voice chanted a poem.

I seek a city throughout all the world's estate
That has an angel standing at the gate
It is his wing that I carry, broken,
Upon my shoulder blade, a grievous weight
And on my brow, his star as seal and token.

It was Else Lasker-Schuler, Germany's greatest woman poet, cel-ebrating Berthe's role as witness of God's baffled, baffling love.

With the bull cradled in his arms, the angel slowly retraced the Path from Madrid across France to Germany. He placed the dead animal on top of a tremendous pyre composed of blackened tanks, ruptured hulls of submarines and other warships, the smashed fuse-lages of planes and thousands upon thousands of ruined artillery pieces and machine guns and rifles. Fire gushed from the round O of the angel's mouth and the pyre became a volcano of flame that flick-ered eerily across Europe.

The angel turned his stupendous head and gazed at Berthe. "LOVE CALLS US TO THE THINGS OF THIS WORLD," he said. His voice was like the music of a gigantic cello, playing at the center of the universe. Joy leaped in Berthe's heart. She knew she had been forgiven for her betrayal of Ernst, her abuse of Jonathan's love. Her mission as God's blundering messenger was almost over.

Berthe woke to find Jonathan sitting beside her bed, his eyes swimming with anxiety.

"Did you mean what you said to me in Ernst's car about carrying faith through time?" she asked.

"Yes."

She sank into a dreamless darkness this time. Awakening again, she found Annie Talbot sitting beside the bed. She was no longer the angry woman in the jeep, but her expression was far from friendly.

"Do you wish me dead?" Berthe murmured.

"I did, until quite recently."

"You must understand something. Jonathan no longer loves me. I destroyed our love with my blind worship of Germany."

Annie's eyes remained coldly skeptical. "You never loved him?" she asked.

"Oh I did. How can a woman not respond to a man like him when he offers you his love? There was a purity, a simplicity to it that is so rare. I felt the same thing for Ernst until history—Germany's history—destroyed us."

"Something similar happened to me and Zeke—with America's history," Annie said. "He's escaped it, thanks to you. The bitterness, the rage, the compulsive superpatriotism are gone."

Was she saying she could love Jonathan again, if Berthe von Hoffmann were not so blatantly, pathetically visible? "It would be simpler for us all if I died," Berthe said. "I only want to live for my children's sake."

"You're not going to die," Annie said.

Invoking her political power as a congressman's daughter, Annie wangled an ambulance and an escorting nurse and doctor from the Ninth Army. They drove across chaotic, prostrate Germany to an American hospital in Paris. There, Berthe watched concern about her imminent death slowly decline on the faces that hovered around her bed. But she still remained extremely weak and gained weight with excruciating slowness.

Jonathan visited every day, bringing her terse reports on the final days of the war, Hitler's suicide, Germany's unconditional surrender. Annie, pressured by deadlines, was a less frequent visitor. But she was the sponsor of what she called "new medicine"—Jonathan's appearance with Georg and Greta. At first they recoiled from the sight of their mother as a grisly skeleton. Greta burst into tears. But they soon calmed down and admitted they were glad to escape from their grandmother.

"Mother," Georg said. "Is Father dead?"

"Yes," Berthe said. "He died in the battle for Berlin. I saw him just before he went to the front. His last words to me were of how much he loved you and Greta."

Georg fought back tears. "Did he die with his face to the enemy, like a true German?" he asked.

He looked so fierce, so much like Ernst, proclaiming the need for hardness, Berthe's heart was filled with dread. "I'm sure he did. He was a brave man. When you're older we'll talk about why these terrible things have happened to us and to Germany. For now let's simply love each other. That's what Father wanted us to do."

Greta pressed her blond head against Berthe's shrunken breasts. "I never stopped loving you, Muti, no matter what Grandmother said."

"Neither did I," Georg said, after an ominous hesitation.

A new resolve to live for their sakes swelled in Berthe's heart. She started gaining weight at a pace that finally satisfied the doctors. She began to walk the hospital's corridors, which were full of wounded Americans, many of them amputees or blinded. It was not easy to face the price America had paid to rescue Europe from Nazism.

From Berlin via Jonathan came an anguished letter from Helen

Widerstand. The Russians were turning their part of Germany into the very opposite of the paradise Helen had envisioned in her Marxist dreams. Everyone who was a member of the former ruling class—shopkeepers, landowners, business executives—was being ruthlessly eliminated and a ferocious thought control was being imposed on writers and intellectuals. "It's Nazism with a red face," Helen wrote. "Class hatred instead of Jewish hatred."

Berthe found it painful to think she would be an alien in the city of her birth. She had no desire to expose her children to more ideological warfare. Where could she go? She could only wait and hope and trust in the Path.

Later that same day, Jonathan visited her with a guilty look in his eyes. "Annie went back to the states today. Her father's had a heart attack. She told me she still loves me—"

Berthe realized he was half-hoping she would tell him she loved him too much to let him go—and simultaneously wishing she would release him. The wound she had inflicted on their love in Spain had never healed—and probably never would. But his sense of honor and obligation to her still dominated him.

As she wrestled with an answer, Berthe glimpsed one of the amputees struggling past the door on his crutches. With stunning force she realized that would be the image of their love, if she kept Jonathan in Europe at her side. She had the power to keep him, once she regained her health and beauty. But she would be forever contemptuous of herself.

She had to give him up. She managed to stumble out words of sympathy and concern for Annie and her father. "You should go to America and offer your help," she said.

"Who'll take care of Georg and Greta—and you?" he said.

"The Marquesa," Berthe said. "I'll telephone her today."

The answer came to her so naturally, Jonathan assumed she had been thinking about it for days. In fact, it was almost an unpleasant surprise. She had very little desire to put herself in her Spanish mother's power. But there was no other choice.

The Marquesa persuaded General Franco to send a Spanish Air Force plane to pick up Berthe and the children. She greeted them at the Madrid airport with cries of joy, sweeping Georg and Greta into her arms with a maternal possessiveness that almost frightened them. How could they know they represented the future of a Europe that had slain its best sons and daughters for two generations?

That night, after the children were asleep, the Marquesa came to Berthe's room with a glass of warm, sweet milk and an inevitable question. "Where is Jonathan Talbot?"

"In America," Berthe said.

Tears streamed down her face as she told her Spanish mother the rest of the story. "I have to give him up. Do you see that? Or are you going to tell me I'm a fool?"

"I always knew you'd have to give him up," the Marquesa said with astonishing matter-of-factness. "Whether a love lasts for a lifetime or a few years or a month is not as important as what it achieves in the soul. Your love achieved a great deal. Even duende."

"I ruined that," Berthe said. She told her of that night in Granada, the exaltation—the sense of the eternal—and her terrible refusal of it in Germany's name. "But I'm not that way any more," she sobbed. "I love him absolutely now—without reservations or limitations!"

"That's what your heart says. But an amputee walking by your door forces you to confront the other side of that truth. Your love would be forever crippled by his guilt—and your guilt."

In the Marquesa's hooded eyes Berthe saw the ramifications of that scabrous word. It would be more than the guilt for destroying Jonathan Talbot's marriage. It would be guilt for betraying Ernst and Germany.

"I suppose I should be grateful for having Georg and Greta to love," Berthe said. "But I don't want to become one of those women who lives vicariously through her children. Perhaps God has other plans for me, but they're not visible at the moment."

"Granted you may never love another man the way you loved Jonathan," the Marquesa said with infuriating complacency. "But there are other men who will be eager to love you—and you can find room in your heart for them."

For a month Berthe refused to listen to her Spanish mother. They talked of other things, they played card games with Georg and Greta, they taught them Spanish. Berthe's body began to regain its flesh and shape. Her hair grew back, without its golden sheen—more straw-colored and without a trace of natural curl. From America came cryptic letters from Jonathan, reporting that Annie's father had died and he and Annie were "talking things over."

Finally, the Marquesa consulted the Tarot cards. This time she laid them out in the form of a Greek cross. In the center was Berthe's significator, the card that symbolized the character of the seeker—the somber Queen of Swords. The first card Berthe drew was Death, a grinning skeleton in armor, on a white horse.

"That signifies a decisive change in your nature," the Marquesa said, laying it across the Queen at right angles.

The next card Berthe drew was the nine of swords, depicting a woman with bowed head against a background of nine swords. "That means the fate you dreaded is behind you," the Marquesa said, laying it on the right of the Queen of Swords.

The next card was the Knight of Cups, a young man holding a golden cup, riding a white horse. "He signifies continued spiritual aspiration in your future," the Marquesa said, laying it to the left of the Queen.

The next card was the the Ace of Pentacles. The Marquesa beamed at the oversized diamond suspended in a giant hand and laid the card beneath the Queen's feet. "That means a foundation of worldly wealth will sustain you."

The next card was the Sun. The Marquesa laid it above the Queen of Swords, completing the cross. "That signifies a fortunate marriage," the Marquesa said, looking more and more pleased.

Next came four cards laid swiftly beside the cross. Each of the first three was benevolent, but ambiguous. The fourth was the crucial one, the destiny card. The Marquesa's breath grew short as Berthe drew it. "The World!" she cried. "I was praying for it."

Berthe stared at a painting of a naked, dancing feminine figure, with a purple sash draped strategically around her body. She floated inside a large wreath. At the four corners of the card were the heads of a man, an eagle, a lion and a bull—the same symbols that appeared in the vision of Ezekiel, in the cathedral of Santiago de Compostella. "This is the last card of the Tarot," the Marquesa said, her voice croaking with excitement. "The Queen of Swords has reached the end of her journey."

The symbols were very old, she said. They stood for the principal signs of the Zodiac as well as the four seasons and the four elements. The Lion was Leo—summer, fire. The Eagle was Scorpio—autumn, air. The man was Aquarius—winter, water. The bull was Taurus—

spring, earth. The dancer was a figure of joy, declaring the seeker's ability to harmonize all things now.

The next day, Berthe sat in the Marquesa's garden and wrote the most difficult letter of her life.

Dearest Jonathan:

Your letters reveal something to me that I had always suspected. In the midst of your love for me, you never stopped loving your wife. You heard what I said to Ernst in the Grunewald—I never stopped loving him either. Let us be realistic. I can never live in America with you. Europe is my natural home—and the home of my children. I want them to become Europeans—to contribute to an era of new understanding and mutual respect. I can't ask you to stay in Europe with me and struggle to earn a living in a world in which you would never be completely at home. Perhaps it would be best if we said goodbye now while our hearts are full of mutual affection.

With deepest devotion,

Berthe

For a moment she thought she heard Admiral Canaris whispering: *What a clever combination of lies and half-truths. You may master the art of worldliness yet, my dear Berthe.*

The next day, the Marquesa asked, "You've written to Jonathan?"

"Yes!" Berthe snapped. She still found it hard to take her Spanish mother's advice.

The following day, Rafael Sanchez sent Berthe a huge bouquet of flowers. The following day another bouquet arrived. The message was too clear to be evaded. "I could never love him," Berthe told the Marquesa.

"Not as much as you loved Ernst or Jonathan," the Marquesa said. "But I never loved the Marques de Montoya a tenth as much as I loved your father. He never knew the difference. Remember your powers, my dear. The powers of womanhood. They can make you the next Marquesa de Montoya. The family has immense amounts of money. You can become a force for good in Spain—and Germany."

Rafael began coming to dinner. He took Berthe to the opera, the theater, on which he was remarkably well informed. He seemed to know the history of every painting in the Prado. He introduced her to families with children close to Georg and Greta's ages. He talked brilliantly about European history, which he continued to study with the eyes of a professional diplomat. Berthe found warmth stirring in her mind, if not her body.

Rafael repeatedly expressed his admiration for Canaris and Helmuth von Moltke. He had spent five years in the Spanish embassy in Berlin and felt Spain and Germany were linked by history and national temperament. "Spain will never forget the help Germany gave us to defeat Bolshevism," he said. "Although the aid was tainted by Nazism, German soldiers shed their blood on Spanish soil. That is a sacred bond between our countries. A bond between the Spain that exists beneath Franco and the Falange and the Germany beneath Hitler and his SS."

Berthe was amazed by how much this testament moved her. She never dreamt this shy, taciturn man concealed such deep feelings.

Late one night there was a call from America. Jonathan Talbot's voice sounded strange and distant, but his emotion filled the room. "Your letter hit me pretty hard," he said. "But every word of it is true."

Words tumbled from Berthe's lips. "I want to see you one more time. I want to make a pilgrimage with you—to Santiago de Compostella to give thanks for the whole thing. But you must bring Annie."

"She's covering the war in the Pacific. Maybe when it's over."

A week later the Japanese surrendered after a terrible new weapon, an atomic bomb, convinced them further resistance was futile—and President Harry Truman modified the policy of unconditional surrender, permitting them to keep their emperor, and assuring them that the United States would not destroy their nation. The next day a cable arrived from Jonathan, telling Berthe he and Annie would be arriving via Pan American in exactly two weeks.

When he appeared at the Marquesa's palace, Jonathan was alone. "Annie's trying to save her column," he said. "Anyway, she's afraid she'd be out of the loop for this celebration."

With a wry grin he added: "She says she trusts us."

Berthe reported Annie's defection to the Marquesa while Jonathan was unpacking. Her old eyes danced with good-humored approval. "She has no desire to spend any time with you now that you've regained your looks. And what better way to guarantee your behavior than saying she trusts you! A very shrewd woman."

Bernado Moorman and Rafael Sanchez joined them for dinner. Jonathan talked enthusiastically about the new American president, Truman, who had already won his admiration. Moorman discoursed on Spain's current difficulties. The U.S. State Department and the British Foreign Office, urged on by Stalin, were demanding Franco's resignation and the restoration of democracy—which Moorman saw as nothing more than a code word for communism.

Rafael Sanchez said the Caudillo was unbothered by the uproar. He predicted the day would soon come when the United States needed Spain—and Germany—and Japan—to stop the spread of Bolshevism. Jonathan agreed. He gave them a marvelous inside account—obtained from Annie—of how the professionals in the State Department had won the new president's confidence with their unillusioned view of Soviet Russia. Truman was already exhibiting a cool dislike of Stalin's demands and threats.

Moorman said communism was more dangerous, more evil than Nazism. Berthe noticed he directed most of his remarks at Jonathan. She saw he was trying to lure him into this new struggle, which extended far beyond the borders of Europe. She recoiled from the thought, knowing how hard it was to grapple with evil without becoming tainted by it.

"I believe Europe—and the entire world—will eventually repudiate communism," Berthe said. "Nothing founded on hatred can endure."

"Your faith is an inspiration to us all, Frau von Hoffmann," Moorman said. "But I hope the United States and Great Britain don't disband their Army and Navy and secret services."

He was as charming as ever. But he could no longer stir Berthe's German antipathy. She even had to admit the fiercely intelligent little man might have a point.

The next day, Berthe and Jonathan prepared to depart on their pilgrimage in the Marquesa's Hispano-Suiza. She declined to accompany them. "Now that Spain is safe, I have nothing to pray for," she said. Instead, Rafael Sanchez would be their escort.

From the side parlor where Berthe was saying goodbye to Georg and Greta, she overheard the Marquesa in the entrance hall. "Rafael's grown so fond of Berthe and the children. He's visited her every day. He fills her bedroom with flowers."

Rafael's voice betrayed a certain uneasiness about Jonathan's reaction. "She's a remarkable woman," he said.

As Berthe walked into the hall, she realized Jonathan was being assailed by one of his prophetic flashes. He foresaw she was going to marry Rafael Sanchez and become the next Marquesa de Montoya. He recognized it was the perfect ending to her journey—a union that would enable her to become neither German nor Spanish but simply European—the only answer to the continent's ancient feuds and fears. But it was an acknowledgment riven with pain.

She glimpsed all this in a kind of blazing fusion of her mind with Jonathan's. Was there better proof of the reality of their love? For a moment, as she confronted the pain on his face, she could not bear the idea of surrendering him.

In a few hours, they were crossing the mountains into green rainy Galicia. Rafael discoursed in his learned way about the future of religion. He predicted a new age of faith after the collapse of communism—something he called a "second religiousness," which would be less doctrinal and more mystical than the previous era. "The task will be formidable—to bring the best gifts of the old civilization to the children of the new civilization," he said. "But I have no doubt now that it can be accomplished."

They arrived in Santiago de Compostella's immense square to find it filled to overflowing with people. It was the height of the pilgrim season, Rafael explained. As they made their way through the crowd, a familiar figure fell in step beside them.

"Can an unbeliever join this procession?" Bernado Moorman asked.

"Of course he can," Berthe said.

"What brings you here?" Jonathan said.

"Canaris. I want to admit I was wrong about him—and ask someone's forgiveness. Maybe God's, if He's listening."

"You have mine," Berthe said. "And the Marquesa's."

"And mine," Rafael Sanchez said.

"And mine," Jonathan said, holding out his hand.

Together they entered the western door and gazed up at the Portico de Gloria. Once more Berthe was dazzled by the overflowing mixture of beauty and humor and joy on the stone faces from the age of faith. She lifted her eyes to the tympanum above the Tree of Life, where the sculptor had carved Ezekiel's vision of Jesus surrounded by a bull, a lion, an eagle and a man, emerging from God's cleansing fire. The Savior had replaced the Tarot's carefree dancer here, mingling joy with sorrow—but exalting both with a promise of transcendent love.

With quiet authority, Rafael Sanchez took Berthe's hand and led them through the vast vaulted interior of the church to the high altar, where Saint James sat above a blaze of gold and gilt and candles. "He could be any saint," Berthe said. "The important thing is the way he's presiding over Compostella—the countryside where the star shone."

"The star of hope," Rafael Sanchez said.

"The star of faith," Berthe said.

"The star of love," Jonathan said.

"That's one hell of a star," Moorman said.

Now Berthe knew why she had come here. It was the one place where she could find the strength to part from Jonathan. As he raised her hands to his lips in a farewell kiss, she asked God to enlarge the spark of faith that love had ignited in his soul. She wanted him and his clever wife to become American lightbearers, bringing their country's special gifts to the searching hearts and minds of the new civilization. It would require a struggle, of course. There would always be a struggle against the evils of ignorance and fear and hate. But the spark would endure.

A NOTE ON SOURCES

For a thorough background on the diplomatic, strategic, and military impact of the policy of unconditional surrender, Anne Armstrong's book, *Unconditional Surrender*, is a solid, unsparing account. Harry C. Butcher's *My Three Years With Eisenhower* and Stephen Ambrose's *Supreme Commander* describe Eisenhower's disagreement with the policy and his reluctant submission to Roosevelt's orders. For vivid details of Roosevelt's hatred of Germany, the basic book is *The Morgenthau Diaries*, edited by John Morton Blum.

For the ruinous effect of unconditional surrender on the German resistance movement, Allen Dulles's long forgotten *Germany's Underground* is still one of the best witnesses. The definitive story of that splintered group has been told in encyclopedic detail in Peter Hoffmann's *A History of the German Resistance 1933–1945*. For those who want to know more about Count Helmuth von Moltke, *Letters to Freya*, edited and translated from the German by Beate Rhum von Oppen, is a marvelously intimate portrait of this extraordinary man. Life among the less prominent resisters to Nazism is well dramatized in *Berlin Underground* by Ruth Andreas-Friedrich. Another book that reveals the surprising amount of resistance to Hitler among ordinary Germans is *Contending With Hitler*, edited by David Clay Large. Also valuable is *Berlin Diaries* by Marie Vassiltchikov, a White Russian woman who lived in Berlin throughout the war and was involved in the Schwarze Kapelle conspiracy.

For background on the agony Nazism inflicted on German Jews such as the great poet, Else Lasker-Schuler, *Prophets Without Honor* by Frederick Grunfield would be difficult to surpass. Gerald Reitlinger's *SS: Alibi of a Nation* is unsparing in its depiction of evil infecting the German soul. For the role of Ernst Kantorowicz's *Fred-*

erick II in the rise of Hitler, Norman F. Cantor's *Inventing The Middle Ages* is an eye-opening account.

For those who want to get beyond the hagiographic school of Franklin D. Roosevelt biography, Frederick W. Marks III's *Wind Over Sand* is guaranteed to clear the sinuses. Mr. Marks is unsparing in his criticism of FDR's diplomacy, before and during the war. A shorter, more balanced account is *American Diplomacy During The Second World War* by Gaddis Smith. Also helpful is *Roosevelt and World War II* by Robert A. Devine, who does a good job of untangling the strands of isolationism, pragmatism and realism in Roosevelt's worldview.

For a graphic account of the New Dealers' struggle to seize control of the State Department—and their ultimate defeat—*A Pretty Good Club* by Martin Weil is insider history at its best. Invaluable for the ideological struggles that raged in the wartime capital is *Washington Dispatches 1941–1945*, edited by H. G. Nicholas, with an introduction by Isaiah Berlin, who wrote most of these shrewd reports from the British embassy. Also illuminating is William L. O'Neil's *A Better World*, which details the incredible lies some Americans told to themselves and to others in a desperate attempt to believe in Stalin's Russia.

A number of books contain good accounts of Roosevelt's undeclared war against Germany in the North Atlantic during 1941. Among the best are *Mr. Roosevelt's Navy: The Private War of the U.S. Atlantic Fleet* by Peter Abbazia and *Hitler Versus Roosevelt* by Thomas A. Bailey. Books on the diplomatic and intelligence failures that led to the debacle at Pearl Harbor are legion. Jonathan G. Utley's *Going to War With Japan* is especially good on the role of the State Department. *And I Was There* by Edwin T. Layton is probably the best account of the intelligence failure.

The author's article, "The Big Leak," published in the December 1987 issue of *American Heritage*, explores the long forgotten but once sensational leak of Rainbow Five, the Americans' top secret plan for waging war against Germany and Japan—and examines the evidence that Franklin D. Roosevelt was probably the man who leaked it.

On the U-boat war, there is, again, an embarrassment of riches. *Iron Coffins* by Herbert A. Werner is a vivid, early account by a German commander who survived. *U-boat Ace, the Story of Wolfgang*

Luth by Jordan Vause is an interesting biography of a commander who succumbed to Nazism. Peter Padfield's *Dönitz: The Last Führer* is an even more riveting exploration of the way Nazism infected the thinking of the Ubootwaffe, leading to the decision to make war on crews, not ships. Best of all, for its vivid evocation of life aboard a U-boat as well as a scarifying examination of the U.S. Navy's inept response to the Germans' 1942 offensive, is Michael Gannon's *Operation Drumbeat.* For the code-breaking war David Kahn's *Seizing the Enigma* is the definitive book. Equally definitive for the moral dimensions of the air war against Germany is Ronald Shaffer's *Wings of Judgment.*

For Spain's role in World War II, a good place to begin is Willard Beaulac's *Franco: Silent Ally in World War II.* A coolly objective view, it was published in 1986, when the Caudillo was in his grave and Spain had achieved democracy. Beaulac was second in command of the American embassy during most of the war. Ambassador Carleton J. H. Hayes's *Wartime Mission in Spain* supports Beaulac's view—including his disapproval of the OSS's early antics in Spain. For an opposing view of Franco, British Ambassador Sir Samuel Hoare's account, *Complacent Dictator*, seethes with animosity.

Another book readers might find useful is D. J. Goodspeed's *The German Wars, 1914–45*, which offers the fruitful perspective that the two World Wars were really one extended conflict. It also includes a devastating critique of the policy of unconditional surrender. V. E. Tarrant's *The U-Boat Offensive, 1914–1945*, takes the same unifying point of view. Nowhere is the interrelationship of the two wars more visible than in Charles Bracelen Flood's magisterial *Hitler: The Path to Power.*